RETURNING TO PARADISE

KIM FARLEIGH

MINERVA PRESS
WASHINGTON LONDON MONTREUX

RETURNING TO PARADISE

ISBN 1 85863 593 4

First published 1996 by
MINERVA PRESS
195 Knightsbridge
London SW7 1RE

Printed in Great Britain by
Antony Rowe Ltd., Chippenham, Wiltshire

RETURNING TO PARADISE

ONE

The city of Perth is a bastion of modernistic glass and concrete on the edge of vast deserts, ancient forests and monumental seas. Scarcely a mile of the Western Australian coastline has been scarred by the Industrial Revolution: it has not changed for millennia. Great upheavals have taken place in altogether more pressured places – climactic wars, pestilence, inhuman injustices – and this coast has seen little of it.

Often white and uninhabited, populated by sweeping bays, it has remained ignorant of mankind's indiscretions. It only knows the natural processes of water and air, that, with imperceptible ebbs and flows, have secretively altered the face of things with a dignified aspect of unhurried grace. No tumultuous urgencies from other worlds have arrived to speed up this lackadaisical disinclination for rapid transience. Its austere beauty, too inhospitable and unworldly for the manicured tastes of European sailors, has the picturesqueness and mystery of eternity; yet it was too strange, too unrevealing and far too perplexing for those, who, armed with their short-lived whims – those merchants of the high seas – had begun Batavia, and had seen in the green fertility of the Spice Islands the chance for a quick buck; they were unimpressed by the broad sweeps of Western Australia's coves which offered little protection from a blazing sun; they were not moved by the bare orange mountains that fall into the ocean, and by the blood-red deserts that encroach upon the sea. Such appreciation was the preserve of an ancient culture too aesthetic and appreciative to leave any obvious marks upon this wild perfection and, because of this, the city of Perth creates the illusion of being an artificial and modern enclave in a den of prehistoric beauty.

Within it, glass monsters rise inside thickets of brightly-painted buildings of bygone eras whose façades show the taste of those now gone. The educated eye can spot examples of the French influence on British architecture – steeply sloping roofs ingrained with windows surrounded by carved stone with little iron balustrades: a tiny concentration of European experience on the vast silent plains of untamed longevity.

On the edge of this plane there is a place where the frozen sea of sand makes contact with the sea. At this place, one can turn one's back on the ocean and see yellow flowers on red dunes beneath a deep blue sky. It is the only place on earth I have seen the three primary colours together, and nothing else, fused into the natural world. This vision, a moral end in itself, held no pertinence to Europeans before the days of tourism: it could not be exploited for commercial gain; it was worthless; therefore, it was left untouched as it had been since the great forests of the carboniferous breathed their last breaths, alone since the continents split to make their own way in this world; and, when places like Perth have been wiped from this earth, it will still be alone, unmarked by all the haste and anguish and determination of that consciousness so different from itself.

In many places along that coast you can sit on a boat on the water and see a strip of blue – the sea – from which mountains of white dunes rise beneath the blue sky. For miles and miles sailors from other lands were greeted with this silent wonder of blue and white; their leaders saw no other virtues in it than silence and solitude. It is a landscape that engulfs, that holds no pecuniary promise; it excites other forms of imagination, ones impractical to the scheming dreams of men. It is an environment that does not support human enterprise: it is infertile, hot, unforgiving; and it is beautiful.

In the south, where different beauty exists, smoke from great fires within the huge eucalyptus forests once blocked out the coast to the men of galleons and clippers. Where the smoke was thin, in the mouths of rivers, the banks were invisible beneath canopies of gum leaves. No civilisations were present along these banks to attract the avaricious hopes of desperate men. Nothing, it was said, could survive in this interminable jungle of gums. It was a cauldron of uncivil heat, a death-trap of strange creatures, and within it was carved the city of Perth.

Perth sits in a basin bordered by a range of hills, thick bush – and the vast expanse of the sea. It is the European dream within the oldest landscape on earth; a speck of Romanesque roads and detached houses surrounded by an agricultural belt of wheat and sheep that gives way to the sanguine sands of the colossal deserts. The closest contact one feels with something foreign in a place like this is so foreign as to be too mysterious for pragmatic meaning – the universe and the ethereal silence of the ancient lands. It is a feeling of detachment not felt unless your sense of familiarity has been altered by being away.

Mine had been destroyed. I had been away for six years, on the other side of the world, and now I was going home. Below me, the earth appeared as a uniform black cloak upon which the occasional light shone in recognition of the existence of some remote outpost of life. It was impossible, in the darkness of night, from the aircraft, to distinguish between the land and the sea.

During the day the same view yielded a wonder of blue and red, divided by a strip of white. Within the red, exotic patterns, like the designs of Chinese fabrics – the dry beds of creeks and rivers – were like symbols of aesthetic inhospitability. What clumps of white-trunked vegetation existed there were dwarfed by a magnitude of space so vast that one could be forgiven for thinking the aircraft was cruising over the fiery surface of some wild planet closer to the sun.

Suddenly the red earth gives away to green at a point just north of Perth. Here farmlands of green fields containing patches of eucalypti create the promise of civilisation and then one sees the neat rows of houses, different coloured roofs, square patches of garden and the blue of swimming pools before the plane feels the earth again in the dead of night.

Beyond the airport the road is dark, seemingly swimming in a plethora of space. Everything is quiet, distant. No life pulsates. It feels as though the inhabitants have suddenly departed, leaving everything intact, carried off by some mysterious promise into the pellucid wilderness with its untampered practices of which only the stars are aware.

The streets are new and often straight. They seem to contain little of significance to an eye accustomed to concentrations of teeming populations. There is the feeling that nothing is there other than the black sky, the road, and the yellow eerie light of street lamps ridiculously high above the ground. A few houses appear. They are set back an absurd distance from the road. Narrow footpaths run between the road and the front gardens of properties sitting in the phosphorescent glow of dim lights enveloped by the huge immensity of the impenetrable and ebony sky. It is surreal. Slow. The radiance of another set of headlights swims towards us. It is a world of two distinct nocturnal sensations: intense concentrations of artificial light and absolute black. This is home. I am back. I feel worried.

* * * * * * * * * * *

If you travel for a long time with a friend and then resume a normal existence, the experience lives on in conversation, and becomes richer. With experience you can understand more clearly the temperaments and motives of those met along the road. Many years ago, as a young man, green in the ways of the world, I travelled around Australia for eight months with a school friend. Along the way, we worked for a fishing family who were viewed by the town we were living in as being a happy, cohesive unit; the reality, which had to be pointed out to us, and the gravity of which, at the time, was probably beyond me, was significantly different. The husband had been emotionally unfulfilled and professionally frustrated for thirty years. Due to our youth – and what is youth, but the age of retrievability – we could not appreciate the regrets he had built up through a turgid life of silence and solitude. We did not know what schemes this seemingly simple man was conjuring up as he stared through the windscreen of his trawler out on to the same blue ocean he had seen with pitiless monotony, week in and week out, for three insipid decades. It was unimaginable for us that his time was spent contemplating the reckless act he was about to undertake, one which would release him from the burdens of his past mistakes. He felt that he had wasted his life by not taking advantage of possibilities presented to him in his youth, and his existence, as a symbol of what life means, was beyond us. It was only when our lives became constricted as well – opportunities became irretrievable, decisions crucial, time of the greatest importance – that we could then see something immense in his being. I did not realise then how important were the things I was observing: the knowledge now that anything you experience may be of some future value, that we are effectively ignorant of what we may require, is the lesson of experience.

It was also the attitude I was to take with me on returning to Australia some years later. I had not been to the country of my childhood for six years and was determined to observe in the belief that my perceptions would be given greater meaning by intense rumination. If I had to make this journey to Australia, I was at least going to gain something from it, other than the reaffirmation that I am completely different from the rest of my family. As the plane touched down, Jeremy looked at me and said, "You must be really looking forward to this."

He was surprised when I drolly replied, "Not really."

No one looks forward to seeing people with whom they have very little in common. I knew that my family would not have the slightest interest in anything I had done over the previous six years: all the information I had gathered on architecture, different foods, history, music, painting, geomorphology, different cultures, social practices, politics, cinema, photography - the human condition itself - would hold about as much relevance to them as the idea of becoming a concert violinist does to a central African pigmy. I really was faced with the following dilemma: 'What the fuck am I going to say to these people? And who the hell are they anyway? And what incredible assumptions would they make about me?'

I can't imagine what went through Jeremy's mind; my attitude was obviously a mystery to him. I never spoke about my family. The concept of homesickness was a foreign one. There was one thing of which I was conscious, however, and that was independence. I felt as though I were about to lose it. For six years I had cosily pursued a life in London of cultured, hedonistic anonymity, carefully selecting my company, and now I was about to be thrust into the midst of wild beasts, masquerading under the guise of being members of my family. How I was supposed to act in front of them was not clear; the stress created by this prospect gave me an unhealthy aspect of morbid timidity. I was in no rush to get off the plane. The aircraft was the last bastion of mature security I felt that I was going to see for a month. The irony of being fearful in this situation, after I had deposited myself in insecure situations in many places around the world, was not lost on me. It was certainly going to be lost on my family though.

I was surprised by the diversity of racial heritage within the customs officers. Jeremy, for some reason, got agitated by their polite intrusions into his fiancée's bags. Through the open door, leading into the arrival lounge, groups of people were amassed behind a barrier, waiting for those on our flight. Invariably, members of my family would be out there amongst all those innocent people. I saw one of them. It was my elder brother. Fortunately, he did not look much older. A stint in prison and a few job retrenchments probably had no effect at all on his cavalier attitude towards life. Those minor inconveniences, tumultuous to any normal human being, had been shrugged off by him with the serene resignation of a Buddhist monk. I had rung my father up, during my brother's fall from grace, and my father, who had just visited him in prison, produced a gem of hypocrisy by announcing: "The silly prick still thinks life's a party." I could imagine my brother saying this about my father. In fact, I could imagine anyone saying this about my father.

My father, of course, was not there. This would have been too much to ask. The term "self-indulgent" was too mild an expression to use on a man who, while his three children were growing up, had spent more money on women and alcohol than the United States government had planned to spend on the Star Wars missile program. The fact that he was still alive was a biological miracle. Doctors at the Queen Elizabeth II hospital in Perth were stunned by the news that the man with a haemoglobin red blood cell count below that which normally induced death wanted to check himself out, after a tumour – the product of thirty-five years of unmitigated hedonism – had burst in his stomach. His third wife – thirty years his junior – had found him dying on the toilet in a pool of blood. A week later, he was back at work. The doctors, still mesmerised by the shock that this 'freak' had survived and appeared actually to be well, had advised him to give up smoking; and, with the disdain he usually showed for academic opinion, my father continued gorging himself on cigarettes – the first one was always lit the instant he woke up in the morning – galvanised by the belief that these things were determined by genetics.

"Take a look at Clem," he said, during his brief convalescence. "The bastard drank and smoked like a cunt for fifty years – never hurt him."

Everyone looked as though they had hardly aged at all, apart from my youngest cousin. She had gone from being an adolescent into a gorgeous young woman. I actually felt like screwing her. We hugged as if we knew each other, but this was ridiculous. We were complete strangers. The last time I saw her, she had been ten years old. She was as uncertain in her affection towards me as I was towards her.

Next to her, her father beamed happily. I wondered how he would have felt if I had said, "Brian, do I have your permission to seduce your daughter?" He probably would have said, with his usual brash, protective pessimism, "Jesus Christ, yar farkin should see what the farkin tart's wearin these daze! Hell of a bloody job tryin tar getta tar dress properly. Halfa tits are always hangin out."

Jeremy joined his family, my brother saying to his sister, a poised, pretty woman of thirty, "You play yar cards right, and ya could be in there."

This was a reference to me. Sarah and I smiled at each other with rueful embarrassment.

In my brother's car, I observed a detached intensity of expression on his face. The night outside was clear and black and there was an all-pervading sensation of space. Reversing the car, he remained silent, as if I had just come back from a week's holiday in Bali. When we got through the barriers, and were out on the open road, he eventually said, "The old man gets worse by the day. He's absolutely on the bones of his arse."

Most families probably begin with: "It's great to see you. How was the flight?"

Then he said, "He is just such a cunt. He hasn't seen Nanna for about a year. The last time they saw each other, they went to a restaurant and she had to pay. The only reason he saw her was to keep in her will. But she's not falling for that. He hardly said a word to her at all during that lunch. Just sat there. He was supposed to pick her up last Christmas to take her around to Brian's place, but the bloody idiot forgot. As usual, he was totally pissed and Brian had to go and get her. You can imagine what that was like."

I stared out the windscreen, looking out into a well-lit road which seemed to float in the darkness. Two days previously, I had been at the Royal Albert Hall seeing Eric Clapton. A few weeks prior to that, I had been gliding up the Nile on a felucca. I was not prepared for the quagmire of domestic trivia the next month was due to bring. Next to me, my brother's vitriolic assessment of our father's character continued unabated. It was as though I had never left the place. My brother seemed to take the attitude that I had not gone anywhere at all. It was as if the last six years had been erased from his memory, as if I had been there yesterday.

"And the silly cunt", he said, "is completely unable to communicate without trying to take the piss out of someone. He's got nothing. Every cent he's ever earnt he's pissed up against the wall. He has one drink, and he's got to dredge up all this shit. I suppose he wrote to you and told you that he was going to become a millionaire?"

My father had in fact done this.

"Well," my brother said, "you can forget that shit."

The avalanche of abuse continued all the way to my brother's house. I felt supine from it.

"Anyway," my brother said, pulling into his driveway, and taking a rapid change of conversation, "what have you got in the way of presents?"

He was delighted to discover that I had got him something. It was mid-December. I intended to give it to him for Christmas.

Inside the house, I was intrigued by the decor. It felt as though I had never seen anything like it before. The walls were a glowing lemon-yellow. Everything seemed bright, unnaturally cheerful. I realised that I was looking at something previously familiar in a new light. I was having the experience of a European.

My sister-in-law emerged from the bedroom wearing a pink night-gown. Her tired smile showed genuine affection. I felt sorry for her as her husband, a thirty-five-year-old man, was prancing around, excitedly saying, "He's got presents. He's got presents. He's got presents."

"Come on," he said, digging at my bags, "out with 'em."

Kay shook her head and said, "For Christ's sake, Wayne, are you going to get him a drink, or what?"

This was the first sensible thing I had heard since I had landed; but Wayne persisted. It was clear that no talking was going to take place until Wayne got his present. I could not believe what I had just seen. Even from him. Even a ten-year-old would have showed greater mature restraint.

He ripped the present open with childlike ruthlessness. It seemed to calm him. He was pleased with his discovery. To use his phraseology, he was a "mad keen West Ham supporter". I had got him an away shirt. He put it on immediately, poured himself a port and then began telling me, in great detail, about the progress the local team had made in the Australian football league.

Listening to this barrage, it became apparent my brother was either bereft of curiosity or was willing himself to take the position that I had not done anything, ever, of any relevance. Eventually, he got on to rugby union. The World Cup had just finished. He assumed that I knew nothing about the game – Perth is not a rugby city – and when I dryly announced that I had been to the World Cup final, I was surprised by his reaction: he seemed to receive this information like a stab in the heart, before dropping the subject completely, allowing his wife the opportunity to ask me some questions about life in England.

During the discussion about the old country, Wayne pointed out that he knew several people, his next-door-neighbours for example, who had emigrated from Britain "because they detested the place". All the people he cited "were so glad to be here – the lifestyle's much better; they all say that. None of them ever want to go back."

It was apparent that anyone living in Britain, who could have been in Australia, needed to have their heads examined. On that note, we went to bed. Lying down, I stared up at the ceiling, wondering how I was going to endure the finicky politics of my splintered family for the next six weeks. I was even surprised at the accuracy of my predictions. From what I had seen so far they were, in fact, even worse than before; but this impression, I was to realise, existed because I had developed so much and they were just the same.

Then I closed my eyes, wondering if I was going to find anyone at all in this town to whom I could speak. I was not hopeful.

* * * * * * * * * *

When I woke up in the morning, I knew that it was time to meet my niece. She was four years old. The experience of meeting children was usually an unfortunate one, as my mysterious emotional disposition was usually interpreted by them as a sign of my repressed hostility towards them. They had a tendency to see me as I had been when I was their age: depressed, anguished, stunned, fraught with astonishment at the cruelty of this world, the emotionally corrupt victim of divorce; and I could see no reason why this situation should be any different from all those others, in which the worried stare of some petrified child reinforced the fact that I was the embodiment of all evil.

I had remained in my bed as long as possible to delay our meeting. When people meet the offspring of their closest relatives they normally rejoice in the occasion. However, they probably respect their closest relatives; I was in a position in which I was about to meet a child whose father was about as stable as strontium-90.

In the room next to me, I could hear the television. Going out to investigate, I saw my niece – a tall slim girl with an elegant neck –

swaying in front of the screen. I looked at my smiling brother who said, "She does this every day."

Emma was singing and dancing to the video of a musical.

"She's obsessed by it," Wayne said, grinning proudly. "She knows every word."

Emma was absolutely transfixed by the screen. My brother's love and pride were clear from the gentle expression on his face - a face usually marked by angered, piercing brown eyes which could stare at you as if all the outrage ever experienced by man was mere indifference in comparison to the savage bitterness of his fiery demeanour. I knew that expression was not going to last. The evening before made it plain to me that Wayne was sliding along a razor's edge. The only psychological experience my brother was incapable of experiencing was indifference. When he was around there was either great joy, scandalised resentment, barbaric insolence or insulting cynicism. The prospect of laid-back, polite pleasantries was absolutely nil. And indifference? I don't think he knew it existed.

"Hey, Emma!" he yelled out. "Look who's here."

Emma spun around and looked at me with a face of crinkled glee. She waved, then resumed her absorption in the musical. Wayne went into the kitchen to continue preparing his breakfast.

I walked over to Emma, feeling obliged to take some interest, and said, "Who do you think I am?"

She smiled up at me and said, "You're Daddie's brother."

"And why don't you know me?"

"'Cos you don't live here."

"Where do I live?" I asked.

"In England," she replied.

"Where's England?" I asked.

"On the other side of the world," she replied.

"What does that mean?" I asked.

"Far away," she replied. "So you can't get to us by car."

I stroked her head and walked off, smiling. In the kitchen, I said, "Apparently I live too far away to get to you by car."

"Gorgeous, hey?" Wayne said, expecting me to agree wholeheartedly.

"She seems very bright", I replied, "and mature."

This was not a lie.

"She thinks", Wayne said, "that she knows everything. She always pretends she understands. It's incredible; even at her age there are things you can't tell her, because she's already got her own idea. She doesn't want to appear ignorant."

This was a trait that ran all the way through our family. I was surprised that my brother was so surprised by this. He said it as though this characteristic of his daughter's was an entirely new phenomenon, disassociated from any psychological proclivity known to man. The inability of parents to see the pitfalls of their children's personalities as products of their own weaknesses was, to me, the greatest and most dangerous achievement of the human ego. I could not possibly recall the number of times I had heard my father say, when discussing the negative aspects of my elder brother, the following cliché, said time and time again with emphatic peremptoriness: "He's just like his bloody mother!" The fact that my elder brother and father were, in virtually every respect, identical seemed, to my father, to be beside the point. I was certain that, over the next six weeks, I was going to hear this comment with unerring frequency.

As I prepared some toast, I began listening to a radio discussion between four articulate men about an aspect of Australian Rules football called handball. I appreciated that Australia was a nation gripped by sport, but this placed things firmly into perspective. Those four men went on and on and on, on prime-time radio, with a clarity and inventiveness normally associated with the dissection of vast issues, as though Australian rules football was the prime and sole reason for any of us existing. It was interesting – I liked the game – but I had been away long enough to appreciate that the intellectual intensity of their debate may have been better used elsewhere. People were given the opportunity to ring up and offer their opinions on the areas covered by the haranguing foursome. This led to some surprisingly sharp exchanges of views. Passions began to run high. One woman was told that she did not have the faintest idea of what she was talking about. Someone else vehemently disputed that handball had improved the game.

"It", this outraged individual said, "has destroyed the high mark."

The fact that this game was elevated to the plateau of significant intellectual debate by the electronic media was symptomatic of an isolated society, determined to detach itself from the real problems of this earth. Had I commented to the producers of this program, and its listeners, that it was more in the common interest to have a two hour debate on environmental or political issues instead of a serious analysis of an insignificant recreation, I, no doubt, would have been met with the grim looks of people convinced that they were beholding an idiot.

On the subject of idiocy, I became witness to more of it when Wayne attempted to persuade Emma to wear a certain article of clothing. It was here that the inevitable trouble began. She wanted to wear a specific dress. He wanted her to wear another. He also wanted her to wear a cardigan. She did not want to wear it. She was an asthma sufferer and Wayne was concerned about her getting an attack.

"No, no, no," she kept screaming out, as the discussion on handball became even more heated.

"Yes!" he blurted out. "Bloody well wear it!"

"No!" she wailed, bursting into tears.

"Okay," Wayne said, "that's it. I've had enough. I don't care less. Get sick. See if I care."

He came storming out of the bedroom with a look of grim resolution. His aggrieved daughter came running after him, naked. She was hysterical.

"No," he said, rushing past me, waving his hands up in the air in a mock gesture of indifference, "I'm not interested. Cry as much as you bloody well like. I don't care. You know better. We all know that."

"Go away," he then said, as she tried to gain his caring attention, bursting with delirious tears, craving love. But he was not interested. The child, naked, a screwed-up mournful face, looked like a victim of war. Her desperate attempts for affectionate recognition became so frustrated that she began stomping her feet into the floor. Deep gulps between high-pitched wails exploded from her twisted mouth when she finally realised that she was not going to receive the benevolence which she so desperately required. This knowledge made her inconsolable. There was nothing I could do. I stood there looking at this as though I were witnessing a tragedy. I longed to be away from this sort of nonsense. I could have been in a Parisian café discussing Impressionism with a beautiful woman, or running my fingers over the glorious depictions of heaven in funeral tombs in Egypt. But here I was looking at this!

I realised my aesthetic and intellectual indulgences, pursued with selfish determination for over a decade, had made me ignorant of what constitutes life for so many. I also realised that my lifestyle, sensible and fulfilling, had given me a repugnance for the constricting trivialities of domestic life. It was incredible, with all the noble experiences available to one on this earth, that human beings, in their droves, made decisions that could lead them into this! But they did – each day – with ruthless naivety, as if building a house with someone would reduce the grand possibilities of existence to insipid trifles.

I felt that the insensitive way my brother had defied his daughter's ambitions was destined to leave a vile scar upon a soul already confused by the meanness of this violent world. The unnecessarily brutish method my brother had employed to exert his authority and the potential repercussions of these actions filled me with an alienation which I had not experienced for twenty-five years. It was that feeling that made you say to yourself: 'I could not allow this to happen to any child of mine.' It seemed so immature, unnecessary, unjustified, useless – these brash explosions of frustrated seriousness that caused such pained reactions in small children. But they were repeated, everywhere, each day, like an incurable disease, without the faintest concern for consequences.

I had tried my utmost to build a life away from them. I felt no need to contribute to this vicious cycle of emotional instability, and I doubted if anyone in my family could perceive how warped and abnormal these experiences were now for me. The scene I was witnessing made me determined to leave my brother's house as quickly as possible. I was in no mood to be the calm eye in a whirlpool of domestic violence. My brother, seemingly incapable of communicating without reverting to puerile gibes, had taken it upon himself to blame everyone else for the limitations of his own life.

As his daughter wailed before him, he screamed out, "Why do we always have to fight? Go away! I'm not interested! Do what you like!" causing such a wave of tumultuous hysteria to run through Emma that she screamed out: "I hate you! I hate you!" before charging out of the room and out of sight.

Wayne glumly attended to doing the dishes while I sat in the lounge-room wondering what to do with myself. I felt imprisoned;

being in the company of someone gripped by prickly silence was uncommon for me. I stared out into the spacious back garden and found myself associating the wide expanses of lawn, the space, with something sterile and desolate. The garden was surrounded by an asbestos fence, a barrier that could induce death. For the first time in years, I was with someone who saw life as entrapment. Psychologically, we had nothing in common.

When he got Emma organised to go shopping and I refused to come he made some sarcastic remark about my 'sociability'. I ignored this and felt a great sense of relief when I heard the front door slam. I knew that Kay would be home from work shortly and this was one of the reasons I had elected to stay. I wanted to talk to her. I wanted to express my bewilderment at Wayne's immaturity; I knew the subject would be of profound interest to her.

When she came home she went into the kitchen, unpacked some bags and said, "Sorry about Wayne: he's a complete bastard."

"He seems", I replied, "to have regressed to the point of no return. I offered him some money before he went shopping to get some food and he grabbed it off me and said, 'Hah, don't often get this out of you!' He's about as pleasant as a full-scale nuclear attack. It's impossible to speak to him without being insulted."

Kay said that this was not surprising "when you look at the company he keeps." She explained that every time they went out with Wayne's friends there was always an undercurrent of derision in the conversation.

"They", she said, "cannot talk to each other without being insulting. I can't possibly explain the shame I felt one night when we went to a barbecue with Ian Cook and Damien Kelly and their wives. It was so puerile. No one could say anything without them taking the piss. It was a real embarrassment for me to discover that I'm married to someone who's so immature. It was one of the worst nights of my life. They niggled each other so badly, eventually the inevitable happened. Cook brought up Wayne's prison sentence and after a scuffle in which dishes were smashed, Wayne charged out, me in tow, obviously screaming, and he hasn't seen Cook since."

On the drive from the airport, I had asked Wayne if he had "seen much of Ian Cook recently" and Wayne had gruffly said "No," and quickly changed the subject.

"He's got so few friends now," Kay continued. "We lost so many because of what Wayne did at the bank. I've tried telling him that it's not all due to his prison sentence either, but the immature way he berates people in conversation. He just doesn't seem to understand this."

She made coffee and sat down with me on the settee in the television room. I told her how I had asked Wayne if he had seen much of a friend of mine around town called Ana Sharrin. Wayne said that the last time he saw Ana was in a service station about a year ago driving a Porsche.

"Not a Lancia?" I had asked.

"No," Wayne had replied, "a Porsche."

"It wasn't a Lancia?" I had persisted.

"No," Wayne had growled, "a Porsche. I think I know a bloody Porsche when I see one."

"You sure it was a Porsche?" I had continued.

"Look," Wayne had snapped, "how many bloody times do I have to tell you? I think I know a fucking Porsche when I see one!"

What had begun as a simple inquiry had led very quickly, as it always seemed to with Wayne, to pathetic acrimony.

"That's typical," Kay said. "He's not going to change either until he changes his friends. This Damien Kelly's unbelievable. There's something bizarre about him. I came home from work one day – Wayne didn't hear me – he was on the phone. I was about to yell out when I heard him say, 'Does she groan very much when you give it to her?' It was Damien Kelly. He was telling Wayne about his sex life with his wife. Imagine that! I was petrified, frozen. I didn't want him to know that I had accidentally overheard. I started thinking: What's he going to say about me? He actually said, 'Kay does that as well.' I was so annoyed, I charged in here and yelled out: 'Wayne! Get off that bloody phone!' You can't imagine the look of surprise on Wayne's face. He said to Kelly, 'Missus's just arrived. Must go', and we had an almighty bloody row."

She looked down at the carpet. I was speechless. Wayne's got a friend who gives him details of his wife's idiosyncrasies in bed! Maybe I wasn't open-minded enough. Was it the thing to do in California these days?

"We haven't", Kay continued, "slept with each other since. How can I? How do I know he's not telling people what I do?"

She took a sip of her coffee and said, "On the day you marry someone, the last thing you expect them to do is tell people about your behaviour in bed. I just can't believe it."

Even I was finding it difficult to believe. I knew that Wayne was capable of most things, but I had thought that he was bright and sensitive enough to draw the line on that most absurd of indiscretions.

"I thought something was bizarre about Kelly well before that, though," Kay remarked. "Wayne thought I was just being paranoid. I used to let the Kellys baby-sit Emma, until one day I walked into their place and found Emma on her knees with one of the Kelly kids sticking a vacuum cleaner end up her bum. I was horrified. There's no way Emma's going into their house again."

Kay's blue eyes sparkled with sensitive astonishment.

"Something happens on television", she said, "and either Wayne'll ring or Kelly will, and they'll have some secretive conversation, usually about some woman on the box that they've just seen. What a way to go on!"

"I know what I would do," I replied.

"What?" she asked.

"Leave him", I replied, "before it's too late."

"Believe me," she said, "I think about it every day. But it's so difficult when you've got a child. It would mean splitting her between her parents. That'd be very traumatic."

"It's", I replied, "going to be very traumatic anyway. If she sees you two fighting all the time, it's going to be murder for her."

"I know, I know," she said, staring past me out into the sunlight which seemed inappropriate in a place like this. "Maybe he might just grow up. We can only live in hope."

She seemed resigned and realistic enough for me to make the following comment: "It's a hope I wouldn't take too seriously."

She smiled with rueful bafflement. It was as though she had once borne a grudge against those forces which had convinced her that it was imperative not to live in sin, to marry without living with someone, to remain virginal, innocent for as long as possible, and then had cast this animosity aside with mature resignation, in the belief that effort could redeem her from the consequences of naive thinking. I felt that there was something courageous and dignified in the way she struggled to overcome the insidious pitfalls of her marriage, and I wondered how unjust it was that someone with maturity and common sense could have fallen for someone so irresponsible and petulant as my brother. But I had seen intelligent women do this everywhere. The fiery glow in an exciting man's eye could burn away any consideration of the negative aspects of character. It was a problem that no amount of upbringing or experience seemed to change.

Then we heard the front door being opened. We were expecting my other brother to make an appearance. He walked in with a big smile on his still youthful face. It had been about seven years since I had last seen him. He seemed as calm and sensible and relaxed as ever.

"Wayne still being a complete idiot?" he asked, with flippant accuracy.

"What do you think?" I replied, shaking his hand.

He was bulky, but not fat and exuded a quality of unruffled affability, the absolute opposite of his eldest brother. He began rolling himself a cigarette, saying, "My poor lungs haven't had any nicotine for at least five minutes."

This was his only vice. Within a few minutes I was hearing about his sporting career.

"Got sucked into bloody playing football last year," he said. "Never do that again. Australian Rules football has got to be the most stupid game on earth. It was murder. All the umpires in this competition seemed to get off on the sight of violence."

Kay and I began giggling.

"It was incredible," he continued. "I actually won the Fairest and Best, playing at fullback. Fullback - can you believe it? Not surprising really; when you play fullback in a team that has an average of twenty-five goals kicked against it each game you do find yourself in the play a bit. Either that or you're continually doing this."

He then bent his head back and looked up at the ceiling; then he quipped, "I had to get my neck rubbed at the end of each game."

After we told him about Wayne's latest antics, he made no apologies for his escapes as a teenager. He would disappear out the back door and go down the road to a friend's house who had a family to whom he could relate. He did so to escape from the "immature turmoils" of his own home. My grandmother was constantly having to ring up to find out where he was. The fact that he now lived in the country was because his friend's family were farmers. He had found refuge in the country; I had gone further afield, to the other side of the world.

Our descriptions of escapism seemed to comfort Kay, who, although she could rationalise it intellectually, still required some justification for the way she felt. I perceived that she did not want to be regarded as someone acting unreasonably by leaving her husband. The tales of abscondment Mark and I produced helped her to feel better about her own escapist feelings. They were also a revelation to her, for she was now able to link our experiences in childhood to our present predicaments. She could now see that, in Mark's case particularly, a desire to retreat from emotional sterility and fractious immaturity in adolescence had led to a vocation in life. In my case, it had created a wanderer keen to find fulfilment across the oceans. She could now see why I was a photo-journalist and why Mark was a farmer.

She said that she found it a tragic revelation, however, that people's ambitions could be bred from negative experiences and not from benevolent nurturing; but the real tragedy, I told her, "occurred when there was no adaptability - like Wayne; when someone meets these appalling experiences, that you cannot do anything about, headlong, like a wild bull - that's the real tragedy.

"I can imagine", I added, "that Wayne'll still be smashing his head into every solid object possible in thirty years' time, just because someone's upset him. The justified outrage he experienced as a young child, he keeps wishing to repeat. He doesn't have the self-awareness to break this vicious cycle because he's got such a deep-seated mistrust of academic thinking. And you know where he gets that from, don't you?"

We were now outside, under a pergola, and the pencils of shade ran across Kay's face, rectangles of light and dark, which enhanced the sad beauty of her smile, as she looked up at me and said, "Absolutely."

Mark chuckled at this reference to our father; then he brought up the subject of Wayne's kleptomania. This was in response to a remark I made about my fears concerning the cash I had left in the guest room.

"Wayne wouldn't do that," Kay said, after I implied that Wayne would be tempted to steal it.

"Oh yes he would," Mark replied.

Kay was shocked when Mark told her how Wayne had stolen so much money from us when we were kids that we had to hide it from him by placing it in plastic bags and putting it behind pictures hung on the wall. Even then he found it. He had no scruples at all. He showed all the brash hedonism of a drug addict.

Kay shook her head and mumbled, "Oh God," then she sombrely remarked that Wayne had recently lost his temper so badly (over "some trifle") that he had thrown a curry dinner into the Venetian blinds.

"I know", Kay said, with real fear in her eyes, "that this sort of behaviour usually pre-empts something infinitely worse."

I was not conscious, until that moment, that the build-up to domestic violence formed a set pattern, but even I found it difficult to imagine Wayne hitting his wife.

"If that happened", Kay said, "that would be it immediately. No going back. It would be over. I couldn't live with anyone who did that."

The pertinacious resolve in her eyes signalled to me the gravity of her belief. It was imperative in life to have these immovable parameters; otherwise, what would you be able to achieve? She had drawn up in her mind a yardstick of certainty amidst the confusion and I was openly prepared to admit that her yardstick was considerably more tolerant than mine.

"Your tolerance," I said, "I have to admit, is astonishing, but, then again, I've already experienced so much nonsense in my life that I'm not prepared to be subjected to another nanosecond of it. And I don't think Mark is either."

"No way," Mark said, "not for me."

* * * * * * * * * * *

I was eating a bowl of Coco Pops when Wayne and Emma returned. Emma saw me eating the breakfast cereal and wanted to try it. She wedged herself between my legs. I handed her single pellets of crunchy, chocolate-coated rice. We were fascinated with each other. She had an expression of naughty intrigue on her tiny face. I was captivated by the minuscule size of her hands and features. It was charming watching her carefully reach into the bowl to retrieve the pellets that she placed between her perfect little teeth and crushed.

She giggled each time she crushed one; I soothed her by swaying her with my legs. Her small, thin lips were cherry red, almost unnaturally so. Her round brown eyes, deep and penetrating like her father's, seemed disproportionately large for the size of her head. Children enjoy eating more when it involves play, but this seemed a new experience for her – the idea that eating could involve sensuality. A contradictory feeling – something like demulcent mendacity – overcame me, for I could see that she felt there existed no viciousness in my heart. The fascinated gleam in her eyes made me feel as though she thought that I was spiteless; she was young enough to assume that I had her best interests at heart – an assumption to which I was unaccustomed – and when I began placing the pellets in her mouth her body relaxed, seemed to flop between my legs, as she gave herself up to this new condition of peaceful docility, as if this revelation that sensuous pleasure could exist without fierce action had befallen her like a hypnotic, perspicacious dream.

And a revelation it was for me too. I realised that parenthood involves the rediscovery of your own lost experiences through observation of their repetition in your offspring. Something intimate and soothing like this, at a time when joy meant action, must have also floated into my life as well. But when? And with whom? From time to time, I saw images of a day, when I was about Emma's age, of being given a box full of fluffy yellow chicks: it was a sight that stopped the frenetic machinations of unbridled play and induced a new sensation, which my niece was currently experiencing, of languorous, aesthetic appreciation.

Unfortunately, her father was not having the same experience. Mark had begun watching English football on television, and Wayne, on his way out to go to work – he managed a bottle shop – said to me, "Are there still problems with hooligans in England?"

"Not now", I replied, feeling as though I had to make a special effort to be agreeable, "the police have introduced such a draconian regime."

"Draconian!" he gasped. "Christ, all I wanted to know was yes or no."

That was it. The time for fire had arrived.

"Yes," I said, "draconian, you pathetic moron. As I've discovered you can't understand English, in future I'll try and keep things simple for you. How about grunts? Do you think you'll be able to understand them?"

"You read too many books," he retorted.

To this pitiful response, he added, "Bloody intellectuals. What books have you been reading lately, anyway?"

"I know the book I should have read," I said, as he went out the door. "It's called *How to Resist the Temptation of Pissing All Over an Immature Loser Whose Life is a Mess.*"

Wayne disappeared as Mark said, "Together again after six years, and, as usual, they fight."

"I'm going to Brian's," I said to Kay. "I can't take this any longer. I didn't come here for this. I haven't experienced anything as ridiculous as this for years. I'm sorry, Kay, but it's pointless my staying here. You've got my deepest sympathy."

"I don't blame you," she replied. "I'm not sure I can put up with it any longer myself."

Emma looked at us all, dumbfounded.

* * * * * * * * * * *

It was time to leave and see the place I had left behind. Mark and I had arranged to see our grandmother. I did not know what to expect, other than an experience I had never had before. I was keen to discover what tricks memory had played in my now limited perception of a place once so familiar, and, when we reversed out of the driveway, the first sensations I experienced were those of space and flatness. Everything was only one storey high, the streets, straight and smooth, were devoid of people, and the cloudless sky was royal blue.

Beneath it, clay-tiled roofs in blue- and orange-lined streets of green. One could be forgiven for feeling that we were driving through a park, interspersed with low-ceilinged bungalows surrounded by lawn, gum trees, thick, tall bushes splashed red, and those unusual blue roofs, that I, six years thence, had forgotten existed.

This tampering with memory gave birth to a surreal feeling of childhood discovery. The old was now new. I found that memory incorporates language. I discovered that memory is effectively the semantics of speech. What I remembered to be high was, in fact, low. Low was now really low. Density had become spacious. Spacious was like a desert.

At one point, we drove past some flat-roofed monoliths with large dark windows and white walls. Two houses, side-by-side, were perched on a small hill overlooking the ocean. I was appalled by the tastelessness that had allowed those two structures to come into existence. They were roughly in the shape of hexagons and were devoid of any of the delicacy that characterises more pleasing residential architecture. I knew that many people in this city would look upon those houses as symbols of wealth; but wealth now had a new meaning for me. It meant style, overwhelming, sumptuous abundance, unrestricted opulence, the feeling that all one's wildest imaginings could be brought to fruition by the wanton and careless dispensation of piles of easily-acquired cash, but that had dispensed with an appreciation of finery which can only be brought about by centuries and centuries of refined spending.

When I think about wealth these days, I think of the great palaces that dot the English countryside not these ridiculous dolls' houses bereft of soul and history. But the environment was exceptionally pleasant. Almost in a vacuous sterile way. Apart from the monoliths, no two houses were exactly the same. This seemed to create a pretension of individuality amidst a suburbia whose desolate decency produced a worrying homogeneity of values and, therefore, emotions.

I knew that my brother, sitting next to me, in many ways was the embodiment of the place: law-abiding, respectable, fair, honest, humorous, would not have the faintest appreciation of or sensitivity towards the esoteric beguilements currently running through my mind. And I did not care. I expected it. How can anyone expect to find emotional complexity in a place anaesthetised from old, ludicrous conflicts, by sameness, by large patches of green lawn whose upkeep results in absurd time-wasting, expenditure and concern? It was a fact that the sociological achievements of this place were a bane to imagination and enterprise. In this place, it was almost against the law to be introspective or depressed. But it was of no concern to me now. Fate had placed me in a position to see a world I knew inside out from the outside. I was looking at it like a European would, and I was transfixed by the vegetation, the colours, the lines of pleasant houses, and by the insular absorption of the place in its own materialistic ideals.

Everywhere was green, usually splashed with colour: white against green, flushes of red against green, palm trees rising out of clumps of green, different shades of green, silvery-white fountains of water sprinkling dark green, green upon green, green golf courses, and green tennis courts, with green bushes embedded in sand dunes held together by green, in an environment of greenery. A lot of the unique vegetation I saw I had forgotten existed. A blackboy, whose gnarled, rising stem was topped by burnt black, seemed covered by the perfect wig of green; small fern trees, growing close to the ground, brought back memories of their unique capacities to hide tennis and cricket balls. Bottle brushes lay like discarded hand grenades on patch after patch of immaculately-kept lawn. I felt as though I was in a great garden; I dreaded to consider all the toil and time and energy that had been dispensed here maintaining this veneer of environmental respectability. If only a fraction of it had been diverted to the creation of more complex things, great jazz musicians or even sophisticated industrialists may have emerged from this opulent wilderness. But I knew who was there.

'If', I thought to myself, 'one of these people had devoted as much of their time to playing the trumpet as they did to their gardens, this joint could have produced Louis Armstrong.'

This was a thought I could not convey to my younger brother, or, in fact, to virtually every other individual who lived in this place. Gardening, although it may be enhancing making something grow, gets in the way of personal growth. I had seen intelligent human beings here reduced to petulance by the thought of someone else's leaves blowing across their precious gardens. The decaying leaves were like new and vile ideas drifting, unwanted, across the green symbols of their materialistic success. I had witnessed the mind-boggling sight of people devoting their weekends to depositing yellow sand on their lawns, and when I considered the absurdity of this now a feeling of pity enveloped me, contemplating the talents wasted or departed that this country now so desperately needs.

Mark pulled the car over to go to a public toilet. The car park overlooked the ocean. I got out of the car and stood looking at the sea. This gave me the opportunity to enhance the experience I was having – the experience of seeing old things with a fresh perspective – for I was amazed by the wonderful colour combinations, the smells, the sounds that befell me.

In the foreground bushes of different shades of brown and green contained chirping cicadas. I had actually forgotten of the existence of these creatures – I had been away for so long – and, when I approached them, the nostalgia of childhood enveloped me as I heard their rhythms slow down, then speed up again as I backed away. The colours were richer than any I had seen for years. The sky was unnaturally blue: puffy globules of snow – the clouds – were painted upon it; and, beneath this dramatic contrast of colours, the sea, so imbued by colour itself – green, blue, deep blue, white-green – seemed like a sheet of taffeta upon which waves broke in lines of swirling cream. White seagulls flickered above the ocean, whose outer rim, a smooth, inviting horizon, divided two vast shades of blue in an immensity of water and sky, which created a beauty so extreme that it appeared artificial, like an enhancement of nature, a painting or an unblemished tapestry hung like a sheet, blocking out the rest of this desperate and scheming world.

Upon the water, in an area darkened by reef, three surfers in black wetsuits vied for the thrill of riding waves whose breaking came to me like a crackle of distant flames, followed by a sharp crack as the sheets of painted glass broke into rolling foam, metres from the shore. This was a place born to produce people obsessed by physical exhilaration, and, with envy, I observed the absorption that those three young men showed for a task which enabled them to eradicate all consideration of the unfortunate realities of life. In their minds, in this instant, there would be no thoughts of loneliness, of inadequacies, of difficult intellectual pursuits, of the need to solve the complex dilemma of professional and economic security; they were lost in this immensity, were engulfed by it, as though anything outside its picturesque tranquillity was an irrelevant chaos. I could have walked through the bushes and down on to the beach wearing a pin-striped suit clutching a briefcase and my existence would have appeared about as sensible to them as the sight of greyhounds flying around a track did to me.

Back in the car, we had now entered the older suburbs. Within them there existed residential architecture the equal to anything I had seen anywhere in the world. The sloping iron roofs of verandahs were held up by ornately-carved timber posts. Stained-glass, like gems encrusted into doors, were visible through painted wrought-iron gates. Weeping willows overhung the frilly eaves of slanting roofs.

Splashes of dazzling bougainvillaea seemed to ignite in front of pastel-coloured walls. Each house seemed to have a unique letterbox, as if they too were status symbols, or symbols of pride. Was it possible here that your entire attitude to life could be judged by the things which you did not possess? And should have? This was entirely possible: Perth was one of the worst places in the world to be if you wanted to achieve something difficult and unusual - there was very little sympathy for those who did not achieve some sort of immediate economic success. The idea of driving an old beaten-up car and living in relative squalor, sacrificing your time to the pursuit of some outlandish artistic or scientific goal, almost certainly meant that you were a pretentious, dreamy, nonsensical, irresponsible fool. The simple solution was just to leave.

Mark decided, as he had not been in Perth for a while himself, that we should go for a drive through some of the premier suburbs. He was keen to show me a house which had been built prior to my departure. It was owned by a mining magnate, who, two months previously, had died. The mining magnate had discovered vast tracts of iron ore in the north-west of Western Australia and had, at one stage, suggested that nuclear weapons be used to speed up excavation work on large-scale civil engineering and mining projects. His consideration for the environment was on a par with his taste in architecture. The pile with which he had scarred the face of the earth possessed a garish hideousness, the likes of which were unparalleled in the history of modern residential construction. Spanish arches and mock Ionic columns proliferated in an excessively rough sea of unnecessarily salient bay windows. It was the sort of place you build to take the piss out of Hollywood - who knows? maybe the guy had a sense of humour - but one thing was certain: I knew that there would be several people here who would look with pride at that misuse of money and feel that that was what could be achieved here, right here, in the State of Excitement.

The rest of the area was magnificent. Every blade of finely-cut lawn looked as though it had been polished. Pot plants hung from the eaves of spacious timber verandahs. Clusters of boats sat on the blue waters of the river. High brick fences ensured the privacy which created the illusion that everyone was afraid to step out into the blazing sun. Everyone was probably down at the beach or playing tennis.

Mark then decided that a little drive past our old school would be appropriate on this day of luminous nostalgia.

He drove as slowly as he possibly could past the playing fields on which I had been bullied, had tried to impress the girls with miraculous sporting feats, and had been about as knowledgeable of this world as a two-month-old chimpanzee suffering from dendrite failure.

"Fucking glad", Mark said, "to be away from there."

His education had been so different from mine. While I was studying calculus and trigonometry, he was learning how to drive tractors and build fences and shear sheep. We were poles apart – aesthetically and practically – I could hardly tie a knot – but we shared a genuine enthusiasm for warm interaction and passivity. We also deplored violence. Particularly towards children. I had not met his yet, but I knew they were receiving the kind, loving, witty attention of which we as young children had been deprived. He was sensible enough to realise that the forces that had conspired to infuse him with escapist feelings should never be allowed to influence the thinking of his children. He was determined to make sure that the nonsense which had enflamed his early years should go no further.

"Anyone", he said, with a rueful growl, "who wants to get pissed and fight, I don't want to know."

I was quite impressed by this pronouncement, for I detested the glorification of violence. I had heard too many people talk, with a kind of amused pride, about the prickly temperaments of their associates, as though this behaviour represented something positive – like individuality or strength of character.

We went down a street named after a village in Scotland. On that street, when I was at school, I knew a family whose name was also derived from that of a Scottish village. The house this family had occupied possessed a dubious significance: it was the place where all those in my year at school whom I wished to befriend congregated for informal, alcoholic, marijuana-smoking gatherings. I was not popular but they were sociable enough not to slam the door in my face when I invited myself around; however, it was clear that my presence was barely tolerated, and when I saw that house of ill-repute, that symbol of adolescent insecurity, I chuckled, glad that such problems were now largely in the past and that, if I ever met any of those people again, it would be I who would be striking fear in them and certainly not the other way around.

Mark turned his car into our grandmother's driveway; the house looked smaller and lower than I had remembered it. But that applied to everything. As the car bobbled down the quaint, lumpy driveway, I saw the two giant gum trees rising above the house – the ones that had caused so many leaves to fall; then I realised how little I had known about this world the last time I had seen those trees.

However, there would be still those, I knew, who would say: "He hasn't changed."

* * * * * * * * * *

My grandmother may have been one of them, but I was not worried about that. I was just relieved that her hair was still snow-white and that her eyes had retained that steely, penetrative sparkle which, as a young child, had sent shock waves of trepidation through me, a soul already in turmoil after the spiteful divorce of my warring parents. I had been concerned about seeing a haggard old woman – a withered remnant of the woman I once knew. But that was not the case. She could still move with some agility and the first thing she said to me, as always, was: "You look terrible."

I always looked "terrible". Ever since I was about fifteen I had looked "terrible". I was more concerned about how I felt and that, on the whole, had been terrible. But, I now realised, it was not as terrible as she must have felt for the majority of her adult life.

She had outlived two husbands by the time she was forty-five. The second, who died three months before I was born, had gone into hospital to have a simple ear operation. The anaesthetist had delivered the wrong dose. They told her over the phone that "something bad" had happened and that she should "get to the hospital as quickly as possible". I could only guess, through the stoic façade which hid a soft core, what sort of devastation that must have caused. Her first husband, after making some shrewd real estate deals involving the sub-division of prime land, was struck down by tuberculosis at the age of forty-four. Husband number two had revolutionised photo-finish photographic techniques for horse racing and had taken beautiful portraits of all of Perth's leading luminaries before fate robbed my grandmother of a man whose ability with a camera was clearly unlimited.

I too had been robbed of the opportunity of learning from this man; but the real consequence of his death was that I would never be able to get to know the woman who had brought me up. There were occasions, as now, when the humourless anguish of her demeanour would be swept aside to reveal a sweet, vulnerable, giggly, uncharacteristically flippant creature unburdened by the savage indictments of fate. But that was rare. I had seen this state of mind in her on possibly five occasions in twenty years. This one was brought about by her charming great-granddaughter – Mark's daughter, a chubby, fresh-faced sweetie – trying to cling to her ankles.

"Dadda, dadda," she waved, gleefully, on seeing Mark.

Mark's daughter smiled with felicitous diffidence and shrugged her shoulders shyly when Mark told her who I was. She was too young to attach any significance to this and quickly diverted her attention again to the task of attempting to scale my grandmother's legs. Mark grabbed her and gave her some toys to play with; this led to my grandmother's normal expression returning – a distant, weary, pained stare, dominated by iridescent-blue eyes which, apart from the deaths of two husbands, had seen the fiery divorces of her two sons, the Depression, the fear on the faces of those petrified by the possibility of Japanese invasion, the seedy deaths of several friends, political corruption and the slow, strange, manic, delirious demise of her mother from Alzheimer's disease.

But that was really only the tip of the iceberg. In an age when women were supposed to stay at home she had taken over her second husband's photography practice while bringing up the three children her eldest son had dumped on her, as he chased women and nearly drank himself to death. If only a mere fraction of her loyalty and sense of stoic responsibility had been transferred into gregariousness, she would have been one the most sociable people on earth.

I watched her looking at her great-granddaughter with a resigned countenance; the contrast between her expression and that of Hannah's, whose face was marked with innocent wonder, brought home to me the demeanours of age and youth, of introspection and outwardness. Both were on the threshold of going on into new states – one death, the other life – and I, with the benefits of both youth and experience, wondered if any envy filled my grandmother's heart as she stared at someone so lively and young, someone without regrets, who was impervious to bad decisions and who enjoyed the emotional fulfilment my grandmother must have missed.

On the verandah a few minutes later, where we sat to take in some air, I got the answer.

"I can't stand the thought," my grandmother said, "of living past ninety. Why get any older than that? I'm quite looking forward to dying."

I was too young to appreciate anyone saying this. This, I initially felt, was the pronouncement of someone who had given up. It was a way of thinking that was anathema to my youthful disposition, which demanded a future littered with wondrous things. No one, I thought, in my inexperienced arrogance, had the right to treat the miracle of life like this. Not in front of me; not in front of someone determined to believe that life held such grandiloquent possibilities. I was in love with the smell of it; I swam in its bouquet. I heard rainbows vibrating in the choir of its sunlit cathedral. I was confused; surely, life did not finish like this? Surely, any normally-adjusted human being clung to it with ferocious tenacity in the hope that some splendour, like happiness, would come flooding into it?

"I'm too tired these days," she said, as the wind swayed the vegetation that surrounded her house, surrounding it with a colourful wildness of red, white, purple and blue against green. "I spend half an hour in the garden and then I have to lie down for three hours. I've really had enough."

It seemed like a crime for someone to take this attitude towards their own existence; but it had to be faced. If your body made it difficult for you to achieve anything and your life had been devoid of intellectual pursuits, then death may have been the winged Epicurean our imaginations wished it to be. I had never been in the presence of anyone before so blasé about dying; but was she indifferent to non-existence? That was a totally different question.

"Oh sometimes", she said, with a refreshingly ironic carelessness, "you think it's impossible. Maybe there's an angel looking after me. Sometimes I even feel immortal. There's so much we don't know."

When she spoke, she looked straight ahead upon a scene whose every detail must have been indelibly painted upon her mind. She had lived in this house for fifty years. It was the first house in the area. She and her first husband had built the place in the forest of eucalyptus now long departed. They had toiled for the privilege of not being able to afford the luxury of going out, had fought over political issues and made love with the windows open to the sounds of the now vanquished trees. Who knows what memories and sentiments lurked in every square inch of turf she called home? She had lived there much longer than I had been alive. How could I possibly imagine what the sight of any one of those bricks must have meant? She could probably recount conversations and incidents of universal significance just by looking at a certain patch of carpet, while I had no such attachments to anything, was a wanderer, a bohemian of spurious respectability, whose indulgences and whims had acquired, in my consciousness, a significance well out of proportion to anything that had occurred here, in my past.

"In England", I said, "I saw dead people for the first time. One moment someone's alive, then they're dead. All that consciousness must go somewhere."

"If it does", she replied, "and I live again, I hope it makes sure that my first son is a little better."

She looked past me towards the rose garden over a brownish lawn. The lawn looked unnaturally worn. Red, white and apricot roses bobbed in the afternoon breeze and, beyond them, a line of trees separated her property from the road. Past the trees, Jeremy's mother's house was surrounded by red driveways, an array of different vegetation and patches of lawn; various shades of green and brown coloured the grass and the sound of the wind was ever-present, like falling water, due to the abundance of leaves. I felt as though the place had a tardiness to it that did not match my recollection of its pristineness. A sort of luminous weariness, made clearer by the sunlight and the paucity of movement, enveloped the area, as though change were impossible, or painful, or unnecessary. I dreaded to think what excitement might do to a place like this. Everything seemed to be in a state of abeyant domesticity, slowly withering, as if there had been an invasion by some new and audacious principle into a sea of rigid values. I felt disorientated. The light was surreal. I had spent fifteen years in this place and it was as foreign to me as the day I was born.

"He", she said, without malice, with the objectivity of refined consideration, "is out of my will. He complained about it. Said he would contest it in court, but he's got no chance. Came storming in here one day saying he'd taken legal advice. I didn't pay any attention at all. Went straight over my head."

The fact that she did not appear to be even remotely interested in my life did not concern me. When I thought of the reasons anyone returns to the place of their childhood, it has nothing to do with impressing anyone with worldliness. A sense of duty to your family perhaps; and certainly a curiosity to discover if some pertinent revelation about yourself can be found in the obscure memories cast up by intense recollection; but, above all, it is a process that allows you to measure change – the yardstick by which you can determine a phenomenon which, in normal circumstances, occurs too stealthily to allow one the opportunity to see it vividly, like a supernova in the breathless sea of stars.

I wondered what supernovas had come into my grandmother's life; I knew, however, that there was one which could not: it would never, in the full stretch of eternity, enter her thinking that she may have played some significant part in producing someone so vile as my father. Experience, usually a great shaper of changes in thinking, is largely ineffectual against inbred delusions and cherished hopes. I had felt for years that my grandmother thought that she was remarkable because of her fierce integrity. Nothing could dent the marble obelisk of my grandmother's egoism. The same characteristic denuded pertinent self-analysis in my father, who was detestable to my grandmother because of his hypocritical disloyalty (when my father was distraught he expected loyalty of the sort he is now not prepared to give to his eldest son, whom my grandmother adores) and abrasive bitterness, a quality she displayed to me in abundance. The venality of my father, therefore, makes him dislikeable to his incorruptible mother, while his most disagreeable characteristic lies within her like a prickly seed. In short, he lacks, completely, her finest virtue whilst being a sordid reminder of her worst weakness. How can two people with that sort of association expect to get along?

My grandmother's philosophical stance crumbled a bit when she said, "He makes no effort, and that's what I can't stand. He can't really accuse me of that, can he?"

I smiled. This was her way of informing me that, at least, she had one positive quality. But he had a few as well. His caustic wit, usually savage, was legendary. He was insulting, brash, often immature, sarcastic, impertinent, disrespectful, occasionally crude, brutally insensitive to esoteric ideals, abusive, insolent, mendacious, thieving and bad-tempered – a lot of which he got from his mother – but he was never dull. To say that he was competitive would be putting it mildly: one day when I was living with him he came home with cuts on his face, saying, proudly, that he had "just put three young bastards in hospital." He was overjoyed by this. Someone had driven his car into his and then had tried to flee. My father chased them, no doubt full of the spirit of justified indignation, and had caught them in the driveway of their home. In the ensuing mêlée, heads were punched, headlocks applied, girlfriends terrified, cars kicked and, finally, the licence number of the offending vehicle taken. As my father related the tale to me an hour after the event, I thought to myself that this violent capturing of the licence number represented something more than just the protection of a small financial interest within the stormy confines of his competitive imagination. His victory acquired the grandiose dimensions of a clear and refined sentiment, rising above the seedy trivialities of human affairs. He was clearly separated from the passive, unadventurous milieu, incapable of taking the law into their own hands.

Remembering this, I then thought it ironic that my grandmother, responsible in the extreme in most instances, was incapable of accepting any responsibility for these aggressive acts by her eldest son. But there was nothing to be gained by pressing this point. Even in her now acquiescent state of philosophical abandonment, it was pointless, and harshly intrusive, getting her to admit something that was painfully obvious to me; she had experienced enough anguish in her life. Some peace was what she deserved and, if such a place as heaven exists, then I knew she warranted a place there as much as any. No one could doubt her contribution: in a century in which women had dragged themselves off the floor to find something pertaining to equality, their struggle had meant that someone like me – self-indulgent, autonomous, ambitious – could, within reason, virtually do whatever they liked. I would probably never understand the sacrifice.

Possibly my younger brother, who emerged with his sleeping daughter in his arms, could. Hannah's hair, in fresh blonde sheets, fell down her back; her limbs, like putty, flopped down my brother's body and her face was buried into her father's neck.

"I think", he said, "it's time to go."

"Yes, yes," my grandmother replied. "She needs a long sleep."

It was clear also that my grandmother did as well: the sleep of ages, the sleep from which no one is spared and from which no one ever wakes. It was heartening, in a bizarre way, to see someone feel that death was peace, was a release from toil into a realm in which no decisions would have to be made, where no work would have to be done and where the conscience was free from nagging responsibilities and loyalties which, even in the purest, are not fulfilled without some regret or anguish or care.

On the way to the car, I was accused of not eating enough meat. My diet in London was obviously "appalling". I giggled when I told her that the proprietor of Quo Vadis, one of the finest restaurants in the West End, where I went frequently, would be "disgusted by this absurd accusation."

Mark, never incapable of perceiving humour, laughed uproariously.

"I can't imagine", I said, "what the chef would do to you if he heard what you just said."

Dryly, my grandmother replied, "He would probably tell me to tell you to eat more meat."

In the car, I told her that I would ring her in a few days. I intended to go around there with Brian. She said that she would prepare a decent lunch, "involving meat."

"Good," I said, as Mark started the car. "Until we meet again."

This caused a flicker of a smile to rush across a weathered face which had seen more storms than I wished to perceive. She could be counted on in a crisis; and, as the car reversed up the driveway, I watched her ambling languidly across a lawn that she had fought to maintain for half a century. The fight to upkeep a garden she had nurtured for decades was really, in a deeper sense, the struggle to maintain dignity; and hers was gargantuan. It imparted to her a detestation of laziness and ineptitude. Her fierce independence made her fearful of the stagnation of old age and this was why she did not wish to live much longer. She detested the idea of being a burden to anyone and this, I felt, would cause her, selflessly, when the time was right, so that money was not unnecessarily wasted maintaining a crippled life – money that could be better used cementing a future for her great-grandchildren – to take her own life.

And she would make it look natural too.

* * * * * * * * * *

We travelled along a road I had travelled along many many times before, but never in this frame of mind. The wind blew with strong but languid grace through the crying swathe of vegetation and seemed to add something like experience or self-awareness to the swishing intonation of its ageless voice. I had seen those afternoon winds on countless occasions rush in and bring to life the sleeping trees and turn the blue dish of the water into a bowl of agitated cream and make the sands on the beaches dance upon the emptied white floor of a shore left bare by this force that had brought opposing civilisations together, and had turned everything towards the east, had capsized yachts on the howling river and had transformed the fuming acquiescence of day into a blast of sands and whistling leaves. I had seen it churn oceans and uproot huge gums and I had witnessed the effects it had wrought by bringing new ideas from Europe into the oldest place on earth; but those things were familiar. This was new - a melancholic, foreboding concentration on the past. I felt, for the first time in my life, truly nostalgic, on the surreal discovery of lost innocence: street names came back to me. It was amusing to think how ignorant I had been the last time I had walked down some of those streets. I now saw something ethereal in them, something previously unrecognisable, like history, a sense of desperate toil behind the respectable façades of detached houses and pretty gardens. I now saw drama beneath the pristine façade, for it was the first time in my life that each perception evoked the past. Houses into which I had been invited caused associations to form of old friendships, of lost causes with women, of delusions, and indiscretions. I was driving through my past; it was unreal, dream-like; revelations my mind tried to suppress came at me as a mixture of pain and pleasure, the wind crying out beneath silk-velvet blue. Coruscations of light from this azure blaze from above gleamed with the weariness of age and with the ebullience of youth upon the chrome bars of unmarked, resplendent cars and within the fresh glass of windows studded into colourful properties. Experience gave me the curiosity I had lacked when last here. The thrill of rediscovery, the pleasure of progressing from that time when this was all I knew of the world, blew through me like a breathless cry, like a gasp, a gasp of pain and wonderment; and, through this gasping, the sunlight sang like angels.

I had spent twenty-five years here, trying to grow up, and now I felt like a foreigner. It was exciting and sad - surreal - to be an outsider in a place once so recognisable. The opportunity to see a familiar place for the first time can also be despairing. It would have been so much easier had I been able to fit into this soporific wealth, but that was not my destiny. The missed pleasures that quirk of fate would have brought mixed with the euphoria of knowing that I had learnt so much by being away. It was a clash of sensations which the flashing wind, that flowed and ebbed and streamed, epitomised with its pitch of shrill lassitude. Its cutting song played with a detached wildness over the gardens of mortals who had assumed an aspect of permanence against its desire for change. I had just floated with it into places where volcanoes erupted, where great sporting events take place, where strange cultures exist in the sparkling gloom of ancient forests; I had drifted with it down murky rivers and over difficult peaks, into villages where Europeans had never been before, had been swept up by the music of its raw, peripatetic passion, and now I was finding it uncomfortable to be within the plush confines of so much uneventful suburbia. What really happens here? Did it actually mean anything? Was anyone's life here going to be of any long-term significance to humanity? It seemed extremely unlikely.

These were questions I felt that I should not ask my brother, who turned the car on to a highway which linked the suburb of my youth with the ocean. It was a busy thoroughfare, straight and undulating, upon which I had ridden on countless occasions; but never in this light - a light from a sun that reigned like a king over the lives of courtiers of the beach - and the realisation that the tennis court's proclivity to remain off the streets symbolised the necessity this city placed on ownership of the car. Without one you were lost, almost ostracised. The streets here were not places where people lived and breathed, but rather functional appendages to a transport system designed to shift this mass of sun-drenched people with as much independent isolation as possible. And shift them it did, with the privacy not accorded to those on foot. Walking was considered an almost absurd activity, the preoccupation of eccentric failures, a fact most Europeans would find remarkable. Walking symbolised poverty, modest means, a condition frowned upon by this fun-seeking populace whose lives were intricately woven around the successful combustion of petroleum liquid fuels in the pursuit of constant pleasure.

I was determined to take in as much information as possible. It was impossible not to: everything breathed memory, recollection, inertia, change, hope, futility, staidness; a feeling of separation from this place had come into my thinking and I knew that I would meet those whose attachment to their upbringings was so strong that the feelings I was currently experiencing would appear to them as the nebulous vagaries of a ludicrous dreamer, warped by the esoteric inanities of being away for so long, of being on the road, of having the audacity to see some other ideal.

The vegetation continued to intrigue me. White-trunked gum trees had deep-green crowns; roses bloomed in the front gardens of low houses. Huge red flowers sat in large green bushes like jewels encrusted in mounds of emerald. The purple of jacaranda lay around the lawn of a house whose roof was a maze of gargoyles and slanting ceilings. Green parrots sat on the power lines. Nothing animate graced the empty streets. It was a world of opulent abeyance, through which this teeming wind of spiritual frustration rushed, as if trying to escape the luminous melancholy of the place it had blown through for an eternity.

Then we went down a street where I had lived. I knew the exact whereabouts of the house, but could not visualise its existence. I had lived in that house eleven years ago for twelve months and had no recollection of its exterior. The interior was as clear as the day I had left it; however, its exterior was now an absolute mystery to me. I must have seen it a thousand times, but had no recollection of it at all. It had been obliterated from my mind by a barrage of pressures and experiences and when I saw the place in which I must have lived, it was as though I were seeing it for the first time. If I had been given a photograph of the front of that house, no amount of persuasion could have convinced me that I had lived there. In the days I lived in that house, a decade ago, I was certain that my memory was infallible. I was convinced that I could remember every minute detail, every face, every experience: what naivety! It may have been true at one stage, but the memory that you can remember everything lingers on long after the reality quietly dawns.

Around the corner from this house was a shop. After university one day I had gone in there to buy a loaf of bread. An old woman was in the shop. She had looked at me with a gleam of cheerful melancholy in her eyes and said, "You look like my two sons. They had hair just like you. They were both killed in Vietnam."

I was speechless before her smiling face. What was I supposed to say to this?

"Really?" I had garbled.

"You have a good life now," she had then said, happily, behind a mounting torrent of tears, as she went out the door.

With a kind of stoic emptiness I ordered the now famous loaf. The proprietor of the shop, a Justice of the Peace in his seventies, a man who had served me on numerous occasions, got irate when I told him that there was no need to wrap it as I only lived "just down the street".

He blurted out, "Of course I'm going to wrap it! It's against the law not to!"

I stood in front of this rude, outraged old fool, dumbfounded, as his wife chastised him severely for his "outrageous behaviour".

Overcoming the shock of this unexpected abuse, particularly as I was trying to be helpful, I weighed in with, "How many Australians were in the presidential palace when the North Vietnamese rolled their tanks in there? How many? You silly old tosspot! You tell me!!"

It was his turn to experience shock. The answer was one. He didn't appear to know it. The loaf of bread then travelled a very short distance, but very rapidly – from my hand straight into the side of his disbelieving head, his wife screaming as the following remark emerged from my mouth: "Here's your fucking loaf back, you silly old cunt – unwrapped!!"

I had been outraged. I could name fifty thousand useless occupants of this place who didn't know a thing about Australia's military history, or cared, and that arsehole had picked me. I made certain in future that he was going to be more selective. I was a touch fiery in those days. I told Mark the story and he chuckled, knowingly.

Then we came upon a house whose significance could not be under-rated, for that house had contained Ross. Ross and I had lived there together for about eighteen months. It had been common for us to buy copious amounts of expensive champagne on a whim, invite people around, get stoned and then watch Ross perform the songs he had created. Ross was tall and lithe, with a feminine grace, and had disproportionately large green eyes that oozed with a flamboyant naughtiness. The creation for which he was best known was called 'Fish-fucking in the Waters of Hell'. This astonishingly sensitive ode to love-making could only be performed by one individual – no one else could give it the justice it so thoroughly deserved. Needless to say who that individual was. When the time was ripe he would rise to his feet, salaciously run his hands up between his thighs and then, in a mellow jazz-blues, laid-back fashion, would unleash: "Fish-fucking in the waters of hell, fish-fucking will cast a spell, fish-fucking everyday, hey baby, float my way. Fish-fucking down somebody's throat, fish-fucking without a boat, hey baby, rub my scrote. Fish-fucking, fish-fucking away…"

It would then proceed with: "Fish-fucking in the middle of the day, think I'll go out and get a lay, no need to think about success, I can get anything in a dress." Eventually, the audience would be treated to: "Fish-fucking in the middle of June, hey, low tide, here's a full moon," before the final crescendo of: "Fish-fucking will cast a spell, when you find yourself boiling in the woe woe woe woe woe woe woe woe woe woe warders uh uh uh uh off-heh heh heh heh heh e e e e ele lllllllllll!!!!"

A highly select group would be left quivering on the floor.

One night we were driving home from a party (there isn't enough space to describe what Ross had done at the party) and we saw a blank advertising billboard on a main road that ran beside the ocean. A friend of ours was at the time in the process of spray-painting his car. In the early hours, Ross broke into the friend's garage and appropriated some bright red spray paint. At three o'clock that night, in full view of a group of drunk people eating hamburgers in an open-air takeaway food store beside the road, Ross boldly strode forth with painting gear and inscribed: *WHITEOUT!!! The hallucinogenic Tippex that only Eskimos have the guts to eat.* From a safe distance, I watched the people standing in front of the food store tottering around like skittled pins. Their laughter, in the quiet air, came to me like cracking whips. That inscription managed to last for nearly twenty-four hours. In that time, the whole city got to hear about it. There were many, I was to discover over the ensuing weeks, who had driven down that road the following day and had recognised the handwriting immediately. For years afterwards Ross was known as 'Whiteout'.

I preferred to call him 'Skyrocket'. He had a flair for writing poetry, something he did not take too seriously, but occasionally he would have a moment of inspiration. One of his more memorable lines, born from his fascination for conflict, came during an evening in which he displayed his considerable propensity for public masturbation. (I mean literally.) After leaving our invited guests stunned by a fine display of "self-orgiastic induction", he rose to his feet, did up his fly and said, "The time for poetry has arrived." He dashed off into his bedroom, returned with a sheet of paper, cleared his throat and announced: "War places places on the map by blowing them off it. Thank you."

We were accustomed to this type of behaviour. We expected it. Total strangers found it difficult to appreciate. He bore a natural detestation for conservative individuals, and the feeling was mutual, but I can recall several occasions when this irresponsible, flippant, decadent, wayward, promiscuous wag would confound straighter mortals with his profound grasp of the stock market. For a layman, his knowledge of military affairs and armaments was second to none. And women could not leave him alone. If I was interested in anyone, he was the last person she was going to meet. He screwed his best friend's girlfriend solidly for a week while the friend was away in Canberra. When the friend discovered this, I had to restrain him from murdering Ross, who, revelling in his triumph (he had a boyish competition with Geoff over their respective powers of seduction), suggested that he could seduce anyone interested in Geoff; Geoff stoutly refused to accept this. The number of women with whom they had affairs in the pursuit of self-esteem would have left the National Bureau of Statistics floundering in a sea of astonishment. I was nowhere near their league, but I wasn't complaining, as women would speak to me in the hope of getting to know the dubious twosome. I was famous for sharing that house with them. Occasionally, very occasionally, one of those women would end up deciding that they liked me instead and these rare, mysterious twists of fate were even more of a mystery to me than they were to them.

I remembered coming home from a six week trip to Indonesia, while living in that house, to discover that the mother of a young New Zealander was still camped in our lounge-room. A New Zealand couple occupied one of the rooms of the house and the mother of the son had arrived from New Zealand about a month prior to my departure. The first thing Ross said to me, ruefully, was: "She's still here. Geoff and I have had to use my bedroom as the lounge-room. It's incredible."

The woman was a hypochondriac. Using her husband's money, she had visited every city in Australia seeking professional help for her 'ailments', and every time she had received a clean bill of health. She refused to leave our lounge-room - our house, our lives! - because she believed that she was ill and needed help. This was true; however, it was psychological help she required. Understandably, the son was unable to see that his mother was insane and when I explained the situation to my shocked grandmother, she, with her disdain for those who do not pull their weight, declared, aptly, that "that woman obviously has got no dignity."

It was a house I will not forget. There were many warm, eccentric, intricate conversations about obscure, but fascinating experiences, usually whilst under the weather from various stimulants. We had real trust and friendship. We learnt a lot from each other and the inevitable break-up of that situation was precipitated by my desire to travel and by Geoff's desire to live the ultimate professional and hedonistic existence in New York. If ever there was a time I would like to relive, it was that; if there was ever a moment in history to be recreated, it was that time, but it would never happen again and the realisation of this tinged me with the sadness of age, the melancholy of bygone youth, and with the loneliness that attaches itself to the ephemerality of all things.

It was this loneliness that seemed to have subsumed itself into the wind. It was as though the universe were issuing a warning to the gleaming domesticity that surrounds us. Every foundation in my life had been swept aside by an uncompromising need for change. Perfectly acceptable situations had been relinquished in pursuit of knowledge; it was as if I had been unable to appreciate how precious were the transient moments of life. Going back into my past made me see the beauty of things I had not fully seen, how whimsical I had been and the opportunities I had failed to recognise. And the wind screamed, delicately, through this, with strength, a wild, untamed force that drove men away from security in search of wealth, experiences and failure. That wind, sad and desperate, had always blown in me.

I giggled when we went past a house where a school friend of Mark's and mine used to live. One day Ross and I and a few other people dropped into that house for a visit. Ross was keen to make the acquaintance of a young lady who had just moved in. The lady in question talked to us for a short time, then disappeared into her bedroom. Some time after this Ross vanished. Initially, we assumed that he had gone to the toilet. Then we assumed that, on a whim, he must have gone home. (We lived nearby.) When we left, I glanced down the driveway to see Ross standing on a rubbish bin looking through a thin gap in the curtains at the bedroom antics of the creature who was later to see him gawking at her. When this happened, Ross fell off the bin, its contents spilling out; then he raced past us, paranoid, whispering loudly, "Quick, let's fuck off. She's seen me!" All of us were laughing too much to move while Ross ran out of sight.

During that time, events such as this occurred weekly. They were boyish, beautiful and necessary; and now they were gone, gone with time, with maturity, with concern, with the preciousness that experience brings to all things; gone, with the onset of responsibilities and adulthood, never to be seen again.

We then passed the house of my first sexual experience in Perth. It was the first shared house in which I ever lived. It was a time of self-deception, deceit, immaturity, unconsciousness of irretrievability, irreverence towards human endeavour, immortality, ignorance; tall stories of sporting and sexual conquests coloured my bland conversation. Philosophical abstractions were more impressive than the simple, dramatic realities of existence. It was the time of fear – fear of exposure. I was surrounded by people who appeared well-adjusted, who seemed to know what to say; I was at my most awkward and felt under great pressure not to express it, for everyone else seemed so socially adept. Did women appreciate vulnerability? Of course they didn't. They wanted confidence, wit, excitement, waggishness; I believed this and did my utmost to show it. Usually, it emerged as rude insensitivity. They wanted confidence all right – the confidence to express weakness, the confidence of self-deprecatory wit; and why? Because it was exciting. It just took a long time to realise this. It was an age of quiet pain beneath the boisterous surface, of innocence and benightedness beneath pretentious lies, of depression after the security and easy euphoria of adolescence – and thank God it was over.

The other occupants of that house began their disillusionment with me after a day of drinking at an outdoor rock concert. Arriving back at the car, the others discovered that a window had been smashed and someone's handbag taken. The owner of the car was doubly upset, as he could see what a devastating blow it had been to the girl whose personal belongings – her sentimental attachments – had been swiped by some desperate arsehole. The owner of the car stood with his head bent – I had never seen him look so annoyed – while the girl's pretty face reddened to the point of tears. Despite obvious visual evidence, it did not register with me that they were truly disconcerted; it seemed ridiculous that people could react like this just because a silly window had been smashed and some insignificant handbag taken; consequently, I continued with my puerile immature ravings and was abruptly halted in my ranting tracks by the owner of the car who blurted out, "Jesus Christ, do you know the meaning of the word 'sympathy', you immature fool?"

And so I had been.

Then I caught a glimpse of the house of a girl with whom I had been desperately in love at school. I had actually lived down the road from her at one stage while I was going to university. I had chased her down that street, out of her house, clutching a cockroach in my hand. That was love. I had recorded, on a calendar, every conceivable form of contact we had had in our final year of school. An empty circle meant that she had looked in my direction. One half filled in indicated that she had smiled at me. A full circle, or a 'stamp', as I secretly referred to it in my love jargon, meant that she had spoken to me. A stamp with an asterisk meant that I had made her laugh. Regularly, I would extricate that calendar from the dusty recesses of a cupboard in my bedroom and peruse it in the hope of seeing it so laced with moons, circles, asterisks and stamps that I would be able to convince myself it was irrefutable evidence of her undying love for me. The delusion, the hope, the wish that this was so, dissipated approximately two years after school, although my love didn't. The realisation of the long-obvious reality came as a blessed relief. So much time had been wasted contemplating her existence when I could have been ruminating upon more pertinent matters; so many journeys had been made just so I could see her, so much effort and thought wasted in the pursuit of the unattainable.

But it had not all been a waste. There had been days when the sunlight, rich enough, had had a tinge of iridescent gold, gold golder than gold. The days when euphoria was quick and fresh and everything positive was a cause for great hope; even the smell of cut grass meant joy, the breaking of a wave, the days of physical exhilaration, the waft of white wings over the mirror laid by the shore – and she had been amongst it. She with that smile, with those blue eyes, she whose glint of refined sensitivity was so intense; she was a piece of exquisite jewellery come to life.

But she was gone. Gone with the wind. Gone for ever. Never to be seen again.

Then another one of Ross's songs filled my mind. Why I didn't remember it before was beyond me. It was one of his greatest classics: "She left her uterus in Vegas, she left her arse in 'Frisco, she left her tits in Phoenix, and her clit in Chicago, she left her thighs in 'Jersey, she left her womb in Houston, she left her tongue in Dallas, and her groans in Boston, she left her husband in Miami, and her groin in Cincinnati, she left her vagina in Seattle, and her pussy in Des Moines, she left her buttocks in Berkeley, and her cunt juice all over me; she left me quivering orgasmically."

Such poetry. He could actually sing this stuff seriously, without raising a smile. It just about murdered me. And I wasn't the only one.

"She left my prick rigid, I tell ya, she wasn't frigid. She left her arse all over my face, and when I came, I did not leave a trace."

He was pure sex and women knew it. They could take it or leave it. Usually they took it. One of the reasons I found it amusing was because it came from him. He managed to infuse such personality into his crudity. It made it acceptable. It was expected that he produce it; and he did in abundance. He could get away with it. One felt in those days as though one had to get away with something. Life didn't seem worth living unless you were getting away with something dubious. But it was now gone – away; away, away, away; away in a slashing breath of infinite change. It had been the dying, flashy spark of immaturity in a growing, smoother blaze of spirited confidence, and now it was gone.

And what had replaced it? Something like an appreciation of value, preciousness, a need for constant, constructive input, a disillusionment with being a spectator; the growing prospect of non-existence inflames the heart with a passion for the simple things in life: reading a book, writing a letter, making a meal, as long as it means passionate involvement.

I was more involved in this place than I had ever been in my life. I dreaded not being involved. I did not wish to rest. Time had become so valuable. Each moment had to breathe achievement, no matter how small. A docile day could mean that I was a failure; and I had become demanding. I took offence at paying money and having my time wasted. I was now too interested in constructive entanglement to suspend my judgement for the sake of being entertained. I could entertain myself. I was doing it now. This was far superior to going to see any ludicrous Hollywood movie.

I was intrigued by the spartan nature of Brian's abode. A large, unnatural, empty expanse of brown lawn stood before a low rectangular dwelling. A tree that used to exist in the front garden had been cut down. A patch of yellow sand, half overgrown with strands of lawn, sat like a lump where the tree used to be. A straight, flat driveway ran down one side of the front garden and house. Rectangular windows without flair faced the street. Low green plants sat in a garden before the brick façade. A red path curled from the driveway, through the lawn, to the steps of the verandah. People here had a tendency to paint their concrete verandahs red. At the head of the driveway a brick letterbox sat beside the only piece of vegetation rising above ankle height. It was a scene bereft of ornamentation. Middle-class functionalism at its most unimaginative. It was the last place in the world I expected to see a Salvador Dali print or a grand piano. I felt that all the money in the world would not affect the sense of cultural destitution: it was like rich poverty.

An iron gate protruding from the side of the house extended across the asphalt driveway to the next-door-neighbour's asbestos fence. The driveway was clean, without a leaf, a contrast to the fallen leaves on the lawn next door. Reticulation holes punctuated the grass. The edges of the lawn had been clipped. Everything was in order. Nothing bloomed or showed individuality. The letterbox itself, a rectangular brick block, had been made to standard specifications. It was the norm in this world of salient letterboxes. Nothing could match its conformity to the principles of utilitarian regimentation. The postman must have suffered years of sensory deprivation by being forced to look at it. It even had those glass iridescent numbers screwed on to it. Even those! (I had forgotten about them.)

Mark dropped me off. Brian greeted me at the front door. His eyebrows had that family characteristic of flaring into tufts. He was bald with a large, round face, a broad, protuberant nose and gleaming green eyes. His mouth, wide and cavernous, housed a perfect set of bone-white teeth. It was those teeth that greeted me. They were ablaze with kindness. His hands were large and strong. We shook each other's; then he led me off into a bedroom as spartan as the world from which it looked out over the dry rectangle of ageing grass. A bed and a set of drawers were the only objects in a room that had once been occupied by his two sons. I dropped my bags in there, then followed him into the lounge-room.

He gave me a beer and said, "Things are tough here now. The government's having all sorts of problems. They're useless. The opposition have produced a good package that the government can't find holes in. It's just a matter of time before they'll be out."

Two days later, he was to return from a barbecue and say, "This GST is so unpopular. People in middle range incomes are going to suffer because things'll cost more and they won't get much in the way of personal income tax cuts."

The Goods and Services Tax was the platform on which the opposition had built its attack on the government. He had been unconscious of his own enormous contradiction. I remained silent. I was certainly not going to jeopardise my stay in his house by belittling him.

Then he began talking about his ex-wife; how, during the course of their sordid divorce, she had attempted to get possession of the property. He told me that she had been asked a series of questions, in front of him, by her own solicitor: Did your husband hit you? Abuse you? Come home drunk? Have other women? Hit the children? No, no, no. "Well, Mrs N—, you've got two choices: move into one part of the house, or move into an old people's refuge." She had left him.

Brian then said, with boyish gusto, "You should've seen her! Christ! She went wild! The look in her face! She was furious! She went fucking insane! She started screaming out, 'Shit! Christ! Blah, blah, blah.' It was incredible. She screamed out, 'He's driven me out of my own home! It's bloody unfair!' Absolutely bloody red in the face she was. She thought she was going to get the lot. Incredible –

she pisses off with some bloke, leaves her kids and then expects to get her hands on a two-hundred-thousand-dollar property. It was amazing."

I feigned a smile. I was not interested in felicitous revenge. I even suspected that he thought I might be amused by this. His hands were flailing around his head. He was animated with bitter mirth.

"I can't ever imagine getting married again," he said. "Out of the question. I know some poor bastard who lost everything. I was bloody lucky. This bloke lost the lot. House, swimming pool, a car, the furniture. All up in smoke. Don't get married, whatever you do. Financial suicide. Women are bloody dangerous."

Divorce was wonderful for nurturing of antagonism towards the feminist movement.

"They're trying to take over the ABC," he said, as if affronted by the idea that women had something to offer. "Look," he continued, with a sudden air of reasonableness, "I think it's better for women if they're promoted on the basis of ability. Surely, that's better for them. In the ABC they've introduced a policy of positive discrimination. Women without sufficient skills have been shoved into positions above their ability. Some of them here even suggested getting rid of the furniture and using beanbags. Beanbags! Let's face it, only a woman could come up with an idea like that."

I had not heard anything like this for years. He was serious. I'm not suggesting that any greater virtue exists in Britain – that would be outrageous – it's just that there, I was able to choose my company. Here that choice had been cast to the winds. I realised that over the last six years I had been protected from attitudes that existed more in the media, like abstract concepts, than in my own realm. This trip was going to expose me to prejudices usually only discussed by people with well-rounded views. I had to get used to the idea.

Brian then started talking about his mother.

"She's slowed right up in the last few years," he said, with real concern. "Any effort makes her so tired. All the hard work's finally taken its toll."

He spoke with a kind of impassioned worry. His sentiment, fear and respect for a woman whose unflappable probity he had constantly tried to appease was in sharp contrast to the indifference and insolence of my father, whose interest in my grandmother was only pecuniary. Brian was the sensitive, conquered soul, my father the disrespectful radical, the fireball incapable of expressing weakness or acknowledging defeat; Brian, subjugated by the fierce will of his mother, had always been anxious to please. His interest in my grandmother had never been financial. When he suggested that my grandmother sell her house and move into something smaller, a suggestion devoid of economic consideration, my father, on discovering this, had shaken his head and said, "The stupid, fucking wood-duck hasn't got a clue. That house'll be worth a fortune in ten years' time and he's trying to get her out! Absolutely fucking unbelievable!"

Brian's concern about my grandmother's welfare held no virtue in my father's selfish mind. It was even interpreted by my father as being a indication of Brian's stupidity. The irony that Brian, and not my father, was going to benefit financially from the continued existence of my grandmother in that beautiful old house had, I had to admit, provided me with one or two moments of dubious delight. There appeared, on the face of that, to be some justice in this world.

"What do you think", I asked, "is going to happen to her house when she dies?"

"God knows," he replied. "Don't really want to think about it."

"You're already thinking about it though," I said.

"Not that much," he replied. "There's still a few years left – hopefully."

There was no doubt in my mind that my father had a plan for that house. The fact that my grandmother's egotistical dignity was going to deny him the opportunity of initiating it was, I felt, going to lead to some potentially nasty battles in the future; they would be outstanding to observe. They would also be symbolic of the desperation my father was sliding towards; it appalled me to think that someone of his age was depending upon a financial windfall from his own mother's death, just so that he could survive. His existence was a lesson to us all. He had always subscribed to the theory that nice guys don't get anywhere. This masochistic belief, foreign to me, was probably born from his inherent desire to wish that no one else's existence mattered in comparison to his own. His life had been coloured by the delusion that he could achieve notorious power. He imagined surrounding himself with people of similar ilk; but time was running out for him.

In contrast, his brother, at the other end of the philosophical spectrum, was on the threshold of having time in abundance. He explained to me that he had received a substantial redundancy package from the Australian Broadcasting Commission – he named the figures – and that I was to keep the exact amount away from my father. I was not certain why he wanted this – I could only presume that it was because he thought my father would consider it an insufficient amount to live on for the next thirty years. I was intrigued by this, but feigned understanding, something I did when feeling insecure. I was in his house and did not wish to do anything that could be interpreted as a sign of disrespect. Somehow I convinced myself that a lack of comprehension of his fears and feelings would be an indication of indifference. I suspected, without conviction, that he felt that my father would deride him if the information regarding his financial affairs became available, for Brian knew that he lacked the piercing spite required to defend himself against the searing derision of his brutal brother. I could not blame him. Any sensible human being does not relish the prospect of having to endure immature cynicism. My father was the embodiment of it.

Then he spoke of his plans and dreams. He intended to demolish his property, subdivide the land and then build two home units upon it. The resulting cash would be used to travel around Australia. He had friends who were interested in making the trip. He painted a picture of harmonious adventure. The bookshelves behind him were full of books about Australia. All this was going to take place after Vanessa's education had been completed. He went to great pains to point out that all this was being delayed for Vanessa's benefit. His sense of responsibility, presumably heightened by the favourable outcome of his divorce, in which he had been clearly shown to have been the righteous party, seemed, to me, in my analytical imagination, to have soared to sanctimonious dimensions. His protective instincts seemed to have convinced him that this rigid adherence to family responsibilities would lead him to the path of freedom, a thoroughfare he wished, he hoped, he dreamed that his ex-wife, through her selfishness, irresponsibility and greed, would never see.

"It'll take a few years", he said, "but I've got no intention of abandoning Vanessa. She's my main concern at the moment."

The instant I had entered his house I knew that all the experiences of my life were of no concern to him. I could not imagine that he would stop to discover anything his nephew had witnessed over the last six years. There was something in my character responsible for this. I rarely spoke about myself; I detested people feigning interest. This meant that others seemed to feel I was particularly interested in their lives. Many had made this mistake. I was not complaining. There was no reason for him to think that I did not possess anything other than a genuine interest in my family.

'If you demolish this house', I thought about asking, 'where are you going to live?'

Brian was not a person known for his ability to turn plans into action. I was feeling too polite to ask this question. I suspected how the other members of my family - particularly Wayne - would feel about that: they too had designs on that house. I could see some alarming conflicts developing in this family in the future. I planned not to be amongst it. I also assumed that my grandmother was shrewd enough to design her will to limit the potential bickering. She was under no illusions of how much of that there was going to be and the only thing I knew with any certainty was that, whatever she did, a certain amount of envy and jealousy was inevitable.

I was not hoping for these events to occur; I was just sufficiently pessimistic to assume that they would, and just sufficiently optimistic to believe that I could learn something from them. I suspected that my interest would be intellectual rather than emotional. I intended to remain an outsider. There were better things in which to become involved. I dreaded the thought that the continued smooth running of my life could become dependent upon the favourable outcome of such spurious contingencies. This was a warning. The huge red light of unsavoury personal interest pours its eerie glow upon us all. I could do without it.

* * * * * * * * * *

Brian dashed off to a job interview. This gave me the opportunity to let an unsuspecting world know that I had returned. Apart from Ross, whose whereabouts was a mystery to me - he could have been repairing parachutes in Zanzibar for all I knew - I was uncertain as to how this would be received back here in the land of milk and champagne. The first to react was Ana. Apart from a brief spell, I never really got along with him that well. But I went for him because his sense of cultural awareness and his gregarious curiosity probably would outweigh all the intrinsic realities that separated us. I quickly established that he wasn't married, but was living with a twenty-year-old American girl. I was under no illusions as to the physical characteristics of this creature. She would be gorgeous. Every woman he managed to seduce for the right reasons had the physical appearance of the geographical equivalent of the Himalayas. He told me that he was in love. I tried, initially, through insecurity, to subtly impart the knowledge that I had changed. This was probably the only air I possessed. I realised people would not make that assumption; but that it was ridiculous to try and prove it. Just let events take their course.

He was happy and friendly. I too was happy and friendly, because he was. I was just glad that he had rung. His call was not based on any absurd fear of repercussion. To my surprise he said that he would come around now and see me. It was about two o'clock in the afternoon on a Thursday. This, I presumed, was one of the advantages of self-employment.

When he arrived his car appeared to me as a gleaming, sumptuous, white object, like a futuristic jewel on wheels in the driveway. Sinking into the smooth, soft leather upholstery I said, glancing over my shoulder, "Was it difficult prising your lounge-room out through the front door?"

His Grecian face exploded into a felicitous frenzy of boyish dimples; then he unleashed that characteristically sonorous chuckle. I found out it was a Porsche.

"This thing", he said, reversing out of the driveway, "has caused me to be on the receiving end of some incredible abuse. You have to be really careful driving something like this about, with people mouthing off out the window. You drive a car like this and you're a yuppie. One day down in Dunsborough I pulled into a parking spot on the main street – I got there just before some other bloke did – and got: 'Yuppie cunt! Why don't arseholes like you just fuck off?' I get the works: prick, cunt, wanker, arsehole, shithead. It's par for the course."

When he spoke he screwed up his face into a brilliant evocation of unjustified vitriol. There was no need for him to explain to me that his values were not as apparent as some of his tormentors believed. He possessed a genuine love of cars. His passion for them was equal to my infatuation with painting or literature. This was a country where a passion for anything would always create a philosophical enemy – particularly cars. They were the traditional symbols of egoism, wealth and power. The average idiot failed to comprehend that there was a minority who saw them as beautiful objects, works of art.

I found out that he had become an insurance broker. I was impressed with his denunciation of those who used the current recession as an excuse for failure. When I told him about my feelings concerning the maintenance of all that manicured space he laughed and said, "Too many people around here have got more space than ideas."

Devoid of a formal education, he was intuitively streetwise. His father, now dead, had emigrated from Macedonia with nothing other than a fierce desire to succeed. With a pittance, and possessed of the single-mindedness that determined immigrants to a rich new world have, his father, who had fought as a partisan against the Germans, eked out a living as a market gardener, before buying up a string of food stores and becoming rich. The tough experience of survival in a new land, prejudice and homesickness, became imbued into his son. This trait of fiscal consciousness is best illustrated by a certain discovery that Ana's grandmother made one morning whilst watering the tomato patch. Some of the more exotic leaves within the crop had risen above the height normally associated with the blooming of the succulent red fruit. On investigation, Ana's father plucked some of the suspect leaves, rolled them around in his hand, approached his son and asked, "How much for this?"

On hearing the answer, Ana's father's eyes spun around like a fruit machine. This was the sort of lucrative agriculture that he long dreamed existed. A study of fertilisation and plant growth led Ana to produce the perfect crop. The proceeds enabled him to take his mother and two of his sisters around Europe for nine months in a Mercedes-Benz. The car was left with all doors open at Athens airport. When I told him that Wayne believed his wealth was due to the sale of illicit substances, he laughed ruefully and said, "I haven't seen a bag of dope for fifteen years."

He never wasted his money. By the time he was twenty-five, he had the finest assortment of music and stereo equipment I have ever seen. In a place like Perth, where access to a wide variety of music is impossible, this was an achievement. His taste, well in advance of his years, symbolised the maturity that comes from early exposure to the existence of an adroit, enterprising mind. His sense of relevance was natural and unerring.

We were driving down to the beach and he asked, "What's your uncle intend to do with that house?"

When I told him, he was intrigued. There was no question that he was considering offering Brian a price and then developing it himself.

"I could do wonders with that land," he said.

This was not idle boastfulness or overconfidence but sharp intuition.

"Offer him a price," I remarked. "He wouldn't know how to go about it himself."

"I just might," he replied.

It was no ordinary beach where we went, but North Cottesloe, the home of the chic. It had undergone some fundamental changes since I had last seen it. Two cafés along the beach front had been built. They overlooked the water, a silent blue expanse of ocean near the horizon that had become suddenly foaming and active, dotted with people, against the shore. The shore stretched in one direction into a haze of sunlight; in the other, distant headlands, miles down the coast, created the illusion of slowly disappearing into an abyss of misty green and blue. The only object that stopped the horizon from drawing a vast straight line beneath the sky was an island, clear and green, about ten miles from the shore. This stretch of turf appeared weightless, floating immobile, as if suspended like an oasis in a great void of blue, which, like a monumental crown, folded over the world to be a burning jewel that drew us out in droves, filling the beaches, pouring its light on to those whose social existences were dependent upon its ability to concentrate them in this single place. There was no doubt that the vast majority of people were here because they expected to see someone else. The beach was a great information-gathering institution; the idea of relaxing on it was a mask for a deeper concern.

As we walked from Ana's car along the pavement, I was awe-struck by the confident beauty of the women. Each one I saw, no matter how ordinary to look at, dressed sensuously to enhance what positive qualities they had. One woman, with large pouting lips and porcelain skin against a rich downpour of brunette hair, unconsciously ran her hands up her neck as Ana and I passed, a public and sensual act beyond the paranoid considerations of most English women; then I laid eyes on a spectacular redhead emerging from an apartment across the road. This creature, six feet tall in high-heeled shoes, possessed a fiery torrent of enflamed follicles that fell from her head in golden-reddish clusters, all the way down her back, a waterfall of satin that gleamed life and sensuality in the blazing light. The dark sunglasses matched the colour of her shoes and between those two extremes of black was a silky, emerald ensemble, short-sleeved, figure-hugging, which finished just above her knees. Ana and I, fascinated, watched her sling a briefcase on to the back seat of a sports cars; then we saw her drive away.

"That", I said, "is power."

I had not seen anything like that for years.

"I don't know why", Ana said, half seriously, "you bother to live where you do."

"Neither", I replied, "do I."

On my right-hand side, two people disappeared down a track that weaved through the high sand dunes to the beach below. The dunes were kept intact by small green plants which dotted the slopes like silent observers of the turquoise boundlessness of the sky and sea. Indiscriminate, mobile groups of seagulls squawked and pecked in white clumps on the footpath. On the road cars moved slowly, their drivers in pursuit of scarce parking spots; the air still, the light clear, the sun ferocious, the sky like a gargantuan arch of blue marble, stretching over the opulent tranquillity of a world devoid of old conflicts, pestilence, poverty and the pressures of a more competitive life.

Above our heads a pair of seagulls hovered and squawked and then swirled off in a rapid swoop over the sand dunes to the shore below. The frenetic loudness of those creatures, their untrammelled cries, were the only signs of the existence of a desperate world in this rich, easygoing and fantastically lazy place. I doubled whether there would he one person here able to say that they had really worked - night and day - unrelenting in the pursuit of some audacious desire. And why should they? There was absolutely no need for it. If you wanted to do that, you went to the other side of the world.

In the café we got a table beside a glass wall that enabled us to gaze out over the sea. The Greek salads took some time arriving but, when they did, they were worth it. Around us, people clad in lurid but tasteful splashes of colour, often with bare feet covered in wet sand, chatted away, as though they were on holiday. Beneath us, down some concrete steps, I could observe the beach fauna sunning itself on the long bone-white strip, a frame of ivory to a canvas of interminable blue; a painting which depicted silence, peace, pleasure, permanence; and, with its smooth, unmarked wash of impenetrable blue, suggested a serene longevity beyond the dynamism of modern life, an astronomical disinclination for radical change.

Ana and I amused ourselves over the behaviour of those on the beach. Beaches, quite the opposite to what they should be, were not platforms on which spontaneous events occurred. The rigidity of beach behaviour was astonishing. The first act one performed when stepping on to a beach was the placing of the towel perpendicular to the shore. Across the white sand, in observance of this rule, colourful strips of wool ran parallel to each other, as though they were prayer mats owned by those bowing in deference to the god of pleasure, whose blue domain had the power to effect a highly ridiculous polarisation of towels, an alignment of conformity easily instigated in a place where people came to observe, rather than exhibit. The second fundamental principle of beachidity was: never move too quickly towards the water. Anyone who actually had the temerity to run perpendicular to the ocean clearly had the social graces of an intellectually handicapped Australopithecus; however, it was more than acceptable to run parallel with it. In fact, it was openly encouraged. Anyone, though, who had decided to indulge in parallel-running had to be careful that they did not run at an angle to the shore first. Very few people made that mistake.

After the laying of the towel, it was mandatory to sit on it, knees up, arms wrapped around the legs and just casually observe. The ability to create an air of unperturbed detachment was essential. Anything less could lead to an hideous intrusion on other people's attention. When that time arrived for the first signs of excessive relaxation, the protagonist would spend a few moments on his elbows, glance around, before falling prostrate on to the carefully positioned mat. Some time later, after a generous application of lotion, our hero would then rise from the carpet of his conformity and move, as disinterestedly as possible, with a subtle hint of an unflustered swagger – do you think I care if half the fucking world is watching me walk almost fucking naked towards a destination I have to get to as slowly as fucking possible? – before stepping into the chilling sea, tentatively, delicately, each foot placed with meticulous precision into the foaming waters before that moment of diving elegantly, with a perfectly formed arched of the back, under an oncoming wave.

It was a process repeated constantly, without variation; a finely-honed mode of action with which no one tampered, unless, of course, they were working class. The working classes had that unsavoury habit of chasing each other over the soft sand, spraying it in all directions (having white sand glued to one's sun-oiled body is no laughing matter), before grabbing their girlfriends and attempting to dump them, often head first, into the shallow water. This kind of unsophisticated behaviour was brutally frowned upon at North Cottesloe, where any sudden, quirky, spirited act was deemed to be the work of an immature fool whose presence, unfathomable on the golden, jet-set sands of 'North Cott', was usually found in abundance on the beaches further north - like Scarborough or Sorrento - where the average girlfriend receives concussion four times a week and loves it.

Apart from the less-educated classes, there was one other phenomenon known for its ability to show scant regard for the norms of beachology. That creature was Ross. Ana and I, laughing hysterically, recalled a day in which Ross deliberately broke every rule in the book. After he announced his intentions, a large huddle of us waited for him on the beach. To our uproarious astonishment, he strode past us wearing a pair of red wellington boots, proceeded to lay down his towel at an obtuse angle, did a headstand - the boots, shiny, red plastic-looking things, were still on - before charging at full tilt, in a swathing, circuitous route, through the soft sand and into the water. In the water, he thrashed around for a few minutes like an epileptic seal, from which he emerged in an endeavour to drag a young lady, whom we all knew, into the boiling seas. That woman, embarrassed beyond all redemption, screamed with fear and excitement, as the staid, unmoved, sophisticated North Cott beach-goers retained their reserved air of uninvolvement while the woman's arms were flailing, her dignity destroyed, as the vile breaker of unwritten precepts completed his evil task. He then dashed from the water, along another absurdly circuitous route, to his towel, which he grabbed and with which he disappeared, not to be seen again at North Cottesloe for well over a year.

The laughter did not subside as Ana brought up the day that he and I strode out to bat and were unable to face a ball, we were both chuckling so severely from a welter of sharp jokes cracked on our way to the wicket. The umpires and fielding side were incredulous as they saw the man at the striker's end - Ana - erupt with bellowing laughter as the bowler came charging in, fully expecting to be treated seriously; that bowler, in full flight, pulled up at the wicket, as the man to whom he had intended to bowl staggered as though in a drunken fit out to short square leg where his head went up, his mouth shot wide open, and, through a tortured grimace, came the sonorous crackles of unfettered hilarity. Never, in the entire history of the game has an innings begun in this fashion. The speechlessness of both umpires and fielding side was increased substantially by the antics of the strange individual at the non-striker's end. He was doubled over his bat as though attempting to vomit.

The umpire looked at me and said, "What'd you two guys take on the way out here?"

This comment caused me to unleash an uncontrollable fit of guffawing as I reeled up to the wicket, put my arm around Ana and said, "Guess what the fucking umpire just said?"

Through a veil of tears I saw Ana's face virtually tear itself apart as he found out the answer. As I had my arm around him and had walked the length of the wicket to speak to him, the members of our team made the logical assumption that he had suddenly fallen ill and was unable to bat. This caused our captain to yell out from the boundary in an endeavour to establish the seriousness of Ana's affliction. Neither of us was able to answer. The opposition's captain approached us from the slips and politely inquired whether it was possible to take up our rightful positions "and bloody well get on with it."

His team was in a strong position - they led comfortably on the first innings - and the fact that he assumed we were indulging in some sort of bizarre time-wasting in order to avoid an innings defeat only served to make matters worse.

"Sorry, sorry," Ana managed, through a gleam of happy tears.

What had begun as innocent gibing about our respective incapacities to deal with the new ball had led to this. I made my way back down the wicket and, when Ana finally got his act together, we both knew, as he bent over his bat, that, had I so much as moved my face, the whole thing would have been repeated, this time probably with our captain - not known for his rarefied appreciation of irresponsible behaviour – bursting out on to the field of play and unleashing a fiery paroxysm of outraged vituperation.

Earlier in the game, he had hurled our scorebook at a member of the opposition after it was revealed that they had not been scoring in our book as well. The captain was a man who operated on a short fuse; he had sent Ana and me in to avoid going in himself – a lot of the jokes were about this – and, when we were both dismissed cheaply and he was padded up a good deal before he wanted to be, he snarled at me and said, as we collapsed at 7 for 27, "I suppose you fucking find this fucking hilarious as well?"

The captain then went out and played a superb innings, one that enabled us to avoid an innings defeat.

As we recalled the incidents of that day, the glee on Ana's face, a parallel to the overjoyed mirth I had seen on numerous occasions, caused me to study his appearance with a scrutiny I had never done before. The single eyebrow was still nice and healthy. It was really two eyebrows joined above his hooked nose. It ran across his forehead like a schematic representation of a bird. His brown eyes looked as they always had – young, sensitive, passionate – but his face, ever so slightly, had aged. The lines that formed in tight ripples around his mouth when he smiled were more pronounced. Plentiful gorges sat within the lightly-tanned forehead. As he spoke, his hands, in traditional southern European style, composed a lively tune of amused and often sentimental remembrance. "Do you remember that time?" was asked constantly; "And what are you up to now?"; "Oh really…" – a progression of intriguing delights.

Often irritating events are the cause of great amusement. This is one reason why the contemplation of the past resonates with such a gentle hush. When Ana and I were simultaneously unemployed about ten years ago, we began doing gardening jobs together. Our most lucrative assignment was a day we will never forget. It was a Friday and we both needed the cash to enjoy ourselves on the forthcoming weekend. After completing the job, our client, whose integrity was not in doubt, declared that he would send us a cheque. Sombrely, Ana and I returned to his parent's house, where his father, sceptical to the point of outrage, insisted we go back and demand our cash. After speaking to his wife, we found the said man in a local pub. His astonishment at our insistence, while he was trying to have a quiet drink with some friends, led him to blurt out, with an intensity of bewilderment, unforgettable for the querulous passion in his eyes, "Jesus Christ! This is unbelievable! Never ever have I ever done business like this before! Never!"

"Well," Ana laughed, "you fucking well have now!"

That day, composed of frustration and labour, and then relief, was now a source of mutual merriment. Our client had even nursed me after my top lip had been turned blue by the bite of a wasp. At that stage in my life I was too inexperienced to appreciate the mentality of a man decent enough to accord us the unwarranted virtue of professionalism. As far as I was concerned, we were unemployed bums without the slightest comprehension of the niceties of polite business practice. We just did not have the experience at that stage in our lives to request, politely, on the spot, if it was possible, with all due consideration, bearing in mind the circumstances, whether - and this is in no way an attack whatsoever on your integrity, which is beyond all doubt - whether we could get a little cash up front?

But that had changed. And so had I. However, because I felt too conscious of this fact, and because I assumed that non-peripatetic people are denied the opportunity of perceiving great, and often imperceptible transitions, I thought that I was the only one here who would know it. I felt as though I were surrounded by individuals philosophically opposed to the idea that someone can undergo a fundamental change. It was a fear that made me vulnerable. I dreaded the thought that everyone I knew here would be too immune to change themselves to perceive it in others. The last thing I wanted was someone to think that I was the person I had been six years in the past. But it would happen.

In an endeavour to ward off this prospect in Ana, I said, "We were too inexperienced then to know how to ask, politely, for the things we wanted. Now we don't hesitate. It's the quiet sign of ever-increasing maturity."

I saw his often gleaming and wondering eyes stop momentarily, in an instant of wonderment.

"We begin in life", I said, taking advantage of this, "by asking constantly for everything, noisily, without the faintest tact; then we reach the adolescent phase where we don't have the social skills to ask, properly, for the things we need, so we often don't ask. This is the phase of morbid timidity. (The phase I am still in emotionally).

Then we start to ask for everything again, but with great diplomacy. This, Ana-baby, is what I call the Cycle of Requests."

Ana, too down-to-earth, was not inclined to make generalisations or philosophical observations himself, but this did not preclude him from appreciating them. His conversation, often anecdotal, was always spiced with specifics.

"I know someone", he replied, "who's definitely still in the child phase."

He was referring to the ex-boyfriend of his present lover. It transpired that Ana had been asleep one night with Jennifer. They had collapsed into bed after a hard night on the town. The ex-boyfriend broke into the house and climbed on to the bed saying, "Jennifer, Jennifer, I love you."

Ana, hungover, got the shock of his life and tried to be polite; but the jilted lover refused to go; so he said, "Look, she obviously doesn't want to speak to you so just get out of here." The ex-boyfriend threatened to annihilate him ("he was an enormous cunt") and began fingering him in the chest. By this time the two of them were standing up, facing each other. Ana went for him, tripped over a telephone cord and came up swinging. This was after the ex-boyfriend had referred to his competitor in the game of love as a "gorilla", a reference to Ana's hirsute appearance. Ana had struck the unwanted intruder in the chest and his distraught rival had quipped, with immature savagery, "How can you go out with a gorilla like that? Come on, gorilla, hit me again."

Ana did. The ensuing mêlée resulted in Jennifer's hurling a porcelain mug into the skull of her previous gentleman caller, a fairly blatant hint that his services were no longer required. He apparently took this subtle reference to his surplusness to requirements and left.

"Because of that night", Ana said, ruefully, "we've had security windows installed."

"But", I asked, "has your consumption of bananas mysteriously increased?"

"Funny you should say that," he replied. "I woke up one morning and found myself lying naked in the gorilla pen at Perth zoo."

I discovered, after questioning, that this incident with the ex-lover had occurred not long after Jennifer and Ana had begun living with each other. It made me wonder if she was as pure as Ana believed. It was easy for women, pristine and smooth, eyes glinting with sensitive vulnerability, to hide successfully behind a mask of delicate moral incorruptibility; they even believed themselves that it was their right to choose whoever they wanted, at any given time, and be absolved of the consequences. No individual, unless he is insane, bursts into someone else's house in the middle of the night in the vain hope of securing love without some incentive; for fear of creating the impression that I was casting aspersions upon his judgement, I kept this notion to myself.

Then he referred to another little difficulty that had coloured his recent history. He had had another altercation with another man over another woman. His rival on this occasion was a former Australian hockey player, with whom I had gone to school, by the name of Peter H—. Ana had asked H—'s girlfriend out; he had been given cause to believe that she and H— had parted company. A series of public separations between H— and the lady had ignited the flame of Ana's hopes. When H— discovered that Ana, someone whom he had felt was a friend, was openly attempting to seduce someone whom H— believed was still his, the resulting anguish led to another finger-pointing confrontation in a popular and crowded pub. The coming together of these two opposed and infatuated forces had failed to resolve the conflict. Ana said, that as a result of H—'s fury, H— had begun spreading a rumour that Ana was gay. Ana believes that H— did this not simply from spite, but because he believes H— is a closet bisexual himself. The two had now patched up their differences. The whole thing seemed remarkably absurd to me. Ana went to great pains to inform me that "it was not my fault if he was having problems with his girlfriend. Does he own her?"

I knew that, if Jennifer temporarily left him, he would be deeply upset if one of his friends tried to seduce her. I knew as well that it would be pointless reassuring him with the magic words: "But you aren't going out with her any more."

I was not perturbed by this hypocrisy. I believe it is essential to be morally deluded: without this fundamental basis of illusory propriety, we would not be free in our actions, constantly hampered in a quagmire of brooding self-analysis. It was just helpful to be aware that one was capable of venality; that at least allowed one to see the justifiability of someone else's pain.

Ironically, H— appeared on the concrete steps beneath us. It was possible to slide the window open. This enabled H— to speak to us.

He too, like everyone else I had seen again, appeared evergreen. He had a broad, triangular face with small, round brown eyes that gazed at Ana and me with polite inquisitiveness. His demeanour, European in its serious complexity of openness, was at opposite poles from the flippant gaiety of expression that marked the behaviour of scores of people in a place obsessed with the goal of constant euphoria. His mature curiosity belied the shallowness by which some believed he operated. He was genuinely interested in Ana's business life; his happiness about the success of Ana's relationship with Jennifer was, I felt, proper and not due to relief born of mistrust of Ana's possibly dubious intentions. He was intrigued and fascinated by my development as a photographer. He had some unusual achievements under his belt and was therefore appreciative of the necessity of sacrifice in the pursuit of difficult ambitions.

When he left, Ana looked at me and said, "He's okay. No problems now."

I watched H— deposit his towel in the traditionally accepted fashion; then I saw him lie down prostrate with an abandonment that displayed the full extent of his contentment. He created the impression of being as pleasantly indifferent to those around him as that prodigious, blue immensity was before us all, a colossal sheet of unblemished sapphire forever unmarked by the passions and dreams and catastrophic upheavals of this deluded earth. No amount of intrigue and drama had ever tampered with the austere beauty of its impenetrable façade; all the sweat and toil of the ages had done nothing to enflame its unruffled temper; its concern for the sacrifices and agonies of those it enveloped was as minuscule as their existences yet, I knew, there were some out there, by the law of averages, sunning themselves on that elongated strip of dazzling white, who believed that they would achieve some sort of eternity. Given the obviously morally dispassionate consciousness which had created our world, it was beyond me how anyone could possess the egotism necessary to believe that they were destined for the annals of permanence, but many did and they would continue to do so, despite the fact that our world was one small island in the endlessly protracted and voluminous ocean of stars that, over the full weight of eternity, would house an infinity of civilisations, the vast majority of which are probably going to be of far greater significance than our own. Low on the scale of importance, our civilisation will most likely not even cause a flicker of consideration within the crepitating soul of that which determines all, and yet we go about our lives with a rapacious desperation way out of proportion to the eventual futility of our dubious cause. I was obviously not an atheist, but I saw no value, in the long run, in stringently maintaining a moral existence.

I was also incapable of achieving the aesthetically powerful purity of indifference which emblazoned itself upon us with its mystifying delicacy of unengagement, and realised that my sudden introspective countenance had caused a touch of concern within the mind of my passionate interlocutor.

"How's Peter Bull?" I asked. "Has he got a girlfriend?"

Peter was someone who, I remembered, displayed a certain impartiality towards the dramas of Perth's social life. His endeavours to seduce women were nowhere near as frenetic as those of his friends and this made him appear, despite the contradiction, a gregarious outcast.

I discovered that he was still a postman.

"This", Ana said, "is not a winner with women. He's told me numerous times that a woman's asked him what he does for a living, then, five minutes later, she's disappeared. He just can't bullshit."

This unintended denunciation of the emotional depth of Perth's women caused a sudden pang of astonishment within me that quickly disappeared as rapidly as it had arrived. The idea that it was necessary for a man to prove his intellect and wit to women through occupational intrepidity was a repugnant but an unfortunately real one. It was particularly pertinent in Peter's case, as he was a man of genuine intellect and wit, with a phenomenal capacity for the mimicking of accents. One night, in a local tavern famous for its Monday evenings - Mondays were known as Poms' nights - he thoroughly and utterly fooled every English person in the place into thinking that he was a tough, no-nonsense, resilient product of East Lahhndun. Every one of the people he met was as ignorant of the fact that he had never set foot upon the hallowed shores of Blighty, as I was as to the future shape of my inevitable death. He, it was alleged, had seen every "'kin game the Hammers had played at Ahhhptun Park for the last 'kin ten 'kin yeaerrs, mate." Half the people he met that night probably assumed he was on their committee. Women in this place probably found him too eccentric for their conservative tastes, which was a pity, because he had so much to offer.

Then I asked about someone else. The person in question was someone with whom I had lived many years ago in a house famous for some of the social escapades that had transpired within it. It is rare in life to receive a genuine revelation, something that confounds your accepted view of actuality and possibility, but I was on the threshold of getting one. David, who, up to the time of my domestic association with him, had never laid hands on a musical instrument, was now a successful recording artist. His music had appeared on television documentaries and he was now well-known on the Perth music scene. Unbeknown to me, he could sing. When I lived with him, I was the one, who, without the faintest glimmer of talent, had played the guitar. David had even said to me, whilst watching me one day, "for someone who normally does things so well, you're useless." This, I thought, was rather strong coming from someone who had not even tried to do it himself. But it appeared as though his observations were justified. When I knew him, he was an overtly sensitive individual cynical towards the insincerity which he felt existed around him. His vindictiveness towards those he often described as "ephemeral" regularly led him into confrontations with the privileged classes who were disinclined towards his serious, and usually aggressive, regaling of his highly principled social morality. His track record for being thrown out of parties because of this was legendary. I could only presume that he had finally learnt to channel his fiery passion for justice into something beautiful. That, after all, is what it's all about. Time had revealed it was he who possessed the gift of music. This was heartening to discover, as his prickly ferocity towards injustice and insincerity was, with a passion furious, like a frenzy of outraged winds, so intense, that, unless he had found refuge in a creative consciousness, his sense of disenchantment with humanity would have probably led him to suicide.

Ana told me that David now plays other instruments as well; then something I had been dreading occurred. Ever since arriving in Perth I had been plagued by an awful feeling that I was going to run into a lot of people I knew six years ago, with whom I did not get along then, who knew me in a way that now does not exist. Such an individual appeared at the window. His grievance against me was that I was thick.

To describe his acknowledgement of my existence as dry would be putting it mildly. His estimation of my intellect was due in part to jealousy – I had publicly embarrassed him once in an argument – and in part to the paranoiac gloominess that had characterised me for months in the build-up to my departure from these fair shores. On the threshold of effecting the most far-reaching decision yet of my life, my personality dissipated into a brooding introspection of sepulchral vagueness. I reached a point where normal social interaction was often impossible, as my mind, like a grey sea on the periphery of a violent clamour, tossed and swayed with the innumerable possibilities that a reckless abandonment into a tumultuous abyss can produce. I knew that a lot of things would become irretrievable by my sudden dislocation from my life in Perth, and the thought, although appealing to a young adventurous imagination, of casting myself to the wolves of fate in pursuit of photographic excellence, was still a decision fraught with potentially depressing consequences. But I would not have expected this individual to have understood. The path of his life had been marked by a careful and sensible progression from school days to the safety of a lucrative profession. Not a single risk in the hope of satisfying a bold desire had flustered the smooth, insipid waters of his conservative transition from the cot to middle age, and when he left, after a discussion about his nephew's chances of succeeding in first class cricket, I knew that the uncomfortable experience which I had just had was going to be an unfortunate feature of my agenda for the next six weeks.

It was an experience which made me realise that I was in a place where the chance meeting was the norm of everyday life. This was great if you were popular. It was a nightmare if you were not. I realised that living here meant one had to endure a bizarre complexity of relationships that did not exist so saliently in a larger and altogether more complex place. Here, due to these unforeseen meetings, often between people who were not that interested in each other, there existed a multitude of different forms of interaction. There were people who subliminally agreed to ignore each other; there were people who just acknowledged each other and nothing else; there were those to whom you spoke for five minutes; there were many to whom you only spoke about specific subjects; there were many with whom you made silly one-liners and never dared probe through the surface, and there was occasionally, very occasionally, someone to whom you could actually talk. The ability to choose your company in social situations was here often ravaged by the relatively diminutive size of the place, and by the fluidity of Australian social life. Your social privacy was therefore attacked, in a pincer movement of sun and alcohol, from both directions, and this, for a uniquely disagreeable and distinctly unpopular individual such as myself, who dreads the discomfort of the worried eye and the pathetic safety of those inclined towards rash judgements, bereft of sensitive insight, was a formula for constant and tense vulnerability. This is how I had felt since my arrival. How I adored the anonymity of the big city; there, you choose who you wished to be with, consequently avoiding, to a significant extent, the dark glances of those incapable of comprehending the esoteric vagaries of your existence.

The fact that Ana made no reference to the silence between myself and the man with whom he had just communicated, indicated to me that he was aware of the disrespect which had just hung in the air like haunting birds of prey, circling with uneasy presence, in the hot dry winds of contempt. People in the United Kingdom suffer from the delusion that Australians are straightforward. In Britain, the coolness of the last exchange would have been commented upon with fascinated avidity, but Ana, diplomatic and fearful, like most Australians, of disagreement, chose to ignore it, as if those high-flying creatures of incivility had soared over his head unseen, lost in the distant, baking thermals of insolent disregard, where only fools, bent on dismantling the smooth machinations of social interaction, choose to tread. Everyone lies to ensure a smooth passage through the tricky waters of collective fraternisation, and the most placid and rewarding thoroughfare is often achieved by silence.

Such was the case when two people, both known to Ana and me, entered the café and sat next to us. A short exchange transpired between Ana, myself and the man, one born of necessity to ensure that we could then ignore each other, but none occurred between myself and the woman he was with, someone with whom I had spent twelve years at school. Her capacity to feign non-recognition was remarkable. As sixteen-year olds we had kissed, passionately, under a street light one night in front of her home; I had chased her for months, fascinated by her healthy thighs and succulent lips, and was overawed by her intellect. At university, in front of a full lecture house, the lecturer described her analysis of *Wuthering Heights* as rivalling the work of T.S. Eliot. The instant the lecturer made this glowing reference to one of his students, I was under no illusions as to whom he was alluding. She got the top marks in the state of Western Australia in French and German in the year we graduated from school, and on that evening, when she allowed me the pleasure of caressing her salacious physique, I knew that her motivation was not due to mutual respect, but to the awakening of libidinous curiosity. It was an awakening of which I was thrilled to have been a part.

I glanced at her long enough for her to make a decision. She chose not to make it. She stared at her friend, engrossed in animated conversation. To have acknowledged me could have opened up unsavoury possibilities. There was no reason for her to assume that I was not still a rampant chaser of women. In her imagination there was every chance that my honeyed phrases were still ringing in the ears my tongue had so lasciviously swirled within. The fact that I had mercilessly molested and then disposed of one of her friends was another factor significant in her ignoring of my visual inveiglements. My seduction of her friend, vile and unforgivable, was, in the feminine imagination, too profound and revealing an occurrence to consider the prospect that its protagonist may have changed. Once a womaniser, invariably always.

The prejudice by which others were going to view me was probably mutual. I could see no reason to assume that the majority of people I knew in the past would have undergone fundamental shifts in thinking. I was as arrogant about my perceptions as anyone else. This brought me on to Ross. He was one individual who had had to change. No anatomy was sufficiently hardy to withstand the existence he had led without some compromise between mind and body. Ana reaffirmed that Ross had indeed changed. He had become an amateur actor who shunned the party scene. This did not surprise me. The party scene in Perth is not the most fascinating on earth; what I did not suspect, as I was to discover, was that the change was due to moral disillusionment. I told Ana a story which I correctly assumed he had not heard.

Ana was oblivious of Ross's predilection for the creation of lewd song lyrics. I told him that the hypochondriac left a day after Ross, dissatisfied with the state of his domestic affairs, and decided to take matters into his own hands. Completely off his head, he went into our lounge-room and gave the woman concerned a personal viewing of that great classic about the woman predisposed towards the racy dispensation of parts of her body in some of the world's most hedonistic locations.

"He stood before her," I said, "and began singing a song about a woman with, shall we say, a liberated moral perspective, possessed of a proclivity for leaving various parts of her anatomy in American cities. After passionately describing how this woman left her breasts, arse, clitoris, rectum, tongue, et cetera, in a string of cities from San Francisco to New York, he thrust his lower abdomen region into the astounded hypochondriac's face and blurted out, 'She fucked me all day and night in Vegas, Christ – she was fucking outrageous – she left huge welts on my back in Dallas, oh God – she was so callous. She was a whore, a slag and a slut, and, oh God, could she fuck.' (Ana was now beside himself). Anyway, this woman wasn't too thrilled about this. She could hear me laughing from the kitchen, which didn't help; but the real crux came when he finished things off with: 'She was the greatest fuck I've ever had by far, and that fucking slag was a New Zealander!'"

Between Ana's chuckles and my own, I said, "She left the following day ranting on about 'the nasty taste' in her mouth. It meant, that after three months, we could use our lounge-room again."

By this stage, Ana and I were chuckling uncontrollably. The laughter compounded itself. Every chuckle caused another in the other. The situation described was probably humorous enough; what really infused it with hilarity was the sound appreciation each of us had of the character involved. It was so easy for us to imagine Ross doing something like this. It was a wickedly pleasant reaffirmation of our knowledge.

After the laughter subsided, Ana announced that he had to go. I declined a lift back to Brian's place, preferring to stay down at the beach to reminisce and watch the gathering sunset. He invited me to a party tomorrow night and we agreed to meet in a certain pub at about eight. I told him not to tell anyone I had returned. I preferred to blow into places unexpectedly and leave them with the same mysterious air with which I had arrived. It was a desire with a philosophical root in diffidence. I knew that it would cause no practical difference to my enjoyment of the impending meeting I was to have with all those with whom I had been once so familiar, but the principle of coming and going without drama appealed to my belief that more pertinent things were unfolding elsewhere. I was not certain of how much I wanted to see those people anyway and the converse also applied, so it seemed dignified and appropriate to reduce the scale of my return to the level it deserved. It would have been nice to have been invisible and wander into that impending party and be able to judge its virtue without having to submit myself to what I suspected would be a paucity of mature, intelligent conversation. I did not feel like going into a place where I would be expected to unleash tales which did not exist of the wanton impregnation of copious quantities of women from Dublin to Bangkok. Others could gain that thrill; I was now absorbed by the beautiful, prosaic features of obscure cultures and by the intricacies of the people I had befriended elsewhere.

I felt that it was not correct for me, though, to express my reservations to Ana. The last thing I wanted to do was create the impression that I had a superior sense of cultural sensitivity. I had seen others return from Europe in the misguided belief that they possessed a more cultivated perception than their childhood contemporaries. It may have been true – their perception had no doubt been altered – but it was insulting to start picking out the limitations of other people's lives.

Ana and I parted on the pavement outside the café. His smile was as beaming as ever. This was one positive thing I was glad was immune to change. I walked past the café towards a patch of greenery which sat above the sand dunes, overlooking the beach. A track ran down the grass to the sand. I chose to go down there to avoid the prospect of unplanned encounters. This path would enable me to bypass the congregation on the beach at North Cottesloe; with my back to them, I wandered along, hearing the ebb and flow of water against the shore. As it fell back off the sand, I saw clear, rapidly disappearing reflections of the sky in the glassy sheets left by the lazy withdrawal of the foaming water. A glimmer of a seagull, reflected as though flying beneath the sand, flickered a distorted image of white wings before the water, instantaneously blue, was sucked away by the illuminated presence of the ocean, a monumental passageway that had both aided and hindered the hopes and passions of scheming men. Only when an ocean is mountainous does it take on, in the aesthetic imagination, the qualities that we, in our cerebral vagaries, ascribe so easily to the striking features of the land. But in my imagination now, after having been away from it for so long, this vibrant vastness of water, air and sand had attained a resonance of beauteous perfection usually only reserved for high mountains, volcanoes, rainforests and glaciers, for on its azure surface, ever-changing globules of burnt orange, ringed by black, swam with a kind of languid frustration over this immensity, as if they had been deposited, like droplets, from the glowing candle of the sun.

On the sand, tinged orange by that descending blaze, indiscriminate couples lay in close contact, side by side, as if their intimate relationships were being blessed by that king of the skies, who brought down upon them the tranquil sanction of his fiery maze. This, I realised, would be a perfect place to have a relationship. It was like living in a holiday resort. The accumulated antagonisms of the centuries had left their savage hooks on the other side of the globe; families would not be split here by pressing issues of conflict and racism. People here could choose their beliefs without the repercussions that, in other places, afflicted millions, and the sun, with its peachy air of mirthful radiance, seemed to affirm this, as though its coruscations of kindness lit up wispy clouds and sprinkled upon the sands a delicate mist of tranquil and orange haze.

Lying on the sand, I faced this pageant of colour and watched it celebrate equality with a dignified silence fitting for such regal magnificence. There are very few situations in nature in which profoundly beautiful changes occur silently; those that do all involve light, and very few ever would have been able to rival the quiet splendour unfolding before my eyes; for, across the waters, peaceful and docile, as though representative of a smiling God, four arms of symmetrical light burst forth from the sun with a powdery brilliance of strength and delicacy and transformed the high white clouds above me into glowing globules of dreamy bliss; spidery wisps of vapour burned with golden iridescence, like electrified epaulettes, on the burnt red cloak of the sun, that, swathed in the fabric of kings, as if possessed of divine miracles, created a pathway across the water in which the droplets of luminous oil quivered in an inviting thread of fiery light. The taffeta this thread was sewn within lay unmoved in its worship of a scene it had witnessed with unpredictable demeanour for billions of years. Smooth and unafflicted, it absorbed the beauty above it with a serenity of indifference idyllic in its calm rejection of all earthly desires. Not one act by man had ever disrupted the unpredictable flow of its unfathomable ways. Like all things beautiful, the consciousness behind its motivations was the subject of infinite discourse and its existence, as an example of the peace to be extracted from the refutation of frenetic aspirations, infused within me a detachment not dissimilar to the magnitude of self-contained imperturbability burning away upon the flaming extremities at the far edge of the world.

Not one thought about London or my ambitions or desires caused a ripple to ruffle the glassy waters of my repose. I felt as unconcerned about my place in the world as that boundlessness of water and sky did about us. No amount of begging would ever unlock it from its serene self-absorption, from its kindness and ferocity, from its wishes that seemed without moral sense; I assumed freedom was a kind of disassociation from moral imposition, and my present detachment (I was unconcerned about God or higher consciousness) although fleeting, created the delusion that I was devoid of difficult hopes and unfulfilled passions. Lying on this beach I almost felt as though I were in love. Something of the unhurried transcendence which characterises that condition enveloped me with the sweetness of the balmy air. Possibly the sudden disconnection from responsibilities had something to do with it, and certainly the intense sensation of reflection did.

On the very waters before me, I had spent some of my most exhilarating days. A reef, dark and mysterious, formed the spot where the waves had broken; a spot sought after by absorbed teenagers in pursuit of the perfect ride. Hordes of us had huddled there together for the opportunity of being lifted, with a surprise that never went away, on to our feet by the momentum of the sacred wave. This experience, still without parallel, is the purest example I have yet to feel of those rare moments in which one is absolved from the unpleasant realities of life. On those waves there was no responsibility, no ambition, no work, no loneliness, no inadequacies – only the free rush of a perfect thrill, over clear water, beneath a dazzling sun, toward a vast sense of exalted achievement.

Being here now before the sunset, amused by my past ignorance, seemed also like an achievement. I presumed it was because I felt that I had made the right decision. I had learnt about life in two worlds and now I was going to learn a lot more. I was in the right frame of mind for discovery and the knowledge I would acquire could, I felt, create unforeseen opportunities. There was something about knowledge that resembled the sight I was witnessing, of light being so gloriously absorbed into vapour. It created a beauty of contentment, continually awe-inspiring with its changing and sensuous complexity of colours. The undersides of the unmoving clouds had now gone an iridescent purple and behind them, beneath the sun, a tinge of orange ran along the horizon and fell from an elongated cloud of gold, as though it were a magic dust falling into a transcendent blaze.

The sky above me had gone a deep ocean blue and, as I followed it from its zenith to the light blue near the horizon, I saw the first stars twinkling in the satin shroud of fabric wrapped over a peaceful world. This appearance of the dazzling existence of other worlds was the starting point from which our sun, now an enflamed peach, began its disappearance by changing shape, spreading itself out along the horizon, as if casting itself into the placid waters which rolled out a welcoming carpet of orange for this king whose light gave life to us all.

As this monarch began his arrival in the old world, other masters of dominions much older revealed their powers with a clarity and simplicity of expression that belied the cataclysmic furies transpiring within their cores. The ocean blue above me was now black and nearer the horizon the hue of an halcyon sea lay washed over the edge of the sky, where the sun's rays, in a lantern-like effect of orange haze, lingered, momentarily, with melancholic luminosity and then disappeared, the final throes of an extravagant demise.

Death in nature is always fascinating, often savage, frequently beautiful and never dull. Its attraction lies in the inevitable destruction of that which is most precious and most mysterious; its sombre necessity, particularly after a blazing sunset, produces an anti-climax, one which, in a country like this, does not last for too long; for here, in a triumph of cultivation, the night sky blossoms with the blooming of the stars.

From the ebony of its impenetrable bed sprang a conflagration of light so profound that it appeared as though the seeds of this flowering radiance had been spread in an orgy of generous disregard. At the zenith of the hemisphere, the concentration of stars was so thick that a shimmering cloud of translucent haze quivered beneath the darkness in a delicacy of gentle resplendence, hiding, like a woman, the passion by which she gives life. From a young age I had marvelled over the complexity of this feminine incandescence; it had awed my tender eye;

it had been a stable force of beauty at a time when family relationships were so tense. Many an evening was spent lying on my back, with my younger brother, studying the patterns and shapes of the sky. Those nights were so clear that we were able, although we did not know it then, to see light which had travelled for two million years. The distraction of these night skies helped ease us away from the emotional constrictions of family life. Its detachment, like an absorption in its own splendours, was so complete that none of our petty indiscretions committed, relatively, in the blink of an eye, would ever affect its beatific aloofness. Its presence rescued us from the chaos of our grandmother's humourless and petulant ways. It made sense, this mathematical exactness of luminosity which offered mysteries and peace, and it opened up our minds.

One evening, while observing the easy glide of American and Russian satellites, we saw something that, had I been by myself, would have remained unmentionable. It came towards the earth at a terrific rate, flashed across the hemisphere with unbelievable speed, then charged off in the direction from which it had come. On those evenings we had seen numerous meteors eaten up by the earth's atmosphere but we had never seen anything like this.

"Jesus," my brother had slowly drawled, "what do you think that was?"

"That", I replied, "was not natural."

It seemed impossible that a heavenly body could do what this object had just done. The speed of approach was too sharp to allow it to just clip the earth's gravitational field and then change direction, as it so radically had. Some intelligence had manipulated its mysterious course. We even wondered whether secret technologies, created by the superpowers, existed. In those days, no Voyager spacecraft travelled the cosmos. Man had yet to bounce his own creations of the earth's own gravitational field. The light show had finally produced some hint of the existence of superintelligence. But how could something come from so far? Relative to the earth's surface, that thing had flashed by at thousands of miles per second. We knew this because we could compare its speed with those of the satellites. It was in one hell of an almighty rush. Its flashing glimpse of this planet probably enabled it to take a high-resolution video of us with equipment a billion years in advance of anything we may ever know.

The astonishment on our faces was of no relevance to my grandmother. She came to the back door and insisted that we come inside. Her temper, usually at boiling point, was on this evening particularly severe. Mark and I had just witnessed the probable existence of another sentient life-form - of intelligence incomprehensible - and we knew, in the storm of her fury, that any attempt at expressing this would lead to a quake of violent uninterest.

Not a word was spoken. We never suffered from the delusion that anyone was particularly interested in us and this was a pity for it is a wonderful delusion to have.

Inside the house Mark, eight years old, and still bewildered, said, with grave wonderment, "It came from another place."

It was then that he realised how minuscule he really was; something about this place led me to believe that there were very few people here who shared the same philosophical perspective.

* * * * * * * * * *

The feminine qualities of the universe - radiant impeccability, coupled with indifference towards those who admire its glowing mysteries - are the antitheses of those possessed by Wayne. Any sensation of indifference he experienced occurred so fleetingly that it was usually undetectable. On the very rare moments it may have been noticeable, perhaps for a freakish nanosecond here and there, its existence in him appeared positively weird. No amount of experience would ever lead him to have prolonged moments of cool, philosophical, reflective introspection. This, biologically and psychologically, was out of the scope of possibility. The news of my premature departure from his house was greeted with barbaric disdain. The fact that he may have had something to do with it was also out of the scope of actuality. His outrage was only matched by his deluded sense of righteousness. The latter quality was so profoundly ingrained within him that it made him appear innocent. To some extent he was. Unconsciously, presumably for reasons of defence, he constantly repeated the justified anger he had experienced when younger. In his morally impregnable imagination, the scale of my departure was lifted to the dark heights of murder.

When glancing into the room I had occupied, the emptiness with which he was greeted was symbolic of the cruel void that clearly characterised my twisted soul. Not even a word of goodbye? The evidence was clear. I was obviously the most ungracious, unsavoury, ill-bred, inconsiderate, unfeeling, disrespectful, obnoxious, impolite, rude, vile, arrogantly superior bastard into whom God, in his/her viciously unfathomable ways, had had the audacity to breathe life.

"The wanker", he shouted, "goes and lives in Europe for six years and thinks he's too bloody good for us now, does he?"

"Us?" Kay asked, satirically.

She was exasperated by her attempts to get him to experience guilt. It confused her well brought-up sense of justice and logic as to why her husband was incapable of connecting his obstreperous fits with other people's peeved actions. It amazed her delicate sense of propriety as to how someone as unruly as her husband could sustain such an indomitable delusion of faultlessness. Her innocent upbringing, like a lot of people's, saved her from being able to comprehend the dubious logic of the classically warped mind. This was a privilege that God had so generously extended to me.

The day after leaving his place I rang up to ask him if he wanted to go to the cricket. Mark and I had decided to see a one day international on the weekend. I was expecting a frosty reception. I was not disappointed. He gruffly refused to be expansive while insinuating that my family priorities were suspect. When asked about his intended plans on the forthcoming Saturday he said, sarcastically, "I intend to spend it with my family."

"Because", I replied, ironically, "you're a family man?"

"A lot", he said, "you'd know about that."

He then hung up.

Infuriated, I rang back straight away and said, "How long do you intend to be so fucking immature? Is it my fault that you don't think? Haven't you got anything better to do than to drive your wife and daughter nuts? Do you honestly expect me to hang around in a place dominated by a whining, oversized kid, incapable of behaving like an adult? Who do you think I am? Some sort of punching bag for your pathetic gibes—"

Just when I was getting into full flight, Kay grabbed the phone. Through her tears she said, "Don't worry about it, Knubs. I'll sort it out."

"He's crazy," I said. "You and I both know you can't live with him for the rest of your life. He's insane."

"I know, I know," she replied.

There was a kind of dignified resignation in her anguish.

"He's incapable", I said, "of connecting his behaviour to the past because he can't remember it. Even if he wanted to, he would not be able to offer an explanation. Do you understand?"

"It's okay," she cried. "You did the right thing."

"He will never grow up," I persisted.

Fighting the tears, she told me "not to worry about it."

She then hung up after I had wished her luck. Her emotional turmoil was a mixture of bemusement, pain, relief and self-pity. The agony of her husband's ridiculous behaviour was balanced by the moral justification my searing intolerance gave to her position. Her understandable ignorance of her husband's psychological state created the sanctity she required to help her through this absurd experience.

I put the phone down and wandered around, staring out the windows. Outside I saw the luminous blueness pour its sheet down upon the uncomplicated richness; the air was so still that hanging bedsheets in the sun gained the consistency of timber, but the radiance of snow. The green bushes were without blemish, shaped, untroubled by harsh turbulences, manicured symbols of self-respect. Only ants moved in this brilliant acquiescence to the sun. Not even the air had the audacity to quake beneath that which controlled all; here, that phenomenon had no consciousness - it was just there! - and one day it would be gone; and it will take all this with it.

In a way, though, it was a tragedy that this environment had not been given over to those whose daily lives were superior as a result of the accumulated experiences of the ages; it was slowly happening, but it hadn't happened yet.

Brian had heard my telephone conversation. He emerged from the lounge-room, startled.

"Problems between Wayne and Kay?" he asked, surprised.

I was amazed.

"Are you telling me", I began, "that you hadn't noticed?"

"I thought", he said, with real perplexity, "that they had patched their differences up."

'Jeezuss Christ,' I thought.

"I've witnessed", I replied, "over the last two days the operational definition of the word 'incompatibility'. If the World Health Organisation wanted to produce a documentary on its existence, they could have sent a video team in there for the last forty-eight hours and used it as the bible for marital breakdown."

"Nanna", he said, "is going to find this hard to believe."

'Even she,' I thought. Wayne was profoundly convincing at times.

"Are you telling me", I began, "that this would come as a shock to her?"

"Totally," he replied.

"Incredible," I said.

"They were at her place for dinner", he replied, "only a few weeks ago and she said everything seemed great."

I clearly wanted to talk about Wayne and Kay, but Brian used their situation as a means to talk about his own. I was suddenly on the receiving end of a tirade against his ex-wife. Hands were waving. Expressions of moral amazement plastered his face. His eyes suggested that the listener could not have any other purpose but to be interested in this verbal bludgeoning. I felt angered, at first; then I accepted the fates: he was incapable of perceiving a lack of interest; his ability to objectively take in information had gone. I knew that absolute reticence was the only solution.

As my mind contemplated the gravity of Wayne and Kay's incompatibility, I saw his righteous face undertake a number of dramatic sways. The opening of his mouth was often accompanied by the sharp raising and opening of his hands. I could tell that he was beginning to run out of information; some of it was staggering in its puerile conception: "She was so cocky. She thought she was going to get everything. She forced her husband to sell one of his properties, and also one of his cars, so she could travel around Australia, Japan and the South Pacific. She's bleeding this bloke dry. One morning at breakfast about five years ago she threw a tantrum and screamed out: 'Why don't we have two properties and a Mercedes?' This, of course, is what lover-boy had when she first met him. Of course, the guy didn't have anyone to support. He could afford it; but, now she's with him, he's feeling the pinch. I get this information from Vanessa. Of course, bloody Lois was too stupid to realise he wasn't that rich. His bloody Mercedes was seventeen years old! Seventeen years old! Vanessa told me that Lois had said to her: 'I don't love him, but he's generous.' I can't understand how any woman could love that bloke. He's a mess. When I first saw him, I couldn't believe it. Short, fat, bald, terrible. It was a bloody joke. He tried coming around here a few times and I threatened to kill him. Of course, you know, Greg clobbered him. Took me a while to really work out what she was up to. It wasn't just him, you know. He wasn't the only one. She gave me a non-specific urinary tract infection. The doctor said to me, 'Brian, have you been playing up?' 'No, no, no,' I said. 'Why?' 'Well,' he said, 'I'll leave it to you to come to your own conclusions.' Of course, Lois denied everything. I found out later that she was getting laid virtually every day after work in the car park at the Education Department. Her boss was giving her one every day after work in a van. One day at the front door here I heard one of her sugar daddies saying, 'He's not good enough for you.' There were so many things I wanted to say to her face, but didn't. I did everything to retrieve the situation – everything. I gave her a chance."

Then he began regaling me with tales about men who had thwarted their ex-wife's attempts to "ruin them financially":

"I know a bloke who knew his wife was having an affair and that she was planning to leave him. She left, and he got the property in the settlement. About a week after the divorce his girlfriend moved in with him – into their property. She was still paying the mortgage at that stage. Apparently she went berserk. Nothing she could do about it, though. What'd she expect? She leaves him and expects to still control his life. Incredible! I know another bloke whose wife was having an affair. He packed her bags and dumped them on the front verandah and refused her entry. Within two weeks she was back. Obviously, the boyfriend wouldn't live with her. I know of another bloke – this one's a bit of a famous story – who burnt down his house and factory to deny his wife any property in their settlement. He worked for it; why should he give it to someone else? So many blokes lose houses and cars. That bloke who burnt down his factory – he got done for arson – said he wasn't the slightest bit interested in the insurance money. Made sure though that the wife got nothing. There was probably no point in receiving insurance money anyway; it'd probably've all gone to her. So many blokes lose the lot. No way I'm ever going to get married again. Not a chance. Won't happen. I was lucky though. I came out of it all right. The kids say I'm too conservative – but I've still got my house and car. I'm much better off now than I expected to be at this age. People say I'm bitter, but I'm not. Things are okay."

I didn't agree. All I saw before me was bitterness. He was unable to see mine. No doubt his ex-wife had had these frustrations compounded to the point of hysteria as well.

"No way am I bitter," he reiterated, with a glint of resolve in his eye which did not exist in his character. "Things could be much worse. She was a financial nightmare."

There was no doubt in my mind that, if it were possible for him to revert back to the situation within which he had existed previously, he would not hesitate to accept this opportunity to have his emotional fulfilment returned. His dignity was immature enough to stop him from acknowledging bitterness, but it was not strong enough for him to be more considerate of other people's feelings.

I had stared at him blankly throughout his ill-timed rant and the only thing that had formed in my mind during the course of his unwanted harangue was a bleak and sad picture of my elder brother's questionable future. But my interlocutor was desensitised to that.

"During our divorce", he continued, without the slightest consideration for my sanity, "she was told by her lawyer that my behaviour had been too good to enable her to get the things she wanted, so do you know what the bitch did?"

"What?"

"She deliberately undressed in front of me to try and tempt me to do something she could take advantage of. I was sleeping in the lounge and she came in there and stripped off in front of me; she virtually shoved her arse in my face. But I wasn't having anything of it. She knew she was facing an uphill battle and she started to get desperate. No way was I going to lay hands on her. No way. I knew when she did that, that I had her. She hung around in the lounge-room for about fifteen minutes and I just rolled over and ignored her. Then she just started screaming. She said she was going to get the lot. She said I had driven her insane. I just waved my hand and said, 'I'm not interested.' I slept like a baby that night, I can tell you."

My anger had now been replaced by a sort of determined righteous resolution. I was going to talk about Wayne whether he liked it or not.

"Kay", I said, "will not be sleeping like a baby."

"When Wayne lived here", he replied, "he drove everyone nuts. I always had to be careful of what I said for fear of upsetting him. Me! In my own home! The only reason I didn't throw him out was because of Nanna. She would have been pretty upset about that. There were times when Wayne's behaviour was unbelievable. He could suddenly throw unpredictable tantrums in which cutlery would be strewn all over the floor. I had to endure this because they had to live here to get themselves back on their feet financially again, and he treated me like that. He was impossible. The bloody abuse he can dish out. When I was building the swimming pool, he reversed out of the carport and ran over a cable I'd laid across the driveway. He ruined the bloody thing and I said, 'Don't you ever look in the rear-vision mirror? One day you'll run over a three-year-old child.' And Wayne, in his typically argumentative, never-accept-the-blame style said, 'I suppose you nicked it from the ABC. Wouldn't put it past you.' If he ever apologises for anything, I'll eat my car."

I was quickly getting the impression that Brian's repressed outrage at those who had compromised his self-esteem and deluded sense of moral impeccability was going to be poured out all over me over the next six weeks.

"Wayne", I said, slowly and dryly, "is definitely headed for a disaster."

* * * * * * * * * *

Brian got his second phone call in two days before nine in the morning from someone who must have known that he had retired. The fact that I was next door on the other side of a paper-thin wall made me feel that, if this was retirement, then I'd rather work for ever.

"Ah God," he gasped, "they have to do that themselves! If he can't talk to his wife and repair the damage – THEN WHO CAN!!!"

I felt like creating the ultimate dance of frustration called the Hucancan. It was Nanna attempting to persuade him to have a barbecue so that Wayne and Kay could undertake a reconciliation. My grandmother's impulsiveness, born from love, was only rivalled by my own. All concern for Brian appeared to have momentarily been wiped away by the flood of her irresistible demands. Have you ever heard of sacrifice she could've easily asked: "Well? Have you?"

"Yes," I would have replied, "my whole childhood was sacrificed. Fortunately, however, not before nine in the morning."

Unfortunately, this kind of dry appreciation had the effect of sharpening my grandmother's attack and, because of this, Brian was rigidly fearful of employing it.

"Okay, okay," he said, "I'll ring – today."

Bleary-eyed, Brian explained to me that Wayne was not coming home from work. Apparently, he'd been "driving off in huffs and Christ knows what. Bloody Wayne. He's such a bloody irresponsible child. And I'm supposed to do something about it! Me! What about your father? Why doesn't she ask him? Wh—"

"Because, Brian," I interrupted, "she's got faith in you as a human being and none in my father. Maybe she wants to believe in you more. Sometimes she must say to herself, when thinking about my father, 'Was I really responsible for that?' At least you can reassure her. And also because she's ignorant of one very significant fact, of which my father, disgusted by its existence, is totally and utterly aware."

"What fact?" he asked.

"Something", I replied, "regarding one of Wayne's previous employments."

"You don't mean the bank?" he asked.

"No," I replied. "Something else."

"Does Kay know this?" he asked.

"No," I replied. "She's got an inkling, but she doesn't know for sure."

When my father told me the facts, it was the first time that I had felt sympathy for his outraged dismissiveness.

"On the day he got sacked", my father said, "he came around here acting as if he was amazed by what had happened. He tried telling me he'd been retrenched. The idiot was going home early. He was spreading yellow sand on his lawns when he should have been working."

My father had got Wayne out of prison and given him a job, assuring Wayne's employers that Wayne would behave.

"He's finished," my father said, emphatically. "That's it."

On discovering these facts, I was uncertain of how my grandmother would react if she knew. I was to unearth the answer before departing from the land of my birth. It was a pleasant, but melancholic, realisation.

"I wonder if Nanna knows?" he asked, as though I were not there.

"Not a chance," I replied. "And I'm certainly not going to tell her."

* * * * * * * * * *

Back in London twelve months later, after having not contacted my family, I realised how much remorse, despite everything they did and had done, I would suffer if one of them died: guilt, regret, self-analysis, unsatisfied curiosity – all at once. This was an experience that yet awaited me – the departure of one's close ones from this world – and it would happen, eventually, in mounting waves, in compounding textures, across nationalities, continents, hundreds of them, all just gone. How much time would there be to think about anything else? There were obviously a great many strong people out there holding back a lot.

* * * * * * * * * *

He came in through the glass sliding doors and ignored them both, completely. The piercing outrage in his brown eyes suggested a wild depression lying ready to explode into violence. A mood of ferocious intolerance enveloped the air around him. The bright light outside seemed a mistake, a trifle, in comparison to the tenebrous fury that lurked within.

He went to the refrigerator and got a beer, almost walking over his confused daughter in the process. She looked up at him with bewildered eyes.

"Daddy," she began, as he went straight past her.

She watched him go out on to the patio and sit down. She walked up to the glass and saw the inexplicable anger of moral outrage and entrapment work devilish tricks on someone upon whom she was dependent for emotional support. There was something dangerous and incomprehensible in his pain, something permanent and recurring; long periods of aggressive hysteria were beyond her comprehension. There was nothing tangible to which she could relate this mood. Nothing had been knocked over. Nothing had been said. The house was clean. Mummy had not said anything. No arguments about dress or television had occurred. It was painful in its nefarious unpredictability.

She began opening the sliding doors and he told her to leave him alone. The tone of cruelty in his voice suggested something new and iniquitous had entered this world. The atmosphere reeked of a surreal uncertainty. All the trust on which she had relied was now dissipated by this dangerous complexity of fuming viciousness. For the first time in her life the world had become a truly evil place.

She pressed her face against the glass and watched with a mixture of grave concern and hope as her father stared distantly into the back garden at a point way beyond the fence. Alienation from the simple pleasures of life induced within her a sensation that certainty was an illusion. The glass that separated her from her father was solid, impenetrable, but, as though in a deliberate attempt to make her see, it was transparent, beyond doubt. She was being left in no doubt that her father's life was more important than her own.

Unbeknown to her, her father had had the same experience thirty years previously. Wayne had attempted to get into bed with his parents. I was already in the bed. For some inexplicable reason they did not allow him in. He was thrust out and shoved on to the floor. He was too surprised and shocked to make a sound. The expression on his face that day paralleled that of his daughter's helpless disbelief.

While he was on the floor looking at us, our parents began laughing at him. They even found his pained confusion amusing. It was impossible to judge what he would do to someone now if they laughed at him in the same way. Someone who knew him well could not rule out the possibility of unrestrained violence.

Conscious of his daughter's gaze, he got up and moved around the patio and out of sight. Kay was in the kitchen watching Emma staring through the glass. Both of them were unconscious of the repressed hostility Wayne bore towards those he considered responsible for the thwarting of his hedonistic goals. From a young age the easy pleasure others received, constantly, was denied to him; it only came to him in unpredictable fits and starts; his whole life had been an attempt to have this experience on a more normal and permanent basis - in a sense to have the childhood he had been denied. Forces had now conspired to inhibit this desire - his wife was not sleeping with him, friends had deserted him, his professional future was not overtly going to be interesting, contemporaries had travelled - and the intensity of this ineluctability was enhanced by the pertinacious self-belief of his wife.

She opened the glass doors, angered that he was not paying any attention to their daughter. Her demands were justly born from the idea that parenthood has to be shared. Wayne was not fulfilling his part of the bargain. His immature denial of responsibility grated on the simplicity of her emotional and moral foundation.

She burst out on to the patio and said, "You know the reason why I don't sleep with you."

This caused Wayne to throw the can of beer on to the ground and storm off along the side of the house to the front garden where he got into his car and drove away.

Inside the house, after hearing the car, Emma said, "Mummy – what happened?"

"Daddy had to go back to work," Kay replied.

"Now?" Emma asked, bemused.

"It's a special night," Kay replied.

"Why special?" Emma asked.

"Oh Emma," Kay snapped, impatiently, "it's hard to explain."

The fiery tone of her mother's voice caused Emma to feel as though her curiosity were indecent. Her absolute ignorance of the background to her parents' behaviour gave her a feeling of abandonment. Life now was like a forced march along a deadly precipice. Goodness seemed to have no reward. Perplexing reprehensibility seared dark shadows into the light of her existence.

She followed her mother into the kitchen and said, "Can we go and see Daddy at work?"

"Not tonight," Kay replied. "I'm afraid your father wants to be alone."

Emma had never seen her parents in such a state of agitated detachment. It was frightening. The idea that one of them wanted to be alone scared her. But it didn't scare her as much as the idea of both of them being like this at the same time.

She went into her room and was alone, against her will, for the first time in her life. It was not going to be the last.

* * * * * * * * * * *

I rang Kay to see if any normality had descended upon her abode. There was an air of resignation in her voice; Wayne was "beyond redemption." He was still ignoring them both and "being horrible to Emma."

"She", Kay said, "is totally confused."

I assumed Kay was as well. I could imagine that Wayne, in his current mood, would be interpreting any tentative attempt to placate him as a sign of weakness.

"The best thing to do with Wayne", I said, "is to point the facts out to him, and then ignore him."

"The thing that upsets me most", she replied, "is his total inability to admit blame. He's just like your father."

I laughed and said, "My father's always told me he's just like his mother."

"Who do you believe?"

"My grandmother told me once", I replied, "that my mother was a calm, polite individual. That is towards her, of course. She was violent towards us. I would say that my parents were as bad as each other. Wayne managed to acquire the negative aspects of both of them."

"If he", she calmly said, "lays a hand on Emma, I'll kill him."

"He won't do that," I replied. "You've seen the worst of him and you have to decide if that's too bad for you."

"Domestic violence", she said, "would definitely be the end. These things usually begin with violence towards an inanimate object first; he's already done that. I'm a bit on edge."

"He's mad", I replied, "but he won't do that. He'll drive you nuts in a more unpredictable way. I was totally opposed to your marriage because he's the sort of person who should never be married. He can't cope with responsibility. He'll cause all sorts of problems continually – and you have to decide if you can live with that."

"He said", she remarked, "that he isn't going to spend Christmas with us. He charged off one day saying he was going to spend it at Rottnest with some friends. In a way, I hope he does."

"Are you prepared for a divorce?" I asked.

"Yes," she replied.

I was glad about this.

"My father told me", I said, "that he had tried to convince your mother that your marriage should not go ahead. He told me your mother assumed this was an attack on you – that you weren't good enough for Wayne. My father told me he had said, 'It's not your daughter, it's my son – he's mad!' Is this true?"

"Yes," Kay replied. "A party was arranged to bring the two families together. Your father acted disgracefully. He was really pissed. He swore like hell. He said that he would do everything to stop Wayne getting married. He destroyed the occasion."

"Not the first time he's done that," I said.

"No," she replied, ruefully; then added, "Wayne's just pulled up here. He's recently shown signs of wanting a reconciliation. He suggested that I ring Brian to organise a barbecue at his place, but I can't ring someone to ask if we can have a party at their house. Can you get Brian to ring?"

"No problems," I said.

'Nanna', I thought, 'has obviously been hard at work.'

* * * * * * * * * *

The barbecue was eventually arranged. It was an occasion monumental for Wayne's charismatically derisive jocularity, the disinclination some women possess toward contentious debate and, lo and behold, communication. If someone had lifted the roof off Brian's house and listened to the conversations transpiring in two different rooms – one the lounge: a house of debating, beer-swilling men – the other, the kitchen: a group of annoyed women performing mundane domestics – then the voyeur would have been treated to parallel scenes of dramatic power the rival of anything in Harold Pinter. Prosaic the occasion may have been, but there was an underlying veracity to it which appealed to that unshakeable aesthetic sentiment at the core of my person. For this reason I longed to know what the ladies were discussing. I could imagine it: 'Bloody men! Why do they have to argue? Is there one on earth capable of listening? How long are they going to sit there for, squabbling about the world's problems? As if any of them really care!'

A few days later, I asked Kay. I knew that her reluctance to elaborate was due to a fear that I would spread the information freely amongst the male members of my family. It was hopeless trying to explain to her that my motivation was born from some noble sense of dramatic sensibility and not an idle interest in gossip; I was unconcerned, in a sense, by the personalities involved; it was the situation that intrigued me. The scenario of two groups, defined by sex, herding themselves together into separate rooms to perform completely different tasks was a phenomenon fundamental to this society, and therefore fascinating to the anthropologically-inclined mind. However, I never found out. She was too proud to satisfy my intellectual curiosity. And how could I expect anyone to appreciate my motives? They were too vague, too esoteric. Not everyone – and this was a good thing – is motivated by the slice of ice in the soul more commonly known as "an infatuation with the truth".

The evening began carefreely enough. I was stretched out on an easy chair on the patio when Wayne came bounding in through the side gate carrying a cardboard box full of meat and drinks. An aura of chirpy open-mindedness marked his arrival. The incivility of his previous behaviour was as distant as the first stars, gleaming above in the azure and tranquil heights that stretched for ever in a luminous testimony to aesthetic morality, to fineness, to power and delicacy, to the very foundation of our souls. I had been enjoying the still splendour of the twilight, the silent music of the gathering night, when Wayne thrust a beer in my hand and said, "I'm under strict instructions this evening from the War Office to behave. Me!? Can you believe it?"

His self-derision indicated to me that he intended to be thoroughly agreeable. His daughter was overjoyed with this attitude. She came charging out of the house with her bathers on and grabbed Wayne by the leg in an endeavour to drag him into the pool. Hanging from Wayne's leg, she giggled as he spun around and said to me, "The tart'll never learn to tackle properly. And it's all her fault."

He was now pointing at Kay who emerged with the steaks. She looked at me and said, "It's always my fault."

She dropped the steaks on to the barbecue and soon the sizzle of cooking filled my ears.

"Thank God for that," I replied, stretched out. "I was beginning to worry that I would have to undertake the indecent and thoroughly displeasing act of having to insist that someone hurry up and cook for me."

She smiled and said, "I wonder how long his sense of humour will last this time?"

"It's a pity", I replied, "that he possesses such a profound ability to lose it. Such is life."

In the distance we could hear Emma giggling and splashing with her jovial father in the pool.

"You don't have much faith in him, do you?" she asked.

"No," I replied. "But I don't think he's going to get any worse either."

"You're probably right," she said.

"On the subject of a sense of humour," I began, "I was in this restaurant the other day and twice this waitress had to ask me to get up so she could get these brandy glasses out of this cabinet which happened to be right next to me. The second time I got up she said, 'Sorry, I won't bother you again. I promise,' and I said, 'That's exactly what my first wife said,' and she fell down on to the table absolutely killing herself laughing. I knew it was good, but it wasn't that good. She seemed to take about five minutes to get up."

Kay laughed generously at this anecdote.

"That's not a bad one," she then said, chuckling.

Her laughter was arrested by Greg's arrival. My cousin swaggered in slowly with a look of cheery naughtiness on his handsomely-chiselled face. He was expecting to be the recipient of some good-natured derision: he was not wrong. From the swimming pool, Wayne gave him the option of getting him a drink or "having his head used as a mallet to soften up the steaks."

"I can cope with that," Greg smiled. "My head loves coming into contact with nice, soft, red flesh; you know that."

Greg was not known for his shyness in matters prurient.

Kay spun around and said: "Oh Greg!"

Greg and I laughed at her prudish anger. It was short-lived, for she quickly took Greg's remark in the spirit it was intended; then Greg's girlfriend entered the patio carrying further refreshments as Wayne yelled out, ironically, from the swimming pool, "Do you think I want to listen to the sordid details of your disgusting sex life? Who do you think I am? Get me a bloody drink. Man's not a camel."

Greg and I laughed at Wayne's sardonic temerity.

"Such a master", Greg said, "in the art of diplomatic requests."

"He gets it from his mother," I said, "according to his father."

His girlfriend got Wayne a drink.

"A man", Wayne finally said, with mock outrage, as everyone laughed, "can't even rely on members of his own family in a crisis. You're all out of my will."

Greg and Danielle then went inside to see Brian. I lay back in the chair and looked at the pellucid sky and marvelled at the alluring distances. A pale band of sky was crowned by the dark blue of the encroaching night. So perfect was the configuration of air and stars that it seemed artificial, too unblemished, in the mind of one now influenced by the attractive tardiness of the old world. Nothing stirred. The buzz of insect calls had departed with the loss of day. The wind, as though daunted by the appearance of so much intergalactic light, had gone. Everywhere beneath this intrusion of arcane possibilities houses stretched uniformly in a converse reflection to that which rose over them, as though this universe were only compromised of two things: suburbia and the stars. This empirical distortion of mystery and security enhanced the sense of isolation that fell on this place in the blackness of night. There was no sense of outside influence, other than things too mysterious and distant to be of any relevance, for they were too implausible to leave a mark on people bent on simple, hedonistic pursuits; but I did not care. I was set free in a warm succulence of irresponsibility.

Later, we were sitting around the dinner table when the stirring debate began. Its inspiration was Brian. He was convinced that the current economic recession could be laid squarely to blame on the current prime minister. The instant this comment was uttered, the women disappeared into the kitchen. They moved with such quiet rapidity that it seemed as though their departures were expected. The mere smell of political debate enters the nostrils of some people here like a putrid redolence capable of causing cancer. Its introduction into conversation is sufficient to cause the transmigration of millions. I responded to Brian's charge – that the deregulation of the banks was the main cause – by suggesting that Australia's current situation had arisen as a result of "historical factors" born "from a lack of enterprise" and an appalling attitude towards "intelligent management and investment". The deregulation that caused an absurd tidal wave of badly invested credit was just a catalyst for the exposure of a much deeper problem. Brian was not overtly opposed to this. Political debate is often merely a platform on which people can step to air their prejudices. Maybe this was the reason the women left so quickly. A debate about personal feelings may have been more in their interest, but these debates cannot always occur.

In front of a collection of empty beer cans, Greg was next to step on to the platform of bias. He was adamant that "all New Zealanders should be kicked out." They had "just taken jobs that Australians could do." As he spoke, Danielle silently collected the empty beer cans and left without the slightest reaction to her boyfriend's radical remark. Moments later, she reappeared with four more cans and deposited them on the table before us. I was amazed by this. I felt as though I were in some remote enclave in Saudi Arabia. She left with an air of dutiful disenchantment. In the kitchen I could hear the sounds of conversation and the clattering of dishes. The debate about immigration had raged on without the slightest fillip as Danielle had silently performed her domestic sacrifice. How I longed to discover what was being said in the kitchen. I felt that I would never know.

Wayne and I dismissed Greg's remarks by agreeing that "Australians had been too lazy." The jobs taken by New Zealanders were there because Australians, Wayne said, "had been too busy surfing. There are thousands of young blokes around this country more interested in their surfboards than in getting a job."

Greg's ideas on immigration were given universal denunciation. During the raucous arguments against his hard-line views, Wayne, with a look of sentient involvement, opened one of the beer cans virtually the instant it had been placed on the table; he began his tirade against work-shy Australians as though Danielle were a waitress in a club frequented by men glad to be away from women. She did not expect a response and she got none. I felt rather awkward about this. This degradation was foreign to me. It had happened naturally, as a matter of course. I stared at her face during this episode and was met with an expression of phlegmatic resignation. Pride alone would have stopped me from being treated like this. I would have thought, 'Let the bastards get their own!' But she was kinder than I, and obviously more accepting.

Brian then introduced the subject of American foreign policy. American warships had for years come and gone from Fremantle, their personnel pouring millions into the coffers of the Western Australian economy. Now they were gone. Brian was convinced that Washington had changed its policy as a result of pressure applied by "aggressive, shit-throwing lesbians" on the docks at Fremantle. I was so astonished by this theory that I got him to repeat it. Even though I had acoustically perceived his comment, intellectually my neo-cortex was unable to process it. A handful of foreign lesbians had been responsible for the American government re-examining its foreign policy! What a concept! The utterance was remarkable enough, but, in a situation where a geographic schism had already developed based on sex, it was positively inflammatory. With a disregard for the facts brutal in its biased unreality, he stepped on to the platform of jaundiced preconception and attempted to tell me that, because American servicemen had been attacked by "huge lesbians wielding plastic bags full of shit", the American government had altered its strategy in the Indian Ocean. This caused some laughter to burst out of me. I was overjoyed with the thought that some clean-shaven, square-jawed, prickle-headed, broad-shouldered, red-blooded American seaman had been so upset about his pristine uniform being smeared with faeces that the steely, rigid hand of American foreign policy had been lifted from the shores of Western Australia. Brian's detestation of lesbians, of feminists, of women who altered the safe status quo was so profound that it affected his view of international politics. It further warped his already warped mind.

After my laughter receded, I explained that American foreign policy in this part of the world had been changed as a result of the cessation of the Cold War and the growing American budget deficit.

"It is neither economically nor politically feasible", I said, "for American warships to land on these shores. Just imagine how much it costs – and for what?"

This comment caused Greg to say, "No more jobs for the boys."

Greg's remark was accompanied with an expression of pretentious certainty. The idea that American naval personnel enjoyed the ride on warships and then get a genuine thrill out of spending a week on shore in a place as boring as Perth was not worth the merest hint of consideration. However, there was a sort of diffident peremptoriness in the tone of his voice that embarrassed Brian who looked at me, unprepared, although feeling it, to admit that his comments about lesbians were ridiculous. His eyes were filled with stunned dismay. I felt that he was undergoing self-analysis. He may have even been undertaking the realisation that his insights were too regularly affected by absurd prejudices. That would have been a breakthrough in personal thinking which I could not seriously assume was occurring.

His failure to equate harsh economic morality with America's relationship with other countries actually said more for his cherished dream for perspicacity – a dream that led to some weird insights and made him appear even less knowledgeable than he actually already was – than any particularly negative feelings he may have possessed about women. Too often he spoke without thinking, applying a tone of serious austerity to his speech, one designed to add veracious conviction to his eccentric platitudes, and one that only belittled him in the eyes of his listeners. His main problem was his own credulity. He possessed too much unfounded respect for people. In this regard, he differed markedly from everyone else in my family. There was, however, no vindictiveness in his silence. He knew, correctly, that I had not disagreed on grounds of personal bias. He was not ridiculous in that respect; other members of my family were. Wayne assumed it as a matter of course.

It was he who broke the silence by saying that Vanessa was looking "too fat". He blamed this on Brian's insistence that Vanessa should not play sport. The playing of sport, in Brian's view, impinged upon study time. Wayne was appalled by this suggestion.

"Everyone in my day", he said, "did it. It's part of your education. It's a way of getting to know people. It improves you as a person. It makes you competitive. It actually helps to improve study because it stops you from becoming lazy. Let's face it, how often does she sit around here doing nothing when her friends are out playing sport?"

He then leant forward over the table and beseeched Brian passionately with a glare of assertive righteousness. Brian, keen not to inflame the debate, maintained a look of unruffled calm. He pretended that he had heard all this before.

"If she played sport," he said, with a gentle assurance belying his true feelings, "she would waste even more time."

"Rubbish!" Wayne quipped. "Look at her – she's enormous."

This was an exaggeration. Vanessa was plump but shapely. She possessed the statuesque femininity of the Australian wench. She charged out of the kitchen, clutching four cans of beer, and said, "No, no, no. It's study, study, study. No time for anything else. Just study, study, study."

"No time", Wayne smiled, "for showing off those great legs on the hockey field."

"You should see her", Brian said, "in her Elle Macpherson underwear. She doesn't need sport—"

"Come on, Brian," Wayne interrupted, "you're talking about my cousin here. Here I am, interested in her education and welfare, and you have to reduce this discussion to a puerile debate about women and underwear. I'm shocked."

"Here at the dinner table as well," I added, equally amazed.

"Exactly," Wayne replied. "What a comment to make in front of two former members of the Church of England Boys' Society. Quite frankly, I'm disgusted."

"Didn't you know", Greg smiled, "he keeps incest magazines under his bed?"

"If he did", Wayne said, "you'd probably know."

Brian was chuckling happily on the other side of the table.

"Can't you wait", Wayne continued, "until we leave?"

"Obviously not," I said. "Has the man no shame?"

"And my cousin, too," Wayne added.

"I wonder", Greg said, "where the photography gear's stashed?"

"I can't afford to pay for her sporting career," Brian said. "The underwear costs me a fortune. She can't get enough of it."

"Well," Wayne said, "she's a member of this family, isn't she?"

I wondered what sort of reaction our boyish gibes were inducing in the kitchen.

"Hey, Vanessa," Wayne yelled out. "Put your underwear on – your old man's got a point to prove."

"That underwear", Vanessa said, emerging from the kitchen, "is only to be viewed by a special man. Not a drunken pack of sexist louts."

"My beer", Greg smiled, "has just run out. Do something constructive for a change, will you, and get me another one. Man's not a camel."

"You can get up", Vanessa said, "and get one yourself, you lazy bastard. Then you can help us dry some of these dishes."

"Okay," Greg replied, "but only if you put your underwear on."

"Now hang on," Wayne cried, maintaining his pretence of light-hearted propriety, "here I am – former member of the Church of England Boys' Society, a man confirmed into the Protestant Church, a caring family man with the sort of values that have helped forge the upright backbone of this community – and I'm surrounded by those whose gutter-like temerity extends to suggesting that members of the same family should make love. Outrageous!"

Leaning towards me and whispering, he then said, out of the corner of his mouth, "Just quietly, I got some last night. Wasn't bad either."

"Missus?" I asked.

"Just for a change."

Later, in an atmosphere of irreverent banter, all of us went into Vanessa's bedroom to extract Emma, who was asleep, from the bed. A long discussion had preceded our entry. Wayne and Kay knew that Emma would be annoyed about being woken up. However, there was no way anyone would be able to get her home in the morning. They jointly faced the inevitable abuse.

Apparently, in the car on the way home, Emma, strapped into the child's chair on the back seat, screamed out, with horrified detestation: "I hate you! I hate you both!!"

Of course, she was too young to appreciate the guilt her parents experienced; she was also oblivious of the fact that the evening had taken place for her benefit. But, then again, what are children for? She was effectively the unsuspecting victim of my grandmother's wisdom.

* * * * * * * * * * *

In the kitchen, the dinner plates had been stacked up with the sort of resignation normally associated with the predictability of something undesirable and unavoidable. They were covered in grease and bits of meat. On one plate, the smear of tomato ketchup looked unreal in the bright, fluorescent light; it was the sort of light one sees in an advertisement involving domestic products being used by some overjoyed housewife thrilled by the prospect of spending years washing the clothes of some gorgeous, caring husband, who, because of the perfection of his relationship with a woman profoundly satisfied with homely chores, never gets to see the kitchen in a state of grease-filled disarray. Everything was bright: the yellow gloves worn by Kay; the shiny white tiles upon the walls; the polished chrome of the sink; the gleaming door of the refrigerator; the white lino on the floor. A television documentary crew could have feasted on the pristine, well-kept delights of this excellent example of advertising bliss. Even the froth from the detergent had a joyous resplendence made more acute by the breaking down of white light as the photons ran through the bubbles, gleaming green, red, and gold. The high-pitched clash of dirty cutlery being tossed into the sink had the timbre of symbols being struck by an orchestra keen to render the positive aspects of domesticity with soaring crescendos and rhythmical chimes; it was an occasion to bring tears to the eyes of those emboldened by the pursuit of traditional roles. Not one advertising executive in the country could have been disappointed with the gusto with which these women attacked the pile of dishevelled plates that lay like some cancerous tumour on the stainless steel sink. How could those dishes not be ecstatic at the prospect of being dumped into the bubble bath that Kay had produced from a liquid the greenness of which was like the symbolic hue of a hangover? Those dishes longed for the frothy waters of cleanliness. You could almost hear them sing. Even the smell of the detergent was like a vaporous elixir sending the user into dizzy heights of warm contentment.

The only thing lacking was the right woman. These ones were a touch ironic to have the acquiescence required to fit the bill.

"Imagine", Kay said, as the rumble of contentious conversation emanated from the lounge, "if God decided tomorrow he was going to reward us with an entirely new opposite sex."

"You mean", Vanessa replied, "one with brains?"

"One", Danielle remarked, "that didn't have to be right all the time."

An advertising agency could at least put women in a better light by producing an advertisement in which the protagonist, chained to the kitchen, says, "The microbiological properties of new Strippo, known to be able to neutralise sodium phosphates, have revolutionised the chemistry of biodegradable polymers. My stupid husband doesn't know what that means either. The idiot forced me to stop my research at CSIRO because he was too fucking lazy to do the dishes, and our kids – God bless them all – all got hepatitis. New Strippo – more than just a detergent: with a husband like I've got, it's a matter of life and death."

"After a while", Kay sighed, languidly wiping grease from a plate, "you get sick of hearing the same old arguments."

"Sometimes", Danielle said, "I wouldn't mind joining in, but what's the point in just being shouted down?"

Danielle was twenty-one years of age. Her blonde hair looked bleached by the sun. It fell over her shoulders and swayed each time she moved. She often hurried around, full of energy, leaping about, continually expressive; her green eyes contained extremely small pupils so that the area covered by the eyes seemed larger and more lively – unmysterious – than they may otherwise have been. The flushed red cheeks on her wide face created the illusion that her face was continually warmed by the glow of a gentle heat. Her most striking feature was her mouth. It was classically formed – perfectly symmetrical – and very large and fleshy. The line of the top lip had the curves of a bass clef. Her ebullience, usually unmitigated, was profoundly wearing. The concept of people passionately expressing different points of view was anathema to her one-dimensional felicity. It was a pity that she did not possess the maturity to apply her great sympathy and enthusiasm to the contemplation of serious issues. Presumably, this experience lay ahead of her.

"The best thing to do", Vanessa said, "is just walk into the room with a shotgun and blow a hole in the ceiling and say: 'Right, you lot, now bloody well listen to this!'"

The three of them began giggling.

"It's incredible", Vanessa continued, "how many times you have to be told the same thing. You can sit down for hours and say absolutely nothing and this is known as a discussion."

The chortling continued.

Vanessa had as much right to her complaints as the other two. She lived alone with her father, a kind man with only a limited ability to perceive that others were conscious. She had heard, for years, a repetitive stream of insipid cautions, as though her short-term memory were non-existent. The pummelling she had received had actually had the effect of increasing her disobedience. She deliberately flouted the constantly-expressed ground rules. But she was no up-and-coming feminist. She, like a lot of young women, had been sharp in quickly realising the value of money. What she did not respect was the art of getting it. This, ironically, was what her father had so uselessly attempted to pump into her. But it was a waste of time. Vanessa believed that she deserved cash, and piles of it, simply because she existed. The crux of the problem lay in her fundamental belief that she was destined to meet a man sufficiently successful to pave the path of her life with gold.

"It amazes me", she said to Kay, "how you put up with what you do. He's such a bastard to you. I could never put up with it. He's so aggressive and rude and— and— and— unpredictable."

Wayne was not destined to be successful. He was never going to drive expensive cars and hurl credit cards at women who refused to work. What he had was passion. Sometimes that extraordinarily fierce impetuosity would be channelled into amicability and bliss, leading to a charisma which very few on earth were capable of displaying. It was this which was more important for Kay than all the status symbols and security that her husband's cousin found so meaningful.

"Unpredictability is the key word," Kay replied. "If I knew – wholeheartedly – that he was not going to get any worse, then I could endure it. I could just live for the good times. But who knows what he's going to do? It's not dull, at least, being with someone so charming and then so vile. My heart rate has never been so high. I know Knubs thinks he's not going to get any worse. I suppose Nanna thinks that as well, otherwise she wouldn't have such faith in him."

"But", Vanessa grimaced, "the things he does! Why bother with it? Surely there are better things to do than put up with that? You never know when he's going to embarrass you next."

Love was something so mysteriously deluded that it was incomprehensible to anyone who had yet to experience it.

"I guess", Kay said, "I have to learn to be less affected. Just ignore him when he regresses into childhood and wait for him to get over it. But it's hard."

Kay's attitude was mysterious to Vanessa because Vanessa had never placed faith in anything and then been forced to examine it. What Vanessa failed to understand was that Kay was no quitter. She had drawn the line of intolerability: she was going to endure it all up to that point; anything else was not going to deter her from giving in.

"Listen to Brian, will you?" Vanessa then smirked.

Danielle and Kay both chuckled. Brian was unleashing his theories on American foreign policy.

"Incredible, hey?" Vanessa remarked. "It's all because of lesbians. I didn't realise that gays had such an effect on international affairs."

Danielle was laughing joyously.

"Greg", she said, "said to me the other day that he was amazed how you put up with him. He said that if he had to live here he'd now be in a mental institution."

"Sometimes", Vanessa replied, "it's fun. At least he can laugh. And he's never really rude. And he'd never be violent or really abusive. He complains a lot, which is sometimes a good laugh, but he's pretty generous. Personally, I'm amazed how you put up with Greg. He's such a bastard to Richard and me. He only ever talks to us when it suits him."

"That", Danielle sighed, "is Greg. When I was out there dumping the sacred beer – the divine amber nectar – on the table, he was having his racist theories on immigration torn to shreds. I almost giggled, but there was such an atmosphere of learned debate going on that I decided, for the sake of respect towards erudition, to keep my insignificant, but lovely, feminine mouth shut."

Vanessa unleashed a compressed burst of hilarity.

"Oh, you did the right thing," she agreed.

The pile of dishes was now down to manageable levels. The satinwood cupboards were now filling up with the glossy porcelains. Our advertisement for the wonders of women's place in the world was beginning to take on, again, the immaculate freshness that so characterises the average woman's domicile. Kay wiped the sink, leaving its lustrous surface to shine with mirth beneath the white light of purity. The glasses were almost transparent. The love that only the undemanding, gentle, unthinking hand of femininity can impart upon glassware caused Vanessa, with bitter jocularity, to say, "Oh, how I would love to do this every night for the rest of my life for the right man."

"The problem with you", Danielle remarked, with cheery sarcasm, "is that you're such an incurable romantic."

"Isn't it like that, though?" Kay smiled. "Surely the advertisements can't be wrong?"

"Advertisements", Danielle remarked, "made by men."

"Imagine", Kay began, "what sort of a mind you'd have to have to be made happy because you use the finest soap powder, and your life is wonderful because of it."

"Only a man", Vanessa said, "could come up with an idea like that."

"It's a marketing fact", Kay smiled, "that the greater proportion of domestic products are purchased and used by women. It also appears", she continued, with a naughty gleam in her blue eyes, "that it's also a marketing fact that many intelligent women are thrilled to pieces by this."

"What about", Danielle cried, "tampons?!"

The two others began laughing as Danielle said, "Bloody hell! It's incredible! Anyone from another planet would think, if they watched an advertisement for tampons, that having a period was like being drunk on fine champagne. It's amazing to think that because you stuff a piece of hard fabric up between your legs, you're going to be floating, blissfully, through serene mountain skies, unconcerned about stomach cramps and searing headaches. What a bloody joke!"

"Oh well," Kay said, "we can't expect them to understand."

"Absolutely," Vanessa replied, "but at least at the end of an advertisement like that, the woman could turn around and vomit and say: 'Christ, this mountain air is terrible for menstruation – but what the hell because I'm wearing cheery old Soakpox. Soakpox – shove them right up your fanny! They soak up all the blood!'"

The three of them were staggering around the kitchen, their faces twisted with glee.

"I'll never", Kay said, "be able to watch one again without killing myself."

Then the discussion about Vanessa's physique began in earnest in the lounge.

"Jesus," she said.

The others giggled ruefully when Brian said that his daughter was not obese.

"It's just puppy fat," Brian said, as Vanessa raised her eyebrows, and shook her head.

"What", she said, "a charming discussion. I'm sure my arse will be next."

Brian's defence of his policy on playing sport caused Vanessa to say, "It's got nothing to do with wasting time. He doesn't want to spend any more money. I'll see you two in a minute."

She extricated some beer from the refrigerator, quipping about "how inconsiderate it would be" if she entered the lounge-room without "the fluid that stimulates all fine debates."

Danielle and Kay smiled at each other warmly as they heard Vanessa flippantly deriding Brian's attitude towards the playing of sport.

"She's so cheeky," Kay said. "My parents would've murdered me for being that disrespectful."

"Brian", Danielle replied, "doesn't appear to be that worried by it though."

"He can't afford to be," Kay giggled. "He gets it from everyone. Wayne was terrible when we lived here."

"Wayne just can't swallow his frustration, can he?" Danielle asked.

"He can't", Kay agreed, "and I'm supposed to."

"You're a woman," Danielle smiled.

"His ability to listen, at times," Kay said, "is absolutely non-existent. And I'm supposed to listen to his complaints without retaliation. I know I'm not unreasonable. But you know what they're like - even when they're in a good mood they can't help throwing shit at each other. It makes conversation impossible. Knubs is so much more mature than the rest of his family, apart from Mark."

"I find him", Danielle said, "quite frightening. Cold. He doesn't react in a normal way."

"Thank God for that," Kay replied. "He stands out so much to me because he can calmly say what he feels. But he isn't going to do that for everyone. It's obvious that he thinks negatively of people at times, because, let's face it, everyone's got weaknesses they refuse to acknowledge. It's amazing the way he talks about Wayne."

Vanessa re-entered the kitchen and, opening the refrigerator, said, "I feel like some wine. Brian's just told me not to drink, so that's obviously a cause for great celebration."

She opened a bottle of Chardonnay and poured out three glasses.

"That feels better," she said, tasting the subtle complexity of flavours offered by the Rosemount Estate, as Kay shook her and smiled, and Danielle said, "Maybe you should go and offer him some."

She did this as the subject of her underwear rose to the surface.

"Brian", Kay laughed, "has got no control over her at all."

When Vanessa left, Kay said, "Knubs used to scare me as well. I had actually never met someone with a university degree until I met him. He was sort of intriguing, but off-putting, because he didn't indulge in the easy-going banter that other men did. It made me feel as if I was being judged."

"It scares me a bit," Danielle said. "I think he's seen straight through me."

"All the way through his childhood," Kay replied, "so I've just discovered, he was appalled by the behaviour of his family. He's under no illusions about humanity being a wonderful thing."

"I'm so used", Danielle said, "to people being happy and lively without any conditions being applied. It's hard to think that that doesn't apply to everyone."

"It doesn't," Kay replied. "Having seen him again, it's made me realise how responsible women are for the way men behave. We do have to take some of the blame for some of what we endure. I realised when I met him that I was much more comfortable having easy-going chats with relaxed, gregarious men - even if they did take the piss out of each other - rather than really using my brain. He suddenly forced me to really think and I was a bit uncomfortable about it. Now I enjoy it. It's a challenge. I look forward to it. He's not being judgmental. He just wants to use his intelligence. I realised that this was a man who really did want to meet an intellectually-gifted, fiery, independent woman - someone he could learn something from - and I should have been pleased about this. But I wasn't. My upbringing caused me to dash into my safe shell, where I would not be forced to look at myself. I'm glad he's back."

Kay knew that Danielle was not experienced enough in the unpleasant realities of this life to see any great significance in this remark. This view was confirmed when Danielle said, "You can't go through life being so intense all the time. It's— it's— it's not human."

Kay smiled and said, "I don't want to sound arrogant or pompous or anything stupid like that. And I certainly don't want you to think I'm attacking you. Unfortunately, not everyone has a heart of gold like you. You've been loved to death since the day you were born. A lot of other people just haven't. And because of this, in a relationship, there are those who've become accustomed to finding solace in other things - intellectual things - and then, for them, love begins."

Danielle was confused by the notion that attraction could take time to really develop. She was so angelic that she loved people immediately. She stared at Kay with the sweetness of bemused vulnerability. A great well of protective concern rose in Kay's heart. She stroked Danielle's face, smiling at the befuddled green eyes of innocence, and said, "Meeting this family has made me realise that those who've been truly victimised by circumstances beyond their control seek each other out for understanding and comfort. Knubs is not terribly concerned by people who've been loved to death. He knows they can look after themselves."

Then Kay dropped her hands and said, "Listen to bloody Wayne!" as her husband began making whimsical asides about moral outrage. The comment about "members of the same family making love" caused a stir in Kay's heart of which Danielle was not conscious. In the ensuing debate in the future, Kay knew that Wayne would say, with astonished blamelessness, that he was "only celebrating" or perhaps "just placing this serious issue into a more harmonious light." Apart from Knubs, no one else knew about the tenuous state of her sex life.

Wayne's flippancy caused Danielle to say, "What a mouth he's got. It would be impossible to convince him of anything. He could talk his way out of just about everything. Mister Never Guilty."

Kay knew that there were a few things her husband would not be able to explain away. The striking of either her or her daughter would never be washed away by a torrent of frenzied apologies. That would be it. No amount of recantation would convince her that this was not an impeachable crime. She dreaded the depths to which she was prepared to descend to protect her marriage. It was like walking through a dark forest, in the blackness of night, suspecting that one of the trees was set to explode - a forest of passionate, tumultuous beauty that could stir the heart with its whispering mottled magnificence of light or cause, in the violent shuffle of chaotic winds, a thrashing of tormented branches, twisted by an unpredictable might. Her daughter's welfare was uppermost in her mind.

When the announcement of her impending departure was made, Wayne made enquiries of Brian as to the chances of Emma being transported back home the following day. Kay considered the possibility of collecting her after work, but this was quickly dismissed as no one would be about to look after Emma during the day. Brian apologetically explained that he would not be able to drive her back in the morning as he had to work. He had just began an important job with a commercial television station and had to leave early in the morning. The only alternative – one her parents accepted was undesirable – was to get her up and take her home now.

All of them went into Vanessa's bedroom to see Emma's tiny head protruding from the fluffy dishevelment of a puffy duvet. Her little face was buried in the soft whiteness of a bulging pillow. The sound of her breathing reminded Knubs of the noise a mouse would make if it leapt on to a tiny bellow.

"How cute," Danielle whispered.

"Oh no," Kay ruefully remarked.

"This", Wayne said, "will not be good."

Kay worked quickly. The duvet was ripped back and Emma's bewildered eyes shot open. Within seconds hysterical tears were exploding from her disgusted face.

"No, no, no, no," she screamed, as Kay whisked her off the bed, her arms and legs thrashing with peeved amazement.

"No, no, no, no," she yelled, as Kay wrapped her arms around her and clutched this horrified child to her breast.

She cried with livid fury as Vanessa stroked her inconsolable brow. The guilt of her parents was hidden behind a shield of pragmatic indifference. They knew in the short time that their daughter had existed that this represented, in the infantile imagination of their offspring, a disaster, an unforgivable act of profound inconsideration, a grave travesty, a cruel and hideous display of wanton disregard from those who should have known better. How her parents could even consider undertaking the immoral and reprehensible step of plucking her, against her will, out of a deep sleep was beyond the bounds of her minuscule comprehension. She was wild with infuriated astonishment. But her parents, without any other choice, ignored this. They knew that her anguish would be short-lived. Anguish it was – extreme in its crudity – but it would be over soon, for it was not the anguish that comes from seeing people dying of starvation in Third World slums, or the pain of divorce, or the sorrow experienced at the news of the death of a loved one; it was not the bitterness that lasts when you see young soldiers blown apart in some futile war, or the anger you feel when someone who does not know you spreads absurd rubbish about your supposed moral inadequacies; it was nothing like the horror you experience when you discover that very few people care, all chasing their little, self-indulgent dreams, as though outside the scope of their small lives exists nothing but an irrelevant chaos, the vast majority of which does not require an ounce of consideration. It was nothing like the disenchantment you feel when you see some collapsed individual lying prostrate on the streets as others, in their hundreds, flock past without the slightest concern, or the agony you see in the eyes of people whose lives have been wrecked by the ravages of drought, fire, theft - the horror you endure at the sight of violence: this experience was appalling enough, but when you see it between your parents you learn the meaning of the word "anguish".

She was not going to see this but, like us all, she would see enough. Despite her current state of vindictive agitation, brought about by the hands of her mother, she was oblivious that Kay was doing her utmost to spare her the scarring dismay of real pain - an experience that had entered the lives of certain other members of her family at an age too young for comfort, and one that will never go away.

* * * * * * * * * *

The first sight of my father was a shock. He looked as though a fine, white powder had been poured over his head. The hair I once knew as black was now a white-silver hue, as if a snowstorm had left an enduring mark upon his skull. His skin was deeply weathered; there were bright capillaries, like streaks of red lightning, across the point of his broad nose. His eyebrows were still tufty, as though someone had roughed them up; they looked as if they had been set with a grey spray. Just beneath them, deeply set, his small, cheeky green eyes seethed with tempestuous irreverence. He was still slimly built and his roguish attitude to life was absolutely intact.

Shaking my hand, he said, with trivial displeasure, "Christ, this joint's like a fucking sauna. Christmas Day's going to be bloody murder."

When pronouncing "murder", he elongated "ur" to a ridiculous length so that it sounded like "muuuuuuuuuurder".

"For Christ's sake," he then said to Brian, whom he had not seen for a year, "why don't yar get yarself some bloody air-conditioning?"

A pleased, nefarious gleam then beamed upon his face as Vanessa jumped up from the lounge-room settee and said, "Yeah Dad, let's get some air-conditioning. Why not?"

"Yeah, Skirts," my father joined in, "do something constructive for a change and get some bloody air-conditioning. For Christ's sake, can't yar see the joint needs some fresh air? Yah poor daughter can't even breathe in here - yar cruel bastard."

My father smiled at me wickedly as Brian tried to remain dignified, despite the fear and anger that registered in his eyes. I was standing in the kitchen and could see him sitting in the lounge-room trying to read a newspaper. The light in the kitchen was almost unreal, it was so bright. The late afternoon sun poured through the open windows, lighting up the white door of the refrigerator with the sharp outlines of the plants that sat on the brick ledge above the sink. It was so still that any movement appeared a dramatic absurdity in the stifling heat.

Brian folded his newspaper, but not quite convincingly enough to suggest indifference. Vanessa was still pontificating about air-conditioning.

"Jesus Christ," my father giggled, as Vanessa, taking this opportunity to rib her father, said, "Michelle's house is beautifully air-conditioned. Why isn't ours?"

Any genuinely unmoved individual would have casually remarked, "Because Michelle's a greedy bitch - just like you," but Brian was too petrified to have his financial inadequacies further exposed by enticing Vanessa to continue her insensitive jibes.

"Come on," my father then said to me, "let's leave her to it."

In the car, I stopped myself from smiling. The interior was air-conditioned. I doubted if my father had taken advantage of the utopian environment of Western Australia for over a decade. He lived an artificial existence that consisted of shutting himself off from a climate that millions elsewhere dreamed of having. It was an attitude that suited the emotional austerity of his bitter ways. He had no regard for kindness, but possessed a simplistic, unquestioning respect for those who had achieved great wealth. His ability to recognise the width of possible aspirations was, however, limited by the place in which he had spent the bulk of his life. He was incapable of realising that people could also make millions quickly without having to be involved in industries directly related to the three basic necessities.

As he drove along, he stared with stone-faced detachment at the road. The rigid silence was expected. His interest in me had never amounted to anything other than the chance for vicarious glory; as he now believed that that prospect was long gone, there was little point in indulging in any conversation. I was of no use to him, and I did not care. What interest the world held for him was diluted, sharply, by the sad desire he possessed to make a fortune through insipid means. The dream of fame through wealth in business had consumed any potential he might have had for any Epicurean appreciation of this life. He was the only person I knew who did not own a single piece of music or a book. It would be safe to assume that, if he had ever purchased anything like this, the memory of it would have now been obliterated by years of alcoholism and the sharp focusing of his wicked brain on financial pursuits. It always intrigued me how both he and his mother could be so bereft of aesthetic sentiments: both were dispassionately unconcerned about the need to listen to outstanding music. The only time I had seen my father lose himself in any form of artistic appreciation occurred when a woman he loved had left him. For a fortnight, my father sat in the darkness of the flat we were sharing, staring out the window, listening to one of my Bob Dylan tapes. The tape had been left in the cassette player I had left on the lounge-room table. At the end of this fortnight, he said, "Who is this guy? He speaks a lot of truth." Then he was back to his old, sterile ways.

During that time that he sat on the settee looking at the bright lights out the window as Dylan's voice echoed around the flat, his introspection, which usually had a fierce aspect to it, became smoother, rounder, less suggestive of vindictive thought. Now as he glared out through the windscreen, uncommunicative, distant, uninterested, the prickly grimness of his countenance was as extreme as ever I had seen it, an impression reaffirmed when he turned his car into the car park of the complex of apartments where he and his wife lived and announced, grumpily, sneering out of the corner of his mouth, that "that bastard's parked on my lines again. The prick."

I was not expecting an evening of unrestrained revelry. It would be a chore, but I would get through it.

After he parked the car, the ungenerous expression remained firmly fixed to his face as we walked across a surface laid with bricks toward his abode; in front of his place – a one-bedroom flat – was a rectangular patch of soil containing a manicured line of small plants. The shadows of a white pergola above this garden cast the front of his flat into latticed slices of light and dark. It was the only apartment that did not have plants dripping from the timber webbing of the pergolas. I was not surprised by this minimalist approach to residential embellishment. It fully reflected his disinterest in visual ornamentation. The harsh pragmatism of his approach to adornment belied the uncultivated impetuosity of his explosive demeanour. If only an ounce of this overly-sensitised expression could have been applied to the playing of musical instruments or the making of intricate sculptures, his creative production could have rivalled the works of recognised geniuses; but he did not have the upbringing in the right place to learn that the mature application of emotional extremes to creative pursuits had enormous value, for his world had been fashioned by the admiration he possessed for his scheming father, a man with a charismatic aspect of taciturn invulnerability; like my grandfather, my father dreamed of being perceived by a wide milieu as one overly endowed with steely perception, a quality my grandmother's first husband had exuded in abundance; and now, as that man's son opened up the door of his apartment, it fully reached me that I was not considered to be amongst this chosen milieu, and I did not care.

My father's wife greeted me with a kind and loving smile. She emerged from the kitchen, where she had been attending to the dinner, and we kissed in a lounge-room whose overriding impression was one of comfortable simplicity. His wife expressed surprise at my youthfulness.

I was taken aback by her obesity. Although she was in her late thirties, she had the aura and physique of someone twenty years older. She wore beige-coloured cotton trousers and a pale, short-sleeved shirt. Her hairstyle was from a different era. It was parted down the middle and curled up over the ears; a reddish tinge filled her puffy cheeks; her skin looked very pale against her dark hair; her eyes were small and slit-like, but they exuded a warm ambience suggestive of someone disinclined towards confrontation. She referred to my father as "darling", a term of endearment bizarre when applied to someone so acerbically recalcitrant as the man who described the majority of the human race as "fucking wood-ducks".

I could understand its use, however: my father's viciousness occasionally contained an endearing pejorativeness. Vileness was sometimes amusing because of the moral ambiguity that lies in courageous expressions. Such was the case when Darling began talking about his brother.

"You should've seen Skirts," he told Sue, who giggled at this demeaning nickname. "What a useless prick! Christmas Day at his place is gonna be fucking muuuuuuuuurder. I said to him: 'Why don't yar get yarself some fucking air-conditioning?' No money, of course; and Vanessa jumps up and said: 'Yeah Dad, get some air-conditioning.' Poor old Skirts. Talk about fucking useless. What the fuck does he do all day? He ought to rewire houses for cash. You know his problem, though? He'd take about five fucking months to do one house – the useless cunt!"

When Darling made this reference to illicit cash jobs, he upturned his cupped right hand to indicate unrecorded payments; then, to my absolute astonishment, Sue said: "Why don't you bring him into your business somehow?"

Over the years, my father could not have made it more blatantly obvious that he considered Brian to be incapable of common sense. He was astounded. His head spun around as he exclaimed, "What?! Jesus Christ! Bring him into my business! Are you fucking nuts? He'd ruin it! I'd get Mario on the phone saying: 'Who the fuck was that dickhead?' No way!"

Despite this undiplomatic denunciation of her suggestion, Sue smiled; the passionate rebuking of her idea had a comic aspect born from the unrestrained temerity of her husband; he and I were sitting side by side on the settee. Above us, on the lemon-coloured wall, three small etchings, which I referred to as "postcards", were hung beside a painting of Montmartre. I suspected that both of them were unaware that this print was an accurate representation of a real place. I had sat on that very street in a cafe called Le Chat. I could see the opening of the café. I longed to be there. It seemed very civilised in comparison to the place I was currently.

As I contemplated this, Sue's sense of humour was given further cause for expression when my father, sipping on a stubbie of beer, announced, "There's been a few changes around here since you've been away. This useless, fucking, commo-boong government has opened the floodgates. They ought to now call Nedlands

'Slopelands'." (Nedlands was the suburb my father lived in). "I feel like erecting a banner across Broadway saying: YOU ARE NOW ENTERING SLOPELANDS - BEWARE!"

Sue chortled happily. The simplicity of her humour was the only explanation I could offer as to why she was married to such a man. Even I was surprised by this unsophisticated attack on Chinese people; for years my father had been a keen connoisseur of Chinese food but that was presumably at a time in his life when his dreams were achievable. He had even owned a Ming Dynasty porcelain. It did not even dawn on him that I had no interest in his racist views. It appeared as though whole populations were being used as scapegoats for his failure.

"As a matter of interest," he then asked, "how much did Brian get from the ABC?"

I was surprised that he was curious about his brother's financial affairs. I assumed it was because he thought that, if Brian had been made financially secure, then a greater proportion of the inevitable inheritance would go to others, instead of 'Skirts'.

"Two hundred or so," I replied, not having the faintest clue.

"He can't live on that," my father replied. "He's going to have to work. What the fuck else is he going to do anyway?"

"I think he'll probably go away somewhere," I said. "Maybe to that place there."

I pointed to the print of Montmartre. I discovered that Sue had bought it from a market. She was delighted that the place actually existed. She was extremely impressed that I was able to give her a brief history of the Church of Our Sacred Lady whose spires rose above the street that contained Le Chat. As I spoke, my father stared grumpily at the wall before him, puffing on a cigarette. Any normal person would have given up after nearly dying. You had to admire his indifference to death.

"He'll travel," I said, perceiving envy in Sue's eyes, "beginning with Australia."

"Travel!" my father acerbically quipped. "What a fucking waste of time."

When I mentioned this remark to my grandmother a few days later, she smiled with malevolent satisfaction and said, "If he had any money, he'd be off like a shot as well."

His wife did not seem to share the same view about travel. Her silence indicated to me, along with her curiosity about the Parisian print, that she harboured a profound desire to see the world. Her husband's grating comment brought the conversation to a searing halt. She sat at the table with an air of resigned repression, a demeanour that made me feel grateful for my own adventurous sense of independence. I also felt some pity; I suspected that she had been given some motivation to give up her job; it was almost certain that my father's enormous mouth - an item that could exaggerate and distort with the dazzling efficiency of a convex mirror - had convinced her innocent mind that her fiancé was a successful businessman destined for early retirement with loads of money. She saw in my father the way to an easy, opulent life full of raucous, unrestrained wit; the shallowness of her dependence and the falsity of her hopes had been vehemently expressed in the savage denunciation by her husband of travel. It was something that would remain an obscure dream for her; she was being reminded by my father that she had no independence. Secretly, it must have shocked her to discover that not only was her husband uninterested in travel, but hostile towards its very existence: I found this hostility pretentious. It only served to enhance my belief that my father could never admit failure. He was going to go to his grave a bitter and disillusioned man, unable, through pride, to admit that his life had been mediocre and largely unfulfilling. He sat on the couch gravely consuming nicotine. I wondered how much money he had squandered destroying his lungs. It could have begun worthwhile businesses; it could have made an excellent pension; it could have been used to finance several trips to Asia; it could have been spent on beautiful objects, but instead it constituted a hapless destruction of piles of finance which my father did not have the flair or aesthetic temperament to spend on more rewarding things.

As if by way of tenuous explanation for the violence of her husband's enmity, Sue said that the recession had stopped them from getting a property. She spoke as though she were an equal in my father's business. She said that, if it weren't for "our overseas sales" then, she said, she would not know what "they would do."

This caused my father to say, "What are you talking about? You don't do any bloody work!"

"Not many people in this country do," I replied.

When I brought up the working hours of several of my friends in London, my father said, "I worked until ten o'clock one night!"

I chuckled at the naivety of this from someone who prided himself on having a sound grasp of affairs. Again, Sue hid her feelings. The only indication that she felt humiliated by this admonishment of her supposed indolence was a sudden and pitiful emptiness of expression, a kind of stone-faced resignation, as though she had become used to the expectation of being treated with disrespect.

My grandmother was to tell me that my father, when working as a travelling salesman, used to come home a day early to have sex with one of his lovers, and then create the illusion that he had returned home at the right time. It was likely, for the better part of his working life, that my father had never done a proper week's work. My grandmother was cynical towards her son's laziness.

"In the fifteen years he lived here with you", she told me at her place one day, "he hardly lifted his finger. The only time he ever did anything was when he knew he was going to be thrown out – and then he just did the bare minimum. He was usually too busy drinking."

In the atmosphere of straightforwardness created by my father, I had no qualms about bringing up the subject of his removal from grandmother's will. This unleashed a tirade of idle threats and a litany of peeved pronouncements, suggestive of one tormented by a harrowing chain of injustices, that culminated in "and I bloody painted her bloody house about five fucking times as well!"

I had it on good authority that he had painted my grandmother's house only once.

Then his fax machine began printing out a message. The machine sat on a bench that separated the living area from the kitchen. Its humble appearance as the only sign that this flat was used as an office imparted to the seriousness with which my father dashed across the room towards it an endearing absurdity that made me giggle. As though to show me that his life was a model of voracious industriousness, a fastidious whirlpool of unabridged conscientiousness, he plucked his reading glasses out of their pouch and began peering over the message with a look of such pronounced gravity that it appeared as if he were assessing the net gain of some shrewd and lavish investments made that day on Wall Street.

His lengthy and intense absorption in this flimsy sheet of A4 paper caused me to say, "Does he stroke his fax machine every night? It looks so cute. Who would be able to guess that this seemingly insignificant device represents the electronic apex of a sophisticated chain of vital commands stretching from here all the way to Hong Kong? Surely, in the history of Australian economics, there has never been such a misleading and grotesquely distorted appearance of business machine and financial import. I believe that we are witnessing a frenetic revolution in business practice, the likes of which could have serious repercussions for us all – the linking of vitamin C with the electronic transferral of information."

My father ignored this remark while Sue chuckled freely. I was amazed by the simplicity of my father's business existence. The machine epitomised this. I was not being absurdly vindictive. There was a genuine stamp of hilarity surrounding that machine's positioning in a kitchen and the almost boyish way my father had approached it. I could not help myself.

"Does he take it to bed with him every night?" I asked. "Surely an object so significant and deserving of such reverence requires all the love and care that only the most noble and generous of human beings can give? After all, we are witnessing the beginning of an era – the I Kitchen Fax Revolution. I believe it is fair to say that the Technical Revolution is over."

My father continued his esurient devouring of the fax message with unwavering determination. Not a feature moved on his absorbed face as Sue chortled happily at the other end of the table.

"Is it possible", I continued, as Sue giggled, "to touch this object whose magnificence surpasses all understanding?"

Still my father's face remained rock-like, unmoved before the captivation created by that sheet of paper.

"During the winter", I asked, "does he wrap it in the finest furs to keep it warm?"

The immersion in erudition of my father's countenance seemed immovable.

"How long will it be", I said, "before astronomers realise that there is, in fact, a fixed centre to this universe?"

Sue was guffawing happily.

"Do you wake up in the middle of the night", I asked her, "wondering what that object is between you and your husband? Or does his fax have its own little cot, kept, with loving care, at just the right temperature?"

Sue was now blissful with laughter.

"A cot", I continued, "lined with only the finest satins and made from only the most magnificent mahogany?"

She chuckled with gregarious gaiety.

"And who is this Mario?" I asked. "Is it because of his Italian background that it was decided that this tour de force of business communication had to be placed next to a bowl of fruit?"

She then unleashed a burst of laughter.

"A bowl of fruit", I added, "chosen from only the finest of market gardens?"

Another chortle erupted from her.

"A bowl—"

"Ah, Jesus Christ," my father then dryly remarked, "are you ever going to shut up?"

The sudden, austere, bitter, harsh, acerbic, sniggering tone of my father's voice – a tone hilarious in its searing familiarity – caused Sue and I to guffaw simultaneously. It was a tone like whispering cynicism, drawn out, staggered, disbelieving, which made "Jesus Christ" sound like: "Jeeeeereeeesuzzz Chuuuurrieistz!!"

"Just shut up?" I pleaded, in response, astounded. "How can I just shut up – as you so insensitively put it – when I've been so unexpectedly confronted by the destruction – by the smashing into tiny fragments – of every accepted norm of working practice – practices that have taken aeons to evolve – destroyed, harshly, savagely, brilliantly, in seconds, by the stunning realisation that the interplay of information conveyed electronically has been revolutionised by the simple but awesome combining of fax, kitchen and fruit bowl? I ask you – I appeal to any sense of decency that may exist within you – how can a man just be expected to sit back and shut up under those conditions? Surely, an impossible task?"

My father glared at me disdainfully then he returned to his avaricious reading of the intricately coded message.

"Never", I said, "has a question ever been so insensitive and so inappropriate: 'Are you ever going to shut up?'"

"I think", my father replied, "it's time to shove some food down his throat. That always used to work before. His bloody appetite just about broke me financially."

This was the one subject I would never bring up with him – his finances. His curiosity about Brian's affairs was evidence enough for me that all was not well with his. Sometimes curiosity is born from a malignant desire to appease one's baser instincts; for once, this was not the case with my father. He wanted to hear that Brian had been given a fortune. He wanted to hear that Brian had become so rich that it would be pointless giving him any more money. My father was going to be disappointed. Brian was destined to get his share.

"Oh what a good idea," I said. "What's for din-dins?"

The meal was served not so long after this.

"A tour de force", I said, "of textures and flavours clashing in the pursuit of excellence - an excellence," I continued, gorging on a lump of roast chicken, "readily achieved by a flourish of finesse only paralleled by the wristy and elegant removal of the A4 sheet from one of the greatest fax machines ever to have been placed within the pristine confines of an office that, to me, looks mysteriously like a kitchen."

Again, Sue was unable to hold back her delight.

"I wonder", I said, "if Alan Bond keeps his fax in his kitchen?"

Even my father smiled at this suggestion.

"Do you think", I began, "that one day they'll have fax machines which look like ovens or refrigerators just so the business person, concerned about interior design, can ensure that their kitchen/office achieves the harmony of visual splendour that one so readily associates with unlimited success?"

An explosion of hilarity emerged from Sue's mouth.

"If they ever do", my father said, "I hope they make one in the shape of a rolling pin so I can shove it up your arse."

"Interesting idea," I replied. "The fax for the industrious, gay sodomite."

"Jeeeeeeeeerreeeezuzzzz Cheeeerieeezzzt," my father whispered as Sue chortled with unrestrained appreciation.

"On that subject," I began, "I reckon that Wayne is probably the most needy I know in that department. I'd certainly recommend a huge boat travelling at the speed of light."

Sue's face suddenly became serious.

"It's extraordinary", she said, "what he did after Keith helped him out the way he did."

"Explain," I replied.

My father crossed his legs and lit up a cigarette. A half-drunk glass of Chardonnay sat before him. His gold-rimmed glasses, which gave him a misleading air of academic appreciation, were still on. One of the legs of the grey-coloured trousers came up to a point halfway up his calf as his right leg folded over the left, exposing a thin, white strip of skin above a black sock. When he spoke, he gesticulated by pointing and waving.

"When he got sacked", my father said, "he came charging in here, startled, acting as if it was a total surprise. The bloody idiot had been falsifying orders. He tried telling me that he didn't have a clue why he'd got the sack. I knew. I knew he was going to get it as well; I told him to get out of here and to never come back."

My brother had been a sales representative for a large wholesaler with whom my father had had close business contacts for decades. My father's name would have been diminished severely by my brother's actions. My father would have gone to considerable lengths to get Wayne employment after the debacle with his previous employers.

"After what you did for him," I said.

"Keith did everything he could," Sue said proudly. "Everything!"

Then the bit about yellow sand and early departures arrived. I felt real sympathy for my father whose inadequacies and weaknesses were largely detestable. He had made an uncharacteristically altruistic attempt to help someone else and had been rewarded with an act of inconsiderate stupidity. I too would have been livid.

"That's it", he then said, waving his arms emphatically, "as far as I'm concerned – he's finished. No more!"

My sympathy was heightened as I knew that my father had not spread around the real reasons Wayne had lost his job. The mere thought of the subject would have been repulsive to his distorted perception of his own worth. I could feel the embarrassment he must have endured: at the time of Wayne's dismissal, my father was still renting floor space in the building in which Wayne had worked.

"Wayne", my father continued, "doesn't think. He's always taken short cuts. He thinks life's a party."

He took another drag on something he should have stopped years ago; then he produced the immortal: "He's just like his mother!"

Wayne was like a few other people as well. His unpredictable disposition could have only come from one individual – his father. This seemed irrelevant to "Darling" who chose to believe that this flippant irresponsibility in his eldest son was the result of forces out of his control. My father lacked the responsibility to accept some blame for Wayne's waywardness but he was right about one thing:

"Wayne", he said, "should never've got married. He should never be married. I said this to Kay's family. They thought I was having a go at their daughter. I said: 'It's not your daughter, it's my son. He's mad!' He's never grown up. He never will. He's always living in the past."

My father spoke with assertive blamelessness. He did not possess the subtlety of mind to consider that the brutal lack of attention Wayne had received from both his parents may have played a part in permanently disturbing any potentially mature outlook his eldest son might otherwise have had; Wayne had always tenaciously refused to accept being ignored. He was never able to resign himself to the existence of mistreatment. He couldn't treat it indifferently, as though it were something else, just there. This was a courageous virtue - he would never lie down in a crisis - but with all courageous virtues there is pathos, and Wayne's life was slowly filling up with this unnecessary self-destructiveness, like a beautiful river being fed by an acrid stream. I suspected that Wayne's life would end in the similar dire circumstances under which it had begun. Trees would lose their bark in the stagnant waters of his explosive ways. He was beyond help. All the injustices that had been wrought upon him could never be forgotten, creating a vicious dignity often in pursuit of unnecessary expression.

The phone rang. Sue answered it. It was Jeremy. He asked me if I wanted to join him in the cinema the following night. I did.

Sue said, "That was Jeremy, wasn't it?

"Yes," I replied, "he asked me if I want to go to the Somerville Auditorium with him tomorrow night."

"Paaahh!" my father sneered.

The Somerville Auditorium was an open-air art cinema set in a pine forest in the grounds of the University of Western Australia.

"Why don't you come?" I asked my father, sarcastically.

"Can't be fucked," he replied. "Wouldn't be able to read the subtitles anyway. Maybe if they put something on in English."

My father was not known for his cultural sensitivity.

"What's on?" Sue asked.

She was genuinely interested. It was a pity in a way for I knew that she did not possess sufficient independence to go there by herself.

This was remarkable since the cinema was only five minutes' walk away.

"A film", I replied, "about fascism in Italy during the thirties."

"Paahh!" my father sniggered. "Big deal."

"Keithio Dictatorialio," I remarked.

"Never liked Mussolini anyway," my father said. "Wasn't tough enough."

Sue erupted with gleeful laughter. I can assure you that my father was not joking.

"Hitler was good," my father continued, stone-faced, as Sue continued chuckling. "Killed six million Jews."

He said this with emphatic pleasure.

"He had the right idea."

A chill of astonishment ran through me. I realised then that to hide from the awareness that he probably faced a desperately uninteresting future, my father was going to absurd lengths to de-fascinate this complicated and divine world. He reminded me of a creature caught in nets, gradually being tightened by the twist of failure; but his wife was overjoyed by his simplistic audacity.

She lacked the perception to realise that her husband's ferocity was the result of suppressed pain and fear, of vast, irreversible loss; she was oblivious that her husband had taken the first step in a radical and egotistical attempt to dissociate himself from any analysis of his insignificance and ineluctability.

"Why bother to see such a boring world," I could imagine his alter ego telling him, "one populated with Jews and communists? Not on. What a fucking waste of time that'd be when I could be sitting here hoping that that fax performs an incredible miracle and gets me out of this desperate rut. Jesus Christ – this is going to kill me. There's no way I can sit around here for the rest of my life. It's gonna be bloody muuuuuuuurder. Come on fax, pull your finger out!"

"I see", I said, "that you've lost none of your diplomatic suaveness."

Sue giggled and said, "You should have heard what he said to one of our neighbours one day. Keith charged across the carport and screamed: 'If your bloody cat attacks mine again, I'll kill it!' The neighbour came over later and asked me, 'Did he mean it?' You should've seen the poor guy; he was really worried."

Sue giggled appreciatively. My father's threats were always idle (he had once threatened "to wrap a baseball bat around my head" if I was not at my brother's wedding in time), but he could look incredibly menacing. His meanness was beyond question. To an unsuspecting individual, well-adjusted, compromising, he could appear violently insane. The raw beauty of this tempestuous and fierceless expression appealed to his wife's humour; it was an appeal based on the loveliness of bold nonconformity, of peerless individuality, uncontaminated with prim pressures and twee expectations. He was alive; and he was also everything that most people avoided for a safe and liberal existence.

"Bullshit!" he snarled, a few minutes later after turning the television on to watch the news. "Jesus, what a fucking wood-duck!"

A news report had come on about the prospect of one year paternity leave. A man who'd been out of work for three years bringing up children was interviewed.

My father said, "Strewth!" when this man, who spoke with a feminine air, said that "employers were becoming more aware of the needs of their employees."

"What a fucking load of crap!" my father gasped, just prior to sipping on a beer. "Yet another example of the commie-boong regime. Bloody unbelievable! Have a kid and get a fully-paid holiday for a year. What a fucking wanker!"

This news report continued, punctuated by expletives issued with disbelieving ingratitude by my father, whose joy in watching the news was born purely from indignation.

"I don't mind people getting crèches at work", he said, "but you've got to work. No one gets a fucking year off in Japan for twelve months to have a kid. Not on."

I was not in disagreement with this. The amusing aspect for me, as the news continued, was the realisation that my father's interest in watching stemmed more from an excuse to express his cynicism, rather than as a way of discovering what points of view existed within the morass of public debate. I burst out laughing after a particularly severe stream of vituperation, involving a series of snarling, unsavoury, ill-mannered expressions emerging from a pair of lips that seemed, in their twisted rage, to have become bloodless, so tightly were they compressed against his nicotine-stained teeth: "Fucking wanker. Absolute cunt. Wood-duck. Stupid prick. Fucking silly, wanking tosspot. What a fucking absolute cunt. Silly bitch. Stupid, fucking wanker," et cetera, et cetera, piled on with an aspect of discourteous and myopic reproachfulness which fuelled his wife's light-hearted appreciation of her husband's vileness. It was so predictable to hear him vehemently refute any point of view, irrespective of how justified, which emerged from the mouth of a Labour politician. His objectivity, shattered by a love of shocking criticism, was further diminished by the polarisation caused by the two party system. Democracy has done as much for cerebral intransigence as any left-wing propaganda: it is effectively two propaganda machines pandering to the instincts of an uncertain electorate. My father was the product of this liberal extremism. He saw no need to enquire about my well-being. I could not be used as a means to rescue his financial situation - his ego. The switching on of the television set was the signal that any more conversation was a useless trifle; with an expression of fierce insularity, he glared at the screen. A permanent cloud of smoke floated languidly above his head. It was ironic that this cigarette smoke reminded me of the way galaxies move through the heavens, for there was something of the void and isolation of the skies about my father, but none of the serenity. His curiosity had no intellectual base: it was aroused either by tales of financial scheming or by the satisfaction of his malicious passion. The only other thing that stimulated him was war. He was fascinated by the climactic drama of this senseless activity, a fascination without pragmatic import in a society where the vast majority of people have hardly seen anyone get seriously injured, let alone seen a head get shattered by flying shrapnel from a distance of two feet.

On the journey in his car on the way back to Brian's place not a word was spoken. I realised that night, if I was not already aware of it, that my father and I could never be friends. Something of the quiet desolation of suburbia, of the spiritless respectability of these plush streets, seemed to haunt the black air between us. He was the perfect example of what I should avoid. He would have liked to have thought the same thing about me - he had already successfully done this with Wayne - but I knew in my case that his disturbed detachment was born from envy and the longing for the freedom which charges the soul, adorned by the hope of audacious success. His life, like the dying flickers of a once erupting sun, was slowly slipping away.

* * * * * * * * * *

The Somerville Auditorium contains rows of canvas chairs surrounded by pine trees. Before the films begin, you see the purple haze of twilight and the first stars. People bring their own drinks, often champagne, and some people will dine on a picnic dinner. A small bar sells goodies and it is common to run into those whom one has not seen for years.

On the night I went with Isabelle and Jeremy and some of Jeremy's friends, I witnessed a murder and a rape within the first ten minutes of the film. These crimes were committed by the same individual. (The crimes took place within the film.) The only crimes I could imagine this audience committing were of a tweely moralistic nature, perhaps the odd financial misdemeanour. After this opening episode, the only images which remained in my mind of that film were fleeting, incomprehensible, as vague and meaningless as a work of abstract expressionism.

At the end of the film, a complicated debate erupted among the other four over the implications of someone else's complex actions. It became apparent to me that the individual they were discussing was a character in the film. There was great contention over the motivations of this strange individual. Jeremy believed this man's attitude towards the Bible had had something to do with some theft alleged to have occurred in a library that housed only extremely expensive leather-bound books. Heather thought that the man's actions were more readily explained by his relationship with his mother. I was absolutely intrigued. Isabelle was convinced that someone else hid from the others the reason for this theft because this perplexing individual did not want to compromise her chances of securing the affections of some local politician. It was a riveting conversation to which to listen. Guy expressed his dismay over the way this local politician was able to win support for his spurious cause by exploiting other people's moral weaknesses. Some differences of opinion arose from this contention. There was a great deal of head-shaking and calm, but assertive, disagreement.

Suddenly, in the midst of it, Jeremy looked at me and said, "What do you think then, Knubs?"

Silence descended. I was suddenly confronted by four pairs of curious faces. The fascination in their eyes suggested that they thought my opinion would be able to place their debate into a more transparent light.

"I absolutely haven't got a bloody clue," I said. "All I can remember is a rape and a murder that took place in the first ten minutes. After that, I was out cold."

Laughter exploded among them. I explained that I had been woken up at the end of the film when the man sitting on my right had moved his shoulder. My head had been on it.

"He was quite nice about it," I said, as their chortling continued. "He smiled at me and said, 'Are you a film critic?'"

Jeremy was particularly amused. His bellowing laughter reverberated around the auditorium in healthy bursts of sonorous appreciation.

He slapped his knee when I said, "But from what I've just heard from you lot, though, it sounds like an interesting film. I might have to come back some time during the week and see it. Anyone interested?"

They gave me a lift down the road to a place where I could catch a taxi. Fascism dominated the conversation. This gave me the opportunity to let them know what I had heard from my father the night before. The part about Hitler, Mussolini and the deaths of six million Jews caused them to look at me, bewildered. The story caused Jeremy to whisper with awed stupefaction, "Jeerreeezuzz Cheeeeeeerieeeiiitzzz!"

He was beginning to discover why I had not been terribly enthusiastic when the plane landed.

* * * * * * * * * *

I met Ana and Jennifer in a bar. The place was quite stylish. A terrace of white-painted iron tables and chairs had plants falling from the roof. A palm tree sat in a large bucket at the entrance to the interior. People were sitting at the iron tables with bottles of wine; nicely presented delicacies – seafood, salads, pâtés – lay before them. It was a very appealing place to bring a cultivated woman.

Inside, the rectangle of the bar was surrounded by indiscriminately placed timber tables and chairs which sat upon a marble floor. People sat around the bar on stools drinking a wide variety of colourful concoctions. A friendly rumble of conversation hummed through the place over some smooth jazz. The waiting staff languidly moved between the tables smiling and serving. Through a doorway next to the bar was a restaurant. From where I sat at the table with Jennifer and Ana, I could see an inviting array of food in an elaborate buffet within the confines of this simple but elegant eatery.

"Been a few changes, I see," I said.

When I was in Perth last, it was uncommon for this type of place to exist.

"For the better," Ana said.

"I agree," I replied.

I concentrated my attention on Jennifer. So this was the creature responsible for causing an innocent man to undertake an illegal entry in pursuit of her heart. She dripped with femininity and with a syrupy and pretentious guilelessness that, strangely, was not in the least annoying. I felt that her disposition could upset less attractive women, for she possessed a girlish coquettishness, alarming to your genuine feminist, which hid the real depth of her intelligence. Her head swayed constantly with languid grace, a characteristic that suited the calf-like cuteness of her enormous brown eyes; her mouth, when she was silent, sat open so that this quality of dreamy naivety was given extra sweetness. In the middle of the fleshy triangle of her open mouth, her tongue would sit, creating a large area of succulent pink at the bottom of her round face, while the eyes would stare at you with dramatic vulnerability, as though she fully expected to be adored, to be rescued, to be looked after by some gorgeous man. She possessed an air of sensitive docility and, when she spoke with interest about something that concerned her, the esoteric vagary of her quietude would disappear to reveal a lively brain.

I wanted to talk to her about the cultural transitions one is expected to undertake when one lives abroad. I suspected that we may have made similar false assumptions.

"Men and women", she said, "relate differently here than they do in Boston. It took a while to learn this."

Her voice had a deliberately adolescent and guiltless timbre, as though she felt that innocence was a trait seductively attractive to men. I did not know why this did not perturb me until I realised that it was her desire to be loved as someone gentle and open-minded which caused her to evoke this image of sweet incompetence, of blameless purity – an image she could get away with, and quite obviously did.

"When I first came here", she said, with big, round eyes, "I was told by other women to be careful. The men here are basically only interested in one thing, and I've discovered that the women are probably worse. So many of them have told me not to speak to men for fear of leading them on. The vast majority of women here only talk to a man if they're interested. It's a bit puerile."

I did not need to be told this: I already knew it. This was one reason I was not looking forward to going to the party to which Ana had invited me; but it was a positive sign that she recognised the pitfalls of the social life she had acquired by living in a place like Perth.

"The women here", she continued, "are quite unbelievable. It's so difficult to form relationships with them because of jealousy."

The jealousy of which she spoke was born of a pathetic failure from which so many young women suffered here: in not being curious enough to be able to intelligently discuss matters not directly related to their social lives. This American from Boston, possessed of sublime beauty, would have been doubly infuriating to the average woman here for her ability to comment on matters more far-reaching than how nice, revolting or gorgeous was some frivolous surfer, standing across a garden strewn with empty beer cans, or how many beautiful Italians someone else had met on their trip to Europe. The most tormenting influence on these women would, however, have been the ethereal girlishness of Jennifer's inherent femininity. Her consciousness of this quality would have inflamed the souls of lesser beings. So aware was she of what she had been given that it appeared as though she had been covered by a honey whose taste would render any man, about to accuse her of impropriety, full of remorse. It did not seem possible that she was capable of any act of vileness, but there would be many women here trying to accuse her of one. Perhaps there were many with genuine grievances.

"When I first came here", she said, "I met these two guys who took me everywhere. They were really good friends, but because of me their friendship split up, because I was naive about their motives. It was incredible. One of them asked me to marry him. We hadn't even laid hands on each other. He kept saying, 'You've got to make a decision'; he assumed, because I had spent so much time with them, that I had to be interested in one of them. This was a strange assumption for me. I didn't say anything to make them think that there was anything romantic in my motives. Then I began meeting other women and being told that I should be careful. It was a bit of a shock. I had thought this place would be easy for forming relationships – I mean real ones – but it's not."

Not all that many places are; particularly one dominated by a sort of conservative hedonism which forces people to act as though each night of their lives is the most euphoric experience that they have had for years. Discussions about the complexity of sensations possible in a multifaceted society were not commonplace here.

"Are you particularly interested in anything – fiercely?" I asked.

The question came as a surprise to her. The bafflement caused her to lose the dreamy pretentiousness of her normal demeanour.

"Fiercely?" she asked.

"Absolutely," I replied.

"I love music," she said.

"How badly?" I persisted. "Do you play a musical instrument? Do you read about it? Do you think about it every day?"

"I listen to it every day," she replied.

"And does it make you dream?" I asked.

She giggled and said, "Why do you want to know that?"

"There are things", I replied, "that make me dream."

"What things?" she asked.

She was now leaning towards me, fascinated. Chestnut hair with gold streaks fell in silky clusters over her shoulders. Her eyebrows were dark half-circles that fell towards the bridge of her quaint, upturned nose. Her skin was like silk. I felt myself smiling with great joy.

"Things", I replied, "so beautiful that they cause such enormous passion which, if you happen to be very good at them, they can give you a power so enormous that you feel eternal?"

She was awe-struck by this. Her face was like a triangle of delicate wonderment.

"What things?" she asked.

"Anything", I replied, "as long as its execution requires great skill and imagination, and its learning can only come about by years of fierce dedication."

"You mean painting", she asked, "or something like that?"

"Anything creative, scheming, intellectual, scientific," I replied. "It doesn't matter. The important thing is friendship. When you do something extremely well with someone else, who also does the same thing extremely well and you both succeed - against great odds - then you can find out about friendship; but you will not find much of that in the circles you mix in around here. Not a chance. I've seen respect built on too flimsy a foundation here to describe its outcome as friendship. Here, it's more like mutual convenience."

"There are people here", she said, "doing difficult things - things that require a lot of knowledge - and doing them well. Lots of people."

I smiled and said, "There's no one here who's risked death for the sake of art. Very few people have also come up with any remarkable ideas. And why should they? There's no need, no pressure to do it. What would be the point?"

She swayed her head in agreement; then she asked,: "Do you know anyone who has?"

I reached into my back pocket and pulled out a six by four inch colour photograph.

She stared at it closely and said, "That's awful. Where is it?"

"Bosnia," I replied. "I took it two months ago. Photographs make the photographer seem cold; but you can't see the tears in his or her eyes."

"You were in Bosnia?"

"Someone had to be. It takes a lot to get me excited. I made a fortune."

She was a bit disgusted by this. I was expecting her to be.

"But—"

I stopped her before I heard all the standard clichés.

"Everyone", I said, "has the right to decide what they think they need to see. A lot of discussion arises from images like this. Some people even care. I don't want to bore you with the outrage I feel, but some of the money I made has been donated to a clinic in Belgrade. This clinic helps devastated children whose parents have lost their lives as a result of this stupid war. I met a lot of fine courageous people there. Other photographers. When you have this experience with someone else, something which requires great skill and great human qualities, then you become real friends, irrespective of personality, tastes, attitudes, finicky preferences. All that nonsense just gets swept aside. Everyone loves each other. Maybe, if you want to find some real friends, you should involve yourself in something like that. Believe me, it's worth it."

"Well, I won't do it here, will I?" she asked.

"I doubt it," I replied.

* * * * * * * * * *

Parties, I find, are usually a frustrating halfway house between a good dinner party and the raging anonymity of an excellent nightclub. They are even worse if your values don't correspond with all those who you know will be there. But I had to satisfy my curiosity. There was also the knowledge that Ross had spread stories, after I had left town, about my alleged kinkiness. I was not too worried about this – Ross was right into discussing kinkiness anyway – but the real problem resulted from the dire prospect of having to stand around watching people getting excited about tedious subjects of conversation that bore little association to the real dramas of this earth. I was a little morose for I expected to be going into a situation where people judge others, or choose their friends, on the bizarre grounds of how suited they are to a party life. If ever a person was in the incorrect mood to see a group of 'old friends' at a party, it was me. Most of these 'old friends' were suspicious of my 'unnatural ways'.

The first thing I heard punctuating the stillness, after getting out of the car, was the rumble of distant conversation. As it was the only sound, seemingly, between here and the stars, it came to my ears with a vivid directness in a sense appealing for its primeval raucousness. Over the top of it, I heard the crack of someone's guffawing, a mirthful cry in the gregarious cacophony of noise, which caused Ana to giggle, confident he was just about to enjoy himself. I envied him. He would flow into this situation like quicksilver across a sheet of polished chrome. He had all the natural attributes: he was good-looking, sensitive (this was useful occasionally), sharp-witted, an excellent listener and an irrepressible raconteur. He possessed in addition the wonderful gift of knowing precisely how much attention to give a woman; he also had a highly developed memory of sense-oriented experiences. There was not a chance that I would enter this place, alone, without him. My pompous dignity would not allow me to be ignored by a group of unambitious individuals with insipid social values without some intelligent crutch on to which fall back.

We walked around the side of the house. A weeping willow hung over the driveway. A group of men were standing in the darkness by the fence smoking a joint. Surprisingly, these complete strangers did not offer me any. Around the corner, I was greeted by the sight of a back garden lit by a bright light. People were huddled in groups, chortling away. The water of a swimming pool looked duck egg blue in the artificial light. The memory that people here keep their drinks with them at parties came back to me. It now seemed like an amusing ritual, rather than normality, to see men with boxes of beer at their feet. It had a comic aspect that appealed to my sense of the absurd. It was laughable to see all these men jealously guarding their alcoholic booty. Profound moral questions could arise if someone reached into someone else's box and took, without permission, someone else's precious beer.

The sight of the first person I recognised caused me to chuckle. The typicality of his situation caused the amusement. He was standing on the edge of the swimming pool, looking like Mick Jagger, surrounded by women, a palm tree rising up behind him. His life was dominated by superficial relationships. He knew about two thousand people, all of whom he probably spoke to for about two minutes each a week. The term 'speaking to' was largely an exaggeration. His capacity for listening was virtually zero. A conversation was worthless unless it was about him. The fact that he was studying to become a psychiatrist was an anomaly as he showed no interest, socially, in anyone else's peculiarities. If anything, it was he who required one.

Then I was standing next to Peter Bull, shaking his hand. It was refreshing to see a genuine smile. He had been standing in the thick of the party, drolly detached from the proceedings; he showed not the slightest interest in anything going on around him. This I considered to be a mark of intelligence. He was a bastion of eccentric maturity in a cauldron of empty gaiety. I admired the way he accepted that this lifestyle was flawed, but not worth getting hysterical about. Soon we were cracking jokes about the prospect of a retired British army colonel attempting to seduce some seductive young creature who was diving in and out of the pool.

"Now look here," Peter said, "I bet it was that chap Higgins who told you I simply adore the sight of a set of fine, young, healthy buttocks glistening in the moonlight. Can't tell you how much it means to me to give something like that three or four good lashings after a glass or two of Napoleon."

Brad Shilkin had come back from the toilet. He was standing in front of Peter, giggling. We shook hands. He smiled warmly. It intrigued me how he could be so openly generous towards someone he detested, although detestation was probably too strong a term for someone with his amiable disposition. He wore glasses and had a hooked nose. He was very sensitive about the subject of Israel. Most Jews I knew who had never been to either the Gaza Strip or the West Bank were. It was not the subject of conversation appropriate for this occasion. He began talking about the girl in the swimming pool. For some reason that totally eluded me, he referred to her as "that map". It was not the first time since my return that I had heard this term used to describe a girl. I ignored it to listen to what he had to say. The woman in the swimming pool was presented as someone from a privileged background who was excessively conscious of her own beauty. She was certainly attractive: she had long black hair, a fine figure superbly displayed in a black bathing costume and an annoying habit of getting out of the pool, walking three steps and then diving back in. It was a pity that Brad wasted his considerably attractive personality in the pursuit of such stupid women. He stood next to me mumbling, making lascivious comments about her physique. Had that woman any ounce of intelligence, she would have found something more constructive to do on a Friday night than parade her body around a swimming pool; irrespective of how gorgeous she looked, her existence, to me, amounted to nothing more than a waste of good oxygen.

"You don't seriously", I said, "find that woman interesting?"

"She's a bit fat, really," he replied.

I suppose it's pointless to say that this was not the comment I was expecting.

"Well, yes," I said.

The girl had become conscious that I was looking at her. It made her glamorise her movements even more. I was intrigued by this. She was under the impression that I found her mysterious. I was in fact staggered by her shallow simplicity. An egotistical individual makes assumptions bereft of doubt. I could not imagine the pain I would suffer if fate forced me to spend an evening trying to speak to this spoilt airhead. She was now standing on the edge of the pool, her head back, running her fingers through her hair. Every moment was laced with dramatic superiority. She was too stupid to realise that my interest in her was purely sardonic.

"Imagine", I said, "the size and power of a microscope required to detect the existence of a brain capable of falling in love with that. It'd have to be about the same size as Mount Everest."

"The lenses", Peter replied, "would have to be about the same size as Mount Everest."

"I haven't seen anything as ridiculous as this for years," I said, as this inflated ego in the shape of a woman continued her eventful parading around the edge of the pool. "It's outstanding entertainment though."

The entertainment continued when she bent over in preparation for another dive and stayed in that position for an unnaturally long length of time, presumably to gloat to herself over our prolonged gawking at her hindquarters. She seemed to take the attitude that I was admiring her beauty. The falsity of her perception caused my gaze to linger. I was supposed to have been awed by her sensuous complexity. I wasn't. She dived in, lingering momentarily before hitting the water with pretentious elegance. There was an unfortunate gulf between her need to exhibit and the style of her act.

Brad forgot she existed and asked, "How many women did you sump in Europe?"

"What?" I replied. "You must be nuts. What woman do you think's going to go to bed with me?"

They started laughing.

"You must be off your head," I continued. "Women have got better things to do than waste their time with me. I thought you had brains."

They were now chuckling loudly.

"I thought", Brad said, smiling, "that you were going to tell us heaps of stories about sumping women in Europe."

"How", I replied, "did you ever come to that conclusion? A lot of women might be thick, but they're not that stupid. Are you aware of the scale of the attack that you've just unwittingly launched upon womanhood? You should be ashamed of yourself."

They were both giggling away with pleasurable astonishment.

"The first day I got back here", I said, "I was walking down the street and some bloke holding a clipboard – I think he was one of these Church of Scientology characters – said to me, 'Excuse me, sir, would you like to do a personality test?' I laughed and said, 'You're wasting your time with me, mate, I haven't got any.'"

The chortling continued unabated.

"If", I said, "the World Health Organisation was given five dollars by every woman who's rejected me, Third World debt would be wiped out overnight."

The giggling hysteria flowed on.

"The main problem is", I remarked, "that it's impossible to respect any woman who shows any interest in me. How can any woman expect to be taken seriously with taste like that?"

"Has it happened much?" Brad asked.

"I doubt it," I replied. "If it has", I continued, as Brad and Peter chuckled away, "I wouldn't notice it anyway. I haven't got the faintest clue how to judge if someone's interested in me or not. Even if a woman's bum was about to come down on my face, I still wouldn't have a clue."

Both of them erupted with boyish appreciation.

"I'd probably think", I said, "that they'd mistaken my head for a toilet."

The guffawing reached another crescendo.

"The last time I discovered", I continued, "that someone was actually interested in me, I asked the person who'd told me this if there was any history of mental illness in this deluded woman's family. Guess what – there was."

They both chortled in their distinct ways. Brad had a high-pitched staccato giggle, as though he were fantastically surprised and overjoyed by discoveries he had previously considered to be well out of the bounds of actuality, while Peter cackled with elongated, droll bursts of appreciative acknowledgement.

"I discovered", I said, "that this poor unfortunate woman believed that she could speak Russian because she thought that she'd lived in Saint Petersburg in a previous life. When I found that out, I thought to myself, 'Now I know why she's interested in me – she's insane.'"

Their laughter rose above the cackling, raconteuring and chortling transpiring around the back garden of a house bordered by a high timber fence. Large green bushes and trees obscured the fence down one side; on the other, a garage sat at the end of the driveway. The ground between ourselves and the garage had been paved with light-coloured bricks. A strip of grass ran between the pool and the garage and finished where the paving had been placed to ensure that one's wet footsies did not acquire any untoward foreign objects on their way from the pool to the house.

The quaintness of this arrangement contrasted with the informality of the socialising occurring under the clear, sparkling sky. A dazzling array of colourful shirts caught my eye. I had become accustomed to the subdued hues of British dress. By comparison, this looked like a fancy dress party. It appeared as though no attempt had been made to spare the casual observer's retinas from being blinded by a lurid kaleidoscope of colour so intense that even rainbows paled into insignificance against the blazing ensembles I saw pasted on to other people's backs. A great number of people showed a quite remarkable sense of colour: brilliant purples, fantastic reds, burnt oranges, eye-catching golds, striking emeralds; it was taste born from liberation. It was certainly no finer than taste born from restraint, just different, a different environment creating a different awareness.

I noted the resplendent hue of Brian's dark-green shirt and said, "The last time I managed to get my hands on a woman occurred in this place in central Turkey called Goreme. All the hotels are the same in this place, so the only distinguishing factor is who's in them. My friend and I would get to the reception areas in these places and say, 'We're looking for someone called Natasha; is she staying here?' And these blokes'd go, 'Natasha, Natasha, she here, she here. You come in.' And we'd say, 'Look, do you mind if we check the register?' We'd then go through it and decide if it was worth checking in. I'd stand there and go, 'A German, a Frenchie, two Dutch,' then we'd move on to the next one. Eventually, we picked the one we wanted: two German girls and a potential Dutch goddess called Eva – just them, no men. These women ignored us for two days before we finally made contact with them in a restaurant. I amazed each one by telling them, after clutching my temples in concentrated effort, what their star signs were. Of course, they didn't have a clue that I had discovered their birthdays by looking at the hotel register."

This caused a chorus of naughty chuckling.

"They were so impressed by this", I continued, "that they decided to share a few bottles of wine with us. We got smashed and decided to go to a nightclub. I got into the taxi first and to my amazement one of these girls just sat on my lap and refused to move. Within about fifteen minutes inside the club we were all over each other. My friend managed to seduce one of the Germans. This caused logistical problems later, back at the hotel, because my friend and I were sharing a room and so were the girls. Tim got the German in our room so Eva and I had to head for the shower. We were in there for so long that the hotel did not have any hot water for the next twenty-four hours, a fact that one of the hotel employees kept reminding me about with absolutely no tact whatsoever for the next two days."

After the laughter died down, Brad said, "In the time you've been gone, I haven't had one relationship with one woman I've really wanted. Missed out completely. I'm starting to wonder if it's ever going to happen."

Real concern fell across his face.

"My going away", I said, "was the worst thing that ever happened to you guys. At least then, women would look at me and think, 'At least they're not as bad as that arsehole', but now the parameters have obviously been reoriented."

Another episode of giggling transpired.

"I've basically given up," I continued. "It was about six months ago that I finally accepted the fact that I've got no chance. After years of bashing my head into a brick wall, I finally accepted that women are not my forte. The feeling's not as bad as I thought it would be though. It's given me the chance to concentrate on other things."

Around us, excited-looking people ebulliently conversed in a brash atmosphere of harsh euphoria, unconducive to the conveyance of genuine feelings. Despite Brad's profound gregariousness, it seemed that he was beginning to feel disillusionment with the aimless production of witticisms and anecdotes required to sustain the usually short-lived attention of these people - people accustomed to meeting others in situations like this. A drunk, smiling woman, about twenty-five, with pale, parched skin, wildish hair, tough-looking, unfeminine, clutching a can of beer, made a comment to Brad that I was unable, in the din, to hear. The comment was conveyed with a shallow joy that suggested a disposition uninterested in the more esoteric or interesting sensations of the human psyche. She looked absolutely unwilling to discuss her deeper feelings while trying to appear warm, friendly and open. She epitomised the character of the crowd.

Brad responded to her flippancy by suddenly dropping his disenchanted countenance and making a vacuous grip that appeased this woman sufficiently to enable her to go on her merry way. I was introduced to her prior to her departure and she showed not a hint of interest. This had nothing to do with me; her lack of real interest in people showed in her flightiness. She was probably bored with meeting people. It happened so regularly here that people got annoyed by it. It was not uncommon even to be sneered at by someone when being introduced to them, so pessimistic were so many people here about meeting yet another individual who appeared uninteresting. I was unconcerned about my supposed inability to be able to entertain. The sort of person in whim I was interested would immediately induce it in me anyway.

As though by way of explanation for his change in attitude, Brad said, "She lives down the street with a group of people we go out with a bit. She's a good laugh. We always let each other know where the parties are on. It's useful."

I was surprised that he thought I would not be aware of the sort of relationship he obviously had with her; his momentary change of state did not require explanation, although I could appreciate his embarrassment. The woman clearly wanted to go to bed with him. It made me feel that his considerably genial personality was an ironic impediment to his desire to find someone with whom he could have a rewarding relationship: he was not intolerant or cynical enough to stop wasting his time with people who frequented places unsuited to his purposes. He spread himself around far too much because he was too affable to concentrate his attacks with the tasteful precision of one blessed with cultivated intolerance. I did not want to tell him this; it was better if he found out for himself. He would not agree with it anyway. It was an idea foreign to his amiable perception of affairs.

"I hear", I said to Peter, "that your employment causes difficulties."

He smiled and said, "Somehow postman doesn't have the same aura as film director. One finds, if one is brutally frank with oneself, that the communications industry lacks a certain je ne sais quoi."

Brad and I chuckled at his wry self-deprecation.

"It can", I replied, "be used to your advantage."

"How?" he asked.

"Refuse", I replied, "to tell them what you do for a living. It immediately arouses enormous interest. They'll become so fascinated that you won't believe the intrigue you'll inspire. They'll say, 'Go on, what is it?' and you'll say, 'You won't appreciate it. I can't tell you; it's too early in our association' and they'll say, 'Oh go on, why not? I want to know,' and you'll say, 'I know you do, but it's too early. You're going to have to trust me.' You won't believe the amount of totally unjustified mystery you'll create. They'll be virtually ripping your clothes off just to find out. And when they get to the point where they're so frustrated that they're about to do something you'll regret – like leave you – relent a little and say, 'Okay, but don't go spreading it around. The only thing I can tell you at this sensitive stage is that I'm involved in communications. I can't tell you any more than that.' And they'll say, 'Why not? Do you work for the government?' And you'll say, 'Yes, but that's as far as I can go right now. I'm afraid at this stage that I don't know you well enough to be able to elaborate. I'm sorry. You're just going to have to trust me.' And if they say, 'Okay, I'm going to ask one of your friends then', always say, 'You'll be wasting your time with them. My friends are all under strict instructions not to answer that question. I trust them implicitly.' By this stage, your persona will have created such an unwarrantedly charismatic presence, you'll have to start preparing yourself for the inevitable backlash: this is the most beautiful bit. Under intense probing, give away the highly sought-after information and then say, 'See, I knew it. You're just as shallow as all the others. If I told you straight away what I did for a living, you would've left me immediately – you're just like all the rest.' Then they'll deny this vehemently, and you'll say, 'Do you really expect me to believe that rubbish? Who do you think I am? Just because I ride bikes around all day and finish work at lunch time and do fuck-all, at least I've got a degree in nuclear physics to fall back on – and I'm human: I don't go around judging people on what they do for a living – like you!' You'll murder them every time."

They cackled appreciatively.

"One thing that pisses me off", Peter said, "is the imbalance in interest between the two sexes on first meeting. Imagine being female and having a pretty face and immediately getting an enthusiastic response every time you open your mouth. It'd be incredible."

"Particularly", I replied, "if you were a genuinely interesting individual and you knew that, every time you were going to make an interesting comment, the response was going to be rapid, ebullient and without the faintest hint of distraction."

"It doesn't bother me", Peter said, "that that situation exists – it's life – but they take it for granted. Some of them think they are interesting because of it."

"A lot of them", I said, "are probably totally unaware that that imbalance actually exists. I'm sure most women think that they find men equally as attractive as we find them. In fact, I've said this to a few women and they always disagree with it: they always go, 'No way! God, you've got to be joking!' as if they know what attraction is. And I say, 'Well, if you went to a crowded place – hundreds of people around – how many men would you find so attractive that you couldn't resist going to bed with them?' And they sort of shake their heads and say, 'One, maybe two per cent,' and I always burst out laughing, and they, of course, haven't got a damn clue as to why."

"One per cent!" Peter laughed. "With me it's one hundred per cent."

"With me", Brad added, "it's about a hundred and thirty per cent."

"I discovered once", I said, "that I really fried out a friend's wife in London by saying to her, 'Think of the most attractive man you've ever seen in your life; think of the effect this man had on you, how much desire he created, then imagine having that tumultuous experience about twenty different times a day and being absolutely useless in being able to do anything about it; then you can start to think about what it's like to be a man.' That", I added, over the din of conversation and music, "apparently shattered a few illusions."

After chuckling, Peter said, "I thought that we were supposed to have it easy."

"Dissatisfaction", I replied, "runs through me like a slowly meandering river, tearing into the sides of immovable cliffs."

"On the subject of rivers," Brad said, "Dob has got himself a yacht. He sails it in The Twilights. He got a letter from the Royal Freshwater Yacht Club warning him about overcrowding. Someone fell off one night after they collided with another boat. The boat was absolutely packed. Everyone was off their heads. It was about the fourth time he had taken it out and he didn't really know how to sail it

- no one else on board did either - they created mayhem. It was a miracle no one got hurt. You should come out with us one night."

"I haven't got any travel insurance," I replied.

Dob was the student psychiatrist. The Twilights occur, usually on Thursday nights, once a week during the summer. All the yacht clubs along the river have informal races. Members invite guests on board their boats for a casual, drunken cruise around the river during sunset. It is a lurid experience in every sense of the word.

"You see that guy over there?" Brad said, indicating a tall, brown-faced man in his late twenties. "He's a corporate lawyer who says, 'Want to come out on our yacht?' when referring to Dob's yacht. I try to keep away from the situation, really."

I watched the corporate lawyer talking to two attractive women. The women had an air of importance. They were in their early twenties and beautiful. The significance they exuded stemmed, I did not doubt, from being with a corporate lawyer who 'owned' a yacht. As women were attracted to success, I had every desire to become famous. Wealth was not as important as fame, for fame created the absurd impression that you were more interesting than those living in obscurity. I wanted it in abundance. I wanted to live this exceptional lie - not for reasons of egotism - but so that I could have the experience of life which comes naturally to a beautiful woman, but from a position of gratitude. That would be bliss. The ability to do whatever you like with the opposite sex must be one of the most powerful experiences a human being is capable of experiencing, particularly when the attention has been earned through guile, grit, courage and enterprise. It was also a necessity for me, for I had neither the personality nor the physical appearance to bring to fruition the situation with women which I so passionately desired: a relationship with a charming, well-educated, stunning genius. Okay, so I'm ridiculously hopeful. What else would you expect? I am an Epicurean - a penalty received as a result of a backlash against the deprivation during childhood that has given me a lust for beauty so profound that all my goals are unachievable, condemning me to perpetual frustration. But at least it drives me to see what's over the next mountain. At least my collection of photographs is going to be a lot better than most other people's. At least I've got that.

Dob was now standing next to me saying: "Kahnubazzz!"

He pronounced my pseudonym with an insincere emphasis which I found inhuman and boring.

"So how's sailor boy?" I asked. "Still trying to find the answer?"

The diction he used when responding was unnecessarily analytically verbose. He sounded like an academic addressing an audience of people trained in the same field - the field of hedonism, Australian style.

"No mortgages, responsibilities," he said, not looking me in the face, "so no point in indulging in the standard-routine syndrome; all that can wait. No unemployment problems to ever face, so the excitement indulgement process is given maximum credence. All possibilities are still living in the contingency spectrum, and that's the way I like it."

The serious expression on his face and the technical loquacity of his speech were, I felt, a product of insecurity. Even the supreme hedonist could have his confidence burnt by that dragon whose flames could parch any optimism. The arrogant pessimism with which he explained away a subtle suggestion on my part that his life had an aspect of immature superficiality was born from his belief that I could offer him nothing in his aspiration towards "perpetual pleasure intoxications".

"What about love?" I asked. "Has the brushstroke of real infatuation coloured the hedonistic canvas of your existence since I left these fair shores?"

I thought that I would add some poetry as a counterpoint to the academic technicalities of his language.

"Or, should I say", I added, in recognition of this, "has the heart-throb impulse caused alterations to all those schedule titillation episodes of which you speak so eloquently?"

A grin did something to unruffle his cool distance.

"I feel", he replied, "that it is about to."

"And who is this angel", I asked, "who has descended from the tenebrous mists of futility to shower light into a place where no light has ever been?"

"An architect," he replied.

"And how old is this nymph", I asked, "whose beauty knows no bounds?"

"A mere", he replied, as if he felt I would sneeringly disapprove, "twenty."

"I see", I replied, "that beauty outweighs maturity in your assessments related to matters of the heart."

"The uninformed," he said, "or perhaps the cynical, may take that view."

I laughed and said, "Dob, you know as well as I do that the instant this creature - whoever she is - opens her mouth for lengthy periods that you are going to get bored."

"What makes you think", he replied, "that you know me that well?"

"What makes you think", I continued, "that you know *me* that well? I'm just repaying you the compliment. Oh," I added, smiling, "the other answer to your question is observation."

This exchange took place with good-natured assertiveness. The subject of love arose again after I asked him about a few people with whom he used to be friendly. The two men concerned were now living in domestic harmony with women.

"Both", Dob said, with obvious disrespect, "have gone under."

This comment indicated to me just how narrow-minded the pretentiously liberated could be.

"What's wrong with that?" I asked. "What do you expect everyone to do? Find this interesting - still - after fifteen years? You must have an exceptionally high boredom threshold after all. Maybe you have changed."

"What are you doing here then?" he asked, with interrogatory glee.

"No choice," I retorted. "I've only been here a few days. Haven't had time to find someone with whom I can share the wonderful things of life yet."

"Maybe", he said, "I can help you out there then. My boat leaves next Thursday at six from Royal Freshie. Be on it."

"You'll forget", I replied, "by then that you've invited me. Let's face it - you've got another two and a half thousand people to speak to between now and then. You won't even remember that I'm here."

"The offer is there," he said. "If you want it, you'll take it."

"It's certainly open to debate", I replied, "as to whether I want it. Maybe by then", I continued, smiling, "my brain may have shrunk sufficiently to enable me to take on the daunting prospect of spending an evening listening to you bedazzle a pack of giggling teenage girls. When I think about it," I added, with sardonic reflection, "it has got excellent documentary possibilities, however. I could sell it to American television networks: 'Australia's answer to Roman Polanski' – and you even look like Mick Jagger."

A huge boyish grin swept aside the uninterested superiority of his previously dry demeanour. It revealed an innocence of self-appreciation endearing in its harmless desire to interpret any suggestion of his social uniqueness in positive and flamboyant ways. He was not flamboyant. He never tried to be; he had no interest in exceptional wines, in great music, in outstanding cars, in penthouses, in truly stylish women: he was just a boy with unlimited energy. He was not entirely unaware of this either. A hint of self-deprecation emerged from his lips when he said, "No time, Kahnubbazzz, to continue this repartee. I'm under a moral obligation now to go to The Other Party."

The emphasis on The Other Party was his playful admission that there was something ridiculous in this lifestyle of constant, informal social gatherings. Invariably, every Friday or Saturday night there was The Other Party. Conversations about The Other Party always sprang up when it became obvious that The Party was not destined to live up to expectations. The analysis given to the pros and cons of both parties was usually debated with an intensity often lacking in the conversations that had transpired previously in the night. Such was the case around me now. Brad and Peter were giving their views on the possibility that The Other Party would have "high mappage".

The woman who had approached Brad before entered the debate and spoke with a seriousness not previously recognisable in her character. She imparted to Brad and Peter the views of her friends. It was suspected that such and such would be there. Dob had now departed with an entourage of men and women; his arrival at The Other Party would give it the credence it required to usurp The Party and turn this party into The Other Party. It was a complicated process of debate and negotiation. Continual exposure to the mechanics of this change in status of one party to another could eventually lead to the development of someone with a keen mind for international diplomacy. It was rip-roaring debate without petulance or egotism; just a healthy exchange of views which enabled people to put their usually dormant analytical brains to work.

In front of me, the girl, whose name was Sue, was doing her utmost to persuade her friends that The Other Party held greater promise. Several people she knew would be there. Her eyes burned with persuasive animation. I wondered, with some doubt, as to whether she ever approached any other subject with the same intensity of feeling. It really seemed as though she were discussing something important. She was not the only one. All around me, on a patio littered with empty wine bottles and cans of beer, the remains of cardboard boxes strewn about the place, discussions about The Other Party erupted in an atmosphere that had suddenly transformed itself from aggressive gaiety into resigned dolefulness. This party had clearly outlived its usefulness. The impression was created that it was now impossible to experience absolute euphoria at this gathering, therefore its worth had been severely dissipated.

As Brad, Peter, Ana and Jennifer debated what they were going to do, I smiled when I noticed the swimming pool girl emerge from the clear, blue waters of mystery, sensitively, with a particularly feminine aspect of pain, expecting that some adoring man would provide her with a towel. A young man was waiting upon her to perform the said task. I was unsuccessful with such women for I had no desire to pander to their superiority. The man placed the towel around her shoulders with gentle care. She stood before him on the pedestal of her egotism and fully expected to be wiped dry. Her servant performed the task as if it was a privilege; upon her face was a look of pampered, momentous gravity. She stood before her valet with a haughty loftiness which, with each wipe, was enhanced as she played out her dream of unsurpassable supremacy. I was so amused by this display of pathetic superciliousness that I burst out guffawing, causing the four others to suddenly halt their discussion and look at me with beguiled curiosity.

"That woman over there", I said, "is labouring under the greatest misconception that has ever managed to grace the surface of this earth."

"The silly girl", Jennifer replied, "relies for her self-esteem on her ability to get men into bed."

I was amazed by the accuracy of her hard-headed perception.

"Getting men into bed", Peter said, "is the easiest thing any woman can ever achieve."

"In my case," I said, "it's an achievement of pity for which there is no other parallel."

This induced Brad's high-pitched giggle.

"I've found", I added, "that there is not a great deal of pity on this planet."

Everyone was amused in their various ways. Ana unleashed a violent, joyous crack of laughter; Peter almost sneered with jovial appreciation; Brad's shrill giggles went up a few notches; Jennifer glared at me with delighted fascination.

"I", I continued, this time seriously, "represent the other extreme from that woman over there. I have to earn everything I get. I do not envy her at all."

"You never", Jennifer accurately commented, "ever have to face the prospect of someone showing an intense interest in you for dubious reasons."

"Absolutely," I replied. "That woman seems unable to dissociate herself from her own perception of herself and why someone displays an interest in her. People like her – and thank God there aren't that many! – are incapable of gauging the genius and worth of those around them. There's nothing wrong with loving yourself – it's great – but it's deplorable if you can't see how remarkable everyone else is as well. She creates the illusion that other people were put on this earth to enhance her unparalleled excellence. I find it incredibly funny."

The girl was now surrounded by three tall, handsome young men – all with blond hair – who were attempting to engage her in conversation. Three heads were talking to one. A set pattern ensued. A comment would emerge from the three heads and the one head would respond. It went on for some time. Each member of the three heads was uninterested in anything that emerged from the mouths of the other two. A subtle competition of wit began. I wondered how my character would be affected if I too were perennially in situations in which attractive members of the opposite sex wanted to swamp me with affection. It would be dreadful, so dreadful that I would probably become the most egotistical, unsavoury, ill-mannered, disrespectful, reprobate, arrogant, self-centred, self-indulgent, conceited, overbearing, imperious, uppish, swaggering arsehole ever to have graced the confines of this earth. Actually, I think that I would be wonderful. She obviously thought that she was. I guess that I would be no different. Her existence was at such opposite poles to my own that it would be impossible for us to share the same perception of ourselves, relative to others. Her beauty gave her an unreal perception of the ease with which it is possible to gain the sort of intimacy that most of us have to work so hard to get. An air of introspective, contented irreverence oozed from her smug face; her egotism stood little chance of ever abating as men were blessed with the capacity of still being able to find someone scintillatingly attractive, irrespective of character. This created complications for men – for men like me particularly who were hopeless in the art of seduction – as we had to accept affection, warmth, comfort, intimacy from whoever was prepared to give it to us; often, in this desperate scenario, the woman's character was of little consequence. We still found her attractive whatever she said or did; there was no escape from it – we were natural losers. The burning rapacity of our lust could not be quenched by mere deficiencies such as stupidity, racism, egotism, dullness. We had to balance our negative feelings with our desire to touch. The simplicity of a woman's sexuality would be a godsend. How convenient it would be to have the natural sense to associate character with physical attraction, to connect an appreciation of someone's remarkable virtues with the desire to touch. Such magnanimous simplicity was, however, not the lot of men. We had the unfortunate capacity to find charm in the most vile of women, a swan in a flock of pigeons, the rainbow in the storm, the shaft of sunlight through a black sky. We could see it with a vision as clear as the obviousness of our concupiscent attentiveness. We were the condemned.

"Whatever women say", I said, "about the immorality of men, nothing's ever going to convince me that women are not partly to blame."

"Confidence", Jennifer replied, "is a source of great fascination for women."

"And men too," I said, looking over at the egotist who was doing her utmost now to use the towel as a means of enhancing her pretentious vulnerability; she wrapped it around her body so that her mouth just managed to rise over the top of it, as though she were cocooned in her own beautiful sensitivity, a waif, strong and wise, who deserved to be handled only with extreme delicacy.

"Women", I continued, "associate it with decisiveness. They need to think they've been chosen by someone whose taste is so well honed through mental strength that they are the greatest thing on earth. Perhaps that's being just a bit too deluded."

"Confidence", Jennifer said, "means mystery. We want to discover where it comes from."

"It's not too difficult", I replied, "to work that out in her case. It comes from undiscerning attention - loads of it. This country breeds it in horrendous quantities."

Peter particularly found this comment amusing.

"There's not much else to do," he smiled. "Hardly the sort of place you're going to spend all day in an art gallery, is it?"

"The potential", I replied, "is awesome."

Behind him, through an open glass sliding door, I could see a group of people prancing around to the music. A series of elastic gyrations and drunken pirouettes were accompanied by huge grins and bursts of cackling, deadened by the boisterous cacophony. It appeared as though the six people in that room had consumed a strange potion that made them undertake epileptic fits while standing up. Some of it was very sensual. A couple were in each other's arms, staring, with smouldering intensity, into each other's eyes while gliding around the length and breadth of the room. Their hips moved with mutually carnal synchronicity. It would take the most persuasive individual on earth to convince me that their lower abdominal regions were not destined to come into prolonged contact. The passion of their communication had risen well above the level of mere chat. Their passionate harmony seemed to my pessimistic envy to exist in another world, a place of security and aesthetic and sentient fulfilment, a world devoid of destructive insecurities and puerile conflicts where every perception, word, thought, rose from sun-drenched flower beds buzzing with fat, woolly bees.

I had seen this world, had seen it too often for cynicism or neglect, but from the outside, as though I were at a closed window, glancing with awakened eyes into the utopian fields; I had accepted, with a sort of flippant resignation, after years of cracking my forehead into the unmoving glass, that that window was forever closed. What the hell. I had seen millions in worse positions than myself. I had seen piles of dead soldiers, their mothers weeping with furious inconsolability, cursing the absurdity of this maddened and avaricious world; I had seen blind people in the teeming streets of Cairo begging, their vision closed by cataracts, gnarled hands raised like twisted branches into the heavens; I had seen toothless old men sleeping on the frozen streets of London and knew people whose entire families had been decimated by war. I was extremely lucky and the instant I realised this, after thirty years of plush, First World living, I developed an immediate resilience to the nagging trivialities of everyday life: to its routines, and petty trifles, to its insignificant squabbles and the desolation of its bland securities; in that instant, I fell in love, not with myself, but with my life – with its potential for learning, with its calculated waywardness and with its mystery. You were not destined to hear me complain. I was on the verge of a vast, tranquil ocean, touched, here and there, by the rippling sunlight, and I knew it.

"It appears", I said, smiling, thoroughly enjoying the romance before me, "as if the flower of love is blooming upon the dance floor."

"A flower", Peter added, "whose bouquet has been sweetened by the consumption of several bottles of champagne."

"A flower", I said, "whose petals have been touched by the sugary poison of infidelity."

"And", Peter replied, "by the bitter honey of iniquity."

Both of us giggled away happily.

"And," I added, "the intoxicating elixir of unrestrained passion."

"A flower", Peter said, "whose luxuriant, exotic petals have sprung from the hot, fertile bed of libidinousness."

The dancing couple were now in a swirling embrace. Then their lips clashed in a frenetic rubbing of pouting flesh. It was absolutely absorbing. I was captivated by public displays of romance. The sight of people kissing filled me with a sensation almost joyous, as though the observation of it acted as a substitute for that which seemed beyond my reach.

"But", Peter commented, "it can be assumed that the petals of this rose of lust will, however, one day surely die."

"But", I said, "will they perish in a sudden, violent storm, or will they wither slowly with age? This is the question."

"A question", Ana quipped, with typically outstanding timing, "very much on both their lips."

We all broke into warm bursts of elated blithesomeness. Ana's face became swathed in mirthful lines and dimples. Waves of naughty jocularity rolled across it. Jennifer beamed with titillated surprise. Brad giggled with overjoyed pleasure, his laughter like an unlimited recoiling of some deeply-implanted and felicitous spring, while Peter, glancing around at everyone with happy acknowledgement, unleashed a handful of sonorous cackles that culminated in his slapping his leg and saying, "What a classic!"

Some drunk girl with gorgeous skin then emerged from the dancing room and accused us, with some seriousness behind her jovial façade, of "not having a good time".

"Why don't you dance?" she asked, as if having a conversation were a poor substitute for experiencing epilepsy.

"Because", I replied, "we've got taste."

"Taste?" she asked.

"The art", I replied, "of discernment."

"That", she said, with an unnecessary toughness, "sounds to me like a pile of shit."

"Do you", I replied, "review opera for *The Sydney Morning Herald*?"

Australian women do not appreciate sarcasm as a weapon of belittlement.

"Do you want me to tell you to fuck off?" she asked.

"Yes," I replied, "but only in Italian."

Ana was chortling. That did not help to calm this aggressive woman's ruffled ego. My aside about the quality of the music was understandably not the most diplomatic of actions, given that it was probably her party. She stood in the doorway glaring at me with an outrage well beyond the significance of the event. She was fuming, I felt, about something that had little to do with me. I was the guilty catalyst of a trauma buried until this moment.

"It's okay," Brad said, trying to appease her.

Despite her overreaction, I felt responsible for her torment.

"Look," I said, "I'm sorry. It's a pity that more people aren't dancing. You're right. The music's quite good, really."

"Then", she replied, "why did you make that comment about taste?"

"I was just joking," I said. "You claimed we weren't enjoying ourselves. I thought I'd try and come up with an excuse."

She began to calm down.

"Sorry," I said.

It was a pleasurable experience being apologetic towards her. She was very pretty and had a despairing vulnerability that appealed to an instinct within me for rescuing women in distress.

"I deserve", I added, "to be told to fuck off in any language you'd care to use."

She smiled briefly and said, "Forget it."

There was in her voice a sweet grudging appeasement; whether or not I was the guilty party was beside the point. I wanted to be. I wanted to soothe this creature's damaged ego. I even felt like saying, 'It amazes me how I could have been so horrible towards someone so beautiful. I obviously need my head examined.'

Instead, I said, "Under normal circumstances, we would probably be dancing, but I haven't seen these people for six years. We've got a bit to catch up on."

"Have you", she asked, smiling wryly, "just been released from prison?"

"Yes," I replied. "I murdered someone on a dance floor. Someone who told me to fuck off."

The more I looked at this creature the more beautiful she became. She had long dark hair and piercing black eyes that stared at me with sensuous fury. She had red cheeks which epitomised the sensual obstreperousness of her impassioned demeanour. It was a pity that, as men, we have to hide the swiftness with which passion befalls us. Women could never appreciate the alacrity with which their beautiful faces can unleash our profound hopes. It is a mystery beyond explanation.

She flicked back her hair so that her fringe became a wave that curled away to the right. A rapid smile increased the size of her full cherry lips so that the edges of her mouth became fine points from which cavernous dimples ran up past the end of her long, elegant nose.

"Had I known," I said, "while I was inside, that you were out here, I would've become so loquaciously persuasive to the probation officer that they would've had no choice but to let me out within three months."

"Do you normally", she asked, "go so quickly from sarcastic abuse to flattery?"

"Only when", I replied, "guilt gnaws at me for being so terrible to someone so sensitive."

"I forgive you," she said.

"Is this your party?" I asked.

"Yes," she replied.

“Your birthday?” I asked.

“No,” she replied. “Housewarming.”

The others were now talking to a group of people I did not know so that I was left alone with her; it was exciting and unnerving, for she was indifferent, and I was intrigued, attracted, under the ever-recurring spell of womanhood. The vast gulf in our desire for each other was beyond our mutual control; this denuded me of my inferior position of pride.

“You’ve got an exceptionally lovely face,” I said.

The expression on her face was a combination of a smile and a sneer.

“What do you expect me to do?” she asked. “Throw my arms around you and be eternally grateful?”

She had placed her left arm along the jamb of the door and was infuriated that someone would assume that she was impressionable enough to be overawed by such a remark. Her action was unconscious and very feminine; because she was so unpretentious I wanted to inflate her ego.

“Of course not,” I replied. “It’s just that its obvious that you’ve got real character. I don’t often come across such charisma. Is this my fault?”

“Why”, she asked, “don’t you just keep it to yourself then? I’m afraid I’m not really in the mood for psychoanalysis.”

“Because”, I replied, “I’m an incurable Epicurean. My aesthetic sentiments are so vast that, if they are not released immediately, it can have an adverse effect on my health.”

A contemptuous snigger emerged from her mouth. I was impressed and amused by her disdainful suspicion.

“Do you sit at home”, she began, “and stare out windows conjuring up these lines? For God’s sake, get a grip on yourself.”

“Get a grip on myself!” I replied. “How the fuck do you expect me to do that? It’s easy for you to go through life absolutely unhampered by your senses - you don’t have to put up with the experience of suddenly being confronted by awesome, unattainable beauty. All you have to do is exist. That must be bloody difficult.”

“Back to sarcasm,” she said, before one of the men with whom she had been dancing came up behind her and whispered something in her ear.

They talked enthusiastically as I stood by myself, feeling victimised by my inappropriately expressed heightened appreciation. A sensation of worthlessness tore into me with each smile and chuckle she produced in conversation with her male friend. The diverse fashion in which she dealt with us both - from amicability to disrespect - expressed to my infatuated mind a complexity of character irresistible to my aesthetic instincts. I was captivated by her erotic vitriol. I wanted more of it.

The opportunity to receive it again occurred when her friend went off to get her a drink. I watched her looking out into the back garden. She eyed the proceedings with a sort of intrigued distance, as though I were non-existent, not part of her environment, beneath her consideration.

"What's your name?" I asked.

She glared at me, impatiently, and said, "Why? What's it to you?"

"Beautiful," I laughed. "I bet your Christian name ends in 'a'."

She stared into my face with passionate disbelief and said, "What does it matter what bloody letter it ends with? Have you ever considered psychiatric treatment?"

"It makes an incredible amount of difference," I replied, smiling. "Anyone can tell you that female Christian names ending in 'a' are without doubt the most sensuous. But some names ending in 'a' are better than others. There's no doubt about the fact that, if your name happens to be Natasha, then I am going to fall in love with you instantly."

"So if my name was Doreen", she asked, "you'd leave me alone?"

"I wouldn't leave you alone", I replied, "if your name was Frank."

"Well, to be frank," she said, "you may as well, because you've got no chance."

"That", I replied, "was exactly what my first wife said."

"Someone actually married you?" she quipped.

"Wonderful," I replied. "Why is it", I pondered, with a look of genuine appreciation, "that, from you, abuse sounds like a Mozart symphony?"

She smiled ruefully and shook her head in exasperation.

"What makes you think", I continued, "that I would begin to assume that your taste is so bad as to consider me as a viable prospect for passion? That obviously is simply not going to happen. So cultivated abuse is the next best thing."

"That", she smirked, "sounds suspiciously like another slimy compliment."

"But", I replied, "a compliment no less."

"I suppose", she remarked, "there've only been a hundred women this week who've had the pleasure of your obsequious flattery?"

"Can you imagine", I replied, "what it's like to be brimming with appreciation - genuine, warm-hearted appreciation - and to be tormented because of it?"

"You poor thing," she said.

"I know," I replied, "and I can tell you something else as well. You see that woman over there by the swimming pool?"

"What about her?"

"She's definitely one woman who'd never get an ounce of it from me. And you know why?"

The expression on her face suggested that she wanted to know.

"Because", I continued, "she's completely opposite to you. She suffers from the delusion of thinking that she's mystifyingly complex. I dread the thought of doing anything to build that bitch's ego up."

"How do you know she isn't complex?" she asked. "Have you ever spoken to her?"

"No need to," I replied. "Her actions speak for themselves."

"Do you always go through life making such rapid conclusions?" she asked, with a hint of appealing disdain.

"Name me", I replied, "one person who doesn't."

"Me," she said.

"You don't honestly expect me to believe that absolute rubbish," I replied, "do you?"

"Why not?" she asked. "You're expecting me to believe yours."

"Now", I replied, "you really are jumping to conclusions. I thought I'd already told you that I had to do it for health reasons. You don't honestly think that for one moment I thought you were actually going to believe it. Has it ever struck you that there's something fantastic for a man in getting the opportunity to express his complicated feelings to a beautiful, suspicious woman? One with obvious strength and delicacy? One whose passionate abuse has the beauty of a wild storm? And one who is absolutely oblivious of the magnitude of her awesome charm? I want your phone number. Give it to me. Whether you like it or not, we're going out."

She exploded with laughter.

"That", she said, through her derisive chuckles, "has got to be the most inappropriate request I will probably ever receive in my life."

"I take it then", I replied, with sardonic inquisitiveness, "that the answer is 'no'."

"I suppose", she said, "that it's about time that you made an accurate assumption."

"Oh well," I replied, "you're only human. You're entitled to make mistakes. I suppose it goes without saying that one day you're going to regret this."

"Oh, I have no doubt," she said, shaking her head with sarcastic agreement.

Her friend returned with some drinks and she turned her back on me.

I wandered over to the others and said to Brad and Peter, "I was just making the acquaintance of our gracious hostess - a charming creature."

"How'd you go then?" Brad asked.

"Hopelessly," I replied, with a playful air of refined dignity. "What else? She's got taste. She hates my guts."

They began giggling.

"It gets tiresome", I said, "having to continually explain to these women that I do not expect them to like me. A lot of them have no regard for the joys of salacious mistreatment. I find that woman incredibly attractive. It'd be great convincing her that she was beautiful."

"There'd be no chance", Peter said, "of ever being able to do that."

"Absolutely zero," I replied. "As far as she's concerned, I'm at the bottom end of the Kelvin Scale. I did not even move a molecule."

Brad laughed with boyish glee.

"It looked to me", Peter said, "as if you were on the receiving end of some useful abuse though."

"Every bit of it", I replied, "was like listening to the harmonic resonance of violin strings."

I felt the elation of having endeavoured. The result was superfluous. That was out of my control. Only fate could dictate that, and only I could give fate the opportunity to express itself. I knew that idle chatter would be a waste of time. It was a chance to have some dubious fun and I had taken it. Doing something naughty with style was always erotic. At least she knew that I existed. It was obvious that she did not possess the faintest interest in polite conversation, unless it came from someone as beautiful as herself. It was exciting causing upheavals to the accepted way of things. It created the feeling that something miraculous was possible. I detested standing around inactively.

Jennifer did too by the look of it. As Ana spoke to two people beside him, she looked about, dazed with boredom. She was too young and inexperienced, and had everything too easily, to feel the need for passionate involvement. She did not have to affect things. Things were usually too busy trying to affect her. Too often unsophistication is mistaken for stupidity. Her pained dreariness came from lack of exposure to ideas, not dullness. She was too young for long periods of concentration. The riches of life fell into her lap with little effort; the intimacy and consideration necessary for contentment comes to people like her with an ease that can cause someone like me to experience sharp moments of bitterness, extended bouts of resignation and, occasionally, a quiet chuckle at the naive ingratitude of such a person's position.

"How come you're in this country?" I asked.

Her face looked up at me and came alive. Her father was a geophysicist who had decided to leave America and see the world. Talking to her, I assumed yet another personality. The experience of communicating with her was vastly different from that which I had felt when speaking to 'Doreen' or whatever her name was.

"He split from my mother", she said, "and wanted to get away from things. He's a wanderer."

I felt swathed in a polite restraint; there was nothing overtly obvious in her character that should have led me to feel the way I did. It was her physical appearance which caused this conservative reaction. I felt as though I had to be a gentleman: unthreatening, virtuous, enquiring, not free to rankle the righteous innocence of such a creature. The mystery of my diversified reactions to people was beyond my consideration. Style comes and goes with an incomprehensibility that I afforded to the existence of the stars. Perhaps it was a twisted form of egotism which led me to believe that my responses possessed a magnitude of width well above the average. In the space of five minutes I had gone from being a dubious rogue of suspect disposition to a safe harbinger of all those insipid qualities that women tried to convince us were of profound significance to their romantic cause. Ideally, I wanted to be accepted as a flawed being uncomfortable and dangerous in an atmosphere of sober politeness. It was difficult to achieve, to grasp; the slither of corrupt magnetism writhes with the wildness of its untamed force, writhing and snapping and jolting, unheld, beyond the capabilities of my fumbling hands.

"And", I asked, "has the same spirit been infused within you?"

"I wouldn't be here", she replied, "if it hadn't been."

"There are definitely some people", ('Should I really say this?' I was thinking to myself. 'How's it going to come out? She's going to be bored by this one.') I said, "who", ('This is going to be perceived as a classic platitude.') "are so infused with it", ('More ill-timed pretensions to a better existence.') "that the more they wander, the worse it becomes."

"And you're one?" she asked.

"No question of it," I replied. "I feel something artificial and eerie in the desolate respectability of suburbia."

She smiled with a grace befitting someone so beautiful.

"Where did you learn", she asked, "to put things that way?"

I was astonished to be asked such a question. Does she really want to know? I had little faith in the collective curiosity of self-indulgent humanity.

I returned the smile and said, "It appeals to my sense of humour."

"If you fell in love", she replied, "your attitude towards suburbia might change."

"You mean", I said, "if I fell in love and it was reciprocated, then my attitude might change."

"Okay," she replied, "I mean that."

"No," I said, "it wouldn't make the slightest difference. It'd only cause me to pursue my designated task with an even greater relish. In fact," ('Thank God, relief, return of confidence. It's that smile. It can melt icebergs.') "I would trudge across the burning, endless desert of audacious ambition even less affected by the potential pain that the blinding sun of failure can afflict."

She had a charming laugh.

"Such nobility," she beamed.

"Knubs," Ana suddenly spun around and said, "you're always trying to chat my girlfriends up. If you lay hands on my sheila I'll rearrange yar farkin front teeth, okay?"

Ana enjoyed deriding the macho attitudes of some Australian men.

"I was just explaining", I said, "to Her Royal Highness, the Princess of Boston, Countess of West Perth, that, if the angel of reciprocated love descended into my existence then I believe that the hot, burning sands of difficult aspirations would singe the exposed souls of my feet even less."

"Is that all?" Ana laughed. "I thought you were saying something relevant like: 'You can't possibly be interested in that ugly boyfriend of yours. Get rid of him.'"

"Imagine walking up to some woman," I smiled, "totally pissed, and saying, 'Look, tart, I accept the fact that you've probably been around a bit, but there is one bit you haven't been around and that's my dick. Be on it before midnight or I'll come all over your face.'"

The three of us chortled away.

"I've heard some ridiculous chat-up lines in my time," Ana said, "but the other night a friend of mine came up with a classic. He walked up to this woman in a nightclub and said, 'I come from a long line of bears; how about a hug?'"

"One night in London", I replied, "I walked up to this woman in a bar – she hadn't even seen me there – and I said, 'Why do you keep staring at me?' She was astounded. 'I haven't been staring at you,' she said. 'Yes, you have,' I said. 'Every time I look away and then look back, your eyes are always right on me. Why?'; and she said, 'I might have been looking at you, but I wasn't thinking about you.' 'Pity,' I said. 'It'd be nice being in your thoughts.'"

"What happened?" Jennifer asked.

"Her boyfriend came back from the toilet," I replied.

Brad and Peter joined us again. They reported that The Other Party was now in the ascendancy. A gradual defection had been occurring towards this magnetism of hope; Brad and Peter were not keen to join it. As the four of them expressed uninterest in moving, I watched Doreen – or whatever her name was – looking up into the face of a man who seemed politely detached from her attentiveness; the expression of animated intrigue in her shining eyes – eyes which could stare at me until the sun exploded in a blinding helium flash – eyes glinting with sensitivity – indicated to me that her cynicism was easily revoked, easily replaced with passion, concern, appreciation, agreeableness. It was rare to suddenly have a profound and unshakeable belief in the greatness of someone else's character; it mattered not a jot what she thought of me. Every aspect of her personality conveyed charm. The apparence of this was instant. The vision of her appearing sympathetic was so arresting that I thought the swirl of noisy interaction had unfurled itself before my eyes like a silken coil connecting my heart to a place my imagination had created solely for the existence for such a being. It was typical of fate to organise itself to my detriment. Her attitude towards me could not have been any more disrespectful; but so what? She existed: this was more important than either of us forming wildly divergent opinions of each other – instantaneously – from what appeared to be a shred of evidence. I know beauty when I see it. I saw it in the devoted nodding of her head each time the man to whom she was talking said something that appealed to her sentiments; I saw it in the line of her smooth cheek and the sheen that graced the generous clusters of her overflowing hair; I saw it in the sparkle of her gracious eyes and the way the index finger of her right hand ran along her cheek as she swayed her supported head and heeded the information she was consuming from someone blessed with that mystifying sense of preoccupation which she no doubt believed did not exist within my soul. I saw it in the sudden explosion of lips and hands as she responded with confident intelligence each time her dreamy interlocutor ceased his talk; and I saw it in the overall way she carried herself with sanguine grace, the truculent swan whose face seemed to explode with light each time a smile registered upon a collection of features crying out to be covered in long, sensuous kisses. I was convinced that her negative qualities stemmed from something beautiful – from a sort of determined certainty – that embodied the righteousness of her views and the charming fury of her passion. Oh yes, I know class when I see it.

The instant I got the chance to speak to her, I was away, like a sensation yearning for its expression.

I came up behind her and said, "You really do have an amazingly lovely face."

She spun around startled, ablaze with fury and disgust, and said, "Oh God! Did anyone ever tell you that there is a fine line between persistence and stupidity?"

"Did anyone ever tell you", I replied, "that appreciation is far greater than both of them?"

She sneered at me with the bitterness of an enraged animal; behind her, the kissing couple were groping each other on a settee and the sweet bitter thought that she had done this herself with someone else was like an awkward theoretical construct in the already impossible scheme of things.

"You can't tell me", I continued, "that you've never ever been in a situation where you've been suddenly overcome by somebody else's charisma; I assume that even you are capable of being human."

She glared at me as though the inappropriateness of my attempt to explode into her life were a vile absurdity, unjustified and naive in its unmitigated intrusion.

"There are ways", she sardonically suggested, "of going about it. Perhaps in future you might like to take this into consideration."

I was thoroughly enjoying the impolite veracity of our interaction. It produced a closeness like the bonds of love, something unrestrained and healthy.

"Spoken", I said, "like a true woman. If I'd walked up to you and said, 'Wow, what a really nice house you live in! Can I use your toaster?' I'm sure you would have been really impressed."

The expression of indifferent disdain on her face – if such a thing is possible – summed up the uselessness of my position. It was programmed in that I had to impress her, but there were limits my dignity would allow me to travel; but, whatever self-possession I had, nothing was going to deter me from appreciating the beauty of her eyes. I saw them multicoloured, different shades from iridescent blue to black. My imagination saw geometric shapes in them. They were catlike.

"I assume", I said, "that it's pointless to inform you of the fact that I actually find your unappreciative, arrogant displeasure rather endearing, because I suspect that this will be taken – horror upon horror – as a compliment."

A brief half smile gave me remarkable pleasure.

"And I assume", she replied, "that you will find it impossible to comprehend that it seems ridiculous to walk up to someone you don't even know and begin giving them inappropriate accolades, as if you'd known them for most of your spurious life."

"This", I said, "indicates two things to me: one, the remarkable effect you've had on me, and two, that you lack self-esteem."

"What?" she exclaimed. "I do not lack self-esteem."

"I think you do," I replied.

"What warped perception", she began, "enabled you to produce that rubbish?"

"Simple," I replied. "Observation. If you were truly conscious of your charisma, then it would come as no surprise to you to be confronted by someone clearly astounded by the fact of your existence. Instead," I added, with a mocking, haughty peremptoriness, a tone that had coloured both our voices, "I find that the bearer of all this alluring attractiveness is, against all predictions, astounded by the seemingly prosaic event of some ordinary man, with wide eyes, acknowledging that which is obvious. Really," I finished, glancing away with lofty disbelief, "I'm quite surprised."

A rueful guffaw of mocking elation erupted from her magnificent mouth. It was a mouth the natural colouring of which was light cherry, the perfect hue. She seemed to be under the delusion that I thought I had every chance of depositing mine upon it. I had no chance whatsoever.

"I don't suppose", she remarked, "that it's entered your quite clearly diseased mind", (I smiled as wide a smile as is humanly possible) "that many a young lady is not moved by the empty dispensation of approbatory nonsense linked to physical appearance."

"It was", I agreed, "approbatory, but to say that it was purely linked to physical considerations is a distortion of the grossest proportions. It was an ethereal reaction."

This caused another eruption of condescending laughter.

"You may laugh," I said, "but it is apparent to me that, if your self-esteem was on the plane which it deserves to be, then, against the dark grain of suspicion that sits in the satinwood of your soul, you would be open-minded about the possibility that what I've just said is true; but, instead, what do we have? Recalcitrance, bellicosity, disrespect, truculence, prickliness, unsavouriness, ill-temperedness – all while I'm being so nice. Whatever you do from now on, don't go around saying there's any justice in this world. Please, at least do me the service of avoiding that."

"What makes you think", she replied, "that I want to be told the obvious?"

"I couldn't help it," I said. "I was overcome."

"Overcome with what?" she asked, sarcastically.

"Absolute appreciation," I replied. "Something", I sighed, "that does not happen very often. Comprehend?"

The sharp, straightforward tone of my voice shocked her. The passion with which I imbued my words was obviously genuine. I was almost furious.

"Do you realise how pointless it is", I said, "for the average man to be nice to women? Do you realise what the average man gets for that?"

She was suddenly vulnerable, speechless.

"Well," I continued, "allow me the privilege of telling you: a lot less than you get for doing exactly the same thing. There is a thing in the universe called work. That is precisely what people like myself have to do. And you?"

I burst out laughing. It was a cynical cackle with mysterious overtones.

"Huh!" I continued, "All you have to do is show up to the office. And even when you get there, you can't even be bothered just momentarily glancing out the window from the plush confines of your leather seat, where you sit so smugly, unscathed, a picture of sensitive certainty, and see the strain that so many others are under. And do you know why?"

"Do I", she replied, "have to find out?"

"Of course not," I said. "Why should you? It's not your problem. But, at least, you could occasionally just glance out the window and wonder. Believe me, it would be in your interest to do that."

"I don't really think", she replied, "that you're in a position to tell me what to do."

"I never", I said, "tell anyone what to do. Occasionally, very occasionally, I indulge in advice."

"Oh," she replied, "so I'm privileged?"

'Cheeky, fucking bitch.' I smiled.

"I'm glad", I said, "I've helped you experience some self-awareness. It's been a privilege."

She unleashed the same smile. A rare wave of restraint stopped her from saying: 'Cheeky wanker.'

"It's time", she said, "that I went and spoke to a friend. Bye."

She went inside and proceeded to speak to the man with whom she had been talking earlier. I watched her for a few minutes; she could leave any situation and any number of opportunities would be waiting for her. I suppose that opportunities are irrelevant without desire. Desire is not, however, irrelevant without opportunities. It's hell. It is the mark of Cain. It is the reminder that your life is short and painful. Unfulfilled desire creates the impression that time is limited. It was rushing away from me.

Through the glass sliding doors, I observed the ethereal 'Doreen' displaying the alluring aspects of the pleasant side of her personality. The mind could only marvel at how it would react if it got the chance of being exposed to the wild, salacious furies of her passions. Fate would no doubt conspire to give me every opportunity to imagine it. I would see it all – see it and never feel it.

I was told on the drive back to Brad's place that he had found out her name was Samantha. I was not surprised by this: the instant I laid eyes on her I knew that her Christian name had to end in 'a'. I just knew it. I knew it! I knew it! As usual, I was bloody right! That sensuous beast had to have a Christian name ending in 'a'. She just had to. There was no other possibility.

And just imagine what condition your brain would be in, Knubs, old boy, if that spark of cosmic genius was called Natasha? Oh my God... And she was Russian and she played the guitar and her great grandfather fought in the principal battles of the Russian civil war, and she had been skin-diving in the Red Sea, and she loved only me? But I would never find these things out. I knew that it would take a miracle for me to discover her secrets, and there were no miracles on this earth (not for me, anyway) other than life itself. Oh well, goodnight.

* * * * * * * * * *

In a taxi going back from Brad's to Brian's, I observed that the streets had a momentous quietude which belied the activity transpiring in the minds of myself and the Iranian driver, whose swarthy, bushy-moustached appearance was not in keeping with the sensitive, gentle ambience in his brown eyes. He was a man displaced. Nothing about him suggested that he was from here. He had real soul for a start. The conversation rapidly got on to Iran.

"If I go home," he said, "I get it."

He slashed a finger across his throat. I turned and looked at his profile, and saw house after house gliding past his head; the lamps of front verandas threw a lemon powder into the darkness. Such safety and security seemed abnormal.

"You would", I asked, "definitely be killed if you went back?"

"Yes," he replied. "Killed. Dead!"

Another slash went across his throat. The reasons for this were not given by him easily. I concluded, after he had told me, that his reticence on the subject was due to modesty.

"I get letters from people", he said, "saying: 'Get me out!' So many letters. What can I do?"

He raised his hands in exasperation. A flash of angered bewilderment filled his eyes; then the passion subsided to the tranquillity of their natural state.

"Nothing," he added, tapping the wheel. "And this will not stop. Not now. Maybe never."

This was a form of frustration to which I could relate. It could have been me talking about women. I knew the feeling well – the helplessness, the bitterness of one's inaction, the uselessness in the face of simple, pleasurable and sensible goals. Except that his adversity was far greater. Everything had been taken from him – country, family, love, profession – everything, but the free will of his thoughts.

"And you know what?" he asked.

"What?" I replied.

"That country could be so great," he said, almost whispering. "But, never."

This was the first time in my life that I had met a political refugee, one who would face execution for 'subversive activities' if he returned to his homeland. I had met others who had left their countries of birth for financial reasons – a new repressive regime wishes to redistribute wealth – but this was the first time I had met someone who had defied a government, courageously, on moral grounds. And what a government to defy! One which killed people, randomly, because its leaders believed they were in contact with God! This was some scenario in which to grow up.

"There's something I'd like to know about Iran," I said; "something trivial in comparison to what you've just been talking about."

"What is it? What is it?" he demanded.

He was happy to have met someone curious about his country.

"Three weeks ago in London", I began, "I was sitting in an Iranian restaurant and I saw a photograph on the wall of a mountain surrounded by desert. It looked like an ancient volcano. It was obviously summer – there were flowers in the foreground and a heat haze. That mountain was half covered in snow."

The driver nodded his head enthusiastically. He was astounded to have picked somebody up able to tell him this. I was very surprised by this. I was accustomed, after years of travel, to these 'international coincidences', and thought nothing of it.

"That mountain", I said, "must be enormous. Why haven't I heard of it?"

He was smiling like an excited schoolboy. I was delighted that he managed to be so charming whilst glowing with pride.

"It's true," he replied. "It's nearly the same as Kilimanjaro. Only a few hundred feet difference. It's called Damavand. It's about one and a half hour's drive from Tehran. I believe it is fair to say – magnificent."

He shook his head with lugubrious worship. There had been days when he had driven there with his wife and they had seen the "great shadow" creeping across the plain in the late afternoon. The peak, covered in snow, was "from another world". Those days were now over. Now it was driving taxis. No love in the protective shadow of beauty.

"Me," he sighed, with amused resignation, "me. Hah! The great journalist is now taxi-driving. Me! Taxi-driving because English not good."

We laughed at his ironic deprecation. His smile was like the day so foul and fair that Shakespeare to which had alluded so many years before. This was a man not impressed by easy security; yet it was something like this which he and people like him were attempting to achieve for us all.

"You can't", he said, "have surprises about anything that happens to you. No surprises," he continued, waving his finger, "not in this world."

We were now parked beside the road in front of Brian's place. The occasional sound of a car in the distance was the only auditory sign that we were in a populated area. Nothing moved in the vast docility of the night. Street lights cast down yellow-white light in silken patches on to grass verges and the smooth asphalt of the road. It was an unnecessary waste of light. So little traversed these opulent streets that it was a wonder anyone had bothered to illuminate them, as though the use of artificial lighting had spiritual significance, was a justification in itself for the profligacy of photons in this staid and tranquil world.

I asked him about his wife. He stared through the windscreen with a look of pained disbelief. I was starting to wonder if I had made the right decision in bringing the subject up. The news was a disgrace to every form of justice imaginable.

"She's still over there," he sighed. "They won't let her out. They watch her every day. My letters are sent through other friends. And I'm so in love."

"Jesus Christ!" I said. "Or should I say Allah?"

He smiled with the resignation of a being whose every fibre was made from the accumulated experiences of the centuries; a being absolved from surprises.

"Who is this Allah?" he asked.

"You tell me," I replied. "I'm still trying to come to grips with God."

"Allah", he said, "is another word for 'excuse'."

It was a problem that some people believed their actions were above mortal considerations, but it was a real problem when these people decided that the world would be better off allowing them to dictate the course of history. These people were responsible for the destruction of so many hearts. I could not imagine what it must be like being in love with a woman who reciprocate your adoration, who's made you what you are, who's filled so many prosaic moments with light, who's given everything the glowing transcendence of childhood, who wants to give you all that attention, and who has nothing but life in her heart - and she is held away from you by politics. If that is divine providence, I would suggest that it may be in the interest of all concerned if God undertook a little reprogramming.

"Can you see a way", I asked, "to get her out?"

He shook his head slowly and said, "There are so many wonderful people. So many. Amnesty International have been working very hard. Not everyone in the Iranian hierarchy is an idiot. There is hope. How can there be anything else?"

"There can't be", I replied, "anything else. While she is on this earth, there is hope."

"We will see each other again," he said. "The world is not that bad."

"I hope it isn't," I replied.

"What else can we hope for?" he asked.

"Exactly," I replied.

The concentration of one's mind on negative possibilities comes naturally enough without having to extend it to the existence of nefarious omniscience. I told him that I wanted to go to Tehran. He was delighted. He said he could "put me in contact" with "virtually anyone I wanted".

"I was hoping you would," I said. "I'm a photojournalist."

This led to a rapid exchanging of numbers. I told him that I had first wanted to go to Iran when I read a story about an Australian many years ago who had left his hotel room "virtually naked". "Within seconds" venomous people in black were hurling objects at him about the same size as "house bricks". It took the said gentleman some time to realise that his physical appearance was an insult to all forms of decency.

"'That', I thought at the time," I said, "'must be so foreign. I'd like to try that.'"

Khalid laughed and said: "The thinking of a journalist!"

"And now", I replied, "the time has come."

"And", he added, "there's also the volcano to see."

"That", I said, "would be a real pleasure."

I told him that I thought volcanoes were the most fascinating of natural phenomena because they represented "vast, prehistoric forces", something "at the heart of transition"; they were objects laced with "metaphysical significance" and they rise "straight out of flat plains".

"They are the earth", Khalid said, "reaching for heaven."

Heaven was a place Khalid had been before; heaven at the bottom of Damavand. I left him in his taxi and wandered down Brian's driveway knowing that tonight two very significant things had occurred. Both were going to widen the parameters and both were dangerous. And both were going to happen.

* * * * * * * * * * *

The voice on the other end of the line was female, eccentric, deliberately transformed and unnaturally deep. I assumed that it was someone with a sense of humour who knew Brian.

"Must speak to great white one," this woman said, in an accent resembling a Hollywood movie adaptation of an American Indian. "Must speak now, O great travelled one!"

I was curious, but it wasn't my business so I just handed the receiver to Brian and said, "Do you know anyone interested in nineteenth century American social history with a flair for travel?"

When he spoke to this person his voice, too, underwent an eerie transformation. The bemusement of his expression quickly turned to sombre intensity as his voice became coloured by a sort of bitter formality. The strange being was after Vanessa.

"It's Lois," Brian said.

He handed the receiver over. Vanessa rapidly became engaged in a discussion with her mother, on a time to meet, as her father, sitting in the lounge-room reading a newspaper, assumed an unnatural air of morbid introspection. He listened to every word. Nothing from the newspaper entered his brain. He was transfixed by cynical curiosity. He was not sufficiently enraptured by the individual activities and thoughts of his own existence to indulge in indifference. He was too much of a social being to be able to ward off the spectre of hapless inquisitiveness. I could relate to the problem.

After Vanessa and Lois reached an agreement, the phone was handed to me.

A laughing Lois said, "Just thought I'd confuse you. How are you, anyway? Are you here for long?"

We hadn't spoken to each other for about eight years. The voice was now unmistakable. We exchanged some of the basic formalities as Brian, tightly gripping his newspaper, was glued to my every word. His eavesdropping made me feel uncomfortable. It was tacitly expected that I be offhand with her. I had no desire to do this – she had never caused me a problem – but I also did not want to get involved in some futile internecine dispute either.

Lois, quite sincerely, had the power to immerse the tone of her voice into the deep waters of concern. It was a strong, motherly tone, alluring, awash with interest and discretion. She was fascinated to know if "the last six years had had a truly profound effect on my life". When she spoke, the timbre of her voice deepened; it was a sort of sophisticated plea. She envied me because she was an intrepid individual whose life, because of the restrictions on her generation, had been denuded of enterprise. She was attempting to flower in late middle age. I gave her the answer she wanted to hear.

"I have learnt", I said, feeling like a robot mouthing out a tape recording, "more in the last six years than in the rest of my life put together."

This appeased her romantic hopes in the greatness of travel and adventure.

"Good," she said. "You've really taken advantage of your opportunities."

This, I felt, was ridiculously inaccurate. Then she wanted to know if I had seen my father. The fascination in her voice made me realise how much intrigued interest she held for the man who, in yet another bewildered fit of exasperation with his brother, had said, "Lois won't last with him. She's too much of a goer. No way."

"In my opinion", I said, "my father is in a desperate financial situation. He's become intolerable because of it."

Lois was saddened and surprised by this.

"But", I continued, "I have to stress that that is only my opinion. Mine may not be the definitive point of view."

"The recession's hit him, has it?" she asked.

"So he said," I replied.

As we spoke, I kept glancing at Brian's morose countenance, careful not to allow the tone of my voice to become too friendly.

It reached embarrassing levels when Lois said, "If you've got time, can we meet?"

The discomfort was acute when I felt it incumbent upon myself to take her number, knowing that Brian would find it offensive if I saw her. She gently implored me to ring her. I told her that I would. Brian remained unmoved.

After sitting back down in the lounge-room, I passed on a message to Vanessa requesting her to ring Lois. Brian immediately, with the vindictive force of a bursting dam, said, “If you don’t like it here, you can always go and live with your mother!”

Vanessa was very hurt by this. Her face went red with astonished anger. She shook her head, speechless, overcome by frustration. It was the first time that I had ever seen her unable to respond. She was furious with peeved exasperation because she knew that nothing she could say would penetrate the subjective crust that had taken root around her father’s brain.

I said, “Brian, you shouldn’t attempt to split her loyalties. She’s got every right to have a relationship with both her parents. And you know that.”

Brian, who was a fair individual, knew this was correct. However, to protect himself, he said, in a tone of impassioned reasonableness, “It’s none of my business but, I have to warn you, if Nanna finds out that you’ve seen Lois, she won’t speak to you for ten years. I’m only warning you.”

I had no doubt about my grandmother’s position on the subject, but I felt that Brian’s warning was a disguise for his own feelings.

Vanessa echoed this by bleating out, “Don’t be so immature!”

Her comment was repeated after Brian looked at me and said, “I suppose Greg’s said to you that I haven’t lived?”

This was true. Greg had said this. Brian then went on to explain, as Vanessa rolled her eyes, that he was “the backbone”.

Waving his hands in fierce moral superiority, he said, with regard to his two sons, “Every time they leave one of their women and they need a place to stay, where do they go? Here! Of bloody course! Where else? Do you think they’d go running back to their mother? Not a bloody chance! No way!”

“Oh Brian!” Vanessa screamed.

There was no doubt in my mind that she had heard this sermon on more occasions than was humanly possible to bear.

Later, after Vanessa went out, I told Brian that I had “no intention of seeing Lois”.

He assumed that my position was based on moral grounds (Lois was, shall we say, a lady with a certain zest for living), and also because I did not want to risk upsetting my grandmother. There was some truth to the latter, but the principal reason for my decision was that I was in no mood to be revered by someone merely because I had “seen the world”. There were many others who deserved that sort of adoration before me, but Brian was happy with his assumption. I was happy to let him have it.

I realised that day that my family was forcing me to be strangely diplomatic; it was a feeling repulsive to my self-perception.

* * * * * * * * * *

That afternoon, Brian offered to give me a lift over to a friend's place. As we were about to drive off, he said, "If you do see Lois, be careful she doesn't put the hard word on you."

I thought that I knew what he meant by this, but it was difficult to accept he could have been referring to that.

"She made a pass", he said, glancing at me, as we reversed out of the driveway, "at Wayne about twelve months ago."

He was referring to that. My family were even more bent than I was currently giving them credit for.

"Well," I said, "if this makes you feel any better, Lois has already made a pass at me as well. She deposited her tongue down my throat on the occasion of my twenty-first birthday party. On moral grounds, I decided on withdrawal."

I was truly surprised when he showed no reaction to this. I assumed that his proclivity for unresponsiveness had climbed to new heights. 'Is anything really capable of puncturing his self-righteous veneer,' I wondered. I realised then the frustration Lois must have endured endeavouring to impart information into his intransigent brain.

What he told me next was a revelation for my innocent mind.

"Lois", he said, with that wild look of moral outrage which entered his eyes each time he mentioned her name, "once left a job she really wanted. This was years ago. She was infatuated with her boss. I found out later that she left the job because she was so distressed at this bloke's unpredictable behaviour towards her. He was probably giving her one and then ignoring her. The same old story, and it was driving her nuts. I didn't question her move. Why should I? I was madly in love. I didn't even stop to think that there was something strange going on. You know – why would she leave a job she really loved? It didn't even enter my head. I was blind. Absolutely gone. She couldn't do a thing wrong. I should've realised then what she was like but I was too in love. I wouldn't have been able to see it. Christ, I wish I had."

It was better just to sit and absorb the inevitable onslaught. It was transparent that there was only one topic of conversation he was interested in pursuing. I presumed that every other member of my family had already made it clear to him, in their own little ways (you know, something like: 'Brian, if you don't fucking shut up now, I'm going to drive a fucking railway sleeper down your fucking throat!'), that enough was enough. But I was now immersed in the sickly algae of diplomacy. I had become the great listener. How bored I was playing a role not of my choosing. I knew, on this occasion, however, that there was a practical limit on the bombardment. This lift was destined, shortly, to come to an end; my patience could endure.

He continued with: "During our engagement, she decided that she wanted to go down south. She had no one to go with, so Nanna went with her. During a dinner, Lois shot through with some bloke and didn't come back so Nanna went looking for her. You wouldn't believe it, but Nanna found her in a bedroom with this bloke - they had been having dinner in the restaurant of a hotel - and they had left the bloody bedroom door open. They were lying on the bed together. Lois tried to make it look innocent. Obviously, they'd been giving each other a good feel up. The amazing thing is, is that Nanna did the chauffeuring. (This was the part that my innocent mind had difficulty enveloping itself around). If Nanna had told me that this had happened, I would've left Lois there and then!"

This I doubted.

"But I was blind," he went on. "Totally gone. It's amazing what you can convince yourself of. I was a completely different person then. No way would I ever get married again. Impossible. Out of the question."

"Brian," I said, "do you mind if I say something?"

He seemed to fall off the plateau of metaphysical bitterness and slide down to empirical consciousness. I took this as a sign that I was being allowed to speak.

"There is a thing", I continued, "known as being philosophical. You should be glad you had all those years of bliss. Millions just do not get it. And another thing: do not interfere in Vanessa's relationship with Lois. It will do you no good. Understand?"

The car was now parked in front of my friend's place. I could see my friend in the front garden of his house. He was bemused as to why I had not extricated myself yet from Brian's car. What the hell could I be discussing which was so important as to detain me from getting out of some car and seeing someone I had not seen for six years? It was a complete mystery to him. The answer was simple - Brian. Despite numerous allusions "to my friend", Brian bludgeoned on, unconscious of my total lack of interest in anything he had to say.

"She's only interested in getting the best deal," he charged on, in relation to Vanessa.

"Yes, Brian, good, but—"

"If Lois could offer her the sort of home she gets by living with me, she'd be gone."

"Yeah, okay, but—"

"She'd be out like a rocket. But Lois can't offer her the things I can."

"Okay, fair enough, but—"

"She really only sees her so regularly because Lois gives her money."

"My friend—"

Ted was now completely puzzled. The smile had gone from his face. He stared as though he were witnessing an inexplicable event of absurd dimensions.

"She's got a reliable stable home where she is now."

The time for action had arrived. As I dragged myself out of his car, Brian's mouth was still producing information that bore no relation to our current situation.

"Thanks, thanks," I said, as his hands continued their wild gesticulations.

When I got over to Ted, he said, "Who the fuck was that?"

"That", I replied, grumpily, "is my uncle."

A rich burst of joy erupted from his mouth.

"Maybe", he said, giggling, "we should introduce him to my aunty. The other day", he continued, as we went inside his house, "she told me, in all seriousness, that she had discovered the answer to the universe. She unexpectedly knocked on my door - I hadn't seen her for years. Before I knew it, she was telling me that she had discovered something profound and intrinsic about the cosmos. She began producing diagrams to illustrate her point. It involved the drawing of circles and the use of such words as heaven and hell."

He said that he had managed to introduce one of his flatmates to her while he escaped into his bedroom.

"If you think your uncle is bad," he said, "you should try and take an interest in that."

Inside, he said, "I had an abysmal hangover as well. Can you imagine it? It was incredible. The first truly insane person I meet in my life and it has to be in my own home and, of course, it had to be a member of my own family. I should've predicted it. To the outside world, it was probably obvious."

We were giggling away as I said, "Maybe she just needs a man. How about my uncle? Genetically, my family possess all the credentials necessary to appeal to a woman whose insights extend to ultimate perceptions. The great houses of insanity could be brought together in matrimonial bliss. You could become my crazy cousin: The One Who Laughs At Everything!"

As we laughed, I realised that cynicism is a kind of release, an irksome liberation. I suppose that I had been forced to endure a lot of release over the years. And a lot more was waiting.

* * * * * * * * * *

I was still finding the once familiar place in which I had been brought up unusual. The streets of this place oozed a sensation in contradiction of those to which I had grown accustomed over the previous six years. The streets of Perth were wide, ultra-clean and the buildings in the city were often tall and glassy. There was no rush; a melancholic lugubriousness emanated from the place in the searing heat. Three-storey Victorian buildings, painted bright colours, emblazoned by intricate stone carvings and classical pediments, sat within the gargantuan monsters of glass which reflected the known world into strange shapes. It was a pretty blend of two distinct types of architecture from two distinct centuries. But the atmosphere had a sedate eerieness that kept me on edge, for there was no anonymity. It was constantly possible, due to a high concentration of employment possibilities in one small spot, to run into someone you knew – someone who probably detested everything for which you stood. There was no control over this. Turning around any corner could result in an embarrassing and unexpected encounter with an ex-lover, with someone whose girlfriend you had defiled, with an ex-opponent on the sports field into whose face you had spat - anyone! You could even run into the magistrate who had requested that you begin making maintenance payments or the policeman who had arrested you for being drunk and disorderly. This, I found, was a shooting gallery of unplanned social interactions, and it was not my style, for it was not a question of whether you liked them or not; you could only hope that it was with someone sufficiently open-minded to cope with the experience - and this was not very likely.

The first person I saw whom I knew tried to ignore me. He was someone with whom I had worked at the Australian Office of Taxation. I decided, probably from a bizarre sort of gregarious vindictiveness, not to allow him to escape. I decided, for the sake of the experience, to make his discomfort as acute as possible by being excessively nice. I realised that this would contradict his perceived vision of me.

"Oh hullo," I said, with a huge, enthusiastic grin. "How are you?"

Prior to my opening gambit, the said victim had been looking down the street past me, attempting to create the illusion that he was in another world. The instant I opened my mouth he looked at me with faked surprise and a dry concern, the kind of expression that someone has when they're about to jump out of an aircraft for the first time. I was enjoying it already.

I doubted if he could remember my name. The random use of the word 'mate' suggested this to me. I noticed that his hair was greyer and his face pallid, the sure sign of an excess of expenditure designed to unwittingly improve the balance sheet of the Swan Brewery. I asked questions about people we used to know. Someone whom I had contemplated contacting cropped up in conversation. The individual concerned had managed to wangle himself out of a potential paternity suit. The only time Barry showed any facial expression readily associated with a comfortable exchange occurred when he said that our ex-mutual associate was a "bit on the casual side. I'm actually going to have a drink with him at lunch time". This comment caused a brief smile; the rest of the time he stared past me, unable to indulge in eye contact. This gave me ample opportunity to examine his eyes. They were brown, impenetrable, wild with unease. I knew that if, hypothetically, I was to live in this place again, I would have to ignore such obvious signs of distaste and just blunder on, irrepressibly.

I then got the story of why he had left the Taxation Department. It was the well-played-out scenario of perceived lack of promotional opportunities due to a perceived build-up of unjustified personal prejudice. There was even a subtle flicker of interest when he, unexpectedly, inquired about my current vocation. The concept of someone taking photographs in strange places was a little foreign to his desires. There was not a great deal he could ask about this with any ebullience because it was not going to have any bearing on the outcome of his life. There was not a chance that I could set the torch of his mind alight with the realisation of a dream of pragmatic relevance. I could give him no tips on the result of any event next Saturday at Ascot. I did not have close personal relations with any footballer he admired. I was not one of the boys. Terrible pity, eh?

When he got his chance to leave, he said, "Well, got to go and see a mate."

I smiled as he walked off. His distaste for me stemmed from the way that I had upset the wife of one of his close friends. This woman had been my senior officer in the Taxation Department. A combination of many unsavoury things - all due to me - had combined to cause this distressed woman to burst into tears in the office. Effectively, an independent arbiter had concluded that she had acted "unprofessionally" in her dealings with me. The reprimand she received was a severe jolt to her cherished self-view of diligent fairness. All those close to her linked this blow to her self-esteem directly to me. I was "The Arsehole". A brief feeling of the regret that I had felt at this time momentarily returned. It was a regrettable thing to have exacted revenge the way I did - she had lied to me about comments she had made about me to a promotion committee, and had not expressed her concerns to me over qualities she believed I possessed that made me unsuitable for the job - and, as I watched Barry strolling off down the street, I knew that I was in a town where one's dubious, suspect, dissolute past lies like a poisonous seed, always ready to flower, in a fertile bed of uncomprehending conservatism.

And what strange petals some of these people must see.

* * * * * * * * * * *

I got the opportunity to tell Wayne and Kay about the awkward situation when Lois rang. We were lying around the edge of Brian's swimming pool. It was late in the afternoon and the pleasant warmth of the day seemed to have had a positive effect on Wayne's usually explosive temperament. He even came across as a thoughtful, sensitive, even-tempered person. It was one of those rare fits of decency he had when it was possible to feel free about speaking your mind, without fear of cynicism or puerile belittlement. I knew that it was a phase not destined for the illuminated manuscripts of permanency, but I appreciated it while it lasted.

I told them about Brian's unerring determination to talk about Lois. I wanted her in the conversation so I could find out why they were no longer in contact with her. Kay expressed surprise about Brian's attitude. She was under the impression that "Brian didn't care".

"No, no! No way!" Wayne and I simultaneously blurted out. "Not a chance!"

"You can't shut him up on it", I added, "once he gets started. He could go on until the bloody sun vaporises."

This caused Kay to ponder.

It gave me the chance to ask, "When did you two last see her?"

"Years," Wayne replied. "And we won't see her again either. We've written her off because she'd tell Vanessa we'd seen her, who'd tell Nanna. This made the situation, as Doug Bigalo [Australian football commentator] would say, in contemporary parlance, untenable."

Being largely free of the subliminal Christian moral values undermining our society, I was able to lie down on the grass and face the deep blue twilight and contemplate the deeper reasons for this severing of diplomatic relations. The mere fact that her grandson was seeing the despised "harlot" who had caused her son such grief was possibly not the sole cause of Wayne's tentativeness to maintain links with that "disgusting trollop". For a fleeting moment, as the exotic butterfly of corrupt thought flickered across the dense foliage of my diseased mind, I wondered whether Wayne, in a stirring moment of passion, had given Lois the absolute shafting of her life. It was not beyond the realm of possibility – it was even a delicious thought – but imagine what would happen if Vanessa found out!

Dear, oh dear, oh dear. Now that would be interesting.

* * * * * * * * * *

I was lying in bed one morning listening to Brian on the telephone asking someone "if it was there". He seemed worried; the tone of his voice indicated that he was suffering from bemused frustration. By now, he should have left for work. He had just begun a job with a commercial television station; it became apparent to me that he was on the line to them.

"Okay, okay," he said, before putting the phone down and whispering: "Jesus Christ, where is that bloody thing?!"

Brian's organisational habits had always been a mystery to us all. They now appeared to be a mystery to him as well.

When I got into the kitchen, I noticed the drawers open and Brian stomping around with that wild look in his eyes; I felt as though I were about to be subjected to another bout of stunned exasperation. This time, however, it did not involve his family.

"I can't", he said, with his hands on his hips, shaking his head, "find that bloody piece of paper. I haven't got a fucking clue where it is."

He was not prepared to blame himself – yet – for its misplacement. Heinous universal forces had perpetuated a cynically baffling event that his self-exculpatory mind, in its vast innocence, could not accept as resulting from his own incompetence.

"I remember", he said, pointing to the open drawer, "leaving it in here. You saw me put it in there. By any chance, you haven't taken anything out of there, have you?"

He suspected correctly that the answer to this question was no. He had two days previously received a phone call from the program controller giving him details of how to use some new equipment. The details were now missing. I was very amused by this. I imagined what the possibilities of this could mean: a total breakdown of one of the principal stations, or the fantastic embarrassment of Brian having to explain to his new employers that he had "lost the details".

I leant up against the sink and watched with smug fascination as Brian, again, plundered the contents of the drawers only to discover a morass of gas, telephone and electricity bills, and a stack of insipid insurance policies. Every square inch of the kitchen was given his single-minded examination. A desperation, born of the fear of embarrassment, began to fill his agitated movements.

"Oh fuck," he mumbled before charging into the dining room, where he began sifting through the bookshelves, hoping, in vain, for a miracle.

"This", he announced, already late for his second day of work, "is bloody incredible!"

I was in complete agreement. It was rare for me to be able to associate veracious relevance with anything that emerged from his mouth.

He then flew off into his bedroom in the vain hope that his dignity could be saved by the miraculous appearance of the highly sought-after details in a place unpredicted. I heard drawers being pulled out and slammed; cupboards doors being ripped open and the shifting of coat-hangers. Mutters of bewilderment accompanied these frenzied attempts to rescue his tenuous position. Then he flew out the back door and began frantically searching through his car. Through the kitchen window I could see his flailing hands probing into every niche of his dashboard and glovebox. As he slammed the car door and stomped back towards the house, I got the distinct impression that things were now rather bleak.

This feeling was reinforced when I was greeted by a pang-filled look of fuming astonishment as he stormed into the kitchen, went straight for the rubbish bin and said, "It could only be in here."

I had to admit that he was probably right. This was the second comment that he had made in the space of a few minutes which had impressed me with its accuracy. He was the sort of person uniquely capable of absentmindedly depositing something of significance in a pile of garbage.

I stood aside and watched as he dug his hands deep into the rubbish of three days of domestic existence. The first probe produced an interesting mix of potato peels, cereal packets, rotting lettuce and two repulsive cotton-wool balls covered in blood. A further penetration into the bowels of the bin yielded yet another rich concoction of waste, all of which bore little resemblance to a certain A4 size sheet of paper, whose existence had now taken on the importance of a spiritual saviour. One unsuccessful probe after another only served to highlight the uselessness of his predicament. He was now beyond reproach.

As he washed his hands in the sink, muttering, I wondered what my father would have thought, felt, said, experienced if he had been where I had stood that morning. It would have represented unparalleled entertainment for my father's bitter mind and, even in the state of mind in which Brian evidently was, I doubted whether he would have retaliated. My father's unrestrained sarcasm would have been too much.

* * * * * * * * * * *

It was a joy and a relief to have my call to an old friend at university returned. I had spoken to his mother earlier on in the day; she had assured me that Mark would be "really thrilled" to hear from me. Natural pessimism made me doubt this; even though Mark and I had been soul mates to the most esoteric and obscure depths, I had no idea of how he had developed over the previous six years. With him – as with most people to whom I had been close – anything was possible.

Instantly, from the moment he said, "Great joy befell me when I discovered that one so beautiful had once again entered my life," I could detect a calmness and decency in his voice that made me feel as though a vast and colourful maturity had fallen, like an exotic rug, on to the marble bedrock of his existence. He had been a legend at university for his comic wit, but sometimes it was tainted by restricting prejudices which made the sensitive feel uncomfortable. No trace of that now filled his speech. He seemed overcome by a desire to be a perfect gentleman. It was an attitude that invited the free interplay of ideas; his voice was the epitome of humility.

I asked him if he was still interested in living in Germany. He said that, "at heart", he considered himself to be a German. I suggested he should try Prague. He said that he had called his daughter that in recognition of a city in which he had "fallen in love". The story of his stay in Prague, many years ago, was a tale of joy and sadness. His cousin – a beautiful girl who had developed an infatuation for him (his grandparents are Czechoslovakian) – burst into tears on the last night he was there for, after announcing his imminent departure, he told her that he was about "to travel around the world" before ending up in Australia, that free and rich and exotic paradise on the other side of the globe. This was not the sort of information a young, adventurous person, victimised by a repressive regime, was particularly thrilled to hear; and it made Mark realise how lucky he was.

When he gave me details of his three offspring, I pointed out that children often bore a hostile reaction to me for they were immediately able to detect my "dissolute demeanour". He said that in our impending meeting, we would have to "get away for an hour or so" so that he could "hang on every word" I said. I said that it sounded as though he thought I was going to leave a religion behind here when I left. He said that I was the only one he knew who was capable of doing this. I informed him that it was "not possible to receive a higher compliment".

Then we had some laughs over a letter I had sent his first son after I had discovered, through a chance meeting at a London party, that his wife had given birth. I had warned his son that, despite everything his father was destined to say, anything which emerged from his father's mouth should be treated "with the utmost suspicion". I elaborated by pointing out to Mark's son, who, at the time, was three weeks old, that, despite anything his father might say, his father "did not shoot down an entire squadron of Mig-23s during the Vietnam War", nor did he "win the World Driver's Championship" after having, earlier on in the season, been cut from a wreck which had "left every bone in his body smashed" and would have "clearly annihilated a lesser man". I told him that his response to my letter had nearly given me "double vision and a dislocated neck" for the sentences on his postcard began on the edges before spiralling into the middle. ('Lots of love' was right in the centre.)

He then laughed and said that when we got together we would "have to make love again".

I told him that "the orgasms I had received at your hands made cocaine seem like torture".

He said that "such appreciation was a rarity in this self-indulgent and avaricious earth".

I told him that "such worship was only the natural response to the only truly great genius".

He insisted that I rig up a system that would enable me to take photographs of our "passionately intertwined anatomies" so that "true love" could be made "readily available to the masses".

I told him that the "depth of our love" was beyond "the scope of ordinary men" and that such photographs would take "centuries of intense analysis and radical psychosociological development to have the remotest chance of ever being understood".

He said that, "despite the ignorance at the core of human perception", the rendering of such images was our "natural duty to He who had made us both so beautiful".

I laughed and said, "Imagine the reaction within the intelligence services if our phones were currently being bugged."

He giggled and replied, "The tabloids would get you at last: 'Notorious Photojournalist Woos Innocent Architect With Seedy Images of Love'."

I said that I preferred to call such publications "the haemorrhoids".

"Knowing you," he said, "you'd still sell the photographs to them as well."

"Only", I replied, "if one of them showed my dick right up your arse."

He blew a kiss down the phone and said that he would have to negotiate with his wife before arranging a date which would be "bursting with the full red apples of romance, ablaze in the orchard of true love".

I told him that I would be waiting with "breathless anticipation" and that my heart would "undoubtedly skip a beat" each time the phone rang.

He said, that for fear of causing "regrettable and unforeseen coronary palpitations in a heart so pure", he would, "with a radical reshuffling of priorities", ensure that his call was made with "the alacrity that only the most worthy and magnanimous could expect".

I said that I had no doubts about the "waterfall of sincerity" which gushed, "with the music of angels, from the eloquent cascade" of his "mouth".

We were both giggling when he said, "It's a pity that everyone doesn't communicate like this."

"Who cares", I replied, "what the rest of the world does, as long as we're happy?"

He erupted into laughter. My comment had a significance not readily apparent, for it was the remark he used to make when pretending to ravish me; each time he did this, I would try to fight him off – he would always make sure that he had an audience when he did this – and he would always say, as my arms flailed around, "He's just like a clam." Eventually, I would be overpowered, usually with laughter; and, simulating passionate grunts, as he pumped relentlessly into my chortling body, he would produce the immortal line: "Who cares about the world, as long as we're happy." This occurred numerous times; each occasion would be as refreshing as the first. It was completely eccentric and peculiar only to our relationship. It was ridiculous and remarkable.

When I put the phone down, I heard the music of birds. I then sat in the lounge-room and contemplated the first thing I had ever heard him say. This occurred at the very first lecture we ever went to at university. We were both enrolled in architecture. He came in late, boldly telling the lecturer, as though he were the dean of the faculty, "not to mind me" and to "carry on". Then this mysterious person sat next to me. Half an hour into the lecture, this bizarre eccentric then stood up and began grunting to attract the lecturer's attention. Dumbfounded, the lecturer glanced up and saw Mark pointing both hands at him and saying, with a look of grave curiosity, "I have to go now; are you right to take over?"

As the lecturer, through stupefied intrigue, did not immediately respond, Mark, with an aspect of impatient irreverence, reiterated his position: "I have to go now; are you right to take over?"

As he spoke, he moved his hands up and down with profound emphasis, demanding an answer.

"Yes," the lecturer smiled, "I am."

"Excellent," Mark replied. "Before I go, I want you all to know that I'm very pleased with your punctuality. I expect to see you all here, sharp, again, tomorrow, at exactly the same time. Please – carry on."

Then he charged off out the door, this mysterious figure, who left us all, including the lecturer, stunned with bamboozled amusement.

He did something like this every day, without fail, for two years.

* * * * * * * * * *

Perth is a city where it is difficult to escape into a milieu unconcerned with material possessions. As very few people in this town make a living from creative pursuits – the preserve of the mad, as my father would say – materialism is the symbol of personal value.

The belief is that only an idiot cannot afford a car; in this climate, the expression of wealth can attain a personal significance well out of proportion to its merit. It was a common belief amongst some, possibly the jealous, that the less successful had a tendency to be more flamboyant than the super rich in an endeavour to bolster their images in a place absurdly infatuated with physical appearance. It was a sad fact that a lot of people here measured the value of their lives by the amount of money they possessed, even if very few of them had the desire or imagination to spend it with flair. The sadder fact was that very few actually earned it with any.

I had met people here who had made money in property deals – not all that difficult in a place where capital gains taxes did not exist for years – and because of it they thought that they were "successful businessmen". I was pleased to return to Perth at a time when the term 'entrepreneur' was being treated with the disdain with which it should have been greeted fifteen years previously. However, money and sport still often dominated conversation, and this was fairly tedious to someone possessed of esoteric aesthetic aspirations. They were subjects that occasionally, however, in view of the significance placed upon them, gave me a quiet chance to snigger.

Such an occasion arose when Kay, with a look of perplexed wonderment, explained to me that my father "has got nothing behind him. I haven't got a clue what would happen to Sue if he suddenly dropped dead."

This comment encapsulated the entire philosophy of the place. My father had had an ulterior motive in marrying a woman whose sister was married to one of Perth's most successful businessmen. In addition, my father believed that his wife's mother – a sprightly and sensitive lady – had enormous, undisclosed wealth. There were two problems with this arrangement: firstly, my father's sister-in-law's husband considered my father to be an embarrassment. Secondly, the mother-in-law was destitute. Her lifestyle was being maintained by the opulent son-in-law. She was a lovely woman who deserved it. My father was an immature drunk, drowning in the stagnant waters of failure, who definitely did not. His scheme to rub shoulders with the financial élite floundered on the rocks of his social ineptitude. The hardest lesson he would ever learn was that it was possible to succeed in this belligerent world by being nice. Philanthropy opened the gates to far distant fields, a belief beyond the narrow webbing of the net which seemed to have tightened around my father's head.

He picked me up once from somewhere and was in a mood of unusual, but agitated, openness. His well-documented ability to distort the magnitude of other people's wealth - people who usually showed some interest in him - obviously extended to his own position. His mendacity in pursuit of ego enhancement caused others to treat his fanciful references to personal wealth with the amused disdain which had affected him so badly on that day. He told me that he had become the proud owner of a mansion in a plush suburb - "an absolute, fucking bargain it was" - and that none of his drinking associates had believed him. When he had boldly announced to them that he "hadn't bought it", he'd "fucking stolen it, it was so fucking cheap", I got the impression that this had led to howls of derisive laughter. Full of warped satisfaction, he then explained that he had driven the disbelievers from the pub to the scene of his miraculous purchase. He then claimed to have shown these stunned individuals the title deeds that he had conveniently stashed in his glovebox - where else does one keep one's title deeds? - and, by way of punishment, he had forced the sceptical out of the car and "fucking made 'em walk all the way back to the fucking pub". When I asked Wayne about the alleged existence of this property, Wayne produced three words that flew out of his mouth with angered peremptoriness: "Absolute fucking bullshit."

I had asked my father to whom he was renting the property.

"An old woman," he said. "The previous owner."

I wondered if his mother-in-law lived in the mystery property.

She did. A nice bit of imaginative fancy that. The property was owned by the son-in-law. Daddy, in his desperation for recognition through wealth, probably imagined that it was going to become his.

* * * * * * * * * *

Early one typically blue morning my eldest cousin Greg came around to clean the swimming pool. Physically, he was the epitome of the handsome, beach-going Australian. His hair was peroxide blond, his jaw square, his cheekbones sculptured, his muscles well defined, and the glint in his green eyes was roguish, streetwise and unwavering. My father, with his usual, diplomatically-inclined economy of expression, had described him, with great venom, as "that absolute cunt". I could only guess why my father was so savagely vindictive towards his eldest nephew. I presumed that it was because Greg, to the outsider, appeared too casual and lazy for the man who had "worked so bloody hard" that he had even worked "till ten o'clock one night! Even ten o'clock!"

Sitting on the patio next to the barbecue, I watched as Greg manoeuvred a long, white pole through the duck egg blue water, naked from the waist up, the sun blanketing the garden in a sheath of glistening light. It was relaxing watching him languidly manipulating a device whose existence would have seemed bizarre to your average Amazon Indian – a spear that cleans water!

Behind him, in the garden, gleaming patches of white light sat on the drooping leaves of small green bushes; a sort of dazzled stillness enveloped the place. It was a contradiction of brilliance and docility, of energy and inertia, a condition which epitomised the determined but insouciant character of my cousin, who, by the time he was twenty-three, had gained a commercial pilot's licence and had tampered with the sensitivities of numerous beautiful women.

I watched him walking slowly around the edge of the pool in a bold light that seemed to replenish things with the sharpness and clarity of its expression. The white edges of the pool were ablaze with snowy reflection. In a strange way, it was fitting that the newness of the surrounds should be born in such light – a light unchangeable and all-pervading, which had an angelic pellucidity and the savage innocence of predictability. Within it, Greg wandered, seemingly unconcerned about the frenetic struggles occurring outside his immediate realm, as though unemployment in a bad recession were a trivial consideration, unworthy of his relaxed consideration. This was a man certain that the future would take care of itself. What other reason had existed for him to assume anything else? He had youth, intelligence, looks, confidence; he had only ever seen opportunities, did not know poverty, had been admired and had had the experience to believe that this world was a hotbed of pleasure – just for him.

When he finished cleaning the pool, he joined me on the patio and began talking about his immediate family. I noticed that a cluster of freckles ran across the bridge of his nose, the product of years in the sun. Everything he said related to his father.

"When you go away somewhere", he said, "and come back, it's great seeing him for a week, then he just begins to drive you insane. I don't know how Vanessa puts up with it."

A smile of disbelief filled his face. I was then informed of something that put a remark made by my father into a clearer light. Greg told me that "the final straw" for his mother had occurred during the time that the swimming pool was being built.

"Brian", he said, shaking his head, "would come home from work each day and complain that things were not being done properly, when obviously they were. He drove the contractors nuts. And my mother too. She eventually told the contractors to ignore Brian completely. At one stage, the contractors refused to work unless Brian left them alone. We had a fucking great hole in the backyard here for about a month with nothing happening to it. My mother went insane."

It was then that I realised what my father had meant when he had said, "Brian would take five fucking months to finish one job. The useless cunt!"

Greg continued, "Once Vanessa said to me, when she was really pissed off, that Richard and I were incredibly lucky because we didn't have to live here. But we lived with him as well for eighteen years. I'm still recovering now. I reckon that I deserve some sort of compensation from the government."

"I don't think", I replied, "I've ever met such a classic fusspot. The day I got here, he showed me how to use all the domestic appliances."

Greg shook his head and said, "He thinks that, because he's just had to learn how to use them himself, then everyone else has got to learn how to use them as well."

"He doesn't seem to realise," I replied, "that I've had to do these things for myself since I was seventeen. He showed me with meticulous perfection. It was fascinating being shown how to use an iron. Really, it was."

"He's learnt everything from Nanna," Greg smiled. "He takes everything she says as gospel. If she said boil potatoes at 312° and you do it at 353°, then you're an idiot. Before he got divorced, he couldn't even boil an egg."

Greg's voice became sharper as he said, "Every time you do something around here, you can't do anything right. His brain is so inflexible, he believes there is only one method – and no other – to achieve a result. He's the sort of person, who, if he was in a managerial position, wouldn't have a clue of how to nurture talent. He crushes it by his mere presence."

Greg then expressed his disillusionment with his father's abstemiousness. He said that he had suggested they hire a plane and fly over to Rottnest Island for the day, but Brian was too concerned about the expenditure. Greg said that Brian has "spent too long in the public service. He can't take risks. He's so set in his ways."

This prompted me to say, "He really surprised me one day by saying that he thought he'd never really lived."

"His children", Greg smiled, "are doing their best to make up for it."

I was then told about Vanessa's social escapades. She invites a friend around "for the night". They "sleep" in the lounge-room and, after Brian's gone to bed, they put their sexy gear on, climb out through the window and head off into town to a nightclub. According to Greg, Brian "can't work out why she's got a hangover in the morning."

"It takes, I suppose, a scheming mind to discern these things. Greg, Vanessa's just a little girl, remember?"

Greg smiled wryly and said, "It's probably good having a father like him. It's taught me the value of rebellion."

It might have been good, I thought, having him as a father, but what a life it must have been being married to him. Since my return, I had felt humbled by the luck I had experienced in being able to lead what, to many, would have appeared an adventurous existence. The limitations of Lois's past life had become clear to me: she had been chained to this place; she did not earn money for herself; she would not have even been able to go to the cinema on a whim. How alluring my life must have appeared to her with its insecurities and volatile uncertainties - its excitement. Just going out socially would have, for her, been a novelty; so many nights in; a sacrifice of drudgery that could not lead to any glamorous fulfilment, a long, featureless tunnel of predictability without any nugget of esteemed recognition at its insipid end. I was beginning to realise that, by being in the position I was, where I could choose my exotic company, that I had separated myself from the staid reality which life represents to millions. By being in this place all those years as a housewife married to a man whose paranoia insulted professionals who were simply attempting to do their jobs (the swimming pool contractors were apparently vehemently aggrieved to have had their professional expertise questioned by a relative layman), her capacity for positive discovery became a spiral into the dark pits of ignorance.

During my formative years, I had thought: 'What difference does it make if you don't own a great house, have great kids and have loads of money in the bank if you have seen volcanoes explode, have dived in the world's most beautiful reefs, had sex with a beautiful woman, been in the storm of revolutions and eaten in the world's most exquisite restaurants?' Really, it did not make any difference one way or the other as long as you were deeply in love with someone or something; but to have neither? To really have nothing remarkable to show for all that struggle? Now that is a tragedy. One, it was becoming increasingly obvious to me, that was going to face more people than I wished to imagine. I was determined not to be one of them.

Greg then said, "It'll be interesting to see what happens after Vanessa finishes school. After that, there'll be no more excuses."

"He'll find them," I replied. "Don't worry about that."

Greg shook his head and smiled and said, "You're right. Undoubtedly."

* * * * * * * * * *

Brian's actions, often so absurd as to defy logical analysis, were a constant source of rueful astonishment. He had been given the task by his mother of discovering what I wanted for Christmas; he and Nanna were going to split the cost. One morning we drove into the city and I picked out a shirt. To my amazement, he asked the shop assistant "to put it to one side". His reason for doing this was so ridiculous as to defy all rational consideration. On the drive back home, the shirt still safely in the city, he said that he had to check the price with Nanna. I knew that she would be prepared to part with forty dollars; however, Brian, insipidly careful to the core, seemed to believe that enormous thought and planning were required to make this significant purchase.

Apart from the fact that my grandmother would obviously be unconcerned about the expenditure, a simple phone call from town would have solved the problem. But Brian was unable, or unwilling (it was very difficult to judge which) to recognise the value in making use of a device the very existence of which meant convenience. Not wishing to get involved in the convoluted workings of his bewildering and bewildered brain, I did not enquire as to why he had not called. The answer, no doubt beyond the limits of my powers of reasoning, probably would have caused such violently unusual synaptic leaps in my neo-cortex that, in a frenzy of electrical befuddlement, a huge tumour, the size of a dinner plate, probably would have wrapped itself around my brain in a devastating flash, leading to involuntary bodily actions and epileptic fits. It was better not to get involved. You have to understand that Brian did not do these absurd things through absent-mindedness, esoteric vagueness, or even just through blissful unconsciousness; he always had what, he believed, was a logical reason. This was what made him so dangerous. He actually thought before he did anything. Unfortunately, the combination of his mind and thought was a lethal marriage whose result, puzzling to the majority, was as eccentric as the self-defeating need he possessed to constantly try and prove himself to a disparaging world.

When I told Vanessa about Brian's actions in relation to my Christmas present, she put her hands on her hips, tilted her head to one side, took a deep breath and, slowly moving her head from side to side, she said, her eyes full of angered mystification, "How bloody ridiculous. He's incredible! He's just unbelievable!"

Most people in my family were. Yet they existed.

* * * * * * * * * *

Greg and I toyed with the idea of going for a drive down south. I suggested to Vanessa that the invitation was open to her as well. Her reaction surprised me.

"I don't really want to go with that bastard," she blurted out. "He only talks to you when it suits him. You ask Richard."

I was taken aback. So much for wide-eyed respect for big brother. I often found that unexpected blasts of vicious confidence caused me to become speechless. This was no exception. I assumed that her answer was no.

Then she said, with embarrassed curiosity, "What did he say when you suggested I come?"

Her question was asked with the diffidence of vulnerability. It was not in keeping with the arrogant dismissiveness that had only seconds before erupted from her mouth. The answer pleased her.

"He seemed very keen," I said. "He really wanted you to come."

She was suddenly relieved. I then realised that the rapid oscillation of emotions which she had just experienced was the product of unrequited love and the effect of being exposed to an indifferent charisma. Sometimes I wondered how many people, if any, had ever had this experience. I presumed, for reasons of self-protection, that the answer was almost nil. Any other answer may have been too heinous for consideration.

* * * * * * * * * *

The opportunity to meet the child of a friend arose for the first time about a week before Christmas. Frances was over from Sydney. A call to her mother, two days after my arrival, had confirmed my suspicions that she would be coming home for Christmas. Her nine-month-old son was making the journey as well.

Frances was someone I had chased with relentless stupidity for years at university; her existence had been responsible for the creation of some of my most memorable lines: 'Look, why don't we just sweep aside all the restricting garbage that so paralyses the potentially awesome limits of human relations and just make love and have a relationship so outstanding that we'll be the envy of all?'

Her response to this question, a proposal, which, to me, reeked of decency and reasonableness, was, "You're too volatile and unpredictable. I couldn't handle it."

The irony was that I was now a model of philosophical consistency. How I longed for those days of fiery passion, the inflamed turmoils, the outrageous bursts of fearless expression. Would they return? Or had they been doused by the tranquil cascades of maturity? It was one of the great mysteries of our time.

When she opened the door of her parent's house, I was a trifle shocked at the aged plainness of her appearance. Six years had taken their toll. Being of Dutch extraction, she possessed a wholesome simplicity that made the lines of her face group together with an unrefinement which did not fit the character. Every memory I had of her face was obliterated by the vision that befell me. The person I knew had smooth skin; the eyebrows were lighter than the ones I now saw; the hair was straighter and silkier; the face was not as angular. But the smile was definitely Frances. It was a smile of insouciant warmth, unrestrained, playful, expecting of eccentricity; an appreciater of waggish wit. She expected to be amused. The way she carried herself, loosely, like a gangly sapling, suggested this; she had a disposition of carefreeness that created a false picture of openness; it was a trait which had enabled her to extract information from people without having to expose herself. The wary were often infuriated by this.

"What are you laughing at?" I asked.

I was feeling a bit reserved, for I was too conscious of her decline in attractiveness; then I realised that the comparison I had drawn between her and the women to whom I had grown accustomed was a result of the disparity in their relative situations. She was not dressing to please herself in public situations. Her present predicament robbed her of the normal vanities of womanhood. She also looked very Australian. This was not something for which I was prepared when considering the appearance of women. I had grown used to seeing women with skin unaffected by the sun, who wore make-up, who were covered from neck to ankles, who wore earrings and displayed some individuality, if only subtle, in their dress. This, by contrast, was straightforward simplicity at its most unpretentious: it was Frances.

"The wild beast", she answered, "who went out and tamed the world."

"Miaow," I said.

Inside, I was greeted by her boyfriend; in Chris's arms was Dylan. The moment I was dreading had arrived. I was not particularly interested in children; usually they detected this immediately since they are very sensitive to even the most well-hidden attempts to hide hostility. I never really knew how to behave in front of them. Often it was tacitly expected that you should be overcome by their cuteness; usually I was not. Often I felt like tormenting them so that they would get the picture, rapidly, that I was not an organism placed on this earth for their inconsiderate convenience. I particularly detested the way adults behaved towards them, as if the little brats represented the opportunity to the outside world for these obsequious fools to show

how sensitive they were to unparalleled beauty. Children brought out the worst aspects of my cynicism.

That was until I met Dylan. This kid had style. There was no way that he was going to be easily amused by some oversized tosspot attempting to be a comedian. The instant he laid eyes on me, he glared with a ferocious and disdainful ruthlessness. His soft little face beamed out a message of disgusted fascination. My every move was given the utmost scrutiny. He was oblivious to the social ramifications of intense staring. Not a single ounce of diffidence affected his absorbed and charmingly tactless expression. He did not expect to be amused. He seemed determined not to be.

When I went towards him, he flailed his tiny limbs about in monumental anguish. There was no way this arsehole was going to get near him. If he could have spoken, he would have said: 'Get that fucking wanker out of here! Now! And who the fuck do you think you are letting this prick in here? And where's my fucking dinner?'

I was delighted by the beauty of his pejorative tactlessness. He was a cute ball of fiery free expression.

"He's been a little tired today," Frances said dryly.

"It appears", I replied, as Dylan yelped with bitter ferocity, twisting and turning in Chris's struggling arms, "as if he's slightly annoyed about being uninformed about the prospect of there being a visitor."

The three of us were laughing away as Chris carried Dylan into the kitchen where feeding time was about to begin. It was here that the real hysterics began. The tormented child was deposited into a high chair where a bib was tied around his neck. The sudden placing in the chair went some way to restoring his equanimity; suddenly he went back to glaring at me as though I were a monster that his parents, in their philanthropic innocence, were unable to see. The first attempts at feeding were ignored, for Dylan, transfixed, would not take his eyes off me. Attempt after attempt was rebuffed, annoyance increasing until Dylan started screaming, hurling the bowl of food before him into the air, his face smeared, huge wails blaring from his mouth. This unrestrained burst of wildness was uproarious.

"Imagine", I said, as Dylan tossed food in a multitude of different directions, screaming with unabraded venom, "walking into a restaurant and seeing about fifty people behaving like that. It'd be incredible."

I was fascinated by the prickly free will of this gorgeous child. The three of us laughed in appreciation. Food went everywhere. His attitude of uncompromising passion made him adorable. He was infuriated that anyone had the temerity to thwart his desires. In a way, he reminded me of his mother.

"Imagine", I said, between bursts of cackling, "the reaction of a chef in a French restaurant if he heard this racket coming from a complete table of people, hysterical that that imbecile in the kitchen had had the audacity to create the pile of disgusting garbage which had been so insensitively shoved before them – it'd be hilarious."

I glanced at Chris and Frances who were beside themselves with joyous exasperation. Chris, particularly, looked tired. I realised then that this ball of shameless caprice represented a full-time occupation, full of the most acute demands. Not a second of his waking time could go unnoticed. From the instant his little eyes shot open in the morning to the second he collapsed in an exhausted heap – who knows how long later – he was alive, destructive, demanding, noisy, extrovert, constantly testing even the patience of those who adored every fibre of his sweet little body. The adult mind, set in its ways, ambitious, experienced, has a desperate need for reflection; the gravity of this need does not become apparent until enormous demands are placed upon it. Right now, it was obvious to me that Chris and Frances could have slept for days or just lain down somewhere under a distant tree and let their minds wander. The wandering of our minds along ethereal paths is the poetry of our lives; we are all poets – unconsciously – and we are all at it far more than we consciously realise; at this moment that vital function had been severely tampered with in the parents of a child whose intense, ever-changing curiosity, whose fascinatingly disrespectful treatment of his immediate environment required constant supervision: his parents were at the point of infuriated collapse.

Generously, so Frances and I could speak to each other, Chris lifted Dylan out of the high chair, and said: "I'll take over for a while, okay?"

He carried the 'bundle of joy' off into the lounge-room. Frances, after giving me some fruit juice, sank into a chair at the dining-room table, and said, "They say the first two years are the worst"; then, smiling, she added, "Let's hope so, hey?"

"He's a beautiful kid," I replied. "Extremely unusual. That incident with the food was hilarious."

We could hear Chris talking to Dylan in the lounge-room. Outside, through a glass sliding door, I could see a back garden, half in shadow; a patch of beautifully kept lawn was lined with gum trees and blackboys and in the centre of it was a white iron table and a group of white chairs. It was an uniquely Australian garden, characteristically enormous for no apparent reason, and engulfed by high timber fences on three sides.

"The most successful people, I think," I continued, "are those with the ability to demand, almost tactlessly, with outrageous audacity."

"A bit like you, hey?" she smiled.

"I've only ever requested", I replied, "politely. You know that."

"How could I ever forget it?" she asked.

"Precisely," I replied.

She smiled and said, "I agree, actually. You've got to nurture that quality, but in a way which still enables them to function normally. It's a challenge. I think, though, that that quality is inherently within Dylan."

"I wonder", I replied, "where he gets it from?"

"It's hard to say," she smiled. "A genetic miracle, perhaps?"

"Simply hereditary", I said, "is probably the answer."

She smiled with self-conscious acceptance as I leant back in the chair, glanced out through the glass doors and said, "Since I got back here, I've been astounded by the amount of useless space that exists here. The most bizarre thing is that people actually waste so much of their lives maintaining it. What a way to go on."

Frances began giggling.

"It's not so bad in Sydney," she said. "People there basically just let their gardens go."

"The other day", I said, "I tried convincing someone that, if all the time they'd spent watering their garden had been applied to the playing of a saxophone, then they could've been the greatest jazz saxophonist of all time."

Frances erupted with titillated amusement. She knew that not a great number of people here, in the depths of hard-earned suburbia, would appreciate the cynicism of such a scathing view. But the facts were the facts.

"People are starting to realise here", she replied, "that it's not too practical to keep extending sewerage pipes further and further out into the Great Sandy Desert. The local councils are beginning to insist that people subdivide their land. It basically reduces the cost of essential services."

"Not before time," I said. "Unwittingly, they'll also be helping to improve the quality of people's minds. People'll have to occupy their brains with something more substantial than whether the camellias are blooming."

Frances gave a quick snap of laughter and said, "So I see you've been occupying yours in a pretty exotic fashion."

I smiled and said, sardonically, "You didn't expect anything else, did you?"

She produced an embarrassed smile and said, "It was a little difficult to judge."

"Don't worry," I smiled. "Anyone with audacious ambitions, no matter how gifted, is going to be considered to be an idiot in a place like this. It's par for the course. My ambitions, and how I intended to go about achieving them, were out of the scope of open-minded discussion. That's the price you pay for esoteric risk-taking. I was prepared to pay it. It's been worth it."

"Were you shot at?" she asked.

"A few times," I replied.

"And?" she demanded.

"It's not like anything you can imagine," I replied. "When a bullet passes close over your head, it sucks the air away with it; as the air rushes into the vacuum of space it makes a sharp crack, like someone cracking a whip above your head. You think, 'Jesus, what would that do if it made contact?' The sound made me think of bones being shattered. It was fantastically frightening. But I've had the experience and that's enough for me. No matter how intense the adrenaline rush, I'm not mad. I never intend to do that again. No way."

Frances was intensely absorbed.

"Do you think it's a moral dilemma—" she began.

"Other people's wars", I interrupted, "are not my problem. I've always said that in these situations a twenty-four hour cease-fire should take place so all non-combatants can be shifted out; the UN should surround those left, not let anyone out and just let them murder each other. Believe me, it's the finest solution."

"You see", she began, "no scope for diplomacy?"

I laughed and said, "You know as well as I do, Frances, that the last thing human beings with delusions of grandeur, in matters dealing with great emotions, are interested in is compromise."

Laughing again, I added, "Just look at you."

Chris burst out laughing from the lounge-room. Frances smiled self-consciously.

"I'll never forget", I said, "that day at university when you told me, emphatically, without compromise, with hard-headed fanaticism, precisely what you were going to do with the rest of your life. One of the key elements, if I can remember, was marriage at the age of twenty-seven, was it not?"

"Yes," Frances admitted, "I believe it was."

We both laughed at this naive pragmatism.

"And I thought", I said, "that I was the one who was supposed to be naive."

"Well," Frances replied, "you'll be happy to know that these days I consider plans to be fairly unstable commodities."

"Good," I said.

I smiled, feeling grateful that she had the grace to accept my point. She knew that I was not affected by the impracticalities, the inhumanity even, of her previous plans. The point had been made clear that I had every right to berate those who had belittled my aspirations. I had demonstrated that it is naive and ignorant to assume that someone does not possess the talent and wherewithal to achieve their goals, as no one else can tell you who you are. If you are unconscious of yourself, then everyone else must be as well; therefore, who is best equipped to judge your capabilities and fathom the ferocity of your determination? Anyone? Would you do it? Do you know anyone that well?

"An Iranian taxi driver," I continued, "who faces execution if he goes home, told me that no change in the weather should come as a surprise. Life is fate, and fate has no regard for plans."

"In your case," Frances smiled, "it had no regard for common sense either, did it?"

"None", I replied, "whatsoever – and thank God for that."

We both laughed at my uncompromising disposition. Then a long discussion, punctured by bouts of chortling, born from the appreciation of esoteric character traits, transpired about the people with whom we had been to university. A discussion about my previous girlfriends then unfolded. This led to a story involving the house where we were currently. One evening, many years ago, Frances had held a dinner party here. At the end of the night, I was put in her parents' bedroom with my girlfriend. I had asked Frances to wake us in the morning.

"Barbara", I said, "had only just finished giving me a blow job, literally had just finished, when you stuck your head in through the door, beaming, saying, 'Time to get up!'"

Frances was beside herself with wicked appreciation as I added, "Well, let me tell you something - before you innocently burst in, two seconds earlier, I had been."

I watched with delight as she screwed up her face in a pained, overjoyed silence, before unleashing a rip-roaring cackle that caused Chris to come strolling into the room, himself laughing, saying, "Sorry, I couldn't help overhearing that. Even now", he sighed, "she doesn't knock."

"If", I laughed, "she'd come in even a fraction of a second earlier, in the frame of mind I was in, I might have even asked her to join us. It would have added a certain piquancy to the breakfast conversation."

Frances was almost in agony. Her face had reddened considerably and her eyes were full of tears. She managed to say, "At the time I wondered why Barbara was so dumbstruck."

"I", I commented, "had to speak for both of us because her mouth was full of, shall we say, the fruits of life. She swallowed it after you shut the door."

"Oh God," Frances chuckled.

Not a thing had changed between us. No time seemed to have elapsed. There was still that hallmark of true friendship - the ability to create a free and flippant mood, the aspect of comic surprise, the rose-coloured voice in the malaise from a sensation of bland wistfulness. I knew then that we would still be telling each other these stories in fifty years' time; and I suspected that her son would be telling us a few too.

"God," Frances continued, "I'm glad you didn't tell me this at the time. How embarrassing!"

I laughed and said, "Believe me, I wanted to; but I couldn't because of Barbara. Basically, I was dying to tell you."

"Anything else you want to tell me now?" she asked.

"If you're a good girl," I replied, "there might be a few things. Why don't we go to the beach?"

She looked at me purposefully, and I knew that her scheming brain had just swung, effortlessly, into operation.

* * * * * * * * * *

A more perfect afternoon for the beach there has never been. Frances was able to use my desire to head for the coast as an excuse to extricate herself from the drudgery of parental responsibility. Her yearning, pleading, whining, pained, tortured, persuasive voice caused Chris to get her to acknowledge that a favour was being done in allowing her to go; she was then given permission to drive me to the refreshing blue waters of the ocean.

In the car, I said, "Frances, do you think that the tone of your voice, rather than the request itself, is the thing that causes such opposition to your suggestions?"

She screwed up her face with the embarrassment of exposure, huge teeth flashing within her cavernous mouth, and giggled; then she said, "It's a privilege just to be able to go to the beach – alone – with a friend. It's just too claustrophobic at times. I can actually only stay for a few minutes as well."

"Being with me", I smiled, "must be light relief after hours of not being able to let your mind wander."

"Exactly," she laughed.

I considered this to be a compliment. She was not too upset about my pointing out to her that intelligent people got infuriated by a tone of voice suggestive of spurious manipulation. She admitted that it was "a bad habit". She had to work on being "more calm and straightforward".

"It helps", I said, "to make people feel that you've got some respect for their intelligence. Take Graeme for example. You used to think that you were manipulating me, but I actually enjoyed talking to him. You even try it on with people you're in love with. You even try doing it to Chris! Hah!"

Graeme was an ex-boyfriend; Frances had required me to attend specific social gatherings so that I would speak to him, thereby enabling her to socialise.

"I used to enjoy" I said, "letting you think that you were being cunning. It gave me a macabre pleasure knowing that you were going to be insistent at some stage in the future on my being at some party, or whatever, because it would be so dull without me. You didn't realise it, but I learnt a lot from you about what not to do when making a request. I wish to extend my thanks to you now. I don't know where I would be without you."

Frances was surprised by my perspicacity; she was even more surprised by her own transparency.

"You may not remember", I continued, "but there were times when I used to pretend that I was undecided about going to one of these parties - there was never ever any intention on my part of not going: I always enjoyed them - but I used to act unenthusiastic about the prospect of attendance just so I could listen to your powers of persuasion. How the hell you didn't realise what I was doing is still well and truly beyond me. But you didn't. The manipulator got manipulated. I used to put the phone down and shake my head at your absurd arrogance. It actually gave me a lot of inspiration. There's something smugly satisfying in being with someone more innocent than yourself who believes that you're prone to credulity; try it some time. I recommend it, if you want to achieve a difficult ambition, as a means of motivation."

Frances's face was a picture of shocked amusement; this caused me to add, "You're the only person I know with whom I've been infatuated and then fantastically bored by. Now it's nice and there's no reason why it shouldn't remain that way, provided, of course, that Chris doesn't kill you in the meantime."

A wry smile fell across my face as I made this last remark.

"I got the feeling today", I said, "that he's pissed off with your obsequious trickery. I don't know why you try it on him anyway. He's a perfectly reasonable individual. He just doesn't need it. It's quite astonishing."

I erupted into surprised laughter on completing my sentence. Frances was not upset at anything I had said. She appreciated the honesty of it for, in her, curiosity and stubbornness usually outweighed fear.

I glanced at her from side on. She was ruthlessly gathering herself for a retort to my onslaught. I could see a steely contemplativeness descend into her often smiling eyes; there were clearly things that I was not prepared to consider. One could quite easily see this. If only I were more conscious of what was transpiring on this earth! Really, I should learn to be more sagacious.

Her grip on the steering-wheel tightened as she said, her eyes now pierced with frustration, "It's a constant battle. To an outsider, without these sorts of pressures and responsibilities, it must appear ridiculous – the gamesmanship et cetera – but everyone, no matter how unjustified, through frustration, feels at some stage that they are being taken advantage of; it happens to everyone who becomes a parent within a relationship. It's not easy – some days you wish it would all just go away but, of course, it doesn't. It's always there, just beneath the surface. You have to experience it to know what it's like."

Frances was pointing out that I was not a model of saintliness. I was glad of this, for I had no time for sanctimonious indulgences. The moral high plane was not for me. And difficult for her it must have been. On the day that she had discovered she was pregnant (it was unplanned), she had already paid for an impending sojourn – yet another one – to the Himalayas. The proposed trip had to be cancelled. In her letter to me, she had philosophically announced: 'If I don't have this child now, I know it will never happen. Otherwise, I could just keep going on and on and on. And for what reason? But fate has intervened.'

In this instance, I was surprised by her attitude; previously she had prided herself on her adventurousness, as though it were a matter of principle. Her ego was unusual insofar it was apparent to me that the greatest compliment she could have received was: you are the most curious person on earth. (How many people actually care if others consider them curious or not?) Frances was overwhelmed by the idea that she was inquisitive; it motivated her to ask questions in such a way that often her innocent interlocutors were led to feel that she was actually interested in them. This is where her curiosity ceased, for her probings were prompted by her need to discover if someone else had done something that she herself should attempt. It appealed to her glamorous sense of destiny to believe that she would invariably be at the apex of human experience. I considered this to be a fine aspiration; but I knew it had little to do with real curiosity; it was merely a vainglorious self-indulgence, bearing no relation to the unconscious fascination that is the true hallmark of genuine intrigue – the fascination that inspires someone to ponder the root causes of disguised motivations and to venture, selflessly, to the heart of cataclysmic events. Frances was not that curious. She was driven more by an egotistical need to be able to favourably compare her own experiences with those of her peers. It was difficult to imagine that she would develop sufficient interest to continually revisit a particular place, overcome by its cultural complexities, charmed by its history (the genuinely curious are always fascinated by past events which have shaped the course of human affairs); I had never heard her make a single reference to any of the principal events of world history: the French Revolution, the two World Wars, the Arab-Israeli conflict, the influence of the Ottomans, the American War of Independence, African colonisation. These events were irrelevant to her, for they were irrelevant to most others. If, for some obscure reason, the average person became absorbed by the Ottoman Empire, by calligraphy, mosque building, the spread of Turkish cuisine, exotic fabrics, then Frances too would also become absorbed; the process of absorption occurred, not because she bore any intrinsic attraction to such matters, like a sadist might for violence, or a poet might for natural events, but because she was fearful of not being able to add intelligently to dinner party conversation. She dreaded the idea of being incapable of making urbane contributions even if the popular subject held only cosmetic interest to a mind driven by the appearance of knowledge.

I was smiling ironically when I said, “I’m sorry, but I’ve been too busy discovering things of such vast relevance that I haven’t had time to have had the experience to which you’ve just so eloquently alluded.”

She knew that I was not being entirely serious. This was the remarkable thing about her. She was superb fun. She also knew that I was having a little dig. This caused her to glance at me with an admonishing smile before shaking her head.

“Now, now, now,” I said, waving a finger, “it’s no good shaking your little heady-weddy. I can distinctly remember you arrogantly announcing some time after your return from Europe – a whole twelve months I think it was, travelling ‘by yourself’ – that because certain people, such as myself, had yet to do this then, clearly, we lacked the curiosity that so obviously separated you from us. Didn't we?"

She laughed ruefully and said, "You really know how to belittle. You should be ashamed of yourself."

"Now come on," I said. "I only belittle those who have already done exactly that themselves. Arrogance is one thing, but hypocrisy is another."

"I was young," she said. "All of you should have been sympathetically amused."

"We were," I replied.

Both of us just started laughing for, once again, her little naughty botty had been thoroughly and deservedly smacked.

TWO

At the beach, the music of floating seagulls emerged from the blue choirstalls of the sky. Semi-naked people wandered in a blaze of light. At the top of the sand dunes, upon a patch of grass, we could see people sprinkled around the bone-white shore; other people bobbed in the foaming waters; past them, the water undertook a smooth transition in hue from green-white to royal blue. Above the royal blue, the duck-egg blue sky swept over to complete a wall so still, impenetrable and so serene that it felt as though we were enclosed in a cathedral of water and sky.

In the nave of this masterpiece of natural architecture, white lines of waves ran parallel with each other in desperate bids to arrive at the shore. Hearing the rumble of these undulations striking the beach, I observed that they seemed to be made up of billions of tiny organisms, rushing over each other to slide in a frenetic scramble across the smooth hard sand, the wet surface of which, reflecting the sky, contained a hint of mauve that disappeared in a flash as the water flowed back into the sea. Time and time again, this inlay of mauve came and went, as wave after wave floated out, with languid grace, from the pitiless immensity, which, in a tranquil sleep of powerful restfulness, mocked with its longevity the passions and dreams of those who lay before it, mocking us with its pride, its quietude and the prodigious certainty of its mysterious ways.

Across its monumentally unconcerned surface, darker hues, like shadows, came and went as faint hints of breeze touched the sea. At one place, a flock of seagulls sat, dived and swirled, creating a striking contrast of white against blue; seething, bone-white splashes of spray flared in the distances where the immensity came to an abrupt halt at a line of cliffs, as though the sudden uprising of the land were an act of defiance against the unjustified batterings of the vitriolic seas; at this point, black rocks jutted from the water, causing the sea to boil, looking as though cream had been placed upon the extremities of an enormous dish of sapphire, whose sudden conclusion at the cliffs, a distinct boundary between two completely different worlds, indicated that the great force of self-respect had risen, with firm majesty, against the tempestuous tides.

Along that coastline, my eye wandered. I was moved aesthetically when I realised that what I was observing amounted to a symbol of the phenomenon that we call the future, an image of a life. The immediate distances were clear – a strip of coast, a headland, a bay – then the coastline became hazier, the purple outline of headlands visible, then disappearing into hues of violet, grey-blue, as though the distant future were shrouded in an ethereal mist of possibilities, none visible, all obscured; the more profoundly hidden, the more interesting the façade and the more astonishing the revelation. Or so the theory went.

But what really was in the ethereal mists? Greatness? More obscurity? The jagged, wind-swept rocks of lost dreams? The long sweep of halcyon bays? Well-protected coves with transparent waters? Or perhaps the reedy quagmire of tangled mangroves, with unnecessary complications, gnarled and wiry entanglements, unshifting in the nagging tides?

In a life indifferent to planning, all was possible. The only certainty was that the future itself was uncertain. This was not quite as absurd as it sounded. Some people could look into the distances and see them cloaked in tenebrous clouds, the fuming mists punctuated by forks of lightning; they could glance into the future certain that they were going to be trapped in a never-ending storm, an ineluctable whirlpool of regrets and failures. But I was clueless, even at the most mundane level, as to what I could expect.

Perhaps as a result of the emotional uncertainties of the first four years of my life, during which my parents did everything except skewer each other with burning stakes, I developed an exotic taste for unpredictable vacillations; maybe this was true, but the answer was still as uncertain as the mystery of those ethereal mists. How could I possibly ever know? I did not even know if one of the possibilities in the surreal wash of faraway vapours contained a dramatic bay of requited love or a bold and tranquil promontory of lasting satisfaction. These possibilities were still as distant as the smothering opaqueness of those outlying airs which transformed the known, with wispy gentleness, into unexpected forms, reshaping, moulding, hiding, blanketing everything in a splendour of celestial haze.

Above this misty testimony to unforeseen contingencies, four puffy white clouds, unmoving near the horizon, each threw a blanket of shadow on to the sweeping bed of the sea. The strange appearance of those four tiny globules of vapour, with their symmetrical imprints upon the water, still, silent and composed, suggested to me that they were like chances in the far-off seas. Opportunities were like that; they stared at you with sublime imperturbability, with the aspect of beauteous, distant fulfilment which you felt their acquisition could give. These four opportunities – perhaps fame, wealth, love, success, whatever – were made more exquisite by the orange glow of the dying sun. Enveloped in an apricot mist, they stared out at me from across an acquiescent sea, the unpredictable truculence of which could arrive the instant I touched its enticing surface to reach out for the beguiling wisps in the purple seas. My belief in the potential sharpness of the change in temper of the sea was due in part to imagination, where anything could easily become anything else, and due in part to the love of that recalcitrance the bold fury of which excites dreams; it is perhaps an unfortunate quirk of the human aesthetic imagination that the beauty it so readily ascribes to the striking features of the land is only afforded to an ocean when it is mountainous. I had seen many of these rumbustious seas. There had been times when I had almost been thrown overboard, but I had clung on. There were times when the ship that carried me on my calamitous journey had smashed headlong into raging seas; and still that ship had ventured on. Only I knew its ultimate destination. Everyone I knew, including the person I was with, was ambivalent towards the inevitability of its arrival; but, on that day that I intended to enter the final harbour, they would all be there, some acting as if they had played their part, others seeing an opportunity, many wishing to be a part of something they had no right to see.

I spun on to my back and glanced up at the sky. It had only been recently that I had discovered the sky is not blue in other worlds. This just showed me how blinkered the human race was, myself included, when so very few of us had not even bothered to escape our self-indulgence and ask: why is the sky blue? Across it, an open-mouthed seagull unleashed a piercing squawk; it seemed like a primeval cry of frustration. Its wings were taut and motionless as it landed in a flock of other birds that pecked and fretted on the grass about five metres from my resting head. The uniformity of goals within that brood of creatures resembled the instinct for security that so colours the actions of this often anaesthetised world. It is perceived as advantageous to share in a common desire; but what if your aspirations are beyond the pale? Have gone off into other worlds? Bear no consideration for the consequences of extremism? Are completely unique? Do not fit into the conveniently constructed moral strictures, born from obsequiously accepted standards of desire, which have no real place in the teeming whirlpool of the human spirit?

Frances was mystified by my silence. In me it is even more of a beguiling quality than it is in many others, due to the usually frenetic machinations of my consistently loquacious mouth. She leant towards me and said, "Are you in love?"

"Only with you," I replied.

We smiled at each other. It was so easy to be flippant with her – too easy in fact.

I thought momentarily, then said, "Can you imagine what it must be like to be unable to express virtually any of your real aspirations to anyone because they're so wild?"

Frances was a picture of confusion as she wondered what this could possibly mean.

I rose on to my right side and added, "I don't really consider you to be lucky or anything, but you represent someone of whom society can be proud. All your desires are perceived as good. They're achievable, sensible, based on common sense; but imagine if you had something which was not, and was as real as anything and was charged by a furious passion?"

"Like what?" she asked.

I laughed into the nitrogen-rich heavens.

"Oh Frances, Frances," I said, falling on to my back.

Then I rose quickly again and said, "Often I've wondered how many truly good people there are out there being chastised because of the uniqueness of their desires. Imagine feeling embarrassed about being asked what it is you really want to do."

"It's better", Frances replied, "just to go ahead and do it and say nothing."

"Exactly," I said. "Besides," I added, smiling, "it comes across as so galling and mysterious when you say to someone who's badgering you severely, 'Sorry, I can't tell you.' The implication that they're not discreet or open-minded enough to receive the information rocks even the most insensitive moron to their very foundations."

"Is there anything you'd like to tell me then?" she asked.

"No," I joked, "you wouldn't understand."

“Aren’t you even going to thank me for driving you down here then?” she asked.

“No way,” I replied. “You used me as an excuse to make an escape. Once again, I am an innocent victim of the nefarious whims of this heinous world.”

“It’s incredible”, she said, “that you possess the fortitude to carry on.”

“I know,” I replied. “Even I’m astonished.”

Frances departed. I went down on to the beach. I put my towel down at right angles to the shore. A great feeling of tentativeness befell me at the prospect of running into someone unprepared for the uncertainties of having to deal with an eccentric, disinclined towards the normal pleasantries of well-adjusted social interaction. The beach was really a venue for the furthering of insipid gaiety. In the dubious history of this strip of affluent whiteness, it was more than likely that nothing of any real consequence had ever been discussed: most of it would have centred around the careers and social lives of the spoilt thousands who frequented its finely-crushed sands. In a sense it was an achievement that so many had been given so many opportunities to indulge themselves. An achievement it may have felt for them, but not for me. The presence of so many staid, well-adjusted people, all beautifully tanned with respectable jobs, filled me with an abhorrence that definitely would have been worse had it not been for the dazzling sight of the huge, burnt-orange sun, ablaze above the far edge of the world, which sat with enflamed serenity as it prepared itself for its graceful descent into the satin blueness of the sea.

This contrast in emotions – sensual pleasure and detestation of tweeness – suggested to me, if I was not already conscious of it, that my actions were shaped by the aesthetic, rather than by moral or commonsensical considerations. I did not desist from doing something because it was evil; I did not do something because it was good: I did things because I wanted to have my senses titillated. The undesirability of being surrounded by people with little respect for the unusual was thankfully eased by the beauty of light that imbued the white sands with an iridescent kiss of orange and caused a pathway of molten iron to run from the horizon to the foaming lips of the gently undulating sea. It was like being in a place cocooned from class consciousness, poverty, oppression, desperation, real intrigue: the masochistic urge to have something for which to fight seemed to have been drained out of the place by its glorious unreality. This did not mean that it was going to escape its turn in hell. Wherever human beings have existed, there has been war. Eventually, as always, there would be a violent reaction here against the shallowness of overfed staidness, a reaction as sharp and as absurd as any that had transpired anywhere else; yet here, now, the picturesque opulence of the place made a mockery of the fact that, on the other side of that enormous sea, innocent people were currently being blown away, thousands were starving and old villages were being destroyed as we lay here, ignoring it, convinced that the seeds of such things would never be blown to us from all the way across that protective sea. The irony of human existence is that at the heart of all conflicts is a joy in destruction, in mangling the status quo, in disrupting that which every sane society is attempting to achieve. The falsity of social systems is that they now take little account of the fact that prolonged periods of safety are inherently insipid. Everyone just feels frustrated. Something snaps. People begin to find excuses for unleashing their unconscious wishes. The preying bird of turbulence then swoops into the calm waters of uneventful respectability, gorging itself on the bloated fish of mindless indulgence.

Okay, so I'm insane. But I knew that I was not the only one who would have been half-delighted had a huey gunship strafed that self-important beach with a healthy dose of machine-gun fire. It would have been beautiful to have seen the surprise on the stricken faces of those turgid sun-worshippers, being sent into a panic by the introduction of a little self-effacing excitement, ripped in with macabre glee, right into the fabric of their smug and gluttonous lives. Society was not surreal enough for its own good. Let there be change.

Picture this. You're on a plush, exotic beach in a wealthy, First World country, surrounded by good-looking, happy individuals – they're all gibbering on about their social lives, giggling, talking about parties, with whom they'd like to go to bed, with whom they have been to bed, with whom they are going to be going to bed next, where to buy a certain article of clothing, the virtues of investing in gold, et cetera – and you're contemplating the causes of war, and the potential destruction of a place that all these other people perceive as good. Would you feel a little misplaced? Do you think that you would be in the frame of mind to have to deal with some shallow ecstasy in the guise of a human being?

The inevitable contact with the local species occurred when my spurious musings were disrupted by the sudden depositing of a shirt and a pair of sunglasses next to me, by Dob, who complemented his arrival with the usual, "Karnabbazzz!" followed by, "Watch my stuff, will you? A few lexters I need to speak to."

He then deposited himself before a young couple. For half an hour he unleashed upon their solemn faces a remarkably self-indulgent analysis of a certain aspect of Freudian psychology. I wondered what it was that made him so certain these two people, enjoying each other's intimate company in the balmy evening, would not mind, uninvited, being used as earpieces for the reinforcing of something which Dob had obviously learnt that day. They endured the situation, presumably conscious that it would not last for ever. The stony, withdrawn expressions on their faces indicated to me that they knew their existences were of little consequence to their interlocutor, whose existence was of mild amusement to some of us because he was so constantly and innocently conscious of himself. His attention span was virtually non-existent with regard to matters dissociated from his own life; this I found a curious phenomenon, as it was so foreign to my own predicament. I naturally presumed that no one had any real interest in me; he seemed to believe that his life was held in messiah-like esteem. Both of us were completely wrong. Our feelings were not representative of reality. Mine were justified to some extent, though, in that I knew I was the only one on that beach that day who would have contemplated the causes of war; his were justified to the extent that he was very entertaining; however, he did not take into consideration the fact that many mature people considered his lifestyle to be superficial and trivial. This was of no consequence to him because it would not have dawned upon him that the majority saw life as an opportunity to discover the intricacies of themselves in the secure framework of finding out about another. He saw the human race as an audience. He took his stage with him everywhere.

He finally got up and took it further along the beach to a ring of young ladies who exhibited that deluded air of mature refinement which I had learnt to associate with a public school education. The four of them were all extremely attractive. One of them had to be called Fiona. One of them no doubt was. The likely candidate was sitting upright, her long, tanned, shapely legs before her, the palms of her hands flat on the sand behind her back. Looking up at Dob, she flicked her long brunette hair away from her face and smiled, unleashing a set of teeth from which a star of sunlight should have bounced. She was about twenty years of age; young and attractive enough to believe that her attentions should only be given to an older, well-educated, urbane swinger. She chuckled as Dob, swaggering, plucked, from the mischievous bouquet of his exotic social life, yet another flowery tale of naughty intrigue. The tweely-held perception of his notoriety was the cornerstone upon which his egotism was built. It led him to believe that perfectly intelligent people were fascinated to discover what he had been doing. It was immature, self-centred, incurious and pathetic, but it got him into bed with twenty-year-olds. He was thirty-three. In doing this, it was irrelevant for him that his actions were of no consequence to someone interested in meeting a thirty-five-year-old international journalist who had scaled Mount Everest and who could speak three languages. It was apparent that if any of these twenty-year-olds were given the opportunity to really express themselves, they would put him straight into a coma. They were just there to be dazzled.

Eventually, he returned to his belongings, one and a half hours later. In that time he had entertained scores of worshipping people with his egotistical repartee. The brilliant lustre of the sun-drenched sand had now been dimmed – the sun had disappeared under the sea – but Dob made up for it with his adolescent enthusiasm. Standing over me, he said, “Party on tonight. The Avenue. You coming?”

I knew that he was not expecting me to answer in the affirmative, so I said, “Yes.”

His concern was kept in check when I added, “And you’re going to have to give me a lift, because I don’t have a car.”

“Okay, okay,” he said, nodding his head. “We’ll leave in half an hour. Right?”

The departure was delayed because he and a friend were considering the prospect of opening up diplomatic relations with some young ladies who Dob suspected were friends with someone he had “once sumped”. I looked up at Dob and his friend and observed the serious looks of intense contemplation that had fallen over their faces: they appeared as though some great decision were about to be reached. As they stared at the intended victims, they mumbled their observations to each other: "Very sumperable. Excellent mappage. Oh, fucking horny."

I glanced over at the three girls they were eyeing up. They had the air of women who expected to be approached. Dob and his friend went over to them and I went and plunged into the water. It was sublime. I did not realise before, when I was living here, what an exquisite pleasure it was to just float around in this superbly unpolluted sea. Circle after circle I described, pirouetting through the water, floating in angelic bliss, gliding, and swimming, diving and surfacing, languidly drifting, turning and sinking, detached and free. Lying on my back, I was able to detach myself sufficiently to create the illusion that I was a celestial body, flying through the universe, the only reference point the first stars that had appeared in the profound turquoise magnificence of the sky. Over and over I tumbled, rotating with mathematical precision, charging serenely between the stars. I could have been gliding along happily at a relatively leisurely rate – perhaps fifty kilometres per second – or I could have been blazing a searing trail up near the speed of light. In the endless spectrum, with nothing to compare, it was impossible to tell. This was what I wanted to do – this was what I wanted to share with someone beautiful. Who cares about parties? For God's sake!

When I got out of the water, Dob was ready to go. The feeling that something of sociological amusement was about to arrive into my life – a feeling usually nearby – overcame me with the clarity which marked the glistening sky. On the landing of the concrete steps leading up to the road, Dob stopped, again, to communicate with yet another group of people, who persuaded him to join them in one of the cafés that overlooked the beach.

Rapid introductions were made; then we went into the café. Just as we were about to sit down, Dob flew off, again, charging across the floor towards two girls sitting at the window. They were delighted when they saw him coming. This left me alone with a group of people I had only just met. Across the blue carpet I saw Dob's flailing hands and flashing teeth. The two girls chortled and giggled and said very little. I looked at the people with whom I found myself and smiled. They showed some sympathy for my predicament. I appreciated their concern. They could have quite easily spoken amongst themselves and ignored me completely. Instead, one of them smiled ruefully and said, "You can't expect much else from Dob, really, can you?"

It was heartening to realise that the social graces which had so profoundly avoided Dob had found some measure in the people with whom fate had unexpectedly placed me. One of them, a beautiful girl, asked me if I knew Greg. During the introductions, Dob had used my surname. I was again astonished by the incestuousness of the place. I was on the point of unleashing a great burst of laughter when this girl described Greg "as a real sweetie", a view of affairs that would have probably caused my father to blurt out, 'What an absolute pile of fucking crap.' (Greg smiled extremely sweetly when I eventually told him this. Vanessa almost vomited.)

When Dob came back, he was just about to sit down when he realised that he also knew the two girls who were sitting at the table next to us. As he flew off again, the people at my table all laughed. We watched as Dob ebulliently invited the two girls to the party. Unbeknown to the people having the party, he had been doing this all afternoon. They were no doubt oblivious of the fact that they had unwittingly solicited the services of a highly loquacious and exceptionally mobile inviting machine. If only a mere fraction of the people he had invited made an appearance, almost two-thirds of the entire population of the city were due to attend.

Outside on the street, as we walked to his car, beside a road bumper to bumper with traffic, Dob suddenly yelled out to a dark-haired man, sitting in an open-top sports car with an exotic, long-haired beauty beside him: "DAVE! PARTY TONIGHT! ONE THE AVENUE! BE THERE!"

Dave spun around impressively in the seat of his car, his dark sunglasses an unnecessary accoutrement in the fading light, and raised his thumb. He was probably under the impression that Dob possessed some interest in him. Dob's comment was made as though he were under a moral obligation to impart all knowledge he possessed of social events.

"It appears", I said, "as if Dave is going to be preoccupied with something else."

This caused Dob to say, "There's no way he's coming. But you've still got to let them know anyway."

This summed up Dob's situation perfectly. He was concerned about maintaining his reputation. In a sense, it was sound thinking. It meant that people already knew him before being introduced to him. This gave him the licence to do what he wanted: it was like fame. He was expected to be mischievously gregarious. People already had it in their minds that they could expect surreal humour, disobedience, enthusiasm, help with the lacing of their diaries with exciting social affairs. Because they had heard of it they wanted it, expected it, encouraged it. And Dob delivered.

In the car on the way to the party, I told him that I used to be a patient in the psychiatry department where he was currently working. It was amusing because, at the time my mind was being examined, I was supposed to be under twenty-four hour supervision. The doctors were mystified as to why I was behaving the way I was. I was only let out to go and play football for one of the local league clubs. This caused us both to laugh. We could imagine a scene where a well-known footballer is unable to attend the post-match presentations because, as the coach would announce, "He's in a psychiatric unit." For anyone wishing to indulge in the practice of Australian Rules football, a psychiatric unit comes highly recommended. Perhaps I was inadvertently predicting the existence of the modern player.

Dob's face brightened up considerably when he heard this news. He had looked a worried man. He had not predicted anyone else being in his car on the way to the party, least of all me. What would he say when his adoring flock saw him enter with me? Who is that guy? Where's he from? Would they realise that the one who came with Dob is a total embarrassment? And how would Dob's reputation be affected by the thought of the masses subliminally associating his remarkable existence with me?

These were just some of the great questions that can befall a man deeply conscious of his position in a society dominated by airy, hedonistic conversation. How could Dob possibly introduce me to anyone? Did he know what I was going to say or do? Would I open my big mouth and unleash upon the world a litany of sordid tales involving the dubious Dob? It was a very worrying mystery. And could my dim humour be trusted? And, worst of all, what would happen to Dob if he was unable to shake me off and I just followed him everywhere, never leaving him alone, popping up at awkward moments, getting in the way, boring his audience, causing embarrassment, cramping his style, perhaps even chatting up his intended belle? My sheer presence had caused a turmoil. The highly rigid structure of his carefully planned social life had been shaken by the unexpected appearance of a suspect social moron. What would he do? Panic? Run? Elicit the services of some poor fool to shake me off? It was all running through his mind. He would find a solution. I was waiting with enormous anticipation to discover what it would be.

I did not have to wait too long. We got to the front garden of a beautiful old house that had a long red driveway running down one side of it. Exotic gargoyles rose out from the obtuse-angled planes of the orange-tiled roof. Baskets containing plants hung from the roof of the verandah. Large, stained-glass windows sat like jewels encrusted into the alluring brooch of the doorway. Their colours were similar to those of the purple and orange flowers with black centres that sprang from the pot plants. The deadened cacophony of human interaction could be heard from a distance which suggested that the noise was not emanating from within the house. The front door was open. The interior was dark. High ceilings and large empty rooms faced us. Dob almost sprinted through it to escape from me. His disappearing figure in the darkness came as a relief, as I had no desire to be seen walking into the party with him. I preferred sliding into parties, blending in, gradually creating havoc. My social intelligence had the elusive qualities of style: it came and went of its own accord and was at its finest only after a lengthy period of confident, esoteric interaction. I was feeling far too self-conscious to suddenly be in a position where a hundred strange faces would all turn simultaneously in my direction. Any entry into a party with Dob was bound to provoke such a response.

I saw him disappear through a distant door. He looked like casualness incarnate. His legs seemed to fly around with a sort of loose sanguinity. His shirt was open and flapping, the sleeves rolled up. A packet of rolling tobacco hung from the pocket. He entered a patio of people dressed in colourful shorts and T-shirts. I went left into the kitchen. I stashed some cans of beer in the refrigerator. Two women, both with sunglasses perched across their heads, were discussing a prospective sojourn to Europe. Being the sarcastic bastard that I am, I felt like suggesting Yugoslavia. I was, and always had been, pessimistic about the chances that the majority had of extracting anything of real pertinence from travel. There was a disturbing self-importance about the way these women stared with serious relish into each other's eyes as they addressed the solemn task of deciding with whom they would be staying in a variety of locations from Vienna to London. It appeared as though numerous people were going to be taking a personal interest in their trip.

Outside, I observed a swimming pool enclosed by a timber fence. Plants and flowers were draped with luxuriant succulence over the ribs of the enclosure. Three people were sitting in the duck-egg blue water sipping on champagne. The pool was lit up by a light that projected its radiance down upon the water from a height of about five metres. Around the edge of the enclosure, fern leaves arose from clumps of green leaves. Across the lawn, groups of people chatted away beneath a clear sky. On the other side of the garden, down a sharp slope, two people were playing tennis. A group of girls were sitting on the edge of the court observing the proceedings. On the patio, Dob was talking to someone to whom I went and stood next. After the introductions, he dashed off and joined a group of people at a barbecue.

Within a few minutes, I realised that he had introduced me to The Most Boring Person On Earth. The Most Boring Person On Earth had a monotone voice connected to a brain unable to comprehend that its owner was not quite as exciting and significant as its owner seemed to believe. For about an hour he peeled off a series of names associated with the Australian film industry – people of whom I had not heard – with whom he had worked on 'sets'. It was explained to me that, on any film shoot involving action, a nurse is required in case an accident transpires. He was the man. Such and such had told him this; such and such had told him that; this and that on such and such a film – none of which I had heard – had gone wrong. Believe me, it was all so important. Never had anything attained such significance. And everybody had confided in him. He had been out on such and such's boat. He had mingled. He was no ordinary nurse. Do you understand? Just because the party was full of doctors, he was not going to feel inferior. His life was more exciting than any doctor's. I can tell you.

I spent the evening enjoying the balminess of the night. When Dob decided that he wanted to go, he offered me a lift.

As he tried to leave, the girl having the party – she was English and about to return to the United Kingdom – grabbed him and said, "Please don't leave. What a great body. Hasn't this guy got such a great body?"

Quite a few of the people watching this were speechless. Dob was confused and embarrassed. He did not know whether to treat her enthusing seriously or not. It was a difficult situation for him because the girl's fiancé was standing next to him. The couple were catching a plane the following day. Dob was a picture of perturbed bemusement, as his "great body" was grabbed and pulled by a woman hoping to have the compliment returned.

In the car Dob said how embarrassed he was by the English girl's audacity.

"Her fiancé was standing there!" he said. "What a tin situation!"

Because he was naturally mischievous, people believed that he was impressed by rash acts of temerity. Such acts were often pretentious, usually ridiculous, always immature and never successful, for they often came from people who were not normally audacious. This woman had turned their parting into a melodrama by grabbing him and saying, "Don't go. I love this guy. Such a nice body." She had flung her head back and was expecting some equally melodramatic retort. Dob had just stood before her, smiling, pretending to be amused, overcome by astonishment. He was paralysed, unable to comprehend that his unconscious sensationalism had inspired this absurd reaction in someone keen to acquire his gift for drama. It was a miserable flop.

Back at Brian's place, another "tin situation" arose. His bleeper had gone off so he had to use the telephone. It was about midnight. Standing in the kitchen, he discovered that one of the patients he was attending wanted to check out. For about half an hour he attempted to persuade the patient to stay.

"Please Mister Gilbert," he said, "it's best for all if you stay tonight and do what Nurse Morgan said. We can discuss the situation in the morning."

As he spoke, he raised his eyebrows at me, annoyed that this idiot of a patient had the stupidity to want to go home, now, at midnight. Dob was in no mood to accept the responsibility associated with acquiescing with Mr Gilbert's wishes.

"That's right, Mister Gilbert," he said, "we can talk about it tomorrow. It's best if you just go to bed."

I wondered what Mr Gilbert would have thought had he had the opportunity to see his doctor now. He would have been greeted with the sight of a man wearing nothing but a pair of jocks and an unbuttoned shirt, raising his eyebrows in annoyance at the childishness of his patient's pathetic ways. This man was his doctor.

After he persuaded Mr Gilbert to stay, Dob asked the patient to hand the telephone over to the nurse. The tone of Dob's voice then changed considerably from one of polite condescension to something laid-back and perfunctory. The words "give him" were used in relation to an instruction to the nurse regarding a dose that Dob wanted administered to the patient.

Dob put the phone down and said: "What a tin situation!"

This man, fascinated by other people's existences, was a psychiatrist. Dob had about as much genuine interest in people as I did in crashing headlong into a brick wall at three hundred miles an hour.

* * * * * * * * * *

My younger brother dropped into Brian's place; he and Brian began discussing Aborigines. Thursday was apparently the day that everyone in Narrogin – the town where my brother lives in – "locks their doors" since this was the day that the Department of Social Security issued their cheques. As my brother spoke, he wandered around smoking a cigarette, an expression of moral outrage on his face. He told a story about a theft from a local bottle shop that had generated a siege mentality in the town on Thursdays. Aborigines would appear in hot conditions wearing overcoats, transparently advertising their thieving intentions. My brother's antagonism towards these people was as noble as it was naive. He saw the behaviour of these people purely in the unquestionable light of his own cultural heritage. He was oblivious and unconcerned about any contribution these people may have had to human thought. It was irrelevant to him that a sophisticated civilisation, built up over fifty thousand years, had existed and that it had been destroyed by people like us. If only these people could learn to be like us! Could learn to live within four walls in a street running parallel to other streets in a house surrounded by thousands of other houses. What was wrong with them? Didn't these damn fools realise the exquisite virtues of suburbia?

Brian listened to my brother with an expression of smug righteousness on his face. My uncle – unconscious of his ridiculous penchant for moral superiority - produced an expression of grave acknowledgement when my brother, revelling in his role of moral arbiter, claimed that those overcoat-wearing Aborigines were "the real boongs", and that there was "nothing wrong with the full bloods", who bore a savage distaste "for dem brown boys". Brian, despite his inexperience in such matters, wholeheartedly agreed with this absurd generalisation. He nodded his head eruditely, an acknowledged expert on a subject about which he knew nothing.

Mark then illustrated his perception of affairs by describing an incident involving a full-blooded Aboriginal at a cricket match. Mark's dog had run on to the cricket field - a black collie - Mark had yelled out: "Come here, you black bastard!" The full-blooded Aboriginal, who was batting at the time, spun around and good-naturedly yelled out: "Don't call me a black bastard, white boy," causing laughter to erupt around the ground.

"Even the full-bloods", Mark enthused, "don't like the half-castes."

The much maligned half-castes then received further chastisement from Brian.

"Yep," Brian said, "it's not the full-bloods."

It appeared as though the half-caste Aboriginal were unjustifiably at the root of all evil. It was bizarre how both Brian and Mark - two extremely kind-hearted individuals - appeased their consciences by ridiculously showering the full-blooded Aboriginal with good, a positive prejudice equally as absurd as the other extreme. Brian showed his gratitude towards full-blooded Aboriginals (he had probably never met one in his life) by explaining that Greg had told him the Aborigines on the station where Greg had worked were "brilliant when sober." It appeared as though sobriety and full-bloodedness were the keys to all things magnificent, a view to which I was unable to contribute.

* * * * * * * * * *

Jeremy and I went to see an Aborigine band. The band were nationally well known and had played in the United Kingdom. Standing out on the street, Jeremy and I giggled at the endearing way a smooth-talking Aboriginal attempted to convince the bouncers that he was "the brother of the lead singer of the band". He was staggered when he was refused entry. He shook his head, outraged, bewildered that the indifferent-looking bouncers were oblivious of with whom they were dealing. When he stopped shaking his head, his face became filled with optimism. A new idea had entered his drunken brain. He poked a bouncer in the chest and explained that he had a right to be given entry "because I am black".

"Are you trying to tell me", the Aboriginal said, "that you white boys are gonna understand what's gonna be goin' down in there? No way! That band is gonna need people like me in there. Who the fuck else is gonna understand? You lot? Jeeesuzzz!"

This comment had no effect on the bouncers. They stared with bored dispassion at the Aboriginal who then tried to buy his way in by offering a sum less than the face value of the tickets. The money was offered with an air of arrogant surprise, as if it was incredible that "the brother of the band" had to stoop as low as this just to gain entry to an event which was effectively a family affair. The Aboriginal was beside himself with disbelief that the bouncers had not been notified of his impending arrival. It was clear that there would be repercussions.

Unsurprisingly, the bouncers were unmoved by these vicious threats. Their faces showed not a glimmer of response. The cute mendacity of the Aboriginal caused not a flicker of amusement to fall across their expressionless faces. Jeremy's was ablaze with warm appreciation. He had a healthy respect for harmless deceit. This Aboriginal was a master at it. He had tried sympathy, arrogance, self-importance, threats, logic, sentiment; he had even suggested that "something very, very good" would happen to these bouncers if they let him in. Even this one caused a subtle hint of amusement to ruffle the stony faces of the doormen. It made Jeremy's light up with overjoyed fascination.

"Amazing character," he said.

It became apparent that this Aboriginal – a man with contacts in high places – had the capacity to give these bouncers virtually "anything you want". Jeremy and I were convinced that this Aboriginal should be given his own television programme. We were fascinated by the way he combined lies with anger in an endeavour to make his unbending interlocutors experience guilt. The ultimate comment then arrived: "When you guys finally get around to really thinking about this, you'll be unable to sleep at night. You'll be forced to say to yourselves, 'There was a night when we stopped a man of true appreciation from coming into contact with his soul. Only a soulless person could do this. I shall wallow forever in the sewers of hell.'"

The loquacious desperation of this individual had the charm of audacious sincerity. It was a pity that he was refused entry. It would have been exceptional entertainment to have seen him giving full vent to his personality inside. But no such luck was to arrive. The deceitful churlishness of this innocently mendacious man was fired by an essentially profound emotion. It was only after I had seen the band and experienced the night that I came to realise this.

He looked a strangely engaging figure as he staggered off into the darkness. He was a charming thief - no doubt about it - and he was a full-blood as well. He must have been quite disgusted that the favour owed to him by white civilisation was not being honoured.

* * * * * * * * * *

The band expressed the sacred myths through a combination of rock and traditional Aboriginal sounds and dance. It was a unique visual and auditory experience. The dances represented various indigenous forms of Australian wildlife. Their metaphysical allusions to the movements of animals were superbly creative; these movements, carefully observed over thousands of years, were performed to reflect various aspects of the human predicament. I realised, whilst watching this, that Aboriginals had devoted a considerably high proportion of their time to producing, over the millennia, a plethora of these wonderful abstract representations of the human condition. I knew that I had to discover more about this; this feeling of having my curiosity aroused, of realising the existence of a fascinating world yet to be discovered, was exciting.

In one of the songs, the dances displayed wallabies preparing the sacred ground. A wallaby is a delicate, gentle and sensitive creature, whose sentient intricacies are reflective of a profound and emotionally stimulating condition. It was the sort of emotional awareness not likely to be recognised as virtuous by a society overrun by suburban blandness and ecstatic materialism. And it was something of which your average, thieving, drunken, full-blood Aboriginal could be proud.

The beginning of the entertainment was signalled by clouds of white smoke; on to the stage came two Aboriginal dancers who moved to the sounds of a didgeridoo. The didgeridoo players were sitting on a platform raised above the stage; cords emerged from the ends of their instruments. The amplification of the primeval rhythms of this instrument were associated with an electronic accompaniment of the sounds of the bush. The dancers moved with the paranoiac vigilance of creatures concerned about the presence of predators; their eyes gave out the wariness of beings torn between fear and curiosity. Sometimes the fear would subside, the movements more confident, and they would shake their shoulders and scamper hurriedly in an unself-conscious release; then they would revert back to fearful alertness, the movements more stilted, each sharp movement associated with the cracking together of two hollow-sounding sticks. Both dancers carried one in each of their hands. When they struck them together, I was puzzled as to how they managed to produce such an abundance of sound. It cracked out like gunshot into the ears of the absorbed crowd, almost made mine hurt and formed an aggressive counterpoint to the suspicious prancings of its perpetrators. Above this, and the swooshing meanderings of the didgeridoo, I could hear the chirping of insects and the subtle rustling of leaves; the stage, awash with smoke, had become a forest. Within it, one of the dancers assumed the characteristics of a wallaby; his legs became the back legs of the marsupial, his arms, extended forward and resting on the ground, became the front paws. Between hops, the wallaby would gather something in its paws, rub it together and then sprinkle it into the sacred ground. At the end of each sprinkling, the wallaby would rise to its feet and violently shake its shoulders before leaping in a free release of energy.

Each action performed by the dancers was built on either sensitive circumspection or eccentric liberation. These two opposites formed the profound extremes of the spectrum of philosophical possibilities; the Aborigines had seen their equivalents in the movements of these delicate creatures. They also equated liberation with the flight of birds, as one of the dancers displayed by floating across the stage, wafting his arms, before suddenly leaping up on to the didgeridoo players' platform and flying off it back on to terra firma. It was an action that thrilled the crowd because it was performed so unexpectedly and with such surprising athleticism. It was also accompanied by a crescendo in the music that signalled the musicians' entrance, much to the delight of the now unrestrained audience, who showed their familiarity with the music by leaping about in fits of epileptic worship. The overall unity of music, band, dancers and audience was maintained throughout the entire night and I was astounded how superbly the Aboriginal language – at least the one employed by this band – was capable of being adapted to rock music. It actually put English to shame.

* * * * * * * * * *

I watched a programme on television about an Aboriginal artist. The artist explained that certain trees – I mean individual ones – have sacred significance. One of the trees is located in the Northern Territory in Arnhem Land. It is a twisted, gnarled, figurative growth known as the Shadow of the Rainbow Serpent. The Rainbow Serpent is the living embodiment of creation. It slid across the Australian landscape imparting life to the world. In the centre of the continent is an outcrop of tall boulders, red and orange; the English referred to them as the Devil's Marbles. The Aboriginals are convinced that they are the eggs of the Rainbow Serpent. It was incredible to my rational, twentieth-century mind that creation was a metaphysical dinosaur which left a permanent shadow. The shadow is a delicate and complex being in a landscape of lush grasses, forks of lightning, stormy skies, glinting rivers; its vein-like tributaries are at the core of oscillation and response. Did you know that creation had a shadow? A visible and eternal reflection of the symmetrical workings of the world? And that it is a tree? It was a revelation to me that a civilisation existed which satisfied its members' aesthetic instincts by combining the subconsciously poetic with the scientific. This came to me when the artist said that, if the shadow loses one of its branches, great storms would be produced elsewhere. I could feel the tension in that tree. I could imagine that, if one of those branches were to break, then something somewhere else would break as well. No surprise really that this comprehension of interrelationships enabled the Aboriginals to realise the existence of the dinosaurs – of evolution – long before anyone else did.

I turned off the television and smiled at the irony that the nearest major centre to that tree is called Darwin.

* * * * * * * * * *

Ross got a shock when he heard my voice on the line. His surprise manifested itself in a laugh of wicked bliss.

"How", he chortlingly drawled, "the pharque are yar?"

The generous enthusiasm he possessed for those whom he considered to be worthwhile was a mixture of boyish worship and playful disdain. I got the impression that my call had broken the sheath of boredom. The instant he heard my voice the sword of his felicity was plucked, with relief, from the trappings of its unwanted cover.

"I gather", he accurately surmised, "that you're just here for a holiday?"

He was implying that I was too interesting an individual to want to waste my time "in a fucking hole like this". He was relieved – in a way – when I verified his theory. It would have been disillusioning for him had I begun spouting the virtues of a place he was obviously keen to deride.

"At least somebody", he said, "has got better things to do than hang around in a fucking joint like this."

"Not in the best bloody place on earth then, hey?" I asked, imitating the jingoistic feelings of the masses.

"Oh fucking paradise," he replied. "Where are you, anyway?"

I informed him of my whereabouts. He told me "to stay right there".

"I'll be along in a few minutes," he said.

"Look out", he added, "for lots of hair and a pair of sunglasses coming down that street to your right."

I waited at an intersection and glanced down the road. It was long and straight. The Romans would have been proud of the rigid adherence that existed here for their conceptualisation of the grid pattern. The streets bisected each other at perfect right angles; their equidistance created the illusion of having been measured to the inch. This street was lined with wide footpaths the concrete slabs of which did not seem to possess a single crack. The unsuspecting would feel something surreal in the sterile appearance of a thoroughfare unpopulated with anything the European mind associates with the pleasantries of everyday living. There were very few pedestrians.

There was a used car lot. There was a newsagent. There was an indoor café. There was a line of small, detached houses, separated from the footpath by a low timber fence. There were tall lamp-posts, equally spaced, holding up the black lines of overhead wires. The odd bird was perched upon them. Across the street, a small supermarket, fronted by a display of fruit and vegetables, added some badly needed colour. All the way down the road, I saw the prongs of ticket meters reflecting the sunlight in starry beams, whose coruscations, progressively fusing into one, wobbled in the sapping heat.

It was from these quivering distances that I saw a tall, thinnish man in a black T-shirt with long dark hair emerging, with his face covered with jet-black shades. The hair of this individual bounced like an elastic helmet in time with his swaggering gait; it was the smile, hidden beneath the glasses, which made me realise it was Ross. His wide mouth was set in a naughty, beaming grimace. He wore a pair of black, slip-on canvas shoes and black jeans. It appeared that his faith in the colour black was as solid as ever. Despite this continued trust in a colour whose overuse by modern society I felt was a mask for fear in the guise of fashionability, I detected immediately that he was a changed individual. Gone was the frivolous exterior. Gone were the prim little touches of clothing and hairstyle that indicated the importance he had once attached to the alluring aspects of his physical appearance. There was an earthy wholesomeness to him not previously detectable. His transformation became obvious when he said, "The social scene in this city is fucking dreadful. Everything here is dictated by image. It's pathetic."

One thing that had not changed was his domestic habits. This, he admitted, was beyond repair. His house, which consisted of four narrow rooms, was a mess. In the room, a duvet was used as a rug. Beside it, for some obscure reason that was probably beyond Ross himself, lay a coil of rope and a car jack. The kitchen, at least free of rotting food, was a forest of discarded bottles and cereal packets. The magnitude of unwashed cutlery and dishes was only matched by the plethora of dirty clothes that spread, in a trail of abandonment, from the laundry, through the kitchen and lounge-room, and into his bedroom. In the lounge-room, a painting lay flat on its face. I had to step over it, along with many other things, to reach the kitchen, where we sat down at a table strewn with magazines and newspapers.

"Too bad", I said, "you don't have a maid."

"If I did," he smiled, "she wouldn't be doing much cleaning."

On the way to his place, we chatted about Perth's social life. I told him how unique it was here to be introduced to people and be ignored immediately.

"Unless you look the right way", he said, "no one's interested in checking you out."

This mature disillusionment was further expressed in his reaction to Jennifer's comments about Perth's women. It set him off on an honest appraisal of his previous ways.

"I've used my good looks", he said, unperturbed about accusations of immodesty, "to telling effect. I know that a lot of women here – probably the majority – are not really interested in who you are."

"That", I replied, "depends on how you behave towards them."

"A good flirtation", he said, "indicates that you're interested in a bit more than just a fling."

The instant this pronouncement fell from his lips – full, red, effeminate lips – a knock was heard on the door. It was a young woman asking local residents to fill out a survey.

After he shut the door, he ran to the window and said, "Could certainly pump that."

Back in the kitchen, he informed me that he could tell the day before she was interested. She had given him the survey then. He had answered the door wearing nothing but a towel.

"She'll be back tomorrow," he said, with an air of flippant resignation, implying that she could not wait to see him again, "you can see it in their eyes."

He was absolutely certain of her intentions.

"I know I could get her into bed," he said. "It wouldn't be any great problem. But I know I've been victimised by the system. Sometimes you have to pull back and realise that they're just not that interested in you. What they're really interested in is fitting in, in parading you before their friends. It's the image. They hope you match it, and usually you don't."

"That's one problem I've never had," I replied. "On the rare occasion that a woman has been, shall we say, peculiarly disposed, it's certainly had nothing to do with my scintillating physical appearance. There's never ever been any doubt about that."

"You're lucky," he said.

I had never thought about my sexual position in that light before, but he was probably right. He then gave me a spiel about his changed views on sex and relationships. He vowed that he would not sleep with another woman again until he had known her for at least "three months". He described with great emotion his love for a girl called Amanda, who had left him after "two years of bliss". The separation had precipitated a massive future crisis, which, with the unfortunate death of his brother, who had choked in his sleep, had fired his transformation.

"I realised then", he said, "the stupid dictatorial ways of my mother. I realised then that all my life had been was an empty attempt to please her. She was forever being demanding. I had been the boy wonder. I was going to be something the world would sit up and see, just so she could experience vicarious glory. I told her to fuck off."

We moved into the lounge-room. It was dark, to keep out the heat. The familiar stereo that I had played numerous times myself lay in the corner. We sat down and Ross began talking about Dob.

"I heard", he said, "that the tosser is in the process of becoming a psychiatrist. What a fucking joke. That wanker is only interested in interviewing young girls. All those guys haven't changed. They're only interested in going to parties to get a fuck."

He sat across the other side of the room from me on a sofa. His feminine face was housed in a muted light. What sunshine crept into the room had little opportunity for reflection, as all the colours in the room were dark. In this enclosed darkness, his large green eyes had lost their elfish sparkle. The elegant curve of his eyebrows was still unblemished by any obvious advancement of his age; the cheekbones, sculptured and smooth, caught the available light that sneaked in through the gap between the window and the drawn curtain that sat above a desk smothered with books and papers. It was a stylish, turn-of-the-century desk with little compartments above the tabletop.

I faced it, lying on the sofa, and said, "Dob is an individual in the process of perpetuating an image born from an immature and empty fame."

This caused Ross to unleash an appreciative snigger.

"But", he asked, "would he be aware of it?"

"It's difficult", I replied, "to imagine Dob being aware of anything else."

Ross chuckled away happily. His amusement increased when I told him about the experience I had had with Dob at the beach. This caused Ross to say that Dob was “completely decadent”.

“What it made me realise”, I said, “is that in all these beach societies there is probably one individual who goes around talking to as many people as possible, not being particularly interested in other people’s views, feelings, et cetera, but doing it because they are conscious that they are being watched; they do this to project an image of popularity, and because they’re excited by the idea of notoriety. If Dob saw you in a café somewhere and he was with some friends, he’d stop to talk to you, even though he wouldn’t have the slightest intention of giving you the time of day when it really mattered, just so he could impress his associates with the vastness of his social network, thereby enhancing his image. It’s done, of course, to impress impressionable young women, and it really is bizarre.”

“With so many people around here”, he replied, “capable of being taken in by it, you can imagine how I feel.”

“What are you doing about it?” I asked.

He pointed to a poster on the wall showing the principles of Kaballah. The poster had a series of symmetrical circles with schematic representations of various animals indicating different states of mind. It was then that I realised how severe Ross’s denunciation of his past must have been. The poster was a reminder to himself that “forces are balanced,” and that “if you know something’s wrong, then react.” He cited the example of Jesus Christ in the Temple of David, suggesting that Christ’s destructive anger was probably much worse than indicated in the Bible.

“Be a law unto yourself,” he said, staring at me with an intensity of purpose which may have been impressive had I not known of the profound indolence of the character.

He glared at me with an eerie force of will, a force struggling to find a pertinent philosophy, one reaching out, like a drowning man, for some solid earth. He was not impressed with this turn-the-other-cheek stuff. I was feeling uncomfortable with the brutish simplicity of his current thinking.

“I get the impression”, I said, “that you think that everyone should take justice into their own hands. What about overreactions? You call someone else’s girlfriend a slut and then six blokes over two hundred feet tall kick your fucking front door down and rape your wife."

Drolly, Ross said, "You have to have perspective."

I said, "The perfect world, Ross. Anyway, I'll tell you one thing. It's important to react straight away so that the receiver relates your actions to theirs."

"Equally", he replied, "and oppositely."

The catharsis of Kaballah had further implications. Ross told me that he wanted to learn to read and write Hebrew so he could go to Israel to look at the scrolls. He said that he wanted to make a film about Jesus Christ. His goals were always unrealistic, romantic, hopelessly beyond his will and determination; only now it appeared as though they had become even more exotic. There was nothing I could say to this. Improbable aspirations are better forgotten in the instant of their discovery. I kept my embarrassment in check.

It rose again, however, when Ross expressed his philosophy on art. He described someone called Mark – I presumed he was a friend – as a "wonder". Ross was already prepared to pay ten thousand dollars for one of Mark's paintings. Mark, the Wonder Boy, was apparently not interested in having exhibitions in Perth. New York was going to be the first. "Where the money is." The Wonder Boy had pronounced: "Most people are not artists, because they don't live their art. All art is a lie, but I'm aware I'm lying. I'm trying to make people see something in the lie."

I did not have a clue what this meant.

"I've always been under the impression", I said, "that life is the lie, and that art is the truth."

"Art is the truth", Ross said, "if you've experienced it."

He went into his bedroom and returned with a folder containing numerous sheets of paper. From the folder he plucked a sheet containing a poem he had written about vanity. The poem described a scene – it was two lines long and basically incomprehensible – in which a motorbike-riding homosexual, without a helmet, began readjusting his highly-prized hair in the mirror of his machine after having gone for a ride. Ross had witnessed this incident while sitting in his favourite café. He said the gay rider had sneered at him after Ross, giggling, had caught him in the act of preening himself.

"I wrote the poem almost immediately," he said. "The mirror of Narcissus was a video of an angel, constantly adjusting his gilded locks."

On completion of this vague allusion to egocentricity, Ross unleashed a chorus of self-congratulatory laughter. I was stone-faced. I could not believe that he thought this was something which warranted a public recital.

My expression did not change when he said, "You've got to live your art."

I did not think it would be in anyone's interest to suggest that far more relevant examples of the association between personal experience and art existed. I assumed his elevation of this obvious relationship between life and abstract representation to the heights of a profound revelation was due to his desire to build his life upon the foundation of an admirable belief. At least it was a step in the right direction. This fact was confirmed to me when I described to him the appalling fascism of my father. His face showed genuine amazement as I told him about my father's theories on Hitler and Mussolini.

"Some people", he said, with a bewildered shrug, "are never going to grow up."

To his credit, this was what he was attempting to do. Although he was still unconscious of the fact that he lacked real focus, at last he had decided that it was time to build. Some day he would probably find a realistic springboard from which to leap into the depths of personal realisation, a prospect which once had not seemed within the scope of his destiny. At that stage, all his personal esteem was derived from his ability to seduce women. The fallacy of this irrelevant method of achieving personal satisfaction was now clear to him. It was part of a transformation, an upheaval, that further expressed itself when he said, "My attitude towards war has changed completely. I now realise how fucked I was in thinking that the experience wouldn't freak me out. What a pile of crap that was. The more I read about it, the more I realise how fucking stupid I was."

Ross had once suggested that leading troops into battle was his "métier naturel". He had read numerous journals on weaponry and had believed that combat would be "the ultimate experience". I assured him that it was, but not for the reasons he had previously assumed. His eyes – containing a seriousness I had not seen before – evoked the stunned speechlessness of his demeanour as I described to him the unnerving experience of taking a photograph of a corpse whose chest had a large circle in it where a shell had passed through on its way to an explosive demise.

"The finger", I said, "on the shutter release seemed to have a mind of its own. I had great difficulty in controlling it. I can assure you that I have not eaten red meat since, and I doubt if I ever will again."

Ross looked at me in a state of confused agitation. Despite all his reading, he had probably not been aware that shells strike people as well. In the movies they always seem to hit solid earth. Not true, I'm afraid.

"You, you," he stuttered, "saw that?"

"And", I replied, "quite a bit else as well."

I recommended that he should read the autobiography of a war correspondent, with whom he was familiar, called Neil Davis.

"This", I said, "will give you a rare insight into the extent a human being can go to gain experience for the sake of art. Perhaps your friend believes art is a lie because the drama of his own existence is less than the amount that he wants to infuse into his own work. I can assure you, art is no lie for certain people."

I suspected that the seeds of Ross's mind, fertilised by a newly acquired maturity, were about to give birth to a new entanglement of thought. This went through his mind: 'Am I prepared to experience the drama required to become a great poet?'

I had my doubts. But vast ambitions always appear absurd in other people.

* * * * * * * * * * *

I was in Brad's car on our way to a party. I was not too comfortable with the prospect that lay ahead. I was never a party person, but the person having this one had shown a malice towards me that on one occasion had nearly led to violence. That, of course, was years ago, but the after-effects of the now famous evening had run fairly deep.

"Do you realise", I said to Brad, "that the person having this party hates my guts?"

He glanced at me, extremely surprised. I, too, was extremely surprised; I had assumed that the malignance of our prospective host towards me was common knowledge. Brad's surprise prompted me to tell him the story of the evening that Gerard and I had almost come to blows.

That evening, ten years previously, was the university tennis club's annual bash. Gerard, the chairman, had held the affair at his parents' sumptuous property. I had gone with Ana and Dave (the left-wing agitator and now famous musician). True to form, Dave displayed his antagonism towards the shallow wealth on display by stealing as much of the barbecue meat as he possibly could. One of Gerard's friends spotted a redhead leaving the proceedings with a box load of steaks. Gerard, probably aware who the thief was, took the opportunity to confront me over the alleged disappearance of "stacks of meat." I was aggressively told that "someone saw a redhead leaving with a box of steaks." I said: 'I'm not the only redhead at this party. I've been standing here for the last hour talking to him.' I followed this up, angered, pissed off, livid, utterly annoyed by his accusing attitude – I took it as symbolic of his feelings toward me – and said, 'Why don't you find out who did it before accusing someone, you fucking arsehole! You call me a thief again – you absolute cunt – and I'll shove every steak left in this joint down your fucking throat!' Several people had managed to get between us. It was not often that I lost my temper and on that occasion he was lucky, and he knew it. I was wild. Wild at this spoilt wanker's arrogance and his righteous smugness that, in a sense, had caused the theft in the first place.

Brad looked at me and said, "For a long time, he didn't seem too interested in me either. He seemed incredibly arrogant. But when you speak to him, there's no problem."

I knew this was correct. Gerard got on with too many people to be as genuinely recalcitrant as he had seemed on that now distant night.

"I know", I said, "that there's nothing wrong with him. He's obviously a very nice bloke. He just doesn't like me. Shows excellent taste, in fact."

Brad giggled at my self-deprecation. His laugh had the air of a naughty schoolboy appreciating something innocently mischievous.

He turned his car into the grounds of a library. The party was taking place in a house across the road. The grounds of the library contained a trust property that was used for social functions and chess tournaments.

Brad stopped laughing and said, "Have you been to a party in Drabble House?"

I replied with, "Come on! Do you think they're going to let me in there?"

He giggled again.

He laughed louder when I said, "The thing that confuses Gerard is the fact that my best friend, Jeremy - a perfect gentleman - is one of his friends. He just can't understand why a perfect gentleman and a complete arsehole - that is, myself - can have such a close relationship. Stuns him completely."

Brad's face was a picture of amiable astonishment. He giggled with the boyish ebullience of a man whose social life was still dominated by somewhat adolescent perspectives. I was under no illusions about the task that faced me. I knew it would be a miracle if I found anyone at this party to whom I'd be able to relate. As Jeremy had once pronounced: "Unpopularity in Perth is probably a sign of mental health."

The party was enormous. The large back garden was swelling with chortling, happy-go-lucky, pleasure-seeking flesh. The racket of conversation created the absolutely misleading impression that something of profound significance was transpiring. I felt immediately that the chances of anything being said that could have been of any interest to a well-travelled, mature, gifted human being were extremely limited. The brief snippets of conversation which I caught as Brad and I made our way towards some acquaintances only served to confirm my pessimistic suspicions: "You were totally pissed", "He's such a bastard", "Why weren't you at Dave's party?"

When we arrived at our destination, Dob, with that grim expression he assumes when organising his future pleasure, was explaining to one of his hedonistic cohorts - the glinty-eyed, womanising Richard 'Dick' Wain - that they required "five curls". Very few people in the world could have understood what this meant. I was one privileged enough to be able to offer an accurate translation. A curl, in the vernacular that arose amongst some of those with whom I went to school, is a lexter, one who curls, sometimes also known as a lard, but more commonly referred to as a bloke or a guy. Most people did not realise that this world is full of curls. I was a member of the tiny minority who knew. It was obvious, straight away, that Dob required five of us to make up the numbers on a boat ride, consisting of the transportation of a certain group of willing young ladies around the more decent areas of the Swan River. It would be a routine exercise for the Prince of Psychiatry to round up the necessary curlment. That task would be performed with ruthless precision during the course of this evening. He would see to it. Richard did not have to trouble himself with either the logistics or the selection process. All Richard had to do was sail the boat. Everything else would just take care of itself. It was going to happen.

As Dob spoke, he put his hands on his hips and bent down to make himself heard. Richard sat on some steps at the rear of the house, listening, rolling a joint. The serious expression of determined reassurance on Dob's face suggested the future realisation of some exquisite reward. I knew, with objective certainty and with a detached feeling of uncaring disinterest, that they would have no problem in securing the necessary curl factor. There would be many willing to spend an evening under a starry sky, attempting to charm a pack of giggly, twenty-year-old girls. There were many around me at this moment attempting to do just that. Scores of them stood in small groups, clutching drinks. In one corner of the garden was a large marquee. Within it were trestles that I presumed at one stage had supported food. A string of lights was hung around the marquee, lighting up about a third of the garden. Around the perimeter of the marquee the crowd was solid; moving away from it, it thinned out. Near the fence, people were seated on chairs. A great cacophony of chattering and laughter created the illusion that a legitimate cause for euphoria existed. Above this inexplicable cause for celebration, the full moon was like a smiling face on the black conscience of the cosmos. It formed a perfect circle of white light, as though a hole had been cut into an impenetrable fabric which covered the vast source of some eternal radiance. Smaller holes in this sheet of unfathomable blackness revealed the lights of more distant worlds, some of which were now probably long gone, creating a falsity of permanence not revealed in this mystery of space and light, which conveyed to me that sense of dreamy mortality I felt was associated with youth, with irretrievability. Many such people suffering from this phenomenon adorned the rear of the house, explaining the unreal atmosphere of unwarranted excitement. Giggles, chuckles, cackles, sonorous outbursts, light-hearted attacks, naughty stories, salacious enquiries, cheeky quips, constant attempts to amuse – they were all there.

Beside me, a teenage woman accused some drunken adolescent of being "disgusting." The adolescent – he was older than he was acting – had clutched her leg. She was being satirical, feigning a sense of morality; the adolescent, considering it a sign of his flamboyant individuality, was proud of her accusations. Similar events were transpiring everywhere I could see. A sameness of facial expression – bland euphoria – characterised events, leaving me with the impression that there was not one individual in the place to whom I could speak.

Brad and I stood next to Richard who lit up the joint. When he saw me, he yelled out: "Karnubuzzz!" His sparking green eyes were as effervescent as ever. An unrestrained grin of boyish cheekiness filled his face – a face of sculptured cheekbones and woolly eyebrows upon a protuberant brow; Brad asked him what he had "been doing today?"

Richard, constantly on the verge of laughter, explained that he had gone clothes shopping with his girlfriend. While his girlfriend tried on clothes, he said he had got "an incredible hard-on" for, in the booth next to his girlfriend he was able to see, through a gap in the curtain, a sixteen-year-old girl trying on bikinis. He said, with a cheeky laugh, that the girl stayed in the booth for as long as possible, deliberately tantalising him.

I smoked the joint, pretending to be amused by this. This prompted him to continue his euphoric outpouring of an event that he presumed must have been one of the most interesting things which I had heard for years. He was sadly mistaken. Apparently, the girl was "an absolute stunner". She had "amazing skin". And her arse! It was "unbelievable".

"And", he chortled, "I was with my girlfriend. She couldn't understand why I just about raped her when she came out of the booth."

I created the pretence of merriment by faking a hollow laugh, whilst thinking: 'Oh God, is there anyone I can speak to in this dreary world?'

"Imagine", he joyously continued, "being with your girlfriend and getting an erection, because she sees some other woman naked! It was incredible. My penis was about to explode!"

Faithfulness was not one of his virtues, mainly because it requires maturity and a seriousness of purpose. These things were beyond him. Genetically they were probably there, but his environment had not provided the fertiliser to germinate their well-hidden seeds.

Out of curiosity, I asked, "How many women do you think you've slept with?"

He became serious, as though he were about to unleash some highly-impressive and profoundly relevant information.

"Definitely", he said, nodding his head with grave solemnity, as if some remarkable milestone had been achieved, "over a thousand."

"Do", I asked, "any of them stand out for any particular reason?"

"There's been a few," he replied; then, smiling, "but I haven't been able to control myself."

The sadness of his immaturity made me speechless. Brad had already made his escape. Most of us manage to dissociate pride from sexual success by the time we have reached our early twenties. Here it was considered a foundation stone for self-esteem.

Richard then told me his future plans. It was a sound idea, that, naturally, contained a sexual element. He was going to sail Japanese tourists on Dob's boat around the river. Hotel chains and travel agents had been contacted. He had connections. Despite his susceptibility to pleasure, he had a great store of energy. A lot of it was wasted on women. He assumed his prospective living would provide him with "a constant flow".

I wished him luck; then I asked him if he employed "any specific technique" when attempting to "beguile the fairer sex".

"Just walk straight up to them", he said, now blasted out of his head, "and say: 'Hey honey, I think I love you.'"

Loneliness was beginning to descend. Marijuana often did not help. It either eliminated insecurities or it enhanced them. Taking it was always a risk, particularly if you were already feeling far too different from the rest. I felt an insurmountable distance from this crowd, who mystified me with their enthusiasms and who staggered me with their capacity for inane chatter. It was unrelenting; amongst it, drunk women were receiving mendacious compliments. At the age that many of these people were, that had to be expected. What dazzled me was how some of the people I used to know here, so many years ago, could still find this interesting. What a path to pursue. I truly felt that they did not, but had no other choice.

Richard was now being engaged in conversation by someone who had remained silent during our brief interlude. Quiet mutterings were going on between them. I left them to it. Feeling the outcast, I wandered through this noisy desert of interaction, perceiving that the surface of amiable openness was a mask for the paranoia and uncommunicativeness that lurked within. This was a boisterous crowd, fearful of quietude, but unwilling to extend. I stopped near two women who immediately became suspicious of my presence. I looked away, lulling them into thinking that I was not a threat. I wanted to overhear their conversation. I had no desire to speak to them. I just wanted to listen. They ignored me and carried on.

"He's only nineteen!" one of them exclaimed. "God, I didn't know that."

"He's not as wankerish", the other replied, "as the usual nineteen-year-old."

They were both about twenty.

"He's trying to grow a beard," the first one said. "Have you seen it?"

"No," the other wailed, titillated. "What's it like?"

"Terrible," the first one replied. "But he's still cute. If he wasn't so young, I'd probably go for him."

She was not that attractive and I wondered what the bearded nineteen-year-old would have made of this. Her unconscious egotism also manifested itself in the arrogant way which she glared at her friend when displaying her concern at my unwanted presence. It was difficult to imagine how much effort would be required to engage either of these people in conversation.

I looked into the marquee. Its interior was bathed in a glaring light. The harshness of radiance had a rough edge and a toughness of luminosity that symbolised the brashness of a place that pressurised people into discarding certain aspects of their personalities. It was an environment of conservative hedonism that stripped the vital and interesting quirks of human nature down to a core of uncomplicated desires. Three hundred people were prattling on about their social lives and none of it would have involved any amusing or fascinating insights into personal existence. It was unlikely that these people were interested enough in each other to do this. This was not my problem.

The person whose problem it should have been went and stood next to me. It was Dob. Looking suitably arrogantly bored, he stared darkly at the proceedings. I wondered what had made him stand next to me. He had no interest in talking. I presumed that he was so used to people trying to impress him that he expected others to speak first. He was not looking very happy. It was ironic to see the great communicator, the fuel of human interaction, the king of blasphemous revelry, looking so withdrawn, while hundreds of his felicitous flock were bursting forth with such superficial euphoria.

It prompted me to say, with the brashness that seemed fitting in a place such as this, "What happened to that architect you were screwing?"

It did not dawn on me that he could possibly be serious about her. It appeared as though I were wrong.

"She's here," he blurted out, clutching his fist in a gesture indicating masturbation. "Can't you tell?"

I was taken aback by his bellicosity. He was obviously sick of people casting aspersions over his intentions. I stared him in the face from close range and said, "If she's left you, what do you expect? What's she supposed to do? Share your life with two million others? Wake up!"

He was speechless at my outburst of aggressive confidence. He stared harshly into the glaring light of the marquee; it was the sort of dry cynical, unnatural light under which a lot of these people deserved to be.

I left him battling with his desire to achieve an adolescent liberation; seeing no point in pandering to the damaged sensibilities of a self-indulgent egotist, I decided it was probably time to leave. This entire crowd gave me the impression of also being engaged in some futile internal battle – one they were not going to win. The noise was like an outcry of a group of conformists, frustrated that the mask for their circumspection was not adorned with the hallmarks of real belief.

Gliding my way through the chirping crowd, I heard someone say to someone else, "Why are you looking so morbid?"

I was not around long enough to hear the answer; but it should have been, "Give me one reason why I should be so happy in a joint like this?"

I was always annoyed by the way people here too readily associated morbidity with introspection. There was extreme pressure here to experience ecstasy when the cause did not exist. I found this to be a denunciation of the human spirit – that refreshing spirit of realistic pessimism which saw death as a mender of all evils, and recognised the dispassion that your insignificant presence evokes on this capacious earth. All around me, I saw people convincing themselves that their lives had real drama, that they were going to affect things; if they stopped to consider that human life in its entirety was more dramatic, was considerably more interesting, then this confrontation of souls could produce something poignant. But it was not to be.

I stood, far too introverted to blend into this mystifying gaiety. I was an alien to the idea of enthusiastic chatter, without a relevant cause. How easily some people are inspired! What would they find to talk about if something really interesting actually happened to them? Or were they already so deluded as to think that this had already occurred? I had no faith in the average person's ability to recognise drama. A lot of these people here probably thought something really dramatic was actually happening to them right now. What a nonsense!

I moved towards the top of the driveway for one last look at the garrulous throng. Down a gentle slope towards a back fence, I saw gaggles of chirping pigeons beating their metaphysical wings. They seemed to feed off the inanity of each other, each crumb of vacuous wind a further inspiration for the forceful lifting of their flighty spirits. It was miraculous to observe: denizens of ebullience without reason.

A friend of Brad's, whom I had met that evening, was suddenly standing next to me. He was astounded when I said, "What the fuck do all these people find to talk about in a place as boring as this?"

He was overcome with uncertainty. Eventually, he said, "I think I'll go and find Brad."

'Obviously', I thought, 'not a man too keen on fresh insights.'

I rang a taxi from a phone booth across the road from the party. It was a relief to escape from a place that created insecurities. I must have appeared a strange creature, because the taxi driver, a robust, thick-set, porcine-looking man in his forties, said, after we had only travelled a short distance, "Look mate, I don't want any trouble, okay?"

I was too stoned to have the faintest clue as to why I had caused him such worry. I was amazed that someone as innocent-looking as myself could cause such unwarranted agitation. He was deeply concerned. I did my utmost to convince him that I had no intention of murdering him.

Eventually, he began to believe this. Then he began to worry again, because I could not stop laughing. I suddenly thought how remarkable it would be if I had in my possession a plastic knife and had suddenly threatened to slit his throat, and then had said, "Don't worry, I only use it to lop off the heads of ants. This is the one I use on people."

The more quizzically the driver glanced at me the more I was unable to control my emotions. It was hilarious. I had never imagined anyone ever considering me capable of murder. Particularly someone twice my size.

I can tell you, that driver was exceptionally pleased to get rid of me.

* * * * * * * * * *

THREE

I saw a green valley. The hills in this valley were bare and steep. A narrow blue river meandered through the grassy floor; small islands containing pine trees sat in the river. Wisps of clouds clung to the peaks. Next to the river was a group of farmhouses with terracotta roofs. Birds swirled high in the air. The river oozed a gentle bubbling. Large boulders covered in moss protruded from the slopes of the hills. Rising above the valley were jagged, snow-covered peaks. The quickly-moving shadows from clouds dashed silently across the land. The walls of the farmhouses were white, their orange shutters tightly closed. I wandered along the river. It was beautiful but safe.

Beyond the boulder-ridden slopes lurked the eerie forest. I crossed over a ledge and entered the dark-light world of leaves and shadow. Sometimes an aircraft would boom overhead. The ground was covered in fresh pine cones. They were like mahogany antiques, strewn by the opulent hand of nature across the carpet of the floor. Each one held an alluring promise of something new, spectacular, memorable and dangerous. I trod delicately between them; one moment was worry, the next exhilarated expectation. My stomach was tight, but I was too fearful of disappointment to linger. The thought of having the ultimate experience drove me on.

Deeper into the grove of prehistoric forms I moved. Sometimes the prongs of sunlight would hit the musky-odoured floor and glint on something potentially lethal and make my twisted stomach run with electric spiders. Then the metal remnants of the gleaming object would be plucked by my unconcerned hands and droplets of dried soil would fall in a slow descent of time past, of an event now gone. These objects were always circular. A round knob always protruded from the top of them. The inability of these now detonated mines to cause death made them lifeless. I was left with the futile feeling of clutching a deceased inanimate object. No terror or noise or violent disruption could now emerge from it. It was safe, and it was disappointing. Its inactivity was predictable.

Many of these discarded objects littered the forest floor. They now held no terrors. Mystery had left them. Often they protruded through the coverage of fallen needles at obtuse angles. Carelessly, I kicked them with the surety of the flamboyantly detached. I saw the rapid shifting of dead pines as my boots unearthed the bottom sides of these mines, causing helmeted insects with trillions of legs and feelers to scurry in panicked disarray. A great scene of carnage had probably been anticipated here; the signs of this anticipation lured me on.

In a gap in the forest, where sunlight transformed the light-brown sheaves of wallowing grass into golden touches of tranquillity, a twisted corpse of metal and rubber lay in a frozen gasp of agonised death. One of the shattered eyes of this creature hung from its socket, held in check by cords whose rubber insulation was torn by the screams of shrapnel. Above this wrecked beast, snow-capped mountains rose with solemn and imperious indifference, silent in the satisfaction of their personal beauty, unembittered by ambitions, serene in their relative longevity which took them above the power struggles that had caused this vehicle to have its existence terminated in such a vituperative way.

I touched the red surface of this broken object and heard the sound of wind through the leaves golden by light rustling as if a fall of water was descending through the shaking boughs. The lighter sides of the leaves were turned as one, waving, as the trees rocked in a gentle submission to the breeze. The destruction of the car had the uselessness that time infuses into everything it allows to occur. The fact that this object now no longer existed, as it should have, meant nothing other than that, in a brief, pointless flash, a cataclysmic contingency had violated the quiet.

Beside the unburied car was a fawn-coloured tank. It was empty apart from a thigh bone that jutted out from the open top. A fishing net with clumps of green bushes was draped over it. I was fascinated by its complexities. Small protrusions stuck out from its armour. I inspected every part of it. It was not as I had expected. It had the mystery of an alien space vehicle. It was hot inside, like a furnace. The interior glowed like molten steel. There was very little room to manoeuvre. I brushed past the bone and the wind howled. It was a lazy, constant, nostalgic cry; it sounded like a dreamy, unfulfilled longing. It made the long grass swish into the sides of the tank which now was an historical object of curiosity rather than one of death. But it had been witness to something extraordinary. The sudden crack-boom of a jet-fighter was testimony to this. Those fighters disappeared between the mountains leaving behind floating paths of cream.

It was the direction I wandered in. Steep mountains rose on both sides. The track was chalk-white and covered in straw. Small orange trees lined the path. Fallen, overripe fruit was rotting in the lush green of the grass. Gleaming droplets of water appeared like diamonds in the drenched undergrowth beneath the trees. There was an air of things having been left. A discarded, wooden, horse-drawn cart, filled with insect-covered apples, sat at the start of a track that led up to a farmhouse ruined by the apocalypse. The white walls of the house displayed the black scars of departed fire. The dead paneless windows looked like black holes. The façade of the house formed an eerie face. The black holes were eyes that could not be penetrated; beneath their lids the black rings of inflammation suggested that a fiery and rapid demise had been precipitated by a weird and nefarious intent. The screams of this catastrophe were frozen by the jagged teeth – splintered timbers – of the front door. A dark bird glided over the shattered roof. The frames of the roof were still intact. Flocks of vultures balanced on the exposed rafters. A twisted metal lintel protruded out of one of the windows. A rustic dream had been destroyed.

Further along the road, the abundance of white flowers made a mockery of this garden of death. The bony shadows of leafless trees suggested that these fields had recently been littered with the skeletons of the victims of this climatic culmination of centuries of mutual displeasure. They sat still, like sinewy webs, on the green sheet of an unmoved earth. Small hills rose, like the undulations of trepidation, away from both sides of the path. It was a path leading into a world of excitement and ignorance, a path the diseased mind of risqué curiosity pursued without the harness of common sense. I was gone, irrevocably, down this irresistible track. A tense fortitude of expectation had its resolution in the knots of concern in my empty stomach. An electric generator had been placed in there.

More wrecked farmhouses appeared. The exposed brickwork of the stripped walls suggested a forced experience of rapid ageing. One of the white walls was smeared with blood. Generously dispersed droplets of it mingled with unintelligible graffiti. Destroyed houses sat in green fields. The black marks of flames licked their walls.

Most of them were roofless – singed shells – baked skeletons of a lost pastoral delight. A stillness had descended. Nothing moved except a raven that circled high before some smoky clouds which rolled through a line of trees sitting on a ridge on some distant hills. It was a strange atmosphere of unsatisfied fascination and intense foreboding, of euphoria and worry, of blue skies awash with the dark-moistured clouds of a livid and dreaded awakening.

All the way down the road, small, burnt-out villages sat beside the path. One smashed dream after another populated this route of white, blown-out boxes, this tumultuous thoroughfare of murdered hopes and unfulfilled passions. A sense of irrecovery was mixed with the need for a new beginning. By moving down this track, the possibility of existing in any previous state was becoming increasingly remote. The risk existed that all previous conditions may have been better. A cord of white-hot paranoia entangled itself around my central nervous system at the realisation of this heinous contingency. The belief that an excess of experience could ruin the most pleasing state achievable, the truly powerful discovery of this, was, I realised, part of the experience itself. I was going to go on. My greed for the perfect condition was unlimited. It had no basis in conditioned expectations. It lived a life of its own.

No roofs existed on the screaming houses. A sudden burst of rain soaked their tender ribs. Patches of luminosity formed weak, pitiful smiles on the sides exposed to the watery light. Broken beams and chunks of plaster and brick filled the grimacing doorways. The distances between the farmhouses were becoming less. The signs of conflict were becoming more extreme. I was stopped in my wide-eyed wonderment by the sight of a wailing skull, perched in a mound of mud. Next to it was a corpse, half buried, its face in its hands, in a pool of muddy water, a quagmire laden with twisted barbed wire and decimated bricks. I was overawed by the world responsible for this. What knowledge could be found in these enflamed extremes?

This question drew me on down a road that curled over a hill and fell into a valley. Purple hills filled the background. Green fields with leafless trees lay before me; the thin ribbon of a glassy river dissected the earth. The river was lined with crosses, each one reflected in the quiet water. Mauve-coloured clouds dotted the sky above the distant hills. The flaming edge of the heavens formed a ring of searing passion around the mystery of an immense stillness. A cloudburst lowered its tentacles through the orange haze. A crying woman in black was draped over a cross. One of her hands was on top of her grieving head. A sound I had never heard before began emerging from her mouth. It was high-pitched, unearthly, something new in the auditory spectrum. With refinement it would be music, the collective wail of the amassed despair of the ages. It shocked me.

Down the road came scores of other women. A mixture of different coloured scarves were wrapped around their heads; they were all carrying their possessions. One of them, with a black veil over her head, was singing: "My son, where have they left your soul?"

Her suppressed cry was like a high-pitched drill. Her flailing arms could not be controlled. Aircraft swooped overhead. A defiant scream was made to these unhearing birds. Several women tried to stop the singing woman from wrenching a brick from a farmhouse and hurling it at the darting jets. The free expression of mourning was a plethora of masochistically futile acts. Nothing stopped its expression – dignity, embarrassment, common sense, all burnt by the fury of an anger fuelled by the great silent absurdity of the abyss.

Into the silence echoed the heartbeats of far-away explosions. They were like thunder – thunder on a clear day with twittering birds. They reverberated over the earth like the sound of an iron door being rapidly closed in a dungeon. Machine-guns sounded like someone hammering, very quickly, on a sheet of metal. The booms of artillery were like the smash of a vast mallet on a hanging, steel bowl. The sounds grew progressively louder. I was drawn to them, thoughtlessly; I sucked in the portentous air when I saw orange-pink tracers charging through the sky. It was surreal to witness these pencils of light-death destroying the roof of a farmhouse in the serenity of a beautiful valley. A cloud of white smoke materialised where the roof used to be. It was a mushroom that filtered away. The sudden distant puffs of white clouds also appeared on the nearby hills, dark green ones covered in leafy green trees. Artillery rounds were plummeting into the pines.

Trapped soldiers under the boughs were waiting with sweat in their mouths for the final moment. A sniper's bullet sang like a jet-propelled wasp. A soldier dashed out of a farmhouse and hurled a grenade. He made it back inside as bullets ripped dark holes into the white of the fragile walls. I rushed inside to see a man with an enormous black beard and piercing blue eyes pouring machine-gun fire out a narrow slit, one carved into the wall. I watched, absorbed, as the bullet holder draped over the barrel jumped like a maniac rushing across a floor of fire. I peered through the slit and saw a street of broken buildings smouldering like withered candles. A thick cloud of black vapour rose up over the street, its orange heart ablaze with fire. Tiny figures darted hither and thither. Sometimes one of them would jolt and fall and twist. Mortar rounds caused the black metal of burnt-out cars and buses to shake like quivering organisms in the last throes of a wretched demise. Broken glass lay everywhere. The air was thick with dust. The drone of tanks hummed under the orchestra of fire.

Down another street I saw the sharp, iridescent-orange flash of a turret pouring death into the remnants of an opera house. It was bizarre to see the Corinthian pillars and the classical friezes of this beauty standing firm against the tirade of searing metal that caused soldiers, like bewildered ants, to scramble over boulder-like chunks of smashed concrete, falling over each other to disappear into smoky black holes in the walls of bullet-riddled buildings. I saw a tank fire an orange flash – then the grey-green murk of the exploding cloud, terracotta tiles flung, willy-nilly, by an eccentric, operating the machinery at a clay-pigeon shoot. I was fascinated. I was in a world you cannot see. It was the dream of a destructive fantasy. It was pure, unrestricted, terrorised, unpretentious, wild, seething with incident, unpredictable, surreal, the wide canvas of the unconscious being made available to empirical observation. And I was alive within it.

I dived into a crevice in the wall of a building and dragged myself into its dust-ridden interior. A group of young soldiers was hiding behind the fallen limb of a concrete lintel, staring down a battle-scarred street.

One of them assumed that I was a journalist and leaped to his feet. He was a macho youth. He wore a singlet and had a red scarf tied around his head. No flak-jacket was good enough for him. He began firing his weapon at nothing, a useless act of bravado from an adolescent living out a dream evolved from boredom. It was a dream he would have to keep living, one that would become witheringly tiresome.

I found myself in a cemetery. I hit the ground as I heard the sound of an incoming mortar. Sounds of pain, sounds like whining lathes, sounds like high-velocity dentists' drills, sounds like the wails of a thousand discordant birds rang out over this triumph of irrational curiosity, as the relatives of the dead writhed on the blood-soaked ground. I saw a photographer dive across the grass and focus on the flailing despair of a mutilated woman. Others flocked around her, vulnerable in their uselessness. I marvelled at the disparity between the dispassion and curiosity of the observer and the despair of the affected. Let no hypocrite tell me that he has never been an observer. To look is to learn, is to rise from the prosaic, is to invent. Some people acknowledge this.

At one end of the cemetery was the arch of a Roman aqueduct. An upheaval of unparalleled dimensions was transpiring on the other side of it. I strolled through it into a wonderland of surreal brutality. Two low-flying aircraft swooped past me. They were involved in a dog-fight. The hatred on the face of the pursuing pilot astounded me with the intensity of its outraged vehemence. It was so vicious that it defeated fear. Tanks ploughed into each other. Wild men with machine-guns were charging through oil fires on the raging streets. The bayonet of a rifle was dug into the heart of a wounded man. Steel and rubber and flesh clashed with each other in a turmoil of deathly chaos. Strange metallic objects, now laced with spiteful animation, sort out victims with reptilian bliss. Individual battles were occurring everywhere. The severed head of a soldier was flung into the air by the flash of a violent eruption. The crack of bullets piercing holes in the bitumen was like the faint patter of rain beneath the thunder of falling shells. Right before me, two bizarre mechanised objects prepared to eat each other alive.

Protruding from their engines were steel battering-rams shaped like the stems of vases. On the bases of these stems were sharp prongs piercing the remains of dismembered soldiers. They charged towards each other in a gluttony of sadism. A huge din of clashing steel rose over the screams of a thousand deaths.

Around a corner, piles of blood-smeared civilians were gazing with overcome fixation at the absurdity of this enduring mess. Corpses in indiscriminate clumps littered the street. A group of axe-wielding maniacs in the guise of soldiers were mutilating the bodies of their enemy's civilian dead. Boots were being crashed into the open-eyed heads of the deceased innocent. They caught me watching. I was pushed up against a wall by a greasy-faced arsehole, screaming some unintelligible vitriol. Someone stuck a bayonet against my throat. A fist was rammed into my stomach. A knee went into my lower-abdomen region. The butt of a rifle came down over my head. I looked up into the dazed world to see pillars of black smoke with orange hearts rising over the bayonet that I saw speeding down towards my chest and, just as it was about to splinter me to pieces, I woke up in a wild-eyed frenzy to find that I was home in bed, beneath a starry, still, unblemished sky, listening to the ticking of the clock.

It ticked and it ticked and it ticked. It ticked in this world of perverted love.

* * * * * * * * * *

The beach was embraced by the unceasing rumble of surf. I lay watching the white water moving towards the shore. People walked within it. The agitated movement of the breaking sea had the sense of a film speeded up. At ground level the ocean seemed to be nothing more than a thin strip separating the sand from the sky, an unblemished border between the ivory and the blue roof, ribbed with wispy vapours, whose serene magnificence was crowned by a medallion of blazing light.

Lying on my back, and feeling deeply contented to be where I was, I glanced up at the slowly moving clouds that resembled white feathers floating across the sky. Between them, a line of birds fluttered over the sea. A distant yacht looked like a triangle of ivory against the immaculate blue porcelain of water and air; a profound stillness in the heavens was balanced by the cacophony of rolling surf. I shut my eyes and listened to this din that did not grate, this sound which sang; then I looked down the beach at the semi-naked congregation that, concentrated in the distance, became a wall of colour and flesh, an unhurried herd of dumb beasts, flocking before the unpredictable plain of an incomprehensible immensity.

Sometimes a member of the herd would wade into the water; when a wave washed past it, it would leap, as if tickled by the naughty sea. Various members of the herd lay in pairs, pruning each other. One man was having oil rubbed into his back by a beautiful girl. Another couple were intertwined around each other, kissing. Another pair were staring into each other's eyes and stroking each other's lightly tanned skins. The woman of this couple was lying on her back, her lips slightly ajar in a sensuous submission to the overwhelming salaciousness of her extreme kissability. She appeared innocent to the gravity of her concupiscent appeal.

Suddenly a blonde woman rose up from her towel and flicked back her wet hair with a look of Nordic, sensual strength. She formed an interesting comparison with an old, overweight, misshapen woman poured into a one-piece bathing costume, who waddled past her, and set up a beach umbrella, one of several, like exotic mushrooms, that rose across the beach, protecting the colony of resting insects, whose noises were drowned out by the constant cry of the sea.

It was a scene of relaxed sociability. Groups of schoolchildren formed tight gatherings with their towels. People strolled slowly in small groups along the shore. Couples wandered, hand in hand. Others stood in groups, chatting. A small boy dragged a surfboard, almost as large as himself, past a couple who were playing with their young child on the edge of a sea, smooth, untrammelled, and restful, unafflicted, tranquil and mighty in the sedate magnitude of its mysterious sleep. Its benign presence cast a spell of contented peace over the teeming flocks, that gathered in the afternoon rays, as though the desire of this overfed herd of creatures for water and light were a necessary ingredient for their continued existence.

Certain intriguing oddities existed within the herd. An unconcerned, hirsute man, with an enormous stomach that spilled out over his pants (there was something beautifully endearing in his total disregard for his appearance in a place where physical appearance was so important), strolled past me, his face covered in black fur, a gold chain glinting around his neck. I presumed that he was the chef in a Greek restaurant. Between the forest of black hair on his torso, I could see the creamy surface of his bloated anatomy. He wore a Panama hat and slip-on shoes and was oblivious – even proud – of his individuality; all the beautiful bodies on earth seemed not to have had the remotest effect on his sense of personal value.

He lay down near a highly-manicured woman who displayed the accoutrements of wealth. Her body seemed to be a display stand for jewellery. Her hair was peroxide; sunglasses sat on top of it. She carefully rubbed a selection of exotic oils into her skin. She worked with a precise delicacy that gave her actions something of the significance of a biological necessity. There was something too planned, too compromising, too affected in the distastefully cultivated and spoilt nature of her appearance. I felt that she was shackled to advertising notions of beauty.

Over the top of her a biplane rolled around in the sky, dragging behind it a pennant informing the herd of the existence of certain drinks. Its easygoing drone was in keeping with the unflustered docility of the grazing flocks, who walked and swam and waddled as one, in the unquestioning idleness of their conforming ways.

Three female members of the languid flock lay before me. They were young and beautiful and formed an unthinking unison of conforming identity. At random intervals, they all unconsciously performed exactly the same actions. Each one would rise up on her elbows and, with a look of vague curiosity, would look around before falling back down, rolling over and then closing her eyes, oblivious that the other two had unwittingly done precisely the same thing only moments before. This almost perfect reproduction of actions, done unconsciously, suggested to me something of the instinctual basis of conformity – the herd mentality and something of the delusion that is individuality.

I got up and walked past them, observing other members of the herd performing similar actions. This standardisation of behaviour seemed to me to result from a short-lived tension between sensual fulfilment and curiosity, a clash quickly snuffed out by visions of predictability. Through it I wandered. I was amused to see a couple lying next to each other in symmetrical harmony. Both were lying on their backs with their right legs raised to form triangles; both wore sunglasses and their faces were raised to the sky. Their hair was blond and they looked as though they were posing for some advertisement displaying a lotion capable of turning snow into an immaculate shade of chocolate brown. I walked near them and noticed that their bags were laced with the standard features of well-equipped beach-going: moisturisers, walkmans, hats, caps and radios. It appeared as though they were planning to move into that little section of beach; certainly their unflinching immobility suggested the permanence of classical forms, a suggestion in keeping with their beautifully sculptured and statuesque appearances. They looked as though they had been carved out of the very sands themselves and, as I went past them, I had to stifle a laugh, for they were so unconscious of their extreme conformity and oblivious of their mindless alignment that they resembled a caricature, a sardonic representation out of the grasp of their limited consideration.

And they were normal.

Strolling along the hard, wet sand between the beach and the sea, I saw surfers darting across the faces of waves, and children allowing themselves to be dragged about by the foaming water. A lot of giggling accompanied the children as they lay on their backs and allowed their bodies to be swirled about by the unrelenting action of the waves. Their behaviour brought back memories of childhood, of days when one of the great considerations was whether the surf was up. As kids we used to charge to the front of a bus that came over a hill affording a view of the sea. That first glimpse of the ocean, in which we could see whether a significant swell existed or not, could lead to groans of disappointment or wails of delight. Each day's happiness was inextricably linked to the sea, to the great beckoning mat laid by an amoral aestheticism as a welcoming to distant lands, as a provider of exhilaration and a tormentor of dreams. It offered experiences outside the realm of everyday life and this was what made it so vital, so beautiful and so fantastic.

Beside it the languorous herd wandered and lay. In a little fortress – a circle of built-up sand – a small boy, armed with a plastic spade, splashed in his clearly-defined territory. Along the beach, the surreal reflections of people quivered in the wet sand, giving the world – this interminable expanse of liquid and vapour – a sense of symmetry, whose pivot, in the vastness of space, occurred at the shore. White water rushed over it. Globules of foam slid with easy grace. Waves curled from sapphire-blue to snow-white. Seagulls darted and rose. The spray from surf shot upwards and dissipated, like misty flames, into the air. Two men armed with bats smashed a ball at each other near the shore. Another man, so somnolent in his laid-back repose, looked like a corpse. Pretty women were spread out on their backs, indifferent to the prospect of a lascivious gaze. This was a place where impatience and enterprise had been snuffed out by an easily-acquired peace.

As I walked along, I watched, in the distance, the spray from surf crashing into a headland, flailing its wispy tentacles into the air. Dramatic outcrops of sculptured rock rose from the sand like classical beings, frozen in moments of triumph, upon a frieze on the white fresco of the shore. Large boulders, surrounded by clear puddles of water, emerged from the hard wet sand beside the sea. The puddles were covered in contours of light. These contours resembled the lines on a geological survey map. I put my foot into one of the these puddles and saw the lines quivering frenetically; charging about, they destroyed the clarity, causing rippling shadows to clash beneath them on the smooth sand of the shore.

When the shadows came to a halt, restoring the contours to their original positions, I sat down in one of these warm puddles and observed the forest of pebbles which existed in the valleys between the rocks. I was astonished by the variety of colour that existed within the overriding grey: orange, ebony, snow-white, grey with streaks of cream, green, burgundy, lemon, ochre – a complexity of hues that made the forest appear, falsely, to be a spectacular of autumnal demise. Each pebble, defined by its colour, shape and size, was a single event in the plethora of contingencies. Some of the events were remarkable, dramatic, alluring, piercing the staid face of things with their surprising beauty; but that was rare. In reality, this forest was a granite equivalent of the herd, a rocky predictability, unhampered by red intimacy and the cool blues of sapphire nights, a uniform phenomenon of conforming grey.

Disillusioned with it, I rose from the puddle and moved down to the headland where the boulders and pebbles rose up an incline to form the face of a cliff. The top of the cliff was covered in a layer of grass, like a cake covered in a passionfruit topping. At the base of the cliff was a cave whose opening was split by a central pillar of rock, creating the impression of an amphitheatre. Before the stage, rocks, like protruding fish scales with curved backs, became the seats of the theatre. Dark-green moss, like silk velvet, filled the stalls, as though upholstered on to the seats by the hand of a theatrical nature. Absorbed children scrambled over these seats in fits of imaginative joy. Tentatively, they negotiated the dark-grey granite of the slippery floor. These children, bent on discovery, were drawn to the stage where the promise of some fantastic revelation lured them on. Fascinated, I decided to follow; careful not to slip in the displaced bodies of water that lay in the depressions of the undulated floor, I moved inside the cave and was met by the sight of a bizarre rock formation – a wicked and dangerous beast with a vast and cynical intelligence. The head of this creature was wedge-shaped. Small, round holes formed the glaring and rabid eyes. A line of protruding rock ran from the snout, curving upward across the face to form the mouth. Yellow rocks within the snarling protrusion created the impression of jagged teeth. Three brains, also wedge-shaped, emerged from the head. They were connected to the skull by strong, thin veins of rock that fanned out towards the ceiling, eventually becoming porous entities with holes and indentations, like teeming convolutions bursting from the mind. Above the brains, through a hole in the ceiling, I saw a seagull disappearing over the cliff against a sky of cobalt blue. An arm of light reached in through the hole and touched a patch of rock just where the gnarled floor rose up to become the flanks of this awesome beast. Small protrusions of limestone – wings – emerged from the sides of this wild-eyed creature whose impending flight – swathed in unrestraint – seemed driven by some calculating and nefarious intent.

Fascinated by its existence, I began to run my fingers over its surface. My eccentric observations caused people to wonder. 'What is he looking at?' I could hear them think. They crowded behind me, bewildered.

Ignoring them, I stepped back and noticed that the body, at its rear, came to a sharp prong, a sting of attack and defence, which prompted me to think that I was in the presence of a reptilian insect, a being of unparalleled physical and mental ingenuity, a being of liberated enmity, free from religion and moral codes, that could fly, that could solve profound problems of celestial mechanics, that was possessed of an unrivalled venom. To me it was the final point of evolution and its future existence was entirely possible.

I was then struck by the force of a great revelation when I realised that Picasso and Dali must have been influenced by the sight of magnificent rock formations such as this. The complexity of these natural sculptures perpetuated the idea in my mind that anything could be used to represent anything else. This creature, with its vile and intriguing cunning, and its guiltless viciousness, therefore became the symbol of a dictatorship.

Overawed by its existence, I began taking photographs of it. This caused more people to stop. I felt invisible waves of confused curiosity flowing towards me. They knew that I was looking at something significant, but what?

I spun around and with a casual wave of the hand, and indicating the ferocity before us, I said, "Picasso."

To my surprise, a member of the group nodded his head knowingly and reiterated the name of that famous painter. He was equally surprised by my observation as I was by his unexpected erudition. He got his answer and moved off, causing the others, still ignorant of our arcane exchange, to follow. Dumbly, they went.

Sometime later I packed my camera gear up and emerged from the cave into the silky translucence of twilight. Orange light kissed the range of boulders that fell down to the sea. The spiky triangles on the edges of the leaves of burgundy-coloured lumps of seaweed made these distributions of aquatic vegetation seem like prehistoric fossils. Ancient shells encrusted in the sides of the moss-ladened boulders also suggested the mysterious and gargantuan presence of time. A perfect and iridescent orange circle was engraved into the blue enamel above. The golden ends of wispy white feathers intensified, the goldness spreading, as the sun fell. Colourful bands blended with each other in sedimentary layers of pastel hues. A powdery orange radiance lay between the smooth blackness of stationary wisps. A streak of black vapour cut the orange disc in half. Gold, orange and mango light fired the sky. The edges of gold clouds were singed black. Gilded lakes in the valleys in the open sky lay between the orange tips of rugged peaks. Across the blue magnitude of the resting sea, a great conflagration of light enflamed the meeting of water and sky, setting alight the far edge of the world. Intense observation of this process revealed that fantastic changes took place subtly, without noise, almost imperceptibly, like evolution. The subsiding of the surf caused the squawks of seagulls to ring with cracking amplification. The clear sound of individual voices sang out in the immense stillness. A small girl playing with a plastic spade was silhouetted at the water's edge. Long, silky clusters of hair fell over her chunky little shoulders. Her father stood next to her, staring into her big innocent eyes. A serene balminess of orange light enveloped them with the peachy delicacy of its gentle touch. Over the top of them, exotic swirls of orange pearl were encrusted into vaporous ebony. The edges of this ebony were singed gold. Puffy apricot bundles filled the air. Distant seagulls quivered like butterflies before the vast flower that bloomed, a way out, on the far edge of the world. The burning core of this lustrous object cast out a luminous pollen that mixed with the grains of sand on the beach and embraced everything in a caress of mango bliss. Globules of molten steel changed shape in the flickering sea; embers were singed charcoal in a liquid fire. A radiant fan of gold light fell through a hole in the cloud and kissed the sea. The concentric rings of splashes from the girl's tiny hands rocked the pathway of orange fire which blazed all the way from the horizon to her feet. She was in a world of opulence and beauty, the only one she knew. Had she been led over that pathway, over the far edge of the earth, she would have encountered another world of poverty and pestilence, one of absurd conflicts and calamitous turmoils, a world of raging disease and the stupidity of enduring struggles. The chances of her seeing these things in her own world in her lifetime were limited; but one day, in the distant future, one of her descendants will. It will happen when someone, bored with all the normal spectacular possibilities of life, seeks to detach themselves as much as possible from the herd-like milieu by attempting to bring all their fantastic visions into existence via political means. It will happen when the country has complicated itself into regional cultures and will therefore be ripe for nationalistic vexations to be stirred up by a tyrant desperate to bring all his egotistical fantasies into being. Untold numbers will be slaughtered, magnificent architecture will be destroyed, families will be split, thousands crippled, millions psychologically damaged. One day, one fine day – who knows when? – this act, this unjustified raising of nationalistic passions for an ulterior and nefarious goal – will be recognised for what it is: the greatest crime a human being can commit, and the instant anyone dreams along these lines they will face immediate execution. It is the only crime worthy of the death penalty and it should be introduced into a system of thinking known as clinical democracy; on one fine day...

* * * * * * * * * * *

Ana arranged a Friday luncheon in a Greek restaurant. The ability to wine and dine throughout a weekday afternoon I presumed was one of the advantages of self-employment. The restaurant had an air of sparkling freshness. Upon its white walls were bright paintings, radiating sunlight. Orange hills rose above terracotta roofs. White birds were plastered against azure blue. Freedom and bliss oozed from these depictions of Grecian summer days.

A plant rose from a pot in a corner and spread its leaves out across the wall. Chairs painted in primary colours sat around satinwood tables. Red porcelain vases in the middle of the tables contained explosions of colourful flowers. The patterns of smiling faces on the exteriors of porcelain mugs and kettles lined the shelving that ran along the shortest wall. Some of the porcelain was decorated with paintings of goldfish. Other pieces were covered in fruit. Sunlight seemed to fill the place, despite the absence of windows. The demeanour of healthy pristineness which emerged from the restaurant's glistening countenance marked the fresh faces of the smiling staff.

I approached two of them and was directed towards a table at which two women were sitting; I was suddenly struck by a piercing bolt of fear and surprise that shuddered my heart. It was her! Jesus Christ, it's her!

I walked slowly to give myself time to recover. The two ladies I was walking towards were facing each other across a table. The one who had caused the shock had yet to notice me. When she did, she glanced at me sourly. This amused me; for some reason, beyond me, I was supposed to be deserving of condemnation. I found this challenging and intriguing. I also found it relaxing. There was no need to maintain a polite façade.

"I didn't know you knew Ana," I said, sitting down.

"I met him", she replied, with a haughty indifference, "last week. He told me all about you."

"Oh," I said, smiling graciously, "what did he say?"

She half smiled at my ironic assumption that it had to be good.

"He", she replied, with a sort of dry weariness, "merely confirmed what I already suspected."

"That I'm a complete angel?" I asked.

"That you", she replied, "make money by immoral means."

"I detect", I remarked, "the stench of a subjective interpretation."

"You can interpret it", she replied, "any way you like."

The waiter came by and we ordered drinks. Ana then appeared with his Macedonian entourage. It consisted of two enormous dark-haired men. Both were married and appeared ready to go to bed with anything. Flippant derision fell from their mouths with the ease of a waterfall. Ana was often the centre of it. Quickly, he became the focal point of conversation. His anecdotal memory was unlimited.

The recollection of one tale always produced another. He was in full flight. Nothing seemed capable of stopping him. With a smile that seemed to have become absorbed into his features, he poured out one amusing story after another. The three other Macedonian people at the table were enraptured. Samantha was not. She glanced away with an unenthused distance, as if the life had been drained from her passionate eyes. This had no effect on Ana whatsoever. He had his audience, therefore he blundered on, deeply amused by his own dubious past.

I leant towards Samantha and said, "I suppose you're going to tell me now that you're not voyeuristic?"

She thought about this momentarily, the life flowing back into her eyes, and said, "I suppose you're going to tell me that you enjoy the sight of people being killed?"

"Have you never", I said, as the Macedonians giggled away, "looked at a picture of a dead body?"

A sudden vulnerability rocked her assertive façade. This surprised me. She could have lied, said that she would never dream of doing such a thing, but she didn't.

"Some people", I added, "are courageous enough to take it a step further. And what have you done to help the victims of war, anyway? Donated tons of money? I doubt it."

"Complete detachment", she said, "is better than exploitation."

"Look," I said, leaning forward, "the personal reasons why someone goes to hell are complicated. I think that too many people take their lives for granted – the fact of their own existence that is – to really be happy. To experience that true and lasting appreciation of your own being, you have to risk death. It's not my fault if that's true."

"Okay," she replied; "but why make money out of other people's suffering?"

"You'd be surprised", I said, "by the number of journalists who give a substantial proportion of their earnings to institutions trying to help those whom you believe are being exploited by media voyeurs such as myself. The victims do appreciate the camera. It means help."

The waiter then appeared with a blackboard showing the menu of the day. The names of the dishes were inscribed on to the board in bright colours that complemented the summery atmosphere of the place. I should have realised that this board was the only thing on earth capable of bringing Ana's amiable raconteuring to a halt; with the culmination of years of refined consumption behind him, he began the task of asking the waiter several questions regarding the multitude of subtle nuances that I was quickly discovering existed within the realm of Greek food. The waiter answered the plethora of Ana's well-educated enquiries with a gracious air of convivial delight.

After he left, Ana immediately resumed his story-telling by saying, "Now where was I?" before launching into another tale.

As the Macedonians continued their banter – Mullethead being a particularly common expression of derision – Samantha cast her dark fiery eyes upon me again ,and with a look of solemn curiosity upon a face containing a mouth like a ripe orchard above the oval of her chin, she asked, "Do you really think it's wrong for people to make a living from other people's suffering – I mean in principle?"

This question was not asked in an unconciliatory fashion; it was put forward with a real determination to discover something unconsidered about this most delicate of questions. I knew a few people who would have asked this question with venomous barbarism and, in an endeavour to define the parameters, I said, "I must admit, I don't torment myself over moral questions. I think that you should realise that I never said gaining exhilaration from the proximity of death was good or evil. It's just a fact. Some people have the courage to experience it – they have the guts to feel this exhilaration – but if you want it to be a moral question, I'll pose one: do you think it's right that people who are prepared to take extreme risks in the pursuit of truth – something totally absolute and unchanging – people who enable us to find out about the world and drag us from our complacency – should get paid so little for doing it, while the directors of multi-national corporations who dump toxic waste in Third World countries, and who really do cause suffering, get paid a fortune for it?"

She burst out laughing.

"Thanks", she said, "for placing it into perspective. In future I'll place it at a more appropriate point on the evil scale; but", she continued, with that contemplative expression fundamental to a questioning mind, her hands, taut, rigid and raised, upheld in a gesture of pained exploration for the correct words, "isn't this how you lot justify it to yourselves? This idea that you are making us all aware?"

"I don't think", I replied, "we need to justify anything to ourselves. We didn't cause the suffering. It was already there. Our actions are only going to help to reduce it. The Vietnam War is a classic example of that. Without courageous, objective reporting that conflict could have dragged on for ever, with who knows what sort of consequences."

I was thoroughly enjoying our battle; because I detected she was as well. I was hoping that she would not agree with anything I said.

Fortunately, she assisted in this endeavour by saying, "But, don't you think it's wrong that people should get their kicks in this way? Should they have the experience at other people's expense and then gloat over it? Don't you ever feel guilty about this?"

The time to really stir her up had arrived.

"Guilty?" I replied, knowing this was going to rock her to the core. "It's just too glamorous an experience to cause me to bother with that."

"Glamorous!" she blurted out, astonished.

This comment ripped out of her in an involuntary release of dismay.

"Yes," I replied, "glamorous. I don't pretend to be nice. Anything that exhilaratingly detaches me from the normal placidity of everyday life is glamorous. And that's what it is – glamorous."

"So glamour", she retorted, with a wry, mocking smile, "overrides the need to feel a proper moral constitution?"

"Glamour", I said, smiling with a whimsical air of didactic erudition, "is a proper moral constitution."

Giggling sarcastically, she asked, "So what's the most glamorous thing you've done? Or should I say: what's the most morally enhancing experience of your life?"

"You wouldn't want to know," I replied. "I would suggest that the answer might be too glamorous for your highly-principled conception of affairs."

"Oh I see," she laughed, mockingly. "Why didn't I think of it before? I'm the one who's supposed to feel guilty, am I? For being too concerned?"

There was a dark edge of humour to this wonderful exchange. I wanted it to go on for a considerable length of time.

In an endeavour to make sure that it did, I said, "Do you really want to know what I've seen? I mean, do you really think that everything I've seen has pleased me immensely? Has it ever struck you that one of the reasons why someone like me might choose to do what I do is because I need to see things for myself, so I know who to blame, and so that I know my opinion is definitive? Has it ever struck you that this might be the case?"

She glanced upward, feigning a magnanimous condescension to agree.

"At last", she acknowledged, flickering her eyelids with noble recognition, "you've said something that suggests there might be some hope for you. I must admit, at one stage, I didn't think that this was possible."

I laughed, overjoyed by her passionate and mocking moral superiority.

"I'm humbled," I replied. "I just can't describe what a privilege it is to be recognised as someone whose dark mind has shining upon it a faint ray from the blazing candle of hope."

"I agree," she said. "You should feel privileged."

I wasn't going to admit it, but secretly I was. I was enjoying her intelligent and combative arrogance. It was novel.

"Is there anything else", I asked, "that you think I might say which you might possibly take the time to condescend to agree with?"

"Probably not," she replied.

I smiled and said, "Is moral enhancement then the driving force of your existence?"

"I have", she replied, "a strong sense of what is right - why?"

"What about", I asked, "subtle niches of thought and belief? Is there a moral basis for every phenomenon? Or are certain things amoral, purely aesthetic, simple joys for the senses? And if morality is supposed to be so important, how far do you take it before it becomes absolutely ridiculous, so you just don't do anything?"

The expression on her face intrigued me. It was a combination of innocence and curiosity.

"There must be some things", she asked, "that make you feel guilty? Surely?"

"I would feel guilty", I replied, "if I stole someone else's idea and it gave me a lot of notoriety, and I was found out. I wouldn't just shrug my shoulders over it."

"And what else?" she asked.

"Not a great deal of things," I replied. "Obviously rape, murder, et cetera, are out: they're pointless and damaging."

"What else?" she persisted.

"Sometimes," I said, "I've made flippant remarks that have caused people to overreact. This makes me feel cheapish - guilty about not being more considerate. But these comments are said when someone else has done something that they regret, and they don't want to face up to it; they get upset if I mention it. Ultimately, they should not have done what they did, but that seems to be beside the point."

"People", she remarked, "suffer enough without having to be reminded of their inadequacies."

"It's actually quite an important question, that," I said.

She looked at me quizzically. Her beautiful eyes were singing with inquisitiveness.

"If you read any great novel," I said, "its author must have gained their knowledge by observing real people. How else could they have done it? A book like that is going to upset someone. The artist should be more interested in truth than popularity. An author can't take responsibility for other people's absurd actions. A book is written or a film made so that people can question themselves more clearly."

"What happens", she replied, "when the person concerned believes they are being misrepresented?"

"That usually", I said, "means that the truth has been exposed. Anyway, let's assume for the sake of argument that that's the case - that the truth is actually being displayed. If it hurts someone, then they should never read a book or ever see a film again, because they should disagree with the entire process of creation in principle. That's what I mean about taking principled behaviour to an absurd level. You either have nothing to hide, or you just keep your mouth shut when you think others are being indiscreet. A difficult act to perform, that."

She smiled at me unexpectedly. A sort of electromagnetic perfume radiated from her face. She fascinated me with her sudden tenderness; then she said, "A truly considerate author might be sympathetic in their assessments as to why somebody has weaknesses."

"Yes," I replied, "but that doesn't mean that the character will appreciate those reasons being made public. The deeper somebody goes, no matter how sympathetically, the worse it can be for someone who's wasted so much of their life creating a false image. No matter which way you look at it, a creative artist will have to deal with this. At the end of the day, I'm not a moralist because I can't blame people for being what they are; there are so many appalling influences on us, it wouldn't surprise me if we all went mad."

The food arrived. This gave Maria, who was sitting next to me, the chance to swap positions with Samantha. I hid my delight at this rearrangement. It was invigorating having this sensuously aggressive creature beside me. It was like having an appealing and morally-outraged presence constantly nipping at my unprincipled laxity.

She took a sample of her meal and said, "A few of the locals stuck in some of the places you've been to must've thought you were mad for being there, when you didn't have to be."

"If you're curious," I replied, "you're curious. What else can you do? You don't get any accolades for not taking the photographs that you should've."

"But you do get abuse though," she said, smiling, "don't you?"

"You haven't abused me," I replied. "You've just stated your point of view. It's a pity there's not more people like you."

"But", she smiled, "if there were more people like me, then there'd be no one to drag us from our complacency, no one to pursue something absolute and unchanging, and getting paid so little for doing it as well."

I erupted into laughter and said, "Brilliant."

She had backbone. I said, "I knew you were going to be an inspiration."

"Thank you," she replied, "but I'm not really interested in compliments."

"What are you interested in then?" I asked.

She surprised me by saying, "Middle Eastern affairs."

She said that she had spent a year in Israel and this had given her a taste for the Arab world. She said that she wanted to learn Arabic and "see more of the East". She was particularly keen on going to Istanbul. When I said that Turkey is a country "with a bewildering array of conflicting attitudes," it caused her eyes to fire, for she correctly assumed that I was referring to women.

"You can go into any village", I said, "and the range of responses you get from women is incredible. One can come up to you, smiling, speaking to you fluently in a foreign language, another will shout abuse, while others will cover their faces and dive for cover. This can happen in the space of fifty yards on any street in any small village. There must be enormous tensions beneath the surface, way beyond what we can imagine."

She seemed to get excited by this idea. I was fascinated by her flailing hands. I almost felt her heart thumping. Her passion for relevant issues was bold and refreshing. Sensations, ideas and feelings seemed to clash within her, like lines of light on a clear and beautiful pool of water.

"That's the reason", she said, with a sort of agonised enthusiasm, "I want to get involved. It's so different. So exotic. I'm appalled and fascinated by the treatment these women allow themselves to be subjected to; there must be a lot of intelligent, self-respecting women just waiting to break free, all over the Arab world."

"And a lot", I replied, "who don't want the system to change at all."

Her eyes seemed to squint at the mere suggestion of this heinous prospect. It was anathema to the way in which she wished to view the world. I suspected that she wanted to believe that it was men - and no one else - who were responsible for the oppression of women. But the time was arriving when responsibility had to be accepted by all.

"There are women in the Islamic world", I said, "who like the idea of being supported for the rest of their lives without having to make a major decision. I've actually met a few in Lombok. I stayed with a wealthy Muslim family on the eastern side of the island many years ago. The women in this family were the envy of all - little work, well fed, no responsibilities. A lazy, unenterprising individual's dream."

"And if you are enterprising?" she asked.

"Then", I replied, "you're gone."

"Exactly," she said.

"But a lot of those women", I replied, "don't know any better."

"Or", she said, "they realise they don't have any other chance, so they make the most of it."

"Which means", I added, "that they can be philosophical about it."

"But imagine", she said, "being an intelligent woman with ambitions in a place like Saudi Arabia."

"Then", I replied, "you'd have to find an intelligent, ambitious man who's also pissed off with the system."

"How many would you be able to find?" she asked.

"Quite a few," I replied.

The waiter came and collected our dishes. The Macedonians were babbling away, wild guffaws emerging from their mouths. The raucous of conversation was so loud that we had to speak very loudly to be heard. Everywhere around the restaurant, people were competing furiously for the next remark.

I glanced at Samantha and wondered how many times she had been in love. I was then taken by her skin. Its purity seemed too unreal for human touch. But it was her eyes. They shone with such audacious verity that they seemed out of place surrounded by something so soft and delicate as her face. I looked into them and, noting their wild intensity, said, "Being an average bloke in an Islamic country – not enough money for marriage – finding the opposite sex scintillatingly attractive and not being able to be seen in public with them, unless married, would be hell."

Sympathy suddenly veiled her face. I was pleased with her understanding.

"In a country like Egypt", I continued, "where the average person is quite poor and the marriage dowry is so high, there are so many men facing a future of emotional sterility and absolute sexual frustration. I felt real sympathy for the men when I was there. Just having this conversation with you today would be impossible. There'd be millions of men in Egypt who, if they saw me now, would be wracked with violent envy. What a pain in the arse that'd be."

"Ironically," she said, "it helps to stimulate fundamentalist beliefs, because it's the only legitimate means of escape. And unfortunately", she continued, those hands beating the atmosphere again, "it's the women who suffer more if they're discovered having an extramarital affair. The shame is not evenly distributed."

"And", I acknowledged, "neither is divorce."

"Exactly," she said.

It was enhancing to feel the fearless relish with which she conveyed her opinions. She had conviction. I found this beguiling and attractive; she was not an individual of half-hearted responses. Great energy had been poured into her contemplation of things. I realised that the apoliticality of someone such as myself could be a potential source of irritation to someone like her. I was a man of wide experience and many views with few convictions. I found life too futile to have anything other than a philosophical intransigence towards the idea of wholehearted involvement. I was a voyeur on the fringe, blessed with profound curiosity, with only a limited capacity for sentient indulgence; I found things too ironic, too hypocritical and too morally pretentious to constantly experience ethical outrage. I was also white, male and educated, and therefore less affected by the prejudices of this paranoid and avaricious earth. But this still did not stop me from admiring someone capable of experiencing something I found essentially vital and alive, even if it was dogmatic, prickly, even narrow-minded, as long as it bore the hallmarks of cultivated fire.

"What do you think", I asked, "about the idea of a man needing four wives and a woman only requiring one husband?"

"How can a man be in love with four women at once?" she asked. "Surely," she added, her right hand cupped in a gesticulation of defiant righteousness, her eyes charged with sanctimonious ferocity, "one of them must take emotional predominance?"

"I couldn't agree more," I replied. "But what do you think of the philosophy behind this arrangement?"

"No man", she said, "needs four wives if he's truly in love with someone."

"I know, I know," I acknowledged. "But..."

I was going to add something, but I giggled, amused at the daunting prospect of attempting to extract a rational, sensitive, well-rounded response from a fiery, intelligent, argumentative feminist over the delicate question of the male sex drive.

"What is it? What is it?" she demanded, those powerful eyes begging an answer, her eyebrows – refined arches of ebony inlaid into the alabaster of her forehead – rising in querulous inquisitiveness.

Her unrestrained and liberating curiosity caused me to chuckle again.

"Oh come on," she said. "Is this going to go on all day?"

"No, no, no," I replied, smiling, shaking my head. "You've got to understand that the question I've just asked is difficult to frame in terms which are not going to cause me to be completely misrepresented."

"Okay, okay," she said, "what is it then?"

I gathered myself. The Macedonians were deep in light-hearted banter. Around the restaurant, gossiping clientele gesticulated with their hands over intense conversations.

I leant forward and said, "The Muslims – the men, that is – believe that a man requires more women, over a lifetime, than a woman requires men. Do you think that's true?"

"It depends", she replied, "on the individual."

"What do you think," I asked, "generally?"

She glanced away, contemplatively. This gave me the opportunity to look briefly at the magnificence of her form. Her neck was strong, rounded and delicate. Round breasts protruded straight out. The pale skin had the unblemished sheen of a fine porcelain or fabric. I noted that things were voluptuously salient where they should have been and tapered inward at those places where fineness and femininity dictated that they had to. It was a masterpiece of anatomical planning. I wanted to shake hands with the great force of nature responsible for this. Maybe one day I would. But it was her mind that allured me. That, too, was forged from some irresistible turmoil of unrestrained creation. Its existence I was grateful for, because it took my mind off her body. There were already enough wasteful distractions in this life; that would have been too much.

She looked back at me and said, "I cannot see any reason why the situation should not be equal. A person's sex drive is a very individual thing."

"What about", I replied, "a person's ability to recognise, register, discern – call it whatever you like – the existence of sexual attractiveness in another?"

"Women", she said, "are quite capable of doing that."

"So capable", I persisted, "that, when it happens to them, they experience a force so overwhelming – I mean someone they don't even know – that it is essential they touch?"

"It's possible," she replied. "Why not?"

"How possible?" I asked. "Would it happen every day? What are the percentages?"

"In a crowd", she replied, "of say a hundred, there'd probably be one or two."

She was perplexed by my sudden chuckle.

"One or two?" I said.

"Yes," she replied. "What's wrong with that?"

"Not a thing," I said. "Sounds fine to me."

"Why do you want to know?" she asked.

Her eyes made it impossible to resist this outburst of curiosity.

"In a man", I replied, "the percentage is quite a bit higher. Probably too high for the comfort of most women."

I saw an aspect of doubt and disbelief creep into those eyes - those slivers of fiery, black marble carved into the silken delicacy of her head. They possessed an expression of forthright incredulity that caused me to elaborate with some misgivings.

"What I am about to say", I said, "will be something you will not have heard before; but it's a fact - one I'm neither proud of or personally responsible for. What I want you to do", I continued, "is to think of the most physically attractive man you've ever met in your life - how you felt when you saw him - and imagine, each day, seeing twenty or thirty replicas in the street - every day, without fail - then you might have some idea of what it's like being a man."

Her face showed the numbed awe I felt was on mine each time someone of her outstanding beauty dispassionately ignored me. The icy scale of their lack of interest usually matched the heated depths of my intrigue.

"That", she said, shaking her head slowly, "would be exceptionally tiring."

"It gives you an electricity", I said, "that never goes away. Every day you walk out the door, you're on fire in expectation at what you're going to see."

Now smiling, her shaking head moved more violently from side to side.

"And", I said, "your expectations are always fulfilled. You are never let down."

"Sex", she replied, genuinely surprised by this, "is on a man's mind more than a wom—"

"Oh, no, no, no," I said, shaking my head. "Wrong. Men are just more conscious of its existence. Women actually think about it more - subliminally. That's why you buy magazines and spend more time looking in shop windows and have such elaborate toiletry and facial accoutrements; it's all sex. You just refuse to recognise it as such."

"I'm not doubting what you say", she said, "and what you've just said is new, but you make it sound as if men are incapable of being happy with one person."

"No, no, no," I replied. "What I said was that men are more desperate to get the sort of intimacy we all crave. We can't hide from it. Surrogate experiences do not work for us. Our needs are just thrust – to use that expression – more obviously into our faces. There's no escape. The mass consumption of chocolates is just not good enough for us. Neither is a nice lipstick. We're just more savagely reminded of what we don't have than you are; that's all."

"But still," she said, "if what you say is true – this thing about replicas – then it's really impossible for a man to be happy with one person."

"No," I replied, "all you need is one person. One person who's right for you is enough to take your mind off all the others. It can happen easily. And it's such a relief from the turmoils created by the finely-tuned and unconditioned receptors of your overloaded senses. What women have to be careful of is the existence of EE-WOC."

"EE-WOC?" she asked, quizzically.

"Intimacy", I replied, "without commitment. EE-WOC," I continued, with a flippant air of grave didacticism, as though I were giving a lecture to a group of eccentric sociology students, "enables the useless, unattached male – and there are quite a few of us around – to gain a well-deserved rest from the chaos – an arrest that can last up to all of, say, if you happen to be lucky, why, even twenty-four hours."

The huge smile on her face, mixed with a touch of embarrassment, suggested that she had some idea to what I was referring.

"I'm sure", I continued, "that Doctor Polverwoski", it was a good name for her, "will be in agreement when I say that the useless male – a fascinating species – gets very few opportunities for the sort of intimacy he so, in his deviant, underdeveloped way, requires; as a consequence, this colourful organism then takes, by way of substitute, any intimacy from the fairer sex that may come along. Of course, it only comes from women in whom the useless male has not the blindest bit of interest; however, this festering scab on the laceration of humanity, known as the desperate unattached male, and, contrary to some of the fine psychological thinking currently being performed in certain quarters today, does, in fact, possess a certain guilt at misleading the EE-WOCETTE; hence, the intimacy must not involve sexual intercourse and, due to the understandable female of the species' disillusionment at the non-consummation of the relationship, the period of EE-WOC – actually spelt IWOC – usually does not, except in very exceptional circumstances, extend beyond fourteen days."

To my delight, this depiction of human existence filled her with astounded hilarity.

"That", she said, "is probably the most bizarre thing I've ever heard in my life."

"All I want", I replied, "is to make some unsuspecting woman – and most are – fully aware of the realities that dominate the lives of significant numbers of people on this planet. I believe that in certain respects women actually have it easier."

"Easier!?" she exclaimed.

"There are certain natural injustices", I smiled, "to which women pay no credence."

Fortunately, this inquiring individual had a penchant for listening.

"And what, if I may be so bold to ask," she inquired, "are they?"

"Women," I replied, "and I say this with the utmost respect, are oblivious of the existence of what I describe as the Great Unfair Imbalance – better known as GOOIE."

She shook her head, disbelieving that someone should be so prejudiced in their perception of sexual politics.

"What about", she began, "fat women? Someone I used to work with – a charming girl – is very overweight and finds it very difficult to get a boyfriend. She probably finds the vast majority of men more attractive than they find her."

"Yes," I replied, ready for this one, "but what about fat men? I can guarantee you that your friend, at least, doesn't get ignored by men on a regular basis. Men will, at least, speak to her. But your average fat man has to battle constantly with women who he knows just want him to lie down and die. Anyway," I continued, ignoring her rueful smile, "the point is, if you've got two people of averagely good physical attractiveness, with the right kind of psychological attributes – one a man, the other a woman – the man, I can assure you, has a lot more work ahead of him if he wishes to achieve the sort of fulfilling intimacy that we, at some stage, all require. And that, I'm afraid, is a fact."

"Possibly", she replied, "it's because women are more discerning."

"Possibly", I offered, "it's because of the existence of GOOIE."

Her laugh filled me with great pleasure.

"Okay," she admitted, "it's maybe because of GOOIE."

"Just maybe?" I persisted.

"Yes," she replied, "maybe. And lust."

"Lust", I said, "is too simple a word. I prefer to call it burning curiosity. You may be interested to know that some strong feelings of desire are, in fact, born from refined appreciation."

She laughed again, a chuckle whose felicity created a considerable amount of it within me.

"Touché," she said.

"I don't want you to think", I said, "that I'm proud of my knowledge of GOOIE. The blatant cruelty of its existence sends me into paroxysms of horror. If I ever met God, I'd strangle him for being so cynical."

I was unsure if she was laughing with me or at me; either way, it was irrelevant. The pretence to a normal view of the world had been dispensed with.

"This world", I continued, "would be an amazing place if men and women were equally attracted to each other. It would be so fulfilling – and it would be fair."

"The way you talk about it," she said, "it makes it sound as though women are never rejected by men."

"Of course they are," I replied, "but I'm talking about men and women of equal, relative attractiveness. Because of their hormones, women are not so sharply confronted by what they don't have. It almost murders us. But we're supposed to keep women in the dark about it. Let's face it, a lot of women'd be pretty appalled if they'd just heard what I'd just told you today. Outraged probably. Particularly women who'd had a relationship with every man that they have ever been interested in. Like you, perhaps."

To her credit, she did not deny this; the fact that she had never seen her relative success in having relationships with people she truly desired as being part of some grand, biological injustice was not her fault. I just wanted to get some satisfaction, born from a love of the truth, in showing someone like herself that her experience was not normal. However, I also did not want her to think that her success was based purely on her physical appearance. That, too, would have been an injustice. The fact that she could have been rubbing shoulders with virtually any man she wanted, but was wholeheartedly engaging me in conversation instead, indicated to me her lack of image consciousness. This was an outstanding achievement in a place like this.

Sipping my drink, I watched her reflecting with profound concentration; then, with a gaze of astounded realisation; she said, "It's funny to think of promiscuity in terms of opportunity, rather than morality."

I felt moved by this remark. That joyous explosion in the soul associated with something new and correct erupted within me.

"Good way of putting it," I said, appreciatively. "There wouldn't be that many highly attractive women who haven't had sex regularly since their late teens. The sheer weight of opportunity must mean that they have to find themselves in that position almost constantly."

"Are you jealous?" she asked, a question surprising for its boldness and disarming frankness.

I laughed and said, "Not about the sex. There's something else I'm a little perturbed about, though."

"So what is it?" she asked, radiating a quality of courageous sincerity, her eyes yearning for something unforeseen and expanding.

"It would be nice", I replied, "if there were a little more gratitude in this world."

"How do you mean?" she persisted.

I had been deliberately vague in the ridiculous hope of subtly suggesting my next controversial belief. But here was a woman who demanded uncensored explanations.

I smiled and said, "I can imagine you at a party surrounded by men, pointing to a table and saying, 'That's a table,' and these men going, 'Oh yes, such magnificent streamlining, such intricate marquetry, such perfect flatness – I mean, have you ever seen such flatness in a tabletop? Why, it's incredible!'

"The point is, the perspicacity or relevance of any comment is usually only determined by the identity of the speaker. Often the comment itself is irrelevant – particularly in party situations. I mean, if I said: 'That's a table,' to a group of women at a party, they'd think I was an idiot. But don't get me wrong – I'm not suggesting that you would even dream of saying anything as banal as that: it's obvious your perspective on things is genuinely interesting – it's just that it must be incredible to know that all the interesting things you've got to say will always find an enthusiastic, sympathetic ear. The other day, for example, I tried to explain to a group of bored people the intricacies of how bees impart complex information to each other – a really incredible phenomenon involving body language. If you'd done that, some of the men I was explaining this to, instead of wishing that I would just shut up and die, probably would have gone out and bought entire encyclopaedias on animal behaviour."

Her chuckle gave me the inspiration to continue.

"Not so long ago," I said, "I met this Bulgarian girl. She was a barmaid in a London pub. Rather attractive. Very intelligent. I got to know her a bit and I asked her out. A few days before we went out I spent about an hour in Foyles studying books in the Bulgarian language section. I wanted to buy an English-Bulgarian dictionary – can you believe that? – an English-Bulgarian dictionary – useful, hey? But I couldn't find one – thank God – but I was still able to offer some erudite observations on the Bulgarian language, however, a subject I've never had any interest in or ever will."

She sighed and said, "That kind of interest can hardly be described as genuine."

"Yes," I replied, "but it's still interest, and interest can be manipulated."

"That's assuming", she said, "that you're interested in manipulation."

"Don't be so sure", I replied, "that there won't come a time when you won't be. You never know what you may want and how badly you may want it. You've got that power. I haven't. The chances of your gaining the sympathetic, enthusiastic ear are far greater than mine. Take advantage of it. You only live once."

Her eyes indicated distaste at the idea of tacit prostitution. She was still too young and self-respecting to believe that people could advance by other means than through ability. Her task, and the task of people like her, was to make the world realise this.

"Women", she said, malevolently, "who do what you just said really piss me off."

I was delighted by this response. I was then told how she had been in situations where she had argued with men over their attitudes towards women, while other women in the group had just sat there "docile and agreeable, frightened to stand up for themselves". As she spoke, her hands, constantly moving, were like spiders of lightning, conveying deeply-felt emotions; when talking about "these women" ("those fucking cows - sorry, I shouldn't've said that"), she made mock allusions to their placidity by sarcastically flickering her eyelids and looking very gentle and pristine. She was in the grip of a passionate harangue that caused her eyes to become charged with a striking expression that made me think, 'Now this creature is really alive.'

"So many women", she said, those eyes now shining with angered perplexity, "are afraid to be labelled as a nagger. If you're opinionated", she continued, those hands gesticulating Italian style, "and a woman, this can take on pejorative overtones. Too many women perceive its eventual meaning as nagging. It's ridiculous."

I was taken aback by the severity of her feelings. Someone like her made me realise how unmoved I was by the appalling injustices of this world.

"How do you get on with your father?" I asked, wondering if the paternal link was the source of all this vehemence.

"Not at all," she replied.

She then unleashed an imprecatory jeremiad of astonishing proportions about her father - how he was embarrassed about showing emotions (she usually just got a little peck on the cheek from him), how his peremptoriness precluded any conversation liable to contradict his undoubted perception of human affairs. When she spoke about him, her writhing hands seemed to conduct the emotion she felt through her fingers, as though the charge searing through them had to be earthed in the atmosphere to stop her mind from short-circuiting. It was explained that he never gave her encouragement; he often described her as "hopeless". She was full of "absurd ideas". She was "a dreamer" who somewhere along the line had "gone funny".

"He's just a classic stereotype", she pronounced, "from his generation."

I was a little worried. Tears were beginning to form in her eyes.

"What's the point", she then continued, with impassioned gravity, "in raising children - spending all that money and time - and not taking any interest in them, just when they get to an age where you can actually learn something from them? It's ridiculous. I just can't get over the stupidity of someone not realising the damage they're doing – damage which is so unnecessary. It's a fact", she then said, composing herself, "that everyone can blame their parents for something."

The ironic truthfulness of this filled me with a sharp jolt of admiration; a beauteous glow of personality resonated from her; it was a fiery glow of perspicacious authenticity that demanded thought and preached the doctrine of outraged justice.

She admitted that, in an endeavour "to trivialise the brittle, egocentric existence" of her father, her feminist leanings were probably born from a desire "to force him to see the stupid austerity of his limited vision".

"I believe", she smiled, "that to some extent I have succeeded."

Her torrent of malign vitriol left me in no doubt as to which attitudes she found detestable.

I gathered myself and said, "This situation between yourself and your father shows how repressed frustrations can lead to feelings and vulnerabilities and personality traits that are totally dissimilar to those possessed by those who brought us into this world. I guess you could call it the reactive personality."

She looked at me with a combination of fascination and appreciation. It was an expression that induced within me a wholesome fulfilment, something akin to a drug that destroys the rationalising function of the brain and shuts out from consciousness any consideration of the unpleasant realities of life. It was a delusory optimism, a reaffirmation of the worthwhile pursuit of living.

Quickly, this expression disappeared, that combination of curiosity and passionate intelligence, and gave way to a look of excited realisation in which her hands flew up beside her face and jolted the atmosphere with their fervid mania – a mania born from the exchange of knowledge – and, with a sudden running of her fingers through that silky, tousled mop of luscious hair, she said, "And that's why some parents aren't as interested in their children as they should be – because they haven't produced a mirror image that they can manipulate and control."

Once again her rebellious individuality rose to a surface made to be stroked and admired, which hid who knows what amount of fantastic depths. Suddenly, like some vast, tropical flower unfurling its petals, her hands rose again in a gesture of symmetrical mushrooming before exploding in rapid quiverings of disgusted ire as she, with another flick through the silk that draped her shoulders, said, "People have children so they can have someone they can control."

"Do you really believe that?" I asked, wondering what other bizarre theories she possessed; I contemplated whether a multitude of these thought-provoking beliefs existed in a dazzling repertoire of veracious insights, like an inward universe flickering behind her face which showed its light through eyes so ablaze with impetuous acuity that, if I were able to hold both of those eyes in the palms of my hands, they - my hands - would have gyrated with such fevered oscillations, in response to the intensity of the buzzing units of energy which they had chosen to embrace, that the joints in my shoulders and elbows would have been under a strain so serious that every ligament, cartilage and tendon in the affected areas of my body would have been ripped, torn and mutilated by the sheer frenzy of motion burning within the struggling enclaves of my fists.

"I mean," I continued, fighting to overcome the stunned supineness that had evolved in my mind in reaction to this onslaught of obdurate, but truthful, sentience, "what about the idea that people have children to strengthen a relationship?"

"Children", she said, with an unflinching certainty that, in someone else, may have disturbed me, "do not strengthen relationships: they tear them apart."

"I realise that," I replied, "but some people believe that by having children they will enhance their relationship by adding another dimension of joy."

"That's because", she said, "they imagine that that child will do everything they want it to do. Do you think that a couple would choose to have a child if they knew beforehand that that child was going to do everything in its power to wreck the wishes of its parents? Somehow", she finished, without a trace of the sort of egotistical relish normally associated with victory in these matters, "I doubt it."

Finding this very difficult to disagree with, I said, "Probably the reason I would make such a useless parent. I have no wish to control - which is probably why I hate horse riding."

This comment threw a gleam of appreciation across her face, as if the molten gems of her eyes had melted before me in a rich evocation of warmth and happiness.

"I hate horse riding as well," she said. "I think it's because I just don't like horses. I can't understand how a creature of that size can allow a human being to get on top of it. How can you have respect for a creature that allows that?"

I laughed and said, "People who ride horses say: 'But some of them have got personality.' Can you imagine being able to get on to the back of a cat, if a cat was the same size as a horse? No way! Besides, the cat'd be able to leap a hundred metres anyway."

"Certainly make equestrian events more interesting," she then said, giggling.

"They'd need to wear spacesuits," I replied, bending forward across the table and chortling.

We giggled together in delight, both of us pleased that we could guffaw over these esoteric considerations.

This inspired me to say, "Imagine being in a 747 and looking out the window and seeing someone else, whose name was probably Sara Copplebottoms-Worth-Carmichael-Johnson, zooming past in silver riding jacket and breeches on a tabby the same size as a Grand National winner, on her way, with a single leap, to Barbados."

On making this comment, I saw her head go back, her chin come up and her face contort itself into a grimace of hilarity before hearing a cute chuckle of gracious responsiveness, an enriching sign of approval that I was able to reciprocate when she returned with, "Imagine if human beings were cats. We'd get up in the morning, eat the equivalent of a refrigerator-load of tuna, drink the equivalent of a forty-four gallon drum of milk and then, from a standing position, leap eighty feet upward to get out a window to go to work."

I laughed, staring happily into those sparkling eyes, those glistening ornaments to a life enriched by emotion, sensitivity, wit, grace and intelligence; each of these virtues were like precious stones encrusting a gilt chalice of voluptuous dimensions, one topped by those eyes that now contained a soft expression which matched the texture of her skin. She could never know the aesthetic pleasure it brought me to look into them and at that face. Women were oblivious to this. They could never know the power their faces held over our hearts. They could never feel the potent delicacy of their features igniting our brazen hopes, like a miracle, like witchcraft. If they did, they would probably be shocked.

"I've been thinking lately", I said, "about power."

"What about it?" she asked.

"I once saw a cop on a London street", I replied, "tell a republican to stop canvassing in one spot. Apparently, it's against the law. 'You have to do it from door-to-door,' the cop said. The week before, Labour politicians had been canvassing on the same spot. They weren't asked to move. Maybe the law changed during the week."

She got excited again and gasped out, "The law!"

She stopped herself from becoming furious; then she said, "No law is reprehensible if it gives a government what it wants – and that's power."

I was intrigued by her outspoken veracity.

"I met somebody once", I smiled, "who, through his desire to bring fairness to every aspect of human life, hunted for abstract generalisations – ideals – to get others to see his vision. In that respect, he was exactly like a megalomaniac."

Before me, that bundle of impassioned femininity erupted again with hand gestures and head-shaking into a blaze of appreciative wonderment. There was something charismatic and charming in the way she responded to these new ideas with childlike zeal. It was as though all the irony, intelligence, observation and pertinence of my remark were perceived in a joyous flash, pounced on instantaneously by the steel trap of her mind.

"Who", she asked, "was this guy?"

When displaying fascination or astonishment, her top lip curved in a half-circle above the fleshy segment of the lower; I could not think of a more desirable place to deposit my mouth.

"He lives in Norfolk," I replied. "Someone who picked me up hitchhiking. He lived with his wife and young daughter in a timber hut-like house he'd built himself. In the back garden was a yellow sand pit. Next to it was a red kennel. The daughter used it for a doll's house. She had long blonde hair and wore flowery dresses. For two hours, I watched her playing in the sand pit, talking to herself, surrounded by imaginary friends, while the father peeled off at me, with a distant, glazed expression on his face, all these unbelievable generalisations about the evils of power. At one point, he even ran inside and came back and gave me four or five foolscap pages of this stuff. I was supposed to follow it while he read it out."

"God," she said, "what did he say?"

"Absolutely can't remember," I replied. "At the time, it struck me as one cliché after another. Who knows what I might think now, though? Probably wouldn't make any difference any way. He was impossible to get through to. There was some emotional vacuum there: there was no fluidity, no change. I suspect he was beginning to drive his wife nuts."

"Why?" she asked.

"Because", I replied, "when I finally got away, as I was leaving, she said to me, with a disillusioned grin, 'We're now even baking our own bread.'"

"Dear, oh dear," Samantha replied. "A dictator of good. I just can't stand these people who have to convince themselves that they care."

"Much better", I said, "to try with complacency. That's what all the smart ones use."

"And", she replied, with piercing insight, "a healthy smattering of mendacious complicity."

"Absolutely," I said. "I wonder what it is."

I then continued, fascinated by her comprehension, "That makes someone want to bring all their fantastic fantasies to fruition via political means."

She did not have to bother to think about this one; it just burst out. "A thrill", she said, "at successfully being able to manipulate which feeds on itself."

She definitely had a thing about manipulation.

"These people", she continued, fixing those spectacular eyes back on me, "have acute desire – something which brings out an individual's will and potential – without conscience."

"Are you suggesting", I asked, "that conscience is a kind of restraint?"

"Yes," she replied. "It's like faith."

"What if," I said, "hypothetically, someone found you so desirable that they were unable to act with it?"

"If they knew me", she replied, "and were genuinely interested, they would."

"I'm glad", I said, "you said that."

"Why?" she asked.

"Because", I replied, "it implies that you're genuinely interested in mature people – and it also supports one of my theories."

"You", she smiled, "certainly are a man of theories."

"Well," I retorted, "that's your theory. Generally, I don't get along with people who don't have a certain mature outlook. Some people are so full of this - ah, shall we say, conscience - you could even call it caring intolerance - that they inadvertently mature me with their presence. Their secure stolidity is uplifting and reassuring."

I was pleased with the clear expression in her eyes. She knew exactly what I meant. It was probable that there were tens of thousands who did not.

In response, she said, "Trust," but to herself, as though she were thinking aloud, an unconscious revelation of her gratitude at my faith in the soothing powers of moral and intellectual certitude that actually astonished me to the point of speechlessness.

"So," she asked, the wonder-struck distance now gone from her face, "what's this theory then?"

"I can't tell you," I replied.

"Why not?" she asked. "What else are you going to do now? Go on a ten mile run? It's against the rules to arouse my curiosity and then not satisfy it. You've got five seconds, or else. Now talk!"

I smiled and said, "The theory is, that it's pointless for a man to make any heavy passes at a woman he may be interested in when all he has to do is ring up; if the woman keeps saying 'yes' each time you ring up, you don't have to do anything. Eventually, if the woman's interested she will do something herself. Women can't help themselves. It's such a rare experience for them to feel real interest in a man - I mean real interest, not just a desire for a relationship - that it burns through them. They will do something; and, besides, they're brilliant at it anyway. They always do it so tastefully. I guess", I added, as an ironic afterthought, "it's because they must know that they've got a more than reasonable chance of success and we", I laughed, "know we've got a more than reasonable chance of failure."

I had decided to go for witty, self-deprecatory tactics. She seemed suitable for this type of attack and I enjoyed doing it anyway. She smiled at my attempt to display inadequacy. I decided to go for the kill.

"That comment", I continued, "I made about the fundamental difference between men and women - that women should try and imagine what it's like seeing twenty or so replicas of their own personal Adonis each day on the street – means you have to struggle to show interest, while we have to constantly pull back the reins for fear of scaring off half the world's population. When you're as unsuccessful as the average man is, this is an excellent recipe for frustration."

"You", she said, "shouldn't put yourself down."

"I don't," I replied. "It's women who do that. Personally, I think I'm brilliant."

I knew that the self-deprecation could not last for too long but it didn't matter: she still found this amusing.

"After a while though," I added, "you get sick of having to prove you're the most wonderful human being on earth, just so you can have a normal, unrestrained conversation with an attractive, intelligent woman."

This remark perplexed her. Before she could seek an explanation, I said, "It would be impossible for the average man to remember how many times, in differing situations, he's had to pretend that the woman he's trying to speak to doesn't really want the floor to open up to have him hurled down into a fiery abyss. You stand there knowing they want you to disappear and you pretend nothing's wrong and that maybe, with a bit of time, you'll go from being an intellectually deficient rapist to someone vaguely resembling a human being."

She erupted into laughter. There was no point in her describing the numerous occasions over the last few months in which she had been involved in situations such as those.

"You probably think that this situation today," I then said, "that is, having a conversation with a man, is normal. You can't believe the amount of work we have to do just to get into this situation – and, more importantly, how desperately we want it to happen. It's quite painful finding the opposite sex so attractive and at the same time so disinterested in intimacy."

It was probably a good sign that she pointed out that women were interested in intimacy as well. However, I elaborated by suggesting that in women it was just a desire that "came and went" whereas in men it was "a necessity that allowed you no rest".

"It's pointless", I said, "my going into a park in this beautiful weather here to relax and enjoy the sunshine. For me, it's hell. All I do is find myself surrounded by happy couples and beautiful women, semi-clad, totally disinterested in their surroundings, draped around the grass in all manner of outrageously feminine positions, their hair spread wide, oblivious of the devastating effect they're having on certain individuals such as myself."

She smiled suspiciously at my nonsense.

"And the thing", I continued, "that really pisses me off is seeing some bloke reading a book or a newspaper amongst that, because you know that that guy is perfectly content. You know that that guy can go to that park each lunch time and not take his eyes from the confounded pages of that bloody book because you know that, somewhere, he's got one of those remarkable creatures, draped on the ground nearby, and he can just lie there, soaking up the UVs in the full knowledge that one of those ravishing beauties is going to be draped around him later that night; and the worst part of it is, unlike those women around him, he knows that someone like me is going to see him looking absolutely unconcerned by the existence of all that beauty, while I'm going to be completely concerned by it; and he's also going to know that his total and utter uninterest and imperturbability is going to make him even more attractive to those women, one of whom he's already got, while I, in a desperate bid to gain even a mere fraction of the contentment he so obviously feels, will become even more repulsive."

By now, she was giggling. I was delighted that she admired my mendacious self-deprecation. I adored anybody who did this.

"You poor thing," she said.

"Miaow," I replied.

"I thought", she said, sardonically, "that a handsome, courageous, thrill-seeking combat photographer such as yourself wouldn't have any problems in seducing gorgeous women."

"I wonder", I said, "if you could elaborate a bit on that part about being handsome and courageous?"

"Oh, I see," she replied. "You really are a poor thing. You never get any compliments."

"Oh," I sighed, "I get a few. People keep telling me that I'm a brilliant photographer, but I'm bored with that one. I want to hear something different. Go on, make something up. Pretend you adore me. If you do, I promise I'll give you ten dollars."

"Ten dollars?" she asked. "Don't you think that my compliments are worth a little bit more than that?"

"I thought I was the one here", I replied, "who was supposed to be fishing for compliments. You really are a cunning little crumpet."

"A cunning little crumpet?" she exclaimed. "How sickly!"

I laughed at her disdain for this vacuous term of endearment. It caused me to add, with a wry smile, "And I suspect that you're also a cute, furry little whelk whose curious, twitching snout often finds itself in places where it shouldn't be."

"Jeesuzzz," she whispered.

Her unrestrained detestation of these gracious absurdities filled me with delight.

"And—" I began.

"Oh, shut up," she replied.

I laughed; then she said, "The last few men I've been out with have told me that they love me within a week. How can anyone be in love so quickly?"

"Maybe", I replied, "it's because they think that you're exceptional."

"Maybe", she said, "there's another reason."

I looked away, then back again, and said, "There is a possibility that these men – whoever they are – are just trying to tell you that they have good intentions. Ever thought of that?"

Men too had the right to be upset by sexist attitudes in the opposite sex; it was hypocritical of women that they felt their simplistic views of men were not chauvinist.

She retreated and said, "The yearning is too often too loud."

"That", I persisted, "is another matter altogether. Why are you so pessimistic about men's intentions?"

"Aren't all women?" she asked.

"No," I replied. "A lot are actually quite open-minded about it. Why shouldn't they be?"

"I suppose", she surmised, "it's because a lot of them secretly love compliments. However, there are some of us, though, who are just a little bit more critical about this than others – that's all."

"Women", I said, "assume you're being sincere when you deliver your compliments with a sense of astonished bewilderment – an amazement that they could actually exist. Maybe you should be more objective about your own qualities. It's a fact that a certain percentage of men are going to find you outstanding. It's also a fact that they are probably going to realise this quite quickly. Certain significant things about a person's character are obvious in a fairly short span of time - particularly if those qualities are seen as being remarkable - and that applies to you as well, so don't let it bother you. It's life."

"But", she replied, "how do they know that these remarkable qualities are only masking a sea of weaknesses, which could lead to someone who thought that they were interested in you being disappointed to find that you are so unattractive after all?"

Her eyes beamed out a message of upright disdain.

"Unlike women," I said, "men are prepared to take more chances in following their instincts. It's a psychological fact that our conditioning tells us that we've got less to lose."

She withdrew to a position of weary diplomacy - a position that did not suit the fire in her veins - by pronouncing, "Oh, it's the old story. Men just fall in love more quickly."

I disagreed with this, hoping to recharge her righteous outrage. I expressed my disagreement in the following way.

"That cliché", I said, aggressively, "is probably the single most inaccurate piece of complete bullshit that I've ever heard in my entire life. Men don't fall in love more quickly - they just realise more quickly that they can do this. Men are more alive to the possibility of being attracted, and are prepared to take more risks in attempting to discover whether there is any foundation to their hopes. We burn", I added, ironically, "with curiosity."

"You mean", she replied, "lust."

I smiled, pleased that she was casting back the vibrant probity which I felt that I was unconsciously emitting, reflecting it back with the jewelled resplendence of sunlight.

Waving her hands about, she added, "Women, despite their weaknesses, have to know they're perfect. This", she continued, her hands conducting the frenetic movements within, "does not mean that I think women are generally egotistical. They have to know that they're perfect to satisfy their protective survival instincts. Women place so much faith in the correctness of their emotions that they have to know that the man they're interested in has got the sort of esoteric, specific, cryptic, beguiling taste which is required for them to find you the most beautiful individual on earth; otherwise, there are problems. It's this thing of faith - faith in the hope that someone can really appreciate you for what you are. When you are so full of emotion, it isn't nice having your faith destroyed."

Her speech, precise and carefully thought-out, was delivered with a strong reassurance that imparted to her words a quality of confident rectitude.

"Can I then", I asked, "take the opportunity of pretending that you're perfect? I've been out of touch lately. I need to sharpen a few skills."

"If you must," she replied, with dry superiority. "Go on, get on with it."

"I wish", I said, "to let it be known that She Who Seems Disillusioned With All Men has an inner beauty so complete that her mere existence must have inspired compliments so rich that her sheer presence on this planet has probably been responsible for significant transformations in the English language."

She glared at me with playful weariness; then she said, "Is that all then? If I'm supposed to have been so constantly and graciously complimented, why don't you give me some more then?"

She looked away, visibly disturbed that I had been so restrained in my eulogising.

I apologised for my insensitivity, then added, in my useless defence, "I didn't wish to be so presumptuous as to assume that you would consider my opinion to be of any relevance. Besides, premature compliments scare people off, remember?"

"I've decided", she remarked, haughtily, "that, as a result of that sort of flippant indifference that only boredom can produce, I may as well listen. Oh, why is life so full of this predictable and futile dreariness?"

I stopped myself from laughing; then said, "At the risk of being tiresomely unoriginal, I would like to officially announce to Her Royal Highness, The Princess of Perth, Countess of Fremantle, that, in my worthless opinion, it appears as if all the vast beauty of this earth has been melted into her remarkable face. It should also be noted that all the indicators at this stage seem to point to the possibility that Her Royal Highness is in possession of a very healthy lust for living, perpetuated by a rich mind sensitive to exotic experiences and the profound issues of our time."

"We must keep in touch," she announced. "You could be of some use in writing my epitaph."

"Preferably", I replied, "in about a hundred years' time, because it would mean that you'd have to be nice to me for a century."

"Not necessarily," she observed, raising her eyebrows in furious disbelief. "I could be completely horrible to you for at least fifty years. That'd give me another fifty years to make up for it."

"It wouldn't be in your interest to do that", I replied, "because there are certain circumstances in which I possess an outstanding memory."

"So you don't forgive easily then?" she asked.

"It's not a matter of forgiveness," I replied. "It has to be realised that, when I've got a pen in my hand, the truth just comes pouring out like an irrepressible tidal wave of veracity, as if I'm nothing but a vehicle for the cerebral whims of a higher force."

She chuckled and said, "What a pleasure it must be to have at your fingertips all the secrets of the universe."

"It has its problems," I replied. "You go to write a thank you card to someone for allowing you to stay at their place while you were on holidays or something, and you end up explaining to them the latest breakthroughs in research in how diet affects the functioning of the thyroid gland. I just have to live with it."

"Imagine", she smiled, "writing a letter of complaint to a local council over their inefficiencies in dealing with waste disposal or something, and you end up inadvertently laying the foundation for an entirely new social and philosophical doctrine destined to shape human thought for the next ten thousand years."

"Yeah," I replied, "I've already done that. Couldn't help it. I did wonder, though, on the plane on the flight over, what Inland Revenue must've thought about my response to their provisional assessment of my affairs. Do you think they'll see any relationship between legitimate deductions and the latest theories on how radiation can actually escape from the event horizon of a black hole?"

"Maybe", she remarked, "your musings might cause them to introduce a Genius Tax. If they do", she smiled, "you'll probably end up having the world's largest disposable income."

The afternoon continued accordingly. At the end of it, I said, "I can't describe what a pleasure it's been being so lavishly complimented by you today. We must do this again."

"Tomorrow night," she replied. "Here's the address of a party."

* * * * * * * * * * *

I burst into a crowded pub late and saw Mark Unger sitting by himself across the other side of the bar and, after having not seen him for about eight years, I announced, "I've just met someone who's absolutely fucking gorgeous!"

I was being serious. He found this very funny.

"Things haven't changed then?" he chortled.

I suddenly realise how funny this must seem to him. I smile and go to the bar and return with some drinks.

He said to me, "Who is she then?"

"Only", I reply, "the most remarkable fireball of personality on earth."

He laughs at my emotional exaggerations. He always did find them unintentionally hilarious. We both chuckle at my sentient excesses.

"I can't remember any time", he said, "when you haven't found somebody gorgeous."

"Yes," I reply, "but each time they get even more amazing."

He smiles with a rarefied warmth; this matches the aura of strength and gentleness that flows from him like an electromagnetic field of love and contentment. He seems so relaxed; he has the disposition of a Buddha. I can't recall meeting anyone so charmingly unruffled. His eyes glow in appreciative reaffirmation of those things that amused him about me all those years ago; something inside me cannot help but appeal to his taste for the unusual. Even serious remarks somehow become ablaze with humour. The soothing electricity between us creates a pleasant quirkiness of thought. In his calmness lies an extraordinary greatness. It contradicts my agitation.

"This experience I'm having now", I say, "is the last thing I expected the day I got here."

His smile is like a candle. Another breath of delighted surprise quivers the light of his soul. His mouth seems to stretch beyond the bounds of normality. The twinkling expression in his green eyes is wild in its dreamy felicity. I feel that I have before me the living embodiment of equanimity.

"If you think", he said, "that she's remarkable, then she must be."

The pleasantness of his attitude glides towards me like a swan over liquid glass; waves of gracious kindness undulate on the smooth pool of appreciation that lies between us. All the noise in the pub is lost in this moment of wonder that not a thing has changed, yet our lives are now so different.

"Ever since I met you", I say, "I've been disappointed about the fact that you're not a woman. By now we could've had five kids and been living in a rambling mansion in the country. A swimming pool the size of a football pitch could have been installed with swans floating across it. We could have had a cinema in the basement showing films we'd made with our friends. The films would have depicted all the great classical themes. But you had to be born a man. What a tragedy!"

* * * * * * * * * *

Before meeting Mark inside the pub, I had run into Brad Henderson in the beer garden. Someone screamed out my surname; it was him. His face was still covered in black fur; the vain habit of closing his mouth when smiling still existed. His teeth - which I considered to be his finest feature - were either missing, coloured or chipped. The hooked nose gave him an exotic ruggedness. When he laughed, silently, because his mouth was always closed, his head bobbed about like a table tennis ball on an agitated sea. It bobbed about even more when he was pissed. Today it bobbed about as if he were in a violent calamity. It was Friday and as usual his drinking had begun at midday.

In a dynamic universe, this process of his Friday drinking was probably the most certain phenomenon from here to the Orion Nebula. I once saw him, after twelve hours of solid consumption, at the end of one of these Friday binges, fall unconscious off a stool. The first thing to hit the deck was his head. When he woke up, he didn't even seem to notice that he had fallen. He just got back up again, amidst howls of protests, and continued his drinking. He then spent two days in hospital with alcohol poisoning.

"I got Les", he beamed, "to try and track you down. I thought to myself, 'I want to go to England. Where's Harley?, But I now realise," he chuckled, "that it's better to just sit in a beer garden and wait for people to come along."

He usually wasn't this talkative. To get him to say anything was usually a miracle.

"I hope", I said, "that your wait wasn't an anxious one."

"Me?" he replied, with incredulous hilarity. "Get anxious?!"

"You seem to forget", I said, "that I'm the master of irony. Has alcohol ruined your sense of humour?"

He looked up like a chirpy pussycat and said, "What are you doing here, anyway?"

"Come looking for you, Brad," I replied. "What else?"

"You're a difficult man to track down," he said. "It was a difficult one between Les and Interpol."

"So how far did he get?" I asked.

"He said", he replied, "that your old man is the most suspicious, grumpiest cunt on earth."

"That," I said, "is about the only thing Les has ever said that's true. Like you, he's basically useless; but he's an excellent judge of character."

His closed-mouthed head bobbed around even more than it had been bobbing around before; then he gave me his card. I was disappointed with the colours.

"Blue and white," I said. "You're letting the side down."

The football team we supported was maroon and gold.

"I try not to hand it out," he replied.

"It'd mean work, anyway, wouldn't it?" I asked.

"I'm", he replied, ironically, "not scared of that."

"I'd be", I said, "if I were you. Anyone with a ticket on the cosy, public service yacht of contentment, gliding along the river of hedonism towards the distant peak of oblivion, must have a natural aversion to effort."

"It's a nice trip," he smiled.

"It got a little boring for me," I replied.

"Each to their own," he said.

* * * * * * * * * * *

I had to go shopping for Christmas presents. This was one of the most absurd things that I had done for years. I was after little girls' dresses. It was a very uneasy feeling shopping for something that either implied suburban uneventfulness or sexual perversion. I, of course, if forced to choose, would have gone for the latter.

I had to confess what I was doing to somebody so I rang up Brad Henderson; the conversation went like this:

HIM: Where are you?
ME: Town.
HIM: Doing what?
ME: Something unbelievable.
HIM: What?
ME: You sure you want to know?
HIM: Up to you.
ME: It's really unbelievable.
HIM: Let me know then.
ME: Get ready for this.
HIM: Okay, I'm ready. What is it?
ME: You sure you're ready?
HIM: I haven't been shocked for years. I'm looking forward to it. Fire away.
ME: Don't say you weren't warned.
HIM: I won't.
ME: Okay, this is it. The man who's crossed swollen, crocodile-infested rivers on nothing more than a broken log; the man who's unexpectedly found himself in vast political turmoils in seething, Third World countries and who's fled from desperate revolutions whilst fighting off vicious Muslim tribesmen, is – and this is bound to bring tears to the eyes of all those familiar with me in the international media – shopping, believe it or not, for little girls' dresses.
HIM: Any particular reason?
ME: I'm into that sort of thing these days.
HIM: Sounds like fun.
ME: It was frightening. I was surrounded by pink, frilly lace and blue-and-white polka dots, involuntarily looking over my shoulder just in case someone like you might've spotted me.
HIM: Are you going to give it to anyone?
ME: I've now got two nieces. Something I've got no control over.
HIM: Who said you had to give them anything?

ME: It's rental payment for free accommodation for six weeks. You never know when I might want to come back.

HIM: Personally, I wouldn't've bothered.

ME: When I got here, I said: 'Don't buy me any fucking presents.' And what do those fucking idiots go and do?

HIM: I bought three.

ME: Not for women?

HIM: No way!

ME: Christ, you had me worried for a moment there.

HIM: A quick stroll to the local record shop was all that was required.

ME: Three records you obviously wanted.

HIM: Yep. All three are now already recorded.

ME: You haven't changed. Still a total arsehole. Imagine this: you haven't seen someone for six years and the first thing they say to you is: 'Glad you're here. I'm going to England next year.'

HIM: Les's family location services left a little to be desired. I knew you'd eventually appear in some beer garden somewhere. It was bound to happen.

ME: Do you want to meet there tonight ?

HIM: Don't like the place.

ME: You ought to. A little ray of sunshine comes back into your life there and you don't like it. You've got absolutely no sentimentality whatsoever.

HIM: Of course.

We arrange to meet, and I wondered if his pretensions at displaying his individuality via total detachment would ultimately bore me.

* * * * * * * * * * *

When I told Brian that I was going to meet someone in Northbridge, he said that Vanessa was going there as well. She wasn't. She was going to a pub known for its gorgeous men. She was under the drinking age and had barely arrived at the age of consent. Northbridge is an area of cafés and restaurants where all generations mix. Young girls are free to go there. When the sister of a friend came to pick her up, Brian said to her, "Wear a jacket," to cover up her breasts, and, "Don't drink." I was always intrigued by draconian attitudes naively implemented to try and stop free spirits from doing whatever they liked. This was yet another example.

Vanessa shook her head in rueful amazement at the overly-protective attitude of her father. He had initially tried to stop her from wearing the "clinging, sexy top", one that made her breasts stand out handsomely.

"Eighty-five dollars!" he screamed, when he discovered its price, before expressing concern about "those Italian guys at Northbridge".

Vanessa replied, "I pinch their bums before they pinch mine."

Brian tried to get aggressive; his threats about stopping her from going, because of this remark, only made her laugh.

The following day she told me that she never suffers from hangovers, "only a dry mouth".

One in anticipation, I thought.

* * * * * * * * * *

The only reason I went to the party was because Samantha would be there. I persuaded Ana to give me a lift. We weren't going to stay long. I was out on an obtain-phone-number mission. It was amusing for both of us when a lady, feigning friendliness, asked us personal details in an endeavour to establish if we had just walked in off the street uninvited. A short, amiable conversation ensued; her insincerity was exposed the instant that she discovered we knew someone with whom she had been to school. When she realised that we were not potentially dangerous elements but invited, her artificial smile dissipated and she just walked off, the façade evaporating in mid-sentence. It was ironically amusing and symbolic of the shallowness of the situation that her pretence to interest departed with the knowledge of our association with one of her friends. I had assumed, initially, that her interest was genuine, born from curiosity, a warm response to human contact. We were both astounded by her arrogance and disrespect.

"Must've thought we were going to fire-bomb the place," Ana said, exasperated.

Samantha then emerged from the swimming pool wearing a bikini and an unbuttoned shirt. Her intense, flashing eyes reminded me of a past love. Her hair, in gleaming, soaked, blue-white/black clusters, was wild with beauty. She was like a fierce, ultra-feminine animal which thrives in an environment of chlorinated water and champagne. I could not imagine such a creature feigning warmth through fear.

She came towards us across a back garden laden with semi-naked people with an expression of anxious detachment upon her face. Quickly, we found ourselves in a conversation about kibbutz life and the PLO. It felt refreshingly bizarre to be having this conversation in this place. I was surprised to discover that she was sensitive to the Zionist cause. It was a little naive and unjustifiably hopeful of me to assume that she was not the sort of person who could be affected by propaganda. A year in Israel had been enough to make her believe that the Israelis had a right to destroy entire villages in neighbouring lands, just because an Israeli soldier was shot at in an occupied territory.

I tried desperately not to look down at her chest. My eyes had minds of their own. Two firm, round soft cups of delicate flesh greeted my leering gaze. The silky smoothness of her breasts was enhanced by the even pleasantness of the apricot light. I had the unnerving feeling of having to move forward very slowly to keep her within acceptable conversational range, for she kept backing away, whilst pouring out her feelings about the Arab/Israeli conflict.

I felt like saying: 'Is it against your principles to discuss international affairs in a single spot or are you just afraid of a bomb attack?'

I then wondered to myself, 'Does this woman do anything that could be described as predictable?'

She then said, "I have to go and change," before running off into the house unexpectedly.

Ana looked at me and said, "Not bad, Knubz."

"Quite a bit of work needs to be done there though," I replied.

"May result", he said, "in some profound job satisfaction, however."

I smiled and said, "Can't see the point in hanging around here though. She feels too uncomfortable about having to entertain me when she knows most of the people in this place. I'm just going to try and grab her phone number. If she says no, then too bad. There's plenty more emus on the plains."

Her return was a long time coming. It had been a little worrying. We ran into her at the side of the house on our way out. She was surprised to see that we were going. She had glamorised her appearance in a manner that contradicted the fiery independence of her character. Her hair was up with curly fronds clinging to the exposed neck. Long, silvery earrings glinted in the subdued light. The unexpected application of make-up made her appear, deceptively, like the empty-headed wife of some superficial entrepreneur.

"Didn't think I'd see you again," I said.

She smiled, slightly embarrassed, and replied, "I just felt like being by myself for a while. You know how it is."

"Don't blame you," I said.

The discomfort level was appalling when I managed, in a voice not my own, to say the following words: "Would you like to go out some time?"

"Yes," she replied.

A warm glow of relief replaced the dread. The number was blissfully extracted. It went straight into the memory like a cowboy branding the hide of a cow. Translucent smoke emanated from my ears. The night's work had been successful. The feeling of achievement at the satisfaction of a vital goal flowed, like a drug, through my veins. It was like being in the grip of an excited peace.

Something now had come into our relationship: embarrassed politeness. I told her how unusual it was to see groups of people so scantily dressed in public. I told her how surprised I was on the first day here when I saw a man riding a bike down the road wearing nothing but a pair of racing bathers and a pair of sunglasses.

"I thought," I said, "'Jesus – that guy's naked. He's going to get arrested.'"

She giggled nervously. The noise from the party was the only animated feature within the sparkling stillness of the night. She moved uneasily before me, a seething beast of restrained passion; I was mystified by the conflict of sensitivity, aggression and detachment that caused the confused fire in her eyes. Perhaps it was my uneasy gregariousness that unnerved her normally stern disposition? Or the ludicrous reference to nudity?

She told me when it was best to ring her. I was pleased with this reaffirmation of my success. I acknowledged it with an uncharacteristic display of unctuous gratitude. The sudden transformation of our association from one of playful and sometimes open disrespect to one of fidgety diplomacy caused us both to act with the sort of tense inanity that resulted in my making a ridiculous pun about her surname and her address. My mind, out of control in a situation that did not warrant it, had leapt upon some eccentric connection it had decided existed between the two. This had occurred after she had, unprompted, provided me with these details as a measure against any memory loss regarding her phone number.

I decided that it was better to go and let fate run its course.

"I'll ring you next week," I said.

"Okay," she replied.

Walking to his car, Ana said, "Those situations are always so awkward."

"Particularly", I replied, "when there's no real build-up to the big question."

In his car, he said, "She's really nice. You should've stayed."

"Don't tell me that," I replied.

"Oh well," he sighed, "it's hardly likely that she'll meet the love of her life over the next few days.".

An eerie feeling of uncertainty about this then descended upon me. 'The man in question is probably at the party,' I thought.

* * * * * * * * * *

The pub in which Henderson and I had agreed to meet had a leafy beer garden covered by a pergola with a square bar in the middle of it. I sat on a stool and waited. Mottled patches of light touched the brick floor of the garden. The afternoon sun threw an orange splendour over the leaves above. The barman rested his elbows on the padded bar and chatted with an obese customer who contentedly puffed on cigars. Clouds of smoke rose slowly from the customer's mouth and curled into the air. Shafts of light illuminated these folds of vapour that dissipated before reaching the leaves. I studied these languidly crepitating veins of mist and imagined them to be free spirits rising upward to nothingness. Each unfurling curl of gas was a further disentanglement from unnecessary concern. These spiralling mists – the metaphysical equivalents of the human spirit before my eyes – suggested to me that I had achieved a state known as "passive intolerance". This condition prompts undemonstrative dissociation from those devoid of a certain attitude. It was unlikely that Henderson would possess the correct one. The chances of him having changed at all were almost zero. My interest in him lay in the satisfaction of a personal curiosity. I wanted to know how I would involuntarily respond to his existence. I could have said to him: 'Do you realise that passive intolerance is a phenomenon designed to stop minor irritations being uselessly compounded into hate through unwarranted involvement, and that tonight I'm going to prove it?' and he probably would have replied, 'Fine.'

My first glimpse of his appearance made me realise how long his hair was now. It was tied back into a ponytail and made him look cool. There were lots of people these days who were looking cool. It was cool to be detached from barbarism (hairdressers).

When he reached me, he said, "Seen Les?"

I should have realised that he wouldn't be able to do this by himself.

"If he is here," I replied, "he probably saw me first."

He sat down. I spoke at length about the experience of change – of suddenly cutting yourself off from one environment and then going back to it years later. It was an experience that gave you the opportunity to gain some measure of awareness about something significant and often imperceptible – that is, how much you had changed. He was proud of the fact that he did not need to do this. He had already achieved the ultimate state; he lived under the delusion that anxiety was an experience for others. It seemed trivial to me to maintain a pretence of calmness when esoteric fears were so entertaining and amusing. To illustrate how proud he was of the possible genetic evidence for the vindication of his vanity he told me a story about his father's return to England. His father had left the United Kingdom forty years ago. All contact between father and family was then severed on departure.

"He hadn't contacted his family for forty years," Henderson smiled. "He gets to the airport and makes a call. One of them came and picked him up from Croydon. Before he left, I said to him, 'Aren't you going to let them know that you're coming?' and he just said, 'What for?'"

Henderson then produced an enormous smile.

"So you see," he said, "that's where it comes from."

Having satisfied himself that he was in perfect mental health, he then refused to indulge in conversation unless it directly involved him. I actually felt some sympathy for him: he was deluded enough to think that this attitude was giving him a fulfilling life. Silence is no problem, but when it is based on a desire to emulate someone else's character it is absurd. To satisfy my feelings about his vain muteness I made a series of contentious comments about AIDS, male-female relationships and history. His responses were limited to changes in facial expressions. Sometimes the lips would forge together and protrude in acknowledgement of a remark that could have been open to debate. But no debate was forthcoming. In deference to his desire to be seen as one already too enlightened for interaction he steadfastly refused to open his mouth. I had made the mistake once of going to New Zealand with him. He did not speak for five days. A year after this, a mutual acquaintance told me, after I came back from a holiday, that Henderson was bored at work and that he felt that he "should have gone to Indonesia with Harley". I was astounded. It was remarkable to think that Henderson actually thought that I would have wasted six weeks of my life in a place like that with him.

Les then arrived. He stood up, tense all night, attempting to please his detached messiah. I could not fathom why someone of Les's intelligence had to submit himself to the pointless task of attempting to befriend a statue. On the brief occasions that one of his too-cynically expressed remarks stirred the features of his master, he would smile with a satisfied relish and a disturbing smugness which reduced, rather than enhanced, his flagging individuality. It was unfortunate that he did not have anything better to do.

They decided that they wanted to eat. The three of us walked separately, in single file, up the street. I brought up the rear. I was smiling in response to the machismo of the predicament. Les, who was between myself and Henderson, was doing his utmost to create an impression of stoic calm. He was failing miserably. His fruitless anxiety made me think that he was a sheep being led by the shepherd of pretentious detachment.

I turned left at the top of the street. Henderson crossed the road. Les whistled. I looked over my shoulder and saw Les wave his arm in a manly gesture of command. He was indicating that they – in fact it was Henderson – were going into a kebab shop. I thought the association with lamb was hilariously appropriate. I saw Henderson disappear through the door. Les the lamb duly followed. I walked slowly towards the entrance. I was expecting the amusing sight I eventually saw. Looking through the window, I saw the seated Henderson staring dispassionately while his disciple, a lonely figure, sat next to him ablaze with agitated concern. I chuckled at the sight of the pair of them. A passer-by was mystified by my amused observations. I was delighted and appalled with the inconsequentiality of such a couple. One believed that they were living with style while the other refused to accept that no real reward was possible for being victimised in these ridiculous ordeals.

I saw a taxi coming down the road and caught it. The following day at lunch I told Samantha about this situation.

She said, with her refreshing openness, that "sometimes it's just easier to leave without saying good-bye". She then wanted to know more about "these two".

She was intrigued by Henderson, because she was at the opposite extreme to his egocentric coldness. I felt profound satisfaction when she was flattered by my pronouncement that "mystery has nothing to do with silence".

"A truly mystifying person", I said, "is someone capable of speaking eloquently and constantly, and with great passion, about a bewildering array of interesting subjects. Someone", I added, with satisfying sincerity, "like you. I'm happy to say that I've now overcome this misapprehension about silence and mystery. A dumbly contented individual is not necessarily an interesting one. A silent person is usually silent because they have no passion and nothing to say. I think it's very important that people realise that."

It was a pleasure galvanising the ego of someone who deserved it. She remarked, with the invigoration of discovery, the revitalisation of a new insight: "that contented people seem gifted and mysterious, because so few of us are contented. We want to try and discover why."

I was thankful to have had an answer to this.

"The human mind", I said, "ignores the hard-bitten, prosaic pragmatist and seeks out the classicist, the egotist, the genius and the fool. It is these four that make life so interesting. Our minds quickly find excuses to slot people into one of these four categories and contentedness, for the reason that you've just given, is the torch that leads so many of us astray down the path of pretentious aptitude, when, in fact, it can mean the reverse."

"I'd better, then," she replied, "to remain a little discontented."

"You will", I said, "anyway. You strike me as being too idealistic and alive not to be."

Fortunately, she was grateful for this. Lunch with her was a fascinating experience. She had already given me an explanation of the proposed attempts to reduce gaps in the ozone layer through oxygen ingestion. This was currently deemed uneconomical. She spent the day maniacally flicking back her lustrous hair. Her eyes were distant - but not in a disturbing way - iridescent, enormous and dark. She was equally indisposed and insecure towards her family. She explained how she had burst out and attempted to sell baby trees to people who owned front lawns in a suburb she described as: "Ahh!! It was..." Fists clenched. "...AWFUL!"

I can assure you that she was not.

FOUR

Everyone had gathered at Brian's place on Christmas Day. It was the first time in years that I was surrounded by people in a social situation whose values I did not share. I planned to say as little as possible and let the day take care of itself.

My father kept referring to his youngest granddaughter, a chubby, little creature, as: "Hoooooooooooge!" (Huge.)

"Christ!" he kept saying, bending over her in drunken wonderment. "She's hoooooooge!"

Everything then became "hooooooge". It was astonishing to discover how many things were actually "hoooooooooge". Sue was particularly amused by her husband's dramatic exaggerations.

She was sitting next to my stone-faced grandmother, giggling, saying, "Oh Keith! Oh Keith!" as her husband's booming voice continued to notify us of the fact that Hannah was "hoooooooooge".

There seemed to be an unnecessary amount of movement. Wayne and Brian wandered around cracking jokes. Vanessa sat on the settee making cynical comments about Brian's fussiness. My father paced up and down in a state of hurried uninterest. His grey-white hair gave him a false aspect of aged graciousness. Richard sat sombrely with his smiling girlfriend. Wayne decided to torment him. Greg sat on a stool in the kitchen chatting to a friend. His girlfriend, Danielle, charged around the house making noisy pronouncements. Kay was in the kitchen adding the final touches to the food. When it was served, everyone scampered to the table. I decided to sit for as long as possible to give myself the opportunity of momentarily being alone. My short-lived peace was shattered when my father, always only too willing to prove his graceless idiocy, stuck his head around the corner – the dining room was tucked away from where I was sitting – and began screaming out my name in an inexplicable outburst of absurd anger.

"Get over here!" he screamed at me.

Everyone was seated at the table waiting.

"Get over here! Get over here!" he wailed.

I stared at him with a sort of inquisitive perplexity. My countenance – a kind of dumbfounded fascination, a gaze of clinical observation – was designed to highlight the disparity in our respective emotional states. This display of passive bewilderment did little to help him see his immaturity.

"Get over here!" he continued screaming, his left arm waving with hysterical inanity, his face burning with peeved outrage.

"Remarkable," I whispered to myself. "The photojournalist, accustomed to the horrors of humanity, is now a five-year-old child again. Truly astonishing."

Due to a macabre desire to see what next he would do, I made my way to the table.

"Have you ever", I began, with sarcastic joy, "considered the prospect of employment as a sophisticated, worldly butler in a country mansion?"

This comment left everyone, apart from my grandmother, in a state of appreciative uproar.

The only spare seat was next to my father. He grabbed me by the head and said, "Just making sure that I got to sit next to my favourite son – that's all."

He then tried to push my head under the table. Lunch, I knew, was going to be absorbing. Painfully so. My father's unrelenting mouth would make sure of that. Before long it caused a paranoiac tension to descend upon the table. The idea of speaking, of putting forward any belief, statement or feeling was crushed under the fear of bearing the brunt of my father's barbaric mouth. The dinner conversation – a grandiose term for the petrified quietude of the occasion – consisted purely of my father's belittlement of his defenceless brother. Fifteen people, all completely different, with very little in common, sat in fearful dumbness as the following exchange occurred:

MY FATHER: So how much are you on? [A reference to Brian's new job.]
BRIAN: Fifty-eight thousand.
MY FATHER: Ha! Yar workin' for nothin'! [Brian greeted my father's sneers with confused restraint. Great silence in the background.]
MY FATHER: Did you approach them, or did they approach you?
BRIAN: They approached me.
MY FATHER: Christ! They must be fucking mad!

This caused Sue to glare at her husband with piercing viciousness. She was down at the other end of the table.

Her searing gaze resulted in my father leaning towards me and whispering, "Christ, I'm gonna cop it on the way home."

Then he said to Brian, "So what are you doing?"

A normal person – a person with real dignity – might have replied, "So what the fuck do you want to know for?" but Brian said, attempting to maintain an unruffled façade, "I'm a producer."

My father then erupted with chortling insensitivity.

"A producer!" he chuckled. "Hah! You haven't produced anything in your bloody life!"

An air of mock and sombre uninterest evaded the place. A pretence of uninvolvement caused a silence rich in its shrill scream for a better world.

In response to her husband's embarrassing behaviour, Sue yelled out, "Keith! Do you have to smoke at the table?!"

My father was the only one smoking. The glass sliding doors were open behind him. The wire of the fly-screen had been pulled across it. He leant towards the open door and held his cigarette up so that the smoke drifted outside.

"Not hurting anyone," he then said, "see?" bringing the cigarette closer to the fly-screen. "No problem."

He then defended his continued smoking, after a serious illness, by saying that he knew of eight people who had died of smoking-related diseases in the past twenty-one months.

"But", he said, "none of them played sport."

He said, as though he were a world authority on the subject, that the determining factor was "genetics" To back his belief in personal immortality – it was almost religious how he placed so much faith in this miracle to prolong his alcohol-and-cigarette-imbibing life – he said that the only person to die young in his family was his uncle "and he jogged until he was forty-nine".

I was astounded by this contradiction.

"How many members of your family", I then asked, "have smoked solidly for thirty years?"

"Doesn't matter", he replied, "if you've played sport."

"What about Theo?" I asked. His uncle.

"An exception," my father conveniently replied.

This was the sort of twisted logic that he so often used to bring a conversation to a grinding halt; the conversation had no future anyway. Bradley, who had received a lethal water pistol – it held about two litres of water and was about two feet long – used it to attack his grandfather's cigarette. He struck from point-blank range. I was buffeted in the ensuing mêlée to grab the pistol. I then attempted to rip it out of my father's hands, causing water to be splattered across the ceiling. This made Brian anxious. He got to his feet, muttering about "appalling behaviour in my house". He then returned from the kitchen with a bucket and swab. He then got up on a stool and began wiping the ceiling.

"What are you worried about?" my father said, smiling sadistically. "You said you were going to demolish the house."

Earlier, Brian had spoken boldly of his plans regarding his beloved residence. My father's comment was a sardonic reference to his belief that "fucking Skirts [Brian] hasn't got a fucking clue of what he's fucking doing."

Brian continued muttering to himself. I heard something along the lines of: "This is the last bloody time! Never again! No way! Not a chance!" while my father smiled with evil relish beneath him, pleased to see his brother so concerned about something so trivial.

"You're okay now, Skirts," my father chuckled, as Sue yelled out his name. "The property's been saved. The water's been overcome!"

"Keith! Keith!"

It was intriguing watching Brian wiping water over water. Did he think that the water from the pistol had special stain-giving powers that the water from the tap did not possess? Why did he bother? He really believed that this event had the potential to affect his future. It was so prosaic and yet so remarkable. His intense concentration had the hallmarks of significant, creative endeavour. Why did he put so much energy into the insipid? As he wiped, he muttered how "bloody careless" we were, causing derisive laughter to break out around the table. Greg, arms folded, shook his head with titillated disbelief, announcing with droll gratitude that he was "ecstatic" about the fact "that I do not have to live here any more." My father smiled with his usual bitter amusement, quipping that "stains can fuck the demolition of any property up. Any developer'll tell you that."

Mark pulled Brian's pants down. This exposed Brian's Y-fronts, which looked so absurd at the top of his gnarled legs. Wayne, Mark,

Danielle, Vanessa and I began to laugh hysterically as I began untying Brian's shoelaces. Mark then took aim with the water pistol and hit Brian in the lower abdomen region. Sue and my grandmother were looking distressed at the other end of the table. On his way back to the kitchen, Brian picked up a glass of champagne, after Wayne had attempted to throw him into the swimming pool, and hurled it into his face. Outraged, Wayne retaliated by grabbing a kiwi fruit, squashing it in his hand and smearing it into the carpet. He then repeated the process with a banana. Even I was astonished by the depth of Wayne's childish overreaction. Brian then emerged from the kitchen bewildered.

"Ahhh! Ker-reist Wayne!" he screamed. "You're such a fucking nuisance!"

Then he grabbed the swab again and began wiping the carpet up, muttering about how "immature" Wayne was. Wayne became defensive.

"Pardon me," he said, with angered righteousness, "but who was it who threw a glass of champagne?"

"Oh, shut up both of you!" my grandmother screamed, as my father laughed joyfully at the other end of the table.

This was not how my grandmother had planned things. It was the last time that we would be gathered together as one for Christmas. It was turning into the nightmare that most of us had expected.

"Christ, Wayne!" Brian continued, bending over the fruit-smeared carpet, as my grandmother yelled out: "Brian!"

"You can throw shit", Brian gasped, ignoring his mother, "but you can't take it!!"

"I beg your pardon," Wayne began, overcome by moral outrage. "I suppose it's all right for people to throw glasses of champagne in other people's faces, is it?"

"I'm not taking any more shit", Brian exclaimed, "in my own home from anyone!"

"That's obvious," Wayne replied, sarcastically, as my father continued to chuckle to himself, while my grandmother continued to scream out: "Brian! Brian!"

Greg's friend looked shocked. He was sitting on the other side of the table from me.

"I take it that Greg warned you?" I inquired.

"Yes," he replied, "but I still wasn't expecting this."

The poor bastard was in a state of genuine disbelief. He stared, open-mouthed, fixedly, dumbstruck; overcome by supine worry, the pained innocence of his expression was a reflection of the depth of the credulity with which his well-adjusted mind attempted to fathom the incredible possibility that someone like Wayne could actually exist. The fantastic immaturity and horrifying petulance of my elder brother was only matched by the labouring triviality and self-defeating concern of my flabbergasted uncle. Together they formed a lethal combination. Each brought out the worst aspects of the other with an ease that delighted my father's cynical mind. Openly pleased with events so far, my father was oblivious of the effect that he was having upon Greg's friend. David was as disturbed by my father's attitude as he was by the events themselves. Hopelessly downcast by an atmosphere that he could not readily explain, David longed for a return to domestic harmony, a desire reflected in Greg's comment: "Probably time you went back to a real family; whadda yar think?"

"Definitely," he mumbled.

He left.

The rest of the day was devoted to observing Wayne's prickly disgust. One irreverent comment after another - all associated with Brian - fell from his cantankerous lips. I walked past as Kay was chastising him for behaving like an idiot; he glared at me with fierce eyes. A great injustice had been done to him.

"He threw a glass of champagne in my face!" he squealed.

"Well," I replied, "you did try to throw him into the swimming pool, and you wouldn't stop when he quite obviously wanted you to leave him alone."

These facts were irrelevant to a mind conditioned to experience shocked desecration at every negative turn. The expression of seething effrontery in my brother's agitated eyes suggested that Brian, himself defiled by years of abuse, had committed an act of the most barbaric proportions. I was seeing a microcosm of the effects of infantile moral superiority. Greed might fuel wars, but it is this philosophical pretence to sacredness that sustains them.

Kay was not particularly forgiving in her denunciation of Wayne's unnecessary bickering. She was not prepared to go beyond the present in a search for the answer to the mystery of Wayne's childish acts of scandalised despair. My grandmother's idea that Wayne should be ignored when he was in this mood could never appeal to the sanity of a woman still perplexed by her belief in normal reactions to normal events. I had experienced sufficient insanity when young, and then had gone to visit it when older, to realise that the pursuit of excuses to undertake destructive fantasies was a normal enough activity, one that did not merit the kind of angered surprise which marked the tormented face of my furious sister-in-law. Her experience had been too well-balanced to enable her to experience the kind of phlegmatism required to ignore such ridiculous occurrences as these. I felt that this quality within her – this mature bafflement – was ironic, in that her well-adjusted standpoint was actually stimulating the continuation of these absurd affairs. She was uselessly inveighing at her husband to cease his spiteful quips, ones directed at an uncle staggered that his mother was admonishing him for being so irate, after having been treated "like this" in his "own home".

"Why can't you just bloody well leave him alone?" Kay hissed at Wayne, who ignored her vehement inquiries and continued his niggling berating of his wilting uncle.

"Hey Brian," he said, "how about a bit of fruit salad?"

"Wayne! Wayne! Wayne!!" Kay pleaded.

"Jesus Christ," Brian replied, "still a fucking child after all these years."

"Brian! Brian! Brian!" my grandmother screamed.

"Go for him, Skirts," my father sniggered.

"Keith! Keith! Keith!" Sue bellowed.

My father smiled wickedly. He was delighted with the events of the day. They were giving him the perfect excuse he required to enable him to avoid ever having to have Christmas with his family again. This – apart from his desire to spend nothing on anyone – was probably the only sensible ambition that he had ever had in his life.

Eventually, Kay got Wayne out the door. They had arranged to visit Kay's parents that evening. Everyone drifted out on to the front lawn for the goodbye ritual. Wayne's mouth was swimming in a raging stream of sarcastic vitriol. His wife dumped him sombrely into the passenger-side seat. He wound down the window and said to Vanessa, "I've left three crayfish in the freezer. Make sure that Brian doesn't get any – right!"

After they drove off, Kay fuming, Brian and I walked up the side of his house along the driveway. We were having a good laugh, largely in admiration of Wayne's defensive persistence.

"Bloody Wayne," he said, giggling. "Even when they go to nail down the lid of his coffin, he'll still be saying, 'You haven't nailed it down properly you fucking, useless cunts!'"

We got to the top of the driveway to say goodbye to my grandmother. I kissed her on the cheek and she wiped her face with her hand in disgust.

'Oh well,' I thought. 'Obviously didn't like my present.'

* * * * * * * * * *

It cannot be described as a happy experience, this fear, this pessimistic emptiness, a belief in the inevitable decrepitude of human intention; someone else would also have to question the motives of an individual attempting to find excitement in this idea that in the end no one should be trusted. With a family like mine, incapable of benign interaction without conflict, these sudden darts, slights, barbarous prongs into the soul, were often perceived as amusing, thrilling, a challenge. Why not shove the euphemistic missile up someone's arse? See how they react. Go on.

It was supposed to be good to confront life. But it was not pleasant always expecting confrontation, attacks, doubts; how could you really care, constantly, if your thoughts are not taken seriously by those who are supposed to listen? It was a struggle to stop that hole of emptiness widening so that futility would not seep into it and erode its edges further. Futility is the emotional pain of having no legitimate excuse of seeing any point in caring. And what is the point in experiencing it? It is a contagious commodity. Parents, only too willing to react more childishly than their children, have a profound ability to spread it. Ever had the feeling of not wanting to go home from school because you are certain that some inexplicable anger will be vented upon you by an idiot overcome by the failure of their frustrated goals? And then the following day staring with wounded eyes into the ignorant faces of your classmates? And imagine being too young to be able to explain this? Too inexperienced to imagine the transience of all despicable things?

It is too easy to believe that injustices have been perpetrated against you. The slightest suggestion of mistreatment can take on associative powers beyond the scope of the event. This applies particularly to the defiant mind unwilling to adapt. The specimen which takes to adaptation - perhaps the natural optimist - has, for reasons presumably to do with a desire to experience constant joy, the ability to connect excitement with brutality. Instead of believing that horrors are being committed, the adaptable creature, at an age prior to moral development, will discover a way of convincing themselves that the crimes being performed upon them are propitious, thrilling, exciting, even beautiful. After all, it is attention from a parent and what is more normal than a child's desire than to receive this?

The human race, too adaptable for its own good, contains many members not prepared to answer in the negative when asked the following question: Is all conflict totally, and without exception, completely bad? So many times I have had the contradictory experience of wishing to see a disaster, whilst being horrified by the prospect of innocent deaths. What can you say about someone who watches motor racing, hoping to see a collision of horrendous proportions? Or someone who visits a fairground and lusts for the ferris wheel to spin of its bearings and fly off into the night? Or someone who finds the personal disasters of others to be side-splittingly hilarious? For one thing, you can say that they are human. And what can you say about someone wishing to thrust themselves into the electrifying unpredictability of warring desecration? Or someone who deliberately places themselves in a position where a bereaving, outraged, mortified, despairing, enraged, tormented, wailing woman shoves her mutilated child into your face and insists that you do your utmost to bring these atrocities to a halt, when you have gone there precisely to see them? Yes, they too are human. And what can you say about someone who is pleased that, on witnessing this unforgivable butchery, experiences such outrageous disgust that they have a blind rage in which the only desire left in their consciousness is the savage ambition of tearing the putrid heart out of the evil maniac who did it, and eating that pathetic excuse for an organ? Or someone who gains a sense of exhilarated gratitude by seeing the primeval savagery of mankind? Need I say it? They too are human. And what can you say about someone so curious, so fascinated and so in love with the visualisation of the broad canvas of the collective unconscious that they are convinced that moral satisfaction is a mere chicane against the addictive power of adrenalin. Or someone who dreams of night skies ablaze with the beauty of iridescent tracers? You guessed it: they, too, are human.

If, in early life, to remain sane, you had to adapt by normalising the abnormal, a fascination for acts that disregard common sense can easily result; it is a lust for the wildness of free expression, the voyeuristic intrigue of existing on the stage of grandiloquent themes, of continuing the perversely conditioned protective process of translating the vicious and ugly into the enriching and beautiful. It is a true fascination for amoral life - and it is human.

If a person is truly altruistic, which is in a sense both anti-aesthetic and anti-intellectual - in that one would not be able to pose oneself certain questions - then I believe that we can look into the glorious eyes of such a being and say: 'You know, you really are truly inhuman.' A much overrated expression is this term "human", and a much underrated one is its antonym.

The beach that Samantha and I lay upon was a surreal place for the expression of such ideas. The air was still and infused with the warm calmness of spiritual contentment. A silken fabric of orange light had been spread over the soft body of the white sand. The perfect silence of the darkening heavens was punctuated by the languid rumble of the swishing seas. A demulcent closeness, like the soothing oscillations of the resting waters, flowed between us.

"Are you saying then", she asked, "that self-analysis eradicates guilt?"

"It is", I replied, "an exculpatory process that must reduce contrition."

She glanced across the fiery ocean to the king of the skies whose crown was imbued with the colourful glory of his radiant magnificence and said, "That means then that if someone has a true grasp of the real reasons for their worst motives, then they have every right to blame someone else for their lack of conscience as they pursue their every ambition."

"I'm afraid so," I replied.

"I can't agree with that," she said.

"I know you can't," I replied.

* * * * * * * * * *

It was Boxing Day and Ross and I were walking down the street to go to his favourite café. As usual, he was in black. The concave shapes of lampposts and shop façades flashed across his dark glasses.

The white flower of the sun burst into life and then disappeared out of the ebony heavens of his dark and sometimes lurid vision. A thin pony-tail protruded from the back of his head. Down the street, power lines converged towards each other in the quivering distances. Lost in a sullen expectancy, they disappeared into a haze of melancholic sterility. A feeling of languid futility gripped the sizzling air. The only shadows were restricted to the frontages of buildings that baked in the high, blazing sun. The sky above, serene and clear, was like a conflagration of blue fire. Nothing dared move quickly beneath it.

Inside the café, the cool air came as a relief. Helicopter blades swirled in the ceiling. A long bar, plated with chrome, curled past groups of people seated on red stools that swivelled noiselessly in the soporific air. The café was in the style of an American fifties diner. Red upholstery adorned the cubicled seats that lay against the walls. We sat at a table at one end of the bar next to a cigarette machine. I told Ross about my father's behaviour the previous day and he screwed his face up and said: "God! Some people just haven't grown up in any way at all."

I took pleasure in describing to him the dinner conversation; he gritted his teeth at the dreadful idea of communication at a family gathering being denuded by fears of cynical abuse.

Then he said, "It's impossible to expect to find someone who thinks and feels exactly as yourself. You've just got to accept that others are not going to be able to understand you."

"Or be unwilling to," I replied.

He then made it clear that sex outside a genuine relationship is undesirable. This still did not stop him from then undertaking a protracted period of boyish sexual innuendoes with respect to the women coming and going from the cafe.

"I feel", he said, philosophically, at the height of this, "that the biological is taking over again."

He then concentrated his lascivious gazes upon a woman sitting at the bar with a man. She was tall and pretty and was flattered by his attention. He would glance coolly in her direction with a sort of calculated indifference, as if idle curiosity had just managed to give him sufficient impetus to make the effort, then he would look back at me, a wry, suppressed smile on his face, and say, "I caught her looking again."

I glanced over at her: it was true. She was intrigued by the chap with the green, sparkling eyes in the corner. Ross was not surprised by this. His life had been dominated by superficial female fascination. This was yet another chapter in a story of mutual, unspoken concupiscence. He did his utmost to convince himself that he was now above such adolescence; he wanted to feel that he had more important things with which to concern himself; but it was difficult.

"There's no way", he said, "that I'm going to do anything here." And then glancing over at her again, "Very tasty though."

The problem with morality (perhaps futile gratification) versus desire could only be solved by falling in love. Ross, like most single men, was in a crisis – a crisis of curves and femininity, a victim of his own highly-developed aesthetic appreciation.

"There's no escape," he muttered, with a sort of grave futility.

His wandering eyes kept gravitating towards the blonde lady at the bar. He was both excited and frustrated by her visual reciprocation.

"Even despite the fact that it's obvious", he began, "she's interested, there's always that problem of being considered something that you're not."

I pointed out to him that the pretentiously cool expression of his itself may have done something to contribute to the perpetuation of an incorrect image.

"Try smiling", I said, "and waving."

"Unlikely," he smiled.

It didn't matter anyway. She left with her man.

"Oh well," Ross muttered, the tense pretension drifting away.

Then his face lit up again. Through the window he could see that she went one way, the friend the other; then she came back inside and dashed off to the cigarette machine where, while reaching down to gather her cigarettes, she spun around and, completely conscious of her actions, almost deposited her bottom in Ross's face.

"Oh my God," I blurted out, titillated by her primeval audacity, as Ross smiled sheepishly.

Then she charged out of the place, embarrassed.

"You really exposed her," he said, giggling. "I saw her face as she went down the street."

"Go after her," I insisted. "She's hurt."

"No way," he said. "I think I'll see her again."

Walking back to his place, he said: "The thing is, you just can't tell whether they want you to do anything about it, or whether they're just playing a little game."

Then back home, as he wandered around his dark flat, he said, "God, I wonder whether I'll ever see that woman again? She was gorgeous."

I remained silent.

* * * * * * * * * *

On Christmas night, Greg invited me to Danielle's parents' place for a feast. Surrounding the family home were bare, rolling fields of scorched brown covered by gums with burnt-orange leaves; we were miles from anywhere. The only sounds, apart from the melancholic screeches of dissatisfied birds, were those of human contact. A large gathering chortled on a patio in the open air. Night fell rapidly around this amiable congregation. Purple streaks gave way to a fantastic black envelope. An immense silence encircled the house. Its verandah was ablaze with the lemon-coloured light of a lamp whose luminosity quickly disappeared into the impenetrable ebony of the night. The light-hearted, harmonious repartee, pleasant chat and cheery derision of the talk was strange to my ears, for it was devoid of cynicism and malicious accusations. The absurdities that torment the interactions of my own family made these people seem eccentric in their weird affection for each other. Was this supposed to be a family?

Danielle's father was distinctly different from the rest. He was a well-known trainer of racehorses who was more interested in relaxed, free-flowing conversation than in convivial hysteria. But the latter did not seem to bother him. Sitting with a beer in his hand, a stomach that curled in a great arc from his neck to his waist, he contentedly absorbed the flippant banter of his female entourage. Often he was the butt of their affectionate jokes. But none of them managed to ruffle the calm waters of his equanimity.

Like the other male members of this country fraternity, he was strangely afflicted by politeness. Greg and I noted the newness of this when one man said to another, as the first one was trying to get past, "'Xcuse Wal." The reply was "No worries, mate." In our family some form of harmless, but pointed, physical interference would have occurred.

Greg said to me, “Can you imagine our family behaving like this?”

“Only”, I replied, “if one of us come into a hell of a lot of money.”

Danielle charged around in a state of hyperactive ebullience. She, her mother and her aunties interacted constantly through wit; one comical remark after another poured from their mouths without the fear of ridicule. It made me realise – I had no doubt that Greg had already discovered this – that this was really the only form of communication in which Danielle felt comfortable in indulging. I wondered how long he would tolerate this vivacious one-dimensionality. I knew that he was keen to leave the country. He would probably take the good with the bad until he got the job he was after, then drift off from there.

Then song exploded on to the scene. Danielle’s mother and her two aunties rose to their feet and sang, with striking concordance, a number whose chorus went: ‘No mother is as sweet as our own’. These three women, all night incapable of a serious comment, suddenly had the passion of the deeply convictioned in their glinting eyes. The grandmother, a robust, easygoing, relaxed lady in her seventies, did very well, despite the gravity of the sentimental onslaught, to hold back the tears. Even I was moved by the blissful sincerity of this beautifully crafted and lyrical attempt to show appreciation.

Then something astonishing occurred. The most repulsive member of the family, Danielle’s fourteen-year-old cousin, became insistent that everyone listen to her “favourite cassette”. She turned the music up and we were treated to a song whose chorus went: ‘Do you fuck on first dates? Does your dad own a brewery? Have yar got nice tits and will yar show ’em to me?’

Other compositions of an equally romantic disposition followed. I was amazed that everyone was guffawing at this stuff that they had heard numerous times before. One song, about an unattractive woman whose ugliness caused a dildo to deflate, produced a particularly raucous response from the listeners. Another song, whose most repeated line was ‘Rooting in the back of the ute with the tailgate down’, also caused a sensation. All the way through these timeless examples of local wit, the cousin stared coldly at her family, pleased she had been able to entertain; knees up beneath her chin, she was sitting on the doorstep next to her grandmother, the occasional flicker of a cool smile forming on her lips at moments of extreme vileness in the music. When I had been introduced to her that evening, I had reached out to shake her hand and she had looked at me straight away with an expression of perturbed disgust.

To my astonishment, the following morning, after we had slept the night, I saw a photograph of this female reincarnation of Klaus Barbie on the shelf. The expression on her face was exactly the same as the one with which she had greeted me. It depicted the heinous tendency which I felt lurked in her soul – and it had been framed and put on the shelf! My only conclusion was that, even in a set-up like this, there was probably going to be at least one genetic quirk. I felt that Danielle's family were too loving and caring to realise that they had a monster in their midst. I could imagine, in the years to come, when this evil adolescent became a serial killer that the other members of the family would be disbelieving, clinging tenaciously to the idea that she was incapable of such sinful acts. But it wouldn't surprise me.

Whilst observing the proceedings, bored severely – it was like being surrounded by fish when diving, the classic surreal experience of the outsider – I fantasised about the gulf that exists between fourteen-year-olds around the world. I saw a scenario in a villa in Italy involving a sophisticated family whose daughter, at a Christmas celebration, became insistent that everyone else listen to her favourite extracts from Mozart. Greg broke my daydreaming by saying that he wanted to go to Europe to fly aircraft.

"Apart from Danielle," he said, "there's nothing holding me here."

I doubted the veracity of this. He would have no compunction at all about leaving her to satisfy his professional instincts. Being with her family – joyous and undemanding – made it apparent as to why.

Before leaving, I kissed one of Danielle's aunties on the cheek and acknowledged her singing.

"Very entertaining," I lied.

She saw straight through this. She was the mother of the monster and she looked at me like a viper. There was little doubt that she had perceived my detestation of her daughter.

Back in Perth, my father, on discovering where I had gone on Christmas night, said, "You what? Why the fuck did you go there for?"

"I'm into contrast," I drolly replied. "You ought to try it some time. It may cause you to have the strange experience of occasionally feeling human."

Or was that inhuman?

* * * * * * * * * *

Oh, I forgot to tell you. When I was at Danielle's parents' house and the fourteen-year-old executionist decided that she wanted to play some music, her mother - sweet thing - said to her, "Play anything but boong music."

So the little darling played what she did, and everyone just loved it.

* * * * * * * * * *

I rang Samantha and she asked me what I had been up to and I said, "Hedonism."

The tone of her voice then seemed to unshackle itself from a fear that our conversation might be plunged into some absurd and insipid abyss. It was intriguing how she managed to be so unwittingly apocalyptically dramatic.

"Some people", she said, suddenly animated, "believe hedonism involves the spending of money. What does it mean to you?"

"Pleasure", I replied, "without regard for long-term consequences. That can be anything from intellectual to physical - and it's got nothing to do with money."

I was about to tell her that the most pleasurable day of my life involved making love to someone with whom I was in love in a rainforest in Queensland, but it was unnecessary because she said, "I'm glad you said that."

"I consider myself", I continued, "to be an Epicurean."

She then said, with a beautiful simplicity, "I like that word."

"Does that mean then", I asked, "that you like me?"

"Of course."

This, of course, could mean anything. We agreed to meet and the elation of this kept me happy for the rest of the day.

* * * * * * * * * * *

Brian came storming in in the middle of my peaceful contemplations and began an outraged tirade.

"Nanna wouldn't speak to me today," he said, livid. He had been around to her place to drop a few things off.

"She thinks", he continues, "that Christmas Day was my fault. You know what Wayne did? He tried throwing me into the swimming pool. Since my accident", he had injured his neck in a car accident a few years earlier, "I haven't dived into the pool. He was determined to throw me in. He tried grabbing me so I kicked him and said: 'You try that and I'll shove your nose down yar arse.' So he backed off. He knew I was serious. And Nanna said, 'He's had a bad start to life.' Okay, but that was thirty years ago. If yar don't stand up to him, he'll get worse. Someone's got to teach him. You know, one day someone's going to thump Wayne and he's going to spend three months recovering with a broken jaw – maybe then he'll have a little think. But Nanna – she thinks he's got to be given all these allowances. But he won't learn unless someone stands up to him. And she blames me! All I was trying to do was defend myself in my own home and Wayne goes blameless! Wayne acts like a four-year-old and she thinks it's my fault! I put up with him here for a year, but not any more. And he keeps going and going. He's always got to have the last say. What was I supposed to do? I tell yar, he came at me determined to throw me in – I was wearing some good clothes too – and I said to him, 'Touch me and I'll smash yar jaw down through yar arse,' so he backed off. I don't mind a laugh. That stuff with the water pistol didn't bother me, but Wayne gets so serious. He's got to outdo everyone. Because Mark's pulled my pants down, Wayne wants to go one step further and throw me into the pool. He just can't be outdone. What was I supposed to do? Let him throw me in because of what happened to him thirty years ago? How old is he now? Thirty-five? Jesus Christ, you'd think he'd know better by now. And how's he going to learn if people just let him do what he likes? Anyway, I've got to go and pick Vanessa up."

* * * * * * * * * * *

Movie time in Perth can mean sitting beneath a starry sky in a pine forest before a huge screen, seated comfortably with over five hundred people. You can bring your own drinks as well. There was never ever any bad behaviour. And it was all so thoroughly enjoyable. The same situation in other places probably would have led to three murders, vicious racist attacks, a mendacious politician trying to dupe the combatants with smiling complicity; who knows what else? But here, miraculously, old world values had blended with aspirant modern thinking in a whirlwind of indigenous and unconsciously unique cultural entertainments. Okay, so I was drunk on champagne, was under the clear spectacle of thousands of stars and just happened to be in the company of a beautiful woman with razor diamonds in her head on a night when satin seemed to be filling the air.

We were sitting on the edge of a pine-enclosed quadrangle. The quadrangle contained a plethora of differently coloured, elaborately hued deck-chairs. British politics were dissected acutely. The universe managed a mention. Movies breezed in. Poetry nipped in with one or two recitals. Exotic cultural adventures formed a lemon wax over the unexplored interplay. Heinous liberal party policies got a scathing hearing. American foreign policy in the Gulf was pierced with savage denunciation. Hands and mouth moved as though both had just been released from years of imprisonment. The processes involved in the production of milk were examined as if this innocuous white substance, as common as air, was an elixir now infused with qualities capable of causing it to be elevated to the position of gold in the world's financial markets. Military expansionism was condemned. Unjustified religious beliefs were treated with disdain. Her parents' attempts to impose upon her the ways of the Catholic Church were, as she said, "as naive as the ideas themselves are ridiculous".

"This substitution", she added, "of facts for faith causes me unbelievable grief."

A heartening revelation was this; it soothes me to be in the presence of those blessed in equal measure with both curiosity and hard-headed pragmatism. The confirmation of these characteristics within her – and the reaffirmation of her charmingly veracious fury – occurred a week later at a dinner party on the quiet verandah of a turn-of-the-century mansion whose ornate timber eaves had hanging from them luxuriant pot plants which blocked out the flickering lights of the night sky. We were plonked in some high cane chairs with curved backs, our bottoms protected by floral-patterned cushions, the tranquil silence of the evening punctuated by our laughter, voices, soft music and the occasional drone of a distant car. Eight of us surrounded an oak table laden with food and drink in an opulent setting of flowers and plush lawn, a garden blooming with the prospect of civil interaction. An American woman, too nice without reason for a cynic such as myself, and attired in the apparel of higher consciousness – reflecting glasses in a lurid woollen waistcoat acquired in Tibet – made the claim that her possessions in India had been stolen because her alertness had been reduced by ill health.

Samantha, thinking as I was, but more inclined to the expression of socially unacceptable feelings, blurted out, "How do you know that? How do you know that you would not have lost your stuff anyway?"

"I just know," this woman reiterated.

"But how", Samantha persisted, "do you know that, even if you were in perfect health, you wouldn't've been ripped off anyway? All it takes is a momentary lapse in concentration at a time when a thief is about, and that's it."

The American, naively assuming that she would dazzle us with an intriguing outburst of psychological insights, claimed that it was "destiny" that she got sick; she was implying that the theft, devastating at the time, was the work of an omniscient being helping her to a position of greater strength. She was adamant in opposition to Samantha's assertion of pure chance and in her belief that the theft had been predetermined to enable her to achieve a higher plane of awareness. Samantha's eyes, piercing and bewildered, expressed outrage at the arrogance of someone who was prepared to believe something so monumental from so little evidence.

"It was a simple theft," Samantha said. "It happens every day."

The American contained her surprise at not being taken seriously. However, she was not prepared to give up her hope of making us see that there was a presence in the universe which could not be explained by rational, scientific means.

"How do you know", Samantha asked, "that such a presence exists?"

We were then treated to a theory regarding Mozart's musical genius. That genius, so it seemed, could not have arisen by any "natural means". His father, you see, was only an "ordinary" musician. Therefore, the expertise of his son had to be due to some miraculous outside influence. It was all so obvious. Samantha was slowly becoming hysterical. Her hair-flicking habit was taking on manic proportions. Even I, nonchalantly amenable to the last, was beginning to become agitated by the fantastic sludge that was starting to pour out of this American dreamer's mouth.

"Crap," I rather impolitely exclaimed at one point. "There is every likelihood", I continued, angered by the imperious babblings of this woman, "that Mozart's ability was the culmination of the accumulation of the repetition of musical skills in Austria over the centuries, leading to the correct neural connections being made from one generation to the next in the brains of those able to play the piano, and who, in the case of Mozart, through unique environmental conditions, had the single-minded relish which comes from the joy of a specific aesthetic appreciation - one that enabled him to enhance this genetic basis as rapidly as possible. The human mind is complex enough to perform these feats - those with true genius will be able to tell you this - without the help of some nebulous and unfathomable influence."

The American shook her head defiantly without compromising her forced equanimity. She explained that, on the scale of scepticism to psychic belief, she ranked at about the three-quarters mark towards the mystic side of the spectrum. Her openness to psychic phenomena had been awakened by a visit to a meeting of psychics on the fifth anniversary of her mother's death. She was asked by the chairperson why she had attended the meeting although I found it ironic that the head of a group of psychics had to ask someone why they were there. Why didn't they know this by other means? Later on, in this now historic evening with the psychics, a woman in the group had interviewed the American with the purpose of impressing her with the powers of the unknown. The American explained that she always liked to do something special on the anniversary of her mother's demise and the visit to the school of mystics seemed appropriate in view of the concerns she was harbouring about the other members of her probably disturbed family. The interviewer had aroused the interest of the American by suggesting that the new acquisition to the group had five brothers and sisters. Despite the fact that the number was actually four, the American was still intrigued. Her interest was aroused even further when the psychic suggested that one of her relatives' Christian names began with J, an astonishing insight, even though J is by far the most popular opening letter in English Christian names. Not many Johns around, are there? Then something really remarkable was exposed: the American had a troubled relative. Now, not many of us have those, do we? It was always amusing how those wishing to believe will believe despite the unearthing of any specific revelations. The American, maintaining an aspect of intense pertinence, a look at odds with the glances she was receiving, then explained that the psychic had said that the number seven was important.

"I keep feeling seven," the psychic had kept saying. "What is this about seven?"

It was revealed by the American that her troubled relative - her eldest brother - was in trauma because his wife had given birth to a child who had died seven months into the pregnancy. The fact that the number seven, a common statistical measure, can be associated with a plethora of different contingencies was of no relevance to someone keen to hear the following from her psychic mistress: "I feel vibrations which suggest that your mother is extremely concerned about your brother's condition."

This was too much for Samantha. Almost leaping out of her chair, she said, "I happen to be a member of an organisation called Sceptics Anonymous. They exist in virtually every First World country. Each branch offers the equivalent of ten thousand US dollars for any psychic to come forth and demonstrate to us that they possess mysterious powers. So far, no one has even tried to win the money. They dismiss the opportunity when asked to perform by saying that they can't do their stuff in front of sceptics. We're not being vindictive: we're just looking for concrete proof. To date we've not seen any. Nothing you've said tonight leads me to believe that the woman who interviewed you is blessed with any extraordinary powers. She was wrong about something extremely simple - the number of your brothers and sisters. She employed basic statistical analysis with respect to the chances of your having a relative whose name begins with J, and she plucked a common figure of seven from the air and then allowed you to associate it with a contingency that probably has numerous sevens connected with it. For example, your brother's child could have been born on the seventh day of the week; the child could have been born at seven minutes past an hour. Seven people may have been in the delivery theatre. It goes on. The point is, the psychic was unable to reveal a simple fact to you - the seventh month of the pregnancy. Had this woman been truly gifted, surely that simple fact would have been revealed by her. We, as scientists, find it degrading that so many people are prepared to believe things simply because they want to, or because they feel something strongly. Just because you feel something strongly it doesn't mean it's true. Everyone makes mistakes with intuition. It's not absolute. It's a psychological response, not a physical one. You want to believe that your mother still exists - and I don't blame you - but what you've just described doesn't constitute evidence. In fact, you want to believe that your mother exists so strongly that you're even prepared to go to any length to find excuses for this to be true. Had the psychic said to you, before you'd even opened your mouth, that you were there because of your mother, even that would not have been conclusive enough evidence to suggest that this woman had exceptional powers, because, after all, our mothers have had a tremendous influence upon us all. Personally I think you've been a victim of suggestion."

The American stared with a sort of infuriated blankness at her effervescent tormentor.

"What makes you think", the American said, "that I don't believe those things have a rational base?"

"Even if they do have a rational base," Samantha retorted, "we don't have the proof to make the judgement. We may never have the proof. There may be a perfectly reasonable explanation for everything, but the human mind may not, ultimately, be complex enough to make the sort of discoveries that too many people believe, presumably for reasons of personal preservation, have already been made. You should really tighten up on what you're prepared to accept."

The advice was dispensed without egotistical malice. They were the words of a fiery atheist with the moral courage to disregard wild hopes and be unconcerned by fiercely ingrained superstitions.

"At this point in history," Samantha added, "we have no conclusive evidence to suggest that the purpose of life is nothing more than the exotic perpetuation of biological functions."

This dazzling comment sent shudders through the vacuous belief system of the besieged American.

"How can you say", the American said, "that something as magnificent as the universe did not have a creator? That to me is absurd."

"Easily," Samantha replied. "If this cosmic being exists, then who created it? And how far do you go with this creative speculation? What are you prepared to believe without concrete empirical evidence? How do you know that God is nothing more than the ultimate sub-atomic particle, the most abundant particle in the universe, the basic building block that nuclear physics is hoping to find?"

"I was told the other day", the American said, "by a nuclear physicist that - is it Brownsian motion? - this idea that it's not possible to predict where a particle might be just after a collision may not be correct."

"It's Brownian motion," I said. "The problem is not just simply that sub-atomic particles don't behave classically in collisions - it may be true that they in fact end up in the positions they're supposed to according to the laws of Newtonian physics - but there is a deeper problem connected to the way we observe. The method of our observations may distort the results. It's something of which we're not sure."

Bemused by this, the American dismissed it as irrelevant by waving her hand before unconsciously producing an ironically revealing comment: "I'm not interested in fine details."

"Exactly," I said. "People like you aren't. That's the reason you're prepared to believe anything."

The shock of this caused a loud silence broken by Samantha announcing that it was time she went.

"Are you coming with me?" she asked.

I leapt out of my seat.

In the car on the way home, she said, "I had to go. I couldn't take anymore of that American psycho-babble. I had a feeling that it was going to lead to something nasty."

Another hurdle had been crossed.

* * * * * * * * * * *

Samantha Cassanetti, 'The Countess of Fremantle', was doing a thesis on the environmental problems of water supplies in the Middle East. For a twenty-five-year-old woman from Perth to be gripped by such an obscure theme was a triumph for the reactionary mind. She was idealistic: she was young enough still to deride the desperation that drives the failed to the compromising of their principles; the loss of idealism to attain personal goals was still as unacceptable to her as ever. I doubted, had I had the courage to suggest it, that the 'Countess Cassanetti' would have been pleased with the notion that nothing is reprehensible if it achieves audacious aims. She would have been outraged by this – a flower firing off a laser beam.

I was foolishly infatuated by this uncompromising probity. I knew that it would cause me nothing but trouble. She was not in the frame of mind to entertain the thought of a new love. I was even petrified to let her know how I really felt. It was too risky. I was only here for a short time. I had another life. My employment was elsewhere. The unwonted exposure of feeling could cause irreparable damage to the delicate membrane that chance had draped over the unexpected bringing together of our separate and wayward lives.

I sat alone for hours in cafés dreaming up excuses to contact her; then I made other excuses to keep my real motives to myself. The past had seen other instances where an insensitive outburst of emotion had torn the heart out of other infatuations; ties had then been severed, regretfully, for ever. That I did not want to risk. It has to be recognised that unjustified declarations of interest are brutish; this I did very well to believe. I also did very well to accept that I had not fully considered the esoteric motives which had driven me to the heart of a wild fracas. Slowly I had begun to accept that it stemmed from a desire to experience dehumanisation. The quiet life in Perth had given me time to reflect, to consider the action-packed dreams, to delve into the complicated responses to deaths and mutilations. I felt that I had escaped to danger in pursuit of a dream of unaffectedness. I wanted to know that any tragedy was not tragic enough for me. I was pleased with dehumanisation; it was refreshing in its destruction of polite façades; it meant strength; it was exciting; it was authentic; it was also miraculous for the development of bizarre humour.

I knew that I had turned the corner after I had overcome a feeling of paranoid beguilement at the sight of death. The first corpses were too mysterious for nefarious contemplation. I felt something so unearthly about them that I imagined a vapour could rise from them and choke me for being so intrusively curious; then I began to ignore certain possibilities – such as the continuation of consciousness after death – because this twee perception did not appeal to my growing toughness. I enjoyed this impenetrable feeling of intractability. Not even the sight of death before my eyes could move me to sentimental contemplation.

I once saw someone in the bus station at Belgrade, after I had survived a period of intense shelling in Sarajevo, suddenly jerk (he was walking in front of me to a toilet), spin around and, with a glazed, panicked expression in his eyes, he collapsed dead. I had to step over his corpse to get into the toilet; at the urinal slab – the door was ajar because the deceased man's head had crashed into it and I could see it from where I stood – I unleashed a burst of unbridled laughter. It was hilarious, truly comical. No one was more surprised by my reaction than myself. When I left the toilet, the dead man had been pulled away from the door and was being attended to by a British doctor who was frantically attempting to revive him. I took one took at the corpse and thought: 'Nah, he's gone. Looks like there's going to be a spare seat on this ride.' Then I had boarded my bus.

I was extremely drunk on gin and tonics. Alcohol had given me a reprieve. For weeks on the edge of an explosive outburst, I had felt myself almost shaking – shaking within. The stupidity of mankind made me shudder. The more deaths the better. The dead man in the bus station had caused me to bellow out: "Good, one less Serb." I had witnessed that "idiotic scum" struggling for lumps of bread in freezing queues and I had been delighted. I had gone mad with flippant dehumanisation. Everything had become a source of cruel humour. I thoroughly believed that on that day – that day of joyous, uncivilised malice – I had climbed the peak of my sordid ambition. I knew, in the bliss of my squalid inhumanity, that I would have been able to endure the sight of people being torn to shreds by wild animals. This untouchability contained the sort of evil transcendence that the Catholic Church ascribes to the devil. On the bus, the British woman who had done her utmost to save another soul was distressed by her ordeal. A kindly American man offered her his sincere condolences. As he did so, I had to place my hands over my smiling face, for I still could not contain my wicked humour.

I had gone crazy on the lust of barbarous indignation. But it had given me a clearer vision. I knew that one day those responsible for the turmoils in the Balkans would face war crimes tribunals. I also knew that those tribunals would be convened by the very people with the power to have halted the conflict in the first place. The morally superior, behind the guise of their cowardly justice, would condemn those distorted by abnormal experiences, and would therefore be able to appease their grand scruples by obliterating from this world the dehumanised victims of a foreign war. I was bad, but at least I accepted it. I also now fully understood tragedy. It was not altogether a bad experience. (Pardon the pun.) It had helped me to wipe idealism from the slate. I was not opposed to idealists in principle – they were just the inexperienced products of a morally superior world – I simply realised that for them it was essential to shout rather than understand. I preferred the decadent path to truth. I was attempting to fill a sphere of experience. At diametrically opposite points were dehumanisation and its antonym. The latter, I believed, would be achieved by the reciprocation of romantic love. The former had been completed. It was all in the name of curiosity. I required no nagging legacies, no impinging vacuums, to fill the chamber of memory. I believed that love would mean the realisation of my most perfect self-image. And this was where the Countess Cassanetti – environmentalist, political commentator, feminist and heroine of international affairs – was supposed to play her part.

Unfortunately I had the uneasy sensation that she did not quite see her role in the way I had dreamed that she would. This unnerving prospect became apparent to me one afternoon under the leafy pergola of a beer-garden in a suburban pub. The light fell in mottled patches over the black waterfall of her silky hair. Gleaming outlines of radiance mingled with the dark. She was even more hyperactive than usual. Her hands were suffering from epileptic fits.

She swayed back and forth and from side to side and finally announced, “I don’t know how to say this.”

Behind my unruffled façade, the chilling prospect of failure, like a slimy river of nitrogen, boiling with torment, sent its futile clouds into the dreamy zones of my deluded brain. When was I going to learn that it is essential to possess only a small, almost minuscule, capacity for illusion?

Then she said, “If a man keeps asking you out…”

Then there was a period of gasping and awkward shuffling, as I sat there, unmoved, thinking: 'Here we go. You are about to receive the coup de grâce.'

I could feel my insides bracing themselves for a horrifying jolt.

"If", she continued, "this happens, you have to ask..."

'Oh God, oh God,' I thought, 'please, please, please, don't let her say it!'

"You just... You have to wonder..."

'Oh please, no, no, no.'

"You don't want to be responsible for..."

"Look," I said, with fake calmness, making sure that she did not have the opportunity to say something I was going to dread, "you don't know what my motives are. You can't just jump to conclusions."

"I know, I know," she said, reeling back, shaking her head. "I was just being unjustifiably egotistical. Sorry."

Despite all the evidence to the contrary, I then proceeded to try and convince myself that all was not lost. She may have been trying to find out if I was interested because she wants a relationship herself. I told this to myself, incapable, unwilling, not accepting the reality of her justified concerns. I was disturbed by the way she suddenly regained her equanimity. She was pleased: she had successfully conveyed her fears without causing embarrassment. And I had the disturbing feeling that she was qualified because I had acted as if I was disinclined towards romance. My concrete disinclination towards the expression of feeling was a mask for the fragility within.

Then she got excited by the sight of a flying insect that landed on the table between us. She was overcome by the beauty of this creature's delicate green wings. They were like iridescent leaves attached to a pair of sensitive feelers. Her hands flew up to her face and she gasped, "Isn't it wonderful?"

I was perturbed by her aesthetic satisfaction. Why the hell couldn't she say this about me? I wondered. What right had that damned insect to be on the receiving end of her precious accolades? I wanted to squash it. Matters were made worse by the fact that that creature was stunning. I was slit by the glassy sheaths of sharp reality. She began to act as if we were just friends. I was tormented by the possibility of her eulogies going elsewhere. She said, with the relaxed air of one confiding to a romantically disinclined associate, that her behaviour changed when she was around a desirable man. She said that under these circumstances she found she could not help fishing for compliments. As I had never detected this in her character, I began to feel vexed by the sort of despairing evidence that I had feared would eventually darken the dazzling lights of my dizzy hopes. She even demonstrated to me the kind of demeanour that she employed when attempting to extract lurid words of adulation from a potential gentleman caller. As I had never detected any facial expressions in her even remotely associated with those that she displayed when demonstrating her seductive techniques, even I had to admit that the future was now looking particularly bleak. Before the expression of her concerns, her behaviour had been restrained, fidgety; she had flicked her hair back unnaturally; her eyes seemed to have been burning with the acrid vapours of unwanted affection. I felt, not necessarily inadequate, but misplaced. Hopelessly unable to reach out to her in a way that would have appeased my steaming instincts for unhampered licence, I had unwittingly created a false pond of uninterest into which the exciting cascade of her personality was now able to safely descend. I could not accuse her of insensitivity. My cowardice, my inveterate fear of the worst, had created the impression that I would be unaffected by anything, apart from the obviously derogatory, that flowed from her luscious mouth. And what a mouth it was! Evolution seemed to have slowly gathered together every molecule of the finest flesh and woven it together into the creation of that perfect orifice. It was beyond belief that anyone had been lucky enough to have had the opportunity to have kissed it. I was delirious with love.

On the way home from the cinema, I was politely accused of possessing all the prejudices of those who "come back from Europe for a short time". Being misjudged is always a hazard. We all judge whimsically, but we all detest being misjudged, particularly by those whose opinions most concern us. Samantha admitted that she had shown the same prejudices on her return from overseas. Her comment about me had arisen in response to an harangue I had delivered concerning the sexism and racism I had experienced on my return to Perth. I said that I had reached a stage where I only wanted to associate with people who are "rational". I was asked to explain what rational meant "in this context". I explained that it meant someone "with a sound idea of that which makes life worth living". I was aghast that she had implied I had been derogatory towards Perth.

I then continued my defence by announcing that, "in the short time I had been back, I had learnt a lot about human nature" because I had been forced, "by circumstances beyond my control", to mix with people (mainly my family) with whom "I would not normally come into contact". I explained that this "could happen anywhere". I said that it could happen in "New York or Vienna – any place; it's just that I've not been able to choose my company. This problem," I continued, pleased with my lucidity, "may have been the case with other people you know who've come back here after being overseas, but it doesn't apply to me."

"I'm glad you said that," she replied. "You had me worried."

At Brian's place, I invited her inside. Brian and Vanessa had gone to Sydney. I prepared a meal and played some South American folk music. Quickly a soothing intimacy formed between us. We spoke freely about our political concerns. I did not feel the need to gain her opinion on personal matters; this was an inclination I had had with other women at this stage of a relationship, ones less interesting, whose lack of suitability needed to be replaced by the excitement of delicate subjects. I was pleased with her enthusiasm for space. There was a genuine atmosphere of friendship between us.

When she left, I walked with her to her parked car where she spun around and tried to hug me. I was incapable of dealing with this spontaneous emotion from someone whose affection I craved. I stepped back complaining of pain. I found a pathetic excuse not to allow our bodies to come into contact; she had accidentally trodden on my foot whilst attempting to put her arms around me. An awkward scene was averted by the creation of another one. She did not hide her disappointment at my inability to show the feeling our evening had warranted. She got into the car with a curt goodbye and drove off.

I went back inside, blaspheming: "Jesus Christ. Shit. Fuck. Cunt. Wanker. Idiot! Arsehole!" not thinking that a phone call the following day with an explanation and an apology may have gone a long way to easing the burden that was developing needlessly in the tormented confines of my diseased soul.

* * * * * * * * * *

Spiritual listlessness… Everything is old… Life stripped bare of fantasy… The dullness of all things… Slowly drifting towards a futile annihilation… There are certain things that will not be done again… That cannot be done again… The pointlessness of life without the intimacy of women… Melancholic authenticity… Everything ever dreamed about is laughable. Ahhh! When will it all end?

* * * * * * * * * * *

The following exchange took place between Vanessa and Brian:

VANESSA:	Dad – can you take me to Floreat [shopping centre] this morning?
BRIAN:	No. Ride your bike.
VANESSA:	Well, give me some money then.
BRIAN:	What? Use the money you've already got.
VANESSA:	I can't. Got to use it for Sydney – and besides, you want me to sew.
BRIAN:	You're going to have to make a decision. It's either put money aside for Sydney or wait to buy stuff for sewing.
VANESSA:	But you want me to get this stuff.
BRIAN:	You've got to learn to make decisions based on what limited resources you've got. That's life.
VANESSA:	Words of wisdom, Brian.

A minute later Brian comes back and says, "Vanessa, you think I'm just a bottomless pit of money."

Vanessa smiles, unaffected, pleased that she's hit a nerve. Brian – true to form – repeats himself, this time with an aggressive sense of dogmatic gravity. This causes Vanessa to smile even more widely.

Later, Vanessa and I are watching a news report about AIDS on television. The story centres around a new drug designed to ease the pain for those in the advanced stages of suffering. My cousin is wearing a sleeveless satin top that nicely displays the spheres of her blooming sexuality. Cosy red circles enflame her soft, voluptuous cheeks. Tight jeans curve around her powerful, generous hips. She was only, in my opinion, months away from her first experience; after that, a crescendo would take place, for she was going to find that sex would assist her desire for radical liberation whilst enhancing her blossoming powers of control. Quickly she would discover that the thrill she received from manipulating her father to perform acts he loathed would be transferred on to others even more willing to forsake their intelligence in the pursuit of her affections. This was the downside of feminism - the destruction of personal moral codes for the gain of an excessive emancipation. (Don't worry, if I were to concentrate on the excesses of malehood, there wouldn't be a page left in this book.)

Outside, the sunshine rained down like an irrepressible reminder of our tired belief in eternal optimism. The dazed light had a weariness to it, as if its radiance could not hide the foibles and unpleasantries that lay within. All the ultra-violet light in the world could not erase the weaknesses and disgraces of this bedevilled life. It could fall like an angelic, gleaming mist all it liked; we were all so unworthy of its graces that its enhancing presence, sometimes sapping, seemed like a sympathetic privilege extended by a natural world forever forgiving of our disparaging ways.

Gaunt, hopeless faces filled the screen. The victims of a disease that bore no prejudices, cultural or ethnic, were strewn over hospital beds. The peace that would soon be theirs was undetectable in their distressed faces. It was not a pretty sight. Some of them appeared as though they had already gone blue. Huge, bulbous eyes protruded from skeletal faces. The prominent eyebrow ridges were unnatural.

"Oh yuk!" Vanessa said, screwing up her unblemished face. "What's the point in keeping them alive? They're no good to society."

I was reading a newspaper and had to put it to my face to hide the outrage that had electrified my features. So what if the relatives of these people were living in hope of a miraculous discovery? Who cares? This unconscious revelation of Vanessa's dismissive attitude (particularly towards her family) did not surprise me. What did was my grandmother's reaction. I told her about Vanessa's comments, and she, missing the point completely, replied that her granddaughter's insensitivity was a product "of her age". Really it was the product of being exposed for sixteen years to our bickering family.

At lunch one day in a vibrant, sunlit restaurant whose walls were laden with amusing drawings of Victorian stereotypes and whose tables contained elegant porcelain amphorae with blooming daffodils and crisp white tablecloths, Brian admitted that he "laboured the point too much". This still did not stop him from doing it though.

Four times in the space of ten minutes he said to Vanessa, "Just pass your exams at school, then you're free. I won't meddle. It's your life then. You can do what you like. You can make your own mistakes then. I won't interfere. That'll be it. I'll be off," as Vanessa's head swirled around as though she were warding off the effects of an incorrectly administered anaesthetic.

Then Brian said, four times in relation to Greg, "I warned him. He loves the good life. That's his problem. When he was twenty he wanted fast cars instead of using the money to study - and he wanted me to give him more! What was I going to do? Give money to someone who was having a better lifestyle than me?" and again, Vanessa, feigning impending unconsciousness, crossed her eyes as though she were on the threshold of blacking out. Brian ignored his daughter's disrespect. He was so used to it that it was natural.

Then Vanessa, regaining consciousness, said, "Dad - do you expect me to spend every day with you in Sydney? It'd drive me nuts! Do you think that Stephen'd like to drive me around?"

Stephen was the flamboyant twenty-three-year-old offspring of the people with whom they were going to be staying. Brian's face became filled with concern. Undoubtedly Vanessa had designs that coincided with the age of consent.

"We'll see," Brian said, realising that he had just discovered a new vehicle for leverage.

Then I made a comment about my father.

This prompted Vanessa to say, "He's such a cold-hearted bastard."

I marvelled at the hypocrisy. I paid the bill by putting the cash into the restaurant wallet. Vanessa then grabbed it out and pretended to stuff it into her pocket.

Brian then said, "Typical female."

All afternoon Vanessa had been dropping unsubtle hints that I should give her some spending money for Sydney. She made it clear that a mere fifty dollars would suffice. I would have done this gladly, but she's devoid of gratitude, so I didn't. Her ungracious disposition was made apparent at the end of the day when Brian thanked me for lunch - I had paid for it - and Vanessa just gave me two fingers in mock derision as she and the car disappeared away. I didn't give a damn.

At the restaurant, after Brian had made some derisive comments about the greed of women – Vanessa's attitude was the catalyst – I said to him, "Did you ever encourage Lois to work?"

His argument had been based on the notion that women who "don't work" have effectively "stolen" from men in divorce. Too bad if Lois had worked her arse off in the kitchen.

He replied, "It was a joint decision."

"Yes," I said, "but did you encourage her?"

He avoided the issue by saying that, when Greg was about to leave school, Lois suddenly said one morning that Greg should not go to university and that she should go instead. He continued by saying, "I told her that if she wanted to go to university, then she would have to pay for it herself," implying that if she ever had those intentions, then she should never have given up "work".

"She", Brian said, oblivious that being a housewife is an occupation, "made a decision to become a wife and a mother and should have stuck with it."

This led to some pejorative remarks about feminism.

"Those bloody feminists," he said. "They want everything."

I tried to pin him down on what he meant by feminism.

He then pontificated on about separate bank accounts; he then tried to tell me that "feminism is different in different parts of the world".

I disagreed by saying that "the principle of feminism is constant around the globe". I then asked him again what, as he put it, "this women's liberation stuff" was.

He explained that it represented equal opportunities for all in the workplace. I was happy with this, despite his inability to recognise that those who remain at home, pursuing domestic necessities are also in full-time employment. He then pointed out that in the ABC "there have been institutionalised excesses caused by the absurd application of feminism". He then told me – although he had already told me this before – that it was agreed by the management committee of the ABC that twenty-five per cent of all management positions within the ABC had to be filled by women. He then expressed his dismay at some of the management decisions that some of those women had made. He claimed that one woman had had all the office furniture on the floor she controlled removed and replaced with beanbags.

"All they did", he said, "was sit on the floor. It lasted about twelve months before the idea was kicked out."

As he spoke, he gesticulated with his hands, reiterating that, "yes, women should get equal opportunities," while Vanessa's head continued to roll around, her eyes crossed, in a picture of malicious disrespect. Earlier on he had said, congratulating himself for the quality of his fatherhood: "I've sat down with Greg, Richard and Vanessa and spoken quietly about everything. Sex, girlfriends, boyfriends, work, et cetera," and Vanessa had quipped, ruefully, "Yeah, and guess who did all the bloody talking?"

I arrived home late one night to find him staring blankly at the television. Three empty beer cans lay on the floor near his bare feet. He was in an uncharacteristically introspective frame of mind.

I sat down.

He suddenly sprang to life and asked, "Why do you think Wayne is the way he is?"

"Good question," I replied.

It was fascinating watching him at last engage in ruthless analysis. I wondered whether it would help him produce something well thought out.

"In the last few weeks," I continued, "I've given it a lot of thought. The only thing I can think of is this: he feels constantly outraged because of the terrible things that happened to him in early childhood. He's not outraged because someone's thrown one-seventh of a glass of champagne in his face – that's just the ephemeral catalyst for his emotions – he's outraged because of what happened to him years ago. He's just repeating that outrage – a justified one born from crimes committed against him in his early youth. The outrage is a release, a substitute for joy, and, every time something untoward happens to him, he again feels that outrage, the legitimate reaction to previous events, because it gives him the moral justification for his aggression. It's that moral justification he feels in conflicts which protected him when he was young and he's still repeating it. Unless he gains some measure of self-awareness quickly, I can't see him breaking this vicious cycle. For one thing, he doesn't believe in the academic solving of problems."

Brian, who was in no mood for sympathy or the basic precepts of psychology as well, said, "But that was years ago."

He was grumpy because of his mother's scathing reaction to his behaviour on Christmas Day and because of her overly protective attitude towards his grand tormentor - Wayne.

"All his friends are the same," he continued. "They communicate through decision."

"What do you expect from Wayne?" I asked. "Look at his father."

Brian shook his head and said: "Keith's unbelievable. He's thrown shit at me for thirty years. For thirty years, he tried to degrade my intelligence. And I'm not going to take it any more. Those two behave the way they do in my place on Christmas Day and I'm the one who gets the blame!"

"I don't know why", I said, "you haven't just clobbered Dad. If anyone gave me the shit he dishes out to you, I'd kill 'em. You should've threatened him on Christmas Day."

"I can't do that," Brian replied, shaking his head. "Nanna'd probably have a heart attack."

"Well, so what?" I said. "Why are you so worried about what she thinks?"

He just shook his head again, angered and confused.

"There'll be no Christmas celebration next year," he then said, defiantly. "It cost me two hundred bucks, just to get abused. Next year I'll just book a restaurant."

That was next year. Then he began on Wayne again: "Bloody Wayne," he sneered. "He's not coming back in here again. I can tell you that now. Christmas Day was the final straw. I came so close to shoving his jaw through his arsehole. He won't show his face around here again."

I was bored with these idle threats. In the morning I lay in bed listening to Vanessa stirring him up again.

"You keep that up", Brian threatened, "and you won't be going to Sydney."

Vanessa then repeated Brian's threats in a tone of sarcastic gaiety, fighting to stop herself from disintegrating into chortling laughter.

"You won't be going to Sydney! You won't be going to Sydney!" she sang, dancing down the hallway, safe in the knowledge that her father's threats were absolutely ineffectual.

She then continued her derision with a series of piercing remarks, mimicking her father, before she finally reached a crescendo of irreverence that culminated in the scornful climax of: "Oh yeah, sure Brian."

I lay down thinking, staring our through the window at the sun-drenched gardens, wracked with cold precision: 'My cousin is the cheekiest bitch on earth.'

* * * * * * * * * *

Jeremy rang me and asked about my Christmas.

"It was confrontational," I replied.

"Wayne and your father?" he asked.

"No," I replied, "Wayne and Brian."

I told him about the water pistols, the fruit, the attempts to throw people into the swimming pool.

Jeremy, in disbelief, said, "Jesus Christ."

Coming from a family noted for its intelligent, harmonious interaction, this description of family immaturity would, for him, be astonishing. I then told him about the dinner-table conversation. My unembellished report of my father's inquiries regarding Brian's latest employment caused him again, with a sort of elongated, bewildered whisper, to gasp: "Jeessuzzz Kerreitz."

I then said, "It's just a classic situation of having fifteen or so people sitting around a table – there for reasons of duty rather than desire – who are all completely different from each other."

He replied, "People should learn to respect each other's differences and enjoy them."

I smiled and said, "Jeremy, the only way my family could do that would be in a war where we had the common purpose of ridding the earth of a mutual aggressor. Then maybe the petty squabbles would disappear. No other way."

I then realised a new aspect of my dubious professional motivations. I realised that I craved the denunciation of cynicism in personal relationships via man's most cynical act.

Jeremy then told me about the problems his mother was experiencing. He was oblivious that my grandmother had already informed me. Living in Britain had trained me in the art of feigning ignorance to protect another's discretion. Everyone talked but no one wanted to feel guilt. Jeremy was powerless to halt the course of nature, but he was contrite about his lack of contribution to his mother's care. I told him that these problems had started after he had "begun another life overseas" and that "no one expected him to make sacrifices" that his mother did not want him to make. He accepted this and then was intrigued to discover that I was on the threshold of ringing a woman I felt "I am in love with", whom I believed was "possibly a little disillusioned with me".

"In five weeks?" he asked.

"The fragrance of love", I replied, "is made from particles of light."

"Why don't you just say", he asked, "that love and photons are interchangeable?"

"Don't be so unsentimental," I replied.

He wanted to know who "this remarkable woman" was.

"Too remarkable", I replied, "for me."

"Is that possible?" he asked.

"She tells the truth", I replied, "with alarming accuracy. It's dangerous."

"Why don't you do something different for a change", he suggested, "and go for someone nice?"

"I hate nice people," I replied.

"You like me, don't you?" he asked.

"Of course," I replied. "You're the biggest cunt I've ever met in my life."

* * * * * * * * * * *

The narrow labyrinth of medieval streets were lined with stone buildings with blue and green shutters. The ground was hard, dusty, and was compacted solid earth. Cows lay around like cats in rare patches of broken light. The desperate charge of humanity blasted past them like refugees, fleeing from the same place all at once. The pitter-patter of stationary, two-stroke auto-rickshaw engines became vicious wails in their fullest, tormented cries. The screams of engines were almost drowned by the cacophony of blaring horns. Blue-white plumes of exhaust fumes burnt my widened eyes. The panicked looks of passengers alighting from moving buses in the middle of this frenetic rush mimicked the fears that lay within. Fingerless hands with dirty faces were thrust into my eyes by beggars with stringy hair risking death at the traffic lights.

"Baksheesh, baksheesh," they screamed, tugging at clothes, climbing in, being pushed out, demanding, overcome by hope, slaughtered by fate, fingers seared by leprosy; then off we went.

My shirt had been ripped open and the blood from the scratches of conscience dried quickly in the burning heat. Beside the road, sleeping dogs with frazzled ears were curled up in the dusty streets. The carcass of one was rotting with bloated flies. Vultures circled above. Streams of milky water in gullies next to the kerbs flowed like diseases through the troubled arteries of the overcrowded streets. A small boy defecated into a stream with the innocent compunction of the pragmatically free. Wiry, cycle-rickshaw drivers winced in deadpan anguish; through the traffic they weaved with bulbous thighs. A shattering whack in the pothole bounce rang in my ears. Irate traffic police smashed the bonnets of cars with bamboo sticks. Line after line of parked cycle-rickshaws were draped with the sinewy bodies of their drivers who were wrapped around them in the sapping heat. Diffident, searching dogs, ribcages exposed, sniffed and sneaked in the grimy haze. The constant march of brown feet, coloured by dust, soil and sun, trampled forth in the din of escape. Filthy linen sarongs concealed the crotches of long-haired gurus dazzled by the lack of consciousness in the teeming throng gone wild in the maze of bustling streets. Aching backs and silent heads diligently transported bulky goods; person after person flowed past with loads seemingly crushing in the ferocious panic. Packages the size of small freezers somehow remained balanced on steady skulls. The wheels of ox-drawn carts splashed through the poisonous liquids that had gathered in the depressions lurking beside the rubbish-strewn streets. Tireless women in lurid saris swept the polluted thoroughfares with straw brooms extracted from the distant trees of lush forests.

The sight of such immaculate fabrics amidst such degradation suggested the seemingly impossible: beauty born from a noxious waste. Impossible loads crammed the small confines of rickety carts. Camels drifted in straight lines through the tumultuous calamity of the contaminated streets. The languid hooves of cows caused ruptures in the dirty puddles that were splashed beneath the besmirched sky. This maddening befuddlement of disregard contained an ironic quality of high-pitched order. The confidence of survival belied the dangers inherent within. The worn out red and blue upholstered seats of the cycle-rickshaws suggested the weariness involved in this constant and hectic retreat.

Herds of people consumed stewed vegetables from bowls made from leaves; the disregarded bowls were attacked by voracious cows and dogs. Their unconditioned hunger mirrored the lust for turmoil that discordantly reverberated through the frantic streets. Every turn was laced with burnt-out faces. A plethora of iron signs, advertising each business, clung to the dilapidated façades of the infected walls. Cracks the size of pythons slithered up the brickwork like harrowed creatures desperate to escape.

I screamed at my driver to turn left. Down the road I had seen her armed with an M16. Her dark features had been set with wicked disdain. She was waiting, waiting, waiting, waiting for me. Her face had contained the confidence of inevitable victory. I charged from it with the desperation born from electric unease. Over potholes we scrambled, spreading the mass, knocking over ovens, turning over baskets, sending roasted peanuts into the mucky fissures that sent a fragrance of oil and salt up through the degraded streets. At a place where the road widened into a small courtyard, a pack of children swamped the rickshaw; then she emerged from the darkness and smiled malevolently into the dim confines of my boiling flight. I saw the devil himself swimming in the great bowls of her impenetrable eyes. Her hair writhed like live wires and gripped the overhead bars of my rattling machine. Frantically the driver hit the throttle and we bounced down a dark street. Small children dived into doorways to avoid our terrorised withdrawal. We flew down the alley toward a patch of distant light, searching in vain for a way out of this maze of irksome streets. They were the streets that she controlled. The treacherous, unpredictable, scathing byways of her fierce intellect. In the patch of light, a woman from a second-storey window poured a stack of putrid garbage on to the roof of the rickshaw. Lumps of rotting food smeared the path over which we hurried, towards the distances, dark, obscured and unending. Out of the rush of a thousand faces she then emerged and stood, lavishly made-up, clad in khakis, her black hair iridescent in a gleaming blue-and-white sheen. A sudden and dangerous swerve to the right enabled us to avoid her, a fact that only made those pouting lips curl in amused cynicism at the absurdity of my useless and desperate attempt at escape.

The rickshaw bounded like a boat on a violent sea down passageways I had to leave; other places she frequented contained palm trees in an orange blaze that burnt where the vast oceans of tranquillity met the sky. I had to find them. Here, in the claustrophobic confines of her dogmatic ferocity, disasters were imminent. Catastrophes were rife. The poverty of misunderstanding and the complicated sewer of false assumptions clung to the flaking walls; everywhere I flew the paucity of relevant education stripped the hopes of positive realisation from these thoroughfares of negative thought. A sweat-ridden insecurity churned the dirt roads to mud. I leapt on to the street and jumped over old women in veils who were selling vegetables and who wailed in disbelief at the careless athleticism of my panicked leap. Down a street soaked in a quagmire of choleric water I rushed in a bid to find the magic corridor leading to the clear streams I sought in the sunlit blue of perfumed days. Such an opening to the worlds beyond became increasingly remote; the harder I searched for them the closer the confining walls of angered perspicacity became.

I turned a corner and gasped in dismay at the sight of her standing upon a platform beneath religious deities whose serenity seemed more in tune with pallid indifference rather than consciousness. She saw me and aimed her weapon; with the steadiness of one certain of the inevitability of her kill, she fired. A chunk of plaster disintegrated beside my head. I dived for cover. A woman balancing a basket of shiny fruit on her head screamed in horror at the awkwardness of my fumbling flight. I shoved her aside and sprinted through the seething turmoil of meaningless humanity, heart pumping, into the slums of my cowardly demise. Strange, whining, fermenting, screeching music filled my ears. The bashing of musical instruments echoed into the redolent shadows. Scrawny men in blue uniforms appeared in the distance. The puffing of cheeks and the smashing of arms occurred with the gyration of hips. Rusting brasses and weathered drumskins came into view. Behind the band, a crowd of people blocked the street. I fought my way through them and arrived in an opening where the crowd swam in a falsity of smiling glee. A man with red-rimmed glasses and frog-like cheeks told me it was the birthday of one of the gods. All pretence of religious precepts were disregarded in the mêlée that ensued when free food – a steaming mound of fried rice covered in vegetables – was offered to the masses.

The collective lust for the satiation of hunger caused small children – helpless, pleading eyes – to be trampled; elbows and tempers were simultaneously raised; pushing and shoving; vituperative shouts; the belligerent throng were so violently impolite in their bid for something in which most disreputable people revel – that is, something for nothing – that the iron-framed food stall was destined for certain collapse. It shook like a sapling in a storm as the greedy crowd fought each other for bowls of rice about the size of a fist. Any thoughts of bad karma were dispensed with in the rapacious desperation of a free feed. I was caught up in the middle of it and could not move. The thought of dying in this avaricious waste caused me to unleash a series of unheard screams lost in the self-indulgent fury of this irreligious haste. People threatened each other with the moronic testimonies of the morally superior, fingers were shoved into outraged faces, foam began to froth around the lips of the tormented; an ironically sweet fragrance of cooking confectioneries filled the stagnant air. The music – a wild frenzy of discordant, pained and frenetic notes – blasted the atmosphere with a passion that matched the recalcitrance of the battling crowd. A sea of lurid turbans collided with each other as the band, exaggerating their movements, tore the heart out of accepted notions of sound by beating pummelled drums and whining with flutes and horns. A scene of trembling disorder greeted the workers in the food store; the iron frames of their tenuous generosity were connected to religious decorations – dazzling strips of glinting aluminium – that were draped overhead, wall to wall across the street. Prints of deities were hanging in them. They shook with the knowledge that the desire to satisfy basic instincts was greater than the desire to emulate their gracious feats. The bellicosity reached such a frenzy that the red and white striped marquee of the food store, rattling in despair, caused the deities, shaking in the fear that their superstitious stranglehold was a sham, to fall to the ground from their absurd heights. It was clear that a full stomach was more important than a clear conscience. Trodden into the dirt, the deities disappeared into the unrestrained impetuosity. Viewing this, the overwhelmed food store workers had their plans for decency shattered by the audacity of this suddenly heathen-like crowd. Rising to their feet, more in fear of being crushed than heard, the workers pranced around the stage of their disrespected beneficence, bewildered, staggered, indignant, for the desperadoes before them had cast aside every ingrained principle of moral acceptability for the spurious reward of four or five handfuls of brown rice. It was chaos, and there was no way I could escape.

She was lurking around here somewhere as well in this fetid crowd, hunting with barbarous, sharply-drawn teeth, fangs that could sing as they bit. The crowd suddenly parted. Through it she rode in black leathers on a motorcycle of polished chrome. The angry faces of dissatisfied people made weird shapes in the convex mirrors of her shining exhaust pipes. Hot orange flames fluttered from this powerful machine's lustrous chrome. This was power and femininity at its most exquisite. A fantastic release of fuel-injected hormones sped in the veins of my dreams as I realised that I had aroused this being's sensuous wrath. I smiled as she rose from the bike; a killer look of abused brutality filled her tigerish eyes. If I were going to die, I wanted it to be like this. I wanted to sacrifice my body to the glories of her unquestionable and distraught sense of vicious probity. She had me up against a wall. This was the end of the line. Such passion and justified ire could only come from woman; and she had it. Her breath glowed with the angelic heat of sensual infuriation. I had the chance to get down on my knees and plead forgiveness. This righteously sumptuous creature, however, was in no mood for apologies and, as she tore me limb from limb, with the rioting crowd murdering each other in the background, I suddenly realised that I had made a terrible mistake. I could not bear the sight of this any longer so my eyes flashed opened in horror, their burning irises fearful in the furious heat of the unforgiving night.

* * * * * * * * * *

I had been warned, internally and externally, to tread carefully. Her volatile nature had the bearing of financial markets in a political crisis. Her concern for investor relations swung wildly. I had seen her stun a group of speechless architects with her scathing views; she had asserted that "a lot of rubbish being built these days - apart from being devoid of any sensible economic environmental considerations - possesses all the visual sensitivity of untreated concrete." The architects were struck supine by this vicious outburst of passionate confidence. Diplomacy was cast aside as she expressed views that sent a chill through an audience numbed by this fierce aggression towards their "fantastically overrated profession". The attitude of the other women in this group – "their ridiculous girlfriends" – almost caused her the same grief.

"They just sit there," she said. "All you ever get from that lot is how much weight they've lost. They just don't realise that the world doesn't care about their absurd weight. The stupid cows."

I had seen her verge on hysteria when expressing her profound fears for a world on a "social and environmental knife-edge". The incredible thing was that she was so genuine. She expressed this by blasting the pomposity of the morally pretentious by declaring, "I'm sick of people who care." I was in awe of her unrestrained scepticism and fire. She almost had to be calmed down when expressing her dismay over what she described as "the delicate Ukrainian question". It was explained to me that the Russian minority in the east of the country "could easily revolt" as the economy of the country deteriorated, as it was doing, "beyond repair".

"The Russians", she said, "could be tempted to move in and try to grab the eastern part of the country under the pretext of protecting their own people. And the Ukrainians – who happen to be the third largest nuclear power on earth – may be tempted to do something deeply regrettable to us all."

She explained that the U.S. State Department had been "following developments closely" and that it was they who had predicted "with pin-point accuracy" the "hideous events" of the "now infamous Balkans disaster". She was a worried woman. It would have been futile for me, and unforgivably absurd, to have said: "Don't worry about it", when it was people like her who were destined to save the rest of us from our monumental stupidity, spineless inaction and self-indulgent frippery. It was bizarre to be hearing such things, expressed with such conviction, in a place where the vices of Epicurean opulence were open to all.

As she spoke, I could see behind her the blue waves of wealth, topped with cream, sweeping over the dozing carpet of an ocean so vast that it melted an interminable distance away, without the faintest effort, into an infinite and unbesmirched silk-screen of azure blue. In the foreground, the lucky and well-fed occupants of this sun-drenched kingdom, spread out on bone-white sand and bobbing happily in the surf, could not be chastised for their ignorance and complacency towards the potentially apocalyptic developments unfolding on distant shores. Why should they? A huge ocean separated them from the disorganisation and desperation of less fortunate worlds. It was over there. Out of the way. On another planet. Largely insoluble. Not worth a second thought.

And she was, a look of intense distance in her contemplative, black eyes, immersed in those foreign concerns. She was ignorant of the attractiveness of her mysterious sense of relevant, universal drama. This ignorance was part of her earthy charm. Her mind, on a plane above those upon whom we looked down, from within the noisy confines of a blue-carpeted café, could not see itself anywhere but in the milieu of cheery party-goers whose principal concerns and most common debates centred around the petty analysis of previous social engagements and the tireless and optimistic contemplation of those that lay ahead. Hardly a word about herself – or that – ever fell from her succulent lips. I was mystified by her constant ability to speak about significant matters without relent; there were those who believed that mystery exists in those who stared silently with arcane wisdom, but I was not fooled by this. Not any more. Any interesting human being, whether they liked it or not, could not help but prove it. Part of her beauty lay in her ceaseless power to do this successfully without ever appearing aware of it. She was as unconscious of her rare talents as she was vitriolic towards those who made "life such a misery for so many". I could not help but wonder that her "critical displacement", as I described it – the separation of her thoughts from the "environmentally expected" – had something to do with her vindictiveness towards her dogmatic father.

"It was sickening", she said, with a mixture of disdain, resignation and anger, "watching my mother being so careful to protect his brittle and unjustified ego. I vowed I would never be like that."

I informed her that she appeared to me to have been "extremely successful" in bringing about this goal. She smiled, a blaze of light in the storm of her grandiloquent ruminations.

"You know", she said, whimsically, "that you can't fool me."

Of this, I had absolutely no doubts.

"This propensity", she continued, "that you've got for danger. It has no moral basis."

I shook my head in wonderment, deeply amused.

"Well, you'll be pleased to know", I replied, "that I've come to the same conclusion."

"This doesn't mean", she said, "that I think you're awful."

"I know, I know, " I replied.

I was fearful of hearing an unwarranted diagnosis of my unacceptability.

"I'm just", I continued, "a typical member of the human race. If a creature from another planet stayed here for long enough, they'd leave believing that man acts as if the attainment of a certain critical level of carnage is absolutely essential to the well-being and perpetuation of our species. Ultimately, under tremendous pressure, most of us are insane. This is ingrained at a young age before we realise the existence of moral codes."

She returned my wonderment with a gaze of child-like beauty.

"That", she said, excited in a youthfully exuberant way, "was a remarkable comment."

"Thanks," I mumbled, stumped by her vivacious honesty.

These sweet and unexpected bursts of aestheticism I found as equally beguiling as her ability to continually dissect important issues with such passion and finesse. It was yet another aspect of her mystifying unpredictability. It left me with the feeling that the journey through the landscape of her existence would be a spectacular one: the fury of volcanic eruptions, the serenity of snow-capped mountains, torrential monsoons, the flaming beauty of blood-red deserts, sudden bursts of mango light. I felt the power of the classic cliché: 'I don't know what she's going to do next.' It was this inability to see an end to her potential that drove my mind to its infatuated distraction.

It also caused the trepidation I felt as I rang her a few days after "the feet-driveway incident". I picked up the phone genuinely oblivious of what to expect. I knew that she was not the cynic which some of her outrageous tirades may have suggested; any negative feelings towards me would be expressed, straightforwardly, and then forgotten. She was not a person heinously disposed to the expression of disgust for the mere sake of it. That would have been unforgivable. But she was not afraid to say what was on her mind and I had no guarantee that I was about to hear something that my delicate, war-torn constitution did not wish to imbibe: 'Maybe it's a good idea if we don't see each other again.'

The phone rang. With each ring, the fear of rejection was slowly replaced with the frustrating emptiness of anti-climax.

'God,' I thought, 'she's not there. Or she's not answering.'

The second contingency – apart from being possibly directly related to me – had an even darker side: She lived in a studio flat and her telephone was right next to the bed. I dreaded the idea of ringing her when some other man was strewn across the paradise of her room. I was too old for this 'so-he's-the-one-chasing-you' stuff. I detested being ridiculed for possessing unjustified illusions. I was vacillating between the fear of a hideous discovery and the dissatisfaction of continued unenlightenment when someone picked up the receiver and did not answer. The silence was as tense as it was mysterious. It seemed to go on for minutes.

'This', I thought, 'is ridiculous. She really is trying to avoid someone.'

I was not used to reality equating unexpectedly with my subconscious fears. Usually my hard-headed, pragmatic conscious mind formed a barrier between these superstitions and the outside world. I contemplated speaking. I had to know the answer. Was it me? Just when I was about to say, 'Samantha, I appreciate the fact that you want to avoid someone. Shall I hang up?' she, tentatively, said, "Hullo."

Her relief on discovering that it was me was not as great as my relief on discovering that it was someone else she was attempting to avoid.

"Sorry, sorry," she said. "Thank God it's you. I made the mistake of having lunch with some fuckwit a few weeks ago and he keeps ringing me up. Sometimes I just don't know what to do."

I felt like saying, 'The answer's simple. Don't answer your phone. Just ring me up every day and just go out with me. Right?' but instead I said, "What's the problem with this guy?"

'This', I thought, 'promises to be enlightening.'

"Ah," she gasped, "half an hour into the lunch he started telling me how beautiful I'm supposed to be. He prides himself on being a bit of a chef, and he'd made quite an effort – all designed for seduction. I doubt whether he listened to a word I said. And his obsequious flattery! How subtle."

'Poor guy,' I thought. 'That's what you get for telling the truth.'

"Samantha," I said, "do you mind if I ask you something?"

"What?" she asked.

"Can you imagine", I began, "what sort of a person you'd be if you showed this sort of rejection to every compliment you ever received?"

"Some compliments", she replied, "are justified and some are not."

"Does it matter", I said, "whether they're justified or not, if they're honest and true?"

Her response was ejected with unerring accuracy.

"Sometimes," she said, "and this is a weakness in us all, the truth is not good enough."

She was referring to good in the biblical sense. I laughed when she followed this up with, "You're absolutely right though - and I make no apologies for it - but I'm probably incapable of objectivity."

I said, "I admire your ruthless honesty."

"Thank you," she replied. "That's what I call a compliment."

"You mean", I added, "a justified one?"

"Touché."

One had to be careful with one's selection and timing as far as compliments were concerned. They could be as damaging as they were constructive. The recipient had to perceive honesty with justification; the honesty was the easy bit. The morality of justification is open to vast interpretation.

'At least', I thought, 'she realises this and probably doesn't take herself that seriously.'

The language she used in our agreement to meet, I felt, was symbolic of her inscrutability. I suggested that we could meet on a particular day in the afternoon. She explained that "this was good" because she "had to do something in the morning" on that day, and that meeting in the afternoon "would make sense". This perplexing way of expressing it may have made sense to her, but it was totally incomprehensible to me, and probably to the rest of the human race as well. However, the semantics of her diction at that point were irrelevant; the feeling of relief and elation as I put the receiver down caused me to clench my fists and prance around the room like an excited schoolboy on the threshold of the greatest adventure of all: the unravelling of the ardent, impassioned, hot-tempered, tempestuous, zealous, stormy, fervent, passionate, enigmatic and superbly human heart. I was about to step over the cliff and had no idea of how I was going to fall.

* * * * * * * * * * *

Ross and I got ourselves invited to a party at Dob McDonald's place. The host – the legendary party attender and giver – had gone to great pains to ensure that only a certain élite number would be in attendance. I was feeling strangely privileged to be amongst them. Dob had decided that a mere one hundred would have to do. Such finicky considerations were not usually a facet of his Epicurean thinking but this still did not stop him with a mysterious air of restraint – an air as foreign to him as fine champagne is to Amazon Indians – from making it clear that he wanted "to keep this one small". Given his deserved reputation in the area of magnitude and excitement with respect to social gatherings, this clarification, from the golden boy of Perth's social scene, was as necessary as it was justified.

Several years ago, when I was last in Perth, he held a party of such vastness that the resulting shock waves almost shattered the city. During the course of fifteen hours of wild interaction – a climactic fracas of unrestrained revelry that attracted well over five hundred to his parents' plush, two-storey mansion – numerous unexpected visitors also made an appearance as well. They consisted of the police, the fire brigade, several outraged local residents and many, who, bored at home and lured by the noise, dropped in, drinks in hand, clueless as to how or why this outlandish testimony to pleasure was transpiring. The fire brigade made the journey because someone set alight an enormous tree in the back garden. The outrage on the part of the local residents did not stem purely from the insurmountable racket – which was unbelievable – but from a highly substantiated fear that their properties too would be engulfed by the fierce blaze. I distinctly remember seeing massive orange flames licking the black sky. The police, overcome by the enormity of the occasion, were constantly frustrated in their endeavours to seek out those responsible, because the vast majority of those there, through drugs or whatever, were also oblivious as well. I saw one peeved elderly woman complaining bitterly to a policeman that a young couple were "doing something unmentionable" on her front lawn. Another woman, wailing hysterically, was screaming that her house – the one behind Dob's – was "about to be destroyed". Dob, who had hired a movie camera, filmed the lot: the before, during and after. When his 'world premiere' was eventually released, the full extent of the mayhem was revealed to all. The incident involving the wailing woman showed that, behind her, great arcs of water from numerous hoses were crashing into the burning tree. My enduring memory from the whole affair was the realisation that it is possible from the one, single, cataclysmic event to witness everything from unbounded ecstasy to inconsolable despair. This fact had given me an unquenchable lust for dramatic events.

Another unique feature of this evening was the fact that everyone whom I knew there got laid. It was uncommon for so many sexy, drunk women to be in one place at one time. Even the completely useless, of which I was proud to be one, and there were several of us, were able, over the ensuing weeks, to regale our friends with lurid stories of libidinous success. The lady with whom I ended up had complained pitifully to Ross and me that she was "too fat". I then produced my now immortal line of: "Good, because I like fucking fat women." Flattery was always one of my more sophisticated weapons. This comment had always caused Ross some amusement - even now.

It was the thing foremost in his mind as we got out of his weather-beaten car in preparation for Dob's latest offering. His whispery laugh, a sort of staccato hiss, swished like a wind of warm and naughty recollection over the gentle rumble of distant conversation. That night of Dob's "megashin", (the word "shin" is derived from the term 'shindig'), Ross had charmed a naive virgin, eventually causing her to go on the Pill and then had proceeded to deflower her by ensuring that his self-esteem and her unquestioning worship rose together in solid harmony with that thing between his legs. This creature's inevitable dismissal - she had gone on the Pill in the belief that Ross was going to have a relationship with her - was done with the usual indifference that only boredom can bring. Her soaked cheeks only left him dry. The term 'bastard' only added to his self-possession. Such proceedings, once standard practice, were now frowned upon by someone struggling to find some new and mature method of attaining the sort of flamboyant self-assurance that had sustained him in his early manhood. The idea of sexual achievements for the sake of boyish, peer-group recognition now made his excessively overused lips curl with disgust. He had reached new heights of respect for the female of the species. He was not going to allow himself to he victimised by "immature temptations". This was all very quaint, and it does become apparent, even to the highly sexed, that the wanton impregnation of women is ultimately an unfulfilling cause, but I also felt that his awkward and too self-conscious separation from his dubious past possessed an element of outrage against a hedonistic society that was slowly rejecting him as it gradually exposed his weaknesses and romantic delusions. It was not very easy sustaining a feeling of prestige if no obvious sign existed for its cause, particularly in a place laced with wealthy young go-getters who, unlike Ross, had made full use of their opportunities. Ross was in desperate need of a legitimate reason to experience a refined self-regard; his employment in a bakery working appalling hours for a relative pittance carried little kudos with the prosperity-conscious children of Perth's luxuriant world. It was a source of embarrassment. It carried no kudos with himself. The past had given him an eminence, the sort of eminence that most of us do not need, but an eminence no less and now he was being left behind in the wake of other people's success. He was unfortunate to have no means of escape from this - something tangible on which to build hope - and, most frustratingly, his intense need to achieve a requited love was a pipe dream in a place whose social life he found, justifiably, to be, with its soporific and shallow conviviality, a nightmare of drunken insipidity. I was able to treat it with complete indifference, but he, for the reasons already stated, and probably from too much exposure, had towards it a certain subtlety of hatred, the kind of abstract but highly-charged emotion found in such things as racism, which caused him within five minutes of being in the party to instruct Dob's housemate - a fellow doctor of high social esteem - to "go and fuck" his "mother".

This was the reward that Pete Bradley had received for attempting to open up relations with someone whom he had not seen for about six months. To say that Peter, after his efforts to be friendly, was astounded would be putting it mildly.

"Fuck my mother?" he gasped, bewildered.

This, after all, was his party as well.

I, in an endeavour to smooth things over, said, jovially, "Yeah, so what's wrong with her?" causing those in the vicinity - so-called friends of his - to laugh rather insensitively.

Peter walked off completely bemused.

The instant we entered the party, Ross began his vindictive tirade against his "shallow" and "sycophantic" host. He mumbled all the way across the back garden with sepulchral anguish at the prospect of having to deal "with an arsehole like that". I was confused as to the precise reasons – that is, the reasons which Ross was trying to project – as to why he was so hateful towards a person who had not done him, nor anyone else with whom he had been even remotely connected, any harm at all. The only crime that Peter had committed was affecting a patronising concern, that Ross, with his newly-found sincerity, deemed to be repulsive as the two of them shook hands. I felt that Ross's belligerent invitation to take up an Oedipus complex was met with an admirable restraint. Ross, hand in hand with his adversary, had imparted his bestial instruction with a smug, but wry grin on his momentarily pleased face. Not many party hosts, I thought, would have been greeted by one of their guests like that. The novelty gave Peter great cause for distressed bafflement. The laughter of his friends, after my remark, only added to his disturbed puzzlement. What the fuck is this? his beguiled face screamed out. This, I thought, is Ross.

Peter left as he had approached, lacking the incentive to indulge in any polite conversation. His eyes had been glazed, distant, unappealing to Ross's proud desire to receive genuine acknowledgement. Ross, however, behind his aggressively-assured façade, was in real need of it. But he was not prepared to act from a position of weakness, describing "image-makers like Pete Bradley" as "people who lacked soul". Increasingly arrogant in his frustration at not being able to find a satisfactory niche, Ross had begun to berate people for characteristics he once so frequently displayed himself; his intolerance – excusable, but hypocritical – was really a rejection of his past, and an ineffective method of maintaining his dwindling dignity. There was a time when he had shown the same uninterest in sincere conversations as his present host had just done. His continually flippant interactions at that time were incurious, not revealing mature considerations. The future did not exist. It was an irrelevance; sometimes I wondered if this demotivation stemmed from his unlimited indolence or from a lack of incentive. Enormous pleasure had come to him easily. The idea that concerted effort channelled into a worthwhile cause could produce an ethereal reward held little promise for a person already blessed with the gift of immediate fulfilment and the satisfaction of ego. There was probably little reason for him, under the sort of immortality which had emerged from vast egotism, to believe that this easily-acquired titillation would not continue. Being worshipped by the uninformed for no profound reason had finally become tedious. Being applauded by the informed for legitimate causes was proving somewhat more difficult. Many people with whom he had associated in the past were now not interested in him because they could see that his self-indulgence had taken a dangerous turn for the worse, or were incapable of taking his transformation seriously; vulnerability and dependence had begun to creep into his increasingly obvious sense of instability. People he once knew well were ignoring him, because they were not interested in his problems when he had previously shown no interest in theirs; they could see that he was beginning to cling at a time when they had sorted their problems out and were pursuing fulfilling lives born from constructive work.

In the café he often frequented, he and I were sitting at the window. It was a Sunday lunch time and the place was packed. An ex-girlfriend of his had walked in carrying her baby. She and her boyfriend pointedly ignored Ross and sat on the other side of the room. Ross then, with forced calmness, expressed his dismay at Sharon's dismissive behaviour; his bafflement contained not a hint of regret for anything that he had ever done. He was oblivious as to what may have caused Sharon to have acted with such severe disenchantment. The poisoned look on her otherwise sweet face had displayed a fury so intense that I was staggered Ross could not, without an ounce of self-righteous mendacity, explain why this woman - probably the only lover of his who had been a true friend - had treated him with such disdain.

"I did so much to help her", he persisted, fighting to remain amiable, "when she was down. Now I get this. And they never ever ever have offered me an explanation as to why! Never!"

Ross's eyes were soaked with sanctimonious lament. He explained that he had "frequently visited Sharon and David" when they were "going through such hard times". He had been the rock upon which their lives had been resurrected. He had been of such "enormous help" to them, and now, when he was "having difficulties" himself, they did not "want to know". For someone with such a genuine cause for outrage, he was being remarkably equitable; he had no choice but to be. He knew that it was he who was in “the position of weakness”.

“They’ve got each other”, he said, “and I’m still trying to recover from my last relationship. They don’t need me any longer.”

I had to go to the toilet; this meant going past Sharon. Her version of events was considerably different. Without hesitation, she explained to me, her new-born baby in her arms, that Ross had shown “no interest whatsoever” in her problems and that they, because of her “bad pregnancy”, were “pretty appalling”.

“He constantly came around”, she said, with an assurance absent from Ross’s voice, “unannounced and uninvited and just whined on incessantly about his break-up with Anne-Marie. It was all we ever got and it was obvious that David and I just wanted to be alone. It drove us nuts. We eventually had to tell him to go. We even had to take the phone off the hook.”

Across the room, Ross was sitting alone, smoking, a forlorn figure, staring blankly ahead. I knew that he would be fascinated to discover what Sharon and I were talking about.

“It’s a real pity”, I said, “because he’s genuinely bemused as to why you don’t want to speak to him any more. It’s incredible, really.”

“I know,” Sharon replied. “But can you imagine it? I was really sick – it was a bad pregnancy – and David was having a tough time at work, and Ross was coming around to our place and bursting into tears. He never showed any remorse at all for these painful intrusions. We just decided we weren’t going to take any more. He had to go.”

Back with Ross, he wanted to know “what all that was about”. I told him that Sharon and I had “only talked about the things that we had been up to”. He accepted this before producing another wail of stupefaction concerning his “unbelievable treatment”. Taking into consideration that he was not completely beyond self-awareness and that eventually he would look with more clarity at his past and benefit from it, I decided to tell him the truth. This predictably led to another bout of measured consternation. It was he “who had listened. She is wrong”. His green eyes sang a charming ballad of mature befuddlement at the astonishing interpretation of events with which I had just presented him.

"Ross," I said, "if you want to speak to them again, then it's you who's going to have to apologise. Whether you like it or not, they don't have the incentive."

Ross was at least realistic enough to accept this. But I knew that his damaged pride would prevent him from taking this bold step. I also knew, however, that it would eventually cause him to do something constructive with his life. Despite his fantastic laziness, it was not as awesome as his profound loftiness; his wounded honour, I knew, would finally drive him to productive heights. Its misuse in the past was soon going to be reawakened by the distant and alluring chiming of the seductive bells of positive recognition. The intensity of their pealing, made euphonious by the desire to prove all these doubting people wrong, was increased by the crossing of rugged mountains. The pain of his present difficulties was making him see that such mountains exist for the better. One day, he would cross one.

Another person similarly disposed towards easy, short-lived pleasures and now in need of something greater was Richard Wain. He approached Ross and me and commented on the "unusual intimacy" of the party. He then produced a comment the philosophical ramifications of which were in direct contrast to his actions: "It's not the quantity that counts, but the quality."

Given that this was the person who, only a week earlier, had told me that he had slept with over a thousand women – and had been proud of this achievement – I thought that this sudden change in perspective, ironic in the extreme, was a transformation in thinking far too abrupt to have any foundation in reality. It was a pity for him that he was so unable to sustain love. A pity because he was genuinely a nice character, full of keen wit, eager, shiny, with warm green eyes, but far too susceptible to simple pleasures for his own good. I had been told that he had recently been the victim of a mysterious illness caused, he had announced, by a sting from an Asian scorpion. This seemed unreal to me, so I remained open-minded about it rather than convinced. What aroused my interest was his sudden desire, and outside context of our conversation, to tell me about it. He seemed anxious to explain. There was an introspection and an unease to him that I had not previously seen. Someone whom I was yet to contact, Paul Humphrey, was adamant that Richard's "sickness" had been a nervous breakdown, due, Paul believed, to Richard's "incapability of sustaining a relationship".

Certainly, Richard's friends had not questioned the scorpion theory. They were in no doubt that Richard had been bitten by a nasty arachnid. It was probably too inconceivable for them to feel that Richard was capable of paralysing self-analysis. They admired his hedonistic successes too much and considered them to be of too much significance in the attainment of happiness to want to believe that they represented a deeper problem, and I was not going to ask what they thought of Paul's view. This could have only stimulated a series of unnecessary and unsubstantiated rumours – and would probably have led to a backlash against me as well.

What intrigued me was whether it was possible for someone to have the experience of love and then to lose it rapidly, and to repeat this constantly with many people. I was fascinated to know whether Richard believed this to be true, but I refrained from asking. The question would have been too embarrassing at a time when everyone was searching for excuses to burst into frivolity. It would have only added to the tension inherent in those people attempting to communicate whilst being sober. Instead, we just glanced around, blankly observing the vivacious hysteria that surrounded us. The paucity of conversation as we stood – Ross, Richard, Peter Bull, Brad Shilkin and myself – engulfed by chirpy packs of prattling party-goers, hoping that something substantial would happen, suggested to me how lonely we all were. Richard was incapable of love; Brad wasted his time on women to whom he was not suited; Ross was far too cynical and too sensitised by his last encounter for any pertinent interaction, while Peter was too eccentric and too interested in relevant matters for the superficial majority, and I was smitten with someone with everything on her mind other than me.

It was agitated yearning, rather than idle curiosity, that caused our divergent gazes to be cast over the chatting throng which had draped itself in small groups over the lawn that stretched a considerable distance, on two levels, from the back of the house to the back fence. A stone path, rising from a shed in the rear corner of the yard, ran all the way across the lawn to the rear of the house. The five of us were standing on this path at a point where it turned into a flight of steps; a sudden plunge down a slope brought this change in the thoroughfare; at the foot of this slope, against the side fence, the purple flowers of a jacaranda tree, the confetti born from the marriage of winter with spring, made an eye-catching carpet in the mottled beauty of late afternoon light. Overhead, quivering white butterflies, like dainty thoughts, swam around the alluring fragrance of the unfallen flowers. Beneath them, a butterfly himself, Dob fluttered, his dark face occasionally bursting into huge grins as he plunged his proboscis into each intoxicated garden of flowers, gorging himself on their pollen, enhancing his notoriety, while denouncing any interest in that from which he had just taken.

Maybe one day he would perceive the absurdity of this ridiculous inflation of an ultimately unfulfilling identity, this need to be admired by people for whom he had no real time, but I suspected that he, too, would not find love. I remember him years ago complaining that he had "never sumped a femme" with whom he was in love. He was so perturbed by his lack of success in this department that he spent about six months going into nightclubs, approaching women in whom he was never going to be interested and telling them that he was a public servant rather than a medical student, because he did not want to scare them off with his intellect. One of the men with whom he was frequenting these clubs, told me, with some concern, that Dob was treating their attempts to communicate with strange women "as if it was a science."

A girlfriend of a mutual friend of ours played a superb trick on him once; Dob had advertised a room in a house he was renting and this woman, whom Dob knew well, rang up pretending that she was interested in the accommodation. Oblivious of who she was, Dob, over a frenetic half-hour, spilled out the entire story of his life, most of which she knew, without ever asking her a single question. Many, many people were amused by this, but I just felt a kind of despairing wanness that someone of Dob's talent could fritter his life away with these one-sided indulgences that led nowhere, which ended with the same futility that he had experienced time and time again. Women have this tendency to skewer themselves on the pitchfork of charm and he and Richard Wain had inflicted more wounds on womanhood than either of them would care to believe.

I remember visiting Richard once to pick something up that he had promised to give me. It was one o'clock in the afternoon when he answered the door, dishevelled, half-naked, a boyish look of beaming excitement on his face, whispering ecstatically, "Knubs, Knubs, five in a row!"

He was enthusiastically referring to his unheralded success in sleeping with five different women on successive nights. Through the gap left by his bedroom door being left ajar, I caught a glimpse of the tousled hair and pretty face of unsuspecting number five. I did not know what to say. It was all too surreal for me. Just one like that would have been enough. 'Didn't these people see any excitement in unearthing the minefield of explosive discoveries that could result from being with one person?' I had wondered. Well, I suppose not. It was a pity, particularly in Richard's case; despite his obsessive unfaithfulness, he was charmingly loyal. I could not imagine, assuming that he could even remember half of them, ignoring any woman with whom he had ever been to bed. He swept women up with his effervescent friendliness. If they became disillusioned with him, it was because they had mistaken his unusual degree of amorous blithsomeness for genuine interest; and it was a pity for all concerned, since it was a road that led into an endless desert of unfulfilment, one dune of perfidious geniality separated by yet another trough of fruitlessness, proceeding to another; one after another, in a pointless ordeal of forgetting through gratification, they swept across the landscape of his frivolous life. He probably wanted to speak about it, but it was almost considered to be immoral in this place to express dissatisfaction.

One of the principal currencies of communication here was vacuous gaiety. It oozed from people's mouths like a debilitating sludge. Thousands were choking on it. Puddles of it were being left everywhere. You could break your ankles on it. And hundreds were willing to dive into it. I felt as though I were standing on a precipice resisting this tiresome force which was trying to shove us all into this swamp the perverse waters of which drowned out all thoughts of aesthetic, enterprising or political contemplation. Our silence, equally as putrid as the empty delirium that encircled us, was broken when a woman, walking up the steps, said, in response to a comment that Ross had made, that "that was a pile of shit".

I was immediately charmed. How could anyone resist such a delightfully whining accent? And such an unattractive face covered by lines from the unrelenting sun, and stringy hair that shot out in a multitude of different directions? I couldn't resist.

"Yeah, bewdy mate," I said, in a broad accent. "Yawrah real top sheila."

This cow's face was suddenly ablaze with outrage. The others again, after another episode of my scathing cynicism, were chuckling with laughter. I was astounded. How could I get away with this? The woman was someone they knew. Why wasn't I being told to shut up? She fired back some coarse comment, just as unsophisticated, in my direction.

Seductively, I said, "You're so feminine. I want to marry you," causing Peter to unleash his sonorous chuckle and Ross to entertain us with his sniggering giggle. Brad's high-pitched chortle of blissful surprise was the real source of this woman's humiliation. Some friend he was, hey?

The disillusioned woman left the scene, allowing Brad to make some comment about "mappage". When the prospects of conversation were dire, references to the party were used to fill the vacuum. Party analysis should have been a university course here. The word "map", in reference to women, had caused me some dismay since the day I realised its derivative – Tasmania's vaginal area shape; possibly preordained by that which creates all, this had given the sexual cartographers of Perth the perfect adjective they sought to describe women. The high concentration of "maps" at this party was apparently "good mappage".

It was an intriguing fact that caused me to say, "I'm amazed that you guys use that expression."

My comment had nothing to do with morality, or even overflowing respect for women; I had no more respect for them than I had for men since they could be just as bad; I was just taken aback by the unadulterated boredom of it.

"It's so funny to us", Brad said, smiling sheepishly, "because it's so adolescent."

Ross and I laughed.

"That's incredible," I replied. "Personally, I hated my adolescence."

And I did. No money. No idea of what to say to anyone, let alone women. Hopeless concern for trivia. No vision. A turmoil of extreme desire without social skills. A constant awkwardness that subjugated life, despite the myths of spontaneity in childhood, with the wretched predictability of anguish. If it hadn't been for sport, I probably would have committed suicide.

"We only use it amongst ourselves," Brad said. "We wouldn't use it in front of women."

"I," I replied, with Ross chuckling in agreement, "wouldn't say it in front of anyone under any circumstances whatsoever."

Ross reiterated this with amused emphasis. The word "whatsoever" was drawn out with jolting accentuation. This was not an attempt to make Brad feel inferior, but its delivery had overtones of pretentious morality. Behind his embarrassed smile, I felt that he realised that the cause of my amazement was the fact he knew that I was not into boyish bonding rituals. They didn't exactly bore me; it was more an indifference that arose from my tendency to pursue sexual or emotional projects secretly. And that did not arise from discretion, but from fear of failure. If I wanted people to find out that my attempts at seduction had failed, I wanted to tell them myself. And anyway, as twee as this might sound, I regarded women as people and mappage didn't fit into the picture.

"I know a few women", I said, "who, if they found out that I had referred to them as a map, would've shoved a handbag down my throat."

I was bemused by what came next.

Brad looked at me, equally stupefied by something else, and said, "Are women in Britain feminist?"

Ross and I laughed and said, simultaneously, "No, they're normal."

I was incredulous that his question had implied that women here would be unaffected by the knowledge that they were being looked upon as one thing - and one thing only - a vagina. Ross and I stood apart observing the peculiar antics of a "map".

The woman concerned was wearing a red baseball cap. She had long brunette hair, was very curvaceous, was wearing jeans that highlighted her womanly figure and was possessed of some absurdly dramatic gestures of hand and head that caused Ross and I to prolong our observations longer than we otherwise would have. The vacuous expression of serene and eventful melodrama on her smug face indicated that she was convinced, like the woman in the swimming pool, on the first night I had ventured to one of these insipid parties, that she was gripped by a compelling and mysterious beauty by which any man with even the faintest appreciation could not help but be captivated. All her movements were calculated to emphasise her bewitching wiles - arching of back, tilted head, the histrionic running of hands through hair, distant, relaxed gazes whilst being addressed, total expectation of receiving intimate attention without the knowledge that it requires mutual effort. This appeared to be someone very much in love with adoration for the sake of it, as though it were an abstract quality, like a classical ideal, that requires no attachment to a real being.

Ross and I looked at her, muttering such things as: "Christ, will you have a look at that!" and "How fucking pretentious!" each time one of her self-indulgent and egotistical movements caused gasps of intrigued disbelief to fall, like barbs of venom against this profligate society, from our gaping mouths. I was fascinated for all the wrong reasons. Ross told me that she had been out to dinner with Pete Bradley. This prompted him to say, "Anyone who accepts a dinner invitation from that wanker must be fucking stupid."

I did not consider this to be an objective judgement.

"She apparently fucked him off as well", Ross added, "and knocked him back several times later."

Now you know why I was not too keen on making my infatuations public. The malicious pleasure people got from hearing about the failures of others was as childish as it was unwanted. The woman then rose to her feet and, pretending to stretch her legs, she pointedly bent over and displayed her buttocks in our direction. She was bent over for a seemingly lengthy period, her arse magnificently poised for intense inspection, her position deliberately primeval and sexual. The man she was with was oblivious as to why she had suddenly assumed this licentious stance.

"Women", I noted, "have a tendency to do this to you."

"The silly cow", Ross replied, "actually thinks we're looking at her because we're interested."

It dawned on me that she may have got up to get some drinks to give Ross the opportunity to speak to her. There was no chance of that happening though. That would have required some enthusiasm for the human race. Observation these days was more rewarding than action. Particularly if the individual concerned was motivated by egotism rather than intelligent curiosity.

She came back and sat down facing us. The position she assumed was geographically absurd. Her back was virtually right up against the legs of the people standing behind her. There was quite a lot of space near where she had been before, but she sat where she did because she was enjoying our attention and she did not want the man she was with to suspect that her behaviour was being affected by anything outside their immediate clique. She was as ridiculous as she was cunning. Her friend was bending towards her, unperturbed that his interest was merely part of her ludicrous game. Because Ross and I were watching her, it presented the opportunity of being admired by three men at once. She naturally took this chance to increase her dubious self-belief. Not an iota of real interest ever crossed her dramatically-affected face. As we gazed at her, she bent forward, returning her friend's attention by touching him with a spurious affectation of affection; her face, tilted to one side with a look of mendacious emotion, was filled, to the careful observer, with a clinical and detached pleasure. She was succeeding with her little game. Ross and I were obviously impressed. Gifted men were clearly leaping over dangerous barriers to get to her. To spread her legs – let's make no mistake about this – you had to be good.

Unbeknown to her, Ross and I were maintaining a barrage of snide remarks, rather than accolades.

"Imagine", Ross said, "what size brain you'd have to have to want to indulge in shit like this."

"Remember, Ross," I replied, "people will do all sorts of silly things for the sake of their precious self-esteem."

"That guy", he said, "thinks she's really interested."

It took me a few seconds to realise that his comment was actually connected to mine. Women had used him for purposes of skin-deep self-enhancement, for their puerile image-making. The character on the ground, so sincere with his appreciative gesticulations, was innocently being victimised in the same way. But he was being earnest. Ross had not been. He had been used as much as he had done the using. It was only in the last few years that he had come to realise it. When the victim leant forward again to impress something of the gravest urgency to the sensual pretender, she appeared to ignore the comment, as if it was irrelevant, preferring to suddenly rip her baseball cap off and to tilt her head glamorously to one side and then back, so that her chin was stuck up in the air, before her hands ran through the clusters of silk that fell in a sensual downpour across her shoulders in a symbolic realisation of her beautiful intricacy. Ross and I giggled at this pitiful display of imbecilic vanity. She did not realise that it was her delusion of personal excellence which was riveting us and firing our dramatic imaginations. Her tinsel presence only served to reinforce our belief in Perth as an image society. She struck me as being an innocent victim of the importance placed upon physical beauty in this trivial and unreal world that preferred mirthful illusion and splendour to reality. The intelligence she may have possessed was very well hidden beneath an avalanche of egotistical fantasy. And there were plenty more like her.

Then Dob appeared nearby. He was being spoken to by someone else. That person, yet another to have to rely on comment about the party to stimulate a conversation, said, "Things are beginning to thin out."

Dob, with a serious took of emphatic gravity, replied, "Anyone still here has a cause."

Ross and I chuckled, conscious of Dob's simplistic interpretation of affairs.

"What cause have I got?" Ross asked, smiling.

"Smut," Dob replied, with brutal emphasis.

He really believed that this was true.

I started giggling when Ross said, "How about simple observation?"

Dob was not able to cope with this, so he left. As he walked off, Ross looked at me, astonished, and said, "Just think, he's going to become a psychiatrist."

He was implying that someone in this position, instead of perceiving action in a Freudian context, should have had a more rounded depiction of human motives.

"Maybe", I said, "it's not possible for people who are not creative to understand the motives of those who are."

Later, after darkness had descended, Brad approached Ross and me with an uncharacteristic air of bemused timidity. He seemed uncertain about engaging us in conversation for fear of experiencing modes of behaviour anathema to his attitudes and good-natured disposition. His natural smile – a real beam of Jewish delight – was, on this occasion, coloured with an uncertainty that caused me to say, in an endeavour to reduce his diffidence, believing that an interest in his life might help him to relax, "What kind of music are you into these days?"

This question only served to increase his disquiet. Too many people here, due to lack of experience, overemphasised the éliteness of the arts. It would have been very difficult to explain to a lot of people here that going to a classical music concert or to the opera, particularly in Italy, was really just good fun. Nothing more mysterious than that.

"I'm not very cultural," he said, as if predicting a conversation with which he would not know how to deal.

He was too paranoically conscious of the difference between himself, and Ross and me. I found this absurd. He was acting as though we did not have anything in common.

"Oh come on," I said. "Don't be so ridiculous."

This helped him to relax. The beaming smile began to overcome the apprehension.

He then said, by way of explanation for his fear of belittlement, with a hint of irony, "Knubs and Ross – the artistes."

He, too, was unconscious of why Ross and I were behaving the way we were at this uninspiring party. I was surprised that the answer to this was not obvious. But it just showed that I had been away so long that I was no longer of this world, and that Ross, desperate to escape from it, was keen to point out the existence of alternative courses of action, even if his abrasiveness in doing so was really nothing more than a mask for his flagging dignity and relative lack of success.

"We find", he said, with sardonic condescension, as if pained at having to highlight the facts to a lesser being, "observing interesting."

He then said, with a frustrated weariness that I found appealing for its truculent presumptuousness, "It gets so tedious having to explain the obvious to people incapable of realising the possibilities for fulfilment that exist on this earth. Ah, but that's life."

The bitter veracity of Ross's speech and the prickly resignation of his demeanour caused Brad and I to look at each other and laugh. A cigarette hung from the corner of Ross's twisted mouth. His growing disdain for a place whose social inadequacies were slowly squeezing the life out of him, I felt, at that moment, might eventually help him to produce the art he really needed to create. It was only now that the compounding of suffering over the years was, in his case, at a stage where a relevant explosion of verse could emerge from his tormented soul. Just a bit more personal honesty, I felt, would do it.

Then another reason for Brad's trepidation became apparent to me. The woman with whom he was having an affair had just arrived and was talking to some friends. He had come over to Ross and me to ask if we wanted to join him and his entourage later at his place for pizzas and videos. He had to go. We told him that we might "drop around later". He got the signal that his friends were leaving and, as his lover walked off, he said, despairingly, "That's her."

The point had been reached where she was no longer required; the tricky phase of extrication, the moment where it was impossible to maintain an emotional pretence, was in the process of rearing its ugly head.

"Good luck," I said.

"I'm not looking forward to this," he replied.

"I don't envy you," I said. "They never understand."

"I know," he replied, wistfully.

He then went off and I wondered why he had failed to realise that a social life like this was not going to yield the fulfilment of his desires; then I concluded that he was probably incapable of making that leap; he had been here too long, was too affected, and that was a real pity. For me, and the rebellious Ross, the pursuit of women in the context of these situations represented nothing more than the hapless rehashing of an undesirable adolescence and, as my adolescence had never been good enough for me then, it certainly was not going to be good enough now.

* * * * * * * * * *

I was waiting on the street when she swayed up the road towards me. It was uncomfortable not being able to see her eyes. They were covered by sunglasses. I did not know whether to break out into a warm smile or not. The feeling that she was conscious of my pitfalls or could interpret my quirks in this way unnerved me; I also hated having to behave. I wanted to be flippant and naughty, to make surreal comments, to indulge in innuendoes, but I also knew that she was still sensitive about my intentions. How I longed to make some bizarre comment that would not dredge up the fears which she harboured about my spurious motivations. But this would not have been very timely.

She removed her sunglasses and did not smile. I would have preferred it had the wind not shaken the tree I was under at that moment; the swirling sight or mottled shadows flashed around my feet. A confused whirl of light and dark sang instead of the tree. Some tensions produce sharp clarity, others made the world opaque. This was a luminous obfuscation.

The blue sky had the effect of indifferent encasement. It gave no sign of ever having been distempered by a flash of evil inspiration; it was one vast sheet of perpetual contentment. Something mocking existed in its sensual passivity. It had made a conscious point not to be of any help. Had I possessed an ounce of its calmness, I would have been able to see that my feelings towards it, buried under a confusion of concerns, were really about her. I would recognise this later.

The stained-glass ceiling inside reminded me of a fascinating mind. The plethora of colours was rich and delicate. Our table was next to a mahogany cabinet full of wine and brandy glasses. Portraits of famous musicians and writers were encased in carved frames upon the lemon walls. A tropical plant climbed up a corner from an oak pot. Cherubs and bouquets of fruit and flowers were carved into the pot's sombre exterior. Between the bottom picture rail and the high skirting boards was a border of burgundy paper adorned with miniaturist depictions of classical antiques. Amongst these depictions of a better world were scenes of nymphs floating in clouds ablaze with omniscient light. The marble head of a curly-haired luminary sat upon a waist-high mahogany stand. A fireplace inlaid with Florentine marble was surrounded by a sturdy grill of finely-cast steel. Above the fireplace was an enormous painting of a mountain range covered in fern and gum trees in a surreal and serene blaze of late afternoon light. Upon a ledge beneath the paining was a Turkish porcelain dish between two amphorae of Japanese imari. Several roses and daffodils had been placed in crystal vases around the room. These indiscriminate explosions of colour gave the place a cheery beauty.

We ordered a glass of champagne each.

"My father", she said, harshly, "used to take us here when he was trying to be impressive."

This unexpected comment was as baffling as it was extraordinary. I had offered to take her out to lunch to a restaurant I wanted to go to again after several years of quiet yearning. I knew that her lack of gratitude was caused by an unwillingness to be moved by superficial charms, but I was uncertain if she considered me shallow enough to believe that she was capable of being affected by flashy attempts to please. The tone of her voice was too scathing for comfort.

'Is she that unconscious of the implications of her remark?' I thought. I doubted it. I had mixed feelings about her forthrightness. Often it was a pleasure. Sometimes her straight talking was based on false assumptions, but that only served to make her even more human.

"I'm here", I said, "because I wanted to see this place again. I would have come here by myself – if I had to."

The tone of my voice was conciliatory. I was disturbed by the thought of being likened to her father, but I dismissed her comment as optimistically as I could by assuming that her unfortunate memories had nothing to do with me. This was not as settling as I would have hoped. She stared at me with a fierce agitation. Her expression suggested that flirtatious episodes were going to be out; believe me, if I knew that that was the price I had to pay for her heart, I would have taken it.

Coolly on fire, she stared at me in a tight ensemble of black velvet. A necklace from a bygone era, silver filigree, made contact with that neck. Strength and delicacy mingled there in fragrant quantities. Her hair contained some maddened, swirling clusters that reminded me of the enlivened vapours of active volcanoes.

I said: "You've got volcanoes in your hair."

"Thank you," she replied.

"Do you like volcanoes?"

"Of course."

"I've always been fascinated by them," I said.

"Good for you."

"I like their fundamental unpredictability."

"Really?"

"And", I continued, "their primeval fineness. They are the thing on earth that my mind best associates with prehistoric time and the existence of great forces."

"Sometimes", she smiled, "I find your epic appreciation rather amusing."

"And how would you prefer to find it?" I asked.

It was certainly going to be one of those afternoons.

"Rising", she replied, "elegantly straight out of a flat plain."

"Definitely dramatic," I agreed. "Perfect."

Then unexpectedly, she said, "So much shape and height coming from something so flat and shapeless. When you see it, you just can't believe it exists. And it makes you feel so glad."

"The unexpected", I said, "with power. When you see something as new as that", I added, "you see again the huge breath of the infinity."

The waiter was a little dumbstruck by what he had just heard. He had a fine line in drinks though. Liked his shirt as well. Cream-white with elegant embroidery. Similar to what I had on. Drolly, she clinked my glass.

"Let's celebrate," I said.

"To what?" she asked.

"The fall of the Holy Roman Empire," I replied.

"No," she said. "What about the existence of great forces?"

I was looking forward to this. She had the ability to add extra dimensions to my own esoteric beliefs. Greater width had just been added to my notion of unpredictability.

"There's a mountain", she said, "outside Tehran. A volcano. The top half of it is always covered in snow."

'Of course,' I thought. 'Damavand. Khalid, the taxi driver. This is incredible.'

"Damavand," I said.

"Exactly," she replied. "It rises straight out of a hot, desolate plain. A sight your eyes would struggle to believe. And very few people have seen it. Without these things", she then added, displaying her passionate responsibility for the protection of irreplaceable beauty, "we would have no defence against personal tragedy and the futility of everyday life."

The beauty of this utterance was heightened because it came from her. I felt that I had known her all my life, while feeling she was perpetually new. It was like discovering a perfection in the real world which you had assumed could only exist in the imagination. Everything, apart from the sharpened clarity of her face, seemed blurred by a whirl of emotions.

"Sometimes", I said, "I wonder about rainforests being turned into bitumen so people can be conveyed along in metal boxes, and it just feels so absurd."

She bent forward in a confiding fashion and said, "Because of that absurdity, I became unbearable. I thought that I had the things I wanted. You know, boyfriends, money, et cetera; but I discovered that my naive, ideal construction of existence was a farce. None of the feelings you experience when seeing an erupting volcano were in my life. And I felt as if I had died."

She looked to me as if she had made an outstanding recovery. I was before a conglomeration of teeming hair and marble skin put together with resplendent mastery.

"I used to look at the concrete", I replied, "and the bitumen and hear the noise and smell the fumes and shudder at the thought that beauty was being sacrificed for such wasteful ambitions. Then I went to war and saw an even more fantastic beauty being destroyed by even more appalling desires, and here I am, shaking."

"Do you have difficulty sleeping?" she asked.

"My subconscious", I replied, "is a bad dream."

"Welcome", she said, "to the collective unconscious of humanity."

"Thank you."

This led to a discussion about "disagreeable tasks" being performed in "artificial surroundings".

It culminated in my saying, "Educated office workers, because of their specialised knowledge, accepted by society as relevant, feel in total control and very important. Yet they experience no great physical challenges or tests of character. They operate in their narrow bands superbly, and that is what I call escapism."

The agreeable austerity of her intense expression was the hallmark of her open-mindedness. This acceptance of new insights in one not credulous made me feel that she could rise easily to a place of significance. My idea made her agitated in a charmingly frenetic way. She seemed frustrated at the fear that she might not be able to get everything out.

"This taste for security", she said, "is making the world insecure. Chemically, we're now on a knife-edge. And, yes, volcanoes don't help."

She had a courageously dignified air about her; then, running her hands manically through her hair, she said, "They affect climate enormously. With ozone depletion, the situation is now becoming perilous."

The force of personality with which she imparted her comments gave them a resonant gravity that made the truth within them more accessible. That force – a mixture of feelings, reflection, maturity and concern – was going to open doors and hearts. It had already started on mine.

"Volcanoes", she added, with that unique quality of veracious sincerity of hers, "produce carbon dioxide that floats into the stratosphere. It reacts with water to produce sulphuric acid. The acid reflects ultra-violet light. This can cool the earth, dangerously, by a about a degree a year. They tracked the cloud from an eruption in Mexico in 1982 and discovered that this acid thins out over the equator. With ozone depletion in the poles, two great – if you like – unnatural forces were squeezing the earth. Not long after – 1984 in fact – Britain had one of its worst ever winters."

"God," I said, "that must've been a shocker."

We both chuckled.

Then I added, "But how do you know that that winter had anything to do with that eruption?"

She seemed to welcome this question. I was in no doubt about receiving a sensible answer.

"The largest volcanic eruption in recorded history", she said, "occurred in 1815 in Indonesia. A place called Tambora. Ten times the force of Krakatoa. The top fourteen hundred metres were blown away. A crater six kilometres wide was left. A vast depression sat over Europe in the summer of 1816. They know that now from essays and poems written at the time and, more importantly," her hands were gyrating up and down, "from sketches. There's more substantial evidence, but I won't bore you with it."

"Bore me!" I protested. "You couldn't do that if you tried."

This erupted – pardon me – volcanically. There was only one direction it was ever going to go, and that was out of my mouth. Fortunately, it failed to cloud the atmosphere. Her exquisite face became a beacon of exposed teeth and cavernous dimples.

"I'm sorry", she smiled, "if I underestimated your interest in things."

"Don't", I replied, "let this dreamy expression fool you. I'm hanging on to your every word."

She smiled wryly and said, "Sorry. I just thought that that was your natural expression."

Her mocking humour equated beautifully with her knowledge.

"If you find it natural", I replied, "that suits me fine."

This exchange was halted by another one of her unexpected bursts of aesthetic appreciation. The waiter had deposited the main course before her overwhelmed eyes. One taste of her Atlantic mussels in cream sauce caused a gasp of surprise that made her hands rise dramatically to her flabbergasted face.

"This, this", she said, staggered, "is magnificent."

I was very pleased by this reaction, but unable to respond to it. Her eyes seemed to become rounder. Their subtle change in shape transformed her face into a new demeanour, the only constant being the face's beauty which held those features together with a sort of delicate magnetism that cast out invisible electromagnetic waves which blurred the sharp edges of the framed photographs and the outlines of distant people some interminable distance away. Sometimes, because of the intensity of my self-indulgent apoplexy, a crepitation of flames in the hell of my potentially unrequited infatuation, I felt as though I were unable to listen.

It was then that I discovered that "frightening information" about the Ice Age had recently "come to light". It seemed impossible for her, in the ferocity of her dramatic convictions, to indulge in puerile frippery. As the Atlantic mussels slowly met their succulent end – I imagined them swimming happily past a place that I longed to touch – she explained that a research station exists in Greenland where "they drill down into the ice cap and bring up ice thousands of years old".

"The ice is laid", she said, "by time", I imagined the ethereal measure of chronology making love to blocks of hydrogen and oxygen, melting them serenely, "in sedimentary layers that can be broken down into individual years. The chemical constitution of each year has been determined back to the Ice Age. Large concentrations of sulphuric acid and other chemicals are associated with low temperatures. These chemicals come down in rain that ends up as ice. The average temperature for each year can be measured from these chemicals. Something alarming was discovered: the average yearly temperature during the Ice Age varied by as much as six degrees centigrade. That is worrying."

It astounded me to meet someone so concerned by something so relevant. It even seemed trivial to me now that so much attention is given to conflicts in the world's press – conflicts that are ultimately irrelevant – when much greater considerations clearly exist. Total social and economic collapse via environmental mismanagement is not as openly dramatic or as deeply personal as being in a mortar attack in Sarajevo, but its significance to humanity is immeasurable. This thought led me to the undisclosed meaning of her information.

"That's worrying", I said, "because no species existed then, like man, to disturb the balance."

"Precisely," she replied. "People don't realise how delicate the system is."

"Thank you", I said, "for informing me."

"A pleasure," she replied, with a deliberately playful and humorous arrogance. "You've been too busy watching people kill each other in stupid wars to find out what's really been going on."

I laughed. The pleasure was increased by the sight of her smile. Her comment had an element of complimentary sarcasm, whilst revealing the profound irony of the situation.

"I'm not trying to trivialise your experience," she said, this time seriously.

"I know, I know," I replied. "But you're right though. I think journalists – particularly war correspondents – although they don't admit it, live in the belief of having had 'superior experiences'. In my case, I wanted to immerse myself in an event capable of producing every possible human reaction, the roots of which were open to everything from merciless corruption to complicated historical analysis. Effectively, I wanted to have a thorough comprehension of one, so-called, dramatic event that encompassed everything, therefore enabling me to arrive at an unchanging understanding of life. But thanks to you I now realise that there are more dramatic things to consider."

She smiled mysteriously.

"What are you smirking at?" I asked, amiably.

"Oh," she replied, "nothing."

"Oh, come on," I said. "You should never arouse a journalist's curiosity and not satisfy it. For people like us it's mental torture."

She shook her head, smiling; then, with a look of gracious sensitivity that made me drop all possible recriminations, she said, "What I'm thinking is definitely not uncomplimentary. I've decided – and you have to trust me on this one – that it's not in your interest to know. Believe me, that's true."

I sighed in frustration and asked, "Do you mind if I am the judge of that?"

She smiled and said, "I never should have opened my mouth."

"Oh, come on," I repeated. "It won't hurt."

"No," she replied, "not yet."

She said this with a sort of emphatic intelligence that I immediately respected. The verisimilitude inherent in the tone of her voice suggested to me that she was right. This realisation calmed me, for it eliminated that churlish, dissatisfied, unfulfilled curiosity which I loathed, replacing it with a mature inquisitiveness, a warm expectation: I was pacified by the belief that the future held a joyous treat. I was not wrong. I was to discover in the ensuing weeks that she was amused by my "constant ability to redefine my complicated motivations". She did not want me to know this for fear of adversely affecting my behaviour. I could respect that, because in her case she had such a healthy disdain for pretension. When she finally told me this, I was glad of her reticence and indebted to her judgement.

"Anyway," she continued, "I don't want you to belittle the value of your own life. Even though I'm sort of against – I mean in principle – the things people like you do, I respect the fact that it takes certain things to do it. And", she courageously admitted, "it often does help – indirectly – and must lead to some incredible experiences."

I took this as an indication that she wanted to know. I was careful not to be self-indulgent.

"It does," I said, "of course."

I was shy about saying anything that would glamorise my experience or present me in a heroically-pretentious light.

"Sorry," she replied. "I don't blame you for not saying anything,"

"That's okay," I said. "Maybe", I smiled, "what I've got to say is probably not best reserved for lunch."

"I'd like to hear it", she gently persisted, "any time you'd like to tell me."

A delicacy surfaced in her voice – a voice whose resplendent clarity was only matched by the sparkling clearness of her face.

"I don't agree with certain things", she added, "but it's pointless to ignore them."

"I can see why you do," I replied.

I then added, after a pause, "I can see why you do because, unlike the vast majority suffering from complacency or small-mindedness, you really are gripped by an even greater drama than anything in which I probably have ever been immersed."

She was flustered by my compliment because it contained no desire to flatter; it was just the expression of a pleasing desire to show admiration without expectation or reciprocation.

"It's quite incredible as well", I continued, "in view of what the average person here is like. In the past few weeks I've seen some unbelievable episodes of vain image-making. I'm getting the impression that there are some people here who believe that only parties and restaurants exist."

She giggled, more in relief than anything else.

"It's outstanding", I smiled, "comparing some of those people to you. They are on another planet – the planet of empty-headed sensuality."

"Don't be so harsh," she said.

"Sorry," I replied, "but the fact is, I'm worse. I can't really tell you precisely what I've experienced. It's arrogant, I know, but I can't expect to be understood. The only thing I can say is that you develop a comprehension of why atrocities take place. You find out that you're capable of reactions, under extreme conditions, which go beyond acceptability. You discover through frustration and anger that it's possible to achieve a toughness which's so strong, it feels like a form of spiritual enlightenment. It's diametrically opposite to being fulfilled in love – I know that this will sound degrading of something considered to be so pure – but it's a very similar sensation of gratified self-esteem. I now know why someone can be so ruthless in one respect and so caring in another. I now fully appreciate this duality. I also now realise that it was an understanding of this that I was after."

Again she smiled in that infuriatingly mysterious way.

"There you go again," I said.

She burst into laughter.

"No, no," she replied, "there you go again."

"What?" I said, dumbly, before saying, "Okay, so I sound a bit dramatic."

Then she assumed that sudden caring disposition that contradicted her proclivity for damning outbursts. Her eyes shone with appreciative amusement. A feeling of happy self-deprecation overcame me at what I thought was a generous reaction on her part to something which she thought was pleasantry ludicrous within me.

"No," she said, reassuringly, "I didn't find what you said to be melodramatic. How would I know? In fact, it was good. What I want to know is – what you actually saw and heard. That I might be able to relate to – in a way."

I chuckled.

"Please, please," I said, "don't take this as an insult, but I doubt it."

She tilted her hair to one side and glared at me with sensuous strength.

"If you don't mind," she smiled, "I'll be the judge of that."

"Touché," I said, imitating the way she had once said this to me. "Let's just say", I remarked, with the seriousness with which she had conveyed her trepidations to me, "that I can't, just yet."

She accepted this sportingly.

"One all," I added.

"Okay," she joked, "so I've just found out that the great photographer – he with experiences in excess of that of the ordinary man – indulges in immature gamesmanship. How surprising."

I adored her sense of humour.

"Call it", I said, "whatever you like. See if I care if you fail to realise that what I'm doing is in your best interests."

She beamed at my unruffled nobility.

"I am prepared", she declared, with suitable dignity, "to accept that, on this occasion, it may be a possibility."

"Thank you."

The truth of the matter was that I wanted to say: 'I want you to fall in love with me, but I feel that if I tell you what I did in Bosnia and how I felt about it that you will run straight out the door, never to be seen again. I actually want to forget all that now – in a sense.'

Instead I glanced at her face and saw within it a sense of moral beauty born from a passion for something remarkable, beyond human relationships. It was this which gave her such a strong sense of identity. It made me feel that she could not experience an ordinary life because her taste for a comprehension of vast dramas, for understanding the forces that shape our destinies – her imagination in effect – would never allow it. She was burning with opinions. They emerged from her as if her soul was expunging itself; she was pitiless towards those who misused power. She detested egotism. She was outraged by duplicity. She oozed indestructibility. She demanded proper treatment. She had vision. She was appalled by injustice. And she looked so ravishing. Around her there existed something pure and ethereal, exciting and vulnerable, an essence of sensual allure, a force of delicate splendour, a salacious tenderness, all emanating from a mind of extraordinary strength and sagacity. I was on edge with anticipation, but numbed by respect. I had a feeling that her moral disposition was an ocean of nitro-glycerine – one meteorite of burning indelicacy into that and a cataclysm of regrettable proportions could easily arise. She had no qualms about being ungracious for the sake of the truth.

I would often find this as amusing as it was fascinating as it was courageous. I once saw her storm down the aisle of a bus to express her outrage at a group of stunned adolescents who were arrogantly smoking in a non-smoking area; this caused others on the bus to congratulate her. I saw her arguing with someone who had employed her for the day. The bemused employer was aghast at the references she was making to various federal government acts; silenced by a barrage of legalities and moral arguments, pummelled into accepting his "unforgivable methods of exploitation", the employer let her have her own way just so he could "bloody well get rid of that unbelievable woman". I was awe-struck by the anger lying politicians could instil in her.

"The Gulf War", she once said, "sorted a few friendships out. I realised then that certain people I knew were actually believing the rubbish being spouted by the Western powers. I was amazed."

She seemed to take things like this personally. She was not someone you wanted to upset. Often, because of this unmatchable emotion, I would experience a feeling of hopelessness at the prospect of ever being able to touch her. I could see myself in a thick fog, amongst a procession of desperate men, breaking ranks on seeing the mist-laden cliffs which had to be scaled to reach her. They were paths of trouble-free delight, but the end always seemed clouded in a mysterious haze.

'Just keep hanging in there,' I kept telling myself. 'You know as well as I do that someone like that must eventually give themselves away.'

But she never did. There was always that inexplicable return, when you least expected it, to a sense of agitated distance, a sense that normal emotional considerations were uninspiring in the greater scheme of things.

Watching her, I felt an expression of resignation come across my face, as she glared down at her food, ruminating; then she stared back at me, with forceful curiosity, and asked, "Do you think that you're motivated by an urge to greatness?"

I smiled. This was an epic philosophy that was not as relevant as many thought.

"An urge", I replied, "definitely for the opportunity of constant self-expression. Whether the products of that are great or not, it doesn't really matter."

There were other urges as well that I did not expect her to understand. They were principally masculine in nature and could be succinctly described as aspects of fear: the fear of frustration, of pain, of emotional dissatisfaction, of finding yourself in a trough without the prospect of excitement in which your leering senses become acutely capable of detecting untouchable beauty, a place where a heightened capacity to recognise splendour coexisted with a debilitating inability to bring that splendour to any pertinent emotional fruition.

This idea caused me to add, after further consideration, the following: "It's important, I think, to keep motivated to stop the naturally pessimistic, distrusting mind from concentrating on negative things."

"But you", she replied, "deliberately go and see negative things."

"That", I said, "depends on what you consider to be negative. In this context it means personal inadequacy."

"Okay," she replied, "that's fine by me."

She looked down again and contemplated. This gave me the opportunity to look at her mouth. It was one of those delicious mouths in which the lips were so full that they curved like fleshy bars and, because the bottom jaw was slightly askew, they met in an alluring displacement which, with the richness of flesh, created a lazy sensuality that belied the sharpness which so often emerged from them. I saw them open, and from that juicy orifice came the following: "I often got this horrible feeling that I'm not going to use what potential I've got."

"You will," I replied.

"How do you know?" she asked.

"Because", I replied, "you've got that horrible feeling."

"The horrible feeling then", she asked, "is not so horrible?"

I chuckled and said, "Who knows? Sometimes," I continued, still smiling, "I wonder how outstanding it'd be to have no ambitions at all. You could then just give yourself up completely to distraction - our most natural urge. It's the reason television's so successful. We can all comment on the relevant issues of the day without ever trying to become knowledgeable about them. We just can't help it. We're drawn to information, like a drug, by way of escape. It prevents the mind from collapsing into disorder."

"And", she added, "it helps to create it."

"That", I replied, "is absolutely true as well."

"You should know," she said.

"I do," I replied.

She drifted off into that intense world of reflection again and broke the spell of her introspection with the following remark: "Have the dreams been more vivid since experiencing the worst?"

"I don't know," I replied. "They just appear that way, because they wake me up. It means I can remember them."

"What are they about then?" she asked.

I felt like saying "You!" but instead I said, "They're about the dividing line between fear and curiosity. I wanted to find out where that line was."

"Why?" she asked.

"Because", I replied, "I think that human behaviour is a compromise between the two. Fear always exists - or usually anyway - but often it's overcome by curiosity. Sometimes, though, it isn't."

"And this", she smiled, "is another one of your motivations?"

"It is," I replied.

I was not able to tell whether she was being satirical or not. I felt aggression rising within. Most of it was directed at myself for being so seriously intellectual without justification.

"Your motivations", she beamed, with a sweetness which then swept my concerns away, "seem unlimited."

Again she had me happily laughing at myself.

"Yes, yes," I replied, waving a finger, "but, sometimes," I was being sardonically didactic, "we do things without really understanding why."

"You don't say," she smiled.

"Yes," I replied, "I believe I do."

"Well," she said, "I feel stretched."

"Good for you," I imitated.

"Thank you," she retorted.

The waiter then removed our dishes from the table. The mandatory silence that accompanied such a ritual ensued. Over the hands of the waiter I looked at her beautiful face – that register of world-shattering concerns – and observed her eyes: they were like two oval-shaped deposits of translucent marble shining above a mouth slightly open as if in expectation, whose top lip, curved above a straight bottom one, formed a triangle of sensuality around her tongue, thereby creating an unnaturally large area of pinkish-red flesh upon that unblemished face whose magnificence I did very well to forget. Behind her, gesticulating people raved on, also oblivious in some shape or form, as though each table, a separate world, represented the boundaries of consciousness; able to perceive, but not understand, the occupiers of each table formed a series of aquaria containing fish floating in the avaricious self-indulgence of their indolent pursuits. Of all the creatures in the room, she was probably the only one motivated by ideas foreign to the attitudes incumbent in each of these chambers that housed the clientele. The realisation of this, however, would have escaped her; she was too modest to see herself in such dramatically individualistic terms. That was left up to admirers, those with an "epic appreciation", such as myself. I was prepared to fill the role.

The waiter left, and she said, "Sometimes I feel the burden of ambition like a form of death. I say to myself: 'Why me? Why have I been chosen to be hounded by an essentially unpragmatic obsession? Why does life have to be made so unnecessarily complicated by an eccentric and thoroughly immovable aspiration? Why me?' I could be doing this or that and feeling free and unconcerned and able to see a rosy future and instead I'm left to struggle with an awkward desire that has no real place in the mainstream of human existence. My illusions disappear and I feel that I'm being made an outcast by my own impulses. What a situation!" Huge grin. "Impulses that could lead me to waste the best years of my life. I worry like hell at times."

I was struck supine again by the passion and intelligence of this remarkable pronouncement. I then realised that she was after advice; I then felt that I might not be able to give her any.

"Go with it," I insisted. "You're lucky—"

"I know, I know," she smiled, shaking her head.

"You're lucky", I continued, "because you've got passion and conviction. All you've got to do is modify your thinking slightly to take advantage of it. I think you should join the foreign affairs department. Do a course in Western-Arab relations; if you just change a few things about yourself - just slightly - you could go all the way."

"What things?" she asked.

"When you hear something absurd", I replied, "don't display exasperation. Go so far at times as to even feign fascination. If you do that, you could easily find yourself in a position where you're able to involve yourself in issues that are of immense significance to yourself. You could - easily."

I was suddenly filled with the emotion that she so constantly displayed. I was not consciously attempting to flatter, but the sweetened expression of dreamy gratitude on her face indicated that I had. Nothing could have been more pleasing to me.

"You have to understand", I continued, motivated by her grace, "that we live in a world dominated by personalities. Often influential people have no real talents other than their outstanding social skills. These people need people like you to help them make decisions. You can do it. I know you can."

"Thanks," she smiled.

She then retreated again into her obsession for inscrutable agitation. I was always affected by these bouts of silence. They were unexpected and mysteriously placed during episodes of sociability. I was troubled by these fluctuations in her attentiveness, because her facial expression appeared to me to be a combination of panic and disdain. Being sufficiently vainglorious, I felt that I must have contributed to this condition. But this was ridiculous. The reality, the heinous, troubling, insidious truth - that horror we all do our best to avoid - was that I was having little impact at all. I was forced, or at least my ego was, to endure the deserts of her arcane speechlessness, that place of high-velocity winds, of tornadoes and dry introspection, where the sounds of my voice dissipated into an endless wilderness of baking indifference. She could find this place at will, and I had to stand out on its perimeter and watch. And it was excruciating.

Then her mouth opened - great relief - and from it came: "For some reason that peculiar combination of environment and genetics which yielded me has ensured that numerous complicated hurdles are deposited before me to make sure that I find it extremely difficult to achieve a satisfying professional identity. It's like a form of punishment for something that I'm not even aware I've committed."

I could not resist the temptation to erupt into laughter. Initially my hilarity appalled her; then she joined in. A self-conscious smile came upon her.

"Sounds big-headed, doesn't it?" she said, sheepishly chastising herself.

"No, no," I replied, shaking my head. "It's funny because, in a way, I see you as a Christ-like figure; someone who's taken on all the evils of this world, with great sincerity, upon their wilting shoulders, while being completely bemused as to why. Sometimes I think that complacency and indolence are probably two of the greatest gifts a human being can ever have. In that regard, you missed out completely. You have my deepest sympathies."

She winced at my grandiose summation. Approbation was both a knife and a feather. Particularly with her.

"Well," she quipped, "I'm thrilled to know that I'm such a grandiloquent figure, and so unconsciously capable of causing humour as well. Maybe someone should put me on a stage."

I burst out laughing again. "I couldn't agree more," I said.

"Are you intending to be my manager then?" she asked.

"Maybe," I replied; "but we'd have to find a specific role for you first, though, I think."

"Exactly," she said. "And that is precisely the trouble."

I was then struck by the notion that thoughts of romantic relationships were so far from her mind because of the strength of this predicament which she had just described. It was difficult to live with the idea that I was besotted with someone indifferent to such trivialities as fulfilment in love; but I was old enough and young enough to appreciate that the future was still a transient enormity of unpredictable possibilities. I could wait.

"This experience", she then said," that I'm having is like a form of identity crisis."

She was unconscious of the fact that it was this which I was experiencing with her, and experiencing it with far greater intensity than is usually the norm.

"I'm glad you said that", I replied, "because virtually every time I meet someone new, I experience one."

It was her turn to laugh.

"You really do", she said, "lead a dramatic existence."

"I'll take that", I replied, "as a compliment."

"Please do," she said.

"I will," I replied.

"Good," she said.

I then collected myself again and continued.

"Every time", I remarked, looking into those judgemental eyes which stared at me with a warning that this had better be good, "that I meet someone new, I experience one of those hurdles that you so articulately referred to earlier. Every person I meet creates a different feeling within me, and the summation of all these feelings is my identity."

"So by going to war", she asked, "it expands your identity, because you come into contact with a wider variety of people existing in a wider scope of experiences?"

"As usual," I replied, "you've got it. The more people you meet", I continued, with those eyes glaring down at me, "the more chance you have of experiencing vastly divergent feelings about yourself. And these feelings are as true as any other."

"And", she smiled, "the sphere of experience grows ever larger?"

"Exactly," I replied.

She smiled at that point at an irony which had just crossed her mind.

"When people think of identity", she said, "they see it as a positive thing."

"Of course," I replied, "but what they see is not their identity, but how they wish to be identified. They're two completely different things."

She pondered this momentarily and said, "In my first year at university I came across quite a few people struggling to be unusual. Some of them had this false self-belief, this delusion that their individuality was, in some shape or form, more individual than anyone else's. Yet they all dressed the same and spoke the same way. Effectively, all they were doing was putting up a barrier."

I smiled again. Her distaste of egotism was both dangerous and entertaining – dangerous because of her savageness towards defensive weaknesses, and because of the moral beauty that accompanied her uncompromising views of human affairs.

"Sounds to me", I said, "as if everyone was caught playing the same game."

She looked at me quizzically.

"You mean", she said, "that everyone was afraid to really express themselves."

"Depends", I replied, "on how you want to look at it."

"How do you look at it?" she asked.

"A person", I replied, thinking of Ross, "begins a game. Precedents are set. Then both parties wait for the other to break. And so the game goes on."

"I think", she said, "that if two people have a special affinity for each other, then it just becomes apparent."

"Any two people", I replied, "can be free and frank with each either, if they want to be."

"Yes," she added, worryingly, "if they want to be."

"Well," I said, "now that we've established that, does the Countess of Fremantle care for dessert?"

"She does."

Our trifles seemed to have been infused with all the sweetness and creaminess that the earth can muster. Lumps of fruit were mixed with cream and fluffiness.

"This", I casually enthused, "is better than sex."

"How would you know?" she asked.

"Intuition," I replied.

"Oh yeah," she said, "I forgot. Sex is not on a man's mind as much as a woman's. Yours obviously finds trifles more interesting than women."

I looked away, shaking my head, ruefully amused.

"Let's just say", I said, "that this trifle is a very special one."

"But", she replied, sardonically alluding to women, "does it have an air of mysterious unattainability? And is it both chaste and chased?"

"Mystery", I pointed out, "exists in talking continually and intelligently to anyone about a wide variety of subjects. It's got nothing to do with silence. So if this trifle has only got quiet, mysterious unattainability, then it would be of no real interest to me."

"It's a pity", she said, "that you can't explain this to people like my father."

"For you", I replied, "I would explain anything to anyone."

"But", she inquired, "would you climb mountains and fight off whole battalions of outraged Kashmiri tribesmen – just for me?"

"If you insisted," I said, "I would even lay all the stars in the heavens at your feet and would row several thousand miles through molten lava just to hear you abuse me – particularly if your father owned a brewery. After all, I am an Australian."

Every chuckle of her laughter caused a wave of joy. Her quaint guffaws echoed through me as though this sound were the cause of all bliss. What a pleasure it was to give pleasure to someone so bright and ravishing as she. But could I keep it up? And did I deserve it? It was as though natural justice had taken a short holiday and would be back soon to redress this blatant quirk in the normal course of contingencies. My time with her was destined to be short-lived – it had to be – this earth was not possessed of opportunities such as these. I had been led to the gates of paradise, the doors unbolted, and had been given a look at the dazzling effulgence of which we all dream. Other men in the place could not keep their wonder-struck eyes off her. I was afraid to go to the toilet for fear that I would find her engulfed by them when I got back.

"On the subject of games and mysterious unattainability," I said, "since I've been back here, I've felt as if I've walked into the world centre of it. It amazes me how people can be so concerned about the impression that they're making, when they haven't got the slightest intention of communicating. Some people here are so unconscious of their total sublimation to the worst aspects of the society which spawned them that they believe they're arousing curiosity because of their alluring complexity; but they don't seem to realise that they're so fascinating because of their ignorance of their own victimisation by the culture that they've stupidly placed so much faith in. They don't seem to believe in the existence of other worlds – that there could be more fulfilling ways of behaving, born from being in other places. They live entirely in the environment that produced them and it's weird and hilarious, like watching stereotypes come alive off the pages of some cartoon created by a wag bent on displaying the ultimate difference between illusion and reality. I'm intrigued for all the wrong reasons. I'm basically astounded."

She nodded her head slowly in agreement, as though spellbound by the gradually increasing significance of some pertinent insight; then she said, "It takes an outsider to see the absurdity that others perceive as being normal."

"Or don't see at all," I said.

"Or don't want to," she replied.

The waiter removed our dishes. He was accompanied by a waitress who wanted me to move so that she could get some brandy glasses out of a cabinet next to my chair. Five minutes later, the same waitress came back and, making the same request, made me move again.

"Sorry," this woman said, genuinely apologetic, as I stood up, "I'll leave you alone after this."

"That", I replied, getting up again, "was exactly what my first wife said."

This comment caused the waitress to explode with laughter. She bent over the table, breathless from giggling. Samantha looked at her, dryly. I was nonplussed as to why she was being so serious. Did she think that I had once been married? How could she possibly think that, I wondered.

Then the waitress left; ignoring Samantha's inscrutable attitude, I said, "So what's an outsider?"

"Someone", she replied, "who believes from a young age that more relevant events have to be occurring away from the place which's caused them so much grief."

I laughed and said, "But then we get old enough and we realise that the gulf between these imagined places and our own world is not so large."

"That's right", she replied, "because travel makes your own place a bit more interesting."

"Experience", I then said, "gives a place a sense of history."

"It'd be a dull life", she replied, "if it didn't."

'Not if I could spend it all with you,' I thought.

She was now so relaxed in her chair that her arms hung languidly down behind the backrest so her biceps were flush up against the edges of the support, allowing her hands to droop underneath the level of her chair, causing her shoulders to be braced back so that her breasts protruded straight out like beacons of sensuality upon the perfectly tapered curve of her form. Her chair had been pulled out from the table, enabling her to cross her legs; the knee of her left leg rose upward, over the knee of the other, in a smooth and round arc, whose uppermost point formed the apex of a triangle, the base of which was defined by her breasts. Her left foot dangled in mid-air, moving up and down, so that her shoe, held up by her toes, moved with it, as if in sensual unison with some casually distracted force that caused the expression of superior and unflappable detachment upon her face. She stared at me with the eyebrow of her left eye arched as though in disdainful wonderment that someone as pathetic as myself could actually exist; this caused a new sensation of surprise at how attractive and challenging she looked with her head tilted to one side, that imperious eyebrow, and all that beautifully formed flesh, observing me with a penetrating glare of lascivious grace.

"It's a pleasure", I said, "being stared at so savagely."

A sort of indolent, appreciative smirk came upon her face, followed by a self-derisory head-shaking.

"I hate", she replied, "people thinking I'm arrogant, because of the way I look."

"You prefer them", I joked, "to think that you're arrogant because of the way you are?"

She was not inclined towards humour, so it seemed, when it was related to arrogance.

"Sorry," I said.

She stared at me very arrogantly. That eyebrow was raised even further.

"Don't worry," she replied. "It's just one of those things that I'm peculiarly sensitive about."

"It's not arrogance," I assured her.

Her face then reverted back to its normal haughty stare of misleading but sensuous superiority. I looked at the smoothness and roundness of her face, the delicacy of its features, and was struck by a feeling that its fineness was ironically anathema to the intensity of expression that so often came upon it.

"You just look that way", I said, "because of the profound nature of your contemplative streak. And it's easier for people to say that you're arrogant so they can have the excuse they need to appease themselves for not really being able to get through to you."

"How do you know that?" she asked.

"Observation," I replied. "You frighten people."

"Do I frighten you?" she asked.

"I'm petrified," I replied.

A huge, glowing smile preceded the following remark, "You don't look it."

"Don't let this artificial exterior of calm reserve fool you," I said. "Deep down inside, I'm quivering like a broken reed in a vicious wind."

"I didn't know", she half-ironically smiled, "that I was so scary."

"The scariest things", I said, ambiguously, "are the most interesting."

"I didn't realise", she replied, "that I was that fascinating."

"I realise", I said, " that you're just too modest."

"Maybe you'd prefer it", she replied, "if I were as arrogant as I look?"

"If you were as arrogant as you look," I said, "believe me, you and I would not be here now."

"You're slowly", she replied, "becoming a master of ambiguity."

"And it would be," I said, "now that you've mentioned it, for both reasons."

"How do you know", she replied, with that dangerous flippancy which I dreaded, "that I might still have been here with you just to appease some sort of macabre, idle curiosity? After all, there's always that indolent fascination about how the other half live."

I was sufficiently unstable and paranoid enough to believe that this was probably the case. It seemed too good to be true that she could be sending up her supposed arrogance. But what more could I expect?

"If you're that macabre", I said, "then there's nothing I can do about it."

"So there's no point in trying too hard, then," she replied, "is there?"

"Probably not," I said.

* * * * * * * * * *

I was beginning to see a painting of my predicament in surrealist terms. I called it: *Man Crushed by the Weight of His Aesthetic Appreciation.* It depicted a sinewy form of myself – huge, gargantuan – a vast figure in the desert-like landscape where I was sprawled out. My skin was purple-grey. I was naked, apart from a linen loincloth. My eyes were bewildered with an existential calamity. They were large, cavernous and dark. I saw no other colour in them but black. They stood out against the gold desert. The sands of this sun-baked wasteland gradually fused into burnt-orange at the horizon. I was engulfed in an enormous sense of space – a boiling ineluctability. I was representative of a being trapped with a massive and all-encompassing desire that I neither needed nor wanted. On this beast's shoulders were plateaux with gnarled, eroded steps containing tree roots that wrapped under this creature's armpits and held him down. The fingers of the man were unable to touch the plateaux, for on his shoulders were his wildest dreams. They were not things stupidly unattainable, but aspirations that most people expect to achieve: fulfilment in love and happiness from beauty. Upon the plateaux were shapely ballerinas and curvaceous women diving from springboards and regal beauties in flowing dresses and contented angelic ladies lying, for figure enhancement, on their sides. Strict, intellectually superior creatures wearing glasses added an extra dimension of disciplined mystique to the untouchable and sensuous contentment. The figures on the plateaux were minuscule in comparison to the man. They were on both shoulders and caused an expression of bulging panic in the man's eyes – a look born from a rarefied ability to perceive beauty and not to be able to ignore it or possess it – which caused a sharpness of incensed futility – the head – from which a stream of broken ideals swirled like a tornado of wrecked hopes, masses of forlorn figures rising in a sweep and disappearing into a fine dot in the empty sky.

It was an experience that she would never know – that she could never possibly know. Biology had seen to that. She had been born to choose. I had been born to wait in the queue and hope to be selected. Waiting is a trial fraught with pessimistic logic. I felt very good with her – on the whole – but how could I expect someone so desirable to be so peculiar as to decide upon me? All statistical measurements pointed to the absurdity of possession hope – that daydream of cynical optimism. Beauty arouses hope and hope exposes flaws. Then flaws are recognised and, after the tears, are worked on. Strength them emerges. The cycle of growth is complete. Thoughts of impending disappointment were made more bearable by the knowledge that good would eventually be born from the overall experience. Whether I wanted it or not, I was again on that precipice between exciting fulfilment and shocking despair. For some reason – known only too well to myself – I always excessively dramatised experiences which others saw as normal and pleasant, a histrionic vision as involuntary as the chaos that screams from order.

You could say it ran in the family. We were all too innocently conscious of the idea that a reason to mistrust has to exist. Surely the more significant a potential ally becomes, the greater is the chance of their displaying their evil unpredictability? Don't all love objects do that? All rational logic, all pretext to sound thinking, born from empirical evidence, is useless in the face of something learned so dramatically in the days when the complex proteins of one's existence were still being formed. No amount of scientific rationales can erase the knowledge acquired prior to formal education. This is one reason – maybe even the only one – it is possible for a scientist to be religious. Enough mistrust in the universe – some personal and uniquely psychological, some cultural – is the spur to a precept known as population control to which we sometimes refer as emotional immaturity, and sometimes we refer to it as war. Even when she said to me that a romantic partner has to find her "perfect", because she "does not trust people easily", I still did not for a moment believe that she could mistrust so profoundly as I or that, because she acknowledged her own fears in this respect, it could lessen her astonishing ability to create it.

It did the opposite, in fact; for she did not associate mistrust with savage inconsistencies. Only a true connoisseur of mistrust is capable of doing that. I knew that I was going to do something regrettable which I could not control, and that she would not understand. It was inevitable.

* * * * * * * * * *

On New Year's Eve Ross and I were splayed out on the floor of a beautiful old house, very, very stoned. I was on that edge that separates enjoyment from a world where everything is just too surreal.

The doorway across the room was now a strange distance away, as if it had, with imperceptible stealth, crept away, making it clear that any movement out of the place was going to take a bizarre amount of time. From the rectangle created by the door being ajar, away on the other side of the room, there emerged a warm lemon shimmering glow of reassuring light, a silky material presence of lustrous satisfaction in the unfamiliar gloom of the lounge.

Ross looked at me with big, red eyes and said, "I wonder if the person sending me strange mail is a maniac."

The concern on his face caused me to recall a story told to me by someone who had once picked me up, hitchhiking in New Zealand. The last thing any person appreciates whilst under the influence of the Devil's Weed From Hell is to suddenly have to be concerned about the prospect of violence. The driver told me that he had been working on a fishing boat in the South China Sea and he had just finished a nice long joint when he noticed that the owner of the boat had doused the light that sits on the top of the mast - a dangerous practice at night in crowded waters.

"Why did you do that for?" he told me he had asked his skipper.

"Pirates," his captain had replied. "There's hundreds of them around here. Didn't you know?"

I sensed that Ross was beginning to endure a similar response to unforeseen circumstances. His letterbox had recently acquired a number of inexplicable artefacts. They consisted of the following: twenty lessons on Christianity, how to join the Victorian state police force, a variety of information about venomous spiders, the reproductive habits of reptiles, and, most alarmingly, a Christmas card which on its cover displayed a picture of a babe in arms: the caption was: *Jesus loves you*. Nothing wrong with that but, turning to the inside, one found the remark: *Even though you are a complete cunt*. A spear had also been struck through the baby's heart.

This card represented the culmination of twelve months of bemusing receipts, and Ross, in his present sensitised condition, had begun to wonder whether his previous theory on the so-called harmlessness of the sender was indeed totally incorrect.

Realising the gravity of his predicament, I said, "God, imagine if you start receiving dead rodents, and it just goes from there?"

He screwed his eyes up, but the information could not be removed.

I continued, "And it gets so bad that you have to go to Zurich to get plastic surgery done and carry automatic weapons with you wherever you go until this freak drives you into a mental institution..."

Ross, shaking his head pleadingly, said: "Oh no, no, no."

"Don't worry," I replied. "I'm only being harmless."

That conversation had taken place on the stroke of midnight when the rest of the world was feigning euphoria. The following day, in the clarity of daylight and sobriety, I assured Ross that he had nothing to worry about.

Relaxed, he said, his equanimity restored, "If I had to, I'd find out who's doing it, and just rub the bastard out."

'The ebb and flow of confidence,' I thought. 'When will it end?'

* * * * * * * * * * *

The long night of New Year's Eve was ended at Ross's place. The quiet and darkness of his lounge-room after the lights went out was difficult to bear. I had removed the cushions from the sofas and settees and was stretched out in the blackness, wondering, fearing, the darkness of the dark too dark to bear. My eyes were having difficulty remaining closed. The absence of light was like an emptiness of air. Too long a period with them shut and they would be flung open like an existential gasping in the thinness of air. I was in a void. All that blackness made my mind concentrate too sharply on one single thing: where were those eyes? Those eyes as dark as this night. And what are they seeing? And where was that pure skin? And had anyone touched its magnificence – on this night – this night so black?

I was in a despair of restless curiosity. All I had were questions – ones I did not want to ask, but ones that were so easily formed. I had felt uneasy all day. In the pub at lunch time her agitation had taken on the quality of distance that this night sky, with its absences of light and sound, had reproduced with a calm vindictiveness that belied the stately magnificence of its unending presence, one which mocked our trivial passions with its indifference and beguiling longevity, a reminder of the futility of all. For an instant – a breathless inhalation in the vacuum of existence – I was only concerned about her; only she was alive, had substance, this talismanic opportunity to experience bliss; and what had she been up to tonight? I dreaded the thought.

There she would have been in some bar, surrounded by intoxicated, predatory charmers, a place she had kept as secret as her heart. And I felt as though I were facing the inevitability of misfortune, for only she could give pleasure: the rest of this world was a sterile construct, a vacuous infrastructure of insipid objects, a series of irrelevant artefacts, bound together by an illusion of achievement. Only she possessed meaning.

How the hell was I going to get through this night?

I was convinced that such darkness could exist only in outer space. I was engulfed in its impenetrability. Time was transformed. I was being made to experience each nanosecond. Every beat of the atomic clock pounded and echoed through the abyss of my brain.

And why had she been so agitated? What the hell had caused that? She had certainly made sure that she wasn't going to be spending tonight with me. There was no friendliness in the way that she had fended off all enquiries on that subject. All was heading for naught. The long, pointless innings without reward. I tried closing my eyes. A swirl of phantoms haunted the gloomy air. I was too irrational to consider that her state of mind may have had absolutely nothing at all to do with me. I wanted to believe that her existence was inextricably linked to mine. Surely I must have influenced her behaviour? Surely?

Then my eyes shot open, and I rose up quickly on to my elbows.

'Of course!' I thought. 'Of course! Of course! Jesus Christ! That's it!'

In an endeavour to redirect conversation on to her, I had said, with regard to the night that we went to the outdoor film, that the movie had begun, and "we were still on a blanket drinking champagne, because she was still prattling on".

'Jesus,' I agonised, 'I had said that she had prattled! Oh God, no! Jesus Christ! Fuck me! And such a sensitive individual – and she's told me that she doesn't trust people either. God, that's it. I'm such a complete dickhead. And when she came along I didn't even offer her a drink either! How fucking useless! I tell you, this night cannot be over quickly enough.'

I rang Samantha the following morning and apologised for the remarks made about her "prattling". I was full of trepidation when I picked up the phone.

"What comments?" she asked, after I had apologised for a remark she obviously did not think was important enough to remember. "You didn't say anything rude," she added. "Not that I'm aware of, anyway."

'Oh,' I thought.

* * * * * * * * * *

The incident in the pub was as follows: Ross and I were sitting in the beer garden with a friend of Frances's. She was due to come along later. We were around one of those portable table/bench facilities with the sun umbrella above, a cloudy sky sending indiscriminate, racing shadows over the grass, a slight, but blustery wind, the sound of surf in the distance across a busy road, seagulls swirling in squawking clusters on the ground and above, and other people languidly drinking in the unsettled humidity of a day undecided on how it wished to proceed.

Samantha suddenly appeared up a flight of steps with the sunglasses that I had left in her car. She smiled nervously, as if gregarious acknowledgement could precipitate something untoward, then said, "Thought I'd drop in and return your glasses. Hah! Just an excuse, really."

Her long hair fluttered haphazardly, like the wings of a seagull in the breeze. Her comment perplexed me. 'An excuse for what?' I wondered.

She sat down as swiftly and as charismatically as she had entered. Introductions were made. I examined her apparel. Her skirt was ablaze with an exotic pattern of birds and flowers – a sea of colours that had swayed with untamed beauty at the top of the stairs; her unexpected arrival was marked by a burst of wind. Across the sky, an inky-grey/blue mass of cloud was forming behind her a small way out over the sea. A fork of lightning, like the skeleton of an electrified tree, suddenly flashed within it; then an explosion of cannon reverberated over the world. Such accoutrements to the entrée of her entry were entirely feasible in one so dramatically ravishing. She was a bundle of nervous, kinetic energy. Those dark eyes were raging with sensuous fire. They turned passion into sharp concentrations of feeling. I was certain that they contained more nuclear energy than a thousand hydrogen bombs. To have grasped them in the palms of one's hands would have caused serious damage to the tissues of one's arms. And what would have happened had the opportunity arisen to have placed one's arms around her? It didn't bear thinking about.

She sat down and Gordon continued to drone on about Brazil. He blundered on in a monotonous harangue, oblivious that the person he had just met was so nervously uninterested in his conversation that she looked as though she were about to self-destruct.

"And when the banks shut..." he bludgeoned on, absolutely unrelenting.

I could see that the only thought which flashed through Samantha's mind was, 'God, I've just got to get the hell out of here!', a message that poured out of those slivers of emotion, cut with such striking effect, into the magnificence of her now bad-tempered face.

Undaunted, Gordon ploughed on. It was impossible to dissuade him from his monotonous course. Ross and I, increasingly frustrated, attempted between the minute breaks in his booming but flat voice to cram in remarks that would help us both simulate a dialogue with the suffering person to whom Gordon had just been introduced. But we were up against a master. Gordon spoke as if he was narrating a documentary on his travelling life. The channel was jammed on prime time Gordon.

Somehow the conversation got on to Bangkok. This enabled me to swing the conversation on to journalism – a topic in which Samantha had a more than just passing interest – by announcing, with Gordon's tacit permission, that I was currently reading Neil Davis's biography. I was allowed to give a graphic description of Davis's death in Bangkok – torn to pieces by shrapnel – upon which Ross elaborated further by describing the news footage of this well-documented and highly charged event.

"Oh wow," Samantha remarked, in response to it, shocked by the gore. "This is turning me off my dream of international journalism."

Ross then attempted to draw her out on this, by asking, without the necessary conviction, "So you want to be a journalist, hey?"

In view of Samantha's defensiveness, he was concerned about accusations of prying. His lack of gusto was contrasted with the frenetic energy of the wind - a tenebrous being as fraught with pang-filled dissatisfaction as the beautiful creature on the other side of the table to him was. Amidst its howls and bursts, its sharp changes of mood, flowed the unruffled, steady, unperturbed voice of Gordon, whose brick-like unaffectedness had, in my subjective opinion, caused the wall of Samantha's curtness to fly up – a wall off which Ross's question bounced like a bait of soggy dough, sliding off it with a deadened thud. It was also a wall that caused the irrepressible sound waves from Gordon's gob to reverberate back like smashing glass.

Except that he did not hear this. He only seemed to hear the slow, sensuous swooshing of feathery wings, the trickling of bubbling streams, the low breath of candlelight, flickering in the warm glow of a summer's night. I was in awe of his optimistic desensitisation. It staggered me that he was so unworried about the emotional states of those who fate, in its malicious workings, had thrown upon him; really, he was impossible to dislike. It was not his fault that he had come upon the unrecognisable lip of a brooding, subliminal volcano of mysterious interaction. He seemed too stolid to be concerned by the petty indulgences of human frailty; therefore, he blundered on.

Despite my attempts to begin a conversation about the film that Samantha and I had seen at the Somerville Auditorium, he somehow – a feat of calm determination if ever there was one – contrived to continue his diatribe about his undoubtedly interesting adventures in Bangkok. Every word that emerged from his lips – something akin to the sounds of smashing bricks – had the effect, in my volatile imagination, of repressing one in the juicy confines of Samantha's mouth. It was ironic that his mature equanimity made him innocent of the pain that he was unwittingly inflicting.

Then Frances suddenly appeared. I looked up to greet her casually swaying frame – a gait that accurately depicted her easygoing personality. Samantha took the opportunity presented by Frances's arrival to depart.

Dashing off quickly, she announced, "I must go now," after I had unsuccessfully tried to find out where she was going to be spending the night.

She flew past Frances who looked at me with a grin of amused astonishment and said, "God, what's wrong with her?"

I marvelled at this interchange of personalities.

Sitting down, Frances then said, with a huge grin, "Not bad though, Knubs. I see that at least your taste has improved."

Her good-natured derision was a welcome change from the inscrutable intensity of my calamitous infatuation. Her presence with her boyfriend and son also helped to redistribute the burden of Gordon's conversation. Ross, even more relieved than I – he had already been pounded into submission well before even Samantha's arrival – took the opportunity to leave the table.

Dylan had become frustrated by his enforced immobility; his screams had echoed out over the beer garden like a wail of horror at the injustices of this benighted world, so Ross carried him off to the sanctuary of a nearby tree. In the shade, under its fantastically tormented and gnarled branches, he began showing the now serenely subdued child little titbits of intrigue, like little birdies fluttering in the leaves; so much fascination appeared on Dylan's face that Frances, oblivious to the conversation at the table, stared on herself with a look of surprised wonderment, every bit as absorbed as that of her son's. Fascinated by the sight of a sensual man captivating her previously inconsolable child, she then said, "Very impressive."

Then Ross returned. The conversation quickly turned into a riveting discussion about technology in the arms race; then the sky opened. A great turmoil of sepulchral mists had been slowly brooding above. When those mists unleashed their tears of a thousand pains and we had to run to safety in the screaming outcry of shattered dreams, I could not help thinking, 'Where the hell is she? Have I done anything to hurt her? And what the hell's going on?'

Being a journalist, I was not pleased with the bitter irony that the more desperately I wanted to find out the less capable of doing so I became.

* * * * * * * * * *

The following also occurred in the telephone conversation I had with Samantha on New Year's Day:

"Bit hard to get a word in edgeways with Gordon," I said, testing the waters.

"I thought he was very interesting," she replied, without the slightest hint of diplomatic insincerity.

'Oh,' I thought again.

* * * * * * * * * *

T'would be a remarkable person indeed who could travel the path of this life without ever having lost their objectivity. Mine had simply evaporated. If you have to continually seek the advice of others when interpreting the actions of a loved one, in the cherished hope of achieving requited love, then you are lost. Such a belief is easily formed in the contented consideration of halcyon days; but, in the single-minded passion of some all-pervading dream, it is rapidly dismissed. It is not even considered. It certainly did not even enter my mind the night that I was lying on Ross's floor: that night was dark with loss. Vivid images had floated into it. I had found myself in a street where patches of fallen plaster had exposed the underlying bricks of a crumbling world. A mountain of tepid garbage was being gnawed at by ravenous dogs. A steamy mist of ghostly vapours, like a spectre of destruction, hung above this uncollected mess, as though the drizzle that fell upon it were the poisoned moisture of life's christening with death.

Above the garbage, on a battered wall, was an American flag beside a poster of the Statue of Liberty, defiant symbols against the Serbian siege. The car parked in front of this apartment had received a direct hit and was now a charred sculpture of black metal, twisted beyond recognition from its sleek and prestigious beginnings into a ruin of complicated configurations, like a well-shaped subconscious brutalised by the viciousness of war. Splinters of shattered glass clung to bullet-riddled window frames, creating the illusion of things long discarded; in the nearby hospital, a sniper victim twisted open-mouthed like a skeleton with burning flesh being electrocuted, screaming unheard in the long avenues or unearthly silence. These emptied streets of uneasy quiet were littered with the fractured thoughts of despairing associations. They created a quiet, like a funereal use of a musical device, a cynical syncopation, anticipating a counterpointing crescendo of pointless violence.

People stared at each other with sunken, manic eyes, alone. I was in a ghost town populated by ghosts. So many of its buildings were glassless, even though their walls remained intact, that it felt as if I were in a giant honeycomb, bereft of sweetness. Trudging people clutching plastic buckets took unbelievable risks to collect their water. The risk of death was seen everywhere in the large circles of mortar holes, great pores full of stinking water, in the wretched skin of the streets. Around them, chunks of bitumen and upheavals of soil were lying about next to the wrecked timbers of damaged houses. Everywhere, the sculptured weirdness of smashed buildings predicted the repetition of heinous events. Piles of blasted timber and plaster were stacked beside houses whose exposed frames were holding up precariously balanced tiles, set to tumble like a fragile peace. In the holes between the terracottas, the unmasked ribs of this decaying world were criss-crossed over the charcoal blackness that lay within.

The remaining touches of surviving architectural sophistication – amphora vases on entry stones riddled with high-velocity depressions and classical stone scrolling on the gilded walls of a lost opulence – only served to heighten the absurdity of hate's victory over a logical peace. Often the painted pastel walls of a distant age's delicacy had been turned black by the foul breath of the dragon's fire. Vast swathes of ebony scorching had defiled the airy splendour of these once glorious streets. Sometimes within the ebony, holes of varying sizes could be seen, gouged across the pastel sensitivity, like a crime the punishment of which will never be complete.

Above this ruined infrastructure, the inky-black-blue-white electrified sky fumed in a grotesque orgy of seething vapours. Away in the distance, the pounding of small-arms fire sounded like someone bashing on the tightly drawn skins of a drum. Some people actually pretended that life was normal. A group of women with rollers in their hair were manicuring each other under a tarpaulin; two men in a doorway were arguing over a game of chess. Someone was washing their clothes in a makeshift laundry consisting of hoses emerging from faucets that ended up in bowls laid upon lumps of timber resting upon bits of metal in an enclave between grey buildings gleaming wet.

The windows of these buildings were like black rectangles in the gloomy faces of the walls. A car with no lights with smashed windows and flaking paint had been left outside the window of a café whose unscathed panes had been kept intact by a ripped pile of sandbags, causing yellow sand to be spewed out over the moribund streets. A cemetery of disused trams lay on the open ground, their seats torn out, their rusting metal roofs rotting in the dreary and tempestuous gloom of a melancholic defeat. Men in blue uniforms, their old masters, walked amongst them; those men, bored, spiritless and saddened, looked on forlornly, as though they were the confused victims of an atmosphere of nostalgia for a life once taken for granted, and now dead.

The spire of a mosque had managed to survive an onslaught that had turned its adjoining buildings into fantastically tormented shapes. The viewer from this tower could look down upon bizarrely futuristic forms, and see the tops of these shell-plastered structures, ironically, as sad and beautiful lines, for these fractured constructions resembled dramatic sculptures to the unforgivable absurdity of a stupid war, vast tombstones to the innocent, unexpectedly elegant testimonies to the fact of sudden death.

A blanket of repressing silence dampened the hopes of a once-thriving earth. Someone keen to reinvoke normality charged between a gap in the buildings; in defiance of his captors, his heart raced with his feet; in sight of the guns, a shot rang out in his mind and then his body was safe. Someone else would try that today and fail.

The pounding of fire in the distance came to an eerie halt. Then I heard the sounds of a piano emerging from a ruined conservatory; dust, plaster fragments, sheets of music, the twisted metal of a leg, the remnants of a broken chair. Then I saw flowers on the graves of the deceased: brilliant colours bloomed in the black soils of death. The same colours could be seen on the balconies of bullet-riddled flats; tulips and daffodils were thriving in these places left waste by the nationalistic excesses of the harbingers of death. Leafless trees stood above stones placed around the perimeters of delicately manicured graves. A woman with a scarf around her head was draped over one of these mounds to the memory of her previous life. Her tears flowed down that raging river whose mountainously egotistical source could not live without its name indelibly imprinted in the pages of history. One day, I swear, all such names will be damned.

The stain of a splash of blood showed the signs of its owner's sudden demise. It formed a half-circle, as though a painter had made a quick half-circular swish on to the grey canvas of the road. The bike that the deceased had been riding was still lying on the bitumen; it acted as a reminder of the prosaic normality that the occupants of this blighted town were trying to maintain against the savage dementia of a distant force – a force born from the basest of instincts, the indecency of which had been legitimised by historical analysis and political will. The pleasure of sublimation has too often been clothed in the fabric of noble virtues, and the denial of its existence is just as much a cause of its ill-effects as the conniving use of it is by salesmen preaching nationalism. Nothing can stand in the way of those innocent enough to believe that they have a cause. They will step on everything as though history has been made for them.

Someone not too keen on starving was tilling the soil of a small park, metres away from where varying size wounds could be seen in a wall. Colourful apparel hung from the railings of balconies in buildings that rose straight out of the grass. Black singe marks on the yellow wall of an apartment block created the impression that hell's fire had rained momentarily in the unexpected flicker of an eye. The shelled-out remains of a building reminded me of a tree, turned into a stump by the fury of a tumultuous blaze. A devastated forest of these gnarled stumps, once people's homes, could be found in a street near the river where the dividing line of barbed-wire made a mockery of suggestions that prewar tensions did not exist. Exposed brick, the sign of aggressive nakedness, formed a dramatic contrast on the façade of a structure whose walls were once adorned with flowering stones and flying cherubs; another building of sloping, orange terracotta roofs and pastel walls remained unscathed amidst a grey street of post Second World War architecture, like a hope that the past could be revitalised, a past made even more significant by the drabness and austerity of those presently unacceptable restraints.

A loud boom of thunder emerged from the unsettled skies. Through it glided the steel dart of an American fighter. Hurtling through the angered wisps it disappeared and then reappeared, and then disappeared again, as it soared over the surrounding hills and then departed into the blackening clouds of the outraged sky. Everywhere, on the ground and in the air, the occupants of this blighted town were trapped by the saturnine forces of some devilish intent. Only the most minimal of movement could be detected from this population whose disillusionment with unwanted attention saw them huddled together in dusty basements, behind the sandbags of cafés and even in the vaults of banks – waiting. Waiting in the cellars of restaurants and in the cocoons of disused refrigeration units and in the sanctuary of protected ground-floor flats, they contemplated or moaned, as if in pessimistic acceptance of an inevitable tumult.

Someone tried another dash between the protecting buildings. A misleadingly innocent-sounding crack of fire, like a balloon popping, punctuated the electric silence. A massive streak of fluorescent veining then ignited the crepuscular heavens. A brilliant flash of white light lit up the world. Another speeding steel bird of immense but shackled power then rushed through the darkening mists. The sniper's target lay dead in the rain-drenched streets. The gargoyles of ancient buildings mocked the immaturity of this histrionic assault. The wide mouths of these screaming creatures of resistance resembled the frozen oval of pained shock that had befallen the white tight lips of the deceased. Shivering in the cold of this ridiculous death, the town then reverberated under the weight of splintering shocks: indiscriminate orange volcanic eruptions exploded around the defenceless streets. Charging, angry whistles carved up the sky. Two people ducked under one, and then, fascinated, glanced towards the place of its fiery demise. A mushrooming boom of grey-white vapour rose from the scene of this maddening crash. Fissures opened up in the earth, as the onrush of cynical magma enflamed the embattled streets. A direct hit on a renaissance building saw a frieze of floral-enveloped gargoyles fall down, as though lowered from above – kept in position by the final threads of artistic decency – before plummeting into an undignified heap. Zinging, smashing, bashing, tumbling, crashing, deafening furies enraged the despairing streets. High-pitched frenzies stormed in from above. The grinding of a thousand steel organisms tore up the air. Death's orchestra played, uninhibited, on the stage of its childish insanity. A wailing scream came to an abrupt halt.

Through a cloud of vaporised plaster, in a pile of crushed bricks, lay the body of a dead child. A sudden shaft of sunlight turned the gloom of the dilapidated room into a chamber of iridescent peace. Enriched particles swam in the cloudy air. A vast funnel of smooth and pure light could be seen bursting through a gap in the black clouds, via a hole in the roof. The sleepy voluptuousness of the dead boy's eyes belied the unsavoury means of his dreadful death. The obscenity of his murder was magnified by the delicate left hand, puffy little fingers at right angles to the wrist. Chipped bone protruded from the arm. I gasped as I realised that the neck had been blown away. I leant up against what was left of the wall and vomited. The ground shuddered underneath. Great booms of outgoing fire echoed above the frenetic swishes of distant mortars, the drilling whines of which disappeared with a chilling thud. The unsteady fingers of my hands caused the dead kid to rock violently within my frame. Two releases were snapped before an inconsolable woman bellowed out in horror at this disgraceful affair. Her hands were firmly clasped around her head. Wild agitation swept, like a blaze, through her piercing eyes. Then she swung her arms up and down, beating the air uncontrollably, screaming, berating, furious, a lunatic of scandalised propriety, a vicious and debauched nutcase of livid resentment. The idea of photographing such a maltreated and deranged psychotic in the instant of her unbridled despair never even entered my mind. Such displays of bitter passion were too personal. They jolted even the most hard-bitten of professionals into supinity, and I was struck dumb.

She stormed around over smashed bricks like a savage beast enraged by the unpardonability of her son's indefensible death. The absolute paucity of justification at the unforgivability of this impeachable crime caused sounds to emerge from her mouth that would have freaked vipers and made dragons hold their burning breath. She wailed and howled and clamoured and shrieked, bewildered by the insufferable impunity of the distant skies; she gasped and bellowed and roared and yelped, mortified by the callous and unnecessary ignominy of this needless war.

"Why? Oh why? Oh why? Oh why?" she begged, peeved by the unanswering void which stretches for ever into unending black.

Hissing like a great fire flying into an unlimited emptiness, she grabbed a lump of rock and hurled it at my head. It came towards me like an asteroid charging, slowly turning through the lifeless vacuum of indifferent space. I watched it gradually becoming clearer in the smoke-ridden haze and, when it became so clear that its accuracy was undoubted, I ducked, her son's image imprinted on my brain, that awful feeling of being drawn to a very private place uninvited playing havoc with my heart, and my eyes shot open on to the silent darkness of the New World.

* * * * * * * * * * *

The unrelenting desire to resolve my curiosity had me waking with such conviction that it felt as though I were fired with amphetamines. I waited impatiently, like an innocent prisoner on the threshold of a possible release, for Ross to wake. The telephone was in his room. I could not let this bad feeling compound itself into a paranoid nightmare. She had to be contacted before she went out for the day. Every minute I spent ruminating on the possible causes of her anger disintegrated fibres in the pulsating organism of my identity. Each moment I had to wait meant another second in which her mind could conceive of some new cause for ill-feeling: I was at the mercy of extraneous events.

And why did I have to make a telephone call like this for, anyway? I detested them, and I also detested telephones as well; but I particularly detested this damned one because it allowed me no excuses for not attempting to satisfy my audacious desires. It just sat there smirking, saying: 'Unless you ring her, tosser, you're never going to find out. Go on, sucker, make an idiot of yourself, or maybe you'd prefer to spend the rest of your life wondering? Imagine that, hey? Wondering for ever.'

Ross woke up. I knocked on his door and he grunted.

He was stretched out, bleary-eyed. His blue pyjamas brought out the red in his eyes.

"Ring her," he said, pointing to the phone.

I was taken aback by the abruptness of his demand.

I sat down on the sofa which lay, covered in discarded clothes, beside his bed. I smiled sheepishly and said, "This isn't going to be easy, you know."

"I know," he replied. "Take the phone out of the room and shut the door."

"I mean," I said, "I think I know why she's so pissed off."

"Why?" he asked.

I told him.

"Jeesuzz," he whispered. "If she's even remotely sensitive, that would not have gone down well at all."

"Exactly," I said.

"Why'd you say it for, then?" he asked.

"Oh," I sighed, "I was trying to introduce her into conversation and I was feeling a bit insecure, so I said something silly."

Ross rolled over and said, "Just say you're feeling guilty about something and see what happens. If she's reasonable, she'll understand."

I removed the phone from his bedroom and lay down on the lounge-room floor. The phone rang and rang. With each ring, tension was replaced by the emptiness of anti-climax. I was now charged up to do something that only minutes before had caused me to see the spectre of bilious failure. Now the same act was alive with appealing unpredictability. Only now, though, I knew that it was impossible to do it because she wasn't there. The titillation of appealing unpredictability, therefore, became replaced by the frustration of having to wait. I had been awake for fifteen minutes and it felt as though the day were already five hours old. I was going to have to wait longer. Jesus Christ.

Ross dragged himself up and we wandered down to his café. The place was packed. New Year's Day had brought out all the local bohemians. It was like having lunch with contented but struggling artists, enjoying the company of their lovers, husbands and wives.

Ross and I sat down and he said, "The phone's over there."

This time I did not hesitate to move towards it. I was prepared for the worst. I had to know. The worst would have come like death, but a death that soothes the pain.

I went around a corner and saw Sharon. Although her appearance was the same – punkish, very pale skin, short ginger hair, mascara'ed eyes – her facial expression was transformed. An air of certainty and maturity had replaced the uncertainty and diffidence of the sweet creature that I once used to know. It was the day that she told me about her disillusionment with Ross. She spoke with an uncompromising and tough realism which suggested that certain priorities and principles had risen like guiding rocks out of the shifting waters of her existence. It was obvious that there was to be no more quiet tolerance of unwanted situations: her now unshifting priorities had been shaped by love and pain.

"How", she demanded, with rhetorical probity, "can you say 'go' to someone when they ask you: 'Am I causing a problem?' It's just so difficult. Eventually, we just had to tell him."

"And", I replied, "he hasn't got a clue as to why?"

"I doubt that," she said. "He hadn't contacted me for years and when it suited him, he decided to re-enter my life. I threw up every day for six months while he just stayed around at my place as long as he liked, burdening me with his problems. There's only a certain amount that any human being can take."

Her report made me feel ill at ease; it was undoubtedly not exaggerated. It was never easy for any of us, particularly someone attempting to rekindle the embers of self-esteem, to have to admit to having caused thoughtless grief to others. Ross would never admit to having made an undignified mistake. This would mean his having to give up his dream of the blame being shared, followed by a reconciliation.

"Day in and day out," Sharon continued, "as I was suffering, Ross just kept going on and on and on about his unrequited love. I could have vomited right into his face and he probably wouldn't've even noticed. It was obvious that, if that woman had come back into his life, he wouldn't've even bothered knocking on my door again. I was just a cog in his emotional wheel. Both David and I were in a bad way and not once did he ever enquire about our well-being. He's lost in his own little self-indulgent world. But I'm sure you already know that."

I did. And I also knew that my interest in this subject was purely intellectual. It stemmed from being able to hear two completely different views of the same rather simple event. The subjective ability of the human mind to add convenient interpretations to uncomplicated contingencies, presumably for reasons of self-preservation, helps all irrational beliefs gleam with possibility. How else has something as fantastic as the *Bible* managed to evade the close, objective scrutiny it so thoroughly deserves? Is it because the reality would be too much for some of us too bear?

Emotionally, my mind was elsewhere. It was on that phone. More specifically it was, of course, on me and my desires. Anybody else's problems, past or present, did not really concern me. They were not my business. They seemed almost unreal. In the state of mind I was in, they represented a gross triviality. Even my own did, let alone somebody else's, for at the heart of all these cerebral disturbances was the knowledge of their transience. It made all long-winded analyses of them seem ridiculous. They were more like personal challenges to overcome rather than something to be shared. But sometimes someone had an interesting one and I liked to think that mine were as well. But then I would, wouldn't I?

The phone became free. A kind of fluttering airiness overcame me as I removed the handset from its holder. Samantha answered almost immediately; it was difficult to tell how happy she was about me contacting her, for music could be heard entering through the half-ajar door of the booth. I was in a British telephone box inside the café.

I asked, "How are you feeling?"

"Fine," she replied, with a surprisingly carefree effect of contented abandonment that left me confused as to whether I should be pleased or disappointed. I felt both relief and concern: relief that she was happy to speak to me, and concern that I appeared to have virtually no effect on her whatsoever. The latter needed to be tested.

"I must admit," I then said, thinking to myself, 'Go on, women are always complaining - completely unjustifiably - about men not expressing their feelings. You've got to do it.'

"I'm feeling a bit guilty about something I said to you yesterday. I thought it might have been the reason you seemed so agitated when you left."

"What?" she asked, genuinely baffled. "You didn't say anything that upset me. And I wasn't agitated either."

I forgot about the agitation. She was either devoid of self-awareness or lying.

"What was it?" she persisted.

"It doesn't matter," I replied.

'Jesus,' I thought, 'she sounds as if she's not putting on an act. This is bad.'

"Are you going to say?" she asked.

"It doesn't matter," I reiterated. "If you weren't upset, then there's no problem."

"I'd like to know," she said. "Otherwise", she added, giggling, "I'm going to go out wondering what it was."

"Forget it," I replied.

Her giggling was disturbing. The inappropriateness of it made her comment about going out with niggling curiosity seem sarcastic.

I asked her what she had done "last night". She said that she had gone to a bar and hadn't really enjoyed it.

"Oh," I said, sympathetically, delighted about this, "that's a pity."

I told her what I had done and she laughed. After a while, she said that she had to go. She was preparing to go to a barbecue. Funnily enough, I wasn't invited. Sharon's comment about the difficulties of telling someone persistent 'to go' was fresh in my mind. We arranged to meet on the weekend, then we hung up.

I stepped out of the phone box disturbed by the beguiling lack of resolution that this phone call was supposed to have avoided. Instead of clearing the misty skies of my brooding ruminations, it simply added another dimension of gloom to the opaque vapours forming in the tenebrous recesses of my unsettled mind. I was honestly not sure if I was worried or glad that she had not been upset by my comment about prattling. However, there was certainly no real relief in it: I was too aware of the sensation of dreary anti-climax that had overcome me for that. In circumstances such as these, we always convince ourselves that something dramatic and definite must take place. When nothing does, we're left with wistfulness.

I stroked the cute face of Sharon's baby. I then marvelled in the irony of her complete detachment from the events which had just transpired in the telephone box only metres away from where she was sitting. We begin life concerned about one thing and that is precisely how most of us end it – concerned about ourselves. Imagine the reaction I would have evoked had I sat down and told Sharon about the problems I was creating for myself with regard to Samantha. Or about the fractured lives I had seen in Bosnia. Or the horrors of war. Or the pain that man inflicts upon his fellow man. She would not have listened to a word of it.

Across the other side of the room, Ross was staring out the window pretending to be unaffected. The only thing on his mind would have been my conversation with Sharon. He would, of course, feign interest in the other conversation that I had just had, but his real concern lay elsewhere. There was no reason why it should not have. He was human too.

Back with him, he swung his head around slowly, with a pretentious casualness, and asked, "So you made contact?"

I told him that Samantha had claimed that she had not felt insecure in the pub the day before.

"Bullshit," he sneered. "She was right on edge."

"If she wasn't feeling insecure", I said, "I'd love to know what it was then."

As Ross was dying to discuss my other conversation, I then added, "Sharon seems to have changed. As you probably realise, I've just been speaking to her as well."

Suddenly, he bent forward enthusiastically over the table and said, "And?"

The overall response to Sharon's claims was, "I was sorting their problems out! Not mine!"

The absolute inaccuracy of this would have been mildly amusing had it not been for his inability to convince himself of its unequivocal veracity. Such a standpoint can only emerge from the unyielding torrents of self-preservation. There was not the slightest admission of guilt as he gasped and moaned and shook his head, unfortunately, however, without the substantial outrage required to be convincing. We all have our moments of pathetic self-indulgence, but not enough of us have our moments of acknowledging it.

"I even", he unconvincingly complained, "drove around to their place to lend them money. I even did that."

This prompted me to tell him that Sharon had made it clear that she was unhappy with the way "his impositions" had made her feel as though she were poor.

"We couldn't even feed ourselves", she had told me, "and Ross expected to be fed."

According to Ross, they had "chips on their shoulders with regards to opulence".

"They", he said, "always equate rich with cold - always."

I felt as though I had inadvertently stepped into a political furnace fired by pride.

Ross then said that "at the time" that Sharon's boyfriend "was having an affair with someone else. I tried to help her through this."

I remained silent. I knew that Ross would have used David's affair as a means of talking about his own. But this possibility was not accorded the gravity it deserved. Slaughtered vanity took care of that. Perhaps he was even innocent enough to feel that, by hammering on about his own experience, it would have helped him shed some light on to the turmoil of Sharon's fragile vulnerability. Such magnanimity was really only the diplomatic face of rapacious self-appeasement. And Ross was full of it.

Across the other side of the room, as a nagging reminder of his past, the smug inaccessibility of Sharon and her entourage echoed like a dull and irrepressible wail through the haunted chamber of Ross's mind. The contented, self-perpetuating righteousness of this impenetrable group was just as intemperate as the breathless screams of the painfully unfulfilled. One form of indulgence was safely twee, while the other was soap operatic with unjustified melodrama. And here they sat, face to face.

It was obvious that Ross was desperate to re-establish contact, but so much damage had been done that the barriers were virtually insurmountable. If it weren't for the fact that I was visiting from overseas, he would have been sitting here alone on one side of this café while his ex-friends would have been on the other, ignoring him, increasing his isolation, making him look an absurd figure against the window in the corner: a stranger to their previously open familiarity.

"You", I said, dreaming about Samantha entertaining flocks of adoring men at that damned barbecue, "have to pretend that it's all your fault. They're in the stronger emotional position so you have to make all the play."

He agreed, reluctantly, but said, "I'm just going to forget it."

This, I knew, was not true. Relationships, I thought, are created when the weaker party – and Ross agreed by saying that they were in a stronger position because "they were a family unit" – is drawn inexorably towards its desire.

"Besides," I said, "once you start blaming yourself in front of them, they'll probably begin pointing out that they haven't exactly been perfect angels either. If they don't, then forget it."

I could see that there was no chance that he was going to do this.

"Oh well," I said, "be a victim of pride."

"We all are," he replied.

'And we're also victims of self-absorption as well,' I thought.

* * * * * * * * * *

My father decided to fulfil some absurd paternal obligation by taking me out to lunch. His bitter silence in the car was finally punctuated by the comment, "Wanker!" when a long-haired motorcyclist glided past. The rider's bike had an abundance of chrome. His helmet was sky-blue. The side of his machine displayed the tongue of a red dragon spiralling out of a body that twisted along the full length of the vehicle. It appeared as though this flamboyant display of self-expression, this harmless addition to the spectrum of human attitudes, did little to appeal to my father's graceful sensibilities.

My theory on this subject attained greater weight when my father completed his in-depth assessment of the full-bearded rider by saying, "Cunt."

It became apparent, however, that this bellicose observation was merely the tip of an iceberg of similar perceptions that my father was forced to embark upon as we ventured down the road. After collecting his wife, he was momentarily held up by someone driving slowly, unsure of where they were going.

"Use yar fuckin' indicator," my father snarled, infuriated that he was going to arrive at his destination ten seconds later than predicted.

"Jesus, cunt, wanker, fucking dickhead," he seethed. "What a fucking, useless prick."

Eventually, we got past the slow driver and I said, "Do you know that the police now have acoustic devices that enable them to detect what drivers are saying in their cars?"

My father glanced at me, seriously, at first, before smiling sheepishly, as I continued, "And quite a few people have already received heavy fines as well. In your case, I can imagine the magistrate saying: 'Mister Harley, in a twenty-four hour period you used the term cunt on two hundred and ninety-five occasions, prick on five hundred and six, arsehole on four hundred and twenty-one and wanker on two hundred and eleven, and that was only when you were driving. What you achieved in general conversation can only be surmised. Despite your mind-boggling deployment of, shall we say, descriptive colloquialisms, the thing that really fascinates me is your proclivity for perceiving a complete lack of finesse in all those who have the misfortune to encounter you. How this belligerent perception then resolves itself so rapidly into the verbal filth that so readily pours from your mouth is, I believe, one of the great linguistic mysteries of modern times. Given the overwhelming scale of your profanity, I have no option but to give you life.'"

My father was now giggling boyishly, proud of his eccentric recalcitrance. Sue was chuckling away in the back seat as well.

My comments prompted her to say, "Keith's a careful driver, though."

Driving into the restaurant car park, my father gleefully added, "Except when I see slopes. Then I just go straight at 'em."

Sue found this extraordinarily amusing.

In the restaurant, a Chinese family made its way through the main section to the terrace where a plant-ridden pergola cast down mottled patches of sunlight on the ground. A small boy from this family stood in the doorway; he looked as though he were going to overbalance and crash on to the paving stones.

This caused my father to hiss, "Go on, Slope, fall over and break yar fuckin' neck."

"Oh darling," Sue remonstrated, weakly.

She had ordered a salmon bagel and was surprised when the waitress presented it to her.

"Is that mine?" she asked, expecting something more exotic.

There appeared to be only a bread roll and a bit of salad on her plate. The waitress took it back to qualify the situation.

Sue decided to do so when my father convincingly said, "You didn't order that. You ordered smoked salmon."

A minute later another waitress returned with the same bagel, saying, politely, "I'm sorry, but this is what you ordered."

"For Christ's sake," Darling sneered, as the waitress walked off, "you dopey bitch."

A sudden flush of red swept across Sue's face. Opening the bread roll, the salmon was revealed within. The harshness of my father's attack was as heartless as it was embarrassing. It was not easy being in the presence of an unpredictable and immature fascist lunatic, but it was unimaginable conceiving of the idea of an innocent person like Sue actually being married to one. There were no doubts that some people felt she deserved it. She had shown insufficient self-respect in the opinions of some and an absolute disregard for the virtues of independence. To be belittled like this so savagely by the person she had married was the inevitable consequence of her actions. However, even I was surprised by the severity of my father's outrageous abuse. His apparent inability to recall that he too had made a mistake – had actually caused the waitress to take the order back – only served to heighten my awkwardness, for it graphically displayed my father's egotistical lack of self-awareness. His return to prickly silence after the bagel incident made it more difficult for me to pretend that no harm had been intended, that it had just been a trivial incident bearing little relation to my father's true feelings.

To my amazement, Sue regained her composure rapidly. An insult that would have caused violent outrage in some women appeared to have only been a minor irritant to someone resigned to being a helpless target for my father's vituperative volatility. The thought that these incidents were probably a normal feature of their relationship was grotesque. But it could not be discarded. Life is pointless – it is effectively a series of inconsequential events with an unfathomable conclusion – but so many people make it even more absurd by their bizarre actions. I shuddered at the realisation that a life's endeavours could come to nothing but the daily abuse of an innocent woman. What a retribution for one's sins that'd be. But he deserved it.

The unfortunate victim – his wife – asked me a series of questions to which I gave reticent answers. Her curiosity about an ex-girlfriend of mine culminated in my telling her that the father of this creature had been paranoid about my marrying her.

"Hah!" my father cynically quipped. "I'm not surprised."

This was the first thing he had said since abusing his wife. In the period between these comments, he had stared sourly around the restaurant as if in anticipation of a financial disaster. His frustration at not being in some imagined place with rich and famous imaginary soul mates gave his intense silences a viciousness that contradicted the sunniness of the location which his dark mind was currently being forced to endure. The smell of blossoms and the kaleidoscope of colours in the garden were misplaced in the presence of this bitchy tormentor of placid souls whose puerile polemics reeked with the pathos of unfulfilment.

This was one lunch that could not end quickly enough. The wind which hissed in the leaves above whistled like the esoteric yearning of lost dreams. It was subtle and elusive, a crying wail of breath, frustrated by the impossibility of resolution; howling in the limbo of its quietly screaming loneliness, the bathos of churning turbulence afflicting my father was gradually becoming stormier as the amount of time available to him to translate a towering self-belief in his own glorious destiny into pragmatic realisation headed towards zero. And I was here, invited by him, because he knew that one day he might become financially dependent upon me. He was therefore churlishly keeping his options open. This was assuming that cigarettes and alcohol didn't kill him first.

When we left the restaurant, I sat in the back seat, quietly dreading the prospect of the goodbye ritual. They were giving me a lift to a main road down the street from where I would make my own way. It was going to be the last time that I would see them for years.

My father pulled the car over at the place where I wanted to get out. I kissed Sue and then he extended his hand, saying, with a sentiment missing from the day's earlier proceedings, "Well, see yar, mate."

"I'll see you", I replied, opening the door so that it overhung the busy road, "in about five years' time."

My father, concerned that the door would be hit by passing traffic, said, "Get out on the other side."

I ignored this, climbing out as quickly as possible, slamming the door behind me, escaping, as I've always done.

* * * * * * * * * *

I contacted Paul Humphrey and we met in a café in one of those fashionable suburbs where women put make-up on to go shopping. It was a cheerful place, airy with light *trompe-l'oeil* paintings of flowers in duck egg blue against the turquoise walls.

We sat down and I noted that he still had his peaches-and-cream complexion, wavy blond hair, chunky torso and his dark-blond beard, features that gave him a gentle ruggedness so attractive to women. Any mention of our past, mutual eccentric indiscretions filled his warm, wholesome blue eyes with sparkling joy. Any suggestion, born from either conversation or appearance, of his once raw and blasé hedonism was now confined purely to the endearing sloppiness of his unpretentious dress. A packet of rolling tobacco spilled out from a long-sleeved, checked shirt on which half the buttons were undone. Tufts of chest hair protruded through the unbuttoned gaps. A determined sternness fell upon his face.

I discovered that he had spent two of the last seven years in prison for possession of heroin; he had then emerged, as a pauper, and within two years had become comfortably rich. This rapid transition from poor drug addict to respectable antiques dealer was almost inevitable for him, for the two extremes of dangerous excess and imaginative enterprise summed up his character.

The story of his renaissance began in New Delhi where he had had to step over a dead body each morning when leaving his hotel. The heroin was cheap, and he was in desperate need of a fix. The relief on acquisition almost caused him to overdose. He described a scene in a New Delhi public toilet that reflected his personal degradation. In great pain, he had staggered into a place, walled off by corrugated iron, to find it "full of shit". He described "mountains of crap" that turned his "blood to pure vomit". It was here that he realised that he did not want to die. The necessity of having to shoot up in a public toilet "so bad that even the flies wouldn't go near it" had driven him to "get on the next plane out". The car he was in after arriving back at Perth airport was rammed by the federal police; one jumped out and put a gun to his head.

"I was absolutely fucking petrified," he said. "I didn't have a clue who these guys were or what they wanted. And I was feeling really sick. Then I thought: 'Fuck, my mother.'"

His mother, a profoundly immature woman with schizophrenia, whom he described as "clinically insane", had gone overboard in notifying the authorities of the danger that her son represented to society. By the time her rantings had penetrated the skulls of the police, Paul had become 'Mister Asia', the head of an international drugs ring stretching from Moscow to Sydney.

"I was just a simple addict," he said. "I went to India for cheap thrills. But they thought that I was definitely the man they had been looking for for years. It was incredible."

"It took some time for the police", he said, "to come back to reality, a place my mother has, unfortunately, never been. But", he admitted, "by contacting the police she actually saved my life and this is probably the only sane thing that she's ever done."

It took nine hours of intense interrogation from the feds before they accepted that they had made a mistake. The magistrate, though, was not so sympathetic. Paul got four years with two years' parole for good behaviour. The cell, he said, without exaggeration "was about the size of a toilet". Apart from the two men who had occupied it, it was also home to rats, mice and cockroaches as well. The walls were smeared with shit. Amnesty International had blacklisted Fremantle Prison, eventually bringing about its closure, describing it as "unforgivably decrepit penal institution in a place so civilised and rich". Paul was one of the last inmates to be admitted to that "outrageous disgrace". The bunks in his cell were arranged perpendicularly so that his feet were at his cellmate's head. Often during the night – they were locked in each afternoon at four o'clock until daybreak – his cellmate, a murderer who had carved up his wife with a chainsaw, would thump Paul's feet because they had come into contact with the head of a man who "regularly threatened other prisoners with knives".

"He threatened", Paul said, "to kill me numerous times. Probably about three times a week."

I was then informed that "two or three people a year" were killed in "that place",

"There was a time", Paul said, "when I was convinced that I was going to be one of them."

He then told a story that really made me wince. There were no toilets in the cells. Portable tin buckets were used. He said that his cellmate had had an accident with laxatives. This caused his cellmate "to spend the entire night on the shit-bucket".

"Not even the rats", Paul smiled, "were around for that."

Someone else – another murderer – had tormented him as well. On one occasion the tormentor, with the help of some "brainless wankers", had pinned him against a wall. The convicted murderer put a knife to his stomach. Paul, after contemplating death, shoved his aggressor aside and walked off; the next day, after months of harassment which led to a vicious crescendo, Paul retrieved a knife from the kitchen and attacked the "arsehole who had menaced me to the point of insanity".

His tormentor had run in fear.

"I realised after that", Paul said, "that that guy was nothing but bluff."

He said that this incident had helped "to improve things".

"People left me alone after that", he said, "because everyone could see that I was capable of killing and, to give you an idea of what that meant in that place, this actually won me respect. Wonderful, hey?"

"Not an ivory tower of intellectual achievement then?" I asked.

"We're talking about underdevelopment", he replied, "on a massive scale."

He wanted to take me to see his antique-filled house. On the way, I told him about my predicament with Samantha.

"Should I risk a move and perhaps upset her and never see her again?" I asked.

"You have to decide", he replied, "if you want a relationship."

The accuracy of this was undeniable.

"You probably won't see her again, anyway," he added, "unless you have a go. So you might as well go for it. And if you did see her again, without having tried, could you tolerate the sight of her with another bloke, wondering what would have happened had you done exactly what he obviously did? Go for it."

There was little I could say to question this. Then he told me the story of his seduction of his present girlfriend. He and two others had been in hot pursuit. She was moving into a flat and required assistance in the transportation of her furniture; therefore, she had elicited the services of the three contenders. Paul described a day of initially subliminal competition that became increasingly overt as the proceedings unfolded.

"While those two went for the refrigerator", he smiled, "I went for her. I was kissing her over the sink in the bathroom upstairs while those two were downstairs installing the fridge. It was", he said, with his dreamy smile that oozed satisfaction, unconsciously highlighting my inadequacies with Samantha, "a golden moment that I will cherish for ever."

The house that he shared with this lady was limestone Victorian. It was three storeys with exquisite stained-glass windows in the landings. The place was full of antiques. A Japanese lacquer chest of drawers sat in the bedroom. Meissen and Staffordshire porcelains sat on the shelves. There was an uplifting luminosity to it in the landings where colourful patches of light were strewn across the timber floors. In contrast, the cool, dark lounge-room, with its abundance of artefacts, had the stamp of cluttered Victorian indulgence; within a patio extending out from this room was a liberty glass spa in the shape of a lotus leaf. It was surrounded by a forest of deliberately overgrown vegetation. Sparkling patches of broken light fell through the forest and were scattered beneath its boughs.

We sat down on some elegant iron chairs and he said, "I wanted to relive our times in Queensland, so I had it built."

He got up and returned with a photo album that I had not seen for years which documented a highly dramatic eight month trip that he and I had taken around Australia as nineteen-year-olds. It was a journey that had opened our eyes to many things.

I glanced through the album, laughing, remembering, re-experiencing, recalling those days when everything was so new, when every undiscovered place on earth reeked with monumental possibilities; I also went through that album with a sense of awe and trepidation, because I knew what I was going to find on one of those pages.

When it appeared, I closed the album quickly, wincing; an explosion of loss welled up within me. On Magnetic Island, Paul had taken a photograph of the most beautiful woman that he and I had ever seen in our lives. I had left Paul to pursue this woman over thousands of miles, finally ravishing her in the bedroom of a house one highly charged afternoon in Bondi. Her boyfriend then arrived from Germany one week later. Things did not go terribly well after that. I lost her for ever as both friend and lover, for I was too young in those days to have the perspective of patience. This experience of unnecessary squandering was currently affecting my restraint with Samantha. It was like the converse of the impulsive Andrea days.

Paul said that I could keep the photographs of a woman he described as being "so beautiful that she makes Grace Kelly look like the Hunchback of Notre Dame". He checked that he still had the negatives. Beneath each photograph in the album he had written a caption. Under the photographs of this stunning beauty, he had written: *Ugly Andrea*. He mentioned, with titillated amazement, that several people had expressed bewilderment that he had written this under the photograph of a creature whose enormous, iridescent blue eyes and olive skin, high cheekbones and long, honey-coloured hair, with little freckles across the bridge of her nose and speckles of gold around her black irises, made her so attractive that it was impossible for anyone not to be overwhelmed by this masterpiece of feminine beauty.

"She's not ugly, they say, " he said, laughing, "and it always causes me to roll around the floor pissing myself. And they don't know why."

I was astounded that anyone could not see the irony. Gaining possession of those photographs again made me feel that a vital part of me had returned. I had accidentally thrown out my copies of them many years previously, not realising then that I had transferred them into a bag that I thought was full of rubbish after I had shown them to someone at my then place of work. I had been furious with myself. I had stormed around the house, muttering. It was like the final departure from a dramatic past when everything was so alive.

The sight of those photographs rekindled an illogical sensation. I had no chance of ever seeing her again – I knew this logically – but it still did not stop the vague flame of hope that such a possibility existed from being ignited.

Paul then began a tirade of disparagement against some of those with whom he and I had gone to school. He was particularly scathing towards Dob McDonald.

"I can't believe", he said, "that that guy is studying to become a psychiatrist. If there's anyone I know on earth who needs one, it's him."

He said that "an obviously ridiculous rumour" had circulated about Dob's sexuality.

"Some people were saying", he said, "that he was gay. I went to a party one day and heard this enormous cheering going on. A large group of people had gathered around this open air spa in the back garden of this place. I walked over to the crowd to see what was going on. I took one look, and then walked away. It was Dob screwing some woman in the spa, being egged on by these morons! What a thing to do, just to prove that you're not gay! I personally don't give a fuck what people think of my sexuality."

"I feel a bit sorry for him", I said, "because he's so affected by his reputation for eccentric hedonism that he feels he constantly has to prove his ability to entertain. He'd much prefer to be an entertainer than a human being."

"He'll never", Paul replied, "be able to have a relationship. It applies to most of those guys."

I was then informed of Paul's theory surrounding Richard Wain's "scorpion bite".

"Got to be", Paul said, "one of the most absurd things that I've ever heard."

I then told him about Richard's story regarding the clothing booth and he shook his head in dismay.

"Imagine", he said, "doing that with your so-called girlfriend around."

"Hardly love," I replied.

I then questioned him about his antique dealing. He had studied antiques in prison to keep his mind "active and to find something beautiful to concentrate on". I got one story after another of the successes that he had had. It seemed as though his serendipity had given him a happy knack of converting one hundred dollar purchases into thousand dollar sales. Someone had given him a Boulle clock, thinking it was "just a piece of family junk". One of his school friends had "virtually given" him a "twenty-four carat gold brooch set with an opal the size of a twenty cent piece". Sotheby's had relieved him of it for an undisclosed five figure sum. The bookshelf in the bedroom was laced with expensive, hardcover books on antiques. The pages of these colourful publications dripped with opulence. He was getting his fair share of it.

"I turn over", he said, "about three grand a week. Not bad," he smiled, "considering my whereabouts not so long ago."

His "whereabouts not so long ago" arrived back in conversation when he told me that he had seen someone get murdered in Fremantle Prison.

"After I got released," he said, "and I had that spa built, I used to sit in it at five o'clock in the afternoon, relieved to be alive myself, and listen to the roll-call from across the road."

The prison walls were only two hundred yards away.

"In the balmy quiet of these often sunlit afternoons", he continued, "the determined, trained ear was able to detect each name clearly. The calling out of each name caused me to erupt with laughter - every time. I knew them all. And here I am and there they are. I raise my glass to fate."

Such satisfaction is rare.

* * * * * * * * * * * *

The lunch I had with my father and his wife gave me the opportunity to experience again the moral subjectivity of the human mind. The proceedings in this department began when Sue voiced her frustration at the unfriendly antics of my grandmother.

"I don't understand it," she said. "She's always done it. Ever since Keith and I got married, I say, 'Hullo,' and she just ignores me."

The sort of outrage that she should have reserved for her husband was being unleashed on to her mother-in-law instead. It was fascinating to listen to; her face was flushed as she said, "I've given up. I make phone calls and go around there and it's always the same response. Always."

An angered air of righteous disbelief swept across her reddened face. The dramatic finality of her comment suggested that she felt some nefarious problem existed with my grandmother. One did but it was beyond her to realise what it was. My grandmother detested people who did not work. Her life of hard graft had given her a disinclination towards wanting to reward a selfish son with an inheritance that would be partly spent on a woman "who refused to learn to take care of herself".

My grandmother and her first husband had built their first house with their bare hands. After my father moved in for nothing with three children, while my grandmother was still running a business, he drank and played around. There was to be no inheritance money for either him or his wife for my grandmother hated laziness and disrespect. She was also spitefully immature when confronting things that annoyed her. Instead of communicating her feelings properly, she either displayed cold silence or went wild. And Sue was oblivious of the source of these strange emotions. Instead of just calming down and saying, "Look Sue, I'm afraid I'm the sort of person who's aggravated by indolent dependence - sorry, it's just one of those little quirks - so no hard feelings," my grandmother had to undertake a series of melodramatic sulks, the constancy of which had caused the obnoxiousness of her son.

The moribund acidity of her eldest offspring was well-known. He was not accorded the name 'Snarley Harley' for nothing, and today had given him several opportunities to prove it, for most of his day had been spent glaring bitterly around a restaurant - as you do - perturbed, even horrified, by the mere concept of conversation. He had married a second time because Sue's family had rich connections and because she was the only woman he knew dire enough to find his appalling behaviour amusing; his interest in me, similarly limited, waned almost to zero when he realised that I was not going to pursue the career in football that he wanted me to undertake; I had unwittingly thwarted his ambitions of vicarious glory. This had left behind a simmering reservoir of muffled antagonism. It showed constantly in my father's belligerent episodes of petulant gloominess. His scathing disregard for most things dissociated from his wallet, that leather ego, worn at the edges, was emblazoned across his face, as his wife continued.

"It's incredible," she said, still referring to my grandmother. "All the others think that she's so wonderful," this I doubted, except in the case of Wayne, and my grandmother was wise enough to appreciate this, hence the protection, "and they make such a fuss of her, but she's not that wonderful, is she?"

"How could she be?" I replied, pointing to my father. "She produced him."

This had the effect of causing a momentary change to my father's vexed facial expression. Sue burst into laughter.

"Nice", I continued, "is not a word I readily associate with my grandmother. After having had the experience of living with her for fifteen years, I can assure you that the last thing she is is nice. She might be many other things but, when the chips are down, she certainly isn't that."

This made Sue feel better. I qualified my comment, though, by saying that my grandmother's obstreperous nature had been enhanced by "her son", who had wasted money on a series of dubious girlfriends, rather than spend it on his family. My grandmother had been put into a position where she was forced to blow money on her three grandchildren while the father of these mites offloaded substantial sums on the pleasures of life. This took Sue very much by surprise.

"He", she smiled, malevolently, "never told me about those women. Who were they?"

My father chuckled proudly. He was always pleased to create an illusion of success, that there was something up his sleeve, that his well-renowned bluntness was a mask for the multitude of fascinating things that he had to hide.

"What women?" he giggled, boasting through innocent humour. "I never had any women. Did I?"

I became as sombre as he had been only moments before.

"Only a few," I mumbled, bored by his self-adoration.

His wife stared at him, pointedly. Enquiries, I assumed, would presumably be made later.

"Anyway," he smiled, suddenly serious, "while I lived at her place, I painted her bloody house five times. Brian did fuck all!"

I did not even consider mentioning that Brian had not spent fifteen years there rent-free, for I was loath to prejudice my pleasure in observing this fantastic delusion of unselfish diligence. I could not wait to tell my grandmother. It would be received like a line of exquisite poetry upon the manuscript of her years.

My father's outburst was lapped up superbly by his sympathetic wife. She looked at him tenderly, as if her sensitive husband had been unjustifiably disregarded by an evil mother. Her blindness – perhaps you could describe it as loyalty – was acute. I had a moment of pity, though, when I tried to come to terms with the idea that there was actually someone alive who looked upon the rubbish which poured from my father's mouth, as though it were born from a blameless tower of insight and probity, rising majestically from within the mendacious waters of teeming dissolution. The reality of this gave me a kind of flustered silence.

My grandmother's response to my father's comments was, "He painted the house probably once. And even then he only did it a bit at a time. Every time he was on the verge of being turfed out, he'd pick up the paintbrush for a day or two. Not a bad deal for fifteen years of free rent. He basically came and went as he pleased."

It was not often that she laughed but my father's exculpatory view of affairs created a brief guffawing.

The smile went from her face though when I brought up Sue's accusations.

"I've always been nice to her," she said, but not as flabbergasted as I would have expected. I found this delusion quaint, and certainly ironic in view of her giggling when presented with her son's illusions. "We rang each other a lot at one stage and talked all the time."

Her defence of her own immense propriety was always done at the expense of accurate self-analysis. This was the thing that aggrieved Sue so badly. It was like a kind of unquestionable moral superiority that destroyed objectivity. I was just amused at how two human minds are capable of being so divergent in their interpretations of one simple event. The vast gap in these interpretations was, as usual, filled with the sickly lacquer of personal preservation.

Later, my grandmother produced something unwittingly revealing.

"She's gone so fat. She won't put herself out for anyone. Your father's had to teach her how to cook. She won't have anyone around. That'd be too much like work."

It was unimaginable that my grandmother's austere sincerity would allow her to be constantly pleasant to someone as unworthy as that. There was no chance of this being possible. That, I can assure you.

* * * * * * * * * *

Samantha and I met in a pub in Fremantle. We were sitting down on a balcony, fenced off with ornate ironwork, overlooking the café-filled road, and I was apparently boring her senseless with stories about my father. She seemed unable to look me straight in the eye.

Her beautiful face was overcome with languid agitation. Her eyes shifted constantly, rarely remaining fixed on any one point for more than a second. Her head would rotate from one side to the other, each rotation being characterised by a quick glance at me. The amount of eye contact we consequently had, during that first hour of our meeting, was absolutely minimal. It would not have represented five per cent of the time that we had been together. She may have been bored but I was getting increasingly annoyed by her lack of interest. 'If she's so unwilling to communicate, what the hell is she doing here?' I thought.

I decided that it was time I either left or she showed a bit more interest. I deposited a copy of a book about the Vietnam War before her and told her to read a certain page while I went to the toilet. The page described a scene in which American MPs gunned down burning prisoners attempting to escape flames after a mortar round had hit the glassworks that the Americans were using as a prison. The author finished that section by declaring that the only corpse at which he would not be able to bear to look would be the one that he was never going to see.

I came back from the toilet, quietly infuriated. I sat down and then unleashed one description after another of the mutilated corpses that I had seen. No details were omitted. Funnily enough, the one that caused most shock was not even related to war. I had had an assignment covering the eccentric proclivities of funeral directorships in England. The embalmer on this occasion had told me that he had a corpse that "was not very nice". A twenty-four-year-old girl had stormed out of a house after having an argument with her boyfriend, charged across the road and was clobbered by a speeding double-decker bus. I told Samantha that the body was under a sheet when I had walked in.

Slowly, the embalmer had pulled the sheet up, exposing the feet first, my teeth grinding, saying, "Do you want to see more?" As the destruction to the body became progressively worse, my teeth grinding even harder, my lips were taut, my firm mouth twisted, saying, "Go on, go on," eyes becoming screwed up and then – oh my God, the head! What a fucking mess!

Probably the most pleasant thing was that one eye was hanging out of its socket, and I won't describe the rest. Eye contact was ninety-nine per cent after that. I pointed out that, unlike a lot of "international journalists", to coin a phrase, I was unable to stop thinking that that "lump of smashed flesh" – her head had caught the bus full on – was once human -- had once been conscious, had had thoughts and feelings. The ability to "sever this association was fundamental for anyone interested in becoming a correspondent".

I was being deliberately aggressive, trying to shock; I felt a touch insulted that I had been forced to be polite to someone who previously looked about as interested in me as a US president would be in wishing to make Marxism compulsory in American schools. The shock tactics worked: she came alive. Suddenly there was the contemplation of the afterlife; then it got on to transvestism and homosexuality. Eventually it reached the subject of writing, creativity, obsession, politics, Nazism, racism, sport, religion, the influence of communism on the Vietnam War, the French resistance, palaeontology, plate tectonics, rainforests, psychoanalysis, hedonism, the slaughtering of refugees in France after the German invasion, skin-diving and then family relationships. I noticed, for over an hour, that her body language had changed. She was bending forward and looking me in the eye; the expression in them had changed as well – it had gone from a distant, wistful docility to an interested, smiling gleam, and all the time I was thinking, 'Christ, I have to leave this country in a few days' time. What a fucking nightmare!'

Then she self-consciously attempted to raise the subject of my dark motives. It was that day that that damned insect was on the receiving end of her precious appreciation. A sensation, like a combination of dread and fear, rose within me. There were numerous harsh realities with which I was prepared to deal, but the thought that she was trying to express concerns about my romantic hopes was unbearable. There was not a chance that I was going to give her the opportunity of saying: 'I hope that you're not interested in me. I would feel very uncomfortable about that.'

Not a chance. This would have been like listening to the auditory equivalent of sulphuric acid being poured into my ears.

She then collected herself courageously and said, "Before, it was difficult to have eye contact with you, but not now."

"Why?" I asked.

"I think", she replied, "there's a bit of gamesmanship going on here."

"Explain," I said.

My curiosity was suddenly outweighing my fear of dreadful discovery again. I was hoping that she would just get straight to the point. I had accepted that it was not going to be good news, but at least it would bring a halt to my unnecessary and debilitating ruminations.

"I was thinking to myself", she said, "'What does this guy want?'"

She raised her hands in taut clutches of passionate frustration; then she continued, "The reason I wasn't keeping eye contact", she was now looking at me intensely, "was that I was worried about leading you on."

"But", I protested, suddenly deciding again that the consequences of this knowledge would be untenable, "you don't know what my attitude is."

"Exactly," she blurted out, spreading her fingers apart, shaking them, saying, "I know, I know. I'm just being presumptuous."

She shook her head, flustered. If I weren't so disappointed, I would have found this tumultuous experience she had just had, that experience of attempting to express her understandable fears, hilarious; but it was no joke. There was not the slightest doubt in my mind that I had just experienced rejection. No other possibility was allowed the luxury of existing. The only explanation for her odd temper was fear - fear of having to deal with my groping attempts to seduce her. What other explanation could there be?

Then she said, "There's another reason I wouldn't look at you as well."

"Yes?" I replied, expecting the worst. "What is it?"

It had been a long time since the prospect of any information had caused me to be so unenthusiastic.

"You", she said, "have the power to see deeply. I was afraid of being caught out. I don't mean", she said, "that you would be able to see into my soul, my deepest thoughts - that's impossible. I was just worried I would be discovered in some way."

I was now completely confused. 'See what?' I wondered but I acted as though I understood. If she was under the absurd impression that I could "see into things deeply", who was I to spoil her perceptions? Why ruin a good compliment with the facts? But it didn't do much to reduce the confusion. I had been happy in my sadness that something definitive had been learnt. I had thought that she had made her attitude clear. I had assumed from the perplexed worry of her sentiments that she was not interested in me and then, lo and behold, I was given again some vague hope, some glimmer of romantic expectation by the troubled, partly embarrassed nature of her delivery and by the ambiguity of her last remark. I thought that I could rest on the knowledge of my failure; I thought that tricky problem of how and whether to show affection had been resolved but obviously not.

Later we got some food and went back to Brian's place. She sat in the kitchen with me and we discussed astronomy, Einstein's theories on the universe, the Hubble space telescope, and her experiences at an observatory where she had seen close-ups of the moon and Saturn. While we ate I played a cassette of South American folk music and dimmed the lights. The conversation was gentle and powerful; there was a quality to it like music. It complemented the velvety blackness that had descended upon the breathless earth outside like a counterpoint of soothing harmony. The melodic whisper of Bolivian pipes gave our serenity an exotic touch. A relaxing intimacy grew up between us. I was being blessed by a rare contentment.

I told her about a wonderful film that I had seen recently about music. Her strikingly tender face, with its giant eyes of transfixed black, relaxed into a gaze of attentive wonderment as I described the plot of a work that contrasted the raw, sentient beauty of the music of suffering Croatian refugees - victims of an early twentieth-century Balkans conflict - with the egotism of famous, bitchy opera singers and musicians on a private yacht owned by the Archduke Ferdinand.

Summoned to the scene of a tempest, in which fires blazed against the dark hills, after numerous episodes of the wealthy musicians attempting to prove their greatness over each other in shallow performances of their overdone repertoires in the sumptuous dining hall of this opulent craft, people in rags climbed on board and, through their playing of traditional instruments and the incredibly euphonious wanness of the women's voices, astounded the superior artisans with the sorrowful magnificence of their heart-rending sounds.

The gravity of this comment on artistic creation induced a pleasing fascination upon Samantha's face. The joy this created within me was enhanced by the gorgeous cries of strings and pipes. Something of the euphoria of camp fires and starry nights, embodied in this music, hushed, like a perfumed vapour, into the room. The thought of repeating this with her constantly, at will, made me see the satisfying self-awareness that could result. But it was really just a dream. For her, this was just another night. Despite that, this one unfolded like a silk ribbon; then, around midnight, she, clutching her forehead - she suffered from migraines - said, "Oh well, must go home and put some pills into my head. How boring."

I was uncertain as to why she had decided to let me know that this prospect was insipid, but I did not question her. I was too overjoyed in the context of my low expectations to want to risk the unusual sensation of wholesome placidity that had descended upon me with the forging of our friendship being decimated by the making of impertinent suggestions. We walked outside to her parked car and she spun around and tried to hug me. Why I made an issue of her foot coming into contact with mine is something the vast majority of normal people would be at a loss as to explain.

Clearly upset at her attempt at affection being thwarted by this absurdity, she blasted down the street and I was left in the darkness of the lonely night.

* * * * * * * * * * *

I visited my grandmother for the final time. She was very worried about Wayne and Kay. Her mission in life now was to keep family relationships intact. The maintaining of my older brother's marriage was proving to be a real challenge. I told her that I did not hold out a great deal of hope for Wayne.

I said, "At his age, he should have a coherent plan for the future. He should be contemplating ways of making money instead of smearing fruit into people's carpets."

This caused my grandmother to become defensive. The loyalty and concern that she showed for Wayne could only be described as love. The bond that had developed between these two could not have possibly been predicted when they were living with each other.

She said, "You have to understand Wayne. You've got to let him get over things himself - and you can't go around agitating him."

"But", I replied, "he should know better. He has to know better. What happened to him happened to him years ago. What he needs to do now is to make some effort to discover himself. But he's got an inane prejudice against academic analysis. And we know where that comes from."

My voice had risen.

My grandmother then said that "the treatment he received as a child from his mother was appalling".

"But", I interrupted, "the treatment he received was no different from what I got."

"But", she replied, "you're different personalities."

I was not swayed; then she said, "When Joan [my mother] used to visit here, after you had all come to live here, Wayne used to become hysterical. He would sit in your father's car and refuse to come out. She used to beat him up badly. Many times he came running into my bedroom in the middle of the night, screaming – you can't imagine the nightmares he must have been having! The expression in his eyes – it was wild, glazed, frightening; he was in absolute despair! He used to lie down next to me in bed and I used to stroke his head. It would often take him hours to calm down."

I was disgusted by the thought of my brother suffering like that. My grandmother was running a business at the time and sleep would have been at a premium. It would not have been easy for her.

"Often", she continued, "Keith used to have to nurse him in the lounge-room when he became hysterical. He did it for hours."

I looked away, disappointed. I should not have been so harsh on someone whose situation had been deplorable.

"It's difficult", I said, "imagining how someone from Kay's background can possibly comprehend Wayne's position. It's like expecting people to understand what it's like being in combat."

"I'm working on her, though," my grandmother replied.

She was confident of her ability to impart understanding.

"I wonder", I said, "what it must be like for my mother. Having three kids and not knowing what they're about."

"She was not the least bit interested," my grandmother replied. "She was glad to get away. She rejected you all."

* * * * * * * * * * *

When I visited Paul Humphrey and told him about Richard Wain's changing cubicle experience, he said, "And he was with his girlfriend!"

"He told me," I said, "proudly, that he had slept with over a thousand women."

"Yeah," Paul replied, "but how many of them were worth having a relationship with?"

After elucidating his scorpion theory, he added, "He's unable to sustain a normal relationship with a decent woman."

I then questioned him about this expression "map", and he shook his head and said, "Those guys are so adolescent – particularly Dob. The last time I went to one of their parties, something incredible happened."

I then got the story about "people milling around, cheering, watching Dob screwing some woman in a spa".

"There were two other people in that spa", he said, "and about ten others looking on."

Paul's face was screwed up in distaste at the recollection of this immature bravado.

"A rumour had gone around", he continued, "that Dob was gay. I suppose he wanted to quell it."

"So what if he was gay?" I said.

"Exactly," he replied.

He then made his comment about Dob requiring a psychiatrist and I said, "He flits around at parties because he's convinced that popularity with the masses will give him some sort of long-term fulfilment – a superficial notoriety. And it's a pity. You would think that he would have seen by now that life was more important than that."

"I can't see any of those guys", Paul said, "having a good relationship with a nice woman. You know, Brad Shilkin walked up to me at that party and said, 'I'm so envious of you. You've always had a girlfriend.'

"'Well, so what?' I said. He got defensive, thinking that I thought he was trying to take the piss out of me. He seemed to think that this was some big deal – a guy like me having girlfriends. I just thought that it was normal."

For some people – yes.

* * * * * * * * * *

As strange as it might sound, the desire to bask in the warm balminess of late afternoon on white sand before a blue ocean beneath an orange sun with a beautiful, interesting woman was an aspiration ironically unfamiliar to me. The last few years had seen little opportunity - even of the consideration - for this. I had the beach, but did I have the woman? The beach had been a revelation: its beauty, its sensuality, the colours and the peaceful swirling in clean water - a place that opened hearts. I wanted to combine its magical tranquillity with the sublime pleasure of lying with a sensuous, intelligent stunner, and I knew that the reason I wanted this was not quite as clear as any normal individual would suspect. The desire to experience demulcent bliss constantly in a land blessed with the light of luck had proven to be more significant than the thrills generated from an involvement in exotic dangers. This transformation in thinking - the transferring of excitement from adventure to domesticity - represented a crisis point in any photojournalist's life, and, for me, the point had been reached. No more tearing between shattered houses to avoid sniper fire; no more invasions into the dank heart of refugee camps to record the bony stares of expiring lives; no more freezing showers, malaria and rat-infested beds. The time for change had arrived.

I rang Samantha and unfortunately she couldn't make it. A Dutch friend of hers had just unexpectedly called. I was definitely going to the beach. Did both of them want to go? She couldn't say, as "he" had yet to arrive. She invited me to her place and I said that I would ring her later "if I want to come around".

"Please do," she replied, with an excessively pleasing friendliness.

The Dutch friend had just arrived in Perth. Naturally, I was egotistical enough at first to assume that Samantha's keenness for me to visit stemmed purely from a desire to see me; but then I realised that she may have required some protection and security. Still, I wasn't complaining about a jovial invitation: her insistence had the effect of wiping out, temporarily, that wistfulness, often present, which caused me to want to be anywhere other than where I was. It was usually not a problem with place but of situation, for most places with the right mood and company are acceptable; but I was forever wanting to be displaced, psychologically. There were moments when this melancholic desire for displacement was so acute that I would not eat the things that I normally enjoyed. Sometimes the motivation to experience pleasure itself seemed like a cynical invention designed to highlight the implausibility of it's ever happening. Even during sex I thought of incongruous things - share prices, the stock market, the chemistry of photography, something that someone had said to me the day before about a game of football, anything other than the person with whom I was. My unsatiated lust for passion and savagery, for rewarding exhilaration, was as much a bugbear as it was a treasure and Samantha was making me experience both.

The beach was an ideal place to be in in a satisfied state of mind. I chose a spot of calmness beside a groyne which separated the end of the beach from that place where the coast became dangerously submerged. On the side of this structure, built from concrete and granite boulders, where I swam, the water was still and green. Its benign clarity made it possible to see the uniform ranges of sandy ripples that ran, like bare mountains, along the bottom, with a serene predictability not found in the foaming clashes of water against rock that were transpiring, in such fury, on the other side. Before entering the seductive equanimity of the quiet side, I had stood upon the groyne and looked out over at the clashing waters, smashing into the exposed reef of the jagged coast. Each frenetic movement of water, inspired by some new tempest, caused a different explosion of mists and liquids to hurtle, in swishing cries, towards the sky. The blueness of this untarnished canopy above infused an array of colours into the turmoil of waters whose restlessness expressed itself in breaths of seething spray. To be amongst that now would have been unnecessarily dangerous beyond all belief. Every time the sea pulled back in preparation for another violent assault on the unyielding rocks, a smooth sheet of gleaming glass would form on the surface, from which the peaks of seaweed-covered reefs would protrude, before being compressed and then shattered by the blasting return of the tempestuous tides. I turned my back on this and went into the water on the tranquil side, where I had the impression of being soothed in a spiritually-cleansing bath of luxuriant sea. Floating on my back and staring up at the heavens, I felt adrift from the transitory nuisances of this bickering world. A brief moment of being uncaring of my own condition swept through me. The sublime forgetfulness of this situation resembled the freezing of desire that takes place when the correct action enters the frame. It feels as though the pulse of life has breathed in and sees no need to exhale again.

I breathed in, and spun over; blue sky was followed by the white bottom and then the liquid glass of the wafting surface. A small child stumbled down the low bank of powdery beach and wobbled towards the hard wet sand. The mother of this child followed her offspring to the water's edge and, gathering her child in her arms, lowered him into the bubbling water that rushed towards the creamy shore. The child's limbs waved about in a frenzy of joy. Together he and his mother giggled in happy separation from the squabbles and aspirations that beset this desperate earth.

In the air above them, a lone gull swooped like a single idea across the vast, azure consciousness of a different world. Taut and motionless, its wings were locked in a certainty of direction enviable for the simplicity and firmness of its aim. The contented sustaining of such purpose is nigh impossible for the grandiloquent, protean mind, but I was just happy at this point to be enjoying a brief respite from the vicissitudes of my grandiose endeavours. Coming to the beach had had the impact of an arresting moment. It was, however, not destined to last. Commitment to a future built on love caused me to withdraw from it, like the seagull, to pursue a natural desire rather than the ethereal constraints of ambitious life.

'Get your emotional life sorted out first,' I thought, 'then worry about the rest.'

* * * * * * * * * *

The block of flats in which Samantha lived was one of those fifties conglomerations, practical, but practically hellish to the eye. Her studio flat, to my mind, was dominated by her big double bed. The royal-blue quilt which adorned it was as vibrant and mysterious as the undercurrent of thoughts that electrified its owner. Around the floor were indiscriminate piles of books – novels and non-fiction works of environmental science – and haphazardly strewn notes, frantically written and cast about. In the far corner, next to some glass sliding doors that led out to a balcony, was a tall plant. Between the plant and the end of the bed was a desk covered in books with notes protruding from them in a plethora of different angles. A print of a Cézanne landscape was on the wall above the telephone, which sat on a small table beside the bed. An air of transience and intellectual activity pervaded the room. The effect of someone keen on learning to the detriment of tidiness was clear. She apologised for the mess. I shook my head, unconcerned.

Her friend was tall and blond. His skin was very tanned. He had been travelling around the north of Australia on a motorcycle. A beetroot patch of burnt skin was on the end of his brown nose. Both Samantha and I warned him of the danger of this but he seemed unperturbed by the prospect of cancer. In fact, he seemed unperturbed by everything. His laid-back open-mindedness made him instantly likeable. When warning him of the hazards of the sun, he smiled, appreciatively, as if his relatives were chastising him to take more care. He felt no need to comment; he was a quiet man who felt little need for idle chatter. I quickly realised that it would have been a chore for someone as frenetically communicative as Samantha to have been with him all night, for her distaste and fear of silences with someone with whom she was not totally familiar could take on neurotic proportions. His answers to her questions were delivered with relaxed, sensible, unhurried brevity. He felt no need to enquire of her anything of which she was enquiring of him. I was astonished and mystified by his easy, gracious detachment, particularly in the face of such inquisitive beauty. Was he blind?

When I first walked in, I had this horrible sensation that the pair of them had just had sex in the shower. Both of them had wet hair but I soon discovered that they had been down at the beach as well. Konrad seemed so disembowelled of insecurities and nagging desires that the experience for which I had craved – the company of this raven-haired creature at the beach under a sky of iridescent peach – would have been completely wasted on him. He was already so stripped of painful aspirations that the idea of ravishing the talkative, succulent, charismatic creature gesticulating furiously before his big, placid green eyes could not have possibly added to his already monumental contentment.

He sat on the floor casually rolling cigarettes. Rivers of bleached gold ran through his hair. Over the course of two bottles of champagne, he remained impeccably helpful in satisfying Samantha's burgeoning curiosity about the people whom they had met whilst living together in a kibbutz in Israel. He was expansive and courteous in his responses to her enquiries. He was equally politely forthcoming when asked about his recent sojourns. He produced an amusing anecdote about a friend – someone whom Samantha knew – who, after several bottles of beer, had attempted to seduce a policewoman who was trying to reduce the noise at a wild party in Port Hedland. The policewoman, increasingly agitated by the unwanted advances, applied an arm lock and then literally threw Konrad's friend out the door. The three of us rolled around the floor, giggling hysterically.

"Typical, typical," Samantha managed, between chuckles caused by this reaffirmation of the amorousness of Konrad's friend, a person famous for eccentric seductions.

This one, however, had gone horribly wrong.

"I vent zoo dar pooloese wan", Konrad said, "and ask ed zem if he koold go if he apologised. Tzey let him go."

Such rare diplomatic skills had, so it turned out, saved the lovestruck friend on a few other occasions as well. While Konrad informed us of these occasions, the wind began to howl so ferociously outside that it felt as though we were in the grip of a calamitous storm. Great cracks of livid air smashed into the flat. We were not more than half a kilometre from the coast. The impression of unrestrained wildness fitted in perfectly with Samantha's loquacious gusto, her emotive gesticulations and her unbridled thought processes which cast up conversation from a seemingly bottomless well of memory, association and experience.

The topic got on to men talking to women about their romantic relationships.

"I think it's lovely when men do this," Samantha said, pointedly looking at Konrad and deliberately avoiding eye contact with me.

She then went on to describe a series of evenings she had had with a man in the kibbutz, whom Konrad knew; this man had often come into her room specifically to talk to her about his relationship with his girlfriend, whom he was missing.

"He used to sit on the edge of my bed", Samantha said, "and cross his legs, and then go into wonderful detail about the things he and his girlfriend used to do. He was lovely."

Her description of this man's love lasted for about ten minutes. Throughout it, I may as well not have been in the room. All her comments were poignantly directed at Konrad. I fell back on to the floor and stared up at the ceiling. My pretence of indifference was fired by an irrational belief that Samantha was trying to tell Konrad something, and certainly not me. Why she had to do it in front of me, like this, I did not know. I don't think Konrad did either. A subtle hint of worried perplexity managed to sneak into his normally unruffled eyes. The directness of Samantha's suggestion caused me pain; every word of her speech was like a hammer cracking into my skull. Her description of another man as "lovely" was deflating enough, but why she then had to go and make it obvious to yet another one, right in front of my face, that he too could attain this elevated status by indulging in the practice of telling her his private thoughts about his lovers was beyond me. Her vindictive behaviour reeked of cruelty. The harshness by which I was being judged transcended the bounds of acceptability. I was not incensed as much as shocked at the childish fashion in which she had chosen to thwart my unjustified ambitions. It was bad enough being made to feel guilty about possessing normal feelings, but why did women have to feel insulted if someone in whom they were not interested showed a desire for them? I was flabbergasted by this arrogant attitude.

Samantha got up to remove her contact lenses in preparation for giving me a lift home. While she was in the bathroom, with the door was open so that she could listen, Konrad and I began talking about loyalty in relationships. I decided, for the benefit of Samantha, to say something openly controversial. The remark could be described as being "the seed of polemicism".

It was: "I would not be particularly concerned if a woman with whom I was having a relationship decided to have an affair with another man, provided that she was still interested in me. I think that the existence of someone else will not influence her ultimate opinion of me."

Then came the real killer: "I think that women are more promiscuous than men," suggesting that I did not know one attractive woman "who had not had regular sex since the age of seventeen".

"It's opportunity", I added, "rather than morality that stimulates promiscuity. And some people get so many opportunities, it must be rather difficult to deal with them all."

Then the inevitable backlash came. From the bathroom, Samantha screamed out, "Knubs, you're so full of shit!"

It was remarkable how I managed to be not simply "full of shit" – oh no – but "so" full of it that it was incredible that "so" much of it could be crammed into "so" small and insignificant a space as my head.

Konrad and I smiled at each other knowingly. It appeared as though Samantha's reputation for spirited bluntness had traversed international borders. I may have shown amusement at this recognition of liberal individuality, but inside I was devastated.

In the car, I tried to remain silent. She enthusiastically tried to begin a conversation. She was oblivious of the hurt that she had inflicted. She started telling me about a very good friend of hers who she had just heard had arrived back in Australia after an absence of several years. Her good-naturedness at the prospect of seeing this woman was detestable. I could not resist the temptation to respond, but I made sure that my comments were short, almost non-existent. This rapidly brought a change in Samantha's behaviour. Infuriated, she raised her left hand and swept it through the air, demanding to know why I was "being so quiet".

"This", she exclaimed, "is not like you. What's wrong?"

I did not say anything. I just looked at her, bewildered that she did not have the faintest idea of why I had become so gloomy. It almost seemed like a crime against humanity – this coupling of unmitigated vitriol with unjustified arrogance. I was clearly an innocent victim of the vile injustices of this impeachable world and she, dispassionately oblivious, wanted to talk about a friend! Someone I did not even know!

Again, she asked, "Why are you doing this? What's going on? What's wrong?" while I remained silent, thinking to myself: 'God, can't a man just sulk in peace?'

She gripped the steering-wheel tightly as if she were contemplating the taking of some difficult and mysterious decision and said, "Look... I was really glad you came along tonight. It would have been really hard just being alone with Konrad. He's a lovely guy [God, not another one] but he's too quiet for someone like me. You're the only guy I know at the moment who's not uneasy with strangers. I invited two other guys along as well, but they're very shy so it's probably lucky they didn't come."

This was not heartening news. All it did was to confirm my suspicions regarding her uncharacteristic friendliness on the phone.

Then she blurted out, "Why this silence? I can't cope with it! You're normally talkative. Please!" as her left hand continued to rise up and down in a pained gesture of irascible confusion.

I kept my mouth shut. What was the point in replying? But I was confused as well. I really did not know whether I had a legitimate right to behave sourly, or whether I was overreacting. But my response was out of my control. Some sick mechanism buried deep within my skull was causing me to behave in this absurd fashion and there was not a thing I could do about it. The entire black soulless universe, stretching into oblivion, seemed like a morbid chamber that choked free expression. Why couldn't I just break this shackle?

Then Samantha said, "Over the last few days I've found you intriguing. That doesn't mean I didn't find you interesting beforehand – because I did – it's just that you've begun talking about your relationships with women. Is there any reason why you've started doing this?"

Even I, in my present mood, knew that this one could not go unanswered. The real answer was: 'I was hoping that it would lead to your saying that you wanted to have a relationship with me,' but I, choosing the cowardly option, said, "When you're with someone for a certain period of time, invariably the subject gets on to relationships."

My comment was made even more guarded by the tone of my voice. It was garnished with a subtle hint of surprise. Surely this was the only reason why a man would bring up a subject like this with a woman? Has there ever been anything more obvious?

Samantha, momentarily accepting my false interpretation of my behaviour, then revealed her suspicions regarding it by saying, "You're much more interesting when you talk about relationships. It's a lot more interesting than fathers. I don't mean to cause offence, but fathers are boring."

Her voice was raised aggressively. Her attempt to shock me out of my sepulchral docility only caused me to become even more introverted and incensed. In response to her allusion to offence, I snapped, "Well, you have!" and this made her go silent.

It also made me experience regret, for my curiosity over her question as to why I had begun talking about relationships was far from dissipated. Time after time after time it is demonstrated to us that sulkiness neither serves problems nor wins respect, yet we still persist in the vain hope that an apology will be made so that our insurmountable lust for victimisation will be appeased. I was rapidly reaching the conclusion that this petulant vanity, this fantastically useless pride, this unavoidable response to the memory of desperate hurts made the idealistic construct of maturity an impossible dream. What the mind learns rationally, I realised, is unlearnt by the powder keg of irrational thought. Everything I had ever learnt about the secrets of success was being discarded in this involuntary return to a time when all ill-conceived acts were evil and grotesque. And now it was her turn.

"Why", I asked, "did you ask me that question about relationships?"

This question came after a lengthy period of mutually accepted stand-offish quietude. She decided to continue with it. I was not the least surprised by this. What else could I expect? Sulkiness breeds like a contagious disease. I tried again.

This time she said, with a philosophical air too intense for my optimistic taste, "Because it helps you to discover things about people."

'Oh dear', I thought. As I had been so desirous of hearing 'Because I'm falling in love with you,' anything else came across as a severe disappointment. Being a kind of phlegmatic optimist, I was even capable of creating bizarre illusions in hopeless situations such as this.

A sensation of proud, unruffled strength seemed to overcome her. Perhaps she was pleased that she was capable of having this experience whilst indulging in uncommunicativeness in the presence of another? How was I to know? Despite her flattering suggestion that I "could see into things deeply", I felt as clueless as the day I was born. All communication between myself and her over the last few hours had, instead of pleasantly demystifying things, only made our increasingly melancholic situation even more arcane. The human mind, forever believing that comprehensive results are close, plunges on relentlessly in pursuit of its vain goals. Disappointments are consequently more common than revealing conclusions.

It was this moribund thought that preoccupied me as she pulled the car up into Brian's driveway. After the tribulations of the journey, we managed, for a time, to be civil to each other; this lasted until she leaned over to kiss me goodnight, and I, stupidly, said, "This way you won't tread on my foot."

The effect was devastating.

The following day I woke up desperate to speak to her. All day I rang and there was no answer. I knew that, had I come into contact with her on that day, I would have given her the truth. This added a further frustrating dimension to my wish to clear the air. All that day the atmosphere was full of luminous surreality. The growing realisation that there was one, and only one, course of action was beginning to loom up clearly through the mists of my dreams. There was no escaping from the fact that only the truth can satisfy and only the truth can bring a sharp end to fool's despair. It is the final resort after all other options are exhausted and I had reached a point where I was desperate to use it, but the chance was not there.

* * * * * * * * * *

I sat clutching my head. I was certain that there would be no end to these disappointments. There only seemed a myriad of possibilities of how I could achieve this disillusionment. I shook my head and wondered how long this feeling of uselessness would last; it had the power of permanency. Small things annoyed me bitterly. At this moment, I had no means of escape. I was forced to face those things that I constantly tried to ignore: the futility of life without an emotional crutch – the impossibility of romantic success. Just when I had reached a stage where excitement should come, despair filled its place. So many times I played over in my mind the event that had led to this, and each time I could not find justification for my lack of opportunism. I doubted if fate would give me the opportunity to apologise. I could see no end to a situation that really, in the deepest psychological sense, was not my fault. I despaired over the waste of this. I was not going to be understood by people who had not had the experience. The last thing women require is to be convinced that someone is capable of sudden, inexplicable fits of nefarious moodiness. I was worried that this feeling of angered futility would get worse. There was no reason why it should not. I felt that there were going to be plenty of opportunities in the near future to make this terrible sensation become the prelude to suicide. I was in desperate need of love and knew that I had no chance of ever getting it. I wandered around the house performing small tasks to help me concentrate on something less dramatic than the terminal free-fall in which I was fated to be. I was detached from the pleasures of this life.

Eventually, I sat at the living-room table and stared out the window at the cold-blue brilliance of the sky. I dreaded the thought of night. All that darkness. I placed my arms on the table and rested my head on them. I imagined how soothing it would be to have her stroking the back of my neck. A simple act that millions receive which would never happen to me. I was powerless to have this hand of birth placed with intimate care on the soft parts of something unused to the mysteries of affection. A miracle would be required for me and there were very few miracles on this planet, other than life itself. But life itself at the moment was a useless exercise in unconscious masochism. Something more powerful than my rational mind was responsible for my regrettable behaviour. All the consciousness of its existence was futile against the brainwashing magnitude of this internal beast, whose awakening from its slumber was caused by the fear that love will hurt. My rational mind was not great enough to overcome an immovable belief that women were made to reject.

I sighed, knowing that despite my knowledge of myself – rationally – I could not control the irrational, and the irrational in my case was truly that – irrational. My actions were remarkably ridiculous to the rational mind. Oh thank you fate. May I have the pleasure of shaking your bony hand? You're a real wonder, and of such use, for you have given me the charming ability to find disdainfulness endearing. What an essential ingredient for personal development. Thank you for the hole you have created.

FIVE

The following night was my last night in the country. Wayne, Kay, Greg, Frances, Ana, Paul, Mark Unger, Samantha and Konrad were invited around. My grandmother had been keen on Brian's having a barbecue so that a harmonious evening out would help to calm Wayne's frazzled disposition. The chances of short-term success in this regard were high: Wayne was in excellent form. He spent a considerable time in the swimming pool entertaining his daughter, whose mirthfulness was inextricably linked to her father's return to normality. Between splashing matches and serene hugs, he would make requests for drinks by using such expressions as: "Don't you lot know that a man can't live on bread alone?" or "How many times do I have to say it? A man's not a camel," and "Strewth, no doubt about it, the war office [the wife] is definitely out of form," while indicating, with the rueful glares of hard-done outrage, his empty beer can. Greg was usually the waiter; he would slowly swagger to the side of the pool, a cheeky gleam in his eye, and ask, with sarcastic reverence, whether "Your Majesty had a preference" and His Majesty would say, "Anything made from amber, as long as it's been chilled to perfection. Now move."

Kay sat on an easy-chair besides the pool. She knew that her husband's current pretence to good-natured derision was fickle; her comments were conveyed with a fear that they would be greeted with cynicism. Her trepidation was equally as capable of igniting Wayne's delicate volatility as any direct attack. When she spoke, Wayne looked at her with a demeanour of enforced repression of his still unquenched hostility and, sipping on his beer with this sudden stare of serious but curbed impatience, would listen, agitated by the pathos of his wife attempting to enlighten him on subjects of which he was already aware. To some people, servility is as offensive as gross belligerence. The important thing was not that Kay was failing miserably in attempting to educate her husband, but that he, unheralded, against all expectations, probably for the first time in his life, was determined to maintain a priority of self-restraint. The brooding, volcanic rivers of fury that scorched his overheated veins when being forced to listen to something old were being kept in check by a tenuous desire for equanimity, born, I assumed, from my grandmother's relentless pursuit of the cause of family bliss. All of it seemed grotesquely fragile to my faithless eyes.

In contrast, Mark Unger was overflowing with gregarious cultivation. His gentle composure oozed with the strength of light-hearted agreeableness. Frances, who had swayed in wearing a sky-blue Laura Ashley ensemble, was very impressed by the quality of approachable peace that flowed out of Mark, like a messianic radiance, subtle and strong, a creature liberated from all evil.

"He's got a real air about him," she said, with a sort of dreamy surprise.

I watched him dealing with his two sons' needs with humorous patience. Then I showed him a portfolio of photographs of incidents witnessed in Yugoslavia and the Middle East. His imaginative quips regarding their contents had me howling with joy. One shot in the back streets of Cairo showed a large group of children responding to the unexpected intrusion of my camera. The full range of responses was displayed. In the middle of this group one of the children, arms spread blissfully at the long-awaited arrival of his inevitable recognition, was flying towards the lens, face ablaze, as though the interest I had showed in him by raising my Pentax could only have been born from the beauty of his extroverted magnificence.

Mark chuckled happily and, pointing to this kid, beamed and said, "There's always at least one in a crowd."

His amused and immediate acknowledgement of someone else's joy reflected his own satisfied state of mind. He told me about the last "existential crisis" that he had had. It was poignant in the context of speaking to me, as he had this frustrating struggle, now resolved, about forsaking his career development for travel, for incident, for the unexpected; but he overcame this traditional clash of youthful exuberance with future concerns by realising that he was "a builder". He said this with the weight of having experienced pertinent self-analysis. The fact of personal realisation had removed a burden from his soul. This realisation had caused him to accept that he had to start a business and "go as far as possible". I then told him that I was on the threshold of making a decision "of similar proportions". My change in direction was due not just to love – although this acted as a catalyst – but to a growing tiredness with "the foolish ways of humanity" and an "interest in recording beauty".

As we spoke, Wayne ventured by and, unusually for him, did not comment. My photographs were spread out on the top of a washing machine next to a sink full of ice and drinks. The photographs had been brought over from Europe at the request of my family but, in the time that I had been back in Perth, none of them had expressed any desire to see them. In Wayne's case, it was jealousy; in the case of the others, it was just a lack of interest. I was not expecting them to be curious about things they could not, and did not, wish to imagine and, in a way, I was glad, for being ignored as a child had given me a distaste for uninvited intervention. My family's lack of interest had freed me from having to explain my eccentric ways, and this meant that I did not have to consider others when making decisions which affected my life.

Such a private and an unsociable condition, however, did not necessarily exclude the converse of invited sharing from being propitious. Sitting in the front seat of his car with the door open, Mark, making it clear that there was an intense excitement behind the misleading veneer of mundane domesticity, said, "I haven't seen my wife and daughter for two hours, and already I miss them."

A look of pained, dreamy wonderment then came upon his face as he added, the streets slumbering in a blanket of balmy air, the following, "It's only been a few hours since I last saw them, and it already feels like months."

Then there was the question of challenges.

"There's so much to consider," he said. "You really need someone else. I'm no genius. I can't think of everything."

His two sons sat silently on the back seat, waiting to leave. It was inconceivable that their small world could encompass the relevance of our conversation or the pertinence of that which their father was about to state.

"Travel", their father said, "presents very few challenges. Probably the major challenge is the arranging of accommodation at the right price – that is, dealing with the street merchants trying to rip you off. But being in one place and trying to juggle a business, a family and a social life is definitely much more difficult. It has far greater depth. And the rewards are therefore much greater."

I smiled and said, "I was once described by someone as being a big issues drifter. Kind of liked it at the time. But I'm starting to come around to the idea that big issues are best confined to dinner parties. Life is about small pleasures of vast magnitude. But I had to try everything first, just to make sure that this was true."

He smiled; then I told him about the challenge I was facing with regard to Samantha.

"I've been out with her on numerous occasions", I said, "and I haven't even dreamed of laying hands on her. I'm besotted by her."

Mark nodded his head and acknowledged my interest by saying, "For you to show that kind of restraint can only mean one thing - love."

"I'm afraid so," I said.

"Good luck," he replied.

"Thanks," I said, "but I feel confused and full of dread."

He chuckled and then remarked, "You really are in love then."

"I'm consumed," I replied. "My state of mind is completely determined by her unpredictable attitude towards me. My emotional state has been swinging for the past few weeks on a thin thread, like a child's. Not really what I had in mind after the pressures of Yugoslavia."

"The best made plans..." Mark said, tilting his head, philosophically. "We all know what can happen to them."

"It was hardly even a plan," I replied. "I just went from one maelstrom into another under the pretext of being a mature individual exerting some measure of control over my personal destiny - but that's just an illusion. We're all fooling ourselves."

Mark giggled in jocund reinforcement of the knowledge that such a sweeping comment could only come from my lips.

"I used to be an existentialist", I continued, "but not now. I used to think that decisions and choices were made on the basis that they were being made wholly independent of the past, as if I were an individual, as if I were really responsible for my preferences and tastes. But that's just rubbish. Even my choice of profession is directly related to past circumstances that were right out of my control."

"But that's you though," Mark replied. "Most people make choices because they can see a long-term benefit. But you needed to do something unbelievably exciting in the short term to compensate for a dismal upbringing. Yours was not a normal decision."

"I know," I said, "but the point is, I had to do it. It was beyond common sense. It had the potency of an instinct."

Mark burst into generous laughter.

"Pure drama," I smiled, "hey?"

"Imagine going to a job interview", Mark pondered, "and being asked why you chose to do your last job and saying, 'There was no choice. I was drawn to it irresistibly. It had the potency of an instinct.'"

I chuckled and said, "I'd love to see the reaction of the interview panel, particularly if you were applying for a job as a financial controller."

"Maybe they just might", Mark replied, "bend uncomfortably over the table, after a period of confusion, and say, 'What do you mean by that?'"

"I'd probably confuse them even further", I said, "by saying, 'It's a phenomenon that cannot be expressed with mere language. Allow me the privilege of creating a visual image that goes some way to exposing the prophetic core of this most beguiling of mysteries.'"

"You'd definitely get the job," Mark replied.

"Particularly", I remarked, "if I said that I considered myself to be in that small minority whose choice of profession was not really a choice – not something based on common sense or the desire to be accepted – but an inevitable response to a profound necessity. Like an artist. Like a delicate flower drawn inexorably towards the dangerous and beautiful rays of a violent sun."

Mark chortled at the underlying arrogance of my remark. Friendship was often based on the ability of both parties to find each other's worst aspects endearing and amusing. He had always found my superior disregard for the values of the majority to be hilarious and I had always found his inherent belief in his own physical attraction to be a source of unbelievable humour.

"So," I said, "do you still think that you're one of the most gorgeous creatures on earth?"

"My children are now," he replied.

"The rose of Albany", I said, "has given birth to three resplendent petals."

I stuck my head through the door and asked, "Do you think that your father's beautiful?"

His sons did not show any reaction.

"Okay then," I said, "do you think that your father's a great father?"

Once again, no reaction.

"Come on," Mark asked, looking into the rear-vision mirror, "am I a great father?"

Again, no response.

"Too young", I said, "to appreciate."

"At least", Mark replied, "I've got future recognition to look forward to."

"I wish I did," I said.

"She must be quite a woman," he replied.

"Out of the ordinary," I said.

"Oh well," he replied, "I'll have to leave you to it."

After he drove off, I wandered back down the driveway. A ring of light blue tinged the sky above the horizon. Slowly, it fused into deep-purple-blue, a porcelain-like backdrop of pristine turquoise, gleaming with the bone-white flowers of blooming stars. The relative youth, against its potential age, of the ancient skies was reflected in the freshness and untarnished perfection of its remarkable colour: the dollops of luminous ivory encrusted on it stood out like splashes of creamy foam on the unblemished, blue surface of a benign sea. The crescent of the moon, its back arched towards the ocean, pointed towards that part of the sky where the orange wake of the deceased sun was unfolding in a sombre glow of breathless remembrance. The quiet of the spacious streets was mirrored in the crepuscular peace of the awakening heavens; what peace may have existed within me was being crushed by the mixed feelings of Samantha's impending arrival. The tranquillity of the evening formed an ironic contrast to the growing turmoil inside me.

Eventually, after Paul had appeared, I took some chairs outside and all of us sat down on the patio beside the swimming pool. The sun had disappeared completely and the still world was now ablaze with stars. A dark blue line ringed the black sheet above us. The feeling of contented dissociation, inherent in the sky, and made apparent to us by the incalculable distances above, seemed infused into the happy throng. It appeared as though only our voices could disrupt the quiet that lingered, like an arcane presence, in the great void of space which separated us from the possibility, way out across the galaxy, of other worlds.

When Samantha arrived with Konrad – Wayne, Kay and Greg had already gone – two seats were available. She got one next to me. She was wearing a red dress with small white flowers, that came up above the knee and ran up her torso to form a large circle around her shoulders. She crossed her left leg over the right. In normal circumstances, I would have been tempted to glance down at the perfect tubes of firm flesh which sprang, like miracles of libidinous growth, from the blazing-red furnace of her attire but, on this occasion, I was so transfixed by her personality, with its welter of contradictions and ideas, that I did not give a damn what lay beneath her neck. All that was irrelevant against the possibilities afforded by the movements of her luxuriant mouth – or it would have been, had I not been so painfully petrified and staid.

She and I got involved in a conversation about impending capitalism in China, hardly seductive, before the discourse moved on to French collaboration during the German occupation. I was appalled by my defensive seriousness and, underneath it, I was thinking, 'Jesus Christ, why can't I just indulge in witty, sexual banter with this glorious creature, and stop being such a complete wanker?' but I was unable to lose my controlled, protective demeanour. This was the prelude, I knew, to failure at the final hurdle.

Then the conversation progressed to a debate on the economic realities of Chile. She took the point of view that Chile was a hotbed of economic disasters, while I, remaining destructively defensive, suggested it was basically "a First World country", in comparison with other nations in South America, citing the fact that it got numerous economic refugees from Argentina. Through this useless intercourse, I was aghast at my argumentative stance; but I felt helpless to change it.

At the first opportunity, she spun around and got herself involved in the discussion that had been going on around us. Throughout the rest of the evening, her body language was indicative of someone uninterested in my existence. Any comments I made were not sent in her direction. I found it exceptionally difficult to look at her when speaking. She ended up dominating the conversation. She never looked at me at all in any of her many, passionate outbursts of information. I was staggered by her knowledge of matters related to conservation, pollution and nutrition.

Inside, Frances said to me, while preparing tea, "A real catch there, Knubs. Her phone must be ringing hot."

I acknowledged this reality with a rueful feeling of inferiority. When we went outside again, I said, to the group, that I thought, "generally", that "English people were more conversational than Australians". I said that Australians were capable of "making a lot of noise", but were not as adept or interested in exchanges of ideas. On making this radical suggestion, I was met with a barrage of disagreement, the most vehement of which came from Samantha, who seemed to take the comment personally, screaming in my right ear, "Rubbish!"

In response to this, I said, not looking at her, but at Paul and Frances, "Well, I have lived for a considerable length of time in both countries, so I feel qualified, at least, to make some comment", as Samantha kept up her abrasive imprecations, which, coming from her, were so passionately beautiful: "Nonsense! Rubbish! Ridiculous! Absolute crap!"

I then said, looking down, deliberately avoiding eye contact with her, "that I didn't say my opinion was the definitive one. It's just been my experience".

Paul then tried to calm things down by saying that it was "an emotive subject" on which "no one on earth" could possibly claim to have "the definitive opinion".

Inside, after Frances left, Paul, Samantha, Konrad and I sat in the lounge-room. I asked Samantha if she wanted to have a look at my black and white photographs of the Middle East. When she saw the first one, she gasped in astonishment. While she and Konrad looked at the photographs, Paul and I discussed the prison system and psychiatry; as we spoke, I felt an uneasy immodesty sweeping through me. I was afraid to look in Samantha's direction. She and Konrad were making comments about my photographs. I felt a great need to do something eccentric but it was a feeling held in place by an equally great impulse to be restrained and aloof. This internal conflict, I knew, was at opposite poles to the serene state in which Konrad appeared to be floating through life.

After finishing with the photographs, he said, "Great photos", with a look of sincere surprise and admiration. Although Samantha agreed with him, she felt uncomfortable about admitting her admiration. I could relate to the experience: it was exactly how I was feeling towards her – admiration kept in check by a need to be distant, independent, unaffected and unconcerned for fear of experiencing an embarrassing rejection.

"People," Konrad added, nodding his head with an understanding that infused his simple remark with a mysterious and penetrating meaning.

Then Samantha asked, "Why did you bring these photographs over here?"

To which I replied, with serious accuracy, "Because my family wanted to see them." Normally, I would have said something like, 'To impress beautiful women like you,' but I was already sensitive about appearing superior.

When the three of them got up to leave, Samantha asked me if I wanted her address. When I told her that I already had it – 16/21 Harvest Road, North Fremantle – to my astonishment, she expressed great surprise by saying, "What a memory!"

This was not a sarcastic comment. Her eyes were laced with intrigue, an expression that bewildered me because they seemed to be saying, 'How did he know that?', an expression that drove me to greater and more repulsive heights of defensive superiority.

"I always remember addresses and phone numbers," I said, before reeling off everyone's phone number who'd been at my place that night. My mouth was moving out of control. Each number was like a sabre through the shattered remnants of my character. I felt like the greatest egotistical fool on earth – and there seemed little I could do about it.

When we went outside, I waited by her door as she stood outside the car, spreading a rug out on the seat. Then she came over to me and hugged me dispassionately. I was hoping for something positive.

I said, "It's been a pleasure."

But she replied sarcastically, "I'll be careful about treading on your feet."

Then she quickly and unemotionally hugged me and got into the car and shut the door. The finality of this closure induced an humiliation of which I was strangely and acceptingly philosophical.

She asked me which was the best way back to the main road and, straight after I told her, she drove off, saying out the window, "I hope that didn't test your memory. I'd hate to dent your incredible ego!"

Strolling up the driveway, it was difficult not to agree with the sentiment of her parting remark. Pure cowardice was the only explanation that I could offer for my appalling behaviour. Having the rare ability to place an enormous wedge between my feelings and the impression that I was giving to the outside world, I was gratified by the knowledge that this trait was not something in which my mind indulged willingly. I was not that ridiculous. However, not a single event of the evening came as a surprise to me. The tedious predictability of everything which had occurred gave me the sort of futility that love is supposed to erase, and the undesirability of these contingencies only reinforced my belief that the level of freedom which can be achieved in someone emotionally impeded is minimal. My life had the appearance of liberation. The reality, though, was quite different. This evening's events had made it apparent that nothing substantial had really changed. Any changes at all in my life were merely superficial, like a veil of diplomacy being pulled over the once warring spitefulness of two rapacious republics. Over the years my tastes had widened; I was more sophisticated at cleverly getting to a certain point, but the end result was always the same - vituperative failure.

I sat down on the edge of the front verandah and gazed up at the sky. Sleep was not a possibility. The nights here were too black, beneath the fantastic calamity of isolated, cataclysmic explosions, to allow my mind to rest in the hope that regrets could be dissolved by a serene and careless slumber. The black dawn of loneliness begins a day of interminable length. It anticipated a void as frustrating as the one above, one which enables you to perceive the dazzling beauty of the heavens but is so vast as to render any chance of benefiting from the existence of such magnificence a theoretical possibility.

Perfect sensual pleasure was nothing more than a hypothetical construct. And didn't I know it.

The phone rang; it could have been her. I dashed inside. It was her.

She said, matter-of-factly, "Look, even though I drove off like that, I want you to know that I still intend to drive you to the airport, as I agreed to do. Okay?"

"Yes, yes," I said. "No problem. No problem."

"See you tomorrow then."

"Okay, great."

I put the phone down and wondered how it was that hope could keep rising from the dead. Then I went to bed and went out as swiftly as the light.

* * * * * * * * * *

The room in which I woke up was in an even worse condition than I had thought possible. Had I appreciated the full extent of the degradation that surrounded me, in the benighted dimness of my somnolence, I would not have even dreamed of entering this blighted chamber of disregarded filth. A murky translucence of morning light enveloped me. A mesh of webs, covered in spiders, ran along a tangled forest of twisted metals down one side of the bed. The horror of seeing all those creepy-crawlies crawling creepily over each other made me shudder at how close I had been to the brink of a sickening disaster. Only my complete unconsciousness of the peril of my predicament had saved me from unleashing a panic-stricken scream in the blackness of the now departed night. It had not even dawned on me, as I had lain on those stained, mite-infested blankets, on that bed of rusting, iron legs, prior to rising, that such a heinous danger had been so near. The shock of discovering the depths to which I had plummeted caused me to charge out of that room – not in hope – but in response to the pointlessness of remaining in that dreadful position.

The next room was almost as bad, but not quite. It was clearly the abode of a pauper but free of the lurking arachnids of unbalanced thought. In it, a sense of dreary hopelessness existed within the definiteness of an emotional poverty. There was even an attempt to maintain some sort of rational order. But everything – every colourless thing – was placed without cause for feeling that their manipulation could lead to any worthwhile reward. It was a room of safe functionalism, of pessimistic acceptance, of servile indolence in the face of endeavour's fears.

A thin crack between the dusty curtains threw a patch of gloomy light, like a misty oil stain, on to the creaking boards of this degraded chamber's floor. A line of busy termites, in a constant stream of ravenous replenishment, gnawed ferociously at a rotting seam in the ageing timbers. An illusion of irreparability oozed from this malignant crevice in the unkept character of the room. Something grotesquely normal exuded from its unacceptable abnormality.

A great feeling that something more profound than this had to exist elsewhere drove me on, even though I knew that I was not going to benefit from any improvement in my surroundings. Venturing forth, I discovered that the magnitude of the establishment in which I had found myself was only now beginning to reveal itself. It was a single-storey residence, an enormous bungalow, with a plethora of mysterious rooms. A feeling that each room that I entered belonged to someone else – each with its own peculiar silence – pursued me, as though I were floating within an ineluctable ether, allowing observation and envy, but little else.

The first room of domestic respectability had the stamp of lurid individuality. A colourful waywardness of expressive thought showed in the deliberately unusual and violent use of clashing hues. Thick, orange silk-velvet curtains, the sort of thing you expect to see in an eccentric cinema, hung from a large Edwardian window. Through it, a crisp, even light flowed in an abundance of cheery, photochemical illumination. The emerald carpets vibrated with the resonance of fulfilled enterprise; the lemon walls radiated an aura of imperturbable peace. I realised that I was in the mind of someone so contentedly distracted from the hopes of unattainable causes that their unusual taste glowed with style. A serene obliviousness to the existence of others, held in the beauteous evenness of rich light, evoked memories of childhood delight. It appeared to me as if the occupier of this room had carried the easily acquired ecstasy of youth into adulthood: everything sang with a foreign optimism. Even the walls seemed to smile.

It came as a shock to me to realise the position I was occupying in the scheme of this emotional architecture. A feeling that my presence in the opulent side of this establishment was that of a temporary uninvolved visitor was enhanced when I entered the next room. This boudoir was much larger than any of the other rooms that I had seen. I got the impression that the owner of this sumptuous chamber – sumptuous in its esoteric tastes – was the owner of the entire house. My presence in their contented kingdom helped me to see what they saw – colour, sensuality, peace – but these things only irked me, for they were not mine: they just emphasised that owned by others.

I opened up the mahogany cupboard doors and tasted the apricot fragrance of the fabrics within. A sparkle of diamanté exploded on the ebony surface of a velvet cloth. A diamond-shaped shadow momentarily engraved itself on to my eye. I felt like an ethereal creature, able to perceive, to comprehend, but not able to take part. I ran my fingers over the silks and taffetas of this flamboyant collection and then I shut the door. Even the movement of the woodwork evoked the sounds of slowly beating wings.

I turned and looked at the bed. A royal-blue quilt covered its bulky expanse. A soft plenteousness of exquisite comfort emerged, like a life-enhancing radiation, from this duvet's lovingly manicured surface. I did not even consider the idea of flopping on to this haven of voluptuous silkiness, for it would have only highlighted the paucity of available pleasure that existed in the denigrated rooms of experience from which I had just emerged, and where I assumed that I was destined to belong. All the magnificence and fineness of careless repletion could be found in this splendour of homely contentment. Bright red lace ran around the rim of the duvet and shone with the gladness of ecstatic life. Scenes of classical beings making love were woven into the fabric of this testimony to the joys of blissful compassion. I bent down and observed the forms of satisfied people, lolling in the Arcadian backdrops of heavenly bliss and felt that such a state of quixotic humour was so near, but so far away. I could sense it; hear about it; observe it; dream about it; be told stories about it; see people wandering about affected by its elixir, but I could never experience it: it was in an unmergable and parallel world. Its existence made me dysphoric yet I was fascinated by it in the same way that peasants are intrigued and anguished by aristocracy; but this was an aristocracy of requited love, of the liberated abandonment of the need to seek a meaningful purpose. I was beset with a feeling of unbelonging. I was unattached to any shared vision of mutual kindness.

I was driven by a desire to peer out of a window. I opened up the burgundy silk curtains, their skin as fresh as a baby's, and pushed open the balcony doors. I stood outside. The sky was blue. Long, fluffy white wisps hung in the air. I glanced along the length of the building. Vast Corinthian columns adorned the façade. The columns metamorphosed out of a red brick wall, starting at the same point where the interior opulence began. Enormous bouquets of luxuriant fruit spilled out from their pinnacles. Scenes of magnanimity, involving wise statesmen, were engraved into the pediments. I looked out across a stretch of manicured lawn to a place where weeping willows enveloped a smooth pond. The still water was deep with the reflections of leafy boughs. A white plaster statue of a woman stood before this calmness of lake and leaves. She was naked. Around her head was a cloth.

I left the balcony and started walking towards her. Her breasts protruded straight out. She was resting her weight on one leg. This caused the curve of her waist and hip to become exaggerated on the other side. I got near her. A great wind began to blow. Huge thrusts of air shook the trees. Maddened waves charged across the pond. Both hands of this statue became raised. Her lips began to move.

Over the din, she screamed: "Stop!"

And then my eyes shot open and I thought, 'Of course! My mother!' and I finally realised why I had been behaving so badly.

* * * * * * * * * *

It was as though a great flash had gone through my mind. The explanation for my behaviour, a form of faith, gave me a clarity of perspective lost in the previous few weeks. I rose from the bed; I was refreshed with the knowledge that certain attributes I appeared to possess were forced on to me by circumstances and hence, with understanding, could be eliminated. At last, I had the platform upon which to build an apology. I was awake with the excitement of a new beginning. I should have been tired from lack of sleep, but the psychological impact of impending air travel and the reprieve of now being able to express love thrilled me into an enthused wakefulness that left me impatient with positive expectation. I could not wait to see her.

I wandered around the house, clearing up the debris from the night before. Intricate patterns of wispy cream sat in the sky. The sun-drenched leaves of quivering branches appeared like diamonds encrusted in the dark emerald of the trees. Resplendent light filled the world. The buzz of insects, a constant rhythm, echoed my feelings of excited impetuosity at the thought of her desperately-awaited arrival.

I rested my forehead against the glass, saying, "Come on, come on."

Then I began tapping it with my head. The greatness of the impending moment caused my eyes to view a still world, rushing, blurring objects already made surreal by a fantastic drenching of light.

I kept peeping out the window. I was so focused on the present that my mind would not allow me to do anything other than watch and wait. I knew now that an incident was going to take place. No other belief had the chance to enter my determined mind. I was going to explain and to express and to give, and nothing was going to stop me. Not even the deeply-ingrained association of pain with beauty; I was not going to blame her for events for which someone else was responsible. She was an individual and deserved to be treated as such.

Her car appeared in the driveway. I was overjoyed because she was so early. I went to the front door and opened it. She stepped out of the car and looked at me.

I could not see her eyes immediately, but it did not matter for she ripped her sunglasses off when she realised that I was moving towards her. She dropped them on the ground. Losing interest in everything else around her apart from me, she started moving more quickly; the ferocity of my determination to consume her as though she were capable of imparting life, of wiping out every misery on earth, was expressed, and matched, by the unrestrained way that her mouth clashed with mine. I found myself, thoughtless, exploding with the desire to deposit kisses on every part of her face and, as I closed my eyes and did this, grasping the sides of her head and planting a long, profoundly-satisfying peck on her forehead, she pleaded, "Don't go."

I picked her up and started carrying her inside and said, "I'll be back in about two weeks. Don't you worry."

I kicked the door shut and laid her down on the nearest bed. I could not believe that someone so beautiful could be this interested in me. I was living in a dream. All the hard edges of this world had become smoothed over in a hazy translucence of perfect light. She was so sharply in focus that everything else was unreal in its unclear luminosity, as though special life-embellishing filters had been placed over my eyes. I swear that I have never kissed such awe-inspiring lips. They were so fresh and so vibrant and so sentient that they appeared to be more than just mere flesh. Every minute sensation of contact with them was felt with such an intensity of feeling that I wondered how it could be possible that the seemingly commonplace touch of lip upon lip could produce such a positive whirl of glorious emotions. I was now fully conscious of the term "beside myself". I was so shocked by ecstatic disbelief – I had convinced myself so thoroughly that this mutual sharing of love could not happen – that I found myself thinking, with an amazement equivalent to that experienced by South Sea islanders when they first saw European ships: 'She actually loves me! She really loves me! Incredible! Amazing! SHE LOVES ME!' as our bodies twisted and groped and writhed, free at last to explore this miraculous wonder of mutual respect.

I lay in her arms and said, "This morning, it just came to me. It's been such a long time since I've felt like this way about anyone that I completely forgot what happens to me when I get into this situation. I woke up this morning realising, again, that the rejection I received from my mother always causes me to think that failure in emotional relationships is inevitable, so I reject the person before they reject me. I couldn't even look you in the face last night."

"You'd be surprised", she said, with a tone of voice as serene as her beautiful face, "how many people are the same. As you've probably noticed, like a conditioned response in having to deal with the rejection that I received from my father, I become hysterically argumentative. You seem to be the gloomy, introverted type."

I smiled and said, "Absolutely. In my case, as far as the argumentativeness is concerned, I don't blame you. I just can't believe that crap that I was spilling last night about Chile. What a pile of absolute rubbish."

She started giggling.

"I", she said, as I realised that she was actually laughing at herself, "naturally took your point of view as an insult, because", she added, kissing me, "I love you and I assumed that you were rejecting me, so I was trying to make you suffer as well."

"You did," I replied.

"You too," she said.

"Sorry," I replied.

"No problem," she said. "So what's this about two weeks? So you're not intending to slip through my clutches then?"

"Not a chance," I replied. "In London I'm going to make plans to ensure that I slip straight into them."

"What are you going to do then?" she asked. "They're waiting to receive."

"They won't have to wait long," I replied. "I'm going to Mount Damavand. I rang the Iranian taxi driver I told you about. I want to do a story on how politics can ruin normal human emotional aspirations. It'll take two weeks. Then I'll be back here. I'm going to work for Reuters in Australia and start a photo agency and make sure that you don't run off with some other man. None of them is going to love you as much as me."

She smiled cheekily; the right-hand corner of her top lip rose up appreciatively and she said, "How do you know?"

"Gratitude," I replied. "Total and complete. No one is going to be more grateful than I am. Have no doubts about that."

We embraced each other more firmly; an overwhelming desire to protect her from all evils, to defend her against all accusations and to ensure her continued well-being swept through me like a potion of magnanimous sincerity.

"That's why", I said, "I made that comment that night in your flat that I wouldn't mind if the person I was having a relationship with needed to sleep with someone else. As long as they wished to be intimate with me, considering my undermining capacity to react badly when I start to feel love, and therefore to ruin it, I don't care. One day you will realise the extent of my gratitude."

Her eyes seemed to lengthen into dreamy slits and her mouth expanded like a cherry sensuous ring of succulent rubber being inflated by the warm airs of appreciation. We hugged and kissed and stroked each other and I experienced tactile sensations that seemed new, but must have been experienced before.

Then she rolled over and looked up at the ceiling and laughed and said, "What a night that was!"

I too began chortling.

"Both teams", I smiled, "gave outstanding displays of defensive organisation. To the casual observer it was apparent that neither team was going to score."

We were both giggling away in mirthful astonishment at the idea that two people, so keen on each other, could be so unwilling to express affection.

"It was Konrad", she said, "who was the catalyst, you know."

"You mean", I replied, "how we talked to each other through him?"

"No," she smiled, "that's another thing. I was prepared to give up, but he was adamant that you were in love with me. He was the reason I stopped last night to call you."

"I liked him straight away", I said, "and now I'm in love with him as well."

"But what do you think", she replied, "about my businesslike approach in making the call to confirm the appointment? Certainly the sort of thing that one does at four in the morning."

"Incredible efficiency," I said. "When I put the phone down, I ran through the house clenching my fists. Even I could work out that something was up, otherwise you wouldn't've bothered."

"I wouldn't've", she replied, "been able to sleep unless I made that call."

"I wouldn't've been able to sleep either," I said. "I would've spent all night thinking about you, bashing my head into a metaphysical brick wall, contemplating all the stupid mistakes that I had made. It would've been hell."

Then I added, laughing, "I would've just lain awake, chastising myself for being such a boring, egotistical bastard."

She smiled sheepishly and said, "Maybe I was a bit of a boring, egotistical bastard myself."

"No, no, no!" I replied. "You were a perfect angel."

She gave me a nice slap.

"Hoom," I said. "Now things are improving."

"I always had the feeling", she replied, "that you were bit of a masochist."

"For you", I said, "I'll be anything you want. Even a boring, egotistical bastard."

"You're not a boring, egotistical bastard," she suddenly smiled with tender graciousness. "You're lovely."

I was struck dumb by this disarming approbation, this unexpected accolade, the caring delivery of which from one so gorgeous sent a wave of pure self-fulfilment through my recently overwrought system. She then placed the palm of her hand on that part of my body unused to such satisfaction and the sensory pleasure of this physical contact was only matched by this unsurpassable contentment of being fulfilled in love. I had the feeling for an instant that the room had been showered in an explosion of dazzling light; I felt as though I were levitating on the precipice of a canyon laced with Epicurean delights, cut into the savage plain of an unforgiving desert.

She rolled over on to her back, swinging her arms above her head, in a display of lustful submission as powerful as any dominant force.

The plainness of her invitation to stroke was really not an invitation but a demand, and the thought that I was the only one receiving this offer from her was remarkable, but insignificant against the realisation that I would be giving such pleasure to someone so beautiful.

She closed her eyes, signalling that I should give that magnificent anatomy of hers the grasping and fondling which it so thoroughly deserved. Between caressing and kissing her breasts and thighs, I deposited long sensuous kisses upon her gaping, accepting mouth, each time completing this loving application of mouth upon mouth with the words: "Eyyyyyyye luuuuuv yuooooooo."

Going into her was so effortless that the impression was created that I had entered something without end. Soon she was writhing around as if her spine were conducting an electric current; I was overcome with disbelief that I could be responsible for producing such a rampant exhibition of wild bliss. Her limbs flailed around, out of control. For one brief and horrific moment, I thought that I was causing her pain. The irony that extreme pleasure wears the same face as agony was quickly forgotten in the frenetic turmoil of our passionate clash. Usually, this sort of surreality was the preserve of hallucinogenic drugs or war but this was actually happening. Not a thing I had ever done in the past could prepare me for this shock of mindless joy. Only combat had provided me with a similar entanglement in a single moment, but that did not carry the illusion of permanency, as this did. I knew that I was going to be able to do this whenever I felt like it, at will, and experience exhilaration, pure adrenaline and not have to worry about death. I could give up worrying about the threat of boredom; the spectre of gnawing self-awareness now did not loom up above my head. I was free of the downside of personal quirks; confirmation been received that my virtues were real. I was released.

We lay in each other's arms, rolling about. The experience had been almost painful. We rolled around shaking and quivering in the aftermath of such a violently fulfilling crescendo. I was on top, swaying her from side to side. We hugged tightly, frustrated at not being able to get under each other's skin. I wanted to get all of my body inside hers. She felt so soft and powerful. I wanted to be linked to her permanently, made inseparable by surgery. I felt as though I were too much in love. I could not avoid smothering her face with kisses.

"It's going to be unbearable", I said, "being away from you for a fortnight."

"Try to avoid trouble," she replied, "for a change."

"Trouble", I said, "is over for me."

"Oh," she replied, squeezing me more tightly, "I don't know about that. I think I might be able to give you some."

"Precisely", I said, "the sort of trouble that I'm looking for."

She relaxed her grip and said, "It'll be you who'll be giving me the trouble though."

I was astounded by her pessimism.

"No chance," I said.

It seemed ridiculous that I give her any problems.

"You've got", she said, "the classic, mystifying, alluring, protean personality."

She started stroking the back of my neck.

"You're capable", she added, "of anything. Promise me one thing."

"What?" I asked.

"That", she replied, "when you want me to go you'll say so immediately. I don't want to be left hanging around."

I was taken aback. The idea that I could reject her, when I knew that she was prepared to give me her love, seemed absurd.

"Promise?" she persisted.

"Yes," I replied, "but I can't see it coming to that."

"You never know," she said.

"Okay," I replied, "the same applies to me as well. If you want me to go, I'll go straight away, without a fuss, and that'll be it."

"Okay," she said. "That's fine by me."

I kissed her reassuringly on both cheeks and said, "I think the reason I won't be so bothered about you rejecting me is because I feel that, every day I'm with someone as beautiful as you, it's just a bonus. It shouldn't've happened. I feel as if I have defied fate."

She burst out laughing, then she hugged me appreciatively and said, "You're so epic. I've never experienced anything like it."

It was a thrill to be so unwittingly impressive.

"Actually," I said, "it's gratitude."

"Okay," she replied, "gratitude. Anyway, it's about time I got you to the airport."

"Trying to get rid of me already, hey?" I asked.

"No," she replied. "I want you out of the country fast so you don't have time to change your mind; then you'll be under an enormous moral responsibility to return as agreed."

"Got an answer for everything," I said.

We dashed into the shower. I rubbed all of her body with soap; then I had the pleasure of drying her. She was amused and pleased by my paternal indulgence. It finally occurred to me that it was this sort of tenderness and attention which she had craved, right from the beginning. I took a mental note and promised myself that I would give her this treatment in abundance.

Back in the bedroom, I made her sit between my legs so I could dress her.

"Come on, now," I said, "stop playing. We have to get dressed."

She was threatening to be naughty.

"You're going to get it", I said, "if you keep that up."

She continued. She became extremely compliant when I spun her over in preparation for a spanking; when I realised that she really wanted me to do this to her, I was both stunned and fascinated.

"Go on," she said, "you promised."

"You really want me to?" I asked.

"Yes," she replied.

I hit her softly.

"Not hard enough," she said.

"I can't do it," I replied.

"Go on," she said.

Then she got up and put her arms around me and said, "Sorry, but I'm a bit kinky. I just thought I'd let you know."

"You really get turned on", I asked, intrigued, "by being spanked?"

"And other things as well," she said.

"This gets more interesting", I replied, "as it goes along. How many times do you need to be hit before it does the trick?"

"Usually", she said, "four or five good ones. Then I'm ready for tender, loving care."

"As long as it just remains a kind of game," I said, "then I'll be right into it. There's no way I want to do anything to you unless it's having a positive effect."

"Believe me," she smiled, "you'll know if it isn't."

She gave me a nice long kiss.

"I gather", I said, "that this is a father thing."

"Of course," she replied.

"Why me?" I asked.

"You're unpredictable," she replied.

"So what?" I asked.

"You're dangerous and also kind," she smiled. "Only you have the power to punish me."

She looked at me with lascivious dreaminess.

"Is it possible", I asked, "to receive a greater compliment?"

"From me," she replied, "definitely not."

* * * * * * * * * * *

The drive to the airport was as sweet a glide as could be imagined. Often we just looked at each other and began laughing. It seemed serendipitously comical that we could be so loving so quickly after having been so spiteful. She said: "One of the problems associated with becoming attracted to someone like you is that, with everything which can be said about you, the opposite also applies. You can be ruthlessly scathing and then exceptionally kind. You can be childish and then very sophisticated and mature. I realised that to be happy with someone like you requires enormous open-mindedness and understanding, and this is why going out with you will be such a significant test of character."

I smiled at the accuracy of her comment and said, "You won't have any problem in passing."

She shook her head and said, "One of the things that people find staggering about you is your self-assurance. It creates the illusion of invulnerability."

I chuckled and said, "And an illusion is all it is. I'm as ignorant as everybody else on this ignorant planet. As far as I'm concerned, it contains two types of people: those who know that they're completely ignorant and just accept the fact that they haven't got a clue of what's going on, and those who actually think that they know. The arrogance and ignorance of the latter group should never be underestimated. I'm, of course, well entrenched in the former, but there is one thing that I'm definitely certain about, and that is that I think that you're absolutely right for me."

"Why?" she asked.

"Because", I replied, "you're so courageous and virtuous; unlike me, you stand up for yourself and what you believe in without the slightest hesitation. Your courage stands out like a skyscraper in a hamlet of low-ceilinged bungalows. And you've got such a fascinating mind. You really are concerned by things that are truly relevant. You're incredible."

She smiled at me with a sensitive aspect of dreamlike graciousness. It was such a relief to feel free enough to make these complimentary pronouncements. An almost tearful sensation of pride, authenticity and gratitude rose within me. I was so thrilled she was so flattered by my sincere observations that an overwhelming desire to caress her caused me to say, "Please! Pull into that driveway."

In the driveway, I put my arms around her and said, "And that's why I love you. The journey through the landscape of your existence is going to be spectacular."

I then deposited a juicy, passionate, luscious, moist, amorous, ardent, sensitive kiss on her mouth-watering mouth, waved to the amused old lady sitting on the verandah of this strange house, made the comment that she – that is, Samantha – "epitomised the moral beauty of a fierce expression", and we were away.

She seemed momentarily lost by the radiant mists of adoration. I told her this; then I said, "You had better get used to it."

"It's so astounding", she replied, "being adored like this."

"You haven't seen anything yet," I said. "What you just got then was abuse in comparison to what I intend to give you when I get back here."

She giggled and said, "Enlighten me. What can I expect?"

"Not telling," I replied. "You're going to have to wait."

"Oh come on," she insisted. "If you really loved me, you'd tell me."

"And if you really loved me", I replied, "you'd trust me and wait."

"Can't," she said. "I'm too impatient. I'm addicted to being adored by you. I need another fix – now!"

"Okay," I relented, "you've made me admit it. It's all your fault. I'm going to have to punish you severely, with my bare hands, for being so cheeky and impatient. You're really going to get it."

"It's about time," she replied. "Hopefully, in abundance."

In the car park at the airport we embraced and she said, "I can't describe how relieved I feel. That look you gave me standing on the verandah this morning just swept all my concerns away."

I put my hands through the twirling silk of her dark hair and said, "At that point, I wasn't really concerned about your feelings – in a sense. I just had to express mine. I just felt that I owed it to myself."

"Please", she replied, "keep it up."

"Don't worry," I said. "I will."

My plane was due to leave in forty minutes.

"Better go, then, darling," I said. "A true Australian can't keep Qantas waiting."

"Don't keep them waiting", she replied, "on the way back."

"No chance," I said.

Then I stroked her soft, round face and said, "Thanks. And I mean thanks."

"Me too," she said.

We kissed one last time and I was then happy to be torn away. I glided towards the departure lounge. Just prior to entering, I turned around and waved and her smile was like sunlight being reflected off leaves on a sunny day. I turned around and continued. The air seemed alive with an ethereal light: all faces seemed appealing – seemed to contain a splendour of which their owners were unaware. I was filled with a rare and refreshing moral satisfaction. Even the affection of contented couples was a godsend. I was an angel of ecstasy hovering before the gates of heaven. I had never felt such a transcendental security.

All the previous pleasures of my life were mere trifles in comparison to this dream that I was now conscious within; this had never happened to me before. All the long days and nights spent despairing were made meaningless by this uplifting, triumphant realisation of what, in the past, would have seemed an illusion – a woman whose face seemed to have had all the wonders of this earth cast within it being in love with me. It felt as though all the serenity that nature could pass into one object had been absorbed by that creature's face, and I was going to be back here in a few weeks' time planting kisses all over it. What a glorious prospect!

It made me feel as if I were above the clouds on the summit of some huge mountain in the grip of an immense stillness. Instead of moving through the unreality of an airport, I felt as if I were floating on a raft of carelessness down a tranquil river of possibilities, mesmerised by the wonders on the banks, where everything was a source of contentment. It was a slowly meandering river that seemed engulfed by a translucent haze of newness.

Around one bend in it, I found the check-in queue - or what remained of it. Any smile that fell on anyone's face seemed to be magnified a thousand times; I was struck by the marvellous efficiency and helpfulness of the people in the place. Everything seemed illuminated by an all-pervading incorruptibility. I was in a world reborn with impeccable intentions. I was enveloped by a surreal cocoon of optimistic one-dimensionality; I was ablaze with a soft but powerful mist that fogged out all consideration of the harsh realities of life. I was unhurried by the dramatic beauty of all things. My mind, morally relaxed, took in more simple pleasures than it had ever known.

Something of the attractiveness that God had so freely given to her had been passed on to me. I could have dashed up to bewildered strangers, shaken their hands and thanked them warmly, just for existing. Everything was imbued with charming irreplaceability; not a thing I saw, as I moved from the check-in counter to passport control, could have been removed or embellished. Even the whining of complaining children had the timbre of a symphony orchestra. The fragrance of polished floors resembled that of the most exquisite perfume. I could have kissed the foreheads of other people's bawling children. It was as though all the pain, loneliness, failures and disappointments of the past were mere devices of preparation for this one triumphant occasion. I was wrapped in a warm blanket of affectionate imperturbability. Packs of vile National Front members could have harassed me and I would have tried to kiss each one. I was so full of the splendours of this earth that I even began to look forward to twenty hours on a plane. Twenty-four hours previously, I had felt that there was nothing which could make me feel like that. Not a thing. This was a true miracle. One that made me feel aloof from ambitions, from every sin that I had ever committed, from every stupid act that I had ever performed. Those acts were now done by someone else, someone with a different state of mind. I was beyond negative self-analysis, amused by my idiosyncrasies, enriched by my regrets. This was the bliss of which others could only dream. It was as though I were in a world of large trumpet flowers with butterflies and huge birds whose wings smothered warm air over fruit-laden trees beside the clear waters of a still river, whose flat surface, reflecting everything with a profound clarity, was fed by an infinite underground spring. I redefined the word diplomacy. I would have gratefully given a mugger all I had, praising him for his well-intentioned efforts to redistribute wealth. Every pejorative comment ever made to me was a cause of forgiveness. Nothing was beyond redemption. I could see nothing but good or potential in everyone who passed me. A wholesomeness and unity seemed to have fallen on a previously fractured earth.

A woman coming in the opposite direction to me received a pleasant surprise when she saw me smiling at her with a detached and unintrusive spontaneity. Her surprise reeked of sweetness. She was an angel in a world of angels. Out there was probably a man whom she was making feel something like I felt now. Not quite as good, I knew, but something similar. It was as if all the good fortune available to this world had been compressed into a tiny unit and been handed to me, a present of such loveliness that it crushed all want. No other gift had the power to do this, but the gift of love. Somehow my awkward, probing proboscis had pierced that elusive vein of beauty that flows through this earth. I was a warm ember of gracious finesse. No concern or worry or absurd error warranted the merest contemplation. Such things were irrelevant. The disappointments and appalling decisions of the past were now laughable. I had been lifted into the clouds on the wings of a bird, rising above the need for gratification, to a vantage point from which even the dullest, most unsympathetic eye imaginable could only see beauty, richness, pleasure, the world of kings, of poets, of realisations. In this world in the clouds, the beating of the great winds was silent. Great changes had taken place without sound, like sunlight breathing life into a gloomy forest; the previously dark parts of my brain had received some of that light as well.

I knew that this could not last, however – everything that begins in bliss finishes with tears – but there was something of the naive immortality of youth in this, a denial of the possibility of lost opportunities, a reckless disregard for consequences that breathed new life into old things, as if my consciousness had been given an indestructibility by the kiss of eternity. This was a state of mind in which the walls of rationality and logic had been swept aside by the raging waters of glee. I was in no mood for pragmatism: this was a moment to be cherished, the moment of victory over frustrated hopes and the nagging limitations of this life, the moment of triumph over all those who arrogantly thought that they knew me. I could see some of them looking at me, wondering, 'God, what's happened to him?' and none of them, I knew, would be able to appreciate the mountain I had had to climb to achieve what came to them naturally.

This ascension was, for me, a privilege. Fate had done its utmost to ensure that I had no right to it and, because it was impossible for me to take this beautiful predicament for granted, it was exactly that: beautiful. I had denied, in a sense, destiny, by gaining the interest and affection of a woman who could be described as almost perfect and, by doing so, I had uprooted the tree of intransigence that drops its dead leaves on futile hopes.

Two days later, as I strolled with casual disregard for the whims of this earth, in St James's Park, I saw the perfect circle of the moon sitting within wispy clouds that floated with peaceful grace across the illuminated sky. It was like a fluorescent button, this moon, on the black cloak of the universe, a torch brightening a dark world. In universal terms, it was just a speck, invisible from most places in the cosmos, but on this night, to me, it was almost blinding. Its light touched the path I walked along with a delicate felicity. Its luminosity imparted an unblemished smoothness upon a tarnished earth. It was like the effect that sunlight has on the follicles of long dark hair, silken clusters of hair through which, within the next fortnight, I would be running my fingers. This was just one sensational possibility in a plethora. Rainbows connected my brain cells together. I could not stop imagining the kaleidoscope of opportunity that had suddenly been thrust before me.

As I neared the bridge that curls over the lake, I saw the reflections of street lamps in the rippling, black hole of the water. Golden concentrations of radiance swam free in an infinite darkness. Couples locked together on the bridge stared along this lake of serenity towards the spires of Whitehall. At last I felt no need to surreptitiously determine the contours of some unknown female's voluptuous form. I had been absolved from the ravages of untouchable beauty. I was now able to appreciate it without feeling an undignified longing. No positive experience, it seemed, was out of my reach. I was in the right frame of mind to assume my potential.

Self-belief stood out like an obelisk of satisfaction. I was dissociated from an earth with which I had never felt so strongly connected. I made a pact with myself that I had to visit as many people as possible before I left and warmly congratulate them for being so wonderful. I believed that all the fruits of the earth should have been heaped upon everyone I had ever met in my life. Subjectively, I felt that they had all unwittingly aided me in helping to deal with a woman whose mind was enriched by vast ideas, by grandiloquent struggles, by relevant issues, a prepossession of imagination that made it impossible for her, like me, to accept the staid respectability of everyday life without some hard-won excitement. Even if most of us could not be world champion surfers or war correspondents, at least we could have a sound appreciation of those forces that created and destroyed great civilisations, so that, if we were unable to live on the edge physically, at least our imaginations could, and that was one step above being a pot plant.

And maybe this was why some of us chose to live in big cities. We were safe from disease and war - this was a downer for those who needed a regular adrenalin rush - but were close to achievement, to history, conglomerations of culture, profound and subtle influences that forced changes on us, that gave us more imagination than we really deserved - and London was no exception. It was a city of desperate people with severe compulsions in which personal situations could change rapidly for the better or worse; in which swift judgements were made; on any given day you could feel like an idiot, a dumb speck of puerile ineptitude - there was a lot to compare yourself with - and then, suddenly, its dispirited skies could open and you could feel like a hero, urbane, dynamic, a champion, a lover and a king.

The sphere of experience was complete.